CAPTURE ME

THE COMPLETE TRILOGY

ANNA ZAIRES

♠ MOZAIKA PUBLICATIONS ♠

This is a work of fiction. Names, characters, places, and incidents are either the product of the author's imagination or are used fictitiously, and any resemblance to actual persons, living or dead, business establishments, events, or locales is purely coincidental.

Published by Mozaika Publications, an imprint of Mozaika LLC.
www.mozaikallc.com

Cover by Najla Qamber Designs
najlaqamberdesigns.com

Print ISBN: 978-163142-179-2

CAPTURE ME

CAPTURE ME: BOOK 1

I

THE ASSIGNMENT

1

ulia

THE TWO MEN IN FRONT OF ME EMBODY DANGER. THEY EXUDE IT. One blond, one dark—they should've been polar opposites, but they're similar somehow. They give off the same vibe.

The vibe that makes me go cold inside.

"I have a delicate matter I'd like to discuss with you," says Arkady Buschekov, the Russian official beside me. His faded, colorless gaze is trained on the dark-haired man's face. Buschekov says it in Russian, and I immediately repeat his words in English. My translation is smooth, my accent undetectable. I'm a good interpreter, even if that's not my real job.

"Go on," the dark-haired man says. Julian Esguerra is his name, and he's a big-time arms dealer. I know that from the folder I studied this morning. He's the important one here today, the one they want me to get close to. It shouldn't be a hardship. He's a strikingly handsome man, his eyes blue and piercing in his darkly tanned face. If it weren't for that chill-inducing vibe, I'd be genuinely attracted to him. As it is, I'll be faking it, but he won't know.

They never know.

"I'm sure you are aware of the difficulties in our region," Buschekov says. "We would like you to assist us in resolving this matter."

I translate his words, doing my best to conceal my growing excitement. Obenko was right. There *is* something brewing between Esguerra and the Russians. Obenko suspected as much when he heard the arms dealer was visiting Moscow.

"Assist you how?" Esguerra asks. He looks only vaguely interested.

As I translate his words for Buschekov, I sneak a glance at the other man at the table—the one with blond hair cut in a short, almost military style.

Lucas Kent, Esguerra's right-hand man.

I've been trying not to look at him. He unnerves me even more than his boss. Thankfully, he's not my target, so I don't need to feign interest in him. For some reason, though, my eyes keep being drawn to his hard features. With his tall, powerfully muscled body, square jaw, and fierce gaze, Kent reminds me of a *bogatyr*—a noble warrior of Russian folk tales.

He catches me looking at him, and his pale eyes flash as they lock on my face. I quickly look away, suppressing a shudder. Those eyes make me think of the slivers of ice outside, blue-gray and freezing cold.

Thank God he's not the one I need to seduce. It will be much, much easier to fake it with his boss.

"There are certain parts of Ukraine that need our help," Buschekov says. "But, world opinion being what it is right now, it would be problematic if we went in and actually gave that help."

I swiftly translate what he said, my attention once more on the information I'm supposed to retrieve. This is important; this is the primary reason I'm here today. Seducing Esguerra is secondary, though likely still unavoidable.

"So you would like me to do it instead," Esguerra says, and Buschekov nods as I translate.

"Yes," Buschekov says. "We would like a sizable shipment of weapons and other supplies to reach the freedom fighters in Donetsk. It cannot be traced back to us. In return, you would be paid your usual fee and granted safe passage to Tajikistan."

When I convey the words to him, Esguerra smiles coldly. "Is that all?"

"We would also prefer it if you avoided any dealings with Ukraine at this time," Buschekov says. "Two chairs and one ass and all that."

I do my best to translate the last part, though it doesn't sound nearly as punchy in English. I also commit every single word to memory, so I can convey it to Obenko later today. This is exactly what my boss was hoping I'd hear. Or rather, what he feared I'd hear.

"I'm afraid I will require additional compensation for that," Esguerra says. "As you know, I don't usually take sides in these types of conflicts."

"Yes, so we've heard." Buschekov brings a piece of *selyodka*—salted fish—to his mouth and chews it slowly, looking at the arms dealer. "Perhaps you might reconsider that position in our case. The Soviet Union may be gone, but our influence in this region is still quite substantial."

"Yes, I'm aware. Why do you think I'm here right now?" Esguerra's smile is reminiscent of a shark's. "But neutrality is an expensive commodity to give up. I'm sure you understand."

Buschekov's gaze turns colder. "I do. I'm authorized to offer you twenty percent more than the usual payment for your cooperation in this matter."

"Twenty percent? When you're cutting my potential profits in half?" Esguerra laughs softly. "I don't think so."

After I translate, Buschekov pours himself some vodka and swirls it around the glass. "Twenty percent more and the captured Al-Quadar terrorist remitted into your custody," he says after a few moments. "This is our final offer."

I translate his words and sneak another glance at the blond-haired man, inexplicably curious to see his reaction. Lucas Kent hasn't said a word this whole time, but I can sense him watching everything, absorbing everything.

I can sense him watching *me*.

Does he suspect anything, or is he simply attracted? Either way, it worries me. Men like that are dangerous, and I have a feeling this one may be more dangerous than most.

"We have a deal then," Esguerra says, and I realize that this is it. What Obenko was afraid of is coming to pass. The Russians are going to get the weapons to the so-called freedom fighters, and the clusterfuck in Ukraine will reach epic proportions.

Oh, well. That's Obenko's problem, not mine. All I need to do is smile, look pretty, and translate—which I do for the rest of the meal.

WHEN THE MEETING CONCLUDES, BUSCHEKOV STAYS IN THE restaurant to talk to the owner, and I exit with Esguerra and Kent.

As soon as we step outside, the frigid cold bites at me. The coat I'm wearing is stylish, but it's no match for the Russian winter. The chill goes straight through the wool and into my bones. Within seconds, my feet turn to icicles, the thin soles of my high-heeled shoes doing little to protect them from the freezing ground.

"Would you mind giving me a lift to the nearest subway?" I ask as Esguerra and Kent approach their car. I know I'm visibly shivering, and I'm counting on the fact that even ruthless criminals won't let a pretty woman freeze for no good reason. "It should be about ten blocks from here."

Esguerra studies me for a second, then motions to Kent. "Frisk her," he orders curtly.

My heart rate speeds up as the blond man comes up to me. His hard face is emotionless, his expression not changing even when his big hands travel over my body from head to toe. It's a classic patdown—he doesn't try to feel me up or anything—but when he's done, I'm shivering for a different reason, the chill inside me exacerbated by a surge of unwelcome awareness.

No. I force my breathing to even out. This is not the reaction I need. He's not the man I need to be reacting to.

"She's clean," Kent says, stepping away from me, and I do my best to control my relieved exhalation.

"Okay, then." Esguerra opens the car door for me. "Hop in."

I climb in and take a seat next to him in the back, giving mental thanks that Kent joined the driver at the front. I'm finally in a position to make my move.

"Thank you," I say, giving my warmest smile to Esguerra. "I really appreciate it. This is one of the worst winters in recent years."

To my disappointment, there isn't even a flicker of interest on the arms dealer's handsome face. "No problem," he says, pulling out his phone. A smile appears on his sensuous lips as he reads whatever message is there and begins typing a response.

I study him, wondering what could've put him in such a good mood. A deal gone right? A better-than-expected offer from a supplier? Whatever it is, it's distracting him from me, and that's not good.

"Are you staying here for long?" I ask, making my voice soft and seductive. When he glances at me, I smile again and cross my legs—the length of which is emphasized by the silky black tights I'm wearing. "I could show you around town if you'd like." As I speak, I look him in the eye, making my gaze as welcoming as I can. Men can't tell the difference between this and genuine desire; as long as a woman looks like she wants them, they believe she does.

And to be fair, most women *would* want this man. He's more than handsome—gorgeous, really. Women would kill for a chance to be in his bed, even with that dark, cruel edge I sense within him. The fact that he doesn't do anything for me is my problem, one I'll need to work on if I'm to complete my mission.

I don't know if Esguerra senses something off or if I'm just not his type, but instead of taking me up on my offer, he gives me a cool smile. "Thanks for the invitation, but we'll be leaving soon and I'm afraid I'm too exhausted to do your town justice tonight."

Shit. I conceal my disappointment and smile back. "Of course. If you change your mind, you know where to find me." There's nothing else I can say without raising suspicion.

The car stops in front of my subway stop, and I climb out, trying to think how I'm going to explain my failure in this department.

He didn't want me? Yes, that would go over well.

Heaving a sigh, I wrap my coat tighter around my chest and hurry into the underground metro station, determined to at least get out of the cold.

2

ulia

THE FIRST THING I DO UPON ARRIVING HOME IS CALL MY BOSS AND convey everything I've learned.

"So it's as I suspected," Vasiliy Obenko says when I'm done. "They're going to use Esguerra to arm those fucking rebels in Donetsk."

"Yes." I kick off my shoes and walk into the kitchen to make myself tea. "And Buschekov demanded exclusivity, so Esguerra's now fully allied with the Russians."

Obenko lets out a string of curses, most of which involve some combination of fucking, sluts, and mothers. I tune him out as I pour water into an electronic kettle and turn it on.

"All right," Obenko says when he calms down a little. "You're seeing him tonight, right?"

I take a breath. Now comes the unpleasant part. "Not exactly."

"Not exactly?" Obenko's voice goes dangerously quiet. "What the fuck is that supposed to mean?"

"I offered, but he wasn't interested." It's always best to tell the truth in these types of situations. "Said they're leaving soon, and he was too exhausted."

Obenko starts cursing again. I use the time to tear open a tea bag, drop it into a cup, and pour boiling water over it.

"You're sure you're not going to see him again?" he asks after he's done with his cursing fit.

"Reasonably sure, yes." I blow on my tea to cool it down. "He just wasn't interested."

Obenko goes silent for a few moments. "All right," he says finally. "You fucked up, but we'll deal with that another time. For now, we need to figure out what to do about Esguerra and the weapons that will flood our country."

"Eliminate him?" I suggest. My tea is still a bit too hot, but I take a sip anyway, enjoying the warmth going down my throat. It's a simple pleasure, but the best things in life are always simple. The smell of lilacs blooming in the spring, the softness of a cat's fur, the juicy sweetness of a ripe strawberry—I've learned to treasure these things in recent years, to squeeze every ounce of joy out of life.

"Easier said than done." Obenko sounds frustrated. "He's better protected than Putin."

"Uh-huh." I take another sip of tea and close my eyes, savoring the taste this time. "I'm sure you'll figure it out."

"When did he say he was leaving?"

"He didn't specify. He just said 'soon.'"

"All right." Obenko seems impatient all of a sudden. "If he contacts you, let me know immediately."

And before I can reply, he hangs up.

~

SINCE I HAVE THE EVENING OFF, I DECIDE TO INDULGE IN A BATH.

My bathtub, like the rest of this apartment, is small and dingy, but I've seen worse. I spruce up the ugliness of the cramped bathroom by putting a couple of scented candles on the sink and adding bubbles to the water, and then I get in, letting out a blissful sigh at the warmth engulfing my body.

If I had my way, I'd always be warm. Whoever said hell is hot was wrong. Hell is cold.

Russian-winter cold.

I'm enjoying my soak when the doorbell rings. Instantly, my heartbeat spikes and adrenaline blasts through my veins.

I'm not expecting anyone—which means it could only be trouble.

Jumping out of the tub, I wrap a towel around myself and run out of the bathroom into the main room of my studio apartment. The clothes I took off are still lying on the bed, but I don't have time to put them on. Instead, I throw on a robe and grab a gun from the drawer in my nightstand.

Then I take a deep breath and approach the door, aiming the weapon at it.

"Yes?" I call out, stopping a couple of feet from the apartment entrance. My door is reinforced steel, but the keyhole is not. Someone could shoot through it.

"It's Lucas Kent." The deep voice speaking English startles me so much, the gun wavers in my hand. My pulse jumps another notch, and a peculiar weakness seizes my knees.

Why is he here? Does Esguerra know anything? Did someone betray me? The questions blaze through my mind, making my heart race even faster, but then the most reasonable course of action comes to me.

"What is it?" I ask, doing my best to keep my voice steady. There's one explanation for Kent's presence that doesn't involve me getting killed: Esguerra's changed his mind. In which case, I need to act like the innocent civilian I'm supposed to be.

"I'd like to talk to you," Kent says, and I hear a hint of amusement in his voice. "Are you going to open the door, or are we going to continue talking through three inches of steel?"

Shit. That doesn't sound like Esguerra's sent him for me.

I quickly evaluate my options. I can stay locked inside the apartment and hope he won't be able to find his way in—or get me when I come out, as I will inevitably have to—or I can take the chance that he doesn't know who I am and play it cool.

"Why do you want to talk to me?" I ask, stalling for time. It's a reasonable question. Any woman in this situation would be wary, not just one who has something to hide. "What do you want?"

"You."

The one word, uttered in his deep voice, hits me like a fist. My lungs stop working, and I stare at the door, seized by irrational panic. I wasn't wrong then, when I wondered whether he might be attracted to me—whether the reason he kept looking at me might be as simple as human biology in action.

Yes, of course. He wants me.

I force myself to start breathing again. This should be a relief. There's no reason to panic. Men have wanted me since I was fifteen, and I've learned to cope with it. To turn their lust to my advantage. This is no different.

Except Kent is harder, more dangerous than most.

No. I silence that small voice and take a deep breath, lowering my weapon. As I do, I catch a glimpse of myself in the hallway mirror. My blue eyes are wide in my pale face, and my hair is messily pinned up, wet tendrils trailing down my neck. With the terrycloth robe wrapped carelessly around me and the gun in my hands, I look nothing like the fashionable young woman who tried to seduce Kent's boss.

Reaching a decision, I call out, "Just a minute." I could try to deny Lucas Kent entry to my apartment—it wouldn't be that suspicious for a woman alone—but the smarter thing would be to use this opportunity to get some information.

At the very least, I can try to find out when Esguerra's leaving and tell Obenko, partially making up for my earlier failure.

Moving quickly, I hide the gun in a drawer underneath the hallway mirror and unpin my hair, letting the thick blond strands stream down my back. I've already washed off my makeup, but I have clear skin and my eyelashes are naturally brown, so it's not too bad. If anything, I look younger, more innocent this way.

More like "the girl next door," as Americans like to say.

Confident that I'm reasonably presentable, I approach the door and unlock it, trying to ignore the heavy, frantic beating of my heart.

3

ulia

He steps into my apartment as soon as the door swings open. No hesitation, no greeting—he just comes in.

Startled, I step back, the short, narrow hallway suddenly stiflingly small. I'd somehow forgotten how big he is, how broad his shoulders are. I'm tall for a woman—tall enough to fake being a model if an assignment calls for it—but he towers a full head above me. With the heavy down jacket he's wearing, he takes up almost the entire hallway.

Still not saying a word, he closes the door behind him and advances toward me. Instinctively, I back away, feeling like cornered prey.

"Hello, Yulia," he murmurs, stopping when we're out of the hallway. His pale gaze is locked on my face. "I wasn't expecting to see you like this."

I swallow, my pulse racing. "I just took a bath." I want to seem calm and confident, but he's got me completely off-balance. "I wasn't expecting visitors."

"No, I can see that." A faint smile appears on his lips, softening the hard line of his mouth. "Yet you let me in. Why?"

"Because I didn't want to continue talking through the door." I take a steadying breath. "Can I offer you some tea?" It's a stupid thing to say, given what he's here for, but I need a few moments to compose myself.

He raises his eyebrows. "Tea? No, thanks."

"Then can I take your jacket?" I can't seem to stop playing the hostess, using politeness to cover my anxiety. "It looks quite warm."

Amusement flickers in his wintry gaze. "Sure." He takes off his down jacket and hands it to me. He's left wearing a black sweater and dark jeans tucked into black winter boots. The jeans hug his legs, revealing muscular thighs and powerful calves, and on his belt, I see a gun sitting in a holster.

Irrationally, my breathing quickens at the sight, and it takes a concerted effort to keep my hands from shaking as I take the jacket and walk over to hang it in my tiny closet. It's not a surprise that he's armed—it would be a shock if he wasn't—but the gun is a stark reminder of who Lucas Kent is.

What he is.

It's no big deal, I tell myself, trying to calm my frayed nerves. I'm used to dangerous men. I was raised among them. This man is not that different. I'll sleep with him, get whatever information I can, and then he'll be out of my life.

Yes, that's it. The sooner I can get it done, the sooner all of this will be over.

Closing the closet door, I paste a practiced smile on my face and turn back to face him, finally ready to resume the role of confident seductress.

Except he's already next to me, having crossed the room without making a sound.

My pulse jumps again, my newfound composure fleeing. He's close enough that I can see the gray striations in his pale blue eyes, close enough that he can touch me.

And a second later, he does touch me.

Lifting his hand, he runs the back of his knuckles over my jaw.

I stare up at him, confused by my body's instant response. My skin warms and my nipples tighten, my breath coming faster. It doesn't make sense for this hard, ruthless stranger to turn me on. His boss is more handsome, more striking, yet it's Kent my body's reacting to. All he's touched thus far is my face. It should be nothing, yet it's intimate somehow.

Intimate and disturbing.

I swallow again. "Mr. Kent—Lucas—are you sure I can't offer you something to drink? Maybe some coffee or—" My words end in a breathless gasp as he reaches for the tie of my robe and tugs on it, as casually as one would unwrap a package.

"No." He watches as the robe falls open, revealing my naked body underneath. "No coffee."

And then he touches me for real, his big, hard palm cupping my breast. His fingers are callused, rough. Cold from being outside. His thumb flicks over my hardened nipple, and I feel a pull deep within my core, a coiling of need that feels as foreign as his touch.

Fighting the urge to flinch away, I dampen my dry lips. "You're very direct, aren't you?"

"I don't have time for games." His eyes gleam as his thumb flicks over my nipple again. "We both know why I'm here."

"To have sex with me."

"Yes." He doesn't bother to soften it, to give me anything but the brutal truth. He's still holding my breast, touching my naked flesh as though it's his right. "To have sex with you."

"And if I say no?" I don't know why I'm asking this. This is not how it's supposed to go. I should be seducing him, not trying to put him off. Yet something within me rebels at his casual assumption that I'm his for the taking. Other men have assumed this before, and it didn't bother me nearly as much. I don't know what's different this time, but I want him to step away from me, to stop touching me. I want it so badly that my hands curl into fists at my sides, my muscles tensing with the urge to fight.

"Are you saying no?" He asks the question calmly, his thumb now circling over my areola. As I search for a response, he slides his other hand into my hair, possessively cupping the back of my skull.

I stare at him, my breath catching. "And if I were?" To my disgust, my voice comes out thin and scared. It's as if I'm a virgin again, cornered by my trainer in the locker room. "Would you leave?"

One corner of his mouth lifts in a half-smile. "What do you think?" His fingers tighten in my hair, the grip just hard enough to hint at pain. His other hand, the one on my breast, is still gentle, but it doesn't matter.

I have my answer.

So when his hand leaves my breast and slides down my belly, I don't resist. Instead, I part my legs, letting him touch my smooth, freshly waxed pussy. And when his hard, blunt finger pushes into me, I don't try to move away. I just stand there, trying to control my frantic breathing, trying to convince myself that this is no different from any other assignment.

Except it is.

I don't want it to be, but it is.

"You're wet," he murmurs, staring at me as he pushes his finger deeper. "Very wet. Do you always get so wet for men you don't want?"

"What makes you think I don't want you?" To my relief, my voice is steadier this time. The question comes out soft, almost amused as I hold his gaze. "I let you in here, didn't I?"

"You came on to *him*." Kent's jaw tightens, and his hand on the back of my head shifts, gripping a fistful of my hair. "You wanted *him* earlier today."

"So I did." The typically masculine display of jealousy reassures me, putting me on more familiar ground. I manage to soften my tone, make it more seductive. "And now I want you. Does that bother you?"

Kent's eyes narrow. "No." He forces a second finger into me and simultaneous presses his thumb against my clit. "Not at all."

I want to say something clever, come up with some snappy retort, but I can't. The jolt of pleasure is sharp and startling. My inner muscles tighten, clutching at his rough, invading fingers, and it's all I can do not to moan out loud at the resulting sensations. Involuntarily, my hands come up, grabbing at his forearm. I don't know if I'm trying to push him away or get him to continue, but it doesn't matter. Under the soft wool of his sweater, his arm is thick with steely muscle. I can't control its movements—all I can do is hold onto it as he pushes deeper into me with those hard, merciless fingers.

"You like that, don't you?" he murmurs, holding my gaze, and I gasp as he begins flicking his thumb over my clit, side to side, then up and down. His fingers curl inside me, and I suppress a moan as he hits a spot that sends an even sharper pang of sensation to my nerve endings. A tension begins to coil inside me, the pleasure gathering and intensifying, and with shock I realize I'm on the verge of orgasm.

My body, usually so slow to respond, is throbbing with aching need at the touch of a man who scares me—a development that both astonishes and unnerves me.

I don't know if he sees it on my face, or if he feels the tightening in my body, but his pupils dilate, his pale eyes darkening. "Yes, that's it." His voice is a low, deep rumble. "Come for me, beautiful"—his thumb presses hard on my clit—"just like that."

And I do. With a strangled moan, I climax around his fingers, the hard edges of his short, blunt nails digging into my rippling flesh. My visions blurs, my skin prickling with heated needles as I ride the wave of sensations, and then I sag in his grasp, held upright only by his hand in my hair and his fingers inside my body.

"There you go," he says thickly, and as the world comes back into focus, I see that he's watching me intently. "That was nice, wasn't it?"

I can't even manage a nod, but he doesn't seem to need my confirmation. And why would he? I can feel the slickness inside me, the wetness that coats those rough male fingers—fingers that he withdraws from me slowly, watching my face the whole time. I want to close my eyes, or at least look away from that penetrating gaze, but I can't.

Not without letting him know how much he frightens me.

So instead of backing down, I study him in return, seeing the signs of arousal on his strong features. His jaw is clenched tight as he stares at me, a tiny muscle pulsing near his right ear. And even through the sun-bronzed hue of his skin, I can see heightened color on his blade-like cheekbones.

He wants me badly—and that knowledge emboldens me to act.

Reaching down, I cup the hard bulge at the crotch of his jeans. "It *was* nice," I whisper, looking up at him. "And now it's your turn."

His pupils dilate even more, his chest inflating with a deep breath. "Yes." His voice is thick with lust as he uses his grip on my hair to drag me closer. "Yes, I think it is." And before I can reconsider the wisdom of my blatant provocation, he lowers his head and captures my mouth with his.

I gasp, my lips parting from surprise, and he immediately takes advantage, deepening the kiss. His hard-looking mouth is surprisingly soft on mine, his lips warm and smooth as his tongue hungrily explores the interior of my mouth. There's skill and confidence in that kiss; it's the kiss of a man who knows how to please a woman, how to seduce her with nothing more than the touch of his lips.

The heat simmering within me intensifies, the tension rising inside me once more. He's holding me so close that my bare breasts are pressing against his sweater, the wool rubbing against my peaked nipples. I can feel his erection through the rough material of his jeans; it pushes into my lower belly, revealing how much he wants me, how thin his pretense of control really is. Dimly, I realize the robe fell off my shoulders, leaving me completely naked, and then I forget all about it as he makes a low growling sound deep in his throat and pushes me against the wall.

The shock of the cold surface at my back clears my mind for a second, but he's already unzipping his jeans, his knees wedging between my legs and spreading them open as he raises his head to look at me. I hear the ripping sound of a foil packet being opened, and then he cups my ass and lifts me off the ground. Instinctively, I grab at his shoulders, my heartbeat quickening as he orders hoarsely, "Wrap your legs around me"—and lowers me onto his stiff cock, all the while holding my gaze.

His thrust is hard and deep, penetrating me all the way. My breathing stutters at the force of it, at the uncompromising brutality of the invasion. My inner muscles clench around him, futilely trying to keep him out. His cock is as big as the rest of him, so long and thick it stretches me to the point of pain. If I hadn't been so wet, he would've torn me. But I *am* wet, and after a couple of moments, my body begins to soften, adjusting to his thickness. Unconsciously, my legs come up, clasping his hips as he instructed, and the new position lets him slide even deeper into me, making me cry out at the sharp sensation.

He begins to move then, his eyes glittering as he stares at me. Each thrust is as hard as the one that joined us together, yet my body no longer tries to fight it. Instead, it brings forth more moisture, easing his way. Each time he slams into me, his groin presses against my sex, putting pressure on my clit, and the tension in my core returns, growing with every second. Stunned, I realize I'm about to have my second orgasm... and then I do, the tension peaking and exploding, scattering my thoughts and electrifying my nerve endings.

I can feel my own pulsations, the way my muscles squeeze and release his cock, and then I see his eyes go unfocused as he stops thrusting. A hoarse, deep groan escapes his throat as he grinds into me, and I know he's found his release as well, my orgasm driving him over the edge.

My chest heaving, I stare up at him, watching as his pale blue eyes refocus on me. He's still inside me, and all of a sudden, the intimacy of that is unbearable. He's nobody to me, a stranger, yet he fucked me.

He fucked me, and I let him because it's my job.

Swallowing, I push at his chest, my legs unwrapping from around his waist. "Please, let me down." I know I should be cooing at him and stroking his ego. I should be telling him how amazing it was, how he gave me more pleasure than anyone I've known. It wouldn't even be a lie—I've never come twice with a man before. But I can't bring myself to do that. I feel too raw, too invaded.

With this man, I'm not in control, and that knowledge scares me.

I don't know if he senses that, or if he just wants to toy with me, but a sardonic smile appears on his lips.

"It's too late for regrets, beautiful," he murmurs, and before I can respond, he lets me down and releases his grip on my ass. His softening cock slips out of my body as he steps back, and I watch, my breathing still uneven, as he casually takes the condom off and drops it on the floor.

For some reason, his action makes me flush. There's something so wrong, so dirty about that condom lying there. Perhaps it's because I feel like that condom: used and discarded. Spotting my robe on the floor, I move to pick it up, but Lucas's hand on my arm stops me.

"What are you doing?" he asks, gazing at me. He doesn't seem the least bit concerned that his jeans are still unzipped and his cock is hanging out. "We're not done yet."

My heart skips a beat. "We're not?"

"No," he says, stepping closer. To my shock, I feel him hardening against my stomach. "We're far from done."

And using his grip on my arm, he steers me toward the bed.

4

 *ulia*

My mind in turmoil, I sit on the edge of the bed and watch Lucas undress.

First, he pulls off his sweater, revealing a tight T-shirt stretched across his muscular chest. Next, he takes off his shoes and pushes down his jeans and black briefs. His legs are as powerful as they'd appeared through his clothes, thick with muscle and as darkly tanned as his face. His cock, already hard again, is jutting out from a nest of brownish-blond hair at his groin, and as he pulls off his T-shirt, I see sharply defined abs and sculpted chest.

Lucas Kent has the body of an athlete, beautiful in its uncompromising strength.

As I watch him, I become aware of a strange urge to touch him. Not in an effort to please him or because it's expected of me, but because I want to. I want to know how his muscles feel under my fingertips, whether his bronzed skin is smooth or rough. I want to lick his neck, tongue the hollow above his collarbone, and find out how that warm-looking skin tastes.

It makes no sense, but I want him. I want him even though I'm sore from his rough fucking, even though he should be an assignment, nothing more.

He steps out of his jeans and briefs and kicks them aside, then comes toward me. I don't move as he approaches me. I hardly even breathe. When he's next to me, he stops and sinks to his haunches. "Lie back," he murmurs, grasping my calves, and before I have a chance to realize what he's doing, he pulls me toward him, not stopping until my ass is partially hanging off the mattress.

"What are you—" I begin to say, but he ignores me, using one strong hand to push me down on the mattress. I fall onto my back, my heart hammering, and then I feel it.

His warm breath on my sex as he pulls my thighs apart.

My breathing quickens again, heat surging through my body as he presses a kiss to my closed folds, his lips soft and gentle. There's barely any pressure on my clit, but I'm so sensitive from my earlier orgasms that even that light touch sends my nerves zinging. I gasp, arching toward him, and he laughs softly, the low, masculine sound creating vibrations that travel through my flesh, adding to the growing ache within me.

"Lucas, wait." My voice is breathless, panicked from the need he's invoking within me. The ceiling blurs in front of my eyes. "Wait, don't—"

He ignores me once again, his tongue sweeping over my slit and delving into my opening. As he begins to fuck me with his tongue, I forget what I was going to say. I forget everything. My eyes squeeze shut, and the world around me disappears, leaving only darkness and the feel of his tongue dipping in and out of my soaked pussy. The fire burning within me is white-hot, my flesh so swollen and sensitized that his tongue feels as big as a cock. Except it's softer, more flexible—and as he moves that tongue higher, circling my clit, I tense, feeling like a string being wound tighter and tighter.

"Lucas, please..." The words come out in a begging moan. I don't know what I'm asking for, but he seems to—because he closes his lips around my throbbing clit and sucks on it. Lightly, gently, using only his lips as his tongue laves the underside of it. And it's enough. It's more than enough. My toes curl, the tension gathering into a pulsing ball in my sex as I arch up—and then I come with a choked cry, the orgasm blasting through me with stunning force. Every cell in my body fills with the pulsing pleasure of release, and my heart gallops in my chest.

Before I can recover, he flips me onto my stomach, bending me over the edge of the bed. Then I hear another foil packet ripping and a second later, he drives into me, his thick cock spearing me, stretching me once more. I gasp, my hands fisting the sheets as he takes me with a hard, fast rhythm, pounding into me so hard it should hurt—except my body is beyond that now. All I feel is need. I'm awash in it, drunk on the sensations he's wringing from my flesh. As he thrusts into me, his movements force my sex against the edge of the mattress, putting rhythmic pressure on my clit, and I explode again, screaming his name. But he doesn't stop.

He just keeps fucking me, his fingers digging into my hips as he drives into me, again and again.

I WAKE UP TANGLED WITH HIM, OUR BODIES GLUED TOGETHER WITH sticky sweat. I don't remember falling asleep in his embrace, but it must've happened, because that's where I am now, surrounded by his powerful body.

It's dark, and he's asleep. I can hear his even breathing and feel the rise and fall of his chest as my head rests on his shoulder. My mouth is dry and my bladder is full, so I try to wiggle out from under his heavy arm—which immediately tightens around me.

"Where are you going?" Lucas's voice is hoarse, roughened with sleep.

"To the bathroom," I explain cautiously. "I have to pee."

He lifts his arm and moves his leg off my calves. "All right. Go."

I scoot away from him and sit up, wincing at the soreness I feel deep inside. I don't know how long he fucked me that second time, but it could've easily been an hour or more. I lost count of how many times I came, the orgasms melding together into one never-ending wave of peaks and valleys.

My legs are unsteady as I stand up, my inner thighs aching from being stretched wide. After fucking me from behind, he turned me over and grabbed my ankles, holding my legs open as he drove into me, thrusting so deeply that I begged him to stop. He didn't, of course. He just shifted his hips, changing the angle of his strokes to hit that sensitive spot within me, and I forgot all about the pain, lost in the overwhelming pleasure of his hard possession.

Inhaling deeply, I force myself back to the present, my bladder reminding me of another overwhelming need. Shakily, I walk to the bathroom and relieve myself. Then I wash my hands, brush my teeth, and splash cold water on my face, trying to regain my equilibrium.

Everything is fine, I tell myself as I stare at my pale face in the mirror. Everything is going according to plan. Great sex is a bonus, not a problem. So what if this ruthless stranger can make me respond this way? It doesn't mean anything. It's just fucking, a meaningless physical act.

Except with him it isn't meaningless.

No. Squeezing my eyes shut, I force that voice away and splash more water on my face, washing away the doubts. I have a job to do, and there's nothing wrong with treating this night as a perk of that job.

There's nothing wrong with letting myself feel pleasure—as long as I don't let it mean anything.

Feeling marginally more like myself, I make my way back to the bed, where Lucas is waiting for me. As soon as I lie down next to him, he pulls me against him, curving his body around me from the back and covering us both with a blanket. I let out a sigh of enjoyment as his warmth surrounds me. The man is like a furnace, generating so much heat that I instantly feel toasty, the ever-present chill inside my apartment forgotten.

"When are you leaving?" I ask softly as he arranges me more comfortably, settling my head on his outstretched arm and draping his other arm over my hip. This is what I need to know from him, what I owe Obenko for my failure, yet something tightens within me as I wait for Lucas's answer.

That pang of emotion—it can't be regret at the thought of him leaving.

That wouldn't make sense.

Lucas nuzzles my ear. "In the morning," he whispers, his teeth grazing over my earlobe. His breath sends a warm shiver through me. "I have to be out of here in a couple of hours."

"Oh." Ignoring the irrational twinge of sadness, I do quick mental math. According to the digital clock on my nightstand, it's a little after four a.m. If he has to leave my apartment around six, then their plane must be departing at eight or nine in the morning.

Obenko doesn't have much time to do whatever he plans to do to Esguerra.

"You can't stay longer?" I turn my head to brush my lips against Lucas's outstretched arm. It's the kind of question a woman who has feelings for a man might ask, so I'm not afraid it would raise his suspicions.

He chuckles softly. "No, beautiful, I can't. You should be glad of that"—his arm on top of me shifts, his hand sliding down to palm my sex—"given how sore you said you are."

I swallow, remembering how toward the end of that marathon sex session I pleaded for mercy, my insides raw from so much fucking. Incredibly, I feel a twinge of renewed sensation at the memory—and at the touch of that big, strong hand between my legs.

"I *am* sore," I whisper, hoping he would stop and at the same time, hoping he wouldn't.

To my relief and disappointment, he moves his hand back to my hip, even though I feel his cock stirring against my ass. The man is a sexual machine, unstoppable in his lust. According to the file I've been given, he's thirty-four years old. Most men past their teenage years don't want to have sex three times a night. Once, twice maybe. But three times? His cock shouldn't harden with so little provocation.

It makes me wonder how long it's been since Lucas Kent's had a woman.

"Are you going to return any time soon?" I ask, pushing that thought aside. It's ridiculous, but the idea of him being with other women—of him giving them the kind of pleasure he gave me—makes my chest tighten in an unpleasant way.

"I don't know," he says, shifting so that his semi-hard erection is wedged more comfortably against my ass. "Maybe one day."

"I see." I stare into the darkness, battling the part of me that wants to bawl like a child deprived of her favorite toy. This is not real, none of it is real. Even if I were truly an interpreter, I'd know this is nothing more than a one-night stand. But I'm not the carefree, easy girl I'm pretending to be. I didn't have sex with him for fun; I did it to get information—and now that I have it, I need to get it to Obenko right away.

As Lucas's breathing evens out, signifying that he's asleep again, I carefully reach for my phone. It's sitting on the nightstand less than a couple of feet away, and I manage to grab it without disturbing Lucas, who's still holding me against him. Ignoring the growing ache in my chest, I type out a coded message to Obenko, letting him know that Kent is with me and what time they're planning to depart.

If my boss is planning to strike at Esguerra, now is as good a time as any, since at least one man from Esguerra's security team is out of the way.

As soon as the text message goes out, I erase it from my phone and put the device back on the nightstand. Then I close my eyes and force myself to relax against Lucas's hard body.

My assignment is done, for better or for worse.

5

I WAKE UP TO THE UNFAMILIAR FEEL OF A SLENDER BODY IN MY ARMS and the faint smell of peaches in my nostrils. Opening my eyes, I see tangled blond hair spread across the pillow in front of me and a slim, pale shoulder peeking out from under the blanket.

For a moment, the sight startles me, but then I remember.

I'm with Yulia Tzakova, the interpreter the Russians hired for yesterday's meeting.

Memories of last night rush into my brain, making my blood surge.

Fuck, it had been hot. More than hot. Scorching.

Everything about her had been perfect, the sex so intense that just thinking of it makes me hard. I don't know what I had been expecting when I showed up on her doorstep, but what happened last night wasn't it.

I had watched her all through the meeting, enjoying the way she translated so effortlessly, her voice smooth and unaccented. It wasn't a surprise that she caught my attention. I've always liked tall, leggy blondes, and Yulia Tzakova is as beautiful as they come, with her clear blue eyes and fine bone structure. She didn't really eat during the meal, just nibbled on a couple of the appetizers, but she drank tea, and I found myself staring at her pink, glossy lips touching the rim of her porcelain cup... at the smooth white column of her throat moving as she swallowed. I wanted to feel those lips closing around the base of my cock and see her throat move as she swallowed my cum. I wanted to strip off her elegant clothes and bend her over the table, to fist that long, silky hair as I drove into her, fucking her until she screamed and came.

I wanted *her*—and she seemed to have eyes only for Esguerra.

Even now, the knowledge that she came on to my boss leaves a bitter taste in my mouth. It shouldn't matter. Esguerra's always been a chick magnet, and I've never minded that. It amuses me, in fact, the way women throw themselves at him, even when they suspect what he's really like. Even his new wife—a pretty, petite American girl he kidnapped almost two years ago—seems to have fallen for him. It's only logical that Yulia would try for him—or at least that's what I told myself as I watched her eye Esguerra all through the meeting.

If she wanted him, she was welcome to him.

Except he didn't want *her*. It surprised me, that last part, even though over the past two years I haven't actually seen him hook up with any woman. He would just go to his private island all the time. It wasn't until a few months ago that I learned he kept his American girl there, the one he ended up marrying. The girl—Nora—must've been taking care of his needs all along. Must still be taking care of them exceptionally well, given that Esguerra didn't spare Yulia so much as a glance.

I was tempted to forget the interpreter as well—except he asked me to frisk her. She stood there shivering in her elegant coat, and I got a chance to feel her, to run my hands over her body in search of weapons. There were none, but her breathing changed as I touched her. She didn't look at me, didn't move, but I could feel a slight hitch in her breathing and see her pale cheeks brighten with a hint of color. Up until then, I didn't think she was aware of me as a man at all, but that moment made me realize that she was —and that she was fighting the attraction for some reason. So when Esguerra turned down her invitation, I made the impulsive decision to take her for myself.

Just for one night, just to appease the craving.

It wasn't difficult to get her address—all it took was one call to Buschekov—and then I showed up on her doorstep, expecting to see the same put-together, confident young woman who flirted with my boss.

Except that wasn't who greeted me.

It was a girl who looked barely out of her teens, her beautiful face devoid of any makeup and her tall, slender body swathed in a decidedly inelegant robe. She let me into her apartment after I explicitly told her what I wanted, but the look in her wide blue eyes was that of a hunted rabbit. For a minute, I doubted whether she wanted me there at all; she seemed as nervous as said rabbit confronting a fox. Her anxiety was so palpable, I wondered if I'd made a mistake coming to her, if I'd somehow misread either the extent of her experience or the level of her interest in me.

Just one touch, I told myself as she took my coat. Just one touch, and if she didn't want me, I'd leave. I'd never forced a woman in my life, and I didn't intend to start with this girl—a girl who seemed oddly innocent despite her corrupt Kremlin connections.

A girl I wanted more with every second.

I told myself I'd stop with that one touch, but as soon as I touched her, I knew I'd lied. Her creamy skin had been baby soft, the bones of her jaw so delicate they were almost fragile. My hand looked brown and rough against her pale perfection, my palm so big I could've crushed her face with one hard squeeze of my fingers.

She froze at my touch, and I could see the pulse beating at the side of her neck. When I'd patted her down earlier, she smelled expensive, like some fancy perfume, but that was no longer the case. Standing there in front of me, her cheeks colored pink, she smelled like peaches and innocence. Logically, I knew it had to be some soap from her bath, but my mouth still watered with the urge to lick her, to taste that clean, fruit-scented flesh.

To see what was hidden under her big, unsexy robe.

She said something about a drink, or maybe it was coffee, but I barely heard her words, all my attention on the strip of pale skin visible at the top of her robe. "No," I said on autopilot, "no coffee," and then I reached for the tie of her robe, my hands acting seemingly of their own accord.

The garment fell apart at a light tug, revealing a body straight out of my wet dreams. High, full breasts tipped by hard pink nipples, a waist small enough to span with my hands, gently curving hips, and long, long legs. And between those legs, not even a hint of hair, just the smooth, bare mound of her pussy.

My dick got so hard it hurt.

She pinkened even more, a flush appearing on her face and chest, and whatever self-control I still had evaporated. I touched her breast, flicked my thumb over her nipple, and watched her pupils expand, turning her blue eyes darker.

She was responding to me. Still scared, perhaps, but responding.

It wasn't much, but it was enough. I couldn't have walked away at that point if a bomb had gone off next to us.

"You're very direct, aren't you?" she whispered, staring up at me, and I told her I didn't have time for games. It was true—if only because the lust I felt was more intense, more violent than anything I'd known before. At that moment, I would've done anything to have her, crossed any line... committed any crime.

"And if I say no?" she asked, her voice shaking slightly, and it took everything I had to ask if she was, in fact, saying no. I managed to keep my tone calm, gently circling her nipple with my thumb as I slid my hand into her hair, but she didn't give me a straight answer. Instead, she asked me what I'd do in that case, whether I would leave.

"What do you think?" I asked, stalling as I tried to figure out the answer, but she didn't reply. She must've sensed the violent hunger brewing within me and decided to stop teasing me. I could see the acceptance in her eyes, feel the way she swayed toward me, as if granting me permission.

And so I touched her, felt the soft, warm heat between her legs.

Penetrated her tight pussy with my finger and felt the wetness there.

She did want me—unless that wetness wasn't for me.

Unless she was thinking of Esguerra at that moment.

The thought filled me with black rage. "Do you always get so wet for men you don't want?" I asked, unable to conceal my irrational jealousy, and she said she did want me. She'd wanted Esguerra before, and now she wanted me.

"Does that bother you?" she asked, and for the first time since my arrival at her apartment, she seemed like the experienced, confident woman from the restaurant instead of the scared girl who greeted me at the door.

The dichotomy both fascinated and aroused me, even as rage continued to burn in my veins. "No," I said, pushing another finger into her slick channel and finding her clit with my thumb. "Not at all."

Her eyes went soft, unfocused, and I could feel her pussy squeezing my fingers, getting even wetter at my touch. Her hands grabbed my arm as though she wanted to stop me, but her body welcomed my touch. I watched her carefully, observing every flicker of expression on her face, listening to every gasp and moan as I worked my fingers inside and around her pussy. She was responsive, so fucking responsive that it took me no time at all to learn what she liked, what made her cream around my fingers. I could feel her body beginning to tighten, see her breathing coming faster, and my cock got so hard it felt like it would burst.

"Yes, that's it." I pressed hard on her clit. "Come for me, beautiful, just like that."

And she did. Her gaze turned distant, unseeing, and her pussy rippled around my fingers. I held her until her contractions stopped, my hand still grasping her silky hair, and then I said with satisfaction, "There you go. That was nice, wasn't it?"

She didn't answer me at first, and for a moment, I wondered again if I'd misread her, if I was somehow forcing her into this. But then she reached out and boldly cupped my balls through my jeans. "It *was* nice," she whispered, looking up at me. "And now it's your turn."

It was all the invitation I needed. I felt like a beast unleashed, but somehow I managed to kiss her in a semi-civilized manner, tasting her lips instead of devouring them, as everything inside me clamored to do. Her mouth was delicious, like warm tea and honey, and for a minute, I was able to maintain some semblance of control, to pretend I wasn't a lust-filled savage.

Except I was—and when her robe fell off her shoulders, I snapped, pushing her against the wall. It was only by the habit of two decades that I remembered to put on a condom, and then I was lifting her and telling her to wrap her legs around me as I thrust into her, unable to wait even a second longer.

She was tight around me, so unbelievably tight and hot that I almost came right then and there, especially when her pussy clenched around me, her body tensing at my entry. Worried that I'd hurt her, I stopped for a moment, waiting until her legs came up to clasp my hips, and then I began fucking her in earnest, driven by a hunger more powerful than anything I'd experienced before. I wanted to be so deep inside I'd never come out, to take her so hard I'd leave my imprint on her flesh.

I watched her as I fucked her, and I knew the exact moment she reached her peak. Her eyes widened, as though in surprise, and then I felt her pussy undulating, spasming around my cock. The sensation was so intense I couldn't hold back my own orgasm. It washed over me uncontrollably, rocketing out from my balls, and I ground my pelvis into her, needing to be as deep as humanly possible, to meld with her in this explosive, mind-bending pleasure.

It was the best climax of my life. I felt high, consumed with her taste, her feel, and for a few moments, I thought it was the same for her—but then she pushed at me. "Please, let me down," she said, looking distressed, and it was like a bucket of ice water thrown over my head.

I gave her two orgasms, and she was looking at me like I raped her.

Like I fucking assaulted her in a back alley.

Something inside me twisted and hardened. Curving my lips in a sardonic smile, I said, "It's too late for regrets, beautiful." Lowering her to her feet, I forced my hands away from her firm, shapely ass. My cock slipped out of her as I stepped back, and the condom, filled with my seed, began to feel loose.

I pulled it off, dropping it on the floor. Her eyes followed the movement, and I saw a flush creep across her face again. She was embarrassed by what happened, I realized, and my anger intensified.

She invited me in, said she wanted me—*her body fucking told me she wanted me*—and now she was acting like it was all some big mistake.

Like she couldn't get away from me fast enough.

Well, fuck that, I decided, my blood boiling with a mixture of fury and renewed lust. If she thought I'd let her get away with that shit, she was very much mistaken.

And for the rest of the night, I dedicated myself to showing her just how mistaken she was. I licked her pussy and fucked her until she begged me to stop, until her voice was hoarse from screaming my name and my dick was raw from pounding into her tight flesh. I made her come half a dozen times before I allowed myself my second release, and then I had to restrain myself from taking her for the third time when she woke up to use the restroom.

I had to restrain myself because somehow, impossibly, I wanted more.

I still want more.

Son of a bitch. I told Yulia I might return one day, but if this insane hunger doesn't go away, I'll have to come back to Moscow sooner than planned—maybe as soon as we're done in Tajikistan.

Yes, that's it, I decide as I get up and start getting dressed.

I'll do my job, and then, if the Russian girl is still on my mind, I'll come back for her.

6

ulia

I PRETEND TO BE ASLEEP AS LUCAS GETS DRESSED AND QUIETLY LETS himself out of my apartment. When he closes the door behind him, I hear the automatic lock click into place. I'm grateful that he set it. In Moscow, it's not safe to leave the door open for even a few minutes. Criminals are bold, resourceful, and seemingly omnipresent.

I lie with my eyes closed for another minute to make sure Lucas is not coming back, and then I jump out of bed, ignoring the twinge of soreness between my legs. Automatically, my thoughts turn to the source of that soreness, and I'm once again cognizant of that strange pang of sadness.

Odds are, I'll never see Lucas Kent again.

Stop it, I scold myself. There's no reason to dwell on him. We had sex, nothing more. What I need to do now is find out if

Obenko had a chance to strike at Esguerra while Kent was out of the way. If so, my gig here will finally be up. My cover is strong, but once the Russians realize there's been a leak, I'll fall under suspicion.

I call Obenko while I'm getting dressed. "Anything new?" I ask when he picks up.

"We have a plan," he says. "We were able to track down Esguerra's Boeing C-17—it's the only private plane of that size scheduled to take off in the next couple of hours. Our contact in Uzbekistan will take care of the rest."

I pause in the middle of zipping up my boots. "What do you mean?"

"The Uzbekistani military will fire a missile when they fly over their airspace," Obenko says. "Accidentally, of course. The Russians won't be pleased, but they won't go to war over one arms dealer. Our contact will get jail time and a demotion, but his family will be well compensated for his trouble."

"You're going to shoot down Esguerra's plane?" A cold knot forms in my throat. I don't care what happens to Esguerra, but the thought of Lucas dying in a tangle of crushed metal or being blown into bits...

"Yes. It would be too risky to attack him here. He has four dozen mercenaries with him. There's no way we can get to him otherwise."

"I see." I feel cold all over, as though someone walked over my grave. "So they'll all die."

"If everything goes according to plan, yes. We'll eliminate the threat in one shot and without any casualties on our end."

"Right." I try to inject a note of appropriate enthusiasm into my voice, but I don't know if I succeed. All I can think about is Lucas's big body burned and broken, his pale eyes staring unseeing at the sky. It shouldn't matter—he's nothing to me—but I can't get that gruesome image out of my mind.

"We need to exfiltrate you," Obenko says, bringing my attention back to him. "If the Russians begin really digging and our Uzbekistani contact decides to talk, it won't take them long to figure out how the information got to us. It's unfortunate, but we always knew this was a risk with this specific assignment."

"All right." I squeeze my eyes shut and rub the bridge of my nose. "Where do I meet the team?"

"Take the train to Kon'kovo. We'll have a car ready for you there." And the phone goes silent in my hand.

IT TAKES ME LESS THAN TWENTY MINUTES TO PACK. I'VE LIVED IN Moscow for six years, but I've acquired few possessions I care about. Some makeup, a hairbrush, a change of underwear, my fake passport, my gun—that's all that goes into my large Gucci handbag. I also make sure that the clothes I'm wearing—designer jeans tucked into knee-high flat boots, a cashmere sweater, and a thick, well-fitting parka—are both warm and stylish. In case anyone sees me leaving the apartment, I'll look much as they'd expect: a young woman heading off to work, bundled up against the brutal cold.

After I'm done packing, I wipe down the entire apartment to erase my fingerprints and walk out, carefully locking the door behind me. I no longer care if thieves break in, but there's no need to make it easy for them.

Nobody seems to be watching the apartment as I exit onto the street, but I still keep a wary eye on my surroundings, making sure I'm not being followed.

As I approach the metro station, thoughts of Lucas intrude again, making me shiver despite my warm clothing. I should be happy—I've been looking forward to exfiltration for months—but I can't get my mind off Lucas's fate.

Will he die fast or slowly? Is it going to be the missile that kills him, or the crash itself? Will he stay conscious long enough to realize he's about to die?

Will he guess I had something to do with what happened?

The knot in my throat expands, making me feel like I'm choking. For one insane moment, I'm seized by an overwhelming urge to call him, to warn him not to get on that plane. I actually reach for the phone in my bag before I jerk my hand away, sticking it in my pocket instead.

Stupid, stupid, stupid, I chide myself as I walk down the stairs into the metro station. I don't even have Kent's number. And even if I did, warning him would mean betraying Obenko and my country.

Betraying Misha.

No, never. I take a steadying breath, ignoring the crush of Moscow commuters all around me. At this point, the operation is out of my hands. Even if I wanted to change something, I can't. Obenko and his team are in control now, and the best I can hope for is a speedy exit from Russia.

Besides, even if Lucas Kent wasn't affiliated with the arms dealer who just became Ukraine's enemy, there's no room in my life for romance of any kind. Whether Kent is dead or alive shouldn't matter—because either way, I won't see him again.

The approach of the train drags me out of my dark musings. The people around me press forward, pushing their way onto the crowded train, and I hurry to make sure I squeeze in before the doors close.

Thankfully, I make it. Grabbing onto a rail, I wedge myself into a space between two middle-aged women and do my best to ignore a leer from an old man sitting in front of me. Another couple of hours, and I won't need to put up with the Moscow metro system.

I'll be on my way to Kiev, where I belong.

I close my eyes and try to focus on that—on coming home.

On being near Misha, even if I can't meet with him in person.

My baby brother is fourteen now. I've seen his photos; he's a handsome teenage boy, his blue eyes bright and mischievous. In all the pictures, he's always laughing, hanging out with his friends and his girlfriends. He's social, Obenko tells me. Outgoing.

Happy with the life they've given him.

Each time I receive one of those pictures, I stare at it for hours, wondering if he remembers me. If he'd recognize me if I approached him on the street. It's unlikely—he was only three when he was adopted—but I still like to imagine that some part of him would know me.

That he'd recall the way I took care of him that one brutal year in the orphanage.

A crackling announcement interrupts my musings. Opening my eyes, I realize that the train is slowing down.

"We apologize for the delay," the conductor repeats loudly as the train comes to a complete halt. "The issue should get resolved shortly."

The passengers around me groan in unison. The middle-aged woman to my left begins swearing, while the one to my right mutters something about corrupt officials pocketing public funds instead of fixing things. It's not the first delay this month; the extreme temperatures this winter have taken a toll on both roads and underground metro tracks, exacerbating the commuting nightmare that is Moscow at rush hour.

I suppress my own sigh of impatience and check my phone. As expected, I have zero bars. The thick walls of the tunnel block out all cell phone reception, so I can't notify my handlers of the delay.

Great. Just great.

I put the phone away, trying not to give in to my frustration. With any luck, this problem is something that requires a little welding, rather than something more serious. Last month, a burst pipe snarled traffic all over Moscow, causing metro delays of three hours or more. If it's something along those lines again, I might not get to my pickup location until late this afternoon.

Against my will, my thoughts turn to Lucas again. By late afternoon, his plane will likely be flying over the Uzbekistani airspace.

He might even be dead by then. My stomach churns with acid as I picture his body torn into pieces, destroyed by the explosion and the crash.

Stop it, Yulia. The churning in my stomach intensifies, turning into an empty rumble, and I realize with relief that I forgot to eat breakfast this morning. I was in such a rush to pack and get going that I didn't have so much as a bite of an apple.

No wonder I'm feeling sick. It has nothing to do with Kent and everything to do with the fact that I'm hungry.

Yes, that's it, I tell myself. I'm just hungry. Once the train starts moving again and I get to my destination, I'll grab some food and everything will be fine.

I'll be safely in Kiev, and I won't think of Lucas Kent ever again.

7

ucas

By the time I get to the plane, the whole team, including Esguerra, is already on board and dressed in combat gear. The suits are bulletproof and flame-retardant—which makes them ridiculously expensive. I'm grateful Esguerra insists on them for every mission; they help minimize casualties among our men.

I'm the last one on board, and I'm piloting the plane, so as soon as I get suited up, we take off for Tajikistan, where the terrorist organization of Al-Quadar has its latest stronghold. Esguerra sniffed it out recently, and since the idiots fucked with him by kidnapping his wife a few months back, he's determined to wipe them off the map. The Russians granted us safe passage—that's what that meeting with Buschekov was about—so I'm not expecting any trouble. Still, I keep an eye on the radar as we get farther away from Moscow and closer to Central Asia.

In this part of the world, one can never be too careful.

Once we're at our cruising altitude, I put the plane on autopilot and check all of my weapons, taking each one apart to clean it before putting it back together. It's one of the first things I learned in the Navy: make sure your guns are good to go before every battle. Esguerra's equipment is top notch, and I've never had it malfunction on me, but there's always a first time.

Satisfied that everything is in good shape, I put the weapons away and glance at the radar again.

Nothing out of the ordinary.

Leaning back in my seat, I stretch out my legs. I can already feel it—the beginnings of the adrenaline burn, the buzz of excitement deep in my veins.

The anticipation that grips me before every fight.

My mind and body are already preparing for it, even though we still have a few hours before we get to our destination.

This is what I was made for, what I love to do. Fighting is in my blood. That's why I enlisted in the Navy right out of high school, why I couldn't stand the thought of following the path my parents laid out for me. College, law school, joining my grandfather's prestigious law firm—I couldn't imagine myself doing any of those things. I would've suffocated in that kind of life, choked to death in the stuffy, elite boardrooms of Manhattan.

My family didn't understand, of course. For them, corporate law—and the money and prestige that comes with it—is the pinnacle of success. They couldn't comprehend why I'd want to do anything else, why I'd want to be anything other than their golden child.

"If you don't want to go into law, you could try for medical school," my father said when I expressed my concerns to him in eleventh grade. "Or if you don't want to be in school for so long, you could go into investment banking. I can get you an internship at Goldman Sachs this summer—it would look great on your Princeton application."

I didn't take him up on his offer. I didn't know at that point where I belonged, but I knew it wasn't at Goldman Sachs, and it wasn't at Princeton or the prep school my parents paid through the nose to have me attend. I was different from my classmates. Too restless, too full of pent-up energy. I played every sport there was, took every martial art class I could find, but it wasn't enough.

Something was still missing.

I discovered what that something was late one night during my senior year, when I was stumbling home drunk from a party in Brooklyn. In an empty subway station, I was attacked by a group of thugs hoping to score some easy cash off a kid from the Upper East Side. They were armed with knives, and I had nothing, but I was too drunk to care. Whatever training I received in those martial art classes kicked in, and I found myself in the first real fight of my life.

A fight where I ended up knifing a man and seeing his blood spill over my hands.

A fight where I learned the extent of the violence living within me.

WE'RE FLYING OVER UZBEKISTAN, JUST A FEW HUNDRED MILES FROM our destination, when Esguerra comes into the pilot's cabin.

Hearing the door open, I turn to face him. "We're on track to get there in about an hour and a half," I say, preempting his question. "There is some ice on the landing strip, so they're de-icing it for us right now. The helicopters are already fueled up and ready to go."

We need those helicopters to get to the Pamir Mountains, where we suspect the terrorist hideout to be.

"Excellent," Esguerra says, his blue eyes gleaming. "Any unusual activities in that area?"

I shake my head. "No, everything is quiet."

"Good." He enters the cabin and sits down in the copilot's seat. "How was the Russian girl last night?" he asks, buckling his seatbelt.

I feel a momentary stab of jealousy, but then I remember how Yulia responded to me all night long. "Quite satisfying," I say, smiling at the images filling my mind. "You missed out."

"Yes, I'm sure," he says, but I can see that he's not the least bit sorry. The man is obsessed with his young wife. I have a feeling the most beautiful woman in the world could parade naked in front of him, and he wouldn't so much as blink. Esguerra's been well and truly caught—and by a girl he's been keeping captive, no less.

The thought makes me grin. "I have to say, I never expected to see you as a happily married man," I tell him, amused by the idea.

Esguerra lifts his eyebrows. "Is that right?"

I shrug, my grin fading. I'm not exactly friends with my boss—I've never known Esguerra to be particularly friendly with anyone—but for some reason, he seems more approachable today.

Or maybe I'm just in a good mood, thanks to one gorgeous interpreter.

"Sure," I say to Esguerra. "People like us aren't generally considered good husband material."

In fact, I can't think of two individuals less suited to domestic life.

Esguerra chuckles. "Well, I don't know if, strictly speaking, Nora considers me 'good husband material.'"

"Well, if she doesn't, then she should." I turn back to the controls. "You don't cheat, you take good care of her, and you've risked your life to save her before. If that's not being a good husband, then I don't know what is." As I speak, I notice a flicker of movement on the radar screen.

Frowning, I peer at it closer.

"What is it?" Esguerra's tone sharpens.

"I'm not sure," I begin saying, and at that moment, a violent jolt rocks the plane, nearly throwing me out of my seat. The plane tilts, angling down sharply, and adrenaline explodes in my veins as I hear the frantic beeping of controls gone haywire.

We've been hit.

The thought is crystal clear in my mind.

Grabbing the controls, I try to right the plane as we plunge through a thick layer of clouds. My heartbeat is rocket fast, its pounding audible in my ears. "Shit, fuck, shit, shit, motherfucking shit—"

"What hit us?" Esguerra sounds calm, almost disinterested. I can hear the engines grinding and sputtering, and then the smell of smoke reaches me, along with the sound of screams.

We're on fire.

Fucking fuck.

"I'm not sure," I manage to say. The plane is nosediving, and I can't get it to straighten out for longer than a second. "Does it fucking matter?"

The plane shakes, the engines emitting a terrifying sputtering noise as we head straight for the ground below. The peaks of Pamir Mountains are already visible in the distance, but we're too far to make it there.

We're going to crash before we reach our goal.

Fuck, no. I'm not ready to die.

Cursing, I resume wrestling with the controls, ignoring the readouts that inform me of the futility of my efforts. The plane evens out under my guidance, the engines kicking in for a brief moment, but then we nosedive again. I repeat the maneuver, calling on all my years of piloting experience, but it's futile.

All I manage to do is slow our descent by a few seconds.

They say your life flashes in front of your eyes before your death. They say you think of all the things you could've done differently, all the things you haven't had a chance to do.

I don't think about any of that.

I'm too consumed with surviving for as long as I can.

Beside me Esguerra is silent, his hands gripping the edge of his seat as the ground rushes toward us, the small objects below looming ever larger. I can make out the trees—we're over a forest now—and then I see individual branches, stripped of leaves and covered with snow.

We're close now, so close, and I make one last attempt to guide the plane, directing it to a cluster of smaller trees and bushes a hundred yards away.

And then we're there, crashing through the trees with bone-shattering force.

Strangely, my last thought is of her.

The Russian girl I'll never see again.

II

THE DETAINMENT

8

ulia

SEVEN AND A HALF HOURS.

The train was stuck in that tunnel for seven and a half hours. The relief I feel as the doors finally open at the next station is so strong, I actually shake with it.

Or maybe I shake from hunger and thirst. It's impossible to tell.

Stepping out of the cursed train, I push through the herd of exhausted, stressed-out commuters and take the escalator upstairs. I need to call Obenko immediately; my handlers must be going mad with worry.

"Yulia? What the fuck?" As expected, Obenko's furious. "Where are you?"

"At Rizhskaya." I name the train station some twenty stops away from my destination. "I was on the Kaluzhsko-Rizhskaya line."

"Ah, fuck. You got stuck because of that idiot."

"Yeah." I lean against an icy wall at the top of the stairs as people hurry past me. According to the last update from the train conductor, the reason for the delay was a hostage situation two trains ahead of us. A Chechen national got the bright idea to strap on a homemade bomb and threaten to blow himself up if his demands weren't met. The police managed to subdue him, but it took them hours to do it safely. Considering the seriousness of the situation, it's a miracle we were able to get off the train before nightfall.

"All right." Obenko sounds a bit calmer. "I'll get the team to return to the pickup location. Are the trains running again?"

"Not the Kaluzhsko-Rizhskaya line. They said it'll resume running later tonight. I'm going to have to take a taxi." I shift from foot to foot, my bladder reminding me that it's been hours since I've had access to a bathroom. I need that, and food, with extreme urgency, but first, there's something I must know. "Vasiliy Ivanovich," I say hesitantly, addressing my boss by his full name and patronymic, "did the operation... succeed?"

"The plane was shot down an hour ago."

My knees buckle, and for a dizzying moment, the station blurs out of focus. If it hadn't been for the wall at my back, I would've fallen over. "Were there any survivors?" My voice sounds choked, and I have to clear my throat before continuing. "That is... are you sure the target's been eliminated?"

"We haven't received the casualty report yet, but I don't see how Esguerra could've survived."

"Oh. Good." Bile rises in my throat, and I feel like I'm going to throw up. Swallowing thickly, I manage to say, "I have to go now, find that taxi."

"All right. Keep us posted if there are any issues."

"Will do." I press the button to hang up and lean my head back against the wall, taking in gulps of cold air. I feel sick, my stomach roiling with acid and emptiness. I have a fast metabolism, and I've never handled hunger well, but I don't recall ever feeling this bad from lack of food.

Pale blue eyes blank and unseeing. Blood running down a hard, square jaw...

No, stop. I force myself to straighten away from the wall. I won't allow myself to go there. I'm just hungry, thirsty, and exhausted. Once I address these problems, everything will be fine.

It has to be.

BEFORE TRYING TO CATCH A TAXI, I HEAD TO A SMALL COFFEE SHOP next to the station and use their restroom. I also get a cup of hot tea and scarf down three meat-filled pirozhki—small savory pies. Then, feeling much more human, I go outside to see if I can find a taxi.

The streets around the station are a nightmare. The traffic appears to be at a complete standstill, and all the taxis look occupied. It's not unexpected, given what happened with the trains, but still extremely annoying.

I begin walking briskly in the hopes that I can get to a less trafficky location on foot. There's no point in getting into a car, only to crawl two blocks in two hours. Now that the plane has gone down, I need to get to my handlers as quickly as possible.

The plane. I suck in my breath as the sickening images invade my mind again. I don't know why I can't stop thinking about this. I'd known Lucas for less than twenty-four hours, and I'd spent most of that time being afraid of him.

And the rest of that time screaming in pleasure in his arms, a small voice reminds me.

No, stop.

I pick up my pace, zigzagging around slower-moving pedestrians. *Don't think about him, don't think about him...* I let the words echo in my mind in tempo with my steps. *You're going home to*

Misha... I pick up my pace some more, almost running now. Moving this fast not only gets me to my destination quicker, but it also keeps me warm. *Don't think about him, you're going home...*

I don't know how long I walk like this, but as the streetlights turn on, I realize it's already getting dark. Checking my phone, I see that it's nearly six p.m.

I've been at it for two and a half hours, and the traffic around me is as bad as ever.

Stopping, I look around in frustration. I've been walking along major avenues to maximize my chances of catching a cab, but that appears to have been a faulty strategy. Perhaps what I should do is get away from the main zones of traffic and try my luck on smaller streets. If I find a car there, the driver may be able to take me out of the city via some more obscure routes. I'll pay him whatever extra money he demands.

Turning onto one of the cross streets, I see a park a block away. I decide to cut diagonally across it, and then go up one of the smaller avenues on the other side of it. I'll still be heading in the right direction, but I'll be away from the busiest area. Maybe I'll find a bus there, if not a cab.

There's got to be some way I can get to my destination in the next few hours.

My phone vibrates in my bag, and I fish it out. "Yes?"

"Where are you?" Obenko sounds as frustrated as I feel. "The team leader is getting nervous. He wants to be across the border by the time the Kremlin learns what happened."

"I'm still in the city, walking for now. The traffic is impossible." The snow crunches under my feet as I enter the park. They didn't bother to clear it here, so all the walking paths are covered with a thick icy layer.

"Fuck."

"Yeah." I try not to slip on the ice as I step over a pile of dog shit. "I'm doing my best to get there tonight, I promise."

"All right. Yulia..." Obenko pauses for a second. "You know

we're going to have to pull the team if you don't get there by morning, right?" His voice is quiet, almost apologetic.

"I know." I keep my tone level. "I'll be there."

"Good. Make sure you do that."

He hangs up, and I walk faster, driven by increasing anxiety. If the team leaves without me and I get caught, I'm as good as dead. The Kremlin isn't known to be kind to spies, and the fact that our agency is completely off the books makes the matters ten times worse. The Ukrainian government won't negotiate to get me back, because they have no idea that I exist.

I'm almost out of the park when I hear drunk male laughter and the sound of shoes crunching on snow.

Glancing behind me, I see a small group of men some hundred meters back, with bottles clutched in their gloved hands. They're weaving all over the walking path, but their attention is unmistakably focused on me.

"Hey, young lady," one of them yells out, slurring his words. "Wanna come party with us?"

I look away and start walking even faster. They're just drunks, but even drunks can be dangerous when it's six against one. I'm not afraid of them—I have my gun and my training—but I don't need trouble this evening.

"Young lady," the drunk yells, louder this time. "You're being rude, you know that?"

His friends laugh like a pack of hyenas, and the drunk yells again, "Fuck you, bitch! If you don't want to party, just motherfucking say so!"

I ignore them and continue on my way, snaking my left hand into my handbag to feel for my gun, just in case. As I exit the park and step onto the street, the sound of their voices fades, and I realize they're no longer following me.

Relieved, I take my hand out of my bag and continue up the street at a slightly slower pace. My legs are aching, and I feel like a blister is forming on the side of my heel. My flat boots are way more comfortable than heels, but they're not made for three hours of speed-walking.

I'm in a more residential area now, which is both good and bad. The traffic here is better—only a few cars pass me on the street—but the streetlights are sparse, and the area is all but deserted. Distant male laughter reaches my ears again, and I force myself to go faster, ignoring the discomfort of tired muscles.

I walk about five blocks before I see it: a cab stopping next to a curb across the street some fifty meters ahead. A short, thin man is getting out. Relieved, I yell, "Wait!" and sprint toward the car just as he begins closing the door.

I'm almost next to the cab when I see lights out of the corner of my eye and hear the roar of an engine.

Reacting in a split second, I throw myself to the side, hitting the ground as a car barrels past me. As I roll on the icy asphalt, I hear the driver hooting drunkenly, and then something hard slams into the side of my head.

My last thought as my world goes black is that I should've shot those drunks after all.

9

ucas

Voices. Distant beeping. More voices.

The sounds fade in and out, as does the buzzing in my ears. My head feels thick and heavy, the pain enveloping me like a blanket of thorns.

Alive. I'm alive.

The realization seeps into me slowly, in stages. Along with it comes a sharp throbbing in my skull and a surge of nausea.

Where am I? What happened?

I strain to make out the voices.

It's two women and a man, judging by the differences in pitch. They're speaking in a foreign language, something I don't recognize.

My nausea intensifies, as does the throbbing in my head. It takes all my strength to pry open my eyelids.

Above me, a fluorescent light flickers, its brightness agonizing. Unable to bear it, I close my eyes.

A female voice exclaims something, and I hear rapid footsteps.

A hand touches my face, a stranger's fingers reaching for my eyelids. Bright light shines into my eyes again, and I tense, my hands bunching into fists as agony spears through me again. My instinct is to fight, to lash out at whoever this is, but something is preventing me from moving my arms.

"Careful now." The male voice speaks English, albeit with a thick foreign accent. "The nurse is just checking on you."

The hand leaves my face, and I force my eyes to remain open despite the pain in my skull. Everything looks blurry, but after I blink a few times, I'm able to focus on the man standing next to the bed.

Dressed in a military officer's uniform, he looks to be in his early fifties, with a lean, sharp-featured face. Seeing me looking at him, he says, "I'm Colonel Sharipov. Can you please tell me your name?"

"Where am I? What happened?" I ask hoarsely, trying to move my arms once more. I can't—and I realize it's because I'm restrained, handcuffed to the bed. When I try to move my legs, I can move my right, but not my left. There's something bulky and heavy keeping it still, and tugging on it makes me hiss in pain.

"You're in a hospital in Tashkent," Sharipov says, answering my first question. "You have a broken leg and a severe concussion. I would advise you not to move."

Tashkent. That means I'm in Uzbekistan, the country bordering our destination of Tajikistan. As I process that, some of the fogginess in my mind dissipates, and I remember what happened.

The screams. The smell of smoke.

The crash.

Fuck.

"Where are the others?" Abruptly enraged, I tug at my wrist restraints. "Esguerra and all the rest?"

"I will tell you in a moment," Sharipov says. "First, I must know your name."

The pounding agony in my skull isn't letting me think. "Lucas Kent," I grit out. There's no point in lying. He didn't seem surprised when I mentioned Esguerra—which means he already has some idea of who we are. "I'm Esguerra's second-in-command."

Sharipov studies me. "I see. In that case, Mr. Kent, you'll be pleased to know that Julian Esguerra is alive and here in the hospital as well. He has a broken arm, cracked ribs, and a head wound, which doesn't appear to be too serious. We're waiting for him to regain consciousness."

My head feels like it's about to explode, yet I'm aware of a flicker of relief. The guy is an amoral killer—some might say a psychopath—but I've gotten to know him over the years and I respect him. It would be a shame if he were killed by some stray missile. Which reminds me—

"What the fuck happened? Why am I restrained?"

The colonel looks at me steadily. "You're restrained for your own safety and that of the nurses, Mr. Kent. Your occupation is such that we didn't feel comfortable putting the staff here at risk. It's a civilian hospital and—"

"Oh, for fuck's sake." I clench my teeth. "I promise not to harm the nurses, okay? Remove these fucking cuffs. Now."

We have a stare-off contest for a few seconds. Then Sharipov makes a short, jerky motion with his head and says something to one of the nurses in a foreign language. The dark-haired woman comes over and unlocks the cuffs, giving me wary looks the whole time. I ignore her, keeping my focus on Sharipov.

"What happened?" I repeat in a somewhat calmer tone, bringing my hands together to rub at my wrists as the nurse skitters away to the other side of the room. The pounding in my head worsens from the movement, but I persist in my questioning. "Who shot down the plane, and what happened to the other men?"

"I'm afraid that the exact cause of the crash is being investigated at the moment," Sharipov says. He looks vaguely uncomfortable. "It's possible there was a... miscommunication."

"A miscommunication?" I give him an incredulous glare. "Did you shoot at us? You know we were to be granted safe passage through the region, right?"

"Of course." He looks even more uncomfortable now. "Which is why we're currently conducting an investigation. It's possible that an error was made—"

"An error?" *The screams, the smoke...* "A fucking error?" My brain feels like a drummer took up residence in my skull. "Where *the fuck* are the others?"

Sharipov flinches, almost imperceptibly. "I'm afraid there were only three survivors besides Esguerra and yourself. They're still unconscious. I'm hoping you can help us identify them." Reaching into his breast pocket, he pulls out his phone and shows me the screen. "This is the first one."

My guts twist. I know the man in that photo.

John "The Sandman" Sanders, a British ex-con. Handy with knives and grenades. I've trained with him, played pool with him. He was fun, even when he was piss-drunk.

He might not be as fun anymore. Not with half of his face cooked extra crispy.

"The plane exploded," Sharipov says, likely in response to my expression. "He has third-degree burns over most of his body. He'll need extensive skin grafts—if he survives at all. Do you know his name?"

"John Sanders," I say hoarsely, reaching up to take the phone. My body protests the movement, my temples throbbing with nauseating pain again, but I need to see the others. Bringing the phone closer, I click to the next photo.

This face is nearly unrecognizable—except for the scar at the corner of his left eye. He's a recent recruit, someone I debated bringing on this mission.

"Jorge Suarez," I say evenly before moving on to the next picture.

This time I can't even venture a guess. All I see is burned flesh. "He's still alive?" I glance up at Sharipov. I can feel the churning in my guts worsening, and I know it's only partially because of my concussion.

The colonel nods. "He's in a critical condition, but he might pull through. If you look at the next picture, it shows his lower body. It's not as burned."

Fighting my nausea, I do as he says and study the hairy legs covered by strips of torn protective suit. The explosion must've blasted through the protective gear; the material is meant to withstand a brief exposure to fire, not a plane blowing up. It's hard to say who the man is from just his legs. Unless... I narrow my eyes, peering closer at the picture, and then I see it.

A tattoo of a bird behind one of the ragged pieces of the combat suit.

"Gerard Montreau," I say with certainty. The young Frenchman is the only one with that tattoo on the team.

Lowering the phone to my chest, I look up at Sharipov. "Why am I not burned? How did I escape the explosion? And what about Esguerra? Is he—"

"No, he's fine," Sharipov reassures me. "Or at least, not burned. The two of you were in the pilot's cabin, which got separated from the main body of the plane during the crash. The back of the plane exploded, but the fire didn't reach you."

The throbbing in my head becomes unbearable, and I close my eyes, trying to process everything.

Five men out of fifty. That's all that remains of our group. The rest are dead. Burned or blown to bits. I can imagine their terror as the fire engulfed the back of the plane. The fact that there are any survivors is nothing short of a miracle—not that the three men in the pictures will see it that way.

An error. What fucking bullshit.

I'm going to get to the bottom of this, but first, I need to do my job.

Forcing my eyelids apart again, I squint at Sharipov, who's cautiously reaching for the phone I'm still holding. What the fuck does the man think I'll do? Strangle him while lying incapacitated in their hospital?

I won't—unless I learn he's responsible for this "error."

"You need to get some bodyguards for Esguerra," I say, gripping the phone tighter. "He's not safe here."

The colonel frowns at me. "What do you mean? The hospital is perfectly safe—"

"He has many enemies, including Al-Quadar, the terrorist group whose stronghold is right across your border. You need to arrange for protection, and you need to do it right now."

Sharipov still looks doubtful, so I add, "Your Kremlin allies will not be pleased if he's killed or taken while in your custody. Especially after this unfortunate 'error.'"

Sharipov's mouth tightens, but after a moment, he says, "All right. I'll have a few soldiers brought in. They'll make sure no one unauthorized comes near your boss."

"Good. Use more than a few. Forty or fifty would be good. Those terrorists have a real hard-on for him." My head is in absolute agony, and the leg that's in the cast is beginning to ache like only a broken bone can. "Also, you need to put me in touch with Peter Sokolov—"

"We've already talked to him. He knows where you are, and he's sending a plane to retrieve you and the others. Now, please." Sharipov extends his hand palm-up. "Give me back my phone, Mr. Kent."

I open my mouth to insist on speaking to Peter myself, but before I can say anything, I feel something sharp prick my arm. Immediately, a heavy lassitude spreads through me, dulling the pain. Out of the corner of my eye, I see a nurse step back, holding a syringe. "What the—" I begin, but it's too late.

The darkness descends, and I'm not aware of anything else.

10

ulia

"I TOLD YOU, I'M FINE."

Ignoring the nurse's squawking protests, I remove the IV needle from my wrist and stand up. I'm dizzy and my head is aching, but I need to get moving. Judging by the sunlight streaming in through the hospital window, it's already morning or later. The exfiltration team likely left already, but on the off chance they didn't, I need to get in touch with Obenko right away.

"Where's my bag?" I ask the nurse, frantically scanning the room. "I need my bag."

"What you need is to lie down." The red-headed nurse steps in front of me, folding her arms in front of her massive chest. "You have an egg-sized lump on your head from bumping into that pole, and you've been out cold since you were brought in last night. The doctor said we're to monitor you for the next twenty-four hours."

I glare at her. My head feels like it's splitting at the seams, but staying here means signing my death warrant. "Where is my bag?" I repeat. I'm uncomfortably aware that I'm wearing only a hospital gown, but I'll worry about clothes—and the headache from hell—later.

The woman rolls her eyes. "Oh, for heaven's sake. If I get you your bag, will you lie down and behave?"

"Yes," I lie, and watch as she walks to a cabinet on the other side of the room. Opening the cabinet door, she takes out my Gucci handbag and comes back.

"Here you go." She thrusts the bag into my hands. "Now lie down before you fall down."

I do as she says, but only because I need to conserve my strength for the journey ahead. It's been less than ten minutes since I woke up here, and I'm shaking from the strain of standing. I probably do need to be under medical observation, but there's no time for that.

I have to get out of Moscow before it's too late.

The nurse begins to change the sheets on an empty bed next to mine, and I take out my phone to call Obenko.

It rings and rings and rings...

Shit. He's not picking up.

I try again. *Come on, come on, pick up.*

Nothing. No answer.

Growing desperate, I try his number for the third time.

"Yulia?"

Thank God. "Yes, it's me. I'm in a hospital in Moscow. I almost got hit by a car—long story. But I'm leaving now and—"

"It's too late, Yulia." Obenko's voice is quiet. "The Kremlin knows what happened, and Buschekov's people are looking for you."

An icy chill spreads through me. "So quickly?"

"One of Esguerra's people is well connected in Moscow. He mobilized them as soon as he learned about the missile."

"Shit."

The nurse gives me a dirty look as she gathers the sheets into a big pile on the empty bed.

"I'm sorry," Obenko says, and I know he means it. "The team leader had to pull his people out. It's not safe for any of us in Russia right now."

"Of course," I say on autopilot. "He did the right thing."

"Good luck, Yulia," Obenko says, and I hear the click as he disconnects.

I'm on my own.

I WAIT UNTIL THE NURSE LEAVES WITH THE PILE OF SHEETS, AND then I get up again, without any interference this time.

The panic circling through me is stronger than any painkiller. I'm barely cognizant of my headache as I walk over to the cabinet that held my bag and look inside.

As I'd hoped, my clothes are there too, folded neatly. I cast a quick look at the room entrance to verify that the door is closed, then strip off my hospital gown and put on the clothes I was wearing earlier. As I do so, I realize the lump on my head is not my only injury. The entire right side of my body is bruised, and I have scrapes all over.

That stupid drunk. I so should've shot him and his hyena friends when I had the chance.

No. I draw in a calming breath. Anger is pointless now. It's a distraction I can't afford. There's still a small chance I may be able to get out of Russia. I can't give up hope.

Not yet, at least.

I pull my hair up into a bun to make the long blond locks less noticeable, and then I do a swift check of the contents of my bag. Everything is there, except cash in the wallet and my gun. But that's to be expected. I'm lucky the bag itself wasn't stolen while I was unconscious. The lining at the bottom of the bag has some emergency cash sewn into it, and the thieves didn't find it, as confirmed by the lack of rips inside.

Gripping the bag tightly, I walk to the door and step out into the hallway. The nurse is nowhere in sight, and nobody pays me any attention as I approach the elevator. Well, one elderly man in a wheelchair gives me an appreciative once-over, but there's no suspicion in his gaze. He's just looking, likely reliving his youth.

The elevator doors open with a soft ding, and I step inside, my heart beating much too fast. Despite the ease of my getaway thus far, my skin is crawling, all my instincts warning me of danger.

My room is on the seventh floor of the building, and the ride down is torturously slow. The elevator stops on each floor, with patients and nurses coming in and out. I could've taken the stairs, but that might've drawn unnecessary attention to me. Nobody uses those stairwells unless they have to.

Finally, the elevator doors open on the first floor. I step out, surrounded by several other people—and at that moment I see them.

Three policemen entering the elevator on the opposite side of the hallway.

Shit. I duck my head and hunch my shoulders, trying to make myself look shorter. *Don't stare at them. Don't stare at them.* I keep my gaze on the floor and stay close to a tall, heavyset man who lumbered out of the elevator ahead of me. He walks slowly and so do I, doing my best to look like I'm with him.

They would be looking for a woman on her own, not a couple.

Thankfully, my unwitting companion heads for the exit, and there are enough people around us that he doesn't pay me much attention. His massive bulk provides some cover, and I use it as much as I can, maintaining my stooped posture.

Walk faster. Come on, walk faster, I silently beg the man. Every muscle in my body is tense with the urge to run, but that would destroy any chance I have of leaving this hospital undetected. At the same time, I know I need to be out of here within minutes. As soon as those policemen realize I'm not on the seventh floor, they'll put the entire hospital on alert.

Finally, the man and I are by the exit, and I see a cab pull up next to the curb.

Yes! I'm due for a little luck.

Leaving the man behind without a second glance, I hurry to the cab and get in just as the woman inside climbs out. "The Lubyanka station, please," I tell the driver as the door is closing. I say it in case the woman is paying attention. That way, if she's questioned later, she'll tell them my supposed destination and, hopefully, muddy the trail a bit.

The driver nods and pulls away from the curb. As soon as we're on the street, I say, "Oh, actually, I forgot. I'm supposed to pick up something at the Azimut Moscow Olympic Hotel. Can you please drop me off there instead?"

He shrugs. "Sure, no problem. You pay, I take you wherever you want."

"Thank you." I lean back against the seat. I'm too anxious to relax fully, but the worst of the tension drains out of me. I'm safe for the moment. I bought myself some time. There's a car rental near that hotel. Once I get there, I'll find myself a disguise and get a car. They'll be watching airports, trains, and public transportation, but there's a small chance I can make it to the Ukrainian border via some less popular roads.

The drive seems to take forever. The traffic is bad, but not nearly as horrible as yesterday. Still, with the driver braking and accelerating every couple of minutes—and the numbing effect of adrenaline wearing off—my headache comes back in full force, as does the pain from all the bruises and scrapes. On top of everything, I become aware of a gnawing emptiness in my stomach and a cottony dryness in my mouth.

Of course. I haven't had anything to eat or drink since yesterday afternoon.

To distract myself from my misery, I think of Misha as he was in the last picture Obenko sent me. My baby brother had his arm around a pretty brunette girl—his current girlfriend, according to Obenko. The girl was smiling up at Misha with adoration that bordered on worship, and he looked as proud as only a teenage boy can.

For you, Misha. I close my eyes to hold on to the picture in my mind. *You're worth it.*

"Well, that's not good," the driver mutters, and I open my eyes to see the cars coming to a complete stop ahead of us. "Wonder if there was an accident or something." He rolls down the window and sticks his head out, peering into the distance.

"Is it an accident?" I ask, resigned. It's like the fates are conspiring to keep me in Moscow. It's not enough that Russia has winters brutal enough to decimate its enemies' armies; now it has spy-detaining traffic, too.

"No," the driver says, pulling his head back inside the car. "Doesn't look like it. I mean, there are a bunch of police cars and all, but I don't see any ambulances. Could be a blockade, or they caught someone—"

I'm out of the car before he finishes speaking.

"Hey!" he yells, but I'm already running, weaving my way through the stopped cars. Whatever discomfort I was feeling earlier is gone, chased away by a sharp surge of fear.

A police blockade. Somehow they triangulated my location—or maybe they just blocked all the major roads in the hopes of catching me. Either way, I'm screwed, unless I can get out of this city.

My heart pounds in a heavy staccato rhythm as I sprint for the street, heading toward a narrow alley I spotted earlier. They'll have trouble following me there in a car, and if I'm lucky, I may be able to evade them long enough to find another cab.

Anything to buy myself more time.

Behind me, I hear shouts and the sound of running footsteps. "Stop!" a male voice yells. "Stop now! You're under arrest!"

I ignore the order, picking up my pace instead. The cold air hurts my lungs as I push my leg muscles to their limits. The alley looms ahead of me, narrow and dark, and I force myself to keep running at the same speed, to keep going without so much as a glance back.

"Stop, or I will shoot!" The voice sounds more distant, giving me a grain of hope. Maybe I'll be able to outrun him. I've always been fast, my long legs giving me an advantage over shorter people.

A shot rings out, the bullet whizzing past me and plowing into the building ahead.

Shit. He *is* shooting. I don't know why that surprises me. The Moscow police aren't exactly known for caring about the citizens they're supposed to be protecting. They're tools of their corrupt government, nothing more. It shouldn't shock me that they'd risk the welfare of innocent citizens to catch me.

Another shot, and the snow explodes off the ground a few feet ahead of me. I hear terrified screams and see people diving for cover on the sidewalk.

Ignoring the commotion, I sprint into the alley. Straight ahead are two large dumpsters, and behind them, a metal fire ladder going up the side of the building.

A third shot, and the bullet ricochets off the dumpster, narrowly missing me. The cop, or whoever's chasing me, has good aim.

I'm almost at the ladder, and I jump up as high as I can, managing to catch the bottom rung of the ladder with my hands. Then, using the momentum of my jump, I swing my legs up and catch the metal bar with my feet. Hooking my knees over the metal bar, I use all my strength to pull myself up high enough to grab the next rung of the ladder with my left hand. It works, and I pull myself up into a sitting position before starting to climb.

Another shot, and the wall in front of me explodes, shards of brick flying everywhere.

Shit, shit, shit. I scramble up the ladder as fast as I can without slipping on the icy metal bars. There are shouts and curses below me, and then I feel the ladder shaking as another person jumps on it.

I guess they decided to try capturing me alive.

I don't look down as I continue my perilous climb. I've never liked heights, so I pretend it's a training exercise and a thickly padded mat is waiting for me below. Even if I fall, I'll be okay. It's a complete lie, of course, but it serves to keep me going despite my heart trying to leap out of my throat.

Before I know it, I'm at the roof, and I jump off the ladder onto the flat surface. The building I'm on is shaped like a square with a hole for a large yard in the middle—a typical Soviet-era structure that occupies an entire block. I pause just long enough to spot another ladder on the other side of the square, and then I start running again, heading toward that ladder.

"Stop!" someone yells again, and I realize with a jolt of fear that they're already up here, right on my heels. Unable to resist, I cast a frantic glance behind me and see two men running after me. They're wearing police uniforms, and one of them is holding a gun. They're both big men, seemingly fast and strong. I won't be able to outrun them for long.

Changing my strategy, I put on a burst of speed and use the two-second lead I gain to zip behind a concrete smoke stack. Leaning against it, I gasp for air, desperately trying not to make any noise as I catch my breath.

Three seconds later, I hear the men's footsteps.

Time to go on the offensive.

As the first cop barrels past me, I stick my foot out. He trips, falling with a loud curse, and I hear the gun sliding across the icy roof.

The shooter's down and disarmed.

Before his partner has a chance to react, I jump out in front of him, my right hand balled into a fist. He automatically ducks to the left as I swing it at him, and I use the momentum of his movement to punch upward with my left hand.

My left fist slams into his chin, and he stumbles back, grunting. Without pausing, I dive for the gun, and see the other policeman doing the same.

We collide, rolling, and for a second, my fingers brush against the weapon.

Yes! I grab it, and as the cop attempts to pin me down, I pull the trigger.

He screams, clutching his shoulder, and I push him off me, the adrenaline giving me almost superhuman strength. I'm already up on my knees when the second cop throws himself at me, his hand brutally squeezing my wrist.

"Drop the weapon, bitch," he hisses, and at that moment, I hear more footsteps.

"You got her, Sergey?" one man yells, and I see five more cops show up, their weapons drawn.

There's no point in fighting anymore, so I let my grip on the gun slacken. It falls to the roof with a dull thud as Sergey spins me around and handcuffs my wrists behind my back.

I'm caught.

Now I can give up hope.

11

ucas

"THEY DID WHAT?"

My voice is a low hiss as I sit up, ignoring the nurse's hands fluttering around me in an attempt to get me to lie still. The rage blasting through me chases away all remnants of wooziness from the drug she gave me earlier. I have no idea how long I was out, but it was clearly too fucking long.

"The terrorists attacked the hospital a few hours ago," Sharipov repeats, his face tense and tired. "It seems we underestimated their capabilities—and their desire to get at your boss. As we didn't find his body among the dead, we can only assume that they took him."

"They took Esguerra?" It takes everything I have not to leap out of bed and strangle the colonel with my bare hands—which are still unrestrained, I note with some corner of my brain. "You fucking let them take him? I told you to put security around him—"

"We did. We had several of our best soldiers standing guard—"

"Several? It should've been several dozen, you fucking idiots!"

The nurse flinches at my roar and jumps well out of my reach. Smart woman. At this moment, I'd gladly strangle her too.

Sharipov's jaw tightens. "As I said, we underestimated this particular terrorist organization. We won't make this mistake again. It was a bloodbath. They wounded dozens of patients and hospital staff on the way out and killed all the soldiers assigned to guard duty."

"Fuck." I punch the mattress so hard, the pillow bounces. "Were you at least able to follow them?" Majid wouldn't be stupid enough to take Esguerra to the Al-Quadar compound in the Pamir Mountains; he must know by now that we've sniffed out its location.

Sharipov prudently steps back. "No. The police were notified right away, and we sent for more soldiers, but the terrorists got away before we could get to the hospital."

"Son of a bitch." If it weren't for the cast immobilizing my leg, I'd be out of bed and punching the colonel's weary face. As is, I have to settle for slamming my fist into the cheap mattress again. My head throbs with the violent movement, but I don't give a fuck.

Esguerra was taken while I lay here, drugged and oblivious.

I failed at my job, and I failed badly.

"Give me the phone," I say when I'm calm enough to speak. "I need to talk to Peter Sokolov."

Sharipov nods and takes the phone out of his pocket. "Here you go." He offers it to me cautiously. "We already spoke to him, but you're welcome to do so as well."

Fighting the urge to grab Sharipov's hand and break his arm, I take the phone and punch in the numbers for a secure connection that takes me through a number of relays. To my annoyance, Peter doesn't pick up.

Sharipov is watching me, so I conceal my frustration as I try again. And again. And again.

"I'll be back in a few minutes," Sharipov says on my fifth attempt. "Feel free to contact whomever you need."

He departs, and I resume trying Peter's number, driven by increasing anger and worry. Esguerra's Russian security consultant always carries his phone with him, and I have no idea why he's suddenly out of reach. Could there have been an attack on Esguerra's estate in Colombia? The mere possibility makes me see red.

Just when I'm about to give up, the call connects. "Yes?" The faintly accented voice is unmistakably Peter Sokolov's.

"It's Kent."

"Lucas?" The Russian sounds surprised. "You're awake?"

"Fuck, yeah, I'm awake. Where are you? Why didn't you pick up?"

There's a short pause on the line. "I just landed in Chicago."

"What?" That's the last thing I expected to hear. "Why?"

"Esguerra's wife. She wants to be Al-Quadar bait."

"What?" I almost jump off the bed, the cast be damned.

"Yeah, I know. That was my reaction too. Turns out Esguerra, that obsessive bastard, implanted some trackers in her. If they take her to use as leverage against Esguerra, we'll have a fix on their location."

"Fuck." The plan is brilliant, and dangerous as hell. If the terrorists find those trackers in her, Esguerra's pretty little wife will pray for death. And if Esguerra somehow survives, he'll dismember Peter—slowly—for using the girl like that. "Nora came up with this?"

"She did." There's a hint of admiration in the Russian's cool voice. "I don't know what hold he's got over her, but she's pretty determined. I was against it at first, but she convinced me."

I inhale and let the air out slowly. I should be surprised—Esguerra did kidnap the girl, after all—but I'm not. However their relationship started, it's obvious that whatever's between them now is mutual. I'm tempted to rip into Peter for going against Esguerra's orders, but that would be a waste of time and energy. What he's set in motion can't be undone. "So what's the exact plan?" I ask instead. "Are you going to hang out in Chicago to make sure they take the bait?"

"No. I'm heading to Tajikistan right away. The rescue team is already on the way there. As soon as Majid's men bring her over, we'll come for her—and for Esguerra."

"You know they might not bring her to him. A video of her getting tortured would be just as effective as the real thing."

"I know."

Of course he does. Like me, he's used to life-and-death gambles. I could point out the risks from now 'til eternity, and it wouldn't change anything. The plan will either work or it won't, and there's nothing I can do about it.

"Did you figure out what happened?" I ask, changing the topic. "Sharipov said it may have been some kind of error on their part."

"An error?" I can hear Peter's derisive snort over the phone. "More like lax security. One of their officers has been in the Ukrainians' pocket for years, and the idiots had no clue until he fired a missile at your plane."

"Ukraine?" It makes sense; now that Esguerra's sided with the Russians, the Ukrainians would want to eliminate him. Except... how could they have found out about our conversation so quickly? Was the restaurant in Moscow bugged? Did Buschekov play for both sides? Or did—

"It was the interpreter," Peter says, voicing my next guess. "I had her detained in Moscow as soon as I learned what happened."

A loud beep sounds in my ear, and I realize I squeezed the phone so hard I nearly crushed one of the volume buttons.

"What the fuck—"

"Sorry. Pressed the wrong button." My voice is cold and steady, even as burning lava moves through my veins. "The interpreter is a Ukrainian spy?"

"It appears that way. We're still digging into her background, but so far at least half of her story appears to have been fabricated."

"I see." I force myself to unclench my fingers before I crush the phone completely. "That's how they were able to act so quickly."

"Yes. They somehow figured out exactly when you'd be passing through the Uzbekistani airspace and activated their agent there."

The phone emits another angry beep as my hand tightens involuntarily. I know exactly how they figured out the timing: I all but told the spying bitch our departure time.

"Lucas?"

"Yeah, I'm here." I can't remember the last time I've been so furious. Yulia Tzakova—if that's even her real name—had played me for a fool. Her initial reluctance, her peculiar air of innocence —it had all been an act. She had probably been hoping to get close to Esguerra, and when she couldn't get him, she settled for me.

"I have to go now," Peter says. "I'll contact you again when we land. Get some rest and heal up; there's nothing else for you to do right now. I'll keep you apprised of any new developments."

He disconnects, and I force myself to lie down, my headache worsened by my burning rage.

If Yulia Tzakova ever crosses my path again, she will pay.

She will pay for everything.

I'M STILL LIVID WITH FURY WHEN SHARIPOV RETURNS TO RECLAIM HIS phone. As he approaches my bed, I sit up and glare at him. "A fucking error, huh?"

Raising his hand, the colonel rubs the bridge of his nose. "We're questioning the officer responsible right now. It's not yet clear whether—"

"Take me to him."

Looking taken aback, Sharipov lowers his hand. "I can't do that," he says. "This is a matter for our military."

"Your military fucked up big time. You had a traitor in charge of your missile defense system."

The colonel opens his mouth, but I forestall his objections. "Take me to him," I demand again. "I need to question him myself. Otherwise, we'll have no choice but to assume that others in your military or your government were involved in the missile strike." I pause. "And maybe even in this terrorist attack on the hospital."

Sharipov's eyes widen at my implied threat. If the Uzbekistani government is found to have ties to a terrorist organization like Al-Quadar, that could be disastrous for the country. I wouldn't be surprised if the colonel is aware of our connections in the US and Israel. By denying me a chance to interrogate one treasonous officer, the Uzbekistani government might be making an enemy of the powerful Esguerra organization and getting a worldwide reputation for associating with terrorists.

"I have to discuss this with my superiors," Sharipov says after a second. "Please, let me have my phone."

I hand it to him and watch as he leaves the room, already dialing someone. I wait, confident of the outcome, and sure enough, he returns a few minutes later, saying, "All right, Mr. Kent. We'll have our officer brought here within the next hour. You can talk to him, but that's all. Our military will handle it from there."

I give him a grim look. The only thing their military will handle is the traitor's body, but Sharipov doesn't need to know that yet. "Bring him," is all I say, and then I lie back and close my eyes, hoping the throbbing pain in my skull subsides in the next hour.

I may not be able to lay my hands on the interpreter right now, but I can certainly get my pound of flesh here.

WHEN THE TRAITOR ARRIVES, THE NURSES GIVE ME CRUTCHES AND lead me to another hospital room. It takes me a few minutes to get the hang of walking with the crutches—the fucking headache certainly doesn't help—and by the time I get there, they have the guy sitting on a bed, with Colonel Sharipov and an M16-toting soldier flanking his sides.

"This is Anton Karimov, the officer responsible for the unfortunate incident with your plane," Sharipov says as I hobble toward them. "You are welcome to ask him whatever questions you have. His English is not as good as mine, but he should understand you."

One of the nurses drags a chair over, and I sit down on it, studying the profusely sweating man in front of me. In his early forties, Karimov is on the plump side, with a thick black mustache and a receding hairline. He's still in his army uniform, and I can see circles of sweat staining his underarms.

He's nervous. No, more than that.

He's terrified.

"Who are the people who paid you?" I ask when the nurses leave the room. I decide to start off easy, as it might not take much to crack this man. "Who gave the order to shoot down our plane?"

Karimov visibly cringes. "N-nobody. Just a mistake. I clean the controls—"

I cut him off by lifting one of my crutches and putting the far end against his groin. Though I apply the lightest pressure to his balls, the man turns sickly pale.

"Who gave the order to shoot down our plane?" I repeat, looking at him. I can see that Sharipov is uneasy with my method of questioning, but I ignore him. Instead, I push the wooden stick forward, applying greater pressure to Karimov's crotch.

"N-nobody," Karimov gasps, scooting back to get out of the stick's reach. "I clean the—"

I lunge forward. He lets out a high-pitched squeal as I pin his balls to the mattress with the stick. "Don't fucking lie to me. Who paid you?"

"Mr. Kent, this is not acceptable," Sharipov says, stepping between me and the prisoner. "We told you, questions only. If you do not stop—"

Before he finishes speaking, I'm already on my feet, propping myself up on one crutch as I lash out at the armed soldier with another. He doesn't so much as lift his M16 before I hit him in the knee and he pitches forward, enabling me to grab his weapon. In the next second, I have the assault rifle pointed at Sharipov.

"Get out," I say, jerking my chin toward the door. "You and the soldier both. Get the fuck out."

Sharipov steps back, his face turning red. "I don't know what you think you're doing—"

"Out." I lift the weapon to point it between his eyes. "Now."

Sharipov's jaw clenches, but he does as I say. The soldier limps out behind him, shooting me a venomous look behind his shoulder. I have no doubt they'll come back with reinforcements, but it will be too late by then.

As soon as the door closes behind them, I turn my attention to Karimov. "Now," I say, my tone almost pleasant as I point the gun at the traitor. "Where were we?"

The man's eyes are wild with fear. "It—it was mistake. I said it before. Nobody pay me. Nobody—"

I squeeze the trigger and watch the bullets tear through his knee. The gunshots and the resulting screaming aggravate my headache, which adds to my rage. "I told you not to lie to me," I roar when the man's screams die down a notch. "Now, who paid you?"

"I d-don't know!" He's sobbing and clutching his knee as his blood soaks the hospital bed. "It was all email! All email!"

"What email?"

"M-my Yahoo! They transfer money to my bank for years and then they ask favors. S-small favors. I not meet them. Never meet them—"

"You don't know who they are?"

"N-no," he sobs out, trying to stop the bleeding with his pudgy hands. "I don't know, I don't know, I don't know..."

Shit. I'm inclined to believe him. He's too much of a coward not to give them up to save his skin, and they probably knew better than to trust him. We'll hack into his email, but I doubt there'll be many clues there.

Hearing shouts and running footsteps in the hallway, I press the gun to Karimov's sweaty forehead. "Last chance," I say grimly. "Who are they?"

"I don't know!" His wail is full of desperation, and I know he's telling the truth. He doesn't know anything, which makes him useless. I'm tempted to save him for Esguerra or Peter's amusement, but it'll take too much effort to get him out of the country.

That means there's only one thing left for me to do.

Squeezing the trigger, I pepper Karimov with bullets and watch his body slam against the wall, blood and bits of brains spraying everywhere. Then I lower the weapon and take a few deep breaths, trying to calm the pounding pain in my head.

When Sharipov's troops burst into the room a few seconds later, I'm sitting in the chair, the empty weapon lying at my feet.

"I apologize about the mess," I say, leaning on the crutches to stand up. "We'll pay for the clean-up of this room."

And ignoring the horror on everyone's faces, I start hobbling toward the door.

12

ulia

"Which organization do you belong to?" Buschekov leans forward, his eyes trained on me with the intensity of a snake hypnotizing its prey.

I stare back at the Russian official, barely registering his question. I can't decide if his eyes are yellowish gray or pale hazel; whatever color his irises are, they manage to blend with the yellowish-gray whites around them, producing the illusion of a complete lack of eye color. In general, everything about Arkady Buschekov is yellowish gray, from his skin tone to the wispy hair plastered against his shiny skull.

"Which organization do you belong to?" he repeats, his gaze boring into me. I wonder how many people have caved from that stare alone; if I believed in x-ray vision, I'd swear he's looking straight into me. "Who sent you here?"

"I don't know what you're talking about," I say, unable to keep my exhaustion out of my voice.

It's been over twenty-four hours since my capture, and I've neither slept nor had anything to eat or drink. They're wearing me down this way, undermining my willpower. It's a standard interrogation technique here. The Russians consider themselves too civilized to resort to outright torture, so they use these "softer" methods—things that mess with your psyche rather than cause lasting harm to your body.

"You know, Yulia Andreyevna"—Buschekov addresses me by my name and fake patronymic—"the Ukrainian government has disavowed any connection with you." He leans even closer, making me want to shrink back into my seat. At this distance, I can smell the salted fish and garlic potatoes he must've eaten for lunch. "Unless some unofficial agency in Ukraine claims you, we'll have no choice but to presume that you're a Russian citizen, as your false background indicates," he continues. "You understand what that means, right?"

I do. If treason is the charge they levy against me, I'll be executed. That's no reason for me to talk, though. Obenko won't come forward to claim me, not even if I expose our off-the-books agency. One operative is nothing in the grand scheme of things.

When I remain silent, Buschekov sighs and leans back in his seat. "All right, Yulia Andreyevna. If that's how you wish to play it." He snaps his fingers at the wall-wide mirror to the left of me. "We'll talk again soon."

He rises to his feet and walks to the door in the corner. Stopping in front of it, he looks back at me. "Think about what I said. This can go very badly for you if you don't cooperate."

I don't respond. Instead, I look down at my hands, which are handcuffed to the table in front of me. I hear the door open and shut as he walks out, and then I'm alone, except for the people watching me through the mirror.

THE HOURS DRAG BY, EACH SECOND MORE TORTUROUS THAN THE next. The thirst that torments me is comparable only to the hunger that gnaws at my insides. I try to lay my head down on the desk to sleep, but every time I do so, an ear-piercing alarm blares through the speakers, startling me awake. The screeching noise is impossible to ignore, even in my exhausted state, and eventually I stop trying, doing my best to zone out for a few precious moments while sitting upright in my chair.

I know what they're doing, but that doesn't make it any easier to bear. People who haven't experienced prolonged sleep deprivation don't understand that it's genuine torture, that every part of one's body begins to shut down after a while. I'm nauseated and cold all over, and everything hurts—my stomach, my muscles, my skin, my bones... even my teeth. The headache from earlier is a blaze of agony in my skull, and my lips are cracking from lack of water.

How long has it been since Buschekov left me alone? Several hours? A day? I don't know, and I'm losing the will to care. If there's any silver lining to all this, it's that I don't need to use the bathroom. I'm too dehydrated, and my stomach is too empty. Not that this saved me from humiliation. Upon arrival, they stripped me and went over every inch of my body. Even now that I'm dressed in a gray prison jumpsuit, I feel horribly naked, my skin crawling at the memory of the guards' latex-covered fingers invading me all over.

I close my eyes for a second, and the screeching alarm blares to life, jolting me awake. Opening my eyes, I attempt to swallow, to gather what little moisture remains in my mouth so I can wet my throat. I feel as though I've been eating sand. Swallowing hurts even more than not swallowing, so I give up, focusing on just surviving from moment to moment. They won't let me die like this, not when they hope to get some information from me, so all I need to do is hang on until they bring me some water.

Until they return to question me again.

My mind drifts, going over the last few days. There's no reason not to think of Lucas now, so I let the memories come. Sharp and bittersweet, they fill me, taking me away from my aching, exhausted body.

I remember the way he kissed me, the way he fit against me and inside me. I recall his taste, his smell, the feel of his skin against mine. He'd looked at me while he was fucking me, his gaze possessing me with its intensity. Did it mean anything to him, the night we spent together? Or was I just a casual lay, a way to scratch an itch while passing through Moscow?

My dry eyes burn as I stare, unseeing, at the wall in front of me. Whatever the answer is, it doesn't matter. It never mattered, but now it has zero relevance. Lucas Kent is dead, his body likely blown into pieces.

The room blurs in front of me, fading in and out of focus, and I realize I'm shaking, my breathing shallow and my heart beating painfully fast. I know it's probably from dehydration and lack of sleep, but it feels like something within me is breaking, the pressure around my chest hard and crushing. I want to curl up into a ball, to shrink into myself, but I can't, not with my hands cuffed to the table and feet chained to the floor.

All I can do is sit and grieve for something I never had—and now would never know.

13

ucas

AFTER MY INTERROGATION OF KARIMOV, SHARIPOV ASSIGNS TEN armed soldiers to stand guard over me and accompany the nurses when they take care of me. I know he's tempted to do more, like throw me in prison, but he doesn't dare. Peter's already worked some magic with his Russian connections, so everyone at this hospital is on their best behavior, the minor matter of armed guards excluded.

I don't mind my entourage. Now that I've had a chance to release some of my rage, I'm a tiny bit calmer, and I spend the time between Karimov's death and Esguerra's rescue learning how to move around on crutches. According to the doctors, it's a clean tibial break, so the cast should come off in six to eight weeks. That gives me a small measure of comfort, lessening my anger and frustration at being stuck in the hospital while others are doing my job.

Peter keeps me updated, so I know Al-Quadar took the bait. Now it's just a matter of waiting for Nora to be brought to wherever the terrorist cell is hiding Esguerra. Feeling cautiously optimistic, I make arrangements for the two of them to be brought to a private clinic in Switzerland after the rescue. I have a feeling they'll need it. I also strategize with Peter about the best way to extract Esguerra out of whatever hole they're keeping him in, and regularly check on the burned men, who are at this point stable but drugged unconscious to ease their suffering. They'll need multiple skin grafts—an expense Esguerra needs to authorize when he returns.

With all that activity, I don't spend much time resting in bed, which upsets the doctors taking care of me. They claim I need to lie still and not stress in order to let my concussion heal. I ignore them. They don't understand that I need to keep busy, that even the worst headache is better than lying there and thinking about *her.*

The Russian interpreter / Ukrainian spy.

Yulia.

Just thinking her name makes my blood pressure spike. I don't know why I can't put her betrayal out of my mind. It's not even a betrayal as such. Rationally, I understand she didn't owe me any loyalty. I came to her apartment to use her body, and she ended up using me instead. That makes her my enemy, someone I should want to kill, but it doesn't mean she betrayed me. I shouldn't give her any more thought than I give Al-Quadar.

I shouldn't, but I do.

I think about her constantly, remembering the way she looked at me and how her breath caught when I first touched her. How she clung to me as I drove into her, her pussy tight and slick around my cock. She wanted me—that much I'm sure of—and sex with her had been the hottest thing I'd experienced in years.

Maybe ever.

Fuck.

I can't keep doing this to myself. I need to forget the girl. She's in the hands of the Russian government, which means she's no longer my problem. One way or another, she'll pay for what she's done.

It's a thought that should comfort me, but it enrages me more instead.

~

"We got them."

At the sound of Peter's voice, I get up, too tense to sit still. "How are they?" It's a struggle to hold on to the phone while balancing on crutches, but I manage.

"Esguerra's pretty fucked up. They did a number on his face—I think he lost an eye. Nora seems okay. She took out Majid. Blew his brains out before we got there." Peter sounds admiring. "Gunned him down cold, if you can believe that."

"Damn." I can't form that picture in my mind, so I don't even try. Instead, I focus on the first part of his statement. "Esguerra's lost an eye?"

"Seems like it. I'm not a doctor, but it looks bad. Hopefully, they can fix it in that Swiss place."

"Yeah." If they can do it anywhere, the clinic in Switzerland would be it. It's known for treating celebrities and the obscenely wealthy of all persuasions, from Russian oil tycoons to Mexican drug lords. A stay there begins at thirty thousand Swiss francs a night, but Julian Esguerra can easily afford it.

"He wants you and the others transferred to that clinic, by the way," Peter says. "We'll send a plane for you shortly."

"Ah." I'd expected nothing less, but it's still nice to hear that. Recuperating at the ritzy Swiss clinic should be much better than being stuck in this shit hole. "He didn't rip into you for letting Nora get taken?"

"I didn't really talk to him. I'm keeping my distance."

"Peter..." I hesitate for a second, then decide the guy deserves a fair warning. "Esguerra's not very rational when it comes to his wife. There's a chance he'll—"

"Rip out my liver barehanded? Yeah, I know." The Russian sounds more amused than concerned. "Which is why I'm dropping them off at the clinic and leaving. They're all yours now."

"Leaving? What about your list?" It's no secret that in exchange for three years of service, Esguerra promised to get Peter the names of people responsible for what happened to his family.

"Don't worry about that." Peter's voice cools to arctic levels. "They'll get what's coming to them."

"All right, man." This is probably my cue to message the guards to detain Peter. Esguerra would undoubtedly praise me for that, but I can't bring myself to betray the Russian like that. Though we haven't been working together that long, I've grown to admire the man. He's a cold-blooded motherfucker, and that makes him excellent at what he does. And frankly, he's dangerous enough that I don't want to risk the lives of any more of our men. "Good luck," I say, and mean it.

"Thanks, Lucas. You too. Hope you and Esguerra heal up soon."

And with that, he hangs up, leaving me to wait for the plane and try not to think about Yulia.

WE STAY AT THE SWISS CLINIC FOR ALMOST A WEEK. DURING THAT time, Esguerra undergoes two surgeries—one to fix his cut-up face and the other to put a prosthetic eye into his left eye socket.

"They said the scars will be barely visible after a while," his wife tells me when I run into her in the hallway. "And the eye implant should look very natural. In a few months, he'll be almost back to normal." She pauses, studying me with her large dark eyes. "How are you, Lucas? How's your leg feeling?"

"It's fine." I've been refusing painkillers, so it actually hurts like a motherfucker, but Nora doesn't need to know that. "I got lucky. We both did."

"Yeah." Her slender throat works as she swallows. "What's the prognosis on the others?"

"They'll live until the next surgery." That's about the only positive thing I can say about the three burned men. "The doctors say they'll each need about a dozen operations."

She nods somberly. "Of course. I hope the surgeries go well. Please give them my best wishes if you speak to them."

I incline my head. There isn't much chance of that, since they're completely doped up, but I don't see any need to tell her that. The petite young woman in front of me is already dealing with enough shit. Esguerra said she's handling it, but I wonder. Not many nineteen-year-olds from the American suburbs blow open a terrorist's head.

I'm about to continue on my way when Nora asks quietly, "Have you heard from Peter?" Her expression as she stares up at me is hard to decipher.

"No, I haven't," I tell her honestly. "Why?"

She shrugs. "Just curious. We do owe him our lives."

"Right." I have a feeling there's more to this, but I don't pry. Instead, I incline my head at her again and continue hobbling to my room.

As I fall asleep that night, the blond spy invades my thoughts again, and my cock hardens despite my lingering headache. It's been like that every night for the past week. Random images from our night together come to me when my guard is down—when I'm too tired to fight them off. I keep recalling the tight clasp of her pussy, the cries that escaped her throat as I fucked her, the way she smelled, the way she tasted... It's gotten so bad I've considered getting a hooker, but for some reason, the idea doesn't appeal to me.

I don't just want sex. I want sex with *her*.

Furious, I get up, grab my crutches, and hobble to the bathroom to jerk off again.

If all goes well, tomorrow we'll be back in Colombia, and this chapter of my life will be over.

Maybe then I'll forget Yulia once and for all.

III

THE PRISONER

14

ucas

My fingers hover over the keyboard of my laptop as I stare at the screen, debating the wisdom of what I'm about to do. Then I take a deep breath and start typing. My email to Buschekov is short and to the point:

Esguerra requests to have Yulia Tzakova remitted into his custody for further interrogation.

I click "send" and get up, reveling in the freedom of moving without crutches. It's been two weeks since I've gotten the cast off, and I still feel exhilarated every time I stand up and walk unassisted.

Leaving my library/office, I head into the kitchen to make myself a sandwich. Cooking is a skill I've never been able to master, so my sandwich is beyond simple: ham, cheese, lettuce, and mayo between two slices of bread.

I sit down at the table to eat, so I don't overtax my leg. Though it's healing well, I still have to fight a tendency to limp. It's only been two months since the break, and the bone needs longer to mend completely.

As I eat, my thoughts turn to the Russians' probable response to my email. I can't imagine Buschekov will be pleased to lose his prisoner, but at the same time, I don't think he'll push back too hard. Esguerra's weapons are the best in the business, and with the conflict in Ukraine escalating, the Kremlin needs our covert deliveries to the rebels more than ever.

One way or another, they'll honor Esguerra's—but really, my—request. Which means that after two months of obsessing about her, I'm going to get my hands on Yulia Tzakova.

I can't fucking wait.

OVER THE NEXT TWO DAYS, I EXCHANGE HALF A DOZEN EMAILS WITH Buschekov. As I'd suspected, he's not too happy, initially going so far as to say he'll only talk to Peter Sokolov about the matter.

"Sokolov is currently unavailable," I tell Buschekov when we get on a video call. The Russian official is once again using an interpreter—a middle-aged woman this time. "I'm the one speaking for Esguerra in all matters now, and he wants Tzakova in his custody as soon as possible, along with whatever information you've been able to uncover about her thus far."

"That's impossible," Buschekov retorts once the translator conveys my words. "It's a matter of national security—"

"Bullshit. All we require are the files on her background. That has nothing to do with Russian national security."

Buschekov doesn't say anything for a few moments after the woman translates, and I know he's considering how to best handle me. "Why do you need her?" he finally asks.

"Because we want to track down the individual or the specific organization responsible for the missile strike." Or at least that's what I tell myself: that I want to interrogate the girl personally to find the motherfuckers who shot down our plane.

Buschekov's colorless eyes are unblinking. "You don't need Tzakova for that. We'll share that information with you as soon as we have it."

"So you don't have it. After two months." I'm both surprised and impressed that they haven't managed to break the girl. Her training must've been top notch to withstand such lengthy interrogation.

"We'll have it soon." Buschekov folds his arms in front of his chest. "There are ways to accelerate information retrieval, and we've just received authorization to use them."

My stomach muscles tighten. I've been trying not to think of what they might be doing to her in Moscow, but every so often, those thoughts creep in along with memories of our night together. I want Yulia to suffer, but the idea of some faceless Russian guards abusing her stirs something dark and ugly within me.

"I don't care about your authorizations." I force my voice to remain calm as I lean closer to the camera. "What you'll do is remit her into our custody. If you wish to maintain our business relationship, that is."

He stares at me, and I know he's thinking this over, wondering if I'm bluffing. And I am—Esguerra didn't authorize any of this—but Buschekov doesn't know that. As far as the Russian official is concerned, I represent the Esguerra organization, and I'm about to pull the plug on what has been a mutually beneficial association.

"It wouldn't go well for you, you know," Buschekov says finally. "If you were to go against us like that."

"Maybe." I don't blink at the not-so-veiled threat. "Maybe not. Esguerra's enemies rarely fare well."

I'm referring to Al-Quadar, which has been completely decimated since our return. We've been at war with the terrorist group for a number of months, ever since they tried to get a certain explosive from Esguerra by kidnapping Nora. However, things have really escalated since we came back from Tajikistan. We've gone after the terrorists' suppliers, financiers, and distant relatives; nobody even remotely connected to the group has escaped our wrath. The body count is coming up on four hundred, and the intelligence community has taken notice.

Buschekov doesn't respond for a few tense moments, and I wonder if he's going to call my bluff. But then he says, "All right. You'll have her within a month."

"No." I hold Buschekov's gaze as the woman translates my words. "Sooner. We're sending a plane for her tomorrow."

"What? No, that—"

"Should be enough time to get everything ready," I interrupt the translator. "Remember, we expect to get her *and* the files. You don't want to disappoint us, believe me."

And before he can voice any further protests, I disconnect from the video call.

THE NEXT MORNING, I TRAIN WITH ESGUERRA AND THE CREW, AS usual. Like me, he's almost back to normal, having kicked ass with our three new recruits. Since my leg is still healing, I'm sticking to boxing and target practice, and I'm more than a little envious that he's able to spar properly.

As we leave the training area, I fill him in on the latest developments with Peter Sokolov. Turns out the Russian somehow got his list from Esguerra, and is now going through the names and systematically eliminating them one by one.

"There was another hit in France, and two more in Germany," I tell Esguerra, using a towel to wipe the sweat off my face. This area of Colombia, near the Amazon rainforest, is always hot and humid. "He's not wasting any time."

"I didn't think he would," Esguerra says. "How did he do it this time?"

"The French guy was found floating in a river, with marks of torture and strangulation, so I'm guessing Sokolov must've kidnapped him first. For the Germans, one hit was a car bomb, and the other one a sniper rifle." I grin. "They must not have pissed him off as much."

"Or he went for expediency."

"Or that," I agree. "He probably knows Interpol is on his tail."

"I'm sure he does." Esguerra looks distracted, so I decide it's as good a time as any to bring up the Yulia situation.

"By the way," I say, keeping my tone casual, "I'm having Yulia Tzakova brought here from Moscow."

Esguerra stops and stares at me. "The interpreter who betrayed us to the Ukrainians? Why?"

"I want to personally interrogate her," I explain, draping the towel around my neck. "I don't trust the Russians to do a thorough job."

Esguerra narrows his eyes, his prosthetic eerily lifelike. "Is it because you fucked her that night in Moscow? Is that what this is about?"

A wave of anger makes my jaw tighten. "She fucked me over. Literally." That much I'm comfortable admitting. "So yeah, I want to get my hands on the little bitch. But I also think she might have some useful info for us."

Or at least I'm hoping she does, so I can justify this insane obsession with her.

Esguerra studies me for a second, then nods. "In that case, go for it." We resume walking, and he asks, "Did you already negotiate this with the Russians?"

I nod. "Initially, they tried to say they'd only deal with Sokolov, but I convinced them it wouldn't be wise to get on your bad side. Buschekov saw the light when I reminded him of the recent troubles at Al-Quadar."

"Good." Esguerra looks grimly pleased. In the world of illegal arms dealing, reputation is everything, and the fact that the Russians backed down bodes well for our relationships with clients and suppliers.

"Yes, it's helpful," I say before adding, "She'll be arriving here tomorrow."

Esguerra's eyebrows lift. "Where are you going to keep her?" he asks. It's a measure of his trust in me that he doesn't question my initiative. Ever since I saved his life in Thailand, he's been giving me tremendous leeway.

"In my quarters," I say. "I'll be interrogating her there."

He grins, and I know he understands. "All right. Enjoy."

"Oh, I will," I say darkly. "You can bet on it."

I'm literally counting down the hours until Yulia is on the plane. I considered flying to Moscow myself to get her, but after some deliberation, I decided to send Thomas, a former Navy pilot, and a few other men I trust. It would've looked strange if I'd gone; as Esguerra's second-in-command, I'm needed on the estate, not handling minor tasks like spy retrieval.

"If there's any trouble, notify me immediately," I told Thomas, though I'm confident there won't be.

In less than twenty-four hours, Yulia Tzakova will be here.

She'll be my prisoner, and nobody will save her from me.

15

ulia

The heavy metal door at the end of the hallway clangs, and I jerk awake, conditioned to respond to that noise as if to an electric shock.

They're coming for me again.

I begin to shake—yet another conditioned response. As much as I want to remain strong, they're getting to me, breaking me down piece by piece. Every grueling interrogation, every humiliation great and small, every day that blends into night as I sit there without food and sleep—it all adds up, destroying my willpower bit by tiny bit. And I know they're only getting started. Buschekov implied as much the last time he had me in that mirrored room.

Trying to control my breathing, I sit up on my cot, pulling a thin, dirty blanket around myself. Outside, it might be May, but in this prison, it's still winter. The chill here is everlasting. It permeates the gray stone walls and rusted metal bars, seeps in through the cracks in the floor and ceiling. There are no windows anywhere, so the sun never warms these rooms. I reside in fluorescent grayness, the cold walls around me pressing closer each day.

Footsteps.

Hearing them, I slide my sock-covered feet into my boots. My socks are dirty, as is the jumpsuit I'm wearing. I haven't had a shower in three weeks, and I undoubtedly stink to high heaven. It's one of those small humiliations designed to make one feel less than human.

"Yulechka..." A familiar singsong voice makes me shake even more. Igor is the guard I hate most, the one with the grabbiest hands and the nastiest-smelling breath. Even with the cameras everywhere, he manages to find opportunities to touch me and hurt me.

"Yulechka," he repeats, approaching my cell, and I see the glee in his beady brown eyes. He's using the most familiar form of my name, one that would normally be an endearment spoken by parents and other family members. On his thick lips, it sounds dirty and perverted, like he's a pedophile talking to a child.

"Are you ready, Yulechka?" Staring at me, he reaches for the lock on the cell door.

I fight the urge to shrink back against the wall. Instead, I stand up and throw off my blanket. He'd welcome any excuse to lay hands on me, so I don't give him one. I just walk over to the metal bars and stand there waiting, my stomach twisting with nausea.

"You're wanted out there again," he says, reaching for my arm. I almost puke as he grabs my wrist, his fingers thick and oily on my skin. He snaps a handcuff on that wrist and then grabs my other arm, stepping closer. "They said you won't be coming back here," he whispers, and I feel one of his hands squeezing my ass, his fingers digging painfully into the crack. "It's too bad. I'll miss you, Yulechka."

Vomit rises in my throat as I smell his breath—stale cigarettes mixed with rotting teeth. It takes everything I have not to shove him away. Fighting means he'll get to touch me even more; I know that from experience. So I just stand there and wait for him to release me. He won't rape me—that's one humiliation I've been spared, thanks to the cameras—so all I need to do is remain still and not throw up.

Sure enough, after a few seconds, he snaps the second handcuff on my wrist and steps back, disappointment darkening his features.

"Let's go," he barks, grabbing my elbow, and I gulp in air untainted by his stench, desperately hoping my stomach will settle down. I've thrown up once before, when they fed me greasy meat after starving me for three days, and they made me clean it up with the blanket that's still on my cot.

To my relief, my nausea recedes as Igor marches me down the hall, and I register what he said.

You won't be coming back.

What does that mean? Are they moving me to another facility, or did they finally decide it wasn't worth it, trying to get anything out of me? Am I about to be executed? Is that what Buschekov was hinting at when he said he was about to get some new authorization?

My heartbeat picks up, a fresh wave of nausea moving through me. I'm not ready for this. I thought I was, but now that the moment is here, I want to live.

I want to live to see Misha.

Except if I give the Russians what they want, I won't see Misha ever again. Obenko's sister and her family will be forced to go into hiding, and my brother along with them. Misha's happy life will be over, and it'll all be my fault.

No. My resolve firms again.

It's better that I die.

At least then I'll be out of this hellhole once and for all.

DESPITE MY DETERMINATION, MY LEGS FEEL LIKE GELATIN AS IGOR leads me down an unfamiliar hallway. We're moving away from the interrogation room, which means the guard wasn't lying.

Something different is happening today.

"This way," Igor says, tugging me toward a set of double doors. As we approach, they swing open for us, and I blink at the sudden flood of blinding light.

Sunlight.

It's warm and pure on my skin, so unlike the cold fluorescence of the prison lights. The air wafting in through those doors is different too. It's fresher, full of scents that speak of city in the spring and have nothing to do with desperation and human suffering.

"Here she is," Igor says, pushing me through the doors, and to my shock, a woman's voice repeats his words in Russian-accented English.

Squinting against the overwhelming brightness, I turn my head to see a short middle-aged woman standing next to five men in a narrow courtyard. Beyond them is a thick wall with barbed wire at the top and several armed guards.

"Who are you?" I ask the woman in English, but she doesn't respond. Instead, she turns to look at one of the men—a tall, thin one who seems to be their leader.

"You can go now, thank you," he says to her, speaking American English without an accent, and I realize she must be an interpreter.

She nods at him and hurries toward the gate on the other side of the courtyard. The man steps toward me, and I see an expression of disgust cross his narrow face. He must've smelled my lack of showers.

"Let's go," he says, grabbing my arm and pulling me away from Igor.

"Where are you taking me?" I'm trying to stay calm. This is not at all what I was expecting. What could Americans want from me? Unless... Could they be with—

"Colombia," the man says, confirming my horrified guess. "Julian Esguerra requests the honor of your presence."

And before I can process this new blow, he drags me toward the gate.

~

I don't know at what point I start fighting—whether it's once we're beyond the prison gate or when we approach the black van. All I know is that a beast wakes up inside me, and I lash out at the man holding me with all my remaining strength.

I have no idea how the arms dealer could be alive, and at this moment, I don't care. The panicked animal inside me cares only about avoiding the terrible torment that awaits at the end of this journey. I've read the file on Esguerra, and I've heard the rumors. He's not only a ruthless businessman.

He's also a sadist.

My hands are cuffed, so I use my feet, kicking out at the leader's knee at the same time as I crouch and twist, breaking his hold on my arm. He cries out, cursing, but I'm already rolling on the ground, away from the five men. I don't get far, of course. Within a second, they're on me, two big men pinning me to the ground and then jerking me up to my feet. I continue to fight them, kicking and biting and screaming as they shove me into the back of the van. It's only when the doors close and the van starts moving that I stop struggling, exhausted and shaking all over. My breathing is harsh and loud, and my heart slams against my ribcage in a terrified tempo.

"Hijo de puta, she stinks," the man holding me mutters, and my cheeks flame with embarrassment, as if it's my fault I've been reduced to this disgusting creature.

They gag me then, probably to stop me from screaming again,

and cuff my wrists to my ankles before throwing me in the corner of the van and sitting down a couple of feet away. They don't touch me beyond that, and after a few minutes, some of my blind panic recedes and I begin thinking again.

Julian Esguerra wants me delivered to him. That means he didn't die from the missile strike. How is that possible? Did Obenko lie to me, or did Esguerra somehow get lucky? And if the arms dealer survived, what about the rest of his crew?

What about Lucas Kent?

A familiar ache pierces my chest as I think his name. I'd only known him for that one night, but I've grieved for him, cried for him in the cold confines of my cell. Could he possibly be alive? And if he's alive, am I going to see him again?

Will he be the one who tortures me?

No. I squeeze my eyes shut. I can't think of that right now. I need to take it one minute at a time, same as I did in that interrogation room. It's likely that the next several hours are my last ones without extreme pain—if not my last ones overall—and I can't spend that precious time worrying about the future.

I can't spend it thinking about a man who's most likely dead.

So instead of Lucas Kent, I think of my brother again, of his sunny smile and the way his small, pudgy arms embraced me when he was little. I was eight years old when he was born, and our parents were afraid I would resent the intrusion of a new baby into our close-knit family. But I didn't. I fell in love with Misha from the moment I met him in the hospital, and when I held him for the first time and felt how tiny he was, I knew it would be my job to protect him.

"It's wonderful that Yulia loves her brother so much," my parents' friends would tell them. "Look how well she takes care of him. She'll make a wonderful mother one day."

My parents would nod, beaming at me, and I would redouble my efforts to be a good sister, to do whatever I could to ensure my baby brother was happy, healthy, and safe.

The van comes to a halt, bringing me out of my thoughts, and I realize with a jolt of panic that we've arrived.

"Let's go," the group leader says when the van doors open, and I see that we're on a landing strip in front of a Gulfstream private jet. I can't walk with my wrists cuffed to my ankles, so the man who complained about my smell earlier carries me out of the van and onto the plane, the interior of which is as luxurious as anything I've seen.

"Where do you want her?" he asks the leader, and I see his dilemma. The wide seats in the cabin are upholstered with cream-colored leather, as is the couch next to the coffee table. Everything here is clean and nice, whereas I'm filthy.

"There," the leader says, pointing to a seat by the window. "Diego, cover it with a sheet."

A dark-haired man nods and disappears into the back of the plane. He returns a minute later with what appears to be a bed sheet. He drapes it over the seat, and the man holding me deposits me there.

"Do you want the gag removed and her ankles uncuffed?" he asks the leader, and the thin man shakes his head.

"No. Let the bitch sit like this. It'll teach her a lesson."

And with that, they turn away, leaving me to stare out the window and try to keep my mind off what awaits me when the plane lands.

16

ulia

"COME ON, LET'S GO." ROUGH HANDS LIFT ME OFF THE SEAT, startling me out of uneasy sleep. "We're here."

Here? My heartbeat jumps as I realize we've already landed. I must've fallen asleep at some point during the flight, my exhaustion outweighing my anxiety.

It's another man carrying me now—Diego, the leader called him. His grip on me is not especially gentle as he holds me in front of his chest. However, I'm glad they're not making me walk. After spending the whole flight with my ankles and wrists cuffed together, I'm not sure my cramping muscles would be up for the task. Not to mention that I'm so hungry I feel sick and dizzy. They took off my gag and gave me some water mid-way through the flight, but they didn't bother feeding me.

As soon as Diego exits the plane, a wave of warm humidity

washes over me, making me feel like I just entered a Russian bathhouse—or maybe a rainforest. The latter is probably a better comparison, given the thick, vine-draped trees surrounding the air strip.

Despite the terror circling through my veins, I'm dazzled by the greenery around me. I love nature—I always have, ever since I was a small child—and this place appeals to me on every level. The air is rich with the scent of tropical vegetation, insects are chirping in the grass, and the sun is bright despite a few clouds in the sky. For a couple of blissful moments, I feel like I'm in paradise.

Then I hear a car approaching and reality crashes in.

The owner of this paradise is going to torture and kill me.

My empty stomach clenches. I don't want to give in to the fear, but I can't help the dread that spreads through me as the car—a black SUV—stops in front of the plane.

The driver's door opens, and a tall, broad-shouldered man steps out, the sun glinting off his short, light-colored hair.

I stop breathing, my eyes glued to his hard features.

Lucas Kent.

He's alive.

His pale eyes lock on mine, and the world around me recedes, blurring out of focus. I forget all about my hunger and discomfort, about the cuffs restraining me and my fear of the future.

All I'm cognizant of is the stark, irrational joy that Lucas is alive.

He starts walking toward me, and I force myself to breathe again. He's even bigger than I remembered, his shoulders wide and thick with muscle. Dressed in a sleeveless camo shirt and ripped jeans, with an assault rifle slung across his torso, he looks exactly like what he is: a ruthless mercenary working for a crime lord.

"I'll handle it from here, Diego," he says, approaching me, and I begin to shake as he reaches for me, his gaze sliding away from mine. Diego hands me over without a word, and my shaking intensifies as I feel Lucas's hands on me again, his touch burning me even through the rough material of my prison jumpsuit.

Stepping back, he turns and begins carrying me to the car, holding me flush against his chest. He evidences no disgust at my unwashed state, and a shudder ripples through me as I feel the heat of his body seeping into me, melting some of the residual chill inside. I should be terrified, but instead I feel that awareness again—that irrational attraction I've only experienced with him. At the same time, a pressure gathers behind my temples, and my eyes prickle, as though I'm about to cry.

Alive. He's alive.

It doesn't seem real. None of this seems real. My reality is a gray, smelly cell in a Russian prison. It's Igor's greasy hands and Buschekov's mirrored interrogation room. It's hunger, thirst, and longing—longing for the life I lost when my parents' car slid on black ice, for the brother I only saw in pictures, and for the man I'd known just one day.

For the man I thought I'd killed—the one holding me right now.

Could all of this be a dream? A fantasy concocted in my exhausted, sleep-deprived mind? Could I even now be passed out at the interrogation table, with that screeching alarm about to jerk me back to consciousness?

Lucas's face blurs in front of my eyes, and I realize I *am* crying, fat, ugly tears welling up and spilling down my cheeks. Embarrassed, I automatically try to wipe them away, but my hands, still cuffed to my ankles, can't reach that far. The motion ends up being jerky and awkward, and I see Lucas's face turn to stone as he glances down at me.

"You fucking bitch," he says so softly that I can barely hear him. "You think you can manipulate me with your tears?" His grip on me tightens, turning hard and punishing as he stops in front of the SUV and glares down at me, as if waiting for a response. When I don't give him one, his features harden further. "You're going to pay for what you did," he promises, his voice filled with quiet fury. "You're going to pay for everything."

And with that, he jerks open the car door and throws me onto the back seat. As my back hits the cushioned leather, I know that I was wrong.

This is not a dream.

It's a nightmare.

~

THE RIDE TAKES ONLY A FEW MINUTES. LUCAS DRIVES SILENTLY, NOT saying anything else to me, and I use the time to compose myself. Strangely, thinking of his threat helps me control my tears, my stunned joy turning into cold fear as I process the fact that Lucas Kent is alive—and that he will indeed be the one to make me pay.

Does that mean the plane crash happened after all? If so, how did he and Esguerra survive? I want to ask Lucas that, but I can't bring myself to break the silence, not when I feel his rage pulsing in the air like a malevolent force waiting to be unleashed. He took off his weapon, setting it on the front seat next to him, but that doesn't lessen the threat emanating from him.

He can kill me with his bare hands if he's so inclined.

As the car leaves the heavily wooded area, I see a big white house in the distance. It's surrounded by manicured green lawns that form a contrast to the untamed jungle behind us. Farther back, I see guard towers spaced a few dozen meters apart. The sight doesn't surprise me; Esguerra's file said that his Colombian estate is heavily fortified despite its remote location on the edge of the Amazon rainforest.

We don't go to the big house; instead, we turn and drive along the jungle to a cluster of smaller houses and boxy, one-story buildings. It must be where the guards and others on the Esguerra compound live, I realize as I see armed men—and an occasional woman—going in and out of the dwellings.

The car stops in front of one of the individual houses, the one with a front porch, and Lucas exits, leaving the gun in the car. He slams the door behind him, and I flinch, trying not to give in to the anxiety choking me from within. The fear is thick and bitter in my throat. It's worse somehow that it's Lucas who'll do those terrible things to me, that he'll be the one to rip out my fingernails or cut me open piece by piece.

It's worse because there were times in that Moscow prison when I used to imagine I was with him, when I fantasized that he was holding me and I was safe in his strong embrace.

Lucas walks around the car and opens the back door. Reaching in, he grabs me and drags me out, still not saying a word as he lifts me against his chest and slams the door closed with his foot. His hold on me is again harsh and punishing, and I know it's only the start.

My fantasies are about to shatter under the weight of reality.

He carries me up the porch stairs, walking as easily as if I weigh nothing. His strength is tremendous, only there's no safety in it. Not for me, at least. Maybe for some woman in the future, someone he'll care about and want to protect.

Someone he won't hate as much as he hates me.

As he pushes open the front door and turns sideways to carry me through the doorway, I catch a glimpse of curious faces staring up at us from the street. There are several men and a middle-aged woman, and for one absurd moment, I'm tempted to beg them for help, to plead with them to save me. The urge fades as quickly as it comes. These people aren't some innocent passersby. They're employees of a sadistic arms dealer, and they're fully complicit in whatever fate is about to befall me.

So I stay silent as Lucas carries me into the house and once again shuts the door behind him with his foot. He's not looking at me, so I use the opportunity to study him, noting the granite set of his jaw. He's still furious, the rage radiating off him like heat off a flame. It makes me wonder why he's so mad. Surely this sort of thing—making Esguerra's enemies pay—is routine for him. I would've expected cold detachment, not this volcanic anger.

Come to think of it, I would've expected him to take me to some warehouse or a storage shed, some place they wouldn't mind dirtying with blood and bodily fluids. Instead, I find myself inside a residential home, albeit one with only basic furnishings. One black leather sofa, a flatscreen TV, gray carpet, and white walls—the room he carries me through is not luxurious, but it's certainly no torture chamber. Could this be Lucas's house? And if so, why am I here?

I don't have time to dwell on it for long because he brings me into a large, white-tiled bathroom. There is a massive tub, a glass-walled shower stall, and a sink next to a toilet.

Definitely not a torture chamber.

"Why did you bring me here?" My voice is hoarse, scratchy from disuse. I haven't spoken since Esguerra's men stopped me from screaming back in Moscow. "It's your house, isn't it?"

Lucas's jaw muscle flexes, but he doesn't respond. Instead, he carries me into the shower stall, sets me down on the tiled floor, and pulls out a key. Grabbing my handcuffs, he unlocks them and detaches them from the ankle cuffs, which he unlocks next. Then he yanks me to my feet.

"You need a fucking shower," he says harshly. "Take those clothes off. Now."

My knees buckle, my leg muscles unable to bear the sudden strain of standing, even as my aching back weeps in gratitude at finally being straight again. My head spins from chronic hunger and exhaustion, and it's only Lucas's grip on my arm that prevents me from sinking back down to the floor.

A shower? He wants me to take a shower? Before I can process that odd demand, he lets out an impatient noise and grabs the zipper of my jumpsuit, pulling it down roughly.

"Wait, I can—" I try to reach for the zipper with one trembling hand, but it's too late. Lucas spins me around, flattening my face against the shower wall, and yanks the jumpsuit down to my knees, leaving me wearing nothing more than a pair of loose, high-waisted panties and a stretched-out sports bra—the only underwear allowed at the prison. Within a second, he rips those off me as well and spins me around to face him.

"Don't make me tell you twice." His fingers catch my jaw in a hard grip as he holds my upper arm with his other hand. "You'll do what I say, understand?" His eyes glint with icy rage and something more.

Lust.

He still wants me.

My heart pounds in a furious rhythm as the fact that I'm naked in front of him again sinks in. I should've expected this, but for some reason, I didn't. In my mind, what happened between us before was entirely separate from the punishment he's about to dole out, but I should've known better.

For men like Lucas Kent, violence and sex go hand in hand.

"Do you understand?" he repeats, his fingers digging painfully into my jaw, and I blink affirmatively, the only movement I'm capable of. Apparently, that's enough, because he releases me and steps back.

"Wash yourself," he orders, stepping out of the stall and closing the glass door behind him. "You have five minutes."

And crossing his arms in front of his massive chest, he leans back against the wall and stares at me, waiting.

17

ucas

She reaches for the faucet, her entire body shaking, and I see the effort each movement is costing her. She's weak and thin, infinitely more fragile than the last time I saw her, and the fact that this disturbs me enrages me even more.

I expected to feel lust and hatred, to revel in her suffering even as I slaked my hunger on her deceitful flesh. I planned to treat her like my fucktoy until my obsession with her faded, and then do whatever it took to find the puppet masters pulling her strings.

I didn't count on this pale, bedraggled creature and how seeing her this way would make me feel.

Did they starve her? Apparently so, because I can see each of her ribs. Her stomach is concave, her hipbones are jutting out, and her limbs are painfully skinny. She must've lost at least fifteen pounds in the last two months, and she'd already been slender.

She manages to turn on the water, and I force myself to remain still as she reaches for the shampoo. She's not looking at me, all her attention focused on her task, and I feel a fresh wave of rage, mixed with lust and that disconcerting something.

Something that feels suspiciously like protectiveness.

Fuck. I clench my teeth, determined to resist the bizarre urge to step into the shower and gather her against me. Not to fuck her, though my body is eager to do that as well, but to hold her.

To hold and comfort her.

Infuriated, I shift against the wall, watching as she begins to lather her hair. Despite her extreme thinness, her body is graceful and feminine. Her breasts are smaller than before, but they're still surprisingly full, her nipples drawn into taut pink buds as she stands under the water spray. I can see soft-looking blond fuzz between her legs; after nearly two months of no razor or wax, her pussy must be back to its natural state. My cock, semi-aroused from stripping her naked, hardens fully, and I imagine myself stepping into that shower, unzipping my jeans, and driving into her tight heat with no preliminaries. Just taking her, like the fucktoy I intended her to be.

And there's nothing stopping me from doing that. She's my prisoner. I can do anything I want to her. I've never forced a woman, but I've never wanted and hated one at the same time either. How would fucking her be any worse than slicing up her delicate flesh to make her talk?

It wouldn't be. She's mine to hurt in any way I please.

Except hurting her is not what I want to do right now. The violence seething inside me is not for her. It's for those who hurt her. When I saw her in Diego's grip, her long hair lank and dull around her pale face, I felt a rage unlike any other. And when she began crying, it was all I could do not to cradle her against me and promise that no one will ever hurt her again.

Not even me.

The urge maddened me then, and it maddens me now. I have

no doubt the witch knew what she was doing to me with those tears, just as she knew how to extract information out of me that night in Moscow. Her frail appearance is just that: an appearance. That beautiful blond exterior conceals a trained agent, a spy who's as skilled at mind games as she is at foreign languages.

"Your five minutes are up," I say, straightening away from the wall. She's washed her hair and her body, and is now just standing under the water with her eyes closed and her head tilted back. "Get out." My voice is harsh, reflecting none of the turmoil I'm feeling.

I won't let her fuck with me again.

At my words, she jumps, her eyes flying open, and reaches back to turn off the shower. She's still shaking, though not as badly as before, and I wonder how much of that is an act and how much is actual weakness.

Pulling open the shower door, I grab a towel and throw it at her. "Dry yourself."

She obeys, toweling off her hair and then her body. As she does so, I notice bruises covering her legs and ribcage and bluish circles under her weary eyes.

Damn her. She's not faking *that*.

"That's enough." Suppressing the illogical pang of pity, I yank the towel away from her and hang it on a hook. "Let's go."

Her eyes plead with me as I grab her arm, but I ignore their silent entreaty, my hold on her unnecessarily rough. I can't give in to this weakness, to this obsession that seems to be completely out of control. Over the past two months, I've come to terms with the fact that I can't stop wanting her, but this is something else entirely.

She stumbles as I tug her through the doorway, and I stop to pick her up, telling myself that it will be easier to carry her than to drag her. As I swing her up against my chest, I feel the soft press of her breasts and smell her scent, now clean and mixed with the aroma of my body wash. Lust surges through me again, pushing aside my awareness of her too-light weight, and I welcome it. This is exactly what I need: to want her and nothing else. And for that, I can't have her as this frail, pathetic waif.

I need her stronger.

The bedroom was my destination, but I change my course, heading for the kitchen instead. I can feel her breathing fast—she's probably afraid—but she doesn't struggle. She undoubtedly realizes how pointless it would be in her weakened state.

When we reach the kitchen, I set her down in a chair and take a step back. Immediately, she draws her knees up against her chest, concealing much of her naked body. Her eyes are big and scared as she stares at me, her wet hair plastered against her back and shoulders.

"You're going to eat," I tell her, approaching the fridge. Opening it, I take out turkey, cheese, and mayo, and place everything on the counter next to the loaf of bread sitting there. As I make the sandwich, I keep an eye on her, making sure she's not attempting anything—which she's not. She's just sitting there, watching warily as I smear the mayo on both slices of bread, slap on some cheese and turkey, and place everything on a plate.

"Eat," I say, putting the plate in front of her.

She runs her tongue over her lips. "May I have some water, please?"

Of course. She must be thirsty as well. Without answering, I walk over to the sink, pour a glass of water, and bring it to her.

"Thank you." Her voice is quiet as she accepts my offering, her slender fingers wrapping around the glass and brushing against mine in the process. A frisson of electricity races up my spine at that accidental touch, and my jeans become uncomfortably tight again, my cock straining against the zipper.

Her eyes flick down for a second before returning to my face, and I see her pupils dilating. She's aware of my lust for her, and it frightens her. Her hand holding the glass trembles slightly as she drinks, and her other arm tightens around her drawn-up knees.

Good. I want her afraid. I want her to know that I may want

her body, but I won't show her mercy. She won't be able to manipulate me ever again.

While she's drinking, I sit down across the table and lean back in the chair, linking my hands behind my head.

"Eat. Now," I order again when she puts down her glass, and she obeys, her straight white teeth sinking into the sandwich with unconcealed eagerness.

Despite her obvious hunger, she eats slowly, thoroughly chewing each bite. It's a smart move; she doesn't want to get sick from eating too much too fast.

"So," I say when she's eaten about a quarter of her meal, "what's your real name?"

She pauses mid-bite and puts down her sandwich. "Yulia." Her eyes hold mine without blinking.

"Don't lie to me." I unlink my hands and lean forward. "A spy wouldn't use her real name."

"I didn't say it's Yulia Tzakova." She picks up the sandwich again and consumes another bite before explaining, "Yulia is a common name in Russia and Ukraine, and it happens to be my birth name. It's the Russian version of Julia."

"Ah." That makes sense, and I'm inclined to believe her. It's always easier to stick close to your real identity when going undercover. "So, Yulia, what is your real last name then?"

"My last name doesn't matter." Her soft lips twist. "The girl it belonged to no longer exists."

"Then there's no harm in telling me what it is, is there?" Despite myself, I'm intrigued. Whether it matters or not, I want to know her last name.

I want to know everything about her.

She shrugs and bites into her sandwich again. I can tell she has no intention of answering me.

My teeth grind together, but I remind myself to be patient. The Russians hadn't been able to get anything useful out of her in two months, so I certainly can't expect to crack her in the first hour.

Priority number one is having her eat and regain her strength. Answers will come later. I'll get them out of her, one way or another.

For now, I mentally go through the information Buschekov emailed me on her. There isn't much that they were able to uncover. All she's admitted is that she's twenty-two, not twenty-four as listed in her fake passport, and she was born in Donetsk, one of the embattled areas in eastern Ukraine. The Ukrainian government refused to claim her as one of their own, so the organization she works for must be private or strictly off the books. Her degree in English Language and International Relations from Moscow State University is apparently real; there is a record of Yulia Tzakova graduating from there two years ago, and Buschekov was able to track down professors and classmates who verified that she did, in fact, attend classes.

Did the Ukrainians recruit her at the university, or did they plant her there? It's not out of the question that she's been working for them since her teens. Agents rarely get recruited that young, but it does happen.

"How long have you been doing this?" I ask when she's nearly done with her sandwich. Her pale cheeks have a bit of color in them now, and she looks less shaky. "Spying for Ukraine, that is?"

Instead of answering, Yulia takes a sip of water, puts down her glass, and looks straight at me. "May I use the restroom, please?"

My hands tighten on the table. "Yes—when you answer my question."

She doesn't blink. "I've been doing it for a while," she says evenly. "Now, may I please pee in the toilet? Or should I do it here?"

The rage smoldering within me flares brighter, and I give in to it. In an instant, I'm next to her, grabbing her by her hair and yanking her to her feet. She cries out in pain, her hands clutching at my wrist, but I don't give her a chance to start fighting. In less than two seconds, I have her folded over the table, her arm twisted behind her back and her face pressed against the table surface. The plate with the remnants of the sandwich slides off the table, shattering on the floor, but I don't give a fuck.

She's going to learn an important lesson right now.

"Say that again." I lean over her, trapping her naked body underneath me. I can hear her fast, shallow breathing, feel the curve of her ass pressing into my crotch, and my cock hardens as dark sexual images invade my mind. In this position, all I need to do is open my fly, and I'll be inside her.

The temptation is almost unbearable.

"Since I was eleven." Her voice is thin, muffled against the table. "I've been doing it since I was eleven."

Eleven? Stunned, I release her and step back. What kind of agency recruits a child?

Before I can digest her revelation, she scoots off the table and faces me. "Please, Lucas." Her face is pale again, her lips trembling. "I really need to go to the restroom."

Fuck.

I grab her arm. "You have five minutes," I warn as I march her back to the bathroom. "And do not lock the door. I have the key."

She nods and disappears into the bathroom, her half-dry hair streaming down her slender back.

Shaking my head, I go back to the kitchen to clean up.

I don't want her to cut her bare feet on the shards of the broken plate.

18

ulia

My knees shaking, I collapse against the closed bathroom door and try to calm my frantic breathing. What nearly happened in that kitchen shouldn't have freaked me out so much, but it was too close to before... too close to that dark place I've fought so hard to escape. The position—on my stomach and helpless, with a man who's determined to punish me on top—had been all too familiar, and I panicked.

I panicked like that fifteen-year-old I thought I'd buried.

Perhaps it wouldn't have been so bad if it had been someone else—anyone else. I could've put up that steel mental wall, the one that kept me sane before. If fear and disgust were all I felt for Lucas, it would've been easier.

If I hadn't had those stupid fantasies about him in prison, it would've been less devastating.

Taking deep breaths, I force myself to straighten away from the door and use the toilet. I have only a couple of minutes before Lucas returns for me, and I can't afford to waste them this way. As I wash my hands and brush my teeth, I stare in the mirror, trying to convince myself that I can do this—that I can withstand whatever punishment he chooses to dole out, even if it's of a sexual variety.

"Your time's up." His deep voice startles me, and I realize I've been just standing there, letting the water run. "Come out."

Panic floods my veins. "Just a second," I call out.

I'm not ready for this. I'm not ready for *him*. For the first time in weeks, I've eaten a normal meal and had a shower, and somehow that makes it worse. Because now that I feel semi-human, I'm keenly aware of my nakedness and how much I am at the mercy of a man who wants to hurt me.

My heart pounding, I scan the bathroom. Lucas wouldn't be stupid enough to leave a weapon lying around, but I don't need much. My gaze falls on the plastic toothbrush I just used, and I grab it. Using both hands, I snap the handle in half. As I'd hoped, one side ends up sharp and jagged, and I clutch it tightly, concealing it in my right hand.

Taking another deep breath, I open the door and step out. "All done," I say, hoping he can't hear the strain in my voice.

"Let's go." Lucas grabs my left arm, and I stumble, on purpose this time. He turns to steady me, and in that moment I strike upward with my makeshift weapon, aiming for his kidney. I shut off the part of my brain that cringes at the thought of hurting him, the part where those fantasies still live, and I let my training take over.

He twists at the last moment, his reflexes razor sharp, and I graze his torso instead of stabbing him. The broken toothbrush catches on his shirt, forcing me to let go of it, but I don't let that stop me. He's still holding my arm, so I drop to the floor, letting my full weight hang on that arm, and kick up with my right leg.

My foot connects with his jaw, the impact sending a shock of pain through me, but he reels back—which gives me the split second I need to twist free of his hold.

Scrambling to my feet, I sprint for the kitchen, desperate to grab a knife, but before I can take more than two steps, he tackles me from behind. I manage to turn, half-rolling as we land on the carpet, and my elbow slams into his hard stomach. The impact makes my arm go numb. He continues rolling without so much as a grunt, and a moment later has me pinned down, his hands capturing both of my wrists and lifting them above my head at the same time as his powerful legs anchor mine to the floor.

I can't move. I'm once again helpless underneath him.

Breathing hard, I stare up at him, my insides squeezing with dread as I wait for his retaliation. Our fight aroused him; I can feel the hard bulge in his jeans against my naked stomach. Or maybe he's still hard from earlier.

Either way, I know how he's going to punish me.

He's also breathing heavily, his chest rising and falling above me. I can see the rage burning in his pale eyes—rage and something far more primal.

To my shock, a tiny tendril of heat snakes through me, my mind transposing the horror of my current predicament with the stunning pleasure of that night. I lay underneath him then, too, and my body doesn't seem to understand that it was different.

That the man on top of me doesn't only want my body.

He wants revenge.

He lowers his head, and I freeze, scarcely breathing as his lips brush my left ear. "You shouldn't have done that," he whispers, the damp heat of his breath burning my skin. "I was going to give you more time, let you get stronger, but no more..." His mouth presses against my neck, and I feel his tongue flicking over the delicate area, as though tasting it. "You've used up all my patience, beautiful."

I shudder, trying to arch away from that hot, wicked mouth,

but I have nowhere to go. He's all around me, his muscular body large and heavy on top of mine. The brief burst of energy I felt after my meal is gone, my strength nonexistent after weeks of deprivation. Exhausted, I stop struggling—and realize that the tendril of heat is expanding in my core, making me slick with unwelcome need.

"Lucas, please." I don't know why I'm begging. I just tried to wound him; he won't show me mercy ever again. "Please, don't do this." My body's irrational response should've made this easier to bear, but it just highlights my helplessness, my complete lack of control. I can't face this with him. It would destroy me. "Please, Lucas..."

He shifts on top of me, his mouth still hovering near my ear. "Don't do what?" he murmurs, transferring both of my wrists into one of his large palms. Moving his free hand, he wedges it between us, his fingers slipping between my thighs to find my sex. "This?" His thumb presses on my clit as his index finger penetrates me.

I jerk at the invasion, the heat inside morphing into a pulsing ache. My nipples tighten, and I feel myself getting even slicker, my body eager for an act that would leave my soul in pieces. "Don't. Please don't." Tears, stupid, pathetic tears, come, and I can't contain them. They spill out and roll down my temples, making me burn with embarrassment at my weakness. "No, please..." His finger advances deeper into me, and the old memories crowd in, taking me back to that dark, suffocating place. My breathing turns into frantic pants, my voice rising in pitch. "Please, Lucas, don't!"

To my surprise, he stills, and then with a curse, he rolls off me, rising fluidly to his feet. "Get up," he snarls, grabbing my arms to pull me up. As soon as I'm vertical, he drags me into the living room and pushes me onto the couch, gritting out, "If you move a muscle..."

Dazed, I watch as he disappears around the corner and reappears a moment later carrying a chair and a coil of rope. He places both in the middle of the room. I haven't moved—I'm shaking too hard for that—and I don't put up any resistance as he picks me up, deposits me into the chair, and binds my arms behind my back, securing them against the chair's sturdy wooden frame. Then he uses additional rope to tie my ankles to the legs of the chair, leaving them spread apart.

When he's done, he stands up and stares at me. The bulge in his jeans is still present, but the heat in his eyes has cooled, turning them into familiar slivers of ice.

"I'll be back in a few minutes," he says harshly. "When I return, you better be ready to talk."

And before I can respond, he strides out of the room, leaving me tied up, naked, and alone.

19

ucas

I ENTER THE BATHROOM AND CLOSE THE DOOR IN A CONTROLLED motion, making sure it doesn't slam too hard. Control—that's what I need right now.

Control and distance from *her*.

My cock is like a spike in my jeans, my balls so full I feel like I could blow any second. I've never come so close to fucking a woman and then stopped.

I've never denied myself something I wanted so badly.

She had been right there, stretched out underneath me, her long, slender body naked and vulnerable. I could've fucked her any way I chose, taking my rage out on her delicate flesh while slaking the hunger plaguing me for so long.

Instead, I let her go.

Son of a fucking bitch.

I stare in the mirror, seeing the fury and frustration on my face. She wanted me—I felt how wet she was, how her body was responding to me—and I still let her go.

Despite my body's burning need, I couldn't bring myself to rape her.

Disgusted with my weakness, I look away, running my hand over my short hair. Rape is no worse than the crimes I've committed in recent years. In Esguerra's service, I've killed and tortured both men and women, and I've felt no qualms. Taking Yulia should've been the easiest thing in the world—I've dreamed of fucking her every night over the last two months—yet I stopped myself.

I stopped myself because the terror in her voice had been real, and I couldn't ignore it.

Gritting my teeth, I lift my shirt and examine my ribcage. There's no blood where Yulia's weapon grazed me, but there is an angry red scratch. She had probably been aiming for my kidney. If I hadn't been fast enough, I would be bleeding out in hellish pain on that floor—assuming she didn't slit my throat immediately. As it is, my jaw throbs where her foot struck me, reminding me how treacherous—and dangerous—she is.

It would've been smarter to leave her with the Russians.

No. As soon as the thought crosses my mind, my entire body tenses in rejection. Now that I finally have her in my possession, the idea of someone else tormenting her is unbearable. Everything inside me screams that she's mine—mine to fuck, mine to punish in any way I choose.

Nobody else will lay hands on her ever again.

Unzipping my jeans, I pull out my engorged cock and close my fist around it. Squeezing my eyes shut, I imagine that I'm inside her and it's her inner walls gripping my dick so tightly.

With the pornographic images filling my mind, it takes less than a minute for me to come, my seed spurting into the clean white bowl of the sink.

20

ulia

I DON'T KNOW HOW LONG IT TAKES ME TO REALIZE THAT THE reprieve is real, but eventually I calm down enough to stop shaking.

He didn't go through with it.

He didn't force me.

I still can't believe it. I know how hard he was—I felt it. There was no reason for him to show me mercy. I'm not some woman he picked up in a bar; I'm the enemy who just tried to injure him. He should've gloried in my pathetic begging and used the weakness I revealed to break me completely.

That's what I would've expected him to do, at least.

Lowering my head, I stare at my naked legs, trying to understand why he stopped. Lucas Kent is not a novice to this life—far from it. According to his file, he joined the United States Navy right after high school and entered the SEAL training program several months later. There wasn't much in that file on his assignments—only that they were usually classified and extremely dangerous missions—but the reason for him leaving was listed.

It was a murder charge eight years into his service. The man holding me captive killed his commanding officer and disappeared into the jungles of South America. There's a four-year gap in the file after that, but eventually, Lucas Kent resurfaced as Esguerra's trusted and extremely deadly second-in-command.

A tingle runs down my arms, and some sixth sense makes me look up.

Two pairs of dark eyes are watching me from the window, one huge and fringed by thick lashes, and the other slightly almond-shaped.

It's two young women, I realize as the owner of the thick lashes ducks out of sight, leaving me staring at the braver intruder. The remaining girl is about my age and looks Colombian, her bronzed, round face framed by smooth dark hair. She's pretty—and extremely curious about me, judging by her arrested stare.

I don't have time to register more because a second later, she ducks and disappears too.

Confused, I continue staring at the window, waiting, but they don't return. Instead, I hear footsteps and turn my head to see Lucas entering the room with another chair.

Placing it in front of me, he sits down on it and crosses his arms in front of his chest. "All right, Yulia." His gaze is hard as it travels down my naked body and then returns to my face. "Why don't you begin by telling me your story."

My reprieve is over.

Trying to remain calm, I moisten my lips. "May I please have some water?" I'm thirsty—and desperate to put off the interrogation for as long as possible.

He doesn't move. "Talk and I'll give it to you."

I swallow, noting the implacable set of his jaw. "What do you want to know?" Perhaps there are some basics I can share with him, just like I shared with the Russians. I can admit to being a spy for the Ukrainians—he already knows that much—and I can give him a little bit of my background.

Maybe that information will buy me some time without pain.

"You said you started at eleven." He watches me coldly, without so much as a hint of the lust that burned between us. "Tell me about them—the people who recruited you."

So much for hoping I can stall him with innocuous revelations.

"I don't know much about them," I say. "They would send me on assignments; that's all."

His eyes narrow. He knows I'm lying. "Is that right?" His voice is deceptively soft. "And was enrolling in Moscow State University an assignment?"

"It was." There's no point in denying it. "They falsified my documents and enrolled me in the university so I could live in Moscow and get close to key people in the Russian government."

"Get close how?" He leans forward, and I see something dark flash in his pale eyes. "How exactly did they want you to carry out your assignment, beautiful?"

I don't answer, but I can see that he knows. How else does a young woman insinuate herself into top government circles?

"How many?" Lucas's voice is sharp enough to slice me into pieces. "How many did you have to fuck to 'get close'?"

"Three." Two lower-level officials and one of Buschekov's friends—which is how I got the job as Buschekov's interpreter. "I had to sleep with three of them." I stare directly at Lucas, ignoring the ball of shame lodged deep in my chest. "Esguerra would've been the fourth, but I ended up with you instead."

His eyes narrow further, and my pulse spikes with cold fear. I don't know why I'm taunting him like this. Getting Lucas angry is a bad idea. I need to be pacifying him, buying myself more time. It doesn't matter that the contempt on his face is like a knife stabbing into my liver.

An actual knife would be much, much worse.

He stands up abruptly, looming over me, and I try not to flinch as I tilt my head back to meet his gaze. His eyes glint at me, rage flickering in their blue-gray depths again. For a moment, I'm convinced he's going to hit me, but he grips a fistful of my hair instead, forcing my head to arch back more.

"Did you want them?" His fingers tighten in my hair, making my eyes sting at the pain in my scalp. "Did your pussy cream for them too?"

"No." I'm telling the truth, but I can see that he doesn't believe me. "It wasn't like that with them. It was just something I had to do." I don't know why I'm trying to convince him. I don't want him to know that he was in any way special, but at the same time, I can't bring myself to lie about this. "It was my job."

"Just like I was your job." He stares down at me, and I catch a glimpse of the dark lust lurking underneath his anger. "You gave me your body to get information."

I don't deny it, and I see his chest expanding as he draws in a breath. I brace myself for hurtful words of condemnation, but they never come. Instead, his painful hold on my hair eases a fraction, as though he realizes my neck can't stay bent like that.

"Yulia..." There is a strange note in his voice. "How old were you when you slept with the first one of the three?"

I blink, caught off-guard by the question. "Sixteen."

Or at least that was when our relationship began. Boris Ladrikov, a short, slightly balding member of the State Duma, had been my first boyfriend, and our affair lasted for the better part of three years. He introduced me to all the important people, including Vladimir, who had become my next assigned lover.

"Sixteen?" Lucas repeats, and I notice a muscle ticking near his ear. He's furious, and I have no idea why. "How old was your target?"

"Thirty-eight." I don't know why Lucas is asking all these irrelevant questions, but I'm happy to answer them for as long as it keeps him away from more important topics. "He thought I was eighteen; the identity I assumed was two years older."

I expect Lucas to drill me on this some more, but to my surprise, he releases my hair and steps back.

"That's enough for now," he says, and I catch that odd note in his voice again. "We'll resume this in a bit."

Without saying another word, he turns and leaves the room. A minute later, I hear the front door open and close, and I know I'm alone again.

21

ucas

A CHILD. SHE HAD BEEN A FUCKING CHILD WHEN THEY PLANTED HER in Moscow and forced her to sleep with sleazy government assholes.

The rage blasting through me feels hot enough to incinerate my insides. It had taken every ounce of my self-control to conceal my reaction from Yulia. If I hadn't left the house when I did, I would've put my fist through a wall.

The impulse is still with me an hour later, so I hammer the sandbag in front of me, channeling my fury into each blow. I can see the other men giving me inquiring looks; I've been at it for the past forty minutes without so much as a water break.

"Lucas, you crazy gringo, what's gotten into you?" A man's voice breaks my concentration, and I spin around to see Diego standing there. The tall Mexican is grinning, his teeth flashing white in his bronzed face. "Shouldn't you be saving some of that energy for your prisoner?"

"Fuck you, pendejo." Annoyed at the interruption, I grab the water bottle off the floor and take a swig. I normally like Diego, but right now I'm tempted to use him as my punching bag. "My prisoner is none of your fucking business."

"I helped deliver her here, so she's kind of my business," he objects, but the grin leaves his face. He can tell I'm in a mood. "She's the bitch who caused that crash, right?"

I wipe the dripping sweat off my forehead. "What makes you say that?" I'd been under the impression that only Esguerra, Peter, and I knew of Yulia's involvement.

Diego shrugs. "We got her from a Russian prison, and everyone knows the Ukrainians were behind it. It just seemed to fit. Plus, it seemed kind of personal for you, so..." His voice trails off as I give him a hard look.

"Like I said, she's none of your fucking business," I say coldly. The last thing I want is to discuss Yulia with the other men. What should've been the easiest thing in the world—revenge—has turned into a mess of epic proportions. The girl tied to the chair in my living room is not what I thought she was, and I have no fucking clue what to do about that.

"Yeah, okay, no worries." Diego grins again. "Just tell me: did you fuck her already? Even with the prison smell, I could tell she's a hot piece—"

My fist slams into his face before he finishes speaking. It's not a conscious action on my part; the fury filling me is simply too explosive to contain. He stumbles back from the force of my blow, and I follow, leaping and tackling him to the ground. My leg protests the sudden movement, but I ignore the pain, raining blow after blow on Diego's shocked face.

"Kent, what the fuck?" Steely hands grab my arms and drag me off my victim, resisting my attempts to throw them off. "Calm down, man!"

"What's going on here?" Esguerra's voice is like a splash of icy water on the flames of my rage. As my mind clears, I realize that Thomas and Eduardo are holding my arms while our boss is standing a dozen feet away, at the entrance of the training gym.

"Just a little disagreement." I manage to keep my voice steady despite the bloodlust still surging through me. Seeing that I'm no longer fighting them, Thomas and Eduardo release me and step back, their expressions carefully neutral.

Knowing I need to say something, I turn to the guard I assaulted. "Sorry, Diego. You caught me at a bad time."

"Yeah, no kidding," he mutters, getting to his feet with some effort. His nose is bleeding, and his left eye is already swelling up. "I've got to put some ice on this."

He hurries out of the gym, and Esguerra gives me a questioning look.

I shrug, as though the problem is too minor to explain, and to my relief, Esguerra doesn't pursue it. Instead, he informs me about a call with our Hong Kong supplier later this evening—he thinks it's a good idea for me to be present—and then heads back to his office, leaving me to shoot beer cans with the guards and try not to think about my captive.

22

ulia

I DON'T KNOW HOW LONG I SIT THERE, TRYING TO FIND A comfortable position on the hard chair, but eventually, a quiet rapping on the window draws my attention. Startled, I look up and see the girl who was watching me before—the one with the rounded face. She's standing outside, her nose pressed to the glass as she stares at me. I don't see her friend, so she must've come alone this time.

"Hello?" I call out, unsure whether she speaks English or would even be able to hear me through the glass. "Who are you?"

She hesitates for a second, then asks, "Where's Lucas?" Her voice is barely audible through the window, but I can tell that her English is of the American variety, with only a trace of a Spanish accent.

"I don't know. He left a little while ago," I say, studying her as thoroughly as she's studying me. It's not a fair exchange; all I see of her is her head, while she's looking at me in my birthday suit. Still, I note her regular features and full lips, filing the information away in my mind in case I need it later.

Who is she? Could she be Lucas's girlfriend? There was no mention of significant others in his file, but Obenko wouldn't know about Lucas's relationships on this estate. For all I know, my captor could have a wife and three kids here. A pretty young girlfriend is a no-brainer; Lucas is a virile, highly sexual man who'd have no trouble attracting women, even in a place as remote as this compound.

The more I consider it, the more it makes sense to me. This, right here, is why he didn't fuck me earlier.

It wasn't because of my pleas—it was because he didn't want to be unfaithful.

"What do you want?" I ask the girl, trying to ignore the irrational sense of betrayal at this realization. She doesn't seem disturbed at seeing me naked and tied up, so she obviously knows what her boyfriend is up to. "Why are you here?"

She opens her mouth as though to respond, but ducks out of sight instead. A moment later, I hear the front door opening and realize why.

Lucas is back.

A hum of awareness flutters through me as I hear his footsteps. He enters the room, stopping directly in front of me, and I see that his tan skin is glowing with perspiration. His sleeveless shirt is plastered against his muscular chest, a V of sweat visible in the middle. He looks powerfully, uncompromisingly male, and as I meet his icy gaze, I become cognizant of a heated ache between my legs.

As unbelievable as it is, I want him.

With effort, I tear my eyes away from his face, afraid he'll realize what I'm feeling. Nothing about my interactions with him makes sense. I just realized he has a girlfriend, and even if he didn't, how can I want a man I fear? And why hasn't he hurt me yet?

My gaze falls on his knuckles, and I tense as I see bruises there.

He just beat someone up.

I want to ask him about it, but I stay silent and look down at my knees. He's still angry—I can sense it—and I don't want to provoke him. I also don't bring up the girlfriend, though I'm dying to confront him about it. For some reason, the dark-haired girl didn't want him to know she was spying on me, and I don't want to sell her out for now.

I need whatever tiny advantage I can get.

"Are you hungry?" Lucas asks, and I look up, surprised by the question.

"I could eat," I say cautiously. I'm actually starving, my body demanding sustenance after weeks of nonstop hunger, but I don't want him to use that against me. I also really have to pee—a fact I've been trying not to focus on too much.

He stares at me, then nods, as though coming to a decision. Turning, he disappears down the hallway to the bathroom, and then I hear water running. Is he taking a shower?

Three minutes later, he reappears, dressed in a pair of black cotton shorts and a fresh T-shirt. His muscular neck is gleaming with droplets of water, and he smells like the body wash I used earlier, confirming my guess about the shower.

Crouching in front of me, he deftly unties my ankles and then walks around to untie my arms. "Let's go," he says, grabbing my elbow to pull me to my feet. "You can use the bathroom, and then I'll feed you."

He leads me to the bathroom, and I walk alongside him, too shocked to think about another escape attempt. "Go on," he says, giving me a push when we get to the bathroom, and I step inside, deciding not to question my good fortune.

As I wash my hands, I see a new, unbroken toothbrush sitting on the counter. For a second, I'm tempted to repeat my earlier stunt, but I decide against it. If I couldn't get him with the element of surprise, I certainly won't be able to overpower him now that he's aware of my capabilities.

Besides, he said he would feed me, and my stomach is doing cartwheels at the mere thought of food.

"Hands," Lucas says, grabbing my wrists as soon as I step out of the bathroom, and I open my palms, showing him that they're empty. He gives me an approving nod. "Good girl."

I raise my eyebrows at his odd behavior, but he's already leading me to the kitchen.

"Sit," he says, pointing at a chair, and I obey, watching as he takes out the same ingredients he used at lunch and begins making two sandwiches. As he works, I quickly scan the kitchen, trying to locate anything that could be used as a weapon. To my disappointment, I don't see a rack of knives or anything along those lines. The countertops are empty and clean, with the exception of the sandwich makings. He's not wearing a gun either; he must have all his weapons stashed somewhere else, like in his car.

"Here," he says, putting a plate in front of me, and I notice that it's paper, not ceramic like the one that broke earlier. The knife that he used to spread the mayo is plastic too. He's being cautious around me now. I have no doubt that if I searched through the drawers, I'd find something, but Lucas would be on me before I so much as opened a drawer.

My hands may be untied, but escape is as impossible as ever.

I run my tongue over my dry lips. "May I please have—"

"Water? Here you go." He pours water from the sink into a paper cup, places it in front of me, and sits down across the table with his own sandwich.

I have a million questions for him, but I make myself drink my water and eat most of my sandwich before I give in to the impulse. The last thing I want is to upset him and lose out on this meal.

Finally, I can't wait any longer. "Why are you doing this?" I ask as he finishes his food. My stomach is full to the point of bursting, and I can feel myself getting stronger as my body absorbs the calories. "What do you want from me?"

Lucas looks up, his features taut, and I realize he was just staring at my breasts—which are visible through my long hair. Heat climbs up my neck, and my nipples tighten, responding to the unconcealed desire in his eyes. I've been naked in front of him all day, and I'm getting desensitized to it, but that doesn't mean the situation isn't intensely sexual. As I hold his gaze, it dawns on me that part of the reason for his silence during dinner must've been the distraction of my unclothed body.

He still wants me, and I don't know if the knowledge terrifies or excites me.

"Tell me about them," he says abruptly. "Tell me about the people who recruited you, who made you do this."

And here it is: the true reason he's being nice to me. He's playing good cop to the Russians' bad one, the savior to their villain. It's so close to my fantasies that I want to cry. Except he's not interested in saving me; he wants to get answers—answers that I can't and won't give.

"What happened that day?" I ask instead. This question has been plaguing me ever since I learned that he and Esguerra are alive. "How did you survive?"

Lucas's jaw hardens, and the desire in his gaze fades. "You mean with the plane crash?"

"So there *was* a plane crash?" I hadn't been sure, though I figured his desire to make me pay meant that *something* had happened.

Lucas leans forward, his hands crushing his empty paper plate. "Yes, there was a crash. Didn't your superiors keep you informed?"

I fight the urge to flinch at the renewed fury in his voice. "They did, but I thought they might've had wrong information."

"Because we survived."

I nod, holding my breath.

He stares at me for a second, then stands up and walks around the table. "Let's go," he says, grabbing my arm again. "We're done here."

And dragging me back to the living room, he ties me up in the chair and leaves again, the front door slamming loudly behind him.

23

ucas

As Esguerra discusses the latest transportation concerns with our Hong Kong supplier, I sit silently, my attention only partially on the video call. I don't understand how one young woman can tie me into knots like this. One minute I want to take care of her, get her strong and healthy, and the next I'm torn between fucking her and killing her on the spot.

A child prostitute.

That's essentially what they made her. They took her at eleven, trained her, and set her loose in Moscow at sixteen with instructions to get close to the highest circles of Russian government.

Just thinking about it makes me sick. I don't know what infuriates me more: that they did this to her, or that she was involved in the plane crash that killed forty-five of our men and left three more burned beyond recognition.

How is it possible to hate someone and want to avenge the wrongs done to her at the same time?

"Thank you for your time, Mr. Chen," Esguerra says, uncharacteristically polite, and I see the wizened old man on the screen nodding as he parrots back the words. It's important to observe the niceties in that part of the world, even when dealing with criminals.

As soon as Esguerra disconnects, I get up, impatient to get back to Yulia. "I'll see you tomorrow," I say, and he nods, still working on his computer.

"See you," he says as I walk out.

It's dark when I step outside—dark, warm, and humid. Esguerra's office is a small building near the main house, which is a bit of a hike from the guards' quarters, where I reside. I could've driven here, but I enjoy walking, and after sitting still for two hours, I'm eager to stretch my legs and clear my mind.

Before I take a dozen steps, I hear a woman calling my name and turn to see Esguerra's maid, Rosa, hurrying across the wide lawn. She's holding what looks like a covered pot against her chest.

"Lucas, wait!" She sounds out of breath.

I stop, curious to find out what she wants. I vaguely recall Eduardo talking about her. He might've been dating her at the time. From what he said, she was born on this estate; her parents worked for Juan Esguerra, my boss's father. I've seen her around and exchanged greetings with her a number of times, but I've never really spoken to the girl.

"Here," she says, stopping in front of me and handing me the pot. "Ana wanted you to have this."

"She did?" Surprised, I take the heavy offering. The aroma seeping through the lid is rich and savory, making my mouth water. "Why?"

Esguerra's housekeeper occasionally sends some cookies or extra fruit to the guards, but this is the first time she's singled me out like this.

"I don't know." For some reason, Rosa's rounded cheeks turn pink. "I think she just made some extra soup, and Nora and the Señor didn't want it."

"I see." I don't see, but I'm not about to argue with what smells like a delicious meal. "Well, I'll gladly eat it if they don't want it."

"They don't. It's for you." She gives me a hesitant smile. "I hope you like it."

"I'm sure I will," I say, studying the maid. She's pretty, with lush curves and sparkling brown eyes, and as I watch her flush deepen under my gaze, it dawns on me that the middle-aged housekeeper might not have been the one behind this.

Rosa's interested in me. I'm suddenly sure of that.

Doing my best to conceal my discomfort, I wish her a good night and turn away. A couple of months ago, I would've been flattered and gladly accepted the invitation evident in the girl's shy smile. Now, however, all I can think about is the long-legged blonde waiting for me at home and the dirty, savage things I want to do to her.

"Bye," Rosa calls out as I resume walking, and I give her a neutral smile over my shoulder.

"Thanks for the soup," I say, but she's already hurrying back to the house, her maid's black dress billowing around her like a shroud.

~

As soon as I get home, I put the pot in the refrigerator and then go to the living room. I find my prisoner exactly where I left her: tied up in the chair in the middle of the room. Yulia's head is lowered, her long blond hair veiling most of her upper body. She doesn't move as I approach, and I realize she must've fallen asleep.

Crouching in front of her, I begin untying her ankles, trying to ignore my reaction to her nearness. With her legs bound apart, I can see the tender folds between her thighs, and I recall with sudden vividness how her pussy tasted—and felt around my cock.

Fuck.

I look down at my hands, determined to focus on my task. It doesn't help. As my fingers brush over her silky skin, I notice that her feet are long and slender, like the rest of her. Despite her height, her build is delicate, her ankles so narrow I can encircle each one with my thumb and index finger.

It would take no effort at all to break those fragile bones. The thought cuts through my haze of lust, and I seize upon it, welcoming the distraction. That's what I need: to think of her as an enemy, not as a desirable woman. And as an enemy, she'd be easy to torment. With just a bit of pressure, I could snap her feet in half. I know, because I've done it. A couple of years ago, a Thai missile manufacturer double-crossed us, and we retaliated by killing his entire family. The man's wife tried to hide her husband and teenage sons, but we tortured their location out of her, breaking every bone in her legs in the process.

We haven't had trouble in Thailand since.

That's what I should do with Yulia: hurt her, make her reveal her secrets, and then kill her. That's what Esguerra expects me to do.

That's what I'd planned to do after I had my fill of her.

Her leg twitches, tensing in my grasp, and I look up to find Yulia awake, her blue eyes locked on my face.

"You're back," she says quietly, and I nod, rendered mute by a brutal spike of renewed lust. My cock, already semi-stiff, turns into an iron rod in my shorts, and I realize that my right hand is sliding up her inner calf, as though of its own accord. Higher, higher... I can feel her tensing even more, sense her breathing changing as her pupils expand, and I know she's scared.

Scared and maybe something else, judging by the color creeping up her face.

Unable to resist the dark compulsion, I let my hand continue on its journey, my fingers trailing over the pale curve of her knee and the softness of her inner thigh. Her leg muscles are so tightly bunched they vibrate under my touch, and under the veil of her hair, her nipples harden, drawing into taut pink buds.

Her throat works as she swallows. "Lucas—"

I don't hear what she's about to say because at that moment, my phone buzzes loudly in my pocket.

Son of a bitch.

Livid with frustration, I yank my hand away from Yulia's thigh and pull out my phone. Glancing down, I see a message from Diego.

Potential problem at North Tower One.

I want to throw the phone against the wall, but I resist the urge. Instead, I get up and walk to my office, so Yulia wouldn't overhear me.

Taking a breath to calm myself, I call Diego.

"What is it?" I bark as soon as he picks up. "What's so important?"

"We detained a trespasser near the north border. He says he's a fisherman, but I'm not so sure."

I tamp down my anger. Diego did well to alert me, even if his interruption came at a shitty time. "All right. I'll be there in fifteen minutes."

I return to the living room and swiftly untie Yulia, doing my best to ignore my raging erection. "Do you need the bathroom?" I ask, pulling her to her feet, and she nods, looking bewildered.

"Let's go then." I drag her down the hallway and practically shove her into the restroom. "Be quick about it."

She comes out five minutes later, her face freshly washed and her breath smelling like toothpaste. I check her hands to make sure they're empty, and then I lead her to the bedroom. Keeping a careful eye on her, I grab a blanket and throw it on the floor near the foot of the bed. Then I reach into the nightstand drawer, take out a coil of rope I'd prepared earlier, and tell Yulia, "Get down on the blanket."

She freezes, and I see her staring at the rope I'm holding.

"Get down," I repeat, reaching for her. "On the blanket. Now."

She tenses as I pull her toward the blanket, and for a second, I'm sure she's going to try to fight me. Instead, she complies stiffly, folding her long legs underneath her.

"Lie down." I release her arm to press down on her shoulder. My dick throbs at the feel of her soft skin, and I have to inhale deeply to fight the urge to take her before I go. With the way I'm feeling, I wouldn't need more than a couple of minutes to blow my load, and the temptation to spread open her legs and fuck her is all but impossible to resist. If I didn't want more than a rough quickie, I would already be inside her.

"Lucas." Her lips tremble as she looks up at me. "Please, I—"

"Lie the fuck down. Now," I bark, losing my patience. If I have to force her down, I *will* take her.

Her face pale, Yulia obeys, stretching out on the blanket. As soon as she's horizontal, I kneel beside her, grab her wrists, and raise them above her head. Careful not to cut off her circulation, I wrap the rope tightly around her wrists and tie the other end of it on the leg of the bed. Then I repeat the maneuver with her ankles and the other leg of the bed, ignoring her stiffness. The end result is her stretched out on her side on the blanket, ankles and wrists tied to the opposite sides of the bed.

Getting up, I view my handiwork. With the bed as heavy as it is, Yulia is even more securely tied than she was in the chair—and she's in a better position to sleep if the trespasser situation takes longer than I expect.

Before I leave, I take a pillow and bend down to stuff it under her head. Her hair is all over her face, so I brush the silky blond strands away, trying to ignore the lust pounding through me. She stares up at me, her eyes like deep blue pools, and I almost groan when her tongue flicks out to wet her lips.

"I'll be back soon," I say, forcing myself to straighten and step away from her.

And before I can change my mind about the quickie, I exit the room and head over to North Tower One.

24

ulia

My pulse racing, I hold my breath as I listen to the sound of Lucas's departing footsteps. He'll be back soon, he said. Does that mean he went to take a shower, or did he leave to go somewhere? No matter how much I strain, I can't hear the front door opening, but that doesn't mean anything. The bedroom is probably too far away from the entrance.

After a few more minutes of silence, I shift on the blanket, trying to ease the strain in my shoulders. With my hands tied to one leg of the bed and my ankles to the other, I can't move more than a couple of centimeters in any direction, and the stretched-out position is only a shade more comfortable than sitting in the chair.

Growing frustrated, I test my bonds. As expected, there's no give in them, and the wooden king-sized bed is so heavy it might as well be welded to the floor. Every pull on the rope makes it cut into my skin, so I stop tugging on it.

Inhaling slowly, I try to relax, but I'm too anxious.

Where is Lucas? Why did he leave me here like this? When he got the rope and told me to get down on the blanket, I was sure he was going to force me, girlfriend or no girlfriend. I could see his erection, feel the intense hunger in his touch, and it was only the knowledge that it would be infinitely worse if I fought that made me comply with his orders.

If I did as he demanded, I hoped he wouldn't be as rough.

Except he didn't touch me. He just tied me to the bed and left me lying here on the blanket. He even gave me a pillow, as though my comfort matters to him.

As though I'm not someone he ultimately plans to kill.

Another few minutes tick by with no sign of Lucas, and I decide that he did leave the house after all. It must be because of that text message he got. Is it work-related or personal? Does it have something to do with that mysterious girlfriend of his? She knows I'm here. She's seen me sitting in his house naked. Could she have called Lucas to her because she suspects something's going on between us? Because she doesn't want her boyfriend toying with his captive like this?

Irrationally, the thought makes my insides twist. I don't know why I care that Lucas has a girlfriend. We're not in a relationship, at least not in a romantic sense. He brought me here to torment me, to make me pay for what I've done. If anyone has a claim on him, it would be that girl, not me.

I'm the other woman—the one he may want, but will never love.

Closing my eyes, I try to relax again. Exhaustion presses down on me like a layer of bricks, but for some reason, sleep refuses to come. The draft from the air-conditioning is cold on my bare skin, and my shoulders ache from having my arms extended up like that. As ridiculous as it is, a small part of me wishes that

Lucas were here—that I were even now lying in his hard embrace.

The fantasy is so alluring that I give into it, like I did in that prison. In my dream, none of this is real. Lucas doesn't hate me. There was no plane crash, and we're not on opposing sides. He's just holding me, kissing me... making love to me.

In my dream, he's mine and I'm his—and there's nothing keeping us apart.

25

 *ucas*

By the time I get to the guard tower, Diego and the others have strung up the trespasser in a small shed nearby. It's pitch-black outside, and there's no electricity in the shed, so I bring a battery-operated lantern with me to inspect the intruder.

As I shine the light on him, I see that he's an average-looking Colombian man, likely in his early thirties. His clothes look cheap and rather dirty—though that could be from struggling with our guards. He's also gagged, likely to prevent him from annoying the guards with his pleading.

I step back and turn to Diego. The young Mexican is sporting a mean black eye—a reminder of my earlier outburst over Yulia. For a moment, I consider apologizing more sincerely, but decide that now's not the time. "Where did you find him?" I ask instead.

"He was by the river," Diego says, keeping his tone low. "He had a boat, and he claims he was fishing."

"But you don't believe him."

"No." Diego glances at the guy. "His boat doesn't have a scratch on it. It's brand new."

"I see." Diego's right to be suspicious. Few fishermen around these parts can afford a new boat. "All right. Ungag him, and let's see what he says."

IT'S TWO IN THE MORNING BY THE TIME THE TRESPASSER FINALLY breaks. I don't enjoy torture as much as Esguerra does, so I let the guards have a go at the guy first. They pummel him, breaking a few ribs, and then I ask him what he's doing here. He tries to lie, claiming he came to the estate by accident, but after I do a few rounds with my switchblade, he begins to sing and tells us all about his employer, a powerful drug lord from Bogotá.

"Do these *cabrons* never learn?" Diego says in disgust when the man's speech devolves into sobbing pleas for mercy. "You'd think they'd know better than to try this shit. Sending this joker to find holes in our security—could they be any stupider?"

"They could." I step toward the blubbering man and slice my knife across his throat, putting him out of his misery. "They could try attacking us here."

"True." Diego steps back to avoid the spray of blood. "Do you want his body shipped to his *patrón* or taken to the incinerator?"

"The incinerator." I wipe the switchblade on my shirt—it's so bloody that an extra stain is nothing—and close the knife before putting it away. "Let his boss wonder."

"Okay." Diego motions to the two other guards, and they drag the body out of the shed. The place will need to be cleaned, but that's a task for the next shift. I wait for the new guards to arrive and give them those instructions before heading out to my car.

Diego walks out beside me, so I ask, "Need a ride?"

"Sure. I was going to walk, but a ride sounds good." He shoots me a grin. "Get myself to bed faster."

"Yeah." Before we get in the car, I take out a rolled-up towel I keep for these occasions and spread it on the driver's seat. Diego isn't as dirty as I am, so I let him get in the passenger seat as is.

It's a short drive, but Diego manages to talk my ear off on the way. He's hyper, like some guys get after a kill. It's as if he needs to reinforce that he's alive, that it's not his body that's about to be incinerated out there. I know how he feels because a version of the same excitement is humming in my veins. It's not as extreme as it was with my first few kills—you can get used to anything, even taking lives—but I still feel sharply alive, all my senses heightened by the proximity of death.

"Listen, man," Diego says when I stop in front of his barracks building, "I just want to say I didn't mean anything earlier today with that girl of yours. You were right—it's none of my business."

"She's not my girl." As soon as the words leave my mouth, I know them to be a lie. Yulia may not be "my girl," but she's mine.

She's been mine from the moment I laid eyes on her in Moscow.

"Yeah, sure, whatever you say." Grinning, Diego opens the door and jumps out. "See you tomorrow."

He shuts the door, and I drive off. Loose gravel shoots out behind my car as I floor the gas, filled with sudden impatience.

I've waited long enough.

It's time to claim what's mine.

BEFORE I GO INTO THE BEDROOM, I TAKE A LONG SHOWER, WASHING off all traces of blood and dirt. The warm water takes some of the edge off, but the dark thrum of adrenaline is still there as I step out of the stall and towel off, my cock hardening with anticipation.

I don't bother to get dressed before I leave the bathroom. The air is cool on my still-damp skin as I walk down the hallway, and my heartbeat quickens as I picture Yulia lying there, naked, tied up, and completely at my mercy. I've never wanted a woman in that position before, but everything about my prisoner brings out my basest instincts. I want her bound and helpless.

I want her to know she can't get away.

It's dark in the bedroom when I step in, so I reach for the light switch. When the bedside lamp comes on, I see Yulia there, stretched out on the blanket in front of me. Her naked body is long and sleek as she lies on her side, her back toward me. Even after her weight loss, her ass is nicely curved, and her pale skin looks like alabaster against the dark blanket. She doesn't move as I approach, and I see that she's asleep, her eyes closed and her lips slightly parted. Her plump, round breasts move with her steady breathing, her nipples soft and pink in her repose.

The lust that's been building all day roars back, more violent than ever. Kneeling beside her, I run my hand over the side of her body, stroking her from shoulder to mid-thigh. Even bruised in a few places, her skin is gorgeous, so soft and smooth it makes me want to taste her all over.

Giving in to the urge, I lean over her, trapping her between my arms, and lower my head to take her nipple into my mouth. It immediately contracts, hardening as I suck on it, and I feel her tensing underneath me, the rhythm of her breathing changing as she wakes up.

Lifting my head, I look down at her, meeting her gaze. There's fear in her eyes, but there's also something more—something that turns me on unbearably.

Desire.

Slowly, using every ounce of willpower to control myself, I trail my right hand over her waist and hip. She doesn't make a sound, but I see her eyes darkening as my hand moves lower to cup the firm, round curve of her ass. Her skin is cool and smooth to the touch, her flesh resilient as I lightly squeeze her ass cheek. She feels good, so fucking good that my cock is all but ready to explode, and my hand shakes with lust as I move it lower, slipping my fingers under the curve of her ass and between her thighs.

Yes, that's it. A savage triumph fills me as I reach her folds and feel the wetness at the rim of her opening. Her pussy's ready for me, just like it was the first time I touched her. Still holding her gaze, I push my finger into her tight heat and feel her shudder as she suppresses a soft gasp.

"You want me, don't you?" My voice is low and hoarse. "You want *this*." I find her clit with my thumb and press on it, watching her reaction. She seems to have stopped breathing, her eyes enormous in her thin face as she stares up at me.

"Say it." I curl my finger inside her and put more pressure on her clit. "Tell me you fucking want this."

She swallows, her pale throat moving, and I feel her pussy squeezing my finger as a long shudder ripples through her. "Lucas, please..."

"Fucking say it," I grit out, but she shuts her eyes, turning her face away from me. She's breathing fast now, her chest expanding and contracting in a frantic rhythm, and I feel her muscles clenching as I push a second finger into her, stretching her tight channel.

She's fighting me, denying me.

My hunger turns dark, lust intermingling with rage and frustration. How fucking dare she do this to me? She's mine—her body's mine to do with what I will. I don't have to give her a choice. She's my prisoner, my spoils of war, and I've been more than patient with her.

"Look at me." Keeping my hand on her sex, I rise up on my knees and grab her jaw with my other hand, forcing her to face me. "Don't play games with me," I growl when she opens her eyes. "You'll lose, do you understand me?"

She blinks, and I feel her inner muscles rippling around my fingers. She's dripping wet, her body welcoming my touch. "Yes."

"Yes, what?" It's all I can do to keep talking instead of fucking her right then and there. My thumb moves over her clit, forcing a gasp out of her. "Yes, what?"

"Yes, I—" She sucks in a breath, her voice shaking. "I understand."

"Good. Now stop lying and answer the fucking question." I curl both fingers inside her, wringing another ripple out of her. "Do you want me?"

Her nod is faint, almost imperceptible, but it's enough.

I release her face and withdraw my fingers from her pussy, my balls ready to burst. I'm tempted to take her right on this blanket, but I've been imagining her in my bed all these weeks, and that's where I want her this time.

Too impatient to bother with the knots in the rope, I get up and go to the laundry room, where I left my bloodied clothes. Thirty seconds later, I return with my switchblade.

Approaching Yulia's legs, I open the knife. Her eyes widen with sudden fear, but I just cut through the rope, freeing her ankles.

"Lie still," I order, getting up to walk around her. A second later, her arms are free too. Not wanting a weapon near her, I go to the other side of the room and put the knife into the top drawer of my dresser before turning to face her.

Yulia's already on her knees, about to get up, but I don't give her a chance. Closing the distance between us, I bend down and lift her up against my chest. I know she can get on the bed herself, but I need to touch her, to feel her. I can see the pulse beating in her throat as I place her on the white sheets, and my lust intensifies.

Mine. She's mine.

The words are a primal drumbeat in my mind. I've never felt so possessive about a woman, have never wanted to claim one so badly. The desire is purely visceral, a need that's as dark and ancient as the urge to kill. I've already had her that one night in Moscow, but it's not enough.

It's nowhere near enough.

Watching her, I reach into the bedside drawer and pull out a foil packet. Ripping it with my teeth, I take out the condom and roll it onto my throbbing cock. Her gaze follows my fingers, and I see her body tensing even more. With fear, with lust? I don't know, and I'm past the point of caring.

"Come here," I order, climbing onto the bed. I don't know what I expect when I reach for her, but what happens isn't it.

The moment I touch her, Yulia wraps her arms around my neck and presses her lips to mine.

26

ulia

I don't know what makes me kiss Lucas at that moment, but as soon as our lips meet, my anxiety melts away, replaced by aching need. I want him—this hard, confusing man who is my captor.

With my fantasies fresh in my mind, I want him more than I fear him.

The panic I felt earlier today is absent, the dark memories quiescent as he bears me down to the mattress, his hands sliding into my hair. I arch against him, and he deepens the kiss, his tongue invading my mouth and exploring it hungrily. He tastes like heat and raw passion, like my dreams and my nightmares. He consumes me, and I consume him in return, my hands moving frantically over his muscular back, his neck, his short hair. I know he'll most likely kill me in the not-too-distant future—I know the hands cradling my head might one day crack my skull—but at this moment, none of that matters.

I'm living solely in the present, where his touch is bringing me pleasure instead of pain.

His lips drift over to my ear, and I feel his teeth grazing my neck before he sucks on the tender skin. My entire body erupts in goosebumps, the pleasure sharp and electrifying as his right hand slides down my side, traveling over the curve of my waist and hip before delving between our bodies to find my sex. Unerringly, his fingers hone in on my clit, and the ache inside me intensifies, the tension becoming unbearable.

I cry out his name, shocked by the intensity of the sensations, but it's too late. I'm already coming, my body having been poised on the edge too long.

He pets me through the shattering waves of pleasure, his fingers stroking my folds until my orgasm ends, and then he grabs my leg and drapes it over his hip, opening me wide. His cock presses against my inner thigh, thick and unyielding, and a tendril of fear invades me again as I meet his glittering gaze.

"I'm going to fuck you," he says, his voice low and guttural. "You're mine, do you understand me? Mine."

Stunned, I attempt to process the claim, but in that moment, Lucas kisses me again and my eyes drift shut, my ability to think evaporating. His body is a warm steel cage on top of me, his scent and taste overwhelming my senses. I can't take a breath without inhaling him, can't feel anything but the devouring force of his mouth and the hardness of his erection at the entrance to my body.

I clutch at his sides, my nails digging into his skin, and then I feel it—his thick cock pushing into me, penetrating me. His left hand tightens in my hair, preventing me from turning away from his mouth, and I can't even cry out as he stretches me, invading my body as if it's his right. He goes deep, so deep it should hurt, and it does—except there's pleasure too, pleasure and a strange kind of relief.

Relief that in this moment, I truly belong to him.

When he's in all the way, he lifts his head, letting me catch my breath, and I open my eyes, meeting his gaze once more. His lips are shiny from kissing me, and his sun-burnished skin is drawn tight over his harshly beautiful features. I can feel him lodged inside me, the heat of him burning me from within, and my body softens for him, embracing him with more wetness.

"Yulia," he whispers, staring down at me, and I know that he feels it too, this pull, this visceral connection between us. He may have all the power, but in this moment, he's as vulnerable as I am, caught in the grip of the same madness.

I don't know whether he realizes it too, but suddenly, his jaw hardens, his gaze growing cold and shuttered. Without saying another word, he reaches down with his left hand to grab one of my wrists and pin it above my head. Next, he repeats the maneuver with his right hand, leaving me stretched out underneath him, unable to move or touch him in any way.

Leaving me helpless under a man who wants to punish me.

"Lucas, wait," I whisper, feeling the dark prickles of panic, but it's too late. Holding my wrists above my head, he begins to move inside me, his eyes glinting with icy fury. His thrusts are hard, merciless, stealing my breath and wringing pained cries from my throat. He's not making love; he's taking my body, claiming it as brutally as any conqueror.

I begin to fight him then, the panic spreading as the old memories flood in, but there's nothing I can do. I'm pinned, invaded, and the man above me has no mercy. His body takes mine, over and over again, and I feel myself sliding into that cold, dark place, the one from which I fought so hard to emerge. The lines between the present and the past blur, and I hear Kirill's cruel, taunting voice, smell the suffocating stench of his cologne as he crushes me into the floor. The horror begins to engulf me, but before I'm completely lost, Lucas transfers my wrists into one of his big hands and reaches between us with the other, finding my clit once more. His touch is skilled, unerring, and the stunning pleasure wrenches me back into the present, making me aware of the tension building within me again.

Squeezing my eyes shut, I try to twist away, to escape, but there's nowhere to go. There's only his cock inside me and his fingers on my clit, pain and pleasure tangling together in a vicious erotic spiral. There was never pleasure with Kirill, never anything but awful pain, and the shock of the dual sensation keeps me grounded in the moment, reminding me that the man on top is not my trainer.

It's Lucas, another man who hates me.

Except my body doesn't know that, doesn't realize that the way he touches me shouldn't cause me pleasure. Despite the roughness of his thrusts, Lucas's fingers on my clit are gentle, and the pleasure intensifies, chasing away the darkness. Gasping and panting, I arch up, frantic pleas tearing from my throat, and he presses harder on my clit, pushing me to that sharp, volcanic edge.

"Come for me, beautiful," he rasps out, lowering his face to my neck, and to my shock, I feel myself peaking. Explosive ecstasy wells up and radiates out to every cell in my body, all of my muscles quivering with sensations as I spasm around his thick cock.

Stunned, I cry out his name, and at that moment, I hear his breathing changing, a low groan rumbling in his chest. His hand tightens around my wrists as he thrusts deeply one last time and halts, his hips moving in a circular, grinding motion. I feel his cock pulsing within me, and I know he came too.

Desperately sucking in air, I turn my head to the side, unwilling to face him or the confusing jumble of feelings in my chest. I'm shattered, undone by both the pain and the pleasure. He's still inside me, his cock only marginally softer than before. I feel the stickiness of sweat gluing our bodies together, hear the harsh bellows of his breathing, and strange, unwelcome tears burn my eyes.

If I had any doubts about the reality of what's happening, they're gone. This act, this soul-tearing thing that happened between us, impresses upon me more than ever the fact that Lucas is alive.

He's alive, and I'm his prisoner.

The tears threaten to spill out, and I squeeze my eyelids tighter, determined to prevent that from happening. I can't allow myself the luxury of crying. Whatever this means, whatever Lucas has in store for me, I have to bear it. I have to be strong because this is only the start.

My captivity is just beginning.

BIND ME

CAPTURE ME: BOOK 2

I

HIS CAPTIVE

1

ulia

PRISONER. CAPTIVE.

With Lucas's heavily muscled weight pinning me to the bed, I feel that reality more acutely than ever. My wrists are restrained above my head, and my body is invaded by a man who just showed me both heaven and hell. I can feel Lucas's cock softening inside me, and my eyes burn with unshed tears as I lie there, my face turned away to avoid looking at him.

He took me, and once more, I let him. No, I didn't just let him —I embraced him. Knowing how much my captor hates me, I kissed him of my own accord, giving in to dreams and fantasies that have no place in my life.

Giving in to my desire for a man who's going to destroy me.

I don't know why Lucas hasn't done it yet, why I'm in his bed instead of strung up in some torture shed, broken and bleeding.

This is not what I expected when Esguerra's men brought me here yesterday and I realized that the man whose death I thought I caused was alive.

Alive and determined to punish me.

Lucas stirs on top of me, his heavy weight lifting slightly, and I feel the cool breeze from the air conditioning on my sweat-dampened skin. My inner muscles tighten as his cock slips out of me, and I become aware of a deep soreness between my legs.

My throat constricts, and the burn behind my eyelids intensifies.

Don't cry. Don't cry. I repeat the words like a mantra, focusing on keeping the tears under control. It's harder than it should be, and I know it's because of what just transpired between us.

Pain and pleasure. Fear and lust. I never knew the combination could be so devastating, never realized that I could soar right after being plunged into the abyss of my past.

I never imagined I could come mere moments after remembering Kirill.

Just thinking of my trainer's name makes the knot in my throat expand, the dark memories threatening to well up again.

No, stop. Don't think about that.

Lucas shifts again, lifting his head, and I exhale in relief as he releases my wrists and rolls off me. The prickling sensation behind my eyes recedes as I take in a full breath, filling my lungs with much-needed air.

Yes, that's it. I just need some distance from him.

Gulping in another breath, I turn my head to see Lucas get up and remove the condom. Our eyes meet, and I catch a hint of confusion in the blue-gray coolness of his gaze. In the next moment, however, the emotion is gone, leaving his square-jawed face as hard and uncompromising as ever.

"Get up." Lucas reaches for me and grabs my arm. "Let's go." He drags me off the bed.

I'm too shaky to resist, so I just stumble along as he marches me down the hallway.

A few moments later, he stops in front of the bathroom door. "Do you need a minute?" he asks, and I nod, grateful for the offer. I need more than a minute—I need an eternity to recover from this—but I will settle for a minute of privacy if that's all I can get.

"Don't try anything," he says as I close the door, and I take his warning to heart, doing nothing more than using the toilet and washing my hands as quickly as I can. Even if I could find something to fight him with, I don't have the strength right now. I'm drained, both physically and emotionally, my body aching nearly as much as my soul. It was too much, all of it: the brief connection I thought we had, the way he suddenly became cold and cruel, the memories combined with the devastating pleasure.

The fact that Lucas took me even though he has that other girl, the dark-haired one who spied on me from the window.

My throat closes up again, and I have to choke back a sob. I don't know why this thought, of all things, is so painful. I have no claim on my captor. At best, I'm his toy, his possession. He'll play with me until he gets bored, and then he'll break me.

He'll kill me without a second thought.

You're mine, he said as he was fucking me, and for a brief moment, I thought he meant it. I thought he felt as drawn to me as I am to him.

Clearly, I was wrong.

A thin film of moisture veils my vision, and I blink to clear it from my eyes. The face staring back at me from the bathroom mirror is gaunt and starkly pale. Two months in the Russian prison took their toll on my appearance. I don't even know why Lucas wants me right now. His girlfriend is infinitely prettier, with her warm complexion and vibrant features.

A hard knock startles me.

"Your minute's up." Lucas's voice is harsh, and I know I can't delay facing him any longer. Taking a breath to calm myself, I open the door.

He's standing at the entrance, waiting for me. I expect him to lead me back, but he steps into the bathroom instead.

"Get in," he says, pushing me toward the shower. "We're going to wash up."

We? He's coming in with me? My insides clench, heat spreading over my skin at the image, but I obey. I don't have a choice, but even if I did, the memory of my showerless weeks at the Moscow prison is still horribly fresh in my mind.

If my captor wants me to take five showers a day, I'll gladly do so.

The shower stall is big enough to accommodate both of us, the glass enclosure clean and modern. In general, everything about Lucas's house is clean and modern, completely different from the tiny Soviet-era apartment in Moscow where I used to reside.

"Your bathroom is nice," I say inanely when he turns on the water. I don't know why I choose this topic of all things, but I need to distract myself somehow. We're in the shower, naked together, and even though we just had sex, I can't stop staring at him. His sharply defined muscles bunch with every movement, and his heavy sac hangs between his legs, where his semi-hard cock is glistening with traces of his seed. He's not the only man I've seen naked, but he's by far the most magnificent.

"You like the bathroom?" Lucas turns to face me, letting the water spray hit his broad back, and I realize I'm not the only one aware of the sexual charge in the air. It's there in the heavy-lidded gaze that travels over my body before returning to my face, in the way his big hands curl, as if to stop themselves from reaching for me.

"Yes." I try to keep my tone casual, as though it's not a big deal that we're standing here together after he fucked my brains out and sent my emotions into a tailspin. "I like the simplicity of your decor."

It makes for a nice change from the complexity of the man himself.

He stares at me, his pale eyes more gray than blue in this light, and I see that unlike me, he's not willing to be distracted. He wanted us to take a shower together for a reason, and that reason becomes obvious as he reaches for me and pulls me under the water spray with him.

"Get down." He accompanies the order with a hard push on my shoulders. My legs fold, unable to withstand the force of his hands pressing down, and I find myself on my knees in front of him, my face at the level of his groin. His broad back deflects most of the water spray, but the droplets still reach me, forcing me to close my eyes as he grips my hair and pulls my head close to his hardening cock.

"If you bite me..." He leaves the threat unsaid, but I don't need to know the specifics to understand that such action wouldn't go well for me. I want to tell him that the warning isn't necessary, that I'm too shattered for battle right now, but he doesn't give me a chance. As soon as my lips part, he thrusts his cock in, going so deep that I almost choke before he takes it out. Gasping, I brace myself on the steely columns of his thighs, and he pushes back in, slower this time.

"Good, that's a good girl." His grip in my hair eases as I close my lips around his thick shaft and hollow out my cheeks, sucking on him. "Exactly like that, beautiful..." Bizarrely, his words of encouragement send a spiral of heat through my core. I'm still wet from our fucking, and I feel that slickness as I press my thighs together, trying to contain the ache within.

I can't possibly want him again. My sex is raw and swollen, my insides tender from his harsh possession. I also remember that encroaching darkness, the memories that came so close to sucking me in. Being with a man like this—when I'm completely in his power and he wants to punish me—is my worst nightmare, yet with Lucas none of that seems to matter.

I'm still turned on.

His fingers fist in my hair as he thrusts into my mouth, developing a rhythm, and I do my best to relax my throat muscles. I know how to give a good blow job, and I use that skill now, cupping his balls with both hands as I create suction with my lips.

"Yes, that's it." His voice is thick with lust. "Keep going."

I obey, squeezing his balls tighter as I take him even deeper into my throat. Strangely, I don't mind giving him this pleasure. Though I'm on my knees, I feel more in control now than I have at any moment since my arrival this morning. I'm *letting* him do this, and there's power in that, though I know it's mostly an illusion. I'm his prisoner, not his girlfriend, but for the moment, I can pretend that I am, that the man thrusting his cock between my lips regards me as something more than a sexual object.

"Yulia..." He groans my name, adding to the illusion, and then he thrusts in all the way and stops, spurting thick jets of cum into my throat. I focus on breathing and not choking as I swallow, my hands still cradling his tightly drawn balls.

"Good girl," he whispers, letting me get every drop, and then he strokes my hair, his touch as gentle as I've ever felt. I should've found his approval humiliating, but I revel in the small tenderness, soaking it up with desperate need. I feel tired, so tired that all I want to do is stay like this, with him stroking my hair as I drift off into nothingness.

All too soon, he helps me to my feet, and I open my eyes when the water spray starts hitting me in the chest instead of my face. Lucas doesn't speak, but when he pours body wash into his palm and applies it to my skin, his touch is still gentle and soothing.

"Lean back," he murmurs, stepping behind me, and I lean on him, resting my head against his strong shoulder as he washes my front, his big hands soaping my breasts, belly, and the tender place between my legs. He's taking care of me, I realize dreamily, my mind beginning to drift as I close my eyes to enjoy the attention.

All too soon, I'm clean, and he steps back, directing the spray at me to rinse me off. I sway slightly, my legs barely able to hold me up as Lucas turns off the water and guides me out of the shower.

"Come, let's get you into bed. You're about to fall over." He wraps a thick towel around me and picks me up, carrying me out of the bathroom. "You need sleep."

He brings me to the bedroom and lowers me to the bed.

I blink at him, my thoughts slow and sluggish. He's not going to tie me up on the floor next to the bed?

"You're going to sleep with me," he says, answering my unspoken question. I blink at him again, too tired to analyze what all of this means, but he's already taking a pair of handcuffs out of his nightstand drawer.

Before I can wonder about his intentions, he snaps one handcuff around my left wrist and attaches the second one to his own. Then he lies down, stretching out behind me, and curves his body around mine from the back, draping his cuffed left arm over my side.

"Sleep," he whispers in my ear, and I comply, sinking into the warm comfort of oblivion.

2

Lucas

Yulia's breathing evens out almost immediately, her body turning boneless as she falls asleep in my embrace. Her hair is wet from the shower, the moisture seeping into my pillow, but it doesn't bother me.

I'm too focused on the woman in my arms.

She smells like my body wash and herself, a unique, delicate scent that still somehow reminds me of peaches. Her slender body is soft and warm, the curve of her ass cushioning my groin. My body hums with contentment as I lie there, but my mind refuses to relax.

I fucked her.

I fucked her, and it was once again the best sex I've ever had, surpassing even that time with her in Moscow. When I entered her, the intensity of the sensations took my breath away. It didn't feel like sex—it felt like coming home.

Even now, remembering what it was like to slide into her tight, warm depths makes my cock twitch and my chest ache with something indefinable. I don't want this with her, whatever "this" is. It should've been so simple: fuck her, get her out of my system, and then punish her, extracting information from her in the process. She killed men I'd worked and trained with for years.

She nearly killed *me*.

The idea that I can feel anything but hatred and lust for Yulia infuriates me. It took everything I had to ignore the softness in her gaze and treat her like the prisoner she is—to fuck her roughly instead of making love to her. I knew I was hurting her—I felt her struggling as I drove mercilessly into her—but I couldn't let her know how she affects me.

I couldn't give in to this insane weakness.

Except I did exactly that when she sucked my cock without a hint of protest, milking me with her mouth like she couldn't get enough. She gave me pleasure after I treated her like a whore, and that damnable need came over me again.

The need to hold her and protect her.

She knelt in front of me, her wet, spiky lashes fanning across her pale cheeks as she swallowed every drop of my cum, and I wanted to cradle her, to take her in my arms and make her promises I should never keep. I settled for washing her, but I couldn't bring myself to tie her up and make her sleep on the floor —just like I couldn't bring myself to truly hurt her earlier.

What a fucking mess. She's been here less than twenty-four hours, and the fury that's burned inside me for two months is already beginning to cool, her vulnerability getting to me like nothing else. I shouldn't care that she's weak and starved, that her body is a shadow of its former self and her blue eyes are ringed with exhaustion. It shouldn't matter to me that she was recruited at eleven and sent to work as a spy in Moscow at sixteen.

None of those facts should make a difference to me, but they do.

Fucking hell.

I close my eyes, telling myself that whatever it is I'm feeling is temporary, that it will pass once I've had my fill of her.

I tell myself this even though I know I'm lying.

It's not going to be that simple, and I should've known it.

A STRANGE NOISE STARTLES ME OUT OF DEEP SLEEP. MY EYES SPRING open, all traces of sleepiness gone as adrenaline rockets through me. I tense, preparing for a fight, and then I recall that I'm not alone.

There's a woman lying in my arms, her left wrist handcuffed to mine.

I exhale slowly, realizing the noise came from her. She shifts restlessly, and I hear it again.

A soft whimper that ends as a choked cry.

"Yulia." I place my left hand on her shoulder, bringing her arm up with it. "Yulia, wake up."

She twists, struggling with sudden ferocity, and I realize she's not awake yet. She's half-crying, half-gasping, and yanking at the handcuffs with all her strength.

Son of a bitch.

I grab her left wrist to stop her from hurting us both and roll on top of her, using my weight to immobilize her. "Calm down," I whisper in her ear. "It's just a dream."

I expect her to stop struggling then, to wake up and realize what's going on, but that's not what happens.

She turns into a wild animal instead.

3

ulia

"It's your fault, bitch. It's all your fault."

A heavy body presses me into the floor, cruel hands tearing at my clothes, and then there's pain, brutal, searing pain as he thrusts into me, telling me that it's my punishment, that I deserve to pay.

"Don't!" I scream, fighting, but I can't move, can't breathe underneath him. "Stop, please stop!"

"Calm down," he whispers in my ear in English. "Just calm the fuck down."

The incongruity of Kirill speaking English jolts me for a second, but I'm in too much of a panic to analyze it fully. The pain of the violation and the shame are like a vise crushing my chest. I'm suffocating, spinning into the cold darkness, and all I can do is fight, scream and fight.

"Yulia. Fuck, stop that!" His voice is deeper than I remembered, and he's speaking English again. Why is he doing that? We're not in training right now. The oddity nags at me, and I realize it's not the only thing that's strange.

He's not wearing cologne either.

Confused, I still underneath him and realize I'm not actually in pain.

He's on top of me, but he's not hurting me.

Reality shifts and realigns, and I remember.

Kirill was seven years ago. I'm not in Kiev—I'm in Colombia, captive of another man who wants to punish me for what I've done.

"Yulia." Lucas's quiet voice is near my ear. "Can I let you go?"

"Yes," I whisper into the pillow. My muscles are trembling from overexertion, and my breathing is labored, as if I've been running. I must've been fighting Lucas instead of the phantom in my nightmare. "I'm fine now. Really."

Lucas rolls off me, and I feel a tug on my left wrist, where the handcuffs still join us. My skin underneath the metal is stinging and raw. I must've been yanking on the shackle during the fight.

He stretches away from me, and a second later, a soft light comes on, illuminating the room. The sight of the clean white walls serves as additional proof that I was dreaming and Kirill is nowhere near me.

Lucas reaches into the nightstand and extracts a key to unlock the handcuffs. When he puts the key back in the drawer, I automatically note its location, though my teeth are already beginning to chatter. I haven't had a nightmare this strong and realistic in years, and I've forgotten how bad it can be.

Lucas turns to face me. "Yulia." His gaze is somber as he reaches for me. "What happened?"

I let him draw me into his lap, so I can feel the heat of his body on my frozen skin. I can't stop trembling, the shadow of the nightmare still hovering over me. "I—" My voice cracks. "I had a bad dream."

"No." He tilts my chin up with one hand, forcing me to look him in the eyes. "Tell me why you had this dream. What happened to you?"

I clamp my lips shut, fighting an illogical urge to obey that quiet command. Something about the way he's holding me—almost like a parent comforting a child—makes me want to confide in him, tell him things I've only shared with the agency therapist.

"What happened?" Lucas presses, his tone softening, and I feel a swell of longing, a desire for the connection I imagined between us before. Except maybe I didn't imagine it. Maybe there's something there.

I so badly want there to be something there.

"Yulia." Curving his palm over my jaw, Lucas strokes my cheek with his thumb. "Tell me. Please."

It's that last word that breaks me, coming as it does from a man so hard and domineering. There's no anger in the way he's touching me, no violent lust. It's true that he hurt me earlier, but he also gave me pleasure and some semblance of tenderness afterwards. And right now he's not demanding answers from me—he's asking.

He's asking, and I can't refuse him.

Not while I feel so lost and alone.

"All right," I whisper, looking at the man I dreamed about for the last two months. "What do you want to know?"

4

ucas

"How old were you when it happened?" I ask, moving my hand to the back of her neck to massage the tense muscles there. Yulia's body is shaking as I hold her in my lap, and a fresh surge of rage knots my insides.

Someone hurt her, badly, and I'm going to make that person pay.

"Fifteen," she answers, and I hear the catch in her voice.

Fifteen. I force myself to remain still and not give in to the volcanic violence boiling within me. I'd suspected it was something like that. Her voice as she screamed had been high-pitched, almost childish, the words tumbling out in either Russian or Ukrainian.

"Who was he?" Keeping my voice even, I continue my little massage. It seems to be soothing her, easing some of her trembling. Her face color matches my white sheets, her blue eyes dark in the dim light of the bedside lamp. She might be twenty-two, but at this moment, she looks impossibly young.

Young and incredibly fragile.

"His name—" She swallows. "His name was Kirill. He was my trainer."

Kirill. I make a mental note of that. I'll need his last name to mobilize a search, but at least I already have something. Then the second part of what she said sinks in.

"Your trainer?"

She averts her gaze. "One of them. His specialty was hand-to-hand combat."

Motherfucker. A fifteen-year-old girl—hell, even a grown man—wouldn't have stood a chance.

"And the people you work for allowed this?" The rage creeps into my voice, and she flinches, almost imperceptibly. Not wanting to frighten her, I take a deep breath, trying to regain control. She's still looking away from me, her eyes trained on some spot to the left of me, so I slide my hand into her hair and gently cup her skull, bringing her attention back to me.

"Yulia, please." With effort, I even out my tone. "Did they sanction this?"

"No." Her lips curl with bitter irony. "That's the thing. They didn't."

"I don't understand."

She laughs, the sound raw and full of pain. "They should've just sanctioned it. Then he wouldn't have been angry like that."

My blood feels both hot and icy. "Tell me."

"He started coming on to me when I turned fifteen, right after I got my braces off." Her gaze drifts away from mine again. "I was an ugly child, you see—tall, skinny, and awkward—but when I grew up, I looked better. Boys started liking me, and men began noticing me as well. It happened almost overnight."

"And he was one of the men."

She nods, returning her attention to me. "Yes. He was one of the men. It wasn't a big deal at first. He'd hold me a little longer on a mat, or he'd make me practice a move a few extra times so he could touch me. I didn't even realize he was interested, not until —" She stops abruptly, a tremor running over her skin.

"Not until what?" I prompt, trying to remain calm enough to listen.

"Not until he cornered me in the locker room." She swallows again. "He caught me after a shower, and he touched me. All over."

Motherfucking piece of shit. I want to kill the man so badly I can taste it.

"What happened then?" I force myself to ask. It's not the end of the story, I can tell that much.

"I reported him." A shudder runs through Yulia's slim body. "I went to the head of the program and told him about Kirill."

"And?"

"And they fired him. They told him to go away and have nothing to do with me ever again."

"But he didn't."

"No," she agrees dully. "He didn't."

I take a breath and brace myself. "What did he do to you?"

"He came to the dormitory where I lived, and he raped me." Her voice is flat, and her gaze slides away from me again. "He said he was punishing me for what I did."

The words knock the breath out of me. The parallels don't escape me. I, too, planned to use sex as punishment, sating my lust on her body and showing her how little she meant to me at the same time.

In fact, that's what I did earlier tonight, when I took her roughly, ignoring her struggles.

"Yulia..." For the first time in years, I feel the bitter lash of self-hatred. No wonder she panicked when I had her pinned on the hallway floor. "Yulia, I—"

"The doctors said I was lucky the other trainees found me

when they did," she continues, as though I hadn't spoken. "Otherwise, I'd have bled out."

"Bled out?" A swell of rage tightens my throat. "The fucker hurt you that badly?"

"I was hemorrhaging," she explains, her face oddly calm as she meets my gaze again. "It was my first time, and he was rough. Very rough."

The motherfucking bastard's death will be slow. Very slow. I picture myself using some of Peter Sokolov's techniques on the trainer, and the fantasy steadies me enough that I can ask evenly, "What is his last name?"

Yulia blinks, and I see some of her unnatural calm dissipating. "His name doesn't matter."

"It matters to me." I clasp her shoulders, feeling the delicacy of her bones. "Come on, sweetheart. Just tell me his name."

She shakes her head. "It doesn't matter," she repeats. Her gaze hardens as she adds, "*He* doesn't matter. He's dead. He's been dead for six years."

Fuck. So much for that fantasy.

"Did you kill him?" I ask.

"No." Her eyes glitter like shards of broken glass. "I wish I had. I wanted to, but the head of our program sent an assassin for him instead."

"So they deprived you of vengeance." I know most people would be glad that a young girl didn't get a chance to commit murder, but I've never believed in turning the other cheek. There's a certain satisfaction in revenge, a sense of closure. It doesn't undo the past, but it can help one feel better about it.

I know, because it helped *me*.

Yulia doesn't respond, and I realize I've hit a sore spot. She resents them for this, this agency she refuses to speak about—this "head of the program," who should've protected her from the trainer to begin with.

Would she give them up if I asked her about them now? She's

raw and vulnerable after reliving her painful past. I would be a real bastard to take advantage of that. Except if I do, I could have the information I need, and I wouldn't have to hurt her.

I would keep her safe, and nobody would hurt her ever again.

Yesterday, I would've pushed the thought aside, dismissing it as a weakness, but no more. I have been lying to myself all these weeks, and it's time to admit it. I won't be able to torture her. When I try to picture myself using my knife on her the way I did on that trespasser, my stomach turns. Even before her nightmare, I couldn't bring myself to treat Yulia like I would a real prisoner, and now that I know how much she's already suffered, the idea of causing her more pain makes me physically ill.

Reaching a decision, I say quietly, "Tell me about the program." This is my best chance to get the required information, and I have to use it, even if it means exploiting Yulia's vulnerability. Still holding her gaze, I move one of my hands to her nape and rub it gently. "Who are the people who recruited you?"

She freezes on my lap, and I see a flash of pain contort her features before they smooth into a beautiful mask. "The program?" Her voice sounds cold and distant. "I don't know anything about it."

And pushing me away, she leaps off the bed and sprints out of the room.

5

ulia

I RUN DOWN THE HALLWAY, MY BARE FEET SILENT ON THE CARPET. Betrayal is a bitter, oily slime coating my tongue.

Fool. Idiot. Dura. Debilka. I castigate myself in two languages, unable to find enough words to cover my stupidity. How could I have trusted Lucas for even a second? I know what he wants from me, but I still gave in to that stupid longing, to fantasies that should've died out the moment I realized he was alive.

The man I dreamed about in prison has never been anything but a figment of my imagination.

The interrogation technique he used on me is beyond basic. Step one: Get close to your enemy and understand what makes her tick. Step two: Lend a sympathetic ear and pretend like you care. It's the oldest trick in the book, and I fell for it.

I had been so starved for human warmth I let an enemy see into my soul.

"Yulia!" I can hear Lucas running after me, but I'm already by the bathroom. Darting in, I close the door and lock it, then lean against it, hoping to keep him from breaking it down for at least a few moments.

"Yulia!" He bangs his fist on the door, and I feel it shaking, echoing the quaking of my body. I feel cold again, the chill from the nightmare returning. Why did I tell Lucas about Kirill? I never trusted anyone but the agency therapist with the full story. Obenko knew, of course—he was the one who ordered the hit on Kirill—but I never spoke about it with him.

Outside mandated therapy sessions, I never spoke about it with anyone until Lucas.

"Yulia, open this door." He stops banging, his tone turning calm and cajoling. "Come out, and we'll talk."

Talk? I want to laugh, but I'm afraid it'll come out as a sob. When I was first recruited, the agency therapist expressed a concern that I wouldn't be sufficiently detached for the job, that losing my family at a young age made me susceptible to emotional manipulation. It was a weakness I've worked hard to overcome, but apparently not hard enough.

A tender touch, a show of anger on my behalf, and I turned to putty in Lucas Kent's hands.

"Yulia, there's nothing in that room for you. Come out, sweetheart. I won't do anything to you, I promise."

Sweetheart? A spark of anger ignites in me, chasing away some of the icy chill. How much of an idiot does he think I am?

Stepping back, I turn and unlock the door. Lucas is right: there's nothing in this bathroom for me but self-recriminations and bitterness. I can't change what happened. I can't take back the fact that I trusted a man who desires nothing more than revenge.

What I can do, however, is turn the tables.

When the door opens, I look up at Lucas and let the tears stinging my eyes finally fall.

6

ucas

SHE STANDS IN THE DOORWAY, LOOKING SO BEAUTIFUL AND vulnerable that my heart squeezes in my chest. Her eyes are glittering with tears, and as I reach for her, she wraps her arms around her naked torso in a defensive gesture.

"No, come here, sweetheart." I unwrap her arms and pull her toward me, doing a quick visual scan of her hands to make sure she's not concealing a weapon. No matter how fragile Yulia appears, I can't forget that she's a trained agent who's already tried to kill me.

To my relief, she's unarmed, so I fold my arms around her, pressing her against my chest. "I'm sorry," I whisper, stroking her hair. "I'm so sorry."

The feel of her bare skin against mine makes my body stir again, and I have to focus to ignore the press of her nipples against my chest. I don't want to get distracted by lust, not after what I've just learned.

I know I'm being irrational. It shouldn't matter that she's been abused. Some of the most twisted individuals I know have had a rough past, and I've never been inclined to cut them any slack. If they fucked up, they paid. Nobody gets a free pass with me, yet that's precisely what I'm planning to give her.

My one-eighty turn is so sudden I want to laugh at myself. She's been here less than twenty-four hours, and my plans for her have already gone up in smoke. I suppose I should've expected this, given that I haven't been able to get Yulia out of my mind for the last two months, but the intensity of my need and the inconvenient feelings that came with it still blindsided me.

She killed dozens of our men and nearly killed me.

The thought that always enraged me now brings up only echoes of my former fury. She was doing her job, carrying out the assignment she'd been entrusted with. I've always known it was nothing personal, but that didn't matter to me before. An eye for an eye—that's the way Esguerra and I have always operated. You cross us, you pay.

Except I don't want to make Yulia pay anymore. She's been through enough, first at the Russian prison, then at my hands. Instead of her, I'll focus my vengeance on the ones who are truly responsible: the agency that gave her that assignment.

"Let's go back to bed," I say, pulling back to gaze down at Yulia. She's stopped trembling, though her face is still wet with tears. "It's early."

She gives a curt shake of her head. "No, I can't sleep. I'm sorry, but I just can't."

"All right." The sun's already starting to come up, so I figure it's not a big deal. "Do you want something to eat?"

She extricates herself from my hold and takes a step back. "Another sandwich?" Her voice still sounds shaky, but there's a tiny note of amusement there too.

"I have soup," I say, trying to keep my eyes off her slim, naked body.

She blinks. "What kind of soup?"

"I'm not sure. I forgot to look inside the pot before putting it in the fridge. It's something from Esguerra's house. His maid gave it to me last night."

A small, surprising smile curves Yulia's lips. "Really? Do they also feed you scraps from their table?"

"No." I chuckle at her not-so-subtle jab. "I wish they would, though. Esguerra's housekeeper is amazing in the kitchen, and I can't cook worth shit."

Yulia arches her delicate eyebrows. "Seriously? *I* can."

"Oh?" I find myself enjoying the unexpected banter. "Did they teach you that in spy school?"

"No, I taught myself some basic recipes when I first arrived in Moscow. I was living off a student stipend, so I didn't have a lot of money for eating out. Later on, I discovered I liked cooking, so I started experimenting with more advanced recipes."

The reminder of the fucked-up nature of her job kills my lighter mood. "You weren't getting a salary?"

"What?" She looks taken aback. "No, of course I was. It was being deposited into my bank account in Ukraine. I just couldn't use those funds—I had to live like a student, else I wouldn't have passed the Kremlin's background checks."

Of course. Undercover living at its finest.

"All right," I say, forcing my tone to lighten. "Let's try the soup for now. Maybe later you can show me your cooking skills."

THE SOUP ROSA GAVE ME IS DELICIOUS, FILLED WITH MUSHROOMS, rice, beans, and chunks of lamb. As we eat, I observe Yulia, wondering what the hell I'm going to do with her now. Keep her naked and tied up in my house forever?

To my shock, the idea holds a certain dark appeal. For the first time, I understand why Esguerra kept his wife, Nora, on his private island for the first fifteen months of their relationship. It's as secure and isolated as one can get—a perfect place for a woman who may not necessarily want to be there.

If I had an island, I'd keep Yulia there, with nothing but her long blond hair to cover her.

Her spoon clinks against her ceramic bowl—I don't have paper plates for soup—and I tense, my gaze jumping to her hand. She's just eating, though, her attention seemingly focused on her meal.

Despite her calm demeanor, I don't relax. She's going to try something, I'm sure of it. I may have decided against making her pay, but that doesn't mean I trust Yulia or expect her to trust me. Even if I told her I no longer plan to punish her, she wouldn't believe me. Given a chance, she'd escape in a heartbeat, and the fact that she's being so docile worries me. It's a good thing I took the precaution of stashing all weapons from my house in the trunk of my car; it would've been too risky to have guns around when I let her eat untied like this.

Naked and untied.

I try not to get distracted by the sight of her nipples peeking through the veil of her hair, but it's impossible. Under the table, my cock feels like it's made of stone. I took the time to throw on a pair of cut-offs and a T-shirt before leading Yulia to the kitchen, but I didn't give her any clothes, and I'm starting to think that keeping her undressed like this is not such a good idea.

As if sensing my thoughts, Yulia tucks her hair behind her ear, causing it to shift and mostly cover her breasts. I let out a sigh of relief and resume eating as my arousal slowly subsides.

"You know, you never told me what happened that day with your plane," she says midway through her soup, and I see that her blue eyes are trained on my face, studying me. Once again, I'm reminded that I'm up against a skilled professional. She might've seemed fragile after her nightmare, but that doesn't mean she doesn't have a deep reservoir of strength.

She must have it, else she couldn't have done her job after that brutal attack.

"You mean after they shot the missile at us?" I push my empty bowl aside. The fact that she can talk so calmly about the crash brings back some of my anger, and it's all I can do to keep my voice even.

Yulia's hand tightens around her spoon, but she doesn't back down. "Yes. How did you survive it?"

I take a deep breath. As much as I hate talking about this, I want her to know what happened. "Our plane was equipped with an anti-missile shield, so it wasn't a direct hit," I say. "The missile exploded outside our plane, but the blast radius was so wide that it damaged our engines and caused the back of our plane to catch fire." Or at least that's the theory our engineers have come up with based on the remnants of the plane. "We crashed, but I was able to guide us to a cluster of thin trees and bushes. They softened our landing somewhat." I pause, trying to keep my fury under control. Still, my voice is hard as I say, "Most of the men in the back didn't survive, and the three who did are still in the hospital with third-degree burns."

Her face whitens as I speak. "So was your boss at the front with you?" she asks, putting down her spoon. "Is that how the two of you survived?"

"Yes." I take another breath to battle the memories. "Esguerra came into the pilot's cabin to talk to me right before it happened."

Yulia's forehead creases with tension. "Lucas, I—" she begins, but I raise my hand.

"Don't." My voice is razor sharp. If she starts lying right now, I may not be able to control myself.

She freezes and looks down at the table, instantly falling silent. I can feel her fear, and I force myself to take another breath and unclench my hands—which had unconsciously curled into fists on the table.

When I'm sure I'm not going to snap, I continue. "So yeah, we were both at the front, and we survived," I say in a calmer tone. "Esguerra was nearly killed afterwards, though. Al-Quadar sniffed out that he was in a hospital in Tashkent, not far from their stronghold, and they came for him."

Yulia's head jerks up, her eyes wide. "The terrorists got your boss?"

"Just for a couple of days. We got him back before they did too much damage." I don't go into the details of the rescue operation and how Esguerra's wife risked her life to save him. "His eye was the main casualty."

"He lost an eye?" She looks stunned, and her reaction awakens the old seedling of jealousy in me.

"Yes." The word comes out sharp. "But don't worry—he got an implant, so he's still as pretty as ever."

She falls silent again, looking down at her bowl. It's still half-full, so I say gruffly, "Eat. Your soup is getting cold."

Yulia obeys, picking up her spoon. After a few spoonfuls, however, she looks up at me again.

"He must hate me a lot," she says softly. "Your boss, I mean."

I shrug. "Not as much as he hates Al-Quadar. Or I should say, *hated* Al-Quadar."

She blinks. "They're gone?"

"We wiped them out," I say, watching her reaction. "So yes, they're gone."

She flinches, so subtly that I would've missed it if I hadn't been staring at her. "The whole organization? All their cells?" She sounds incredulous. "How is that possible? Weren't governments worldwide hunting them for years?"

"They were, but governments are always… constrained." I smile grimly. "When you're trying to be better than the thing you're hunting, it's hard to do what it takes. They have their hands tied by laws and budgets, by public opinion and democracy. Their constituents don't want to see stories on the news about children killed in drone strikes or terrorists' families abused during interrogations. A little waterboarding, and everyone's up in arms. They're too soft for this fight."

"But you and Esguerra are not." Yulia puts down her spoon, her hand unsteady. "You're willing to do what it takes."

"Yes, we are." I can see the judgment in her eyes, and it amuses me. My spy is still an innocent in some ways. "The Al-Quadar stronghold in Tajikistan was one of the last big cells remaining, and from there, it was just a matter of finding the few that were still scattered around the world. It wasn't difficult once we threw all our resources at it."

She stares at me. "I see."

"Eat your soup," I remind her, seeing that she's not eating again.

Yulia picks up her spoon, and I get up to get myself another bowl. By the time I return to the table, I see that she has nearly finished her portion.

"Do you want more?" I ask, and she shakes her head, once again letting me catch a glimpse of her nipples.

"I'm full, thank you."

"Okay." I force myself to start eating instead of staring at Yulia's breasts. When I look up again, she has her knees drawn up and her arms wrapped tightly around them. It makes me wonder if she saw the lust on my face and was reminded of her nightmare.

Thinking about that—about what happened to her at fifteen—infuriates me all over again. I want to dig up Kirill's corpse and shred it into pieces. I know it's ironic as hell that I'm outraged over a rape when I've done things most people would deem a thousand times worse, but I can't be rational about this.

I can't be rational about *her*.

"So, Lucas, what made you decide to work here?" Yulia asks, dragging me out of my thoughts, and I realize she's trying to feel me out, to understand me better so she can manipulate me. I can deflect her question, but she was open with me earlier, so I figure I owe her some answers.

A little honesty will do no harm.

"Esguerra pays well, and he's fair to his people," I say, leaning back in my chair. "What else can one ask for?"

"Fair?" Yulia frowns. "That's not your boss's reputation. 'Ruthless' is how most people would describe him, I think."

I chuckle, inexplicably amused by that. "Yeah, he's a ruthless bastard, all right. However, he generally keeps his word, which makes him fair in my book."

"Is that why you're loyal to him? Because he keeps his word?"

"Among other reasons." I also appreciate Esguerra's loyalty to his own. He's taken care of the people on this estate after his parents' death, and I admire that. But all I say is, "A seven-figure salary helps for sure."

Yulia studies me, and I wonder what she sees. An amoral mercenary? A monster? A man just like Kirill? For some reason, this last bit bothers me. I may not be much better, but I don't want her to see me that way.

I don't want to feature in her nightmares.

"So when did you meet Esguerra?" she asks, still in her information-gathering mode. "How did you end up working for him?"

"They didn't tell you that?" I imagine she must've been briefed extensively on my boss, since he was her original assignment. And possibly on me, since I accompanied him.

"No," Yulia replies. "That wasn't in either of your files."

So she did study up on us. "What *was* in my file?" I ask, curious.

"Just the basics. Your age, where you went to school, that sort of thing." She pauses. "Your discharge from the Navy."

Of course. I shouldn't be surprised she knows about that. "Anything else?"

"Not really." Yulia pauses again, then says quietly, "It didn't even mention whether you're married or otherwise attached."

A peculiar warmth unfurls in my chest. Pushing my empty

bowl aside, I lean forward to rest my forearms on the table. "I'm not," I say, answering the question she didn't pose. "In fact, I haven't been with anyone but you since Moscow."

Yulia gives me an unreadable look. "You haven't?"

"No." I don't bother explaining how I've been too obsessed with her to think about any other woman.

Getting up, I take the bowls to the sink, then turn to face her. "Let's go, beautiful. Breakfast is over."

7

ulia

As Lucas leads me to the living room, I reflect on what I just learned. What Lucas told me about Al-Quadar fits perfectly with the information in Esguerra's file. Lucas's boss is merciless with his enemies, and I'm one of them.

By all rights, I should've already been killed in some gruesome way, yet I'm alive, fed, and unharmed. Now that I'm thinking more clearly, I realize Lucas's decision to manipulate me emotionally rather than torturing me physically is a stroke of unbelievable luck. My feelings may be wounded, but my body is whole, some minor soreness aside. I have no doubt that he's playing me, but it's possible that at least some of his game is real.

It's possible that his desire for me is temporarily stronger than his hate.

I tested that theory when I came out of the bathroom, first by showing vulnerability, then by being subtly friendly. When my captor seemed to respond well to that, I brought up the plane crash, a topic that had provoked him before. The fact that he didn't attack me—that he actually conversed with me, telling me some of his story—is beyond encouraging.

It means that some of the sympathy he displayed earlier may be genuine.

Feeling hopeful, I glance at Lucas as he walks beside me. He has a fresh coil of rope in his hands, and when we stop in front of the chair where he had me tied before, I do my best to assume a vulnerable expression.

"Do you really need me naked?" I ask, letting my eyes glisten with tears. It's easy to bring them up; my emotions are still ricocheting from hurt to anger to lingering longing for comfort. "It's cold when the air conditioning comes on."

He hesitates, and I give him a desperate, pleading look. I'm only half-acting. It's a small thing, clothes, but being dressed would make me feel more human. More importantly, though, Lucas granting me this request would mean that my strategy of playing on *his* emotions is working.

"All right," he says, giving in as I hoped. "Come with me." Leaving the rope on the chair, he takes my arm and brings me to the bedroom.

"Here," he says, handing me a T-shirt. "You can wear this for now."

Trying to hide my ecstatic relief, I accept the piece of clothing and pull it over my head, noting the heat in Lucas's eyes as he watches me do so. It's a man's shirt—*his* shirt—and it's long enough to cover me to mid-thigh.

"All right, let's go," he says when I'm dressed, and leads me back to the chair. As he ties me up, I look at his big, sun-darkened hands looping the rope around my ankles and wonder if he's feeling the same electric tingle that I am. It's fucked up that I still want him, but it may also aid me in escape.

It may help propagate this new, more amicable dynamic between us.

When he's done tying me up, Lucas stands up and says, "I have to get some things done. I'll be back in a few hours."

"Okay, sure," I say, keeping a poker face.

With a lingering glance at me, Lucas departs, and I let my relieved smile break across my face.

AFTER A WHILE, MY EBULLIENT FEELING FADES, REPLACED BY A combination of boredom and discomfort. The chair is hard under my butt, and the ropes bite into my skin every time I try to change my position. The minutes begin to stretch, passing by slowly and monotonously. I keep looking at the window, waiting for the mystery girl to return, but she doesn't. There's only an occasional lizard running over the window screen.

Sighing, I look down and ponder the other tidbit that gave me hope. If Lucas didn't lie, my dark-haired visitor wasn't his girlfriend.

He doesn't have a girlfriend at all.

The knowledge is like a balm to my ragged feelings. I don't know why it matters to me whether Lucas is single, married, or hooking up with a dozen women, but the fact that he's not cheating on that girl with me makes me feel better about last night. I didn't wrong another woman. Whatever's going on with me and Lucas is just between the two of us. Nobody else is going to get hurt.

Of course, I have to allow for the possibility that he lied, that this is all part of his interrogation technique, but I'm inclined to believe him on this. There are no signs of a woman's presence in his house: no decorations or picture frames, no hair dryers or feminine products in the bathroom.

This place is a bachelor residence, right down to the almost-bare fridge, and if I hadn't been so terrified and exhausted yesterday, I would've noticed that obvious fact.

Yawning, I look at the window again. Another lizard runs by. I watch it and wonder what it's like out there, in the jungle beyond these walls. Every part of me aches to be out there, to feel the warm sun on my skin and hear the singing of birds. The small glimpse I got yesterday hadn't been enough.

I want to be outside.

I want to be free.

Soon, I promise myself, shifting in the hard chair. I now understand the game Lucas is playing, and I can play along. I'll be his sex doll for as long as he lusts after me, and I'll seem weak and open. I'll tell him everything except the information he seeks, and I'll let him think that he's prying the secrets out of me, that his soft interrogation is working. This way, he won't resort to harsher methods for a while, and I'll use this time to formulate a real escape plan, something more promising than a desperate attack with a broken toothbrush.

I'll also work on building a bond with Lucas.

Lima Syndrome. That's what they call the psychological phenomenon where the captor sympathizes with the captive so much that he releases said captive. I studied it during training, as there was a high probability I'd be captured one day. Lima Syndrome is not as common as its inverse, Stockholm Syndrome, where the captive falls for his or her captor, but it does occur. I'm not foolish enough to think that I'll be able to get Lucas to release me, but it's possible that I could get him to lower his guard and do little things that would make my escape easier.

Like letting me wear clothes.

Yawning again, I watch yet another lizard scurry across the window, and I imagine that I'm small and green. Small enough to slip out of my bonds and slither through the vents. If I could do that, I'd be the best spy in the world.

It's a silly thought, but it comforts me, taking my mind off what awaits me if my plan fails. My eyelids grow heavy, and I don't fight it. As I nod off, I dream of little green lizards and my baby brother, who's laughing and chasing them around a jungle park.

It's my most joyful dream in years.

"YULIA."

I wake up instantly, my heart jumping, and look up.

Lucas is back—and he's not alone. In addition to my captor, there is a short, balding man standing in front of me, his brown eyes regarding me with a detached curiosity. His clothes are casual, but the bag in his hands appears to be a medical kit.

My stomach drops. I was wrong about Lucas waiting to use the harsher methods.

Before I can panic, the short man smiles at me. "Hello," he says. "I'm Dr. Goldberg. If you don't mind, I'd like to examine you."

Examine me?

"To make sure you're not injured," the doctor explains, undoubtedly reading my confused expression. "If you don't mind, that is."

Right, okay. I take a deep breath, my fear easing. "Sure. Go right ahead." I'm tied to a chair wearing nothing but Lucas's T-shirt, and the man is asking if I'd mind a doctor's examination? What would he do if I said I minded? Apologize for the intrusion and go away?

Apparently oblivious to the sarcasm in my voice, the doctor turns to Lucas and says, "I'd like the patient to be untied, if possible."

Lucas frowns, but kneels in front of me and begins working on the rope around my ankles. Glancing at the doctor, he says tersely, "I'm going to stay here. She's creative with household items."

"But—"

At a hard look from Lucas, the doctor falls silent. Lucas finishes untying my ankles and moves around me to undo my hands. I wiggle my feet surreptitiously, restoring circulation, and think longingly about the bathroom.

I don't know how long I've been tied up, but my bladder's convinced it's been forever.

"I need to pee," I tell Lucas, figuring I have nothing to lose by being honest. "Would it be okay if I went to the bathroom before the examination?"

Lucas's frown deepens, but he gives a curt nod. "Let's go," he says when he's done with the rope. Grabbing my arm, he pulls me up, his grip as rough as upon my arrival. Startled, I nearly stumble as he drags me down the hallway, the gentleness of this morning nowhere in sight.

My anxiety returns. Was I wrong about him, or did something happen? Does this examination have something to do with it?

Before I can analyze my captor's alarming behavior, he pushes me into the bathroom and says harshly, "You have one minute and not a second longer."

And on that note, he slams the door shut.

8

ucas

When I bring Yulia back into the living room, Goldberg has her stand while he feels her pulse and listens to her breathing with a stethoscope. "Good, good," he mutters under his breath, jotting down something in his notebook.

He bends down to look at a big bruise on her knee, and Yulia shoots me an anxious glance. I can see that she wants answers, but I don't give her any reassurance.

I don't want the doctor to know how much I've softened toward my captive.

After a minute, Goldberg stops and gives Yulia a smile. "Just a few scrapes and bruises," he says cheerfully. "You're underweight and a little malnourished, but a few good meals should fix that. Now, I'd like to take some blood if you don't mind. Please, have a seat."

He points toward the couch, and Yulia glances at me again.

"Sit," I bark, doing my best to ignore the distressed look that steals over her face as she complies.

Goldberg pulls on a pair of latex gloves and takes out a syringe with an attached vial. "This won't be too bad," he promises. I wonder if he's trying to compensate for my harsh manner. He's not usually this gentle with the guards—though, granted, none of them have Yulia's fragile beauty.

She doesn't wince or make a sound as the needle sinks into her skin, her expression one of stoic endurance. I, on the other hand, have to fight an irrational urge to tear Goldberg away from her.

I hate to see someone hurting her, even if it's the doctor I brought here myself.

"All done," Goldberg says, taking the needle out and pressing a small sterile pad to the wound. "I'll take this to my lab for analysis. Now, one last thing..." He gives me an imploring look, and I respond with a curt shake of my head.

I'm not leaving him alone with Yulia; he'll have to do the exam with me present.

Goldberg sighs and turns his attention back to her. "I have to perform a gynecological examination," he says apologetically. "To make sure you're okay."

"What?" Yulia's eyes widen. "Why?"

"Just do it." I make my voice as hard as I can. I'm not about to explain that I'm worried I hurt her last night with my roughness. She had been wet, but that doesn't mean I didn't tear her or bruise her internally.

Her face is bright pink as she lies down on the couch, obeying Goldberg's instructions. As the doctor pulls up her shirt and takes out a speculum, I force myself to stand still instead of ripping into the man for touching her. Goldberg is gay, but seeing his hands on her still awakens something savage in me—something that makes me want to murder any man who touches what's mine.

The exam takes less than a minute. I watch Yulia carefully to make sure she doesn't lash out at the doctor, but she lies still, her knees bent and her eyes trained on the ceiling. Only her hands betray her agitation; they're clenched into white-knuckled fists at her sides.

When Goldberg is done, he carefully pulls down Yulia's shirt and steps away. "All done," he says, addressing us both. "Everything seems fine. The IUD is in place, so you have nothing to worry about."

IUD? I frown at the doctor, but he's already explaining, "An intrauterine contraceptive device. Birth control."

"I see." I give Yulia a speculative glance. If she's protected and the doctor determines she's clean, I could fuck her without a rubber.

My cock twitches with instant arousal.

She sits up on the couch, staring straight ahead, and I see that her cheeks are still flaming with color. I want to embrace her and assure her that everything's okay, that I didn't do this to humiliate her, but now is not the time.

As far as the doctor knows, she's a prisoner I despise, and I have to treat her as such.

AFTER THANKING GOLDBERG, I USHER HIM OUT AND RETURN TO THE living room, where Yulia is still sitting on the couch. Her face is back to its normal porcelain shade, but her eyes are glittering brightly. She's upset—I can feel it, even though her expression is outwardly calm.

"Yulia." As I approach, she looks away, her hair rippling down her back in a golden cloud. "Yulia, come here."

She doesn't respond, even when I reach for her and pull her up, forcing her to stand and face me. She also doesn't look at me, her eyes focused on something just beyond my right ear.

Aggravated, I grip her jaw, turning her face so she has no

choice but to meet my gaze. "I needed to make sure you're okay," I say harshly. It still bothers me on some level that I feel this way about her, that I want to heal her and keep her safe instead of hurting her. It's a weakness, this obsession of mine, and I can't help the anger that seeps into my tone as I say, "You could've had internal injuries."

Her eyes narrow. "Bullshit. You just wanted to make sure you don't have to wear a condom."

Her accusation is so close to my earlier thought that I wonder for a second if I said it out loud.

Something must've shown on my face because Yulia lets out a short, bitter laugh. "Yeah, exactly."

"That's not why—" I cut myself off. I don't owe her any explanations. If I want to have her examined so I can fuck her without a rubber, that's my prerogative. I may no longer plan to torture her, but that doesn't mean I've forgotten what she's done. By her own actions, she's placed herself in this situation, and now she's mine.

I own her, for better or for worse.

"I'm clean," I say instead. A better man would undoubtedly leave her alone after what she told me, but I'm not that man. I want her too much to deny myself. "I had all my blood work done after the crash, and I'm completely safe."

Her jaw clenches. "Congratulations."

The sarcasm that drips from her voice sets my teeth on edge and arouses me at the same time. Everything about the girl is a contradiction designed to drive me mad. Compliant yet defiant, fragile yet strong. One minute I want to break her, make her acknowledge that she needs me, and the next I want to wrap her in a cocoon and make sure nothing bad can ever touch her again.

The only thing I don't want to do is let her go.

"Lucas." She sounds anxious as I draw her toward me. "Wait, I—"

I cut her off by slanting my mouth across hers. Cupping the back of her head with one hand, I wrap my other arm around her waist, drawing her flush against me. My balls tighten as my stiff cock pushes against her flat stomach, my ever-present lust for her flaring uncontrollably. I sweep my tongue across her lips, feeling their plush softness, and then I push into her mouth, invading the deliciously warm depths. She moans in response, her hands clutching at my sides, and I drink in the small sound, feeling her slender body softening and melting against mine.

Fucking hell, I want her. Every inch of her, from head to toe. It's wrong, it's fucked up, it's inconvenient, but I can't stop myself. The hunger burns inside me, overpowering whatever scruples I still possess. I know I'm a bastard for coercing her after what she's been through, but I can't stay away. Maybe if she didn't want me, it would be different, but she does. Even through two layers of clothing, I can feel her hard nipples pressing against my chest, can taste the sweetness of her response as her tongue coils eagerly around mine. She's not pushing me away—if anything, she's trying to get closer—and the mindless craving overtakes me, the savage in me taking control.

I don't know how we end up on the couch, but I find myself propped up on one elbow on top of her, her T-shirt bunched around her waist as I slide my free hand down her body to cup her sex. She's already wet, her folds slick and hot as I push two fingers into her, stretching her for my cock. At the same time, I grind the heel of my palm against her folds, putting pressure on her clit. Her inner walls spasm around my fingers as she moans my name, her neck arching and her nails raking down my back, and I know I can't wait any longer.

Pulling my fingers out, I unzip my pants to free my aching erection, and push into her wet heat.

It's like entering heaven. Somewhere in the back of my mind, a warning bell rings, reminding me about a condom, but I'm too far gone to withdraw. The clasp of her body is sheer perfection, so silky and tight that I can't stop myself from plunging in all the way, as deep as I can go. She cries out, arching underneath me, and I lower my head to kiss her, capturing the sound as I take in her taste and scent, reveling in the sensory pleasure of possessing her, of taking her for my own.

Mine, she's mine. The satisfaction the thought gives me is deep and primal, having nothing to do with logic and reason. I've fucked dozens of women without ever wanting to claim them, but that's precisely what I want to do with her. Fucking Yulia is about more than just sex.

It's about tying her to me, binding her so tightly she'll never be able to leave.

Lifting my head, I stare down at her, my cock throbbing deep inside her body. Her eyes are closed, her parted lips are swollen from my kisses, and her skin is glowing with warm color.

She's the sexiest fucking thing I've ever seen, and she's mine.

"Yulia."

She opens her eyes, and I realize I spoke her name out loud. Her gaze is unfocused, her pupils dilated as she stares up at me. She looks dazed, overcome by the same need that's incinerating my insides, and the sight tempers my savage lust, filling me with a peculiar tenderness.

Lowering my head, I take her mouth again, swallowing her needy moan as I begin to thrust in and out, moving slowly so I can feel every inch of her tight warmth. I've never had sex bareback before, and the sensations are incredible. Her pussy is soft and silky, a slick, delicate sheath that appears to have been made just for me. Her inner walls clasp me, embracing me with creamy moisture as I slide in and out, and I focus on the soft clues of her breathing to gauge her response.

The primitive, possessive hunger that gripped me earlier is still there, but now it's reined in by the need to please her, to make her feel at least a fraction of the ecstasy she gives me. Continuing to thrust in a slow, steady rhythm, I move my mouth from her lips to her neck and nibble on the tender skin there. At the same time, I slide my hand under her shirt and gently squeeze her breast.

"Lucas. Oh God, Lucas..." My name is a breathless plea on her lips as I scrape my teeth over her neck and catch her nipple between my fingers, twisting it lightly. She's writhing with need now, her slim legs wrapping around my hips to draw me in deeper as her hands clutch at my sides. I can feel her quivering, her body wound as tightly as a spring, and I pick up my thrusting pace, sensing that she's close.

When her orgasm hits, it's like a quake that reverberates through my body. She tenses, arching beneath me with a cry, and her inner muscles ripple around my cock, the squeezing pressure so strong that it hurls me over the edge. My balls tighten, and then the orgasm sweeps through me, the pleasure dark and intense, shattering in its raw power.

Groaning, I thrust deeper into her and hold her tightly as my cum bursts out into her hot, spasming depths.

9

ulia

Breathing hard, I lie under Lucas, my heart pounding in the aftermath of the devastation that is sex with my captor.

Why is it always like this with him, with this difficult, dangerous man who hates me? I'm far from inexperienced. It's true that I've survived sex at its ugliest, but I've also known its more pleasant variations. My second assignment—Vladimir Vashkov, a trim forty-something FSB liaison—prided himself on being a good lover, and he introduced me to real orgasms, teaching me about arousal and pleasure. I thought I was able to handle anything a man could throw at me in bed, but clearly I was wrong.

I can't handle Lucas Kent.

Maybe it would've been better if he had taken me roughly again. Lust—pounding, punishing lust—is what I expected when he reached for me. And it's what he gave me at first, kissing me by force, using my body's reaction to override my defenses. I was prepared for that after the last time, but I wasn't prepared for his gentleness.

I didn't expect him to treat me like I matter.

"Yulia." He lifts his head, gazing down on me, and my cheeks heat up as our eyes meet. With the fog of lust receding, I become aware that he's still deep inside me—and that I'm holding him there, my legs wrapped so tightly around his hips that he can't move.

My flush intensifying, I unlock my ankles and lower my legs. I also change my grip on his sides to push him away instead of holding on to him. I can't play Lucas's game right now. It feels too real.

He leans down to brush a kiss on my lips and then carefully disengages from me. As he pulls out, I feel a warm, sticky wetness between my thighs.

His seed.

He fucked me without a condom after all.

Irrational bitterness seizes me, chasing away the remnants of my post-coital glow.

"You should've waited for the blood test," I say, pulling my shirt down as Lucas pushes away from me and stands up, getting off the couch. Squeezing my legs together, I give him a hard look. "I have AIDS and syphilis, you know."

"Do you now?" He sounds more amused than worried as he puts away his cock and zips up his jeans. His eyes gleam as he looks at me. "Anything else? Maybe gonorrhea?"

"No, just herpes and chlamydia." I smile at him sweetly, propping myself up on one elbow. "But you'll learn all of that soon, when the test results come back. Now, may I please have a towel or a tissue? I wouldn't want to soil your nice carpet."

To my disappointment, he doesn't rise to my bait. Instead, he laughs and disappears into the kitchen, only to return a second later with a paper towel. "Here you go," he says, handing it to me.

Then he watches with undisguised interest as I sit up and wipe away the wetness on my thighs, doing my best to keep my shirt down as I do so.

"Good job," he says when I'm done. "Now, are you hungry? I think it's time for a second breakfast."

I frown, more than a little frustrated that he's being so calm. I don't know why I want to yank at a tiger's tail, but I do. I hate what he did to me; that impersonal doctor's examination had been humiliating and dehumanizing. And then to come up with that bullshit excuse about potential internal injuries, as though I couldn't see straight through him.

As though I don't know that I'm his sex doll for as long as he cares to play with me.

"I'm not hungry," I say, but right away realize I'm lying. My body is desperate for calories after being starved for so long. "Wait, no, actually—"

Before I can finish my sentence, I hear a faint buzzing sound and see Lucas reaching into his pocket. He pulls out his phone, looks at it, and lets out a quiet curse.

"What is it?" I ask, but he's already grabbing my arm and pulling me off the couch.

"Esguerra needs me," he says, leading me down the hall. "Use the restroom if you need to, and then I have to tie you up again. We'll eat when I return."

And just like that, he's my unfeeling captor once more.

10

ucas

JULIAN ESGUERRA IS ALREADY IN HIS OFFICE WHEN I STEP IN, THE flatscreen monitors on the wall displaying news from all over the world. I take note of the Bloomberg one, where a reputable economist is forecasting another market crash.

It may be time to catch up with my investment manager.

I walk past a large oval conference table and approach Esguerra's wide desk, which is populated with several computer screens. He's on the phone, so he gestures for me to take a seat in one of the high-end leather chairs. I do so and wait for him to wrap up his conversation. Given the mention of Israeli border security, I'm guessing he's talking with his contact at the Israeli intelligence agency, the Mossad.

After a minute, Esguerra hangs up and turns his attention to me. "How's the interrogation going?" he asks. "Any progress so far?"

"A little," I say with a shrug. "Nothing worth mentioning yet." I don't usually keep secrets from my boss, but I don't want to discuss Yulia with him until I figure out the best way to approach the topic. Out of everyone on the estate, he's the only one with the power to take her away from me—which means I need to tread carefully.

Esguerra's harsh reputation is well deserved.

"Good." He seems satisfied with my answer. "Now, on to the reason I wanted you here…"

"An urgent security matter, you said."

"Yes." He leans back, interlocking his hands behind his head. "Nora and I will be taking a trip to the States to visit her family. I'm going to need you to make sure we—and they—are fully protected for the duration."

"You're going to visit your wife's parents? In Oak Lawn?" I'm convinced I must've misheard him, but he nods.

"We'll be there for two weeks," he says. "And I want the security to be top-notch."

"All right," I say. I'm fairly certain Esguerra's lost his mind, but it's not my place to say so. If he wants to enter a country where he's technically wanted by the FBI and spend two weeks with the parents of a girl he kidnapped, married, and impregnated, that's his business.

My job is to ensure he can do it safely.

"The new recruits are already far in their training, so we can take some of the more experienced guys with us," I say, thinking out loud. "Two dozen should probably suffice."

"That sounds about right. Also, I want armored vehicles for all of us, and a good supply of ammo."

I nod, already thinking through the logistics of that. Some would say Esguerra's being paranoid—bulletproof cars are hardly a necessity in the Chicago suburbs—but I don't blame him for being cautious. Al-Quadar may have been squashed for now, but there are plenty of others who'd love to get their hands on him and his pretty young wife.

"I'll make the arrangements," I say, even as my chest tightens at the realization of what this trip will mean.

For two whole weeks, I'm going to be separated from my captive.

"How long do you think it'll take to set everything up?" Esguerra asks. "Nora should be done with her exams in about a week and a half."

"I'm guessing about two weeks." Two weeks during which I'll still have Yulia. "Procuring the cars and all the weapons will take some time, especially if we don't want to set off any alarms at the FBI or CIA."

"Good thinking. We definitely don't want that." Unlocking his hands from behind his head, Esguerra leans forward. "All right. Two weeks should be good. Thanks."

I incline my head and stand up so I can leave and start making calls, but before I can turn away, Esguerra says, "Lucas, there's one more thing."

I stop, my attention caught by an unusual note in his voice. "What is it?"

"I don't know if you're aware of this, but my wife and her friend saw Yulia Tzakova in your house yesterday morning. Nora mentioned it to me today."

"What?" That's the last thing I expected him to say. "Why were Nora and her friend—Wait, what friend?"

"Rosa, our maid," Esguerra says. "They've become close in recent months. I have no idea what they were doing over there, but you need to make sure your house is secure." He pauses and gives me a grim look. "I don't want Nora exposed to anything disturbing in her condition. Do you understand me?"

“Perfectly.” I keep my voice even. “I’ll keep an eye out for any visitors, I promise.”

And the next time I see Esguerra’s maid, I’m going to have a little talk with her.

11

ulia

"Hey."

A quiet rapping on the window draws my attention. Startled, I look up and see the dark-haired young woman from before—the one I thought was Lucas's girlfriend.

"Hey," she repeats, pressing her nose against the window. "What's your name?"

"I'm Yulia," I say, deciding I have nothing to lose by talking to the girl. At least I'm not naked this time. "Who are you?"

"Yulia," she repeats, as though committing my name to memory. "You're the spy who caused the plane crash." She says that as a statement, not a question.

I look at her silently, letting none of my thoughts show. I have no idea who she is or what she wants from me, and I'm not about to say anything that would get me in trouble.

She nods, as if satisfied by my non-response. "Why did Lucas bring you here?"

Instead of answering, I say, "Who are you? What do you want?"

I expect her not to answer either, but she says, "My name is Rosa. I work over at the main house."

Her name sounds familiar. I frown, and instantly, it comes to me. Lucas mentioned a Rosa this morning. She must be the one who gave Lucas that pot of soup.

"What do you want?" I ask, studying the girl.

"I don't know," she surprises me by saying. "I just wanted to see you, I guess."

I blink. "Why?"

"Because you killed all those guards and almost killed Lucas and Julian." Her expression doesn't change, but I hear the tightness in her voice. "And because for some reason, Lucas has you in his house instead of strung up in the shed, where they take traitors like you."

So I'm right to be cautious. The girl hates me for what happened—and possibly has a thing for Lucas. "Do you like him?" I ask, deciding to be blunt. "Is that why you're here?"

She flushes brightly. "That's none of your business."

"You're here to look at me, which makes it my business," I point out, amused. The girl looks to be only a little younger than me, but she seems so naïve it's as if decades separate us instead of years.

Rosa stares at me, her brown eyes narrowed. "Yes, you're right," she says after a moment. "I shouldn't be here." Turning quickly, she ducks out of sight.

"Rosa, wait," I call out, but she's already gone.

At least two hours pass before Lucas returns, and my stomach is painfully hollow by then. According to the clock on the wall, it's one in the afternoon when the front door opens—which means my early breakfast of Rosa's soup was nearly seven hours ago.

Despite my hunger, a prickle of awareness dances over my skin as Lucas approaches, walking with the athletic, loose-limbed gait of a warrior. Like yesterday, he's wearing a pair of jeans and a sleeveless shirt, and his body looks impossibly strong, his well-defined muscles flexing with each movement. I'm again reminded of an ancient Slavic hero—though a Viking raider comparison would likely be more apt.

"Let me guess," he says, kneeling in front of me. His blue-gray eyes glint at me. "You're starving."

"I could eat," I say as he unties my ankles. I could also use a form of entertainment that doesn't include watching lizards, and a more comfortable chair, but I'm not about to complain about such minor things. After my stint in the Russian prison, my current accommodations are positively luxurious.

Lucas chuckles, rising to his feet, and walks around me to free my arms. "Yeah, I bet you could." His big hands are warm on my skin as he undoes the knots. "I can hear your stomach rumbling from here."

"It does that when I don't eat," I say, an inexplicable smile tugging at my lips. I try to contain it, but it breaks through, the corners of my mouth inexorably tilting upwards.

It's bizarre. I can't possibly be genuinely happy to see him, can I?

It's because he's about to feed me, I tell myself, managing to wrestle the smile off my face by the time Lucas removes the rope and tugs me to my feet. It's because I'm subconsciously associating his arrival with good things: food, restroom, not being tied up. Even orgasms, as unsettling as those may be.

It's only my second day here, but my body is already becoming conditioned to regard my captor as a source of pleasure, much like Pavlov's dogs learned to salivate at the sound of a bell. I know that one day soon Lucas may hurt me, but the fact that he hasn't so far has gone a long way toward soothing my fear of him.

There's no point in being terrified if torture and death aren't imminent.

"Come," Lucas says, his fingers an unbreakable shackle around my wrist as he leads me to the kitchen. "We still have some soup, and I can make us a sandwich."

"All right," I say. I'm hungry enough to eat wallpaper, so the sameness of the meals is not a problem. Still, as we stop in front of the table, I can't help offering, "Do you want me to try making something for dinner? I really *can* cook."

He releases my wrist and looks at me, his lips curving slightly. "Oh, yeah. You and knives. I could see that working out." He pulls out a chair for me. "Sit down, baby. I'm going to make those sandwiches."

Baby? Sweetheart? It's all I can do not to react as he takes out the sandwich ingredients and pours soup into bowls. It's a small thing, those pet names, but it's a reminder of what passed between us earlier.

Of the way he caught me at my weakest and tried to make me crack.

Lucas turns away, focusing on microwaving the soup, and I take a calming breath. This is not worth getting agitated about. The invasive doctor exam, yes, but not this. I need to be playing along, acting like I'm starting to trust him. That way, when I slowly open up to him, it will be believable.

The emotional bond between us will feel real.

"So," Lucas says, placing one soup bowl in front of me, "how is it that you speak English so well? You don't have an accent." He takes a seat across from me, his pale eyes regarding me with impassive curiosity.

And so the gentle interrogation begins.

I blow on my soup to cool it down, using the time to gather my thoughts. "My parents wanted me to learn English," I say after swallowing a spoonful, "so I took extra classes, beyond what they taught us in school. It's easy not to have an accent if you learn a language as a child."

"Your parents?" Lucas raises his eyebrows. "Were they preparing you to be a spy?"

"A spy? No, of course not." I eat another spoonful, ignoring the ache of old memories. "They just wanted me to be successful—to get a job in some international corporation or something along those lines."

"But they were okay with you being recruited?" He frowns.

"They were dead." The words come out harsher than I intended, so I clarify in a calmer tone, "They died in a car crash when I was ten."

He sucks in a breath. "Fuck, Yulia. I'm sorry. That must've been rough."

He's sorry? I want to laugh and tell him he has no clue, but I just swallow and look down, as if the subject pains me too much. And it does—I'm not acting this time. Talking about the loss of my parents is like picking at a barely healed scab. I could've lied, made up a story, but that wouldn't have been nearly as effective. I want Lucas to see me this way, real and hurting. He needs to believe I'm someone he can crack without resorting to brutality or torture.

He needs to see me as weak.

"Are you—" He reaches across the table to touch my hand, his fingers warm on my skin. "Yulia, are you an only child?"

Still looking at the table, I nod, letting my hair conceal my expression. My brother is the one piece of my past Lucas can't have. Misha is too closely associated with Obenko and the agency.

Lucas withdraws his hand, and I know he believes me. And why wouldn't he? I've been completely truthful with him up until now.

"Did any of your relatives take you in?" he asks next. "Grandparents? Aunts? Uncles?"

"No." I raise my head to meet his gaze. "My parents didn't have any siblings, and they had me in their mid-thirties—really late for their generation in Ukraine. By the time the accident happened, I had one grandfather who was dying of cancer, and that's it." It's the truth once again.

Lucas studies me, and I see that he already knows the answer to what he's about to ask. "You ended up in an orphanage, didn't you?" he says quietly.

"Yes. I ended up in an orphanage." Looking down, I force myself to resume eating. My stomach is in knots, but I know I need food to regain my strength.

He doesn't ask me anything else while we finish the soup, and I'm grateful for that. I hadn't expected this part to be so difficult. I thought I'd gotten past it after all these years, but even a brief mention of the orphanage is enough for the memories to flood in, bringing with them the old feelings of grief and despair.

When we're done with the soup, Lucas gets up and washes our bowls. Then he pours us two glasses of water, makes the sandwiches, and places my portion in front of me.

"Is that where they recruited you? At that orphanage?" he asks quietly, taking his seat, and I nod, purposefully not looking at him. We're getting too close to the topic I can't discuss with him, and we both know it.

I hear him sigh. "Yulia." I look up to meet his gaze. "What if I told you that I want the past to be the past?" he asks, his deep voice unusually soft. "That I no longer plan to make you pay for following orders and just want to find the ones truly responsible—the ones who gave you those orders?"

I stare at him blankly, as though trying to process his words. I had expected this, of course. It's the logical next move. First, sympathy and caring—some of it genuine, perhaps—then an offer of immunity if I give up my employers. Bringing me to his house, washing me, feeding me—it was all leading up to this. Only sex wasn't part of the equation; the intimacy between us is too raw, too powerful to be staged.

He fucked me because he wanted me, but everything else is part of the game.

"You're going to let me go?" I say, sounding appropriately incredulous. Only a total idiot would fall for his non-promise, and hopefully, Lucas doesn't consider me quite that stupid. He'll have to work to convince me that I can trust him—and during that time, I'll be working on getting him to lower his guard.

To my surprise, Lucas shakes his head. "I can't do that," he says. "But I can promise not to hurt you."

I run my tongue over my suddenly dry lips. This is not what I was expecting; freedom is always the carrot dangled in front of prisoners. "What exactly are you saying?"

He holds my gaze, and my heartbeat accelerates at the dark heat in his eyes. "I'm saying that I want you, and that if you tell me about your associates, I'll keep you safe from them—and from anyone else wishing to harm you."

My insides twist with an unsettling mix of fear and longing. "I don't understand. If you're not going to let me go…"

He looks at me silently, letting me draw my own conclusion.

My pulse is a rapid drumbeat in my ears as I pick up my glass of water, noting with a corner of my eye that my hand is not entirely steady. I gulp down the water, more to buy myself time than out of any extreme thirst. Then I force myself to put down the glass and look at him.

"You're offering me protection in exchange for sex," I say, my voice wavering slightly.

Lucas inclines his head. "You could think of it like that."

"What about your boss?" I can't believe this turn of conversation. "Isn't he expecting you to hack me into pieces, or whatever it is you typically do to make people talk? Isn't that why he had me brought here?"

"*I* had you brought here, not Esguerra."

I gape at him, caught off-guard once more. "What?"

"I wanted you." Lucas leans forward, resting his forearms on the table. "We had that one night, and it wasn't enough. It's true that I wanted to punish you for what happened, but even more than that, I wanted *you*." His voice roughens. "I wanted you in my bed, on the floor, up against a wall, any fucking way I could get you."

"You brought me here for sex?" This goes beyond anything I could've imagined. "You took me out of prison so you could *fuck me*?"

His gaze darkens. "Yes. I told myself I did it for revenge, but it was to get you."

"I—" Unable to sit still, I stand up, no longer the least bit hungry. My voice is choked as I say, "I need a minute."

On shaky legs, I walk over to stand by the kitchen window. The sun outside is bright over exotic tropical vegetation, but I can't focus on the natural beauty in front of me. I'm too stunned by Lucas's revelations.

Is he telling me the truth, or is this just another attempt to throw me off-kilter and get answers? A startlingly different interrogation technique that uses our mutual attraction as the base? I'm used to men wanting me, but this is something else entirely.

What Lucas is saying indicates a degree of obsession that would be frightening if it were real.

As I stand there trying to come to grips with his revelations, I hear his footsteps. The next moment, his large hands grip my shoulders. He's already aroused; I feel his erection pressing into my ass as he draws me against his hard body.

"This doesn't have to be bad for you, beautiful." His breath is warm on my cheek as he bends his head and brushes his lips against my temple. "You could be safe here, with me."

A tremor of treacherous arousal ripples through me, my nipples tightening under my shirt. "How?" I whisper, closing my eyes. His chest is hard, sculpted muscle under my back, his strength terrifyingly seductive. It's as if he's tapped into my deepest desires—into my longing for safety in his embrace. "How can you promise that when your boss could have me killed in an instant?"

"He won't touch you." Lucas's powerful arms fold around me, restraining and comforting all at once. "I won't let him. Esguerra owes me, and you're the favor I'm going to collect."

"Lucas, this—" My head falls back onto his shoulder as he nuzzles my ear, the bulge in his jeans pressing into me more insistently. "This is insane."

"I know." His voice is a rough growl in my ear. "You think I don't fucking know that?" Releasing me, he spins me around and grips my hips, pulling me to him again. Startled, I open my eyes to see savage need tightening his features. He drags me to the right and presses me against the wall next to the window, his lower body pinning me in place. "You think I haven't told myself that a million times?" His cock presses into my stomach as his gaze burns into me. His pupils are dilated, and there's a vein throbbing in his forehead.

He's not acting.

Far from it.

My breath hitches, arousal mixing with a primitive feminine fear. The man in front of me is not about to listen to reason—and my body may not want him to.

"Lucas." Fighting the drugging pull of his nearness, I wedge my hands between us and press my palms against his chest. "Lucas, I think we need to talk—"

"You want to talk about this?" He rocks his hips in a crude, suggestive motion, his cock thrusting against my lower belly through two layers of clothing. His hand catches my jaw, holding my face immobile as he leans in, his lips hovering centimeters from mine. I freeze in anticipation, my heart hammering, and at that moment, a flicker of motion catches my attention.

Startled, I glance toward the window and see a flash of dark hair ducking out of sight.

"What is it?" Lucas's tone is sharp as he registers my distraction. Following my gaze, he looks at the window and lets out a low curse before releasing me and stepping toward it.

As he leans closer to the glass, I slip around him, putting the table between us. My body is thrumming with heat, but I'm glad for the reprieve. I need to digest what Lucas told me, and I can't do that while he's fucking my brains out.

The untouched sandwich on the table draws my attention. I'm no longer hungry, but I pick up the sandwich and bite into it just as Lucas turns to face me, his lips a thin, hard line.

"Who was that?" I ask, my words muffled by a mouthful of food. I need time, and this is the only way I can think of to extend my reprieve. Chewing determinedly, I wave my sandwich at the window. "Did someone come see you?"

His jaw muscle flexes. "No. Not exactly." Lucas stalks around the table and takes a seat on the other side, his pale eyes boring into me. "You saw someone out there. Who was it?"

I swallow, the sandwich dry and tasteless in my mouth. "I don't know. I only saw the person's hair from the back," I say truthfully. What I don't say, however, is that I have a very good reason to suspect who the owner of that hair might be.

"Male? Female?" Lucas presses. "Hair long? Short?"

I deliberately take another bite of the sandwich and chew it as I mull his question over. "A woman," I say when I can speak again. He wouldn't believe me if I pretended not to notice something so obvious. "Hair in a bun, and I think she was wearing a dark dress."

Lucas nods, as if I confirmed his suspicion. "All right," he says, his expression smoothing out.

Then he picks up his own sandwich and starts eating it, watching me the entire time.

12

ucas

We finish the meal in silence, the air across the table thick with sexual tension. As I watch Yulia consume the last crumbs of her meal, my cock strains in the tight confines of my jeans, throbbing painfully.

If Rosa hadn't chosen that unfortunate moment to play stalker, I would already be inside Yulia, nailing her against the wall.

I shocked my prisoner. I can see it in the heightened color of her cheeks and the way her gaze slides away from mine. Did she believe me? Did she realize I was being sincere? The solution to the dilemma of what to do with her came to me as I was walking home, and I knew instantly that was the only way.

I'm going to do exactly as my instincts demand and keep Yulia.

Once, such an action would've been unimaginable. When I was

in high school, if someone told me that I would so much as think about holding a woman against her will, I would've laughed. Even when I was in the Navy, long after I knew I was capable of doing whatever the job required without a flicker of remorse, I still clung to the morals of my childhood, trying to resist the pull of darkness within myself. It was only when I became a wanted man that I fully understood my nature and the extent of my willingness to cross lines I once viewed as sacred.

Keeping Yulia for my own is nothing in the grand scheme of things, and it's certainly better than the fate I originally planned for her.

"So how exactly would this work?" she asks, finally breaking the silence. Her eyes lock on my face. "You're going to keep me tied up in the chair all day and handcuffed to you all night?"

I smile at her, anticipation sizzling through my veins. "Only if that turns you on, beautiful. If not, I think we can work out a better arrangement." I'm already thinking of the tracker implants Esguerra used on his wife. I could do something similar with Yulia, making sure at least one of the trackers is implanted where it would be all but impossible to remove.

First, though, I'll need to make sure the agency she works for is wiped out; otherwise, Yulia could use their resources to disappear, trackers or not.

"You'll untie me?" Her eyes are wide as she stares at me. "And let me go outside?"

"I will." Once her agency is destroyed and I have the trackers in her, that is. "But you need to tell me about your employers first. Who is the head of the program?"

She doesn't answer me. Instead, she rises to her feet and carries both of our empty paper plates to the garbage can in the corner. I watch her, making sure she doesn't try anything, but she just throws out the plates and returns to the table.

Stopping next to her chair, she looks at me. "How do I know I can trust you? Once I tell you what you want to know, you could just kill me."

"I could, but I won't." I get up and approach her side of the table. Stopping in front of her, I run my knuckles over the soft skin of her cheek. "I want you too much for that."

The color in Yulia's face deepens. "So, what? You're going to spare me because you want to fuck me?" There's disbelief mixed with derision in her voice. "Do you always let your dick decide who lives and who dies?"

I chuckle, not the least bit offended. "No, beautiful. Just when he's this insistent."

In fact, I can't remember ever being swayed from my course of action by a woman. I've always enjoyed sex and female companionship, but the need for it has never been a ruling force in my life. My last longer-term relationship—a three-month affair in Venezuela—was before I started working with Esguerra, and I haven't thought about that girl in years. My more recent encounters have been more along the lines of a one-night stand, or at best, a few days of casual fun.

Yulia gives me a dubious look, her eyebrows arching, and I can't wait any longer. She's mine, and I'm going to do what my body's been clamoring for during the past hour.

"Let's go," I say, my fingers closing around her slender arm. "I think it's time we commenced our arrangement."

SHE'S SILENT AS I LEAD HER INTO THE BEDROOM, HER LONG, SLEEK legs drawing my attention as we walk. I suppose I'll need to get her some clothes of her own soon, but for now, I like seeing her in my shirt, as baggy as it is on her slim frame.

I know that by the moral standards of my childhood, what I'm doing to her is wrong. She's my prisoner, and I'm not giving her any choice in this. I'm coercing her into a relationship she may not want, despite her physical response and seeming willingness to accept my touch. It would be tempting to justify my actions by telling myself that her job makes her fair game for such treatment, but I know better.

She was forced into this life by circumstances beyond her control, and I'm a cruel bastard for taking advantage of her.

As I strip off Yulia's shirt, pulling it over her head, I wait for my conscience to rear up, but all I'm cognizant of is a powerful craving for her. The things I've done in the past eight years—the things I've had to do to survive—rid me of whatever morals my family managed to instill, ripping away the layer of civilization that had always been skin-deep. The man who stands before Yulia now bears no resemblance to the boy who left his upper-middle-class home sixteen years earlier, and my conscience remains dormant as I drop the shirt on the floor and rake my gaze over my captive's naked body.

"Lie down," I tell her, my voice roughening with lust. "I want you on your back."

She hesitates, and I wonder if she's going to fight me after all. It would be pointless—even at her full strength, she'd be no match for me—but I wouldn't put it past her to try something anyway.

To my relief, she doesn't. Instead, she climbs onto the bed and lies down, watching me.

I approach her, my cock swelling even more. Though Yulia is still overly thin, her body is gorgeously proportioned, with a tiny waist, feminine hips, and high, round breasts. Her bright golden hair is like a halo on the pillow, framing a face that appears to be straight out of some fashion magazine. With her finely drawn features, thickly lashed eyes, and perfect skin, she's almost too pretty to fuck.

"Almost" being the key word.

Still, I rein in my savage lust. I don't want to hurt her. She's had too much of that, at my hands and at those of others. Just thinking about that—about other men touching her—makes me murderous with fury.

If a man ever lays a hand on Yulia again, he'll pay with his life.

Climbing onto the bed, I throw my knee over her thighs and cage her between my arms. I'm determined to control myself this time, so I hold myself raised on all fours without touching her. Her chest is rising and falling with shallow breaths as she stares up at me, and I know she's nervous.

Nervous and aroused, judging by her erect nipples and flushed skin.

"You're gorgeous," I murmur, bending over one of those tender nipples. She doesn't move, but I can feel the tension in her body as I press my mouth to the pink areola. The nipple contracts further at my touch, and I close my lips around the taut peak, sucking on it gently. She gasps, her hands curling into fists at her sides, and her eyes close, her head arching back on the pillow.

"Yes, utterly gorgeous," I whisper, turning my attention to the other nipple. It tastes like her, like warm feminine skin and peaches. After I suck on it, I blow cool air over the distended bud and am rewarded with a small moan.

I move on to the rest of her breasts then, nibbling and sucking on the plump, delicate flesh, touching her with nothing but my mouth. Her body is a sensuous feast, every curve, dip, and hollow silky-soft, her scent intoxicating. Even with the lust raging inside me, I can't help lingering over the underside of her breasts, her ribcage, her navel… Moving lower, I taste the tender flesh at the top of her slit, and then push my tongue between her pussy folds.

She cries out, tensing, and I feel her hands on my head, her nails digging into my scalp as I find her clit and press my tongue against it. She's wet—I can taste her arousal—and the uniquely female flavor sends a surge of blood straight to my cock. My balls tighten, drawing close to my body, and my arms tremble with the urge to grab her and thrust inside her, to take her as I've been dying to do since the interruption in the kitchen.

"Lucas." The word is a breathless gasp as she twists underneath me, her hips rising in a silent plea as her nails rake over my hair. "Oh, God, Lucas…"

Ruthlessly tamping down my own need, I focus on her, using my mouth to keep her on the edge without sending her over. I lave every inch of her pussy with my tongue, then capture her labia in my mouth and suck on the tender folds, knowing the pulling motion will squeeze her clit. Her cries grow louder, her nails sharper on my skull, and I fist my hands in the sheets to keep from reaching for her. I want to give her this pleasure first, make her feel some of the hunger that consumes me around her.

"Lucas!" She's thrashing now, her heels digging into the mattress on each side of me, and I know she can't bear much more. Sliding my hand between her thighs, I push two fingers into her and suck on her clit at the same time.

Her back bows as she cries out, and I feel her clenching on my fingers, her flesh rippling around me in release. I wait just long enough to feel her contractions begin to ease, and then I move up her body. Holding myself up on my elbows, I push her legs apart with my knees and line my cock up against her opening.

"Yulia." I wait for her to open her eyes, her gaze still dazed and unseeing, and then I give in to my own desperate need, driving into her in a single deep thrust. She gasps, her hands moving up to clutch my sides, and I'm finally lost. Mindless lust descends on me, and I begin pounding into her, taking her hard and fast.

Vaguely, I'm aware that her legs fold around my hips and she starts matching me thrust for thrust, but I'm too far gone to slow down. She's wet, soft, and tight around me, her inner muscles squeezing my cock, and the tension that builds inside me is uncontrollable, volcanic. It grows and intensifies, my heartbeat roaring in my ears, and then the sensations finally crest, the orgasm hitting me with brutal intensity. Grasping her tightly, I groan as I jet my seed into her body in a series of long, draining spurts.

To my shock, she cries out again, and I feel her tightening

around me once more, her body spasming in her second climax. My cock jerks with an answering aftershock, and then I collapse to the side, pulling her to lie on top of me.

There are no thoughts in my mind except one.

I'm never letting her go.

13

ulia

"You fucked me without a condom again," I say when I can find the breath to speak. I'm lying next to Lucas, my head resting on his shoulder as I wait for my galloping heartbeat to slow.

My captor chuckles, the sound a masculine rumble in his chest. "Oh, yes. I forgot about your million diseases. Well, you'll be glad to hear that I got the test results back from Goldberg, and you only have crabs."

"What?" Horrified, I jerk to a sitting position, but he's already laughing, deep guffaws escaping his throat as he sits up as well.

"You asshole!" Furious, I grab a pillow and smack him with it, wishing it had a brick inside it. "That's not funny!"

Laughing even harder, Lucas grabs me and wrestles me back down to the mattress, rolling on top of me to hold me in place. With maddening ease, he captures my wrists, pinning them above my head as he subdues my kicking legs with his powerful thighs. "Actually," he says, grinning, "I thought it was hilarious."

"Oh, really?" Unable to throw Lucas off, I use the only weapon I have left. Lifting my head, I sink my teeth into the muscular junction between his shoulder and neck.

"Ouch! You little animal." Transferring my wrists into his left hand, he fists my hair with his right, pulling my head down on the mattress. To my annoyance, he's still grinning, not the least bit fazed by the red mark my teeth left on his skin. "You shouldn't have done that."

"Is that right?" Despite my helpless position, the old memories are dormant, leaving me free to focus on my anger. "Why's that?"

"Because"—he lowers his head, bringing his mouth close to my ear—"you made me want you." And raising his head to meet my gaze, he nudges his hardening cock against my thigh, leaving no doubt of his meaning.

Incredulous, I stare at him, seeing the now-familiar glow of heat in his wintry eyes. "Are you kidding me? Again?"

"Yes, beautiful." His mouth curves in a darkly carnal smile as he wedges his knee between my thighs, forcing them open. "Again and again."

IT'S WELL OVER AN HOUR BEFORE I'M ABLE TO TAKE REFUGE IN THE bathroom and gather my scattered thoughts. My body is sore and aching, worn out by the endless orgasms, and the residue of sex is crusted on my thighs. After I take care of my most pressing needs, I turn on the shower to take a quick rinse.

Before I can get in, the door opens and Lucas steps in, still fully nude. "Good idea," he says, glancing at the running water. "Let's go in."

Horrified, I gape at my insatiable jailer. "You can't possibly."

He grins, white teeth flashing. "I could, but I won't. I know you need a break. Come here, baby." Grasping my arm, he pulls me into the stall. "It's just a shower, I promise."

He's true to his word, his big hands soaping me without lingering more than a few moments on my breasts and sex. Even so, I'm aware of a slow heated pulse between my thighs as he washes me thoroughly, his fingers sliding between my folds and up into the crevice of my ass. Shocked, I clench my buttocks as the tip of his finger presses into that hole, and he lets out a soft laugh, releasing me when I push at him.

"All right, I can wait," he says agreeably, and I turn away, my stomach roiling at the knowledge that it's only a matter of time before he takes me that way too, regardless of my thoughts on the matter.

Thankfully, Lucas finishes washing himself quickly and steps out of the stall. "Come out when you're ready," he says as he towels off, and then he's gone, leaving me alone in the shower.

Exhausted, I slump against the wall, letting the water beat down on my chest. My nipples are painfully sensitive, as is my swollen, aching sex. Prior to meeting Lucas, I had no idea that pleasure could be so draining, that it could take everything out of me, both physically and mentally. I can't resist him, and it has nothing to do with the fact that he's my captor.

Even if I were free, I'd never be able to deny him.

Protection in exchange for sex. The words circle through my mind, filling me with a confusing mix of outrage and longing. Is it possible he meant it? Did he really bring me halfway across the globe to be his sex toy?

It seems ridiculous—except I felt the strength of his desire for me. Even now, my body aches from his relentless passion. Would Lucas really do that? Let bygones be bygones and simply keep me if I tell him about my agency? When I was thinking of establishing a bond with him earlier, I was hoping to buy myself some time without pain and a shot at escape before I'm killed. However, if what he says is true, my not-so-terrible captivity could go on indefinitely—or at least until Esguerra demands my head on a platter.

No matter what Lucas says about favors owed, I don't believe his boss will spare me forever. Sooner or later, Esguerra will want to get his pound of flesh, and then I'm dead. And even if, by some miracle, Lucas really can protect me, he won't do so for long.

He'll throw me to the wolves once he realizes I'm not going to give him the answers he seeks.

Straightening away from the wall, I turn off the water and step out of the stall. As I towel off, I try to figure out if this turn of events changes anything and decide that it doesn't.

All it means is I've gotten incredibly lucky.

I will have time to plan my escape.

14

ucas

When Yulia comes out of the bathroom, I give her a clean T-shirt to wear and take her back to the living room, my body humming with the bone-deep satisfaction only sex with her can bring.

"Do you like to watch TV?" I ask as I tie her ankles to the chair. I can't remember the last time I felt so relaxed and content. Soon, I'll get the answers I need, and I'll be able to give her more freedom.

For now, the least I can do is alleviate her probable boredom.

"TV?" Yulia gives me a bewildered look. "Sure. Who doesn't?"

"Any preferences? Shows? Movies? News channels?"

"Um, anything, really."

"Okay." Finished with the rope, I turn her chair to face the large television on the opposite wall. "How about *Modern Family*? It's light and funny. Have you seen it?"

"No." She's staring at me like I've sprouted green whiskers.

"Okay, then." Suppressing a smile, I turn on the TV and select the first season of the show from the files I've stored on there. "I have some work to do before dinner, but this should keep you entertained."

"Sure," she says, looking so adorably confused that I can't help myself. Bending down, I press a kiss to her parted lips, swallowing her startled gasp. The delicious warmth of her mouth makes my cock twitch, and I force myself to straighten and step back before I get carried away.

As unbelievable as it is, I want Yulia again.

Inhaling deeply, I turn away, determined to regain control. "I'll see you soon," I tell her over my shoulder and stride out of the house.

As much as I'd like to spend all day fucking my prisoner, there's work to be done.

~

I SPEND THE FIRST COUPLE OF HOURS IN ESGUERRA'S OFFICE, ironing out the logistical details of his Chicago protection with him and the guards I'm planning to bring with us. There's a lot to coordinate, as Nora's parents will need extra protection during and after our visit, in case some of Esguerra's business associates decide that using his in-laws as leverage is a good idea. It's doubtful—everyone knows what happened to Al-Quadar when they tried it with his wife—but it's always good to be cautious.

Some people's stupidity verges on suicidal.

Just as we're about to finish, Esguerra's wife walks in. Her dark eyes widen when she sees us all sitting there. "Oh, I'm sorry. I didn't mean to interrupt—"

"What is it, baby?" Esguerra rises to his feet and comes toward her, his eyebrows drawn together in a worried frown. "Is everything okay? How are you feeling?"

Nora shoots me and the guards an embarrassed look before turning her attention to her husband. "I'm fine. Everything's fine," she says hurriedly. "I wanted to ask you about something, but it can wait."

"Are you sure?" Esguerra's voice softens, as it often does when he speaks to his petite wife. "I can step out—"

"No, please don't. Really, it's not important." Rising on tiptoes, she presses a quick kiss to his jaw. "I'm going to be by the pool. Come find me when you're done."

"All right." Nora steps out and Esguerra gazes after her, frowning. I can see that he wants to follow her, but doesn't want to seem even more obsessed with her than we already know him to be. If he were anyone else, the guards would rib him about this for weeks to come. Instead, we all keep our faces expressionless as our boss returns to the table.

It doesn't take long to finish hammering out the security logistics. As soon as we're done, the guards return to their duties, and Esguerra heads out to find his wife, leaving me alone in his office to catch up on a couple of emails. I decide to use this opportunity to video call our Hong Kong supplier and procure the tracker implants for Yulia. To my disappointment, the old man informs me that he's only going to be able to get them to me in two weeks—exactly when we'll be in Chicago.

"Is there any way you can do it sooner?" I ask, not liking the idea of leaving Yulia unsecured for so long, but the man just shakes his head.

"No, I'm afraid not. The ones Mr. Esguerra got that time were a prototype, and we'll need to manufacture the ones for you from scratch. The coating is highly specialized, so it will have to be custom-ordered—"

"Never mind. I understand." I'll just have to assign some trustworthy men to watch over my prisoner in my absence. "Thank you for your time, Mr. Chen."

Disconnecting from the video call, I get up and exit Esguerra's office.

There's one more thing I have to take care of today.

Ana, Esguerra's middle-aged housekeeper, opens the door for me.

"Hello, Señor Kent," she says in her accented English. "Are you looking for Señor Esguerra? He just went upstairs to take a shower."

"No, I'm not looking for him." I smile at the older woman. "May I come in?"

"Of course." She steps back, letting me into a large, luxurious foyer. "Nora is by the pool. Would you like to speak to her?"

"No, actually." I pause, looking around before glancing back at the housekeeper. "Is Rosa here? I'd like to ask her something."

"Oh." Ana seems startled, but recovers quickly, saying, "Yes, she's in the kitchen, helping me with dinner. Come, this way." She leads me through a set of double doors and past a wide curving staircase.

When we enter the kitchen, I'm greeted by a mouthwatering smell of roasted garlic. Rosa herself is standing next to a gleaming sink with her back turned to us, cutting up vegetables.

"Rosa," Ana calls out to the girl. "You have a visitor."

The maid turns toward us, and I see her brown eyes widen as a flush spreads across her face. "Lucas."

"Hello, Rosa," I say, keeping my tone neutral. "Do you have a minute?"

She nods and quickly wipes her hands on a towel. "Yes, of

course." A bright smile appears on her lips. "What can I do for you?"

I turn to look at the housekeeper, but Ana is already hurrying away, having correctly deduced that I want privacy.

"Thank you for the soup," I say, deciding to ease into it. "It was excellent."

"Oh, good." Her smile widens. "I'm so glad you enjoyed it. It's my mother's recipe."

"Wait." I frown. "You made it, not Ana?"

Rosa turns beet red. "I did—I'm sorry I lied to you earlier. It was just that—"

"Rosa," I interrupt, holding up my hand. I want to spare the girl any unnecessary awkwardness. "Thank you. It was a wonderful soup, but I'd rather you didn't make it again for me. Or anything else for that matter, all right?"

She looks like I just slapped her across the face. "Of c-course," she stammers. "I'm sorry, I—"

"And I need you to stay away from my house," I continue, ignoring the tears pooling in the girl's eyes. I'd sooner face a dozen terrorists than do this, but I have to drive the point home. "It's not safe for you. My prisoner is dangerous."

"I just—"

"Look," I say, feeling like I was just cruel to a child, "you're a beautiful girl, and very sweet, but you're much too young for me. You're what, eighteen, nineteen?"

Rosa's chin lifts. "Twenty-one."

"Right." It strikes me that she's only a year younger than Yulia, but I've never thought of the Ukrainian spy as being too young for me. Still, I continue without missing a beat. "I'm thirty-four. You should find someone closer to your own age. A nice guy who'll appreciate you."

"Of course." To my surprise, the maid regroups, pulling herself together with startling composure. Her tears dry up, and she gives me a steady smile, though a flush still colors her cheeks. "You don't have to worry, Lucas. I won't bother you anymore."

I frown, unsure whether I can take her at face value, but she's already turning away, her attention on the vegetables once more.

II

THE BREAKING

15

ulia

Over the next week, Lucas and I settle into an uneasy routine. He has sex with me every chance he gets—which is at least a couple of times at night and once during the day—and we eat all of our meals together in the kitchen. The rest of the time I spend watching TV while tied to the chair, or sleeping cuffed at Lucas's side.

"Do you think it would be possible for me to read something?" I ask after two days of binging on TV shows. "I love books, and I miss reading them."

"What kind of books?" Lucas appears unusually interested.

"All kinds," I answer honestly. "Romance, thrillers, science fiction, nonfiction. I'm not picky—I just love the feel of a book in my hands."

"All right," he concedes, and the next day, he takes me to a small room next to the bedroom. Like the rest of his home, it's sparsely furnished. However, it's much cozier, boasting a desk, three tall bookshelves filled with books, and a plush armchair next to a bay window that faces the forest.

"Is this your library?" I ask, surprised. I've always thought of my captor as a soldier, someone more interested in guns than books. It's easier to imagine Lucas wielding a machete than peacefully reading in this room.

"Of course it's mine." Leaning against the door frame, he gives me an amused look. "Who else's would it be?"

"And you've read all of these?" I approach the shelves, studying the titles. There must be hundreds of books there, many of them mysteries and thrillers. I also see a number of biographies and nonfiction works that range from popular science to finance.

"Most of them," Lucas replies. "I tend to order in bulk, so I always have something new to read when I have downtime."

"I see." I don't know why I'm so shocked to discover this aspect of him. I've always suspected that Lucas is keenly intelligent, but somehow I've let myself buy into the stereotype of a hardened mercenary, a man whose life revolves around weapons and fighting. The fact that he went straight from high school to the Navy only added to that impression.

I underestimated my opponent, and I need to be careful not to do that again.

Stopping in front of the bay window, I turn to look at him. "When did you manage to acquire all these books?" I ask. "I thought you spent a few years on the run after you left the Navy."

Lucas's gaze hardens for a second, but then he nods. "Yes, I did. I keep forgetting how much you know about me." He crosses the room to stand in front of me. "I got most of these books within the past year, after Esguerra decided we should make this compound our permanent home. Before that, we were traveling all over the world, so I kept a few dozen of my favorites in storage. And before that, I didn't own many belongings at all—made it easier to move around."

"But that's not what you want anymore," I guess, studying him. "You want to own things, to have a home."

He stares at me, then lets out a bark of laughter. "I suppose. I never thought of it that way, but yeah, I guess I got a little tired of never sleeping in the same bed twice. And owning things?" His voice deepens as his gaze travels over me. "Yeah, there's something to that. I like having *things* I can call my own."

My cheeks heat up as I look away, pretending I'm interested in the view outside the bay window. Lucas's extreme possessiveness hasn't escaped my notice. I know my captor believes he owns me, and for all intents and purposes, he does. He controls every aspect of my life: what I eat, when I sleep, what I wear, even when I go to the bathroom. When I'm not tied up, I'm with him, and for much of that time, we're in bed, where he does whatever he pleases with me.

If I didn't want him as intensely as he wants me, it would be hell.

"Yulia..." Lucas's voice holds a familiar heated note as he steps behind me. His big hand gathers my hair to move it to one side, exposing my neck. Leaning down, he kisses the underside of my ear and slides his free hand under the man's shirt I'm wearing as a dress. Delving between my legs, he finds my sex, and I can't suppress a moan as he penetrates me with two fingers, stretching me for his possession.

And for the next hour, as Lucas fucks me bent over the arm of the chair, books are the furthest thing from our minds.

After that time in the library, the quality and variety of my entertainment improves. Instead of watching TV all day, I spend a portion of my alone time reading by the bay window. I also gain the concession of a more comfortable seat and having my hands handcuffed in the front—that way, I can actually hold and read a book. Every morning after breakfast, Lucas secures me to the armchair with ropes, leaving my handcuffed hands just enough range to turn the pages, and I read there until lunch, at which point he comes to feed me and let me stretch my legs.

"You know, I'm not a dog who uses the bathroom on a schedule," I dare to complain one day. "What if I really have to go, and you're not home?"

To my relief, he doesn't point out how spoiled I've become. Instead, later that day, he gives me a small device that resembles an old-fashioned pager.

"If you press this button, I'll get a text," he explains. "And if I can, I'll come to you. Or send someone else to help you."

"Thank you," I say, feeling genuinely grateful and increasingly hopeful.

Maybe one day he really will let me go, or at least give me enough freedom to enable my escape.

Of course, I know I can't rely on that. Every day, Lucas spends a portion of the mealtimes interrogating me, and even though I've successfully stonewalled him thus far, I'm afraid he'll eventually lose patience and resort to more surefire methods of extracting information.

It hasn't been that long, and I can already feel his frustration growing.

"You don't owe them a damn thing," he says furiously when I refuse to talk about the agency for the fifth time. "They took you when you were a fucking child. What kind of bastards send a sixteen-year-old to a corrupt city like Moscow and tell her to sleep her way to government secrets? Fuck, Yulia"—he slaps his palm on the table—"how can you be loyal to those motherfuckers?"

How, indeed. I want to scream at him, tell him that he doesn't understand anything, but I remain silent, looking down at my plate. There's nothing I can say that won't expose Misha to danger and ruin his life. My loyalty is not to Obenko, the agency, or even Ukraine.

It's to my brother—the only family I have left.

To my relief, Lucas lets my non-response slide, ultimately changing the topic to the plot of a post-apocalyptic thriller I read that day. We discuss it in great detail, as we frequently do with books and movies, and we both agree that the author did a good job of explaining why the scientists couldn't prevent the Gray Goo from taking over the world. The meal concludes on an amicable note, but my determination to escape is reinforced.

Eventually, Lucas will get fed up with my silence, and I don't want to be around when he does.

16

ulia

As I plan my escape, I realize that I'm faced with three major obstacles: the fact that I'm tied up when Lucas is not around, the military-level security of the compound, and Lucas himself. Any of those three would be enough to contain me, but when all three are combined, escape is all but impossible.

On the surface, it shouldn't be difficult. When Lucas is home, he usually keeps me untied, letting me eat at the table and even do a few stretches and body-weight exercises to keep fit. However, he always keeps a watchful eye on me during those times, and I know I won't win in a physical battle with him. Even if I managed to grab a knife, he'd probably wrestle it away from me before I could inflict a serious injury. A gun would be a different matter, but I haven't seen anything more deadly than a kitchen knife inside the house. I know Lucas usually carries weapons—I saw him with an assault rifle that first day—but he must leave them in the car or some other location outside.

Contrary to appearances, I'm more likely to escape when he's not around.

To that end, every time Lucas ties me up, I test the rope to see if he left some slack in it, and every time, I discover he didn't. The bonds are always just tight enough to keep me restrained without cutting off my circulation. I don't want to leave betraying marks on my skin, so I don't tug at the rope too hard. Even if I managed to get free, I'd still need to get past guard towers and through a jungle patrolled by Esguerra's men and high-tech drones—assuming Lucas didn't catch me before I got that far.

For me to stand a chance, I need my captor far away, and I need to know the patrol schedule.

I begin by trying to get the latter out of Lucas when we're lying in bed, relaxed and satisfied after a lengthy sex session.

"How did you get this?" I ask as I trace my fingers over a bruise on his ribcage. "The compound wasn't attacked, was it?"

My concern is only partially feigned; the idea of Lucas getting hurt in any way bothers me. He seems invulnerable, every inch of his body packed with hard muscle, but I know that won't save him from a bomb or a gun. In his line of work, life expectancy is much shorter than average—a fact that makes me sick with worry when I dwell on it too much.

"No, nobody would attack the compound," Lucas says, a smile curving his lips. "I got this bruise in training, that's all."

"I see." Acting on some irrational impulse, I press a small kiss to the injured area before looking up to meet his gaze. "Why wouldn't someone attack the compound? Doesn't your boss have a lot of enemies?"

"Oh, he does." Lucas's eyes darken as he slides his hand into my hair and guides me lower, toward his stomach. "But they would be suicidal to come here. The security is too tight. And now"—he pushes my head toward his rising erection—"I want something else that's tight."

Hiding my disappointment, I close my lips around his cock and apply the strong suction he likes.

Lucas is too smart to give me the security details I need—which means I'll have to figure out something else.

As the days drag on without me getting any closer to a viable escape plan, I console myself with the knowledge that I'm using the time to recover from my ordeal at the Russian prison and rebuild my strength. Between sitting most of the day and consuming every bite of food—no matter how boring—Lucas puts in front of me, I'm steadily putting on weight, my body regaining the curves it lost during my weeks of near-starvation. By the time I've been in Lucas's house nine days, I'm no longer a skeleton—and I'm desperate for something other than sandwiches and cold cereal with milk.

"You know, you seriously should let me try cooking," I say after yet another sandwich for lunch. "I can make omelets, soup, chicken, lamb, mashed potatoes, salad, rice, dessert—anything you want, really. If you don't trust me with a knife, you can help me by cutting things up. I'll just add seasoning and things like that. You'll be perfectly safe—unless you store rat poison in your kitchen."

He laughs, making me think he's going to ignore my offer, but that afternoon, he brings in several boxes of food, including all kinds of fruits and vegetables, two types of fresh fish, several whole chickens, a dozen lamb chops, and an entire collection of spices.

"Where did all of this come from?" I ask, eying the bounty in astonishment. There's enough in those boxes to feed five people—assuming one knows how to prepare it all, of course.

"Esguerra gets weekly deliveries, so I took some for us," Lucas says. "I figure it's time to test your cooking skills."

I can't conceal my startled joy. "You'd trust me to cook?"

"I'd trust you to direct me." He grins. "You'll sit there"—he points at the kitchen table—"and tell me exactly what to do. I'll follow your orders, and who knows? Maybe I'll learn something."

"Okay," I agree, more than a little excited by the prospect of ordering Lucas about. "I can do that. Let's start by putting everything away, and tonight, we'll make lamb chops with garlic-dill potatoes and green salad."

17

ucas

As I peel potatoes and chop garlic under Yulia's guidance, she lounges in the kitchen chair, her blue eyes bright with amusement.

"You know you don't have to take half the potato off with the skin, right?" Grinning, she glances at the pile of mangled potatoes on the counter. "Haven't you ever done this before?"

"No," I say, doing my best not to cut too deeply into my current root vegetable. It's harder than it seems. "And now I know why."

"They didn't make you peel potatoes in the Navy?"

"No, that's a thing of the past. We had private contractors who handled the mess halls."

"I see. Well, you need a potato peeler," she says, crossing her long legs. "Like with everything else, a specialized tool helps."

"A peeler. Got it." I make a mental note to order one. I also do my best to keep my eyes off those bare, distracting legs. Four days ago, I finally got Yulia some clothes of her own, but they're of the skimpy summer variety, and I'm now realizing my mistake.

In a white midriff-baring top and tiny jean shorts, Yulia's no-longer-starved body is impossible to ignore.

"Okay, that's enough potatoes, I think," she says, getting up. Her flip-flops—the only shoes I got her—make a slapping noise on the tile floor as she comes toward me. "Now we need to take the garlic, mix it with dill, salt, and pepper, and place everything on a frying pan. You have oil, right?"

"Oil. Check." I grab a bottle of olive oil from a cabinet to my left. "Do I pour it over the potatoes?"

She props her hip on the edge of the countertop. "You're kidding me, right?"

I frown, not appreciating the mockery.

She bursts out laughing. "Lucas, seriously. Have you never fried anything in your life?"

"Nothing that was edible afterwards," I grudgingly admit. "I may have tried it once or twice and given up."

"Okay." Yulia manages to stop laughing long enough to explain, "You pour oil into the *frying pan*. No, not so much—" She seizes the bottle from me before I can pour out more than a quarter of its contents. Laughing hysterically, she grabs a paper towel and dips it in the oil, mopping up the excess. "We're not deep-frying the poor potatoes," she explains when she's able to talk again.

"All right," I say, watching as she picks up the potatoes and the garlic and deposits everything into the oiled pan. Her movements are fast and sure, her slim hands moving with graceful economy.

She wasn't lying when she said she knows what she's doing.

"I wish we had fresh dill," she says, grabbing one of the bottles from the spice rack. "But I think the dried one will also work. Next time, if you like this dish, do you think you could get us some fresh herbs?"

"Sure." *Fresh herbs.* I make another mental note. "I can get us anything."

"Great. Now if you don't mind, I'll season this myself. The potatoes won't be any good if you dump the entire salt shaker in." She looks like she's about to start laughing again.

"Be my guest," I say, moving the knife I used to peel the potatoes behind me. "This mess is all yours."

And for the next half hour, I watch as Yulia whirls around the kitchen, humming under her breath. She seasons and fries the potatoes, bathes lamb chops in some kind of marinade, and washes greens for the salad. She's practically vibrating with excited energy, and for the first time, I realize how little I've seen this side of her—how subdued she usually is in my presence.

It's not surprising, of course. Though I haven't hurt her, she's my prisoner, and I know she still doesn't trust me. No matter how much I push for answers, she either changes the topic or refuses to respond. It frustrates me, but I force myself to remain patient.

Once Yulia realizes I truly don't intend to harm her, she'll hopefully see the light and give up the people who fucked up her life. For now, all I can do is keep her reasonably comfortable—and restrained—until the trackers I ordered arrive.

"All done," she says when the oven alarm goes off. Smiling brightly, she bends to take out the lamb chops, and my cock hardens at the sight of her ass in those tiny shorts.

If the lamb didn't smell so delicious, I would've dragged Yulia to bed right then and there.

As it is, while she carries the dish to the table, I have to take several deep breaths to control myself. It's ridiculous. I've always had a strong sex drive, but around Yulia, I'm like a randy teenager watching his first porn. I want to fuck her all the time, and no matter how often I take her, the desire doesn't diminish.

If anything, it grows stronger.

It takes a few more breaths before my erection subsides enough for me to help her set the table. By then, Yulia's got the salad arranged prettily in a bowl and the frying pan with the potatoes sitting on a neatly folded towel in the middle of the table. I presume the latter is to keep the hot pan from burning the table surface—a clever solution my parents' housekeeper used as well.

Finally, we both sit down to eat.

"Yulia, this is amazing," I say after demolishing half of my plate in under a minute. "The best I've had in a long, long time."

She gives me a happy smile and picks up her lamb chop. "I'm glad you like it."

"Like it? I love it." I can't remember the last time I had a meal this satisfying. The savory potatoes are perfect with the rich lamb and the crisp, lemony greens of the salad. "If I could eat this three times a day, I would."

Yulia's smile widens. "Good. I thought about making dessert too, but I figured we'll be too full from this. We'll just have some grapes instead."

"Whatever you say," I mumble through a mouthful of potatoes. "It's all good."

She laughs and digs into her own food. We eat in easy, companionable silence, and when most of the food is demolished, I put away the leftovers and wash the dishes. I do it automatically, without thinking, and it's only when I sit down to eat the grapes that it strikes me how content I feel.

No, more than content.

I'm fucking happy.

Between the meal, Yulia's bright smile, and the anticipation of taking her to bed, I'm thoroughly enjoying this evening. And it's not just today, I realize as I grab a handful of grapes.

This past week, ever since I decided to keep Yulia, has been my happiest in recent memory.

"So, Lucas," Yulia says before I can digest the revelation, "tell me something..." Her soft lips twitch with a poorly suppressed smile. "How did you get this far in life without ever peeling a potato?"

I pop a grape into my mouth as I consider her question. "I suppose I had a pampered upbringing," I say after swallowing the grape. "We had a housekeeper, so neither of my parents did any chores, and they didn't force me to do them. Later on, when I was in the Navy, we ate whatever was served to us, and after that…" I shrug, recalling the hardscrabble days of camping out in the jungle with small groups of men as lawless and desperate as myself. "I guess I just saw food as sustenance. As long as I didn't go hungry, I didn't think about it much."

"I see." She eyes me thoughtfully. "What made you decide to leave home? It's a big leap to go from a family with a housekeeper to enrolling in the Navy."

"I suppose it was." My parents certainly thought I'd gone insane. "It just seemed like the right thing to do at that point in my life."

"Why?" Yulia seems genuinely puzzled. "You don't have a draft in the United States. Did you feel called to defend your country?"

I chuckle. "Something like that." I'm not about to tell her about the thug I killed in that Brooklyn subway station, or the sick rush I got from seeing his blood spill over my hands. She already fears me; she doesn't need to know I became a killer at seventeen.

"That's very admirable of you," Yulia says, and I can hear the skepticism in her voice. "Very self-sacrificing."

"Yeah, well, someone had to do it." I bite on another grape, letting the cold, sweet juice trickle down my throat. I want her to drop this topic, so I add, "Just like someone had to be a spy, right?"

Predictably, she clams up, her face assuming the shuttered expression she always wears when I get too close to that subject. "Would you like some tea?" she asks, rising to her feet. "I saw there was some Earl Gray in one of those boxes."

I lean back in my chair, watching her. "Sure." I can count on one hand the number of times I've had tea, but I got it because I remembered Yulia drinking it at the Moscow restaurant where we first met. "I could go for a cup."

She puts on some water to boil and readies two cups for us, her movements as graceful as usual. Everything about her is graceful, reminding me of a dancer.

"Did you ever do ballet?" I ask as the thought occurs to me. "Or is that a stereotype about Eastern European girls?"

Yulia turns to face me with a cup in each hand. "It *is* a stereotype," she says, her tense expression fading. "In my case, though, it's true. My parents had me take ballet lessons from the time I was four. They thought it would help me overcome my shyness."

"You were shy as a child?"

"Very." She walks back to the table. "I wasn't a cute kid—far from it. Other children often mocked me."

"Really? I can't imagine you as anything but beautiful." I accept the cup Yulia hands to me. "How does one go from a not-cute kid to the hottest woman I've ever seen?"

Warm color sweeps over her high cheekbones. "I'm not exactly Helen of Troy." She sits down, cradling her cup. "My mom was pretty, though, so I think I got some of her genes. They just kicked in later, after I went through puberty. Oh, and braces helped, too." She gives me a wide smile that shows off her straight white teeth.

"Yeah, I'm sure," I say wryly. "Total ugliness to total gorgeousness, just like that."

She shrugs, blushing again, and I have a sudden mental image of her as that shy child.

"I bet you *were* cute," I say, studying her. "All that blond hair and big blue eyes. You just didn't realize it. That's why they took you from the orphanage, isn't it? Because they saw your potential?"

Yulia stiffens, and I know I ventured too close to the forbidden subject again. My mood darkens as I reflect on the fact that over the last several days, I've made zero progress with her. She may smile at me, cook for me, and willingly take me into her body, but she still doesn't trust me one bit.

"Yulia." I move my tea to the side. "You know this can't go on forever, right? You're going to have to talk to me one day."

She looks down into her cup, her body language all but screaming for me to back off.

"Yulia." Holding on to my temper by a thread, I get up and walk over to pull her to her feet. Holding her arms, I stare into her mutinous gaze. "Who are they?"

She remains silent, her thick eyelashes lowering to conceal her thoughts.

"Why won't you tell me about them?"

She doesn't answer, her eyes trained somewhere on my neck.

My grip on her arms tightens, and she flinches, tensing in my hold. Realizing I'm inadvertently hurting her, I force myself to unlock my fingers and drop my hands. I'm getting angry, which is not good. The fact that I'm not willing to torture her means I have to gain her trust to get answers, and this is not the way to do it.

Taking a breath to regain control, I lift my hand and tuck her hair behind her ear, being careful to keep the gesture gentle and nonthreatening. "Yulia." I stroke her cheek with the back of my fingers. "Sweetheart, they don't deserve your loyalty. They ruined your life. What they did to you was wrong, don't you see that? I told you I'll protect you—from them and from anyone else who wants to harm you. You don't have to be afraid to talk to me. I'm not going to turn on you once I have this information—you have my word on that."

Her eyelashes sweep up as she meets my gaze. "So what are you going to do if I tell you about them? What's going to happen to the agency?"

I suppress my pleased smile. This is the closest she's come to giving in. "We're going to take care of them."

"The way you took care of Al-Quadar?" Her eyes are wide with what appears to be curiosity and hope. "You'll wipe them out?"

"Yes, you'll be safe from them. By the time we're done, nobody connected to the organization will be around to hurt you." I intend my words as a reassurance, a promise of better things to come, but as I speak, I see color leaching from Yulia's face.

She steps out of my reach, her lashes descending to hide her gaze again, and a sudden suspicion stirs within me.

"Yulia." I catch her arm as she turns away. Spinning her around to face me, I stare at her pale face. "Are you protecting them? Are you protecting someone there?"

She doesn't say anything, but I can see the tension on her face, the fear that she's trying so hard to hide. This goes beyond simple loyalty to an employer, beyond concern for coworkers.

She's terrified for them—like someone would be for a person one loves.

Stunned, I release her arm and step back. I don't know why this possibility never occurred to me. I'd been so hung up on the idea that they fucked up her life, I never wondered whether there might be someone Yulia cares about in Ukraine.

Whether she might have a lover who's not an assignment.

I SPEND THE REST OF THE EVENING FUNCTIONING ON AUTOPILOT. Esguerra and I have another late-night call with Asia, so I tie Yulia up in my office, letting her read while I take care of business. She's unusually wary around me, watching me like I might attack her at any moment, and her fear adds to the rage bubbling deep within my chest. It takes everything I have to hand her a book and walk out of the room without grabbing her and demanding answers.

Without resorting to violence that I can't and won't use on her.

As I listen to our Malaysian suppliers argue over the quality of the latest batch of plastic explosives, I try to keep my thoughts from straying to my captive, but it's impossible. Now that the idea is lodged in my mind, I can't push it away.

A lover. A man Yulia cares about and wants to protect.

The mere thought of that fills me with murderous fury. Who is he? Another operative from her agency? Someone she met during her training, perhaps? It's not out of the question. She would've been very young when she met him, but girls that age fall in love all the time. He could've been another trainee, someone she felt close to because they shared the same experiences. Or he might've been older—an instructor or an already-trained agent. Kirill couldn't have been the only one who noticed the ugly duckling blossoming into a swan.

The more I think about it, the more likely it seems. They could've met during her training and continued their romance later on. Just because Yulia's job involved getting close to men for information doesn't mean she couldn't have had a genuine relationship on the side. And if she did have one, another agent would've been the most logical choice for a lover. Someone from her organization would've understood her profession, forgiven her for doing what she had to do.

Accepted that she let me fuck her while she was in love with *him*.

The pencil I've been toying with during the call snaps in my hands, the crack startlingly loud in the pause during the conversation. Esguerra lifts his eyebrows, shooting me a cool glance, and I force my hands to unclench from the broken pieces of the pencil.

I can't give in to this anger. I can't allow myself to lose control. I need to figure out a new strategy, something that doesn't rely on Yulia ultimately trusting me.

If I'm right about her lover, she'll never give me the answers I seek.

She'll protect her agency because he's part of it.

YULIA IS STILL READING WHEN I STEP INTO MY OFFICE, HER BLOND head bent over the open pages of a Michael Crichton technothriller. She's holding the book on her lap—the only position the ropes securing her to the armchair allow.

At the sound of my entry, she looks up, her gaze filled with wariness. She's expecting me to push for information, and her fear is like gasoline on the flames of my fury.

Far be it from me to disappoint my prisoner.

"Why are you protecting them?" I cross the room and stop in front of her. My voice is cold, though the anger coursing through my veins is hot enough to burn. "What do they mean to you?"

Yulia's gaze drops to my stomach. "I don't know what you're talking about."

"Don't lie to me." I crouch in front of her, so we're at the same eye level. Extending my hand, I grip her jaw and force her to look at me. "You don't want us to go after your agency. Why?"

She's silent as she holds my gaze.

"Is there someone there you're protecting?"

Her eyes widen slightly, and I catch a glimpse of panic in their blue depths. "No, of course not," she says quickly.

She's lying. I know she is, but I play along. "Then why won't you talk to me?"

"Because they don't deserve your vengeance." Her words tumble out, fast and desperate. "They were just doing their job, protecting our country."

"So it's all about patriotism for you? Is that what you're telling me?"

"Of course." A pulse is throbbing visibly in her throat. "Why else would I do this?"

"Maybe because they took you when you were a fucking child." My hand tightens on her jaw. "Because the only choice they gave you was to whore for them or rot in the orphanage."

Yulia flinches at my harsh words, her eyes filling with tears, and I stop, fighting a swell of rage. Realizing my fingers are digging into her skin, I unclench my hand and lower it to my lap.

My palm immediately curls into a fist, and she shrinks back against the chair, as if afraid I'll hit her.

I relax my hand with effort. "Yulia." I manage to moderate my tone. "They're fucking monsters. I don't know why you can't see it."

She closes her eyes, and I see a tear trickling down her cheek. "It's not that simple," she whispers, opening her eyes to look at me again. "You don't understand, Lucas."

"No?" Unable to resist, I raise my hand and wipe the streak of wetness off her face. My touch is almost gentle, the worst of my violent anger receding at the sight of her tears. "Then explain it to me, beautiful. Make me understand."

"I can't." Another tear escapes, undoing my work. "I'm sorry, but I can't."

"Can't or won't?" There's only one reason I can think of for her continued silence. My suspicions were correct. Yulia has someone there she's protecting—someone she can't tell me about because she knows what will happen if I learn of his existence.

Because she knows he'll die at my hand.

She doesn't answer my question. Instead, she says quietly, "May I please use the restroom? I really have to go."

I stare at her, my fury deepening. In less than five days, I'm going to Chicago, and I'm still no closer to getting real answers.

I will never get any closer for as long as she loves him.

As I look at her tear-streaked face, an idea comes to me, one I would've once dismissed as too cruel. Now, however, with this new knowledge fueling my rage, I can't see any other way. I can't keep Yulia locked up in my house forever; at some point, I'll have to give her more freedom, and when I do, I need to be certain there's nowhere she can run and hide.

I need to make sure she can't go back to *him*.

Reaching into my pocket, I take out my switchblade and cut through her ropes while she watches me, pale and visibly terrified.

Schooling my face into a hard, impassive mask, I take hold of her slim arm and pull her to her feet. “Let’s go,” I say, my voice like ice.

As I lead her down the hallway, my resolve firms.

It’s time for the gloves to come off.

One way or another, Yulia is going to talk tonight.

18

ulia

My pulse hammers with anxiety as we walk silently to the bathroom. I can feel Lucas's anger. It's different from what I've seen from him before—colder and more controlled. He's both furious and resolved, and that frightens me more than if he had just exploded at me.

He lets me go into the bathroom alone as usual, and I close the door behind me, leaning against it to gather my thoughts and calm my frantic heartbeat. The food I ate at dinner is like a brick in my stomach. I haven't felt the bite of terror in over a week, and I've forgotten how powerful it can be.

He lied. He lied when he promised not to hurt me. I could see the dark intent on his face, feel the barely restrained violence in his touch.

He's going to do something to me tonight—something terrible.

Feeling sick, I use the toilet and wash my hands, going through the motions despite my panic. The knowledge of Lucas's betrayal is like a spear through my chest. In the beginning, I suspected he may be playing me, but as the days went on, I slowly began to lose my natural distrust of him, to believe that the bizarre domesticity of our arrangement might continue for some time.

To hope he truly won't hurt me.

Dura. Dura, dura, dura. The Russian word for fool is like a jackhammer in my skull. How could I have been such an idiot? I know what Lucas is. I see the demons that drive him. My captor is a man who walked away from a good, safe home to embark on a life of danger and violence, and he didn't do it out of love for his country.

He did it because it's his nature—because he needed to find an outlet for the darkness within.

I've known others like him. My instructors. Obenko himself. They all share this trait, this inability to be part of a peaceful society and abide by its laws. It's what makes them so good at their jobs—and so dangerous.

When conscience is nonexistent, it's easy to do what needs to be done.

"Yulia." A knock on the door startles me, and I realize I've just been standing there, absorbed in thought. "Are you done?" Lucas's deep voice breaks my paralysis, and I spring into action, my fear drowned under a wave of adrenaline.

"Almost," I call out, raising my voice to be heard over the running water. "Just need to wash my face."

Leaving the faucet on to mask the sounds of my movements, I kneel and open the cabinet under the sink. There, among extra toilet paper rolls and tubes of toothpaste, is the object I hid for just such an eventuality.

It's a small metal fork I snitched from the kitchen two days ago, slipping it into my shorts pocket while Lucas was washing the dishes. He'd left it inside the kitchen drawer that holds napkins and other small items, likely without realizing it was there. I took it while getting fresh napkins for the table and hid it here, hoping I'd never need to use it.

Well, I need it now. The little fork is not much of a weapon, but it's sturdier than a plastic toothbrush.

Ignoring the part of me that revolts at the idea of injuring Lucas, I take the fork, slip it into the back pocket of my shorts, and close the cabinet.

I can't allow him to break me.

My brother's life depends on it.

LUCAS TAKES ME TO THE BEDROOM, ONCE AGAIN LEADING ME THERE without speaking. I don't make the mistake of jumping him as soon as I come out—I won't catch him by surprise the second time. Instead, I walk as calmly as I can, trying not to focus on the little fork burning a hole in my pocket. I know Lucas always looks at my hands, so I keep them loose and relaxed at my sides, fighting the instinct that screams to protect myself, to strike *now*.

"Strip," Lucas says, stopping in front of the bed. His pale eyes are hooded as he releases my arm and steps back. I can feel the hunger within him. It's dark and potent, despite the cold anger evident in the hard lines of his face.

This won't be a tender lovemaking session. He's going to hurt me.

It takes everything I have to reach for the edge of my short tank top and pull it up over my head, baring my breasts to his gaze. My throat is so tight I can scarcely breathe, but I drop the tank top and face him without flinching. The worst thing I can do is show him how terrified I am—and how desperate.

"The rest," Lucas prompts when I pause. His expression is unchanging, but I see the growing bulge in his jeans. "Get it all off—or I will." His arm muscles flex, betraying his impatience.

I force my lips into a teasing smile. "Oh, yeah?" Slowly, very slowly, I reach for my zipper, praying that my hands don't shake. "And how exactly are you going to do that?"

At my challenge, Lucas's nostrils flare and he does precisely what I counted on.

He reaches for me and hooks his fingers through the top of my shorts, yanking me against his hard body. I gasp playfully, as if excited by his roughness, and while he's distracted, I slip my right hand into my back pocket, grab the fork, and strike.

In a blur of motion, my hand flashes toward his face, the fork targeting his eye at the same time as my knee jerks up, aiming for his balls. Each injury might disorient him for a few crucial moments, and the two together should give me enough time to run.

It should've worked—with any other man, it would've worked —but Lucas is not like any other man. As fast as I am, he's even faster. In a split second, he jerks back. The fork grazes his cheek-bone and my knee hits his inner thigh, and then he's on me, twisting my right arm behind my back in a swift, merciless motion. His fingers squeeze my wrist, making my hand go numb. The fork slips out of my fingers, and in the next instant, I'm on my stomach on the bed, his big body pinning me down. I can feel his erection throbbing against my ass, sense the rage and lust radiating from him, and the old fear flares, the memories washing over me in a sickening tide.

No. Please, no. I can't move, can't breathe. I'm pinned, helpless as rough male hands rip away my clothes. The man on top of me wants to punish me, to hurt me. I struggle, but I can't do anything, and the dark panic engulfs me, sends me spinning out of control.

"No, please, no!" I'm scarcely aware of my screams and cries, of the pleas that tear from my throat. All I can feel are his hands dragging my shorts down my legs and his knees digging into my thighs to hold me restrained. There's no tenderness in his touch, nothing but raw, vengeful lust, and the terror is all-consuming as his fingers invade my body, thrusting in violently as I scream and sob in pain.

"Stop, please stop!" It's no longer Lucas on top of me, no longer the man who gave me pleasure. It's the brutal monster of my nightmares, the one who ripped me apart body and soul. The edges of my consciousness recede, spiraling into the past. "Don't! Please stop!"

The monster doesn't stop, doesn't listen. "Who am I?" he growls, his fingers relentless. "What is my name?"

"No, stop!" I thrash under him, mindless with fear. I don't understand what he's saying, what he wants from me. I need to get away. I need him to release me. "Let me go!"

"Tell me my name, and I'll stop." There's something wrong with that statement, something that should give me pause, but I can't think, can't concentrate on anything but the dark, swirling terror.

"Let me go!"

His fingers push in deeper, his voice hard and cruel. "Tell me my name."

"Kirill!" I scream, desperate for any hope, no matter how slim. I'd do anything, say anything to make him stop.

He doesn't stop. "My full real name."

"Kirill Ivanovich Luchenko!"

"Who am I?"

"My trainer!" The darkness consumes me, destroys me. "Please, stop!"

"Your trainer where?"

"At UUR!"

"What is UUR?" His body presses down on me, suffocating me with its weight. "What does it stand for, Yulia?"

"Ukrainskoye—" The oddity of it all finally penetrates my terror, and I freeze, my mind flitting in agony between the present and the past. It doesn't make sense. Everything is different, everything is wrong. The fingers inside me are rough, but they're not ripping me apart, and there's no cologne.

There's no cologne.

"What does it stand for?" the man repeats, and for the first time, I hear the strain in his familiar deep voice.

A voice that's speaking English.

No. Oh God, no. The realization is like an arrow puncturing my lungs.

It's not Kirill on top of me.

It's Lucas.

It's always been Lucas.

He made my nightmare come true, and I broke.

I told him everything.

19

ucas

YULIA STILLS UNDERNEATH ME, HER SLIM BODY WRACKED BY VIOLENT tremors, and I know she's no longer there, in that old place of her terrors.

She's back here with me.

It should feel good, this victory. Her former trainer's name and the agency's initials are a solid lead. Our hackers will scour the net, and it's only a matter of time before they locate Yulia's bosses and her lover.

I've fulfilled the task I set out to complete.

Except for some reason, it doesn't feel like a victory. My chest aches dully as I withdraw my fingers from Yulia's body, and there's an emptiness inside me, a void where rage and jealousy used to live.

I hurt her. Not much—maybe not at all, in the physical sense.

She hadn't been totally dry, and I was careful not to injure her. But I hurt her nonetheless.

I took the horror of her past and used it to break her. Knowing her fear of sexual violence, I let her get scared enough to attack, and then I retaliated in the way she dreads most.

I recreated the conditions of her nightmare to bring back that terrified fifteen-year-old girl.

"Yulia." I move off her and sit up, the ache in my chest intensifying when she just lies there, trembling. Extending my hand, I gently stroke her back, unable to find the right words. Her skin is cold and clammy under my fingertips, her breathing unsteady. "Sweetheart..."

She twists away, her body contorting into a small ball of naked limbs. Her shorts are still around her knees, but she doesn't seem aware of that. She's just rolling up tighter and tighter, as if trying to make herself disappear.

"Come here, baby." I can't help reaching for her. She's stiff as I draw her into my lap, every muscle in her body rigid with tension. I know my touch is the last thing she wants right now, but I can't let her deal with this on her own.

Even knowing about her love for another man, I can't leave Yulia alone.

Her face is wet against my shoulder as I hold her, stroking her back, her hair, the sleek muscles of her calves. The peach scent of her skin teases my nostrils, but my lust for her is muted for the moment, leaving me free to focus on her comfort. With her knees drawn up to her chest, Yulia seems no bigger than a child, her entire body fitting on my lap. Her fragility weighs on me, adding to the heavy pressure around my heart. I don't know what to do, so I just hold her, letting my warmth soothe her chilled flesh. She doesn't pull away, doesn't fight me, and it's enough for now.

It has to be enough.

"I'm sorry," I murmur when her shaking begins to ease. The words probably sound as hollow to her as they do to me, but I persist, needing her to understand. "I didn't want to hurt you, but we had to move past this standoff. You would've never trusted me enough to tell me about UUR. And now it's over. It's done. I promised I wouldn't harm you if you talked, and I won't. It's going to be okay. Everything's going to be okay."

Once her lover is dead, she's going to be mine and mine alone.

Yulia doesn't say anything, but after a few more minutes, her breathing normalizes and her shaking stops. Even her skin feels warmer, though her body is still rigid in my embrace.

"Are you tired, baby?" I whisper, moving my hand over her back in small, soothing circles. "Do you want to go to sleep?"

She doesn't answer, but I feel her stiffening even more.

"Don't worry, I won't touch you," I say, guessing at the source of her tension. "We'll just go to sleep, okay?"

Still no response, but I'm not expecting any at this point. Cradling her against my chest, I get up and carry her to her side of the bed, then gently place her on top of the sheets. Yulia immediately rolls away from me, wrapping herself in the blanket, and I let her be while I take off my clothes and get the handcuffs.

Lying down beside her, I pull away the blanket and reach for her left wrist. "Come here, sweetheart. You know the drill."

She doesn't resist when I snap the handcuffs around her wrist and mine. It should've been uncomfortable to sleep like this, with our left wrists locked together, but I've gotten so used to it that it feels entirely natural.

As soon as I have Yulia secured, I pull her against my chest, holding her from the back. When my groin presses against her ass, I feel rough material against my bare cock and realize she managed to pull up her shorts while I was undressing. I consider letting her sleep like this, but after shifting a few times in search of a better position, I reach for the shorts' zipper.

"I'm just going to hold you," I promise, tugging the shorts down her legs while she lies rigid and unresisting. "You'll be more comfortable as well."

Kicking the shorts away, I pull her back into the spooning position, marveling at the perfect way her naked body fits into my arms. Before I met Yulia, I didn't get the appeal of cuddling with a woman, but now I can't imagine not holding her as I fall asleep.

Of course, normally I hold Yulia *after* sex, I realize as my cock stiffens against her ass. Sleeping is a lot easier after I've fucked her a couple of times.

Oh, well. I take a deep breath and picture myself crawling through the mud in the mountains of Afghanistan, with icy sleet soaking through my clothes. When that doesn't work, I think of my parents and the way they never touched or smiled at each other, substituting politeness for caring and mutual ambition for a family bond.

The latter memory does the trick, and my erection subsides enough for me to relax. As I sink into the soothing darkness of sleep, I dream of peach pies, angels with long blond hair, and a smile.

Yulia's bright, genuine smile.

20

ulia

"It's your fault, bitch. It's all your fault."

Dimly, I'm aware that the words are strangely distant, but the terror still engulfs me, pressing down on me like a smothering blanket. I can feel him over me, and I scream, struggling to avoid the violation, the awful pain.

"No, please, no!"

"Shh, baby, it's okay. You're just having a bad dream."

Strong arms tighten around me, pressing me against a hard, warm body, and the suffocating terror eases, the cruel voices receding. Sobbing with relief, I try to turn, to face the person holding me, but something hard tugs at my left wrist.

The handcuffs.

"Lucas?"

"Yeah, it's me." Warm lips brush my temple as a big hand

smoothes back my hair. "I've got you. You're all right now. You're fine."

He's got me. Something should worry me about that statement, but at this moment, all I'm aware of is its seductive comfort. Lucas's powerful arms are around me, holding me, protecting me in the darkness, and the horror of the dream grows more distant, sinking back into the mire of the past.

There's no Kirill. There's just Lucas, and nobody can take me away from him.

"Baby, you've got to stop moving like that." His voice is hoarse, strained, and I realize I'm rocking against him in an attempt to burrow even deeper into his embrace. In the process, my ass is shimmying against his groin—with a predictable result.

The horror flickers distantly, the panic returning for a moment, and I try to turn again, to hide my face against his broad chest, but the handcuffs are in the way.

"Shh, it's okay. You're safe." There's a tug and a quiet *snick* as the key turns, unlocking the cuffs. "You don't have to be afraid. It's okay."

It's okay. The panic retreats, especially when I'm able to wrap my arms around Lucas's muscular torso and inhale his familiar scent. He smells like his body wash and warm male skin, like safety, strength, and comfort. Burying my face in his chest, I throw my leg over his hip, wanting to wrap myself around him like a vine, and I hear him groan as his hard cock presses into my belly.

Something about that should worry me too, but with my mind still wrestling with the dream, I can't figure out what. I just want him closer—as close as two people can possibly get.

"Fuck me," I whisper, slipping one hand between our bodies to cup his tightly drawn balls. "Please, Lucas, fuck me."

"You…" His voice sounds strangled. "You want me?"

"Yes, please, Lucas." I know it's pathetic to beg, but I need him. I need him to chase away the horror. "Please"—I grab his cock and try to align it with my sex—"please fuck me. Please."

"Yeah. Oh, fuck, yeah." He sounds incredulous as he rolls on top of me, his hips settling between my open thighs. "Whatever you want, beautiful. Whatever you fucking"—he thrusts in deep—"want."

We both groan when he's seated to the hilt, his thickness stretching me to the limit. I'm not as wet as usual, but it doesn't matter. The near-painful friction, the overwhelming force of his sudden entry—it's exactly what I need. This is not about sex or pleasure.

It's about being his.

"Yulia…" His voice is a tortured groan as he begins to move inside me. "Fuck, baby, you feel so amazing…"

"Yes." I wrap my legs around his muscular thighs, taking him even deeper. "Yes, just like that. Oh God, just like that."

He complies, his rhythm strong and steady, and I forget all about the initial discomfort. As he keeps thrusting, a wild heat ignites inside me, a need that's purely animalistic. I want him to fuck me so hard it hurts, to make me come so much I'll forget my own name.

I want his savagery to destroy my demons.

"Harder," I whisper, sinking my nails into his back. "Take me harder."

He tenses, a shudder running through his big body, and I feel his cock swelling even more. A low growl rumbles in his chest, and he picks up the pace, his muscled ass flexing under my calves as he jackhammers into me, each thrust so deep it almost cleaves me in two. It should be too much, too hard, but my body embraces him, the heat inside me blazing brighter with every bruising stroke. I can hear my own cries, feel the explosive pressure building, and all my fears evaporate, leaving nothing but scorching pleasure.

"Lucas!" I don't know if I scream his name, or if it's only in my mind, but at that moment, he lets out a hoarse cry, and I feel him jetting into me as white-hot ecstasy rips through my nerve endings. The orgasm is so powerful my entire body arches upward and white flecks appear at the edges of my vision. It seems to go on forever, one pulsing spasm after another, but eventually, the waves of pleasure recede, and awareness slowly returns.

Lucas is lying on top of me, his big body covered with sweat, but just as I register the heavy weight of his frame, he rolls off me, gathering me against him so that my head rests on his shoulder. We lie like that, both panting and too drained to move, and as my heartbeat begins to slow, the heavy lethargy of satiation steals over me.

"Sleep tight, baby," I hear him whisper as it pulls me under, and I close my eyes, knowing I'm safe.

I belong to Lucas, and he'll keep the bad dreams away.

~

"MORNING, BEAUTIFUL." A TENDER KISS ON MY SHOULDER WAKES ME up. "How about some tea?"

"What?" I pry open my eyelids and blink to clear the fog of sleep from my brain. I'm lying on my side, so I roll over onto my back and squint up at Lucas—who's standing next to the bed, already dressed and with what appears to be a steaming cup in his hand.

"Tea," he says. His hard mouth is curved into a smile. "I made some for you. I hope I didn't mess it up."

"Um…" My brain is still not fully functioning, so I sit up and try to make sense of what's happening. "You made me tea?"

"Hmm." Lucas sits down on the edge of the bed and carefully hands me the cup. "Here you go. I wasn't sure how long it should steep, but there were instructions on the box, so hopefully, it's right."

"Uh-huh." I take the cup from him and take a few sips. The tea is hot enough to burn my tongue, but the familiar taste of Earl Gray revives me, chasing away the cotton-candy fuzz in my mind. Slowly, in bits and pieces, it all starts coming back to me.

Lucas as Kirill. Telling him about UUR.

The cup tilts in my hand, hot liquid spilling onto my naked breasts.

Startled by the sudden pain, I look down and hear Lucas curse as he grabs the cup from me. He puts it on the nightstand before dabbing at my chest with a corner of the sheet. "Fuck. Yulia, are you okay?"

I stare at him, my skin growing cold despite the burn from the tea. "You want to know if I'm okay?" I remember everything now. The way he broke me. The way he held me afterwards. The nightmare. Clinging to him in the darkness.

Asking—no, *begging* him to fuck me.

Lucas's face tightens. "Did you get badly burned?"

"No." The chill within me deepens, numbing the sick terror flowing through my veins. "I didn't get burned."

Not by tea, at least.

Turning away, I lift the blanket, searching for the pair of shorts he kicked away when we were going to sleep. It's something to focus on, something to do. Besides, I need those clothes. They're a buffer, and I need that.

I need to cling to something to stay sane.

How could I have reached for Lucas after that awful dream, when just hours earlier he made it my reality? How could I have wanted a man who broke me in that manner? It's like I blanked out about what he did, suppressed it all in my desperate need for comfort.

In my weak, selfish neediness, I embraced the man who's going to destroy my brother.

"Yulia." Lucas reaches for me, but I twist away. My fingers finally close around the shorts, and I grab them before jumping off the bed on the other side. I know I have nowhere to go, but I can't let him touch me yet.

I'll shatter all over again.

"What are you doing?" he asks as I shimmy into the shorts and then get on all fours, looking for the top I dropped last night. "Yulia, what the fuck are you doing?"

Ah-hah, there. Ignoring his question, I grab the tank top—if the lacy-edged sports bra can even be called that. All the clothes Lucas got me are like that: casual, yet ridiculously sexy. They're better than nothing, though, so I pull on the tank top and get to my feet, doing my best not to look at him.

That seems to irritate him. In a second, he crosses the room and stops in front of me, his fingers closing around my arm.

"What the fuck, Yulia?" Lucas grips my chin with his free hand and forces me to look at him. "What game are you playing?"

"Me?" As I meet his gaze, a tiny ember of anger flickers in the ashes of my despair. "You're the game master, Kent. I'm just along for the ride."

His eyebrows snap together. "So last night was what? You going along for the ride?"

"Last night was a moment of insanity." That's the only way I can explain it to myself, at least. My voice is hard and bitter as I add, "Besides, what do you care? You have what you need."

"Yes, I do." His expression is unreadable. "I have enough to take down UUR."

A swirl of nausea makes me want to throw up. I don't know if Lucas senses it, but he lets go of my chin and steps back.

"You'll be fine," he says, his voice oddly strained. "I told you I'm not going to kill you or do anything to you once I got the information, and I won't. There's no reason for you to stress anymore. It's done."

I stare at him, struck by the fact that the idea of Lucas killing me didn't cross my mind either last night or this morning. I didn't think about what's going to happen to me at all. Somewhere along the way, I started believing that my captor doesn't want me dead.

I started trusting that his sexual obsession with me is real.

"Look," Lucas says when I remain silent, "things are going to get better. Once UUR is gone, I'll give you more freedom. You'll be able to walk around the estate on your own, go anywhere you please."

"Really?" Despite my despair, I almost laugh out loud. "And what makes you think I won't run?"

The corners of his lips pull up in a dark smile. "Because you wouldn't get far if you tried. I'm going to put some trackers on you."

My heart falters for a beat. "Trackers?"

Lucas nods, releasing my arm. "Esguerra's guys worked out a new prototype. For now, why don't I give you a small taste of what your future will be like and take you outside after breakfast? We'll go for a walk."

A walk outside. At any other point, I would've been ecstatic, but now, it's all I can do to interact with him in a semi-normal manner.

To act as if my whole world isn't about to come crashing down.

"Breakfast first, though," Lucas says when I remain frozen. "Let's go. I'll take you to the bathroom for your morning routine."

Bathroom. Breakfast. I want to scream that he's insane, that I can't possibly eat, but I keep my mouth shut and do as he says. I need to figure out what to do, how to fix the awful mess I've made.

"What kind of trackers are you talking about?" I force myself to ask as we walk to the bathroom. "Implants or the exterior kind?"

"Implants." Lucas stops in front of the bathroom door and looks at me. "Just a few to keep you safe."

And ensure he'd always know where I am.

"When are you going to put them on me?" I ask, trying to keep my voice steady. If the trackers are going to be as difficult to remove as I suspect, escape will be all but impossible.

"When I return from Chicago," Lucas says. "I have a two-week trip coming up in five days. Unfortunately, the trackers won't be here before then, so you'll need to be restrained for the duration."

"You're leaving?" My heartbeat kicks up with sudden hope. If he's going to be gone…

"Yes, but don't worry. I'll have a couple of guards I trust keep an eye on you." He smiles, as if reading my mind. "They'll make sure you're safe and comfortable."

And still here when I return.

The unsaid words hang in the air as I step into the bathroom and quietly close the door behind me. Lucas's plan to chain me to him should terrify me, but the nauseating fear I feel has nothing to do with my own fate.

If Esguerra's men come after UUR the way they've gone after other enemies, nobody connected to the agency will escape their wrath.

Obenko's entire family will be wiped out—and my brother along with them.

21

ucas

YULIA IS SILENT AND WITHDRAWN AS SHE MAKES US BREAKFAST, AND I have no doubt she's thinking about him—the man who holds her heart. She's probably wondering what's going to happen to him, beating herself up with the knowledge that she inadvertently betrayed him. I want to grab her and order her to put him out of her thoughts, but that would just make things worse. If she realizes I know about him, she might plead for his life, and I don't want that.

I'm going to kill the fucker no matter what, and I don't want her unnecessarily upset.

As it is, there's no sign of yesterday's joyous smile, no jokes or laughter as she moves about the kitchen, performing her task. With the fork incident fresh in my mind, I keep an extra-careful eye on her, making sure she doesn't conceal anything else. I suppose it's arrogant of me to let my prisoner walk around like this, untied and with access to things that could be used as weapons. I'm fairly sure I can contain her as long as I see her attack coming, but there's always a chance she might catch me off-guard one day.

She's dangerous, but like a challenging mission, that fact only excites me.

The breakfast Yulia makes is a simple one: an omelet with cheese and a bowl of strawberries for dessert. I could've theoretically made that, except my eggs would've been either rubbery or runny, and the cheese would've gotten burned on the edges of the frying pan. With Yulia, none of that happens. The omelet comes out light, fluffy, and perfectly cheesy, and even the strawberries taste better than I recall.

"This is amazing," I tell her as I devour my portion, and Yulia nods in a quiet acknowledgement of my thanks. Aside from that, she doesn't look at me or speak to me.

It's as if I don't exist.

Her behavior infuriates me, but I contain my anger. I know I deserve her silent treatment. I might not have hurt her physically, but that doesn't lessen the severity of what I did.

I tortured her, used her worst fear to break her.

Annoyed by the sharp prickle of guilt, I get up and wash the dishes, using the routine task to distract me from my churning thoughts. As far as I'm concerned, I'm doing Yulia a favor by getting her lover out of her life. It's clear that he's in no way worthy of her. He let her go to Moscow to sleep with other men, and he left her to rot in the Russian jail for two months. Agent or not, the man is a weakling, and she's better off without him. When Yulia came on to me last night, I thought that by some miracle she forgave me and decided to forget her lover, but now I see that was just wishful thinking on my part.

She'd been too traumatized to know what she was doing.

"Ready for the walk?" I say, approaching the table. Yulia is sipping her tea and still not looking at me. "I have a call in less than two hours, so if you want to come out, we should go now."

She gets up, still silent, and I see that her face is ashen. She's upset. No, more than upset—devastated.

The guilt bites at me again, and I push it away with effort. "Come here," I say, taking her hand. Her slender fingers are cold in my grasp as I lead her out of the kitchen. "We'll go out back."

The bedroom has a door that opens into the backyard, and I use that entrance now to avoid prying eyes. I don't want anyone seeing my prisoner outside and spreading rumors. Until I have something tangible to give Esguerra about UUR, I don't want to broadcast our relationship. My boss does owe me a favor, but it's better if it's a combo deal—the heads of our enemies alongside the news that I want to keep Yulia for my own.

"Sorry it's so hot," I say when we step out. It's only eight-thirty in the morning, but it's already like a steam bath. It'll probably rain within the next hour, but for now, the sky is clear with just a few white clouds. "Next time, we'll go earlier."

"No, this is fine," Yulia says, stopping in a clearing between the trees. Surprised, I glance at her and see that her face has a tinge of color now. As I watch, she closes her eyes and tilts her head back. She looks like a plant absorbing the sunlight, and I realize that's exactly what she's doing: basking in the sun, taking its warmth into herself.

"You like it here." I don't know why that surprises me. I suppose I pictured somebody from her part of the world being acclimated to the cold and hating the humid heat of the rainforest. "You like this weather."

She brings her head down and opens her eyes to look at me. "Yes," she says quietly. "I do."

"I'm glad." Squeezing Yulia's hand, I smile at her. "It took me a while to get used to it, but now I can't imagine living someplace cold."

She doesn't smile back, but her hand feels warmer in my hold as we resume walking, going deeper into the forest that borders the compound. Esguerra's estate is huge, extending for miles through the thick canopy of the rainforest. Back in the eighties, Juan Esguerra, Julian's father, processed vast quantities of cocaine here, but few traces of that remain now. The jungle has already swallowed up the old shack-style labs, nature reclaiming its turf with brutal swiftness.

"It's so beautiful here," Yulia says as we enter another clearing, and I see her looking at the tropical flowers that line a tiny pond a dozen feet away. She sounds oddly wistful.

I release her hand and turn to face her. "It's your new home." Reaching up, I tuck a strand of hair behind her ear. "Once everything is settled, you'll be able to come here whenever you want."

I intend that as a reassurance, a promise of good things to come, but her face tightens at my words, and I know she's worrying about her lover again.

Motherfucker. I wish the man was already six feet under, so she could move on from him.

Reminding myself to be patient, I drop my hand and say, "This is one of several nice places on this estate. There's also a pretty lake not too far away."

Yulia doesn't reply. She turns away and walks over to the pond. Her flip-flops are barely visible as she stands in the thick grass. The sight of the green stalks brushing her ankles makes me realize that I should get her some sneakers for these walks. There are snakes here, and all kinds of bugs. Wildlife, too—some guards have reported seeing jaguars on the grounds.

Suddenly concerned, I join Yulia at the pond and inspect the grass nearby. There's nothing particularly threatening, so I decide to let her be. She appears lost in thought as she gazes into the water, her smooth forehead creased in a faint frown. The sunlight makes her hair glow, and I notice for the first time that some of the strands are a near-white shade of gold, while others are a darker honey color. There are no roots showing, so her color must be entirely natural.

"Were your parents this blond?" I wonder idly, stepping behind her. Unable to resist, I gather her hair in my hands, marveling at its thickness. "You don't often see this shade with adults."

"My mom was." Yulia doesn't seem to mind my messing with her hair, so I indulge myself, running my fingers through the silky mass and then moving it to one side to expose her long, slender neck. "My dad's color was more of a sandy brown, a few shades darker than your hair. He was really light when he was a kid, though."

"I see." I lean down to breathe in her peach scent, but can't resist the urge to nuzzle the tender spot under her right ear. Her skin is warm and delicate under my lips, and as I graze my teeth over her earlobe, I hear her breath hitch. Instantly, desire spikes through me, my body hardening with need.

"Yulia…" I release her hair to cup her soft, round breasts. "I want you so fucking much."

She shivers, her lips parting on a silent moan as her head falls back against my shoulder and her eyes close. She might be upset about her lover, but she still wants me—that much is undeniable. Her nipples are stiff as they press into my palms through her tank top, and her pale skin is painted pink with a warm flush.

Last night wasn't an aberration after all. Yulia might not have forgiven me for my actions, but her body has.

Still kissing her neck, I bend my knees and tug her down to the grass with me. Turning her to face me, I stretch out on my back and have her straddle me, her hands braced on my shoulders. Yulia's eyes are open now, and she stares at me as I hold her hips and rock my pelvis upward, pressing my erection against her sex. Even through the layers of our clothing, it feels good to grind into her, especially when I see her blue eyes darken in response.

"Come here," I murmur, moving one hand up her back. Curving my fingers around her nape, I pull her head toward me and kiss her, swallowing her startled exhalation. She tastes like strawberries and herself, her tongue curling tentatively around mine as I deepen the kiss. I press her tighter against me, needing to get closer, but our clothes are in the way.

Growing impatient, I stop kissing her for a moment and move my hands down to grab the bottom of her tank top. With one smooth motion, I pull it off, exposing her gorgeous breasts—breasts that she immediately covers with her hands.

"Lucas, wait." Yulia casts an anxious glance behind us. "What if—"

"Nobody will bother us here." I reach for her shorts. "We're too far off the beaten path."

"But the guards—"

"The nearest guard towers are too far away to see us here." I unzip her shorts and roll over, stretching her out on the grass. Tugging her shorts down her legs, I add with a dark smile, "We're all alone, beautiful."

I take off my own clothes next, and Yulia watches me with a torn, almost tormented expression. I don't know if she feels like she's betraying him by wanting me, but I'm not about to put up with it. As soon as I'm naked, I cover her with my body and wedge my knees between her legs, spreading them open.

"Look at me," I order when she tries to close her eyes and turn her face away. Holding myself up on my elbows, I capture her face between my palms and repeat, "Look at me, Yulia." Her sex is less than an inch from the tip of my cock, and the lust is beginning to cloud my brain. Before I can take her, though, I need this from her.

I need to know she belongs to me.

Yulia opens her eyes, and I see tears swimming there. She blinks rapidly, as if trying to contain them, but they spill out, streaking down her temples. At the sight of them, something squeezes inside me, a strange ache awakening deep within my chest.

"Don't," I whisper, leaning down to kiss the moisture away.

"Don't, sweetheart. It's okay. Everything's going to be fine." The taste of salt on my lips makes the ache intensify. "Don't cry. You're okay. I'm going to take care of you."

Her tears don't stop—they just keep coming—and I can't restrain myself. The hunger inside me is like a demon clawing its way to the surface. Taking her mouth in a deep kiss, I thrust into her and feel her slick flesh enveloping me, squeezing me so tightly that I shudder with violent pleasure.

She tenses underneath me, a raw, pained sound ripping from her throat, but I don't stop. I can't. The need to claim her is potent and primal, an instinct born in the mists of time. She was made for me, this beautiful, broken girl. She was destined to be mine. Still kissing her, I drive into her, again and again, as deep as I can go, and eventually, I feel her hands on my back as she embraces me, holding me close.

Binding me as tightly as I've bound her.

III

THE RIFT

22

ulia

Over the next four days, we settle into a new routine. When I'm not tied up, I cook, we eat our meals together, and we go for early morning walks in the forest. And we fuck. We fuck a lot. It's as if the knowledge that we'll soon be separated makes Lucas even hungrier for me. He fucks me everywhere—the bedroom, the kitchen, up against a tree in the forest—and so frequently that by the end of the day, I'm raw and aching, my body sore and my soul torn by the knowledge that I'm sleeping with the enemy.

No, not that I'm sleeping with the enemy—that I'm enjoying it. No matter what I tell myself, no matter how much I try to resist, I unravel at the seams the moment Lucas touches me. Maybe if he hurt me again, it would be different, but he doesn't. His passion for me is forceful, even violent sometimes, but there's no anger or intent to harm in it. And often—far too often for my sanity—there's tenderness too.

It's as if he's beginning to care about me, to want me for something more than sex.

I try not to think about that—about his plans for me and the trackers he's going to use, shackling me to him while he destroys everything I hold dear. Lucas hasn't talked much about UUR, but from the little he let slip, I know he's already set things in motion with some hackers. There's a chance his search will set off alarms at the agency and they'll have time to go into hiding, but there's no guarantee of that. Obenko has never been up against an enemy as powerful and ruthless as the Esguerra organization, and there's a very real possibility he's outmatched.

If Lucas and his boss were able to take down Al-Quadar, it's only a matter of time before they'll do the same with my agency. I need to escape, or at least send them a message to warn them of what's coming, but Lucas is as careful with his phone and laptop as he is with his guns. Maybe one day, I'll be able to sneak into his office and crack the password on his computer, but I can't count on that.

There's only one way I can possibly save Misha now.

I have to tell Lucas about him.

It's a terrifying step for me. I don't trust my captor—he's already proven he'll use my vulnerabilities against me—but I don't see any other way. If I stay silent, Misha is as good as dead. I know I won't be able to talk Lucas out of vengeance on UUR, but maybe he'd be willing to use whatever influence he has with Esguerra to spare my brother.

Misha's normal life is already forfeit, but there's a chance I can keep him from getting killed.

Before approaching Lucas with my request, I decide to fix the rift between us, to make things go back to the way they were before he broke me. I do it subtly to avoid raising his suspicions, but by the evening after our first walk, I respond to him in full sentences, and by the next day, I act almost as if nothing happened. I go down on him in the shower, ask him what he would like me to make for dinner, and resume talking to him about the books I'm reading. I even tell him about my first horrendous experience at ballet, when a teacher said in front of the whole class that I have the neck of an ostrich—which, of course, led to the other kids calling me "Ostrich" for years.

Lucas laughs at that story, his light-colored eyes crinkling with amusement, and I smile at him, forgetting for a moment that he's my enemy, that I'm not doing this for real. It's shockingly easy to buy into my own act. When I'm not thinking about Misha's imminent fate, I truly do enjoy Lucas's company. For such a hard-edged man, my jailer is surprisingly easy to talk to—attentive and smart without being arrogant. Though Lucas never attended college, he's well versed in a number of topics and can speak intelligently about everything from world politics and the stock market to cutting-edge developments in science and technology.

"Where did you learn so much about investing?" I ask during a walk when the conversation turns to a finance book I read earlier this morning. Nassim Taleb's *The Black Swan* is a strongly worded criticism of risk management in the finance industry, and it surprises me to discover that it's one of Lucas's favorite nonfiction works.

"Both of my parents are corporate lawyers on Wall Street," he says. "I grew up with CNBC blaring in the background, and on my twelfth birthday, my father opened an investment account for me. You could say it's in my blood."

"Oh." Fascinated, I stop and stare at him. "Do you invest now?"

Lucas nods. "I have a good-sized portfolio. I don't manage it myself because I don't have time to do it properly, but the guy I use is good. He's actually Esguerra's manager as well. I'll probably visit him when we're in Chicago."

"I see." I don't know why I'm surprised. It makes sense. I know Lucas's background from his file. I guess I thought none of his upbringing rubbed off on him, but I should've known better, especially once I discovered all those books in his office.

"Do you keep in touch with them?" I ask. "Your parents, I mean?"

"No." Lucas's expression turns shuttered. "I don't."

His file said as much, but I'd wondered if that was a cover he concocted to keep his family safe. Apparently not. I'm tempted to ask more, but I don't want to pry—it's important to stay in my captor's good graces. For the rest of the walk, I let Lucas guide the conversation, and when we stop by the pond again, I sink to my knees and give him a blow job, using every skill I possess.

His happiness is my top priority these days.

THE DAY BEFORE LUCAS'S DEPARTURE, I DECIDE IT'S TIME TO TELL him about Misha. For lunch, I prepare what I discovered is Lucas's favorite meal: roast chicken with mashed potatoes and apple pie for dessert. I also take special care to brush my hair until it's silky smooth, and wear a short white sundress—the nicest outfit he got for me. When we sit down at the table, I see Lucas devouring me with his eyes, and I know that in this at least, I pleased him.

Now I need to see how far his goodwill extends.

As we eat, I try to figure out the best moment to broach the subject. Will he be in the best mood before or after dessert? Should I let him finish his chicken, or is it okay to bring up my brother now? While I'm debating that, Lucas says conversationally, "I did some research on your hometown of Donetsk recently. Is it true that for most people there, their native language is Russian, not Ukrainian?"

I let out a relieved breath. This is as good a lead-in to this topic as any. "Yes, it's true," I say, smiling. "My family spoke Russian at home. I studied Ukrainian in school, but I'm actually more fluent in English than in Ukrainian."

Lucas nods, as if I confirmed something he suspected. "That's why they came to your orphanage, right? Because the kids there were already fluent in one of the languages they needed?"

It takes everything I have to keep smiling. The reminder of the orphanage and UUR takes away my appetite, even though we're getting closer to the subject I want to discuss. Moving my half-full plate aside, I say as calmly as I can manage, "Yes, that's why. I was a particularly good candidate because I also knew English."

"And because you're beautiful." Lucas's gaze cools unexpectedly. "Don't forget that part."

I gather my courage. "Maybe," I say carefully. "But they're not all bad people. In fact—"

Lucas holds up his hand, palm out. "Yulia, stop. I know what you're going to say."

Stunned, I stare at him. "You do?"

"You want me to spare one of them, right?" Lucas's eyes once again remind me of winter ice. "That's what all this"—he sweeps his hand in a gesture encompassing the table—"is about, isn't it? The dress, the food, the pretty smiles? You think I don't see right through you?"

I swallow, my heart beginning to race. "Lucas, I just—"

"Don't." His voice is as hard as the look on his face. "Don't humiliate yourself. It's not going to work. It's out of my hands."

My stomach fills with lead. "What do you mean?"

"Esguerra will never go for it, and I won't use up my currency with him on this."

I stand up, reeling. "But—"

"There's nothing more to discuss." Lucas gets up as well, his expression forbidding. "The only person from UUR who'll be spared is you."

I step around the table, my shock transforming into cold terror. Surely he doesn't mean this. "Lucas, please. You don't understand. He's innocent. He has nothing to do with this." I grab his hand, squeezing it in desperation. "Please, I'll do anything if you spare him. He's just one person. All you need to do is let him live—"

Lucas wrenches his hand out of my grasp, cutting off my plea. "I told you. There's nothing I can do for him." There's no pity on my captor's face, no hint of mercy. "Esguerra decides these matters, not me. You're shit out of luck, beautiful."

My vision darkens at the edges, blood pounding in my ears. "Please, Lucas—" I reach for him again, but he grabs my wrist and twists my arm upward, preventing me from touching him.

"Do not fucking beg for him." Squeezing my wrist painfully, Lucas pulls me to him, and I see scalding fury in the icy depths of his eyes. "You're lucky to be alive yourself. Don't you fucking get that? If you weren't such a hot lay—" He stops, but it's too late.

I hear his message loud and clear, and the fragile remnants of my fantasies turn to dust.

23

ucas

Yulia's eyes are enormous as she stares at me, her slender wrist caught in my grasp. She looks like I just tore her heart out, and something resembling regret cools the burning fog of rage surrounding me.

Releasing her wrist, I say in a calmer tone, "Yulia, that's not what I—"

"Why don't you just do it right now?" she interrupts, her gaze unflinching as she steps back. "Go ahead, kill me. You will anyway. When I'm no longer such a 'hot lay,' right?"

"No, of course not." My anger returns, only this time it's directed at myself. "I told you—you're safe with me."

"Not if your boss wants me dead." Her upper lip curls. "Isn't that what you just told me?"

"That's not what I meant." I curse myself ten ways to Sunday.

Esguerra seemed as good of an excuse as any to stop her from pleading for her lover, but I should've realized how Yulia would interpret my words. "I promised you I'll protect you, and I'm going to keep that promise."

"Then why can't you protect *him*?" Her gaze fills with desperate hope as she comes toward me again. "Please, Lucas. He's an innocent—"

"Stop." I refuse to hear her beg for him. "I don't give a fuck about his guilt or innocence. I told you—one person only. That's the deal."

I expect Yulia to back down then, to accept that she lost, but she lifts her chin instead, her eyes like blue coals in her starkly pale face. "Then spare *him*. I want Misha to be that person, not me."

Misha. I file that name away even as my ribcage tightens with renewed fury.

She's ready to die for him—for her weakling of a lover.

"What you want doesn't matter." My words are as caustic as the jealousy burning my chest. "I decide who lives, not you."

She reacts like I just struck her. Her lips quiver, and she backs away, folding her arms around her middle.

"Yulia." I come after her, her pain cutting me like a blade, but she turns away to face the window as I approach. I lift my hand to lay it on her shoulder, but change my mind at the last moment. There's nothing I can do to make her feel better, except the one thing I'm not willing to promise.

I want this Misha dead, and I won't let her manipulate me into sparing his life.

Lowering my hand, I step back and survey Yulia's rigid figure. My captive is even more gorgeous than usual today, her short white dress making her look innocently sexy. With her hair streaming down her back in a sleek waterfall, she's temptation personified—and I know it's on purpose.

Like everything else Yulia has done over the last couple of days, her dressing up today is an attempt to save her lover.

The thought fills me with bitter anger. Turning away, I pack up the remainder of the meal and wash the dishes, using the time to cool down. Yulia doesn't move from her spot by the window, and when I approach, I see she's still deathly pale, her gaze distant and unseeing.

Steeling myself against an irrational urge to console her, I reach out to take her arm. "Let's go. " My voice is quiet. "I have to tie you up."

And holding her arm tightly, I lead Yulia to the library.

SHE DOESN'T SAY A WORD AS I SECURE HER IN THE ARMCHAIR, making sure the ropes don't cut into her skin. When I'm done, I step back and look at her. "Which book do you want?"

She doesn't respond, her gaze trained on her lap.

"Yulia. I asked you a fucking question."

She glances up, her eyes dulled with pain.

"What do you want to read?" I repeat, trying not to let her obvious distress get to me. "Which book?"

She looks away, but not before I catch a glimmer of moisture in her eyes.

Fuck.

"All right, suit yourself." I grab a random thriller off the shelves and place it on her lap. "I'll be back before dinner."

Yulia doesn't acknowledge my words in any way, and I leave before the fury simmering inside me boils over.

24

ulia

I DON'T GIVE A FUCK ABOUT HIS GUILT OR INNOCENCE. IT'S OUT OF MY hands. If you weren't such a hot lay...

Lucas's words echo in my mind, replaying on a sickening loop over and over again. He had been so cold, so cruel. It was as if the last two weeks had never happened, as if our time together meant nothing to him.

My heart feels sliced into ribbons, the pain so vast it smothers me. I take in shallow breaths, trying to cope with the agony, but it just seems to grow and expand, sinking deeper into my chest.

I failed. I failed my brother. Everything I've done from the moment Obenko approached me at the orphanage has been for Misha, and now it will all be for nothing.

The man on whom I pinned my last hopes is a merciless monster, and I'm a gullible fool.

Don't humiliate yourself. It's not going to work.

Somehow Lucas knew about my brother. He knew I was going to ask him to spare Misha's life. He knew I was trying to soften him up all these days, and he let me.

He took everything I had to give, and then he drove a knife straight into my heart.

A bitter bubble of laughter escapes me as I think of the genius of his sadistic plan. I have to admit, Lucas Kent's idea of vengeance is exquisite. No physical torture would've hurt as much as his blunt refusal to save my brother.

My laughter turns into a sob, and I gulp it down, choking off the sound. Even to my own ears, I sound mad, hysterical. The agency therapist had been right. I'm not cut out for this job. I'm not like Lucas or Obenko.

I don't have what it takes to remain sufficiently detached.

"Your loyalty to your brother is admirable, but it's also your biggest weakness," Obenko told me a couple of months into my training. "You cling to Misha because he's a part of your past, but you can't have a past anymore. You can't have a family. You need to come to terms with that, or you won't be able to cope with this life. There will be times when you'll need to get close to people without letting them get close to you. You'll need to be in control of your emotions. Do you think you're capable of that?"

"Of course I am," I answered quickly, fearing he'd kick me out of the program and place my brother back in the orphanage. "Just because I love Misha doesn't mean I'd get attached to anyone else."

And I worked hard to prove that. I was friendly with the other trainees, but I didn't become friends with any of them. Same thing with the instructors. I kept my emotional distance from all of them. Even after the incident with Kirill, I did my best to deal with the trauma on my own.

I was such a good, diligent trainee that Obenko gave me the Moscow assignment less than a year after Kirill's assault.

Another sobbing laugh rises in my throat. I swallow the hysterical sound, but I can't control the tears that spill down my cheeks. I thought I was good at what I did. I smiled and flirted with my assigned lovers, but I never fell for them. Even with Vladimir, who taught me about sexual pleasure, I remained cool and detached. No one mattered to me except my brother.

No one until Lucas.

In my effort to get close to my captor, I opened myself up too much. I lost control of my emotions. I let a ruthless, treacherous man get close to me, and he used that closeness to devise the cruelest of all punishments.

He figured out the best way to destroy me.

25

ucas

I HAVE A SHITLOAD TO DO BEFORE WE DEPART TOMORROW MORNING, but I go to the gym because I can't focus on anything, my thoughts occupied by Yulia and the agony in her gaze.

As I pummel the sandbag, I try to push away images of her sitting there, so distant and wounded. She looked at me like I betrayed her—like I hurt her beyond belief.

The bag sways from side to side as I ram my fists into it, landing one hard blow after another. The idea of *her* feeling betrayed by *me* makes me want to beat someone to a pulp. What the fuck did she expect? That she'd give me a couple of blow jobs and I'd happily save her lover? That I wouldn't question her desire to spare this Misha's life?

An innocent, she called him, as if that would matter to me. As far as I'm concerned, the man deserves to die for nothing more than touching her. Add to that his being part of UUR, and he'll be lucky if I kill him quickly.

"Lucas. Hey, man. Are you almost done?"

Diego's question interrupts my mindless punching spree. Wiping sweat from my forehead, I turn to see the young Mexican standing there, his gloves already prepped. Behind him are a couple more guards waiting their turn.

Judging by the looks on their faces and the soreness in my knuckles, I must've been working off my anger for quite some time.

"It's all yours," I say, forcing myself to step away from the sandbag. "Go ahead."

As I leave the gym, I debate going back to my house to take a shower, but I'm not calm enough to face Yulia yet. So instead, I make my way to Esguerra's mansion to use the shower by the pool. He keeps a stash of T-shirts there in case of any unexpected bloody business, and I grab one of them to change into when I'm clean.

I rinse quickly, and as I'm pulling on my shorts and a fresh T-shirt, I catch a glimpse of a familiar dark-haired figure hurrying into the house.

Rosa.

I'd all but forgotten about the maid. She must've taken my words to heart, as I haven't seen her since our talk in Esguerra's kitchen. Hopefully, I didn't hurt the girl too badly, but it couldn't be helped. I didn't want her lurking anywhere near Yulia.

Feeling marginally calmer after my hard workout, I head to Esguerra's office for a call with the Israeli intelligence agency.

~

WE SPEND THE NEXT TWO HOURS TALKING WITH THE MOSSAD ABOUT the recent developments in Syria and the rest of the Middle East. As the call wraps up, I consider telling Esguerra what I've uncovered about UUR so far, but decide it's not the right time. I'll speak to him about Yulia and her agency when we return from Chicago. By then, I should have more concrete information, as the hackers are finally having some success sifting through the coded data in the Ukrainian government's files.

After the call is done, Esguerra and I go over last-minute logistics for tomorrow's trip.

"When we land, we're going to go straight to Nora's parents' house," Esguerra says. "They want to see her right away, even if it means a late dinner."

I'm long past wondering about the insanity of this trip, so I just say, "All right. I'll be with the guard detail tomorrow night to make sure everyone knows what they're doing."

"Good." Esguerra pauses for a second. "You know Rosa is coming with us, right?"

I actually didn't know that. "She is? Why?"

"Nora wants her company."

"Okay." I don't see how that changes anything. Unless... "Do I need to bring extra men to look out for her, or will she be with you and Nora most of the time?"

"She'll be with us." Esguerra seems vaguely amused. "All right, then, sounds like we're all set. I'll see you on the plane tomorrow."

"See you," I say, and head over to the guards' barracks for my meeting with Diego and Eduardo—the two guards I'm appointing as Yulia's jailers in my absence.

"Walk me through it again," I tell Eduardo after I give him and Diego the full list of instructions concerning my captive. "How many times will you visit my house to let her use the bathroom and stretch her legs?"

The Colombian rolls his eyes. "Three times in addition to releasing her during meals. We got it, Kent, I promise."

"And what will you do if she attempts to escape?"

"We'll restrain her, but not harm her in any way," Diego says, his lips twitching with amusement. "You've got to chill out, man. We understand. We're not going to touch a hair on her head other than to make sure she doesn't go anywhere. She's going to have her books, her TV shows, and yes, I'll take her out for a walk once a day."

"And we'll keep our mouths shut about the whole thing," Eduardo adds, parroting my exact words. "Nobody will hear a peep about your spy princess from us."

"Good." I give them a hard look. "And food?"

"We'll bring her products from the main house and let her cook them," Diego says, openly grinning now. "She'll be the most well-fed, well-entertained prisoner in existence."

I ignore his ribbing. "And at night?"

"I will shackle her wrist to the metal post you installed by the bed," Eduardo says. "And I will not lay a hand on her. It'll be as if she's a sack of potatoes—but a really important one," he adds quickly when my hand tightens into a fist. "Seriously, Kent, I'm just kidding. We're going to take good care of your girl, I promise. You know you can trust us."

I do know that. That's why I chose them for this task. Both guards have been working here for the past two years, and they've proven their loyalty. They might find my orders amusing, but they'll do as I say.

Yulia will be safe with them.

"Okay," I say, nodding at them. "In that case, I will see you both tomorrow morning. Be at my house at nine sharp."

And leaving the guards' barracks, I go to the training field to check on our new recruits.

26

ulia

I DON'T KNOW HOW MUCH TIME PASSES BEFORE I GET MY TEARS under control, but by the time I open the book Lucas left for me, the sun is already setting outside. I stare at the words on the open page, but the text fades in and out, the letters jumbling together in front of my swollen eyes.

I failed my brother. Because of me, he's going to be killed.

I attempt to focus on the book, to push the devastating knowledge away, but it's all I can think about. Old memories press in, and I close my eyes, too tired to fight them off.

"Please watch your brother," my mother implores, her blue gaze filled with worry. "Check on him before you go to sleep, all right? He seemed a little feverish earlier, so if his forehead feels unusually warm, call us, all right? And don't open the door for anyone you don't recognize."

"I won't, Mom. I know what to do." I might be ten, but it's not the first

time I've stayed alone with Misha while my parents rushed to my grandfather's sickbed. "I'll take good care of him, I promise."

Mom kisses me on the forehead, her floral perfume teasing my nostrils. "I know you will," she murmurs, stepping back. "You're my wonderful grown-up girl." Her face is tense with stress, but the smile she directs at me is full of warmth. "We'll be back as soon as your grandfather stabilizes a bit."

"I know, Mom." I smile back at her, unaware that my life is about to change forever. "Go to Grandpa. I'll watch over Misha, I promise."

And I tried to do exactly that. When the policemen came to our apartment the next morning, I didn't let them in until they showed me pictures of my parents' bodies in the morgue, broken and bloodied from the car crash. I insisted that my brother stay with me when Child Services tried to separate us, claiming that a two-year-old shouldn't attend his parents' funeral. And when Vasiliy Obenko approached me at the orphanage a year later, offering to have his sister and her husband adopt Misha if I joined his agency, I didn't hesitate.

I told the Head of UUR I'd do anything if he gave my brother a normal, happy life.

Opening my eyes, I try to focus on the book again, but at that moment, a flash of movement in my peripheral vision catches my attention. Startled, I look up and see a dark-haired woman standing in the middle of Lucas's library.

Rosa, I realize, my pulse jumping.

"What are you doing here? How did you get in?" I can't hide the undertone of panic in my voice. My hands are handcuffed, and I'm bound to the chair with a thick layer of ropes. If she means to harm me, I can't stop her.

Rosa holds up a key ring. "In the main house, we have a spare key for every building in this compound, private houses included."

I don't see any weapons on her, which is somewhat reassuring. "Okay, but why are you here?" I ask in a calmer tone.

"I wanted to see you," she says. "Tomorrow, we're leaving for two weeks. Going to Chicago to visit Nora's family."

"Nora's family?"

"Señor Esguerra's wife," Rosa clarifies.

I frown in confusion. I now recall that Nora is the name of the American girl Esguerra kidnapped and married. Lucas didn't tell me the reason for his upcoming trip, but I assumed it was business-related. I had no idea Lucas's sadistic boss has any kind of relationship with his in-laws.

"Anyways," Rosa continues, "I wanted to see you in person before I left."

My confusion intensifies. "Why?"

Rosa steps closer. "Because I don't think you belong here." Her hands are locked together in front of her black dress. "Because this isn't right."

"What isn't right?" Does she want me strung up in some torture shed like she'd implied before?

"You. This whole thing." Her brown eyes regard me steadily. "It's wrong that Lucas has you here like this. That he's leaving you with Diego and Eduardo. They're good guys, both of them. They like to play poker."

"Poker?" I'm completely lost.

Rosa nods. "They play with the guards on North Tower Two. Every Thursday afternoon from two to six."

"They do?" My heartbeat kicks up again. Is Rosa telling me what I think she's telling me?

"Yes," she says evenly. "It's not a problem because the drones patrol the perimeter around the estate, and there are heat and motion sensors everywhere. Anything approaching the border of the estate, no matter how small or big, gets scanned and examined by our security software, and the guards get alerted if the computer thinks there's a problem."

My pulse is now a frantic drumbeat. "I see." *Anything approaching,* she said. That means the computer disregards things heading in the other direction. "How far is the northern border of the estate from here?"

Rosa hesitates, and I kick myself for being too blunt. She clearly wants to pretend she's just chatting with me, and whatever information I glean is something she's giving by accident.

"Two and a half miles," she finally says, and I exhale in relief. I didn't scare her off after all. "There's a river that marks that border," she continues, dropping all pretense. "Farther to the west, a small road crosses the river. It goes all the way north to Miraflores. Occasionally, we get some deliveries via that route." She pauses, then adds, "The next delivery is scheduled for Thursday at three p.m."

"Thursday at three," I repeat, hardly able to believe my luck. "As in, this Thursday afternoon. The day after tomorrow."

She nods. "We're getting some food items brought in."

"Okay." My mind is racing, sifting through the potential obstacles. "What about—"

"I have to go now," Rosa says, stepping even closer. "Lucas will be home soon." She brushes her fingers over the book I'm holding, and her hand touches mine for a second. "Bye, Yulia," she says quietly before turning and hurrying out of the room.

Stunned, I look down and see two small objects on top of my book.

A razor blade and a hairpin.

27

ucas

It's after eight by the time I get home. To my relief, Yulia is calmly reading in her armchair when I step into the library.

"Sorry it took so long," I say, approaching the chair to untie her. "You must be starved—not to mention, needing the restroom."

She looks up at me, and I see that her eyes are slightly reddened, as if she's been crying. She doesn't say anything, but I don't expect her to. I have a strong suspicion tonight's dinner won't be a particularly chatty affair.

Bending down, I untie her and help her out of the armchair, ignoring the way she stiffens at my touch.

"Come. It's getting late." Determined to maintain control of my temper, I lead her to the bathroom.

I wait as Yulia uses the restroom, and then I bring her to the kitchen. I was hoping she'd make dinner despite being upset, but she just sits down at the table and stares straight ahead.

"All right," I say, not letting my irritation show. "You can sit if you want. I'll heat up some leftovers."

She doesn't respond, doesn't even move as I set the table and prepare everything. Luckily, the chicken and mashed potatoes she made for lunch taste great even when warmed up in the microwave.

Given Yulia's withdrawn state, I half-expect her not to eat, but she digs into the food the moment I set the plate in front of her.

I guess her hunger is stronger than her anger with me.

We demolish the chicken in silence; then I cut us each a slice of apple pie for dessert. I'm about to put Yulia's slice on her plate when she startles me by saying, "None for me, thanks. I'm full."

"All right." I conceal my pleasure at having her speak again. "Do you want any tea?"

She nods and rises to her feet. "I'll get it."

With those graceful, efficient movements I've come to know, she makes us each a cup and brings them over. Placing one cup in front of me, she sits down across the table and blows on her tea to cool it down. I do the same before taking a sip. The liquid is hot and slightly bitter, but not unpleasant. I can almost see why Yulia likes it so much.

We don't speak as we drink our tea, but the silence doesn't feel quite as strained as before. It gives me hope that this evening won't be a total disaster.

When we're done with the tea, I take care of the cleanup while Yulia sits and watches me, her expression unreadable. Does she hate me? Wish she could stab me with the nearest fork? Hope I never return from this trip?

The thought is more than a little unpleasant.

Pushing it aside, I finish wiping the counters and approach Yulia. "I arranged for two guards to watch over you in my absence," I say. "Diego and Eduardo. You've already met Diego—he's the one who carried you off the plane."

"Yes, I remember him." Yulia's voice is quiet as she rises to her feet. "He seems like a decent-enough guy."

"He is—and so is Eduardo." I stop in front of her. "They'll take good care of you."

"Jail me, you mean," she says evenly, looking up at me.

"Whatever you wish to call it." I lift my hand to pick up a lock of her hair. "They'll make sure you have everything you need."

She nods and takes a small step back, her silky strands sliding out of my fingers. "All right."

"Come." I catch her wrist before she can step out of my reach. "Let's go to bed. I have to wake up early."

She stiffens, but allows me to lead her to the bathroom without an argument. I let her in there to take a quick shower—I showered earlier, so I don't need one—and then I take her to the bedroom. As we enter the room, my cock rises in anticipation and erotic images fill my mind.

Fighting off the sudden surge of lust, I stop next to the bed and turn to face Yulia. Releasing her wrist, I frame her face with my palms, smoothing errant strands of hair back with my thumbs. She doesn't move, just gazes at me mutely, her blue eyes large and shadowed in her delicate face.

"Yulia..." I don't know what I can say to her, how I can fix the situation, but I have to try. The thought of leaving for two weeks while things are so strained between us is unbearable. "It doesn't have to be this way," I say softly. "It can be... better."

She blinks, as if startled by my words, and I see a fresh sheen of moisture in her eyes. "What are you talking about?" she whispers, her hands coming up to curl around my wrists. "Isn't this what you wanted? To hurt me? To punish me?"

"No." I let her pull my hands away from her face. "No, Yulia. I don't want to hurt you, believe me."

Her eyebrows draw together as she releases my wrists. "Then how can you—"

"I don't want to discuss this anymore. It's done. We're going to move past this. Do you understand me?" My words come out unintentionally harsh, and I see her flinch as she takes a step back.

I take a deep breath. The jealousy is still festering inside me, but I'm determined not to let it spoil our last night together. Forcing myself to move slowly and deliberately, I pull off my T-shirt and drop it on the floor, then remove my shoes, shorts, and underwear. Yulia watches me, her cheeks turning a soft shade of pink as her gaze falls on my growing erection. To my relief, I see the hardened peaks of her nipples through the white material of her dress.

She might hate me, but she still wants me.

"Come here." Unable to hold off any longer, I reach for her, clasping her slim shoulders. She's stiff as I pull her toward me, but I see the pulse throbbing at the base of her throat. She's far from immune to me, and I intend to use that.

One way or another, tonight Yulia won't be thinking of her lover.

I bend my head, wanting to taste her soft lips, but at the last moment, she turns her head and my mouth grazes her jaw instead. I feel her shudder, and then she twists out of my grasp altogether and backs away. Her chest is heaving and her face is flushed, her eyes glittering as she stares at me.

"I can't—" Yulia's voice cracks. "I can't do this, Lucas. Not after—"

"Stop." The unwanted jealousy returns, the pit of my stomach burning with anger as I come after her. "I told you I don't want to discuss this."

She keeps backing away. "But—"

"Not another word." Her back meets the dresser, and I close the remaining distance between us, trapping her there. Placing my palms on the dresser on both sides of her head, I lean closer, breathing in her delicate scent. Every dark fantasy I've ever had slides through my mind, and my voice roughens as I whisper in her ear, "I've had enough of this. You're mine now, and it's time you learned what that means."

28

ulia

The damp heat of Lucas's breath on my ear makes me quiver, my thighs clenching convulsively to contain the growing ache between them. The treachery of my body adds to the tumult in my mind. I thought I'd have to force myself to endure his touch, but revulsion is the last thing I'm feeling.

Even knowing he's a heartless monster, I can't stop wanting Lucas.

His mouth trails over my jaw as he holds me caged against the dresser, and my heart rate accelerates as the hard length of his cock presses against my belly. "Don't," I whisper, my hands bunching into fists at my sides. I can feel the warmth of his powerful body surrounding me, pressing in on me, and my stomach twists with a combination of fear, shame, and longing. "Please… let me go."

Lucas ignores my words, moving his right hand to my shoulder. Hooking his fingers under the strap of my dress, he pulls it down. His mouth is now on my neck, teasing and nibbling, and my arousal intensifies as his hand slips into the bodice of my dress and cups my breast, the rough edge of his thumb rasping over my nipple.

Heat blooms low in my core, my arousal intensifying even as self-loathing fills my chest. I don't want to feel this for my cruel captor. I'm not fighting him because I can't risk jeopardizing my upcoming escape, but I shouldn't be enjoying this.

I shouldn't desire the man who plans to kill my brother.

As if reading my thoughts, Lucas lifts his head to gaze down at me. There's lust in his pale gaze and something else—something dark and intensely possessive.

"No, beautiful," he murmurs, his hand still on my breast. "I'm not letting you go."

I begin to respond, but he lowers his head and slants his mouth across mine. His left hand grips my nape, holding me still, and his right hand moves down to pull up the skirt of my dress. In one yank, he rips off my thong. I hardly register the act; his kiss is too ravenous, too consuming. His lips and tongue steal my breath away, and it takes everything I have to remember why I shouldn't want him. Desperate, I splay my palms on the dresser behind me to keep myself from reaching for him. It's a small victory and one that doesn't last long. Still devouring my mouth, Lucas turns around, dragging me along, and begins backing me toward the bed.

The backs of my thighs hit the edge of the bed, and then I'm on my back, my dress hiked up above my waist and Lucas bending over me. His face is taut with hunger, his eyes glittering. Before I can recover from the kiss, he grips my knees, spreading them wide, and moves off the bed to crouch between my open legs.

"No, please, not this." I try to scramble backwards, but Lucas holds me tight, pulling me closer to the edge of the bed. His lips twitch with an ironic half-smile—he understands why I don't want this pleasure—and then he buries his head between my thighs and swipes his warm, wet tongue along my slit.

The lash of pleasure is almost brutal. My entire body arches up as he latches on to my clit and begins sucking on it in soft, rhythmic pulls. Gasping, I try to close my legs, to move away from the erotic torment, but Lucas's grip is unbreakable and his rhythm doesn't falter. I can feel the slickness of my arousal seeping out, and my nipples draw tight as unbearable pressure builds inside me, intensifying with every moment.

He picks up the tempo of his sucking motions, his lips squeezing my clit with every pull, and a stifled cry escapes my throat as I feel the orgasm approaching. *My brother's killer...* The words whisper through my mind as my body begins to contract in release.

"No, stop!" Without thinking, I jackknife to a sitting position and twist to the side with all my strength, breaking his grip on my thighs. The suddenness of my resistance catches Lucas off-guard, and I manage to scramble on my knees almost all the way across the bed before he leaps after me, his fingers closing around my ankle at the last second.

Acting on instinct, I turn and kick at him, aiming for his face, but he jerks to the side, causing my kick to miss. Before I can try again, he catches my other ankle and drags me across the bed toward him.

"What the fuck, Yulia?" Controlling my flailing legs with his knees, Lucas pins me down and captures my wrists to stretch my arms wide at my sides. His face is rigid with fury, his eyes narrowed into slits. "Are you that crazy about him?"

I stare at him, breathing hard. My body is throbbing with frustrated arousal, and a toxic cocktail of fear, adrenaline, and anger is boiling in my chest. Fighting Lucas was a stupid move on my part, but coming in his arms would've been a horrible betrayal of my brother. "Of course I am," I bite out, unable to restrain myself. "What the fuck did you expect?"

Lucas's fingers tighten around my wrists. "He's nobody to you now." Rage glitters in his eyes. "Nobody. You belong to *me*, understand?"

I gape at my captor, uncomprehending. How can he expect me to forget my brother? I know Lucas is possessive, but this demand borders on insanity.

Before I can gather my thoughts, Lucas's face hardens. Moving swiftly, he drags my right arm over my body, joining my right wrist with the left one. I end up on my side, my wrists held in his left hand as he reaches over me for the nightstand, his heavy weight crushing me into the mattress. Air rushes out of my compressed lungs, but a moment later, he lifts himself up, relieving the pressure on my ribcage. Holding my wrists with his left hand, Lucas looms over me, his lower body pinning mine in place—and in his right hand, I see the reason for his action.

He grabbed a coil of rope from the nightstand.

A chill dances over my skin, my desire dampened by a spike of fear. "What are you doing?" The words come out in a frantic, pleading whisper. "Lucas, you don't need to do this. I won't fight anymore."

But it's too late. He's already winding the rope around my wrists, and the old anxiety rises up, choking me with memories of Kirill. The paralyzing terror of the past rushes toward me, but at that moment, Lucas leans down and whispers in my ear, "I'm not going to hurt you—but I will make you forget him."

I draw in a shaking breath, his words providing the modicum of reassurance I need to stay in the present. Not that my anxiety is lessened in any way; what he's doing and saying is more than a little mad. I begin to struggle again, desperate to get away, but he's too strong. Ignoring my attempts to throw him off, Lucas ties the rope tightly around my wrists and reaches down to grab my ankles. As he does so, his weight briefly lifts off my legs, and I manage to kick him in the side before he seizes my ankles.

"Oh no, you don't." His voice is a low growl as he drags my ankles up, folding my body in half. I strike out with my bound hands, but I don't have much leverage, and the blow glances off his shoulder as he squeezes my calves in the crook of his muscular arm. With his hands free, he loops the other end of the rope around my ankles. His motions are swift and sure, utterly merciless. In a matter of seconds, he has me trussed up like a turkey, my ankles and wrists tied together in front of my body. With my dress flipped up and my underwear gone, my lower body is completely exposed.

The vulnerability of my position propels my heart rate so high I feel dizzy. Blood pounds in my ears in a thundering roar as Lucas forces my bound wrists and ankles up above my head, stretching my hamstrings to their limits. He secures the rope to the metal pole he installed by the bed and moves down my folded-in-half body. His hands grip my quivering thighs, and I see him looking at me—at my wide-open pussy and ass.

"What are you doing?" I can scarcely breathe through the growing panic in my chest. "Lucas, what are you doing?"

He looks up to meet my gaze, his eyes burning with savage heat. "Whatever I want, baby. Whatever I fucking want."

And lowering his head between my legs, he latches onto my clit again.

29

ucas

THE TASTE OF HER IS INTOXICATING, UNBEARABLY EROTIC. HER PUSSY is dripping with cream, and the heated feminine scent of her makes my cock weep with pre-cum. I want to thrust into her, feel her slick tightness cradling me, but I also want something else—something Yulia's withheld from me thus far.

First, though, I need to finish what I started. Ignoring the lust burning in me, I suck on her clit using the same rhythm that brought her to the edge of climax before. I felt her beginning to spasm before she started fighting, and I know I would've had her in another second. She panicked—probably because she doesn't want to betray *him*—but I'm not about to stand for it.

She's going to come tonight, again and again, until her lover is nothing but a distant memory.

It takes less than a minute to bring Yulia to the brink this time;

she's already primed, her pink flesh swollen and sensitized from my earlier ministrations. She pleads with me, begging me to let her go, but I persist until I feel her pussy rippling under my tongue and hear her cry out in release.

Then I begin again, sliding my finger into her spasming channel to stimulate her as I lick her clit. She comes hard and fast, her juices coating my hand, and I go for the third one, even though my cock is ready to burst.

"No more," she moans as I push two fingers into her wet heat, finding the spot inside that drives her wild. "Please, Lucas, no more…"

But I'm not done yet. I'm far from done. Using the two fingers to fuck her, I close my lips around her clit again. My fingers drill her hard and fast, and her cries grow in volume with every second. I feel her inner walls contracting in another orgasm, but I don't stop. I keep going until I feel her come again—and then I scoop out the abundant moisture from her pussy and smear it on the tiny opening of her asshole.

She doesn't react at first, just lies there with her face flushed and her eyes closed as she attempts to catch her breath. With her ankles tied to her wrists and her pussy wet and swollen, she's the epitome of helpless sensuality. Bondage isn't normally my thing, but restraining Yulia is different. It's not about kink; it's about possession.

After tonight, she'll have no doubt that she's mine.

When her asshole is sufficiently lubed, I press the tip of my finger to the tight opening, watching her reaction. The one time I touched her ass in the shower, she tensed, and I realized she either has a problem with anal sex or is new to it. I hope it's the latter, but I suspect it might be the former.

Sure enough, as my finger pushes in the first quarter of an inch, Yulia's ass cheeks clench, and her eyes fly open. "Don't." Her voice is strained. "Please don't."

"Was it your trainer?" I keep my finger where it is, neither pressing forward nor retreating. "Did he hurt you this way too?"

She stares at me, her chest heaving, and I see her mouth tremble before she presses her lips together. She doesn't say anything, but I don't need a verbal confirmation.

The motherfucker did hurt her like this—and she's afraid I will too.

Something squeezes painfully inside me. I don't deserve her trust, but a part of me wants it. It's a desire that directly contradicts my primitive need to subdue her, to keep her at any cost.

Even as I hold her bound and helpless, I don't want her fearing me—not that way, at least.

"I won't hurt you," I say quietly, holding Yulia's gaze. The savage hunger pounding through me dies down to a muted roar as I withdraw the tip of my finger. "I promise you that."

She shudders with relief, her eyes closing, and I lower my head again, licking her pussy with gentle swipes of my tongue. Her flesh is pliant, still soft and wet. I know she's nowhere near an orgasm now, and I don't try to give her one. Instead, I soothe her with my lips and tongue, giving her undemanding pleasure. I do this for what feels like hours, and eventually, I feel the remnants of terrified tension leave her body.

Continuing to lick her, I move my mouth lower, to her creamy slit, and dip my tongue inside, tasting her there. She tenses in a different way, a moan escaping her lips, and I capitalize on her growing arousal by carefully rubbing her swollen clit with my fingers. She's moaning in earnest now, and I move my tongue even lower, to the tight ring of muscle between her ass cheeks.

Yulia stiffens for a second, but I just lick her there, tonguing her back opening and rubbing her clit until she's panting and gasping, her hips rocking in an instinctive rhythm. I can sense that she's on the verge, and I ruthlessly push her over, pinching her clit with a firm, steady pressure.

Her body tightens, and I feel the ring of muscle pulsing and spasming under my tongue as she cries out in release. I lick her one last time, depositing as much saliva as I can, and then, using the distraction of her orgasm, I push my finger in again. It slides in easily before her body clamps down on it, and I keep it there, letting her adjust to the sensation as I sit up and shift closer, pressing my groin against her lower body.

Her eyes are wide and dazed-looking, her lips parted as she stares at me, her chest rising and falling with panting breaths.

"I won't hurt you," I repeat, keeping my finger inside her as I use my free hand to guide my cock to her pussy. "This is as far as we'll go today."

Yulia doesn't respond, but her eyes close, her teeth sinking into her lower lip as the tip of my cock enters her tight, slick heat. With my finger buried in her ass, I can actually feel my cock pushing into her, stretching her inner walls as I go deeper, and I groan at the exquisite pleasure of it, my balls tightening with explosive need.

"Yes, baby, that's it. Let me in deeper…" I'm barely cognizant of what I'm saying, my voice a feral rumble in my chest as her pussy sucks me in, engulfing my entire length. "Oh, fuck, yeah, just like that…"

She cries out as I brace myself on the bed and begin thrusting, no longer able to restrain myself. Being inside her is paradise, and I never want to leave. If I had my way, I'd fuck Yulia forever. But all too soon, the pleasure intensifies, turning into razor-sharp ecstasy, and I feel the boil of incipient orgasm in my balls. My thrusting pace picks up—I'm all but jackhammering into her now—and I hear her cries growing louder, mixing with my own grunting groans. My vision blurs, my entire body seizing with intolerable tension, and through the hammering roar of my heartbeat, I hear Yulia scream and feel her inner muscles clamp down on my cock and my finger.

Dimly, I realize she's coming, and then my own climax is upon me, my cum spurting out into her as my cock jerks uncontrollably, again and again.

30

ulia

I'm dazed and shaking, my heart rate somewhere in the stratosphere as Lucas slowly withdraws his finger from my ass and pulls out of me. I'm so out of it I barely notice when Lucas unties me, lifts me into his arms, and carries me out of the room.

It's not until the water spray hits me that I realize we're standing together in the shower, his arms wrapped around me from the back to prevent me from collapsing. My leg muscles are quivering from being stretched for so long, and my body is throbbing in the aftermath of his dual invasion. Lucas is kissing my neck as he holds me in front of him, and I'm letting him, my head resting on his shoulder as warm water cascades over our bodies.

"Relax, beautiful." His voice is a soft rumble in my ear as I attempt to pull away. His arms tighten around me, holding me in place. "We're just going to take a nice shower together, that's all."

I know I should protest, push him away, but I don't have the strength to fight him anymore. Maybe I never did—because fighting Lucas means fighting myself as well. Something perverse in me is drawn to this cruel, dangerous man, has been drawn to him from the very beginning.

Seeing that I'm no longer trying to pull away, Lucas makes sure I'm steady on my feet and carefully loosens his grip.

"Let me wash you," he murmurs, reaching for a bottle of body wash, and I stand like an obedient child as he lathers my whole body, washing me from head to toe. His soapy hands go everywhere, even into the place his finger invaded earlier, and I close my eyes, giving myself up to his gentle ministrations.

I'll despise myself for this tomorrow, but tonight, I want his tenderness. I crave it.

He kept his promise not to hurt me. I'm still vaguely surprised by that. When Lucas tied me up, I thought he'd do something horrible to me—and when he started touching my ass, I became sure of it. But other than the slight burn of the initial entry, his finger hadn't hurt, and his tongue there had felt… interesting. The sensations had been strange and foreign, but nothing like the terrible pain Kirill had inflicted on me that day.

The water spray stops, and I open my eyes, realizing Lucas turned off the shower.

"Come, baby." He guides me out of the shower stall and wraps a fluffy towel around me before briskly drying himself. "Let's go to bed," he says, stepping toward me. "You're falling asleep on your feet."

He picks me up again, and I don't protest as he carries me back to the bedroom. Even after the shower, I feel like I'm about to fall over. The orgasms Lucas forced on me have depleted me both emotionally and physically, and there's nothing I want more than sleep.

Sleep will be my escape for the rest of the night, and tomorrow, my tormentor will leave.

He'll be gone, and if Rosa gave me good information, so will I.

The thought should fill me with joy, but as Lucas places me on the bed and handcuffs us together, happiness is the last thing I'm feeling. Even now, a part of me mourns the fantasy—the man I'd begun falling for before he shredded my heart.

LUCAS WAKES ME UP IN THE MIDDLE OF THE NIGHT BY THRUSTING into me, his thick cock invading me from the back. I gasp, my eyes popping open at the sudden intrusion. I'm not as wet as before, but it doesn't matter. My body responds to him instantly, my core flooding with liquid heat as he begins driving into me. There's no finesse to this fucking, no attempt to make it anything but what it is.

A hard, basic claiming.

Our left wrists are still cuffed together, and the room is pitch black. I can't see anything; I can only feel as he holds me against him, his arm a steely band around my ribcage. His hips hammer into me, and I take him in, unable to do anything else. My breathing quickens, heat rippling over my skin in waves, and my inner muscles begin to tighten.

"Tell me you're mine." Lucas's hot breath washes over my neck. "Tell me you belong to me."

"I—" The intensity of the sensations overwhelms my sleep-fogged brain. "I'm yours."

"Again."

"I'm yours." I gasp as his cock hits a spot inside me that ups the heat to a volcanic burn. "I'm yours."

"Yes, you are." He moves his left hand to my sex, dragging my wrist along with it. "You're mine and no one else's."

"Yes, no one else's…" I don't know what I'm saying, but with his fingers touching my clit, I don't care. Everything about this feels surreal, like some kind of a sex dream. I can feel Lucas's muscled body surrounding me as his cock pumps into me, and the volcanic heat grows, burning away all thought and reason. Dazed, I cry out as the sensations crest, and then I'm coming, my inner muscles clamping around his hard shaft.

Lucas groans too, and I feel his big body tensing and shuddering behind me. The warmth of his seed floods me, and my sex spasms with aftershocks, sparks of residual pleasure sizzling along my nerve endings.

Breathing hard, I close my eyes, feeling his chest rise and fall against my back as his cock slowly softens inside me. I know I should get up and clean up, or at least reach for a tissue, but I'm too relaxed, too drained by the pleasure. I don't want to do anything but lie in Lucas's arms. He seems to be equally unwilling to move, and my lids grow heavy as my thoughts begin to drift. All my fears and worries feel unreal, distant from this moment and from us. In some faraway world, we're enemies and he's my captor, but I'm no longer in that brutal place.

I'm here, warm and safe in my lover's embrace.

The veil of darkness wraps around me, and as I sink deeper into the haze of dreams, I hear him say softly, "I'm sorry, Yulia. Do you hate me?"

"Never," I whisper to my dream Lucas. "I love you. I'm yours."

And as sleep drags me under, I feel him kiss my temple and hold me tighter, as if afraid to let me go.

31

ucas

Yulia's breathing takes on the steady rhythm of sleep, but I'm wide awake, my heart pounding heavily in my chest. Did she mean it? Did she know what she was saying?

Did she know it was *me* she was saying it to?

I want to shake her awake and demand answers, but I resist the impulse. I don't know what I would do if Yulia told me it was Misha she was dreaming about. The mere thought of it burns me like acid. If I found out she meant the words for him…

No. I can't go there. I don't want Yulia looking at me like I'm a monster again.

Tightening my arm around her ribcage, I brush my lips across her temple and close my eyes, trying to relax. It was most likely a slip of the tongue, something she mumbled by accident, but even if there's some truth to her words, why should I care? Sex is what I want from her, sex and a certain basic companionship.

Just because I want Yulia doesn't mean I need her love.

Forcing my breathing to slow, I will sleep to come, but the thought that she might love me is like a splinter in my brain. No matter how hard I try, I can't seem to let it go—or to suppress the warm sensation that accompanies the idea.

It's an illogical reaction on my part. I know better than anyone how meaningless those words are. My parents used "I love you" as a platitude, as something to say to each other and to me at social functions. It was part of the glossy façade they presented to the public, and I've always known not to take them at face value. Same with the women I've slept with: more than one of them had used the words casually, throwing them out like one might say "hello" and "goodbye." There's absolutely no reason for me to latch onto this one mumbled phrase from Yulia—a phrase that might not have even been meant for me.

Unless it had been meant for me. Is that possible? It wouldn't be casual for Yulia, that much I'm sure of. Given the circumstances, if she did fall in love with me, she'd resist letting me know for as long as possible—which means she probably didn't realize what she was saying.

Fuck. Clearly, I can't let the matter rest. If Yulia loves me, I need to know, so I can stop obsessing about it.

Sitting up, I lean over her and turn on the bedside lamp.

She doesn't so much as twitch at my movements. Her lips are slightly parted, and her lashes form dark crescents on her pale cheeks. With her face relaxed in sleep, she looks impossibly young—an innocent worn out by my harsh demands.

I watch her for a few moments, then reach for the light and turn it off. Lying down, I mold my body against her slender form from the back and breathe in the sweet, peach-tinted scent of her hair.

Soon, I promise myself as I close my eyes. When I return from Chicago, I'll question her and find out the truth.

My captive's not going anywhere, and two weeks is not that long to wait.

~

THE CHIRPING OF MY PHONE ALARM DRAGS ME OUT OF DEEP SLEEP. Suppressing the urge to crush the offending object, I reach for the nightstand on my right and turn off the alarm. Yawning, I take out the key I keep in that drawer and turn back to face Yulia—who woke up from my movements this time and is regarding me with a sleepy, half-lidded gaze.

"Hi, beautiful." Unable to resist, I unlock the handcuffs and pull her into my lap. She's soft and pliant, her skin deliciously warm as I hold her against me, and I have to fight the urge to throw her down for one last fuck. "I have to go," I murmur instead, kissing the top of her head. There are so many things I want to say to her, so many questions I want to ask about last night, but I settle for saying, "Be good with Diego and Eduardo, okay?"

She tenses slightly, but I feel her nod against my chest.

"Yulia, about last night..." I slide my fingers into her hair and gently pull on it, needing to see her face, but she refuses to meet my gaze, her eyes trained somewhere on my chin.

I sigh and decide to let it go. Now is not the time to get into what Yulia may or may not have said to me when she was half-asleep. "I'll miss you," I say softly instead.

Her lips tighten, her gaze dropping even lower, and I remind myself to be patient. I can wait two weeks. Brushing another kiss over the crown of her head, I reluctantly shift her off my lap and get up, doing my best to keep my eyes off her naked curves.

Diego and Eduardo will be here in ten minutes, and I still need to shower and get dressed.

32

ulia

"YULIA, YOU'VE ALREADY MET DIEGO, AND THIS IS EDUARDO," LUCAS says, gesturing toward two young guards. "They'll be watching you in my absence."

I prop my hip against the kitchen table and nod at the two dark-haired men, keeping my expression carefully neutral. Diego is taller than Eduardo, but they're both muscular and in good shape. Handsome in their own way, though I much prefer Lucas's fierce, Viking-raider looks.

"Hello," I say, figuring I have nothing to lose by playing nice.

"Hi, Yulia." Diego grins at me, showing even white teeth. "I have to say, you look much… cleaner today."

His grin is contagious, and I find myself smiling back at him. "Showers have been known to do that," I say wryly, and he laughs out loud, throwing his head back. Eduardo chuckles too, but when

I sneak a glance at Lucas, I see that his face is dark, his eyebrows pulled together into a frown.

Is he jealous of the guards he himself chose?

"You remember my instructions, right?" Lucas snaps, glaring at the two men, and I realize that he's indeed displeased with them. "All of them?"

"Yes, of course," Eduardo says quickly. Diego's grin disappears, and both guards stand up straighter. "You have nothing to worry about," the shorter man adds.

"Good." Lucas gives them a hard look before turning to me. "I'll see you in two weeks, okay?" he says in a softer tone, and I nod, trying to avoid meeting his pale gaze.

I have a terrible suspicion my dream last night might not have been entirely in my imagination.

Lucas pauses for a second, as if he wants to say something, but then he just turns and leaves, walking out of the kitchen. A few seconds later, I hear the front door close.

My captor is gone.

"So," Diego says cheerfully, bringing my attention back to him. He's grinning again, his arms crossed over his broad chest. "What's for breakfast?"

I MAKE AN OMELET FOR MYSELF AND THE TWO GUARDS, BEING careful not to do anything suspicious. They may seem friendly, but I don't mistake their smiles for anything but an amicable mask.

Nice guys don't work for illegal arms dealers, and these two have a good reason to hate me—if they know about my role in the plane crash, that is.

"So, Yulia," Eduardo says, gobbling down his omelet with evident gusto, "how did you learn to cook like this? Is that a Russian thing?"

"I'm Ukrainian, not Russian," I say. Though the difference in my hometown region is slight, I prefer to think of myself as belonging to the country of my employers. "And yes, it's somewhat of an Eastern European 'thing.' Many people there still regard cooking as a necessary skill for a woman."

"Oh, it's necessary, all right." Diego forks the last bite of his omelet into his mouth and glances longingly at the empty frying pan. "Should be mandatory, as far as I'm concerned."

"Sure. Just like cleaning, laundry, and taking care of the kids, right?" I give the two men a syrupy-sweet smile.

"If a woman looked like you, I'd do the laundry," Eduardo says with apparent seriousness. "But cleaning… I guess help with that would be nice."

I laugh, unable to help myself. The guy's not even trying to conceal his chauvinistic views.

"I think what Eduardo's trying to say is that Lucas is a lucky guy," Diego says diplomatically, kicking the other guard under the table. "That's all."

"Right." I suppress the urge to roll my eyes. "I'm sure that's it."

"You bet." Diego winks at me and gets up to throw out his paper plate. "Eduardo's just spoiled," he explains, returning to the table. "First his *mamacita* babied him, then his ex-girlfriend."

"Shut up," Eduardo mutters, glowering at Diego. "Rosa didn't baby me. She was just good at domestic things."

"Rosa?" My ears perk up at the familiar name.

"Yeah, she's Esguerra's maid," Diego says. "Sweet girl. Way too good for this guy here"—he jerks his thumb toward Eduardo—"so she dumped his ass months ago."

"Oh, I see," I say, trying not to appear too interested. If Rosa had dated Eduardo at some point, that explains how she knows about their poker games. "Does Esguerra have many servants?"

"Not really," Eduardo answers, getting up to throw out his empty plate. He's frowning; I guess the memory of being dumped by Rosa is not a pleasant one. "We should get going," he says abruptly, then glances at me. "Are you almost done with your food, Yulia?"

I nod, consuming the remnants of my omelet. "Yes." I carry my plate to the garbage and dump it, then wash the frying pan and place it on a paper towel to dry. "All done."

"Good." Diego smiles at me, his dark eyes gleaming. "Then go use the restroom, and we'll take you on your morning walk."

~

AS THE TWO MEN LEAD ME ON A BRISK STROLL THROUGH THE FOREST, I decide they most likely don't know about my involvement in the plane crash that killed their colleagues. Or if they do, they're excellent actors. They banter with me as easily as they do with each other, their manner friendly and relaxed. They don't seem like killers—except I see the guns stuck in the waistband of their jeans.

If they're ordered to plant a bullet in my brain, I'm sure neither one will hesitate to do so.

Our walk takes about twenty minutes, and then they bring me back to Lucas's house.

"All right, chica," Diego says, leading me to Lucas's library. "Your boyfriend said this is your usual spot. Grab whatever book you want, and then we have some work to do."

"Boyfriend?" Startled, I look at the guard. "You mean, Lucas?"

Diego grins. "That's the one. Unless you have more than one around here?"

I bite back a denial and grab a book at random. Lucas is definitely *not* my boyfriend, but if that's what they think, it could play to my advantage.

It could also explain why the two guards are being so nice to me, I realize as I walk over to the armchair. It's generally smart to show respect to the girlfriend of one's boss—even if that girlfriend is to be handcuffed and tied up most of the time.

Sitting down, I place the book on my lap, take a deep breath, and extend my wrists toward Diego. "Go ahead. I'm ready."

33

ucas

Our flight to Chicago is uneventful. Esguerra stops by the pilot's cabin every couple of hours to check on things, but for the most part, he stays in the main cabin with his wife and Rosa, who's accompanying them on this trip.

"Nora is still sleeping," he says, stopping by again an hour before we land. His dark eyebrows are drawn into a worried frown. "Do you think this is normal, to sleep this much?"

"Pregnant women need a lot of rest, or so I've heard," I say, concealing a smile. Esguerra's acting like no woman has ever carried a baby before. "I'm sure it's fine."

He nods and disappears back into the cabin. *Probably to watch over Nora*, I think with amusement before turning my attention back to the controls.

After the crash, I'm leaving nothing to chance.

We land at a small private airport just outside Chicago, where an armored limo is waiting for us on the runway. I've sent most of the guards ahead of us, and they've scrubbed this airport top to bottom, so I know it's safe. Still, I automatically scan our surroundings for danger before walking over to the limo and getting into the driver's seat.

One can never be too careful in our line of work.

As I drive the limo to Nora's parents' house, my thoughts turn to Yulia. Esguerra is in the back with Nora and Rosa, and everything is quiet on the road, so I decide to use this time to call Diego.

"How's it going?" I ask as soon as the guard picks up.

"Well, let's see…" He sounds like he's on the verge of laughing. "For breakfast, she made an amazing omelet. For lunch, she fed us the best chicken I've ever had, and for dinner, she's grilling pork chops and baking a chocolate cake. So I'd say it's going pretty well. Oh, and we took her for a walk this morning."

"She's behaving? No escape attempts?"

"Are you kidding me? Your girl's a model prisoner. She even taught us a few swear words in Russian at lunch. Like *yob tvoyu mat'—*"

"Excellent." I grit my teeth, battling a swell of irrational jealousy. I know I can trust these two guards, but it still bothers me that they seem to be getting so chummy with my captive. Loyal or not, they're still men, and I know how easy it is to get obsessed with Yulia. "Don't forget to handcuff her to the bedside pole at night."

"You got it, man."

"Good." I draw in a deep breath. "And, Diego, if you or Eduardo so much as lay a finger on her—"

"We would never." The young Mexican sounds insulted. "She's yours, we know that."

"All right." I force myself to relax my grip on the wheel. "Call me if anything comes up."

And disconnecting, I turn my attention back to the road.

Esguerra's dinner with his in-laws passes without an incident until Frank, Esguerra's CIA contact, decides to pay us a visit. He insists on speaking with Esguerra, so I call my boss outside after first making sure our snipers are in position.

If the US agency decides to double-cross us tonight, they'll have a battle on their hands.

Fortunately, Frank doesn't seem to be suicidal. He sends his car away and goes for a walk with Esguerra. I follow at a small distance, keeping my hand on the gun inside my jacket. They don't go far, just to the nearest park and back.

"What did they want?" I ask Esguerra when Frank's black Lincoln pulls away.

"For us to stay the fuck out of their country," Esguerra explains. "Apparently, the FBI is going apeshit—Frank's words, not mine. They're worried about why we're here. Plus, there's the whole matter of Nora's abduction."

"Right. So what did you tell him?"

"That we're not here on business, and that we'll leave when we're good and ready. Now if you'll excuse me, I have a family dinner to get back to." He disappears back into the house, and I head to the limo, shaking my head in disbelief.

My boss has balls, I have to give him that.

It's late by the time Esguerra's dinner is over. Fortunately, it's not a long drive to Palos Park, a wealthy community where Esguerra bought a mansion on my recommendation.

"It'll be more secure than a hotel," I told him when we began planning the trip two weeks ago. "This specific house is particularly good because it's fenced in and has an electronic gate, not to mention a long driveway—optimal for privacy."

When we pull up to the mansion, Esguerra, Nora, and Rosa go inside while I check in with the guards to make sure they're properly positioned and know what to do in case of emergencies. It takes me over an hour, and by the time I finally enter the house, I'm more than ready to hit the sack. First, though, I need to grab a bite to eat; the two energy bars I ate in the car were a shitty substitute for dinner.

I clearly got spoiled by Yulia's cooking.

"Oh, hi, Lucas," Rosa says when I enter the kitchen. Her cheeks flush as she looks at me. I must've caught her on her way to bed, because she's wearing long pajamas and cradling a cup of steaming milk. "I didn't realize you were still up."

"Yeah, I had to do some last-minute security checks," I say, suppressing a yawn. "Why are you awake?"

"I couldn't sleep. Too many new impressions, I guess." Her full lips curve in a wry smile. "I've never flown before—or been to America."

"I see." Battling another yawn, I make my way over to the fridge and open it. It's fully stocked already—I made the arrangements for food delivery myself—so I grab some cheese and a loaf of bread to make myself a sandwich.

"Do you want me to make you something?" Rosa offers, watching me uncertainly. "I can whip up something in a minute."

"It's nice of you to offer, thanks, but you should go to sleep." I slap a slice of cheese on a piece of bread and bite into the dry sandwich. "I'm sure you'll have plenty of cooking to do tomorrow," I say after I chew and swallow.

"Yeah, well, that's my job." She shrugs, then adds, "Though you're probably right—I think Señor Esguerra is hoping to impress Nora's parents tomorrow night."

"Hmm-mm." I finish the rest of the sandwich in three bites and put the cheese back in the refrigerator. "Have a good night, Rosa," I say, turning to leave.

"You too." She watches me walk out of the room, her expression oddly tense, but I'm too tired to wonder about what's on her mind.

When I get to my room, I take a quick shower and fall into bed. Surprisingly, sleep doesn't come right away. Instead, I lie awake for several minutes, tossing and turning on a king-sized mattress that feels cold and far too empty.

It's been less than a day, and I already miss Yulia.

Two weeks, I tell myself. I just need to get through the next two weeks. Then I'll be home, and Yulia will be in my arms every night again.

34

ulia

I STARE AT THE DARK CEILING, UNABLE TO CLOSE MY EYES DESPITE the late hour. It's strange being in Lucas's bed without him... feeling the cold steel of the handcuffs anchoring me to the bedside pole instead of to his wrist. I've gotten used to sleeping tucked into his large warm body, and even with the blanket drawn up to my chin, I feel cold and exposed as I lie there alone, trying to relax enough to go to sleep.

Diego and Eduardo have been good jailers so far. They adhered to the routine Lucas must've laid out to them, letting me eat, stretch, use the restroom, and read in the comfortable armchair. They also kept me company at mealtimes, though I suspect the food I cooked had a lot to do with that. By the time our dinner was over, I decided that I like both of them—as much as it's possible to like mercenaries whose job is to keep you captive. Rosa was right about them being good guys; under different circumstances, we might've been friends.

I hope Lucas won't punish them too harshly for my escape—assuming I succeed tomorrow, that is.

Thinking about tomorrow chases away whatever little sleepiness I was beginning to feel. To alleviate my anxiety, I mentally go over the details of my plan again. It's simple: Right after lunch, I'll use the tools Rosa gave me to free myself and make a run for the northern border of the estate, where the guards at North Tower Two might be distracted with their poker game. Diego and Eduardo will be at that poker game, so they won't come looking for me until after six p.m. By then, I'll be on the delivery truck—which, hopefully, will be far away from Esguerra's compound at that point.

If all goes well, tomorrow evening I will no longer be Lucas Kent's prisoner.

I should be excited, but instead, there's a hollow ache in my chest. The dream from last night—if it was a dream—is still painfully vivid in my mind. For a brief moment, I forgot who we are, what passed between us, and I told Lucas something I didn't know myself until that moment.

"Do you hate me?" he asked, and like an idiot, I said I loved him.

I admitted my terrible, irrational weakness to a man who's hurt me with every weapon I've given him.

Maybe I didn't say the words out loud. Maybe it *was* a dream—or, more precisely, a nightmare. Except if that's the case, why did Lucas bring up last night when he was telling me goodbye? Why did he say that he'll miss me?

Groaning, I turn onto my side and punch the pillow with my free hand. I must be sick, or at least brainwashed by my captivity. I can't be in love with a man who intends to destroy my brother.

I can't be the idiot who's fallen for a killer with an ice rock instead of a heart.

I'll miss you.

His deep voice whispers through my mind, and I squeeze my eyelids together, trying to shut it out. Whatever I'm feeling, whether it's love or temporary insanity, will pass once I'm far away from here.

I have to believe that, so I can focus on my escape.

BREAKFAST AND LUNCH DRAG BY WITH AGONIZING SLOWNESS. BY THE time Diego and Eduardo tie me to the armchair and leave, I'm ready to jump out of my skin. I hope they couldn't tell how anxious I am; I did my best to act normal, but I don't know if I succeeded.

After I hear the front door close behind them, I sit quietly for a few minutes, making sure they're not coming back. When I'm satisfied that my jailers are gone, I begin to move. My heart is beating in a fast, desperate rhythm, and my palms are sweating as I carefully reach into the chair cushions for the items Rosa gave me.

I fish out the hairpin first. With the ropes securing my upper arms to the chair, my range of motion is limited, but I manage to stick the pin into the lock of the cuffs. I'm far from an expert lock picker, but they taught us this during training, so after a few failed attempts, I succeed in opening the cuffs.

The razor blade is next. With my hands no longer stuck together, I wedge the tiny blade under the ropes around my upper arms and saw through them. It's not an easy task—I'm bleeding from several cuts by the time I'm done with one thick rope—but I'm determined, and ten minutes later, I've sawed through enough ropes to be able to wiggle out of the chair.

Step one of the plan complete.

Next, I rush to the kitchen and grab two water bottles and a few energy bars I found in one of the cabinets. I don't expect to be in the jungle for long, but it's best to be prepared. At this time of day, the heat could dehydrate me in a matter of hours. I also take the sharpest kitchen knife I can find and slip the razor blade and the hairpin into the pocket of my shorts, just in case. I put the food and the knife in a backpack I find in Lucas's closet, and then I head for the door in Lucas's bedroom—the one that leads to the backyard and the jungle beyond.

Holding my breath, I open the door and scan the area. There's no sign of the guards, and all I hear are the usual nature noises.

So far, so good.

I step outside and close the door behind me. A wave of humid heat washes over me, making my clothes stick to my skin. I was right to take those water bottles. I'll have to go north for two and a half miles and then west along the river to reach the dirt road Rosa mentioned, and I'll need to drink on the way.

Taking a breath to steady my nerves, I head toward the trees behind the house. My sneakers—the footwear Lucas got me for our walks—make almost no noise as I enter the thick jungle, and I exhale in relief as the canopy of trees closes over my head, concealing me from any potential eyes in the sky.

Now I need to get to the border and locate the road by which the delivery truck will be leaving the estate at some point after three p.m.

Sweat gathers under my arms and drips down my back as I walk briskly, trying not to step on any insects or snakes. Thin tree, thick tree, a cluster of bushes, a fallen log—these landmarks are how I track my progress. Focusing on my immediate surroundings helps me not think about the drones that might be hovering overhead or the guard towers I'll have to pass on my way to the border. Rosa told me North Tower Two is the one where the guards play poker, but I have no idea how I'll distinguish between that tower and some other one.

If there's a North Tower Two, there must be a North Tower One, and if I stumble upon the wrong tower, I'm screwed.

After a half hour, I take out the first bottle and gulp down most of the water, then wipe the sweat off my face with the bottom of my shirt. Even in the shorts and skimpy tank top I'm wearing, the heat is difficult to bear.

Just a little longer, I tell myself. It can't be that far to the river now. I just need to reach it and then follow it west until I get to the road.

It's at most another half hour of walking.

"Alto!"

At the harshly yelled Spanish command, I freeze, instinctively raising my hands. The water bottle falls out of my nerveless fingers. *Oh, shit. Shit, shit, shit.*

The male voice barks another command at me, and I turn around slowly on the assumption that that's what he told me to do.

A dark-haired musclebound man is standing a couple of meters in front of me, his M16 pointed at my chest. He's dressed in camouflage pants and a sleeveless shirt, and I see a radio hanging on his hip.

It's one of the guards. He must've been patrolling the forest and spotted me.

I'm so, so fucked.

Glaring at me, the guard says something in Spanish, and I shake my head. "Sorry." I moisten my parched lips. "I don't speak much Spanish."

The young man's glower deepens. "Who are you? What are you doing here?" he says in heavily accented English.

"I'm—" I swallow, feeling sweat trickling down my temples. "I'm staying with Lucas."

"Lucas Kent?" The guard looks confused for a moment; then his dark eyes widen. "You are the prisoner."

"Um, kind of. But now I'm his guest." I attempt a shaky smile as I slowly lower my hands to my sides. "You know how that goes."

An understanding look comes over the guard's face. "You are his *puta*."

I'm pretty sure he just called me a whore, but I nod and widen my smile, hoping it looks seductive rather than frightened. "He likes me," I say, pulling my shoulders back to thrust my braless breasts forward. "You know what I mean?"

The man's gaze slides from my face to my sweat-dampened tank top. "Sí." His voice is slightly hoarse. "I know what you mean."

I take a step toward him, keeping the smile on my face. "He's away," I say, making sure to roll my hips. "Went on a trip with your boss."

"With Esguerra, yes." The man seems hypnotized by my breasts, which sway with my movement. "On a trip."

"Right." I take another step forward. "I got bored sitting at home."

"Bored?" The guard finally manages to tear his gaze away from my chest. His eyes are slightly glazed as he looks at my face, but his weapon is still pointed at me. "You should not be out here."

"I know." I purposefully bite my lower lip. "Lucas lets me go out into the backyard. There was a pretty bird, I followed it, and I got lost."

It's the stupidest story ever, but the guard doesn't seem to think so. Then again, the fact that he's staring at my lips like he wants to eat them may have something to do with that.

"So, yes, maybe you can point me back to his house," I continue when he remains silent. I risk another tiny step toward him. "It's very hot today."

"Yes." He lowers his weapon and takes hold of my left arm. "Come. I will take you there."

"Thank you." I smile as brightly as I can and jab my right hand up, ramming the heel of my palm into the underside of his nose.

There's a crunching noise, followed by a spray of red. The guard stumbles back, reflexively clutching his broken nose, and I grab the barrel of his M16, kicking at his knee as I yank the assault rifle toward me.

My foot connects with his knee, but the man doesn't let go. Instead, he releases his nose and grips the weapon with both hands, pulling it—and me—toward him.

He may not be as well trained as Lucas, but he's still much stronger than me.

Realizing I only have seconds before he wrestles me to the ground, I stop pulling and push the gun toward him instead, causing him to lose his balance for a moment. At the same time, I kick upward between his legs as hard as I can.

My sneaker meets its target: the guard's balls. A choked gasp escapes the man's throat, followed by a high-pitched scream as he bends at the waist. His face turns sickly pale, and his grip on the gun loosens for a second—which is all the time I need.

Jerking the heavy weapon out of the guard's hands, I swing it at his head.

The rifle makes a loud *thud* as it meets his skull. The impact of the collision sends a shock of pain through my arms, but my opponent drops like a stone.

I have no idea if he's unconscious or dead, and I don't waste time checking. If there are other guards in the vicinity, they might've heard his scream.

Clutching the M16, I begin running.

Tree. Bush. A gnarled root. An ant hill. The tiny landmarks blur in front of my eyes as I run, my breath rattling loudly in my ears. Every couple of minutes, I glance behind me for signs of pursuit, but none are evident, and after a few minutes, I risk slowing down to a jog.

Where the hell is that river? Two and a half miles is about four kilometers; it shouldn't take this long to get there.

Before I have a chance to wonder if Rosa might've lied, the ground in front of me suddenly slopes downward at a sharp angle. I skid to a stop, barely managing to avoid tumbling down the incline, and through the thick tangle of bushes in front of me, I see a shimmer of blue below.

The river.

I'm at the northern border of Esguerra's compound.

My breath whooshes out in relief. I start forward to get a closer look—and freeze again.

Less than a hundred meters to my left is a guard tower.

The trees had obscured it from my view.

I back up and crouch behind the nearest tree, desperately hoping the guards didn't spot me yet. When I don't hear shouts or gunshots, I risk peeking out to look at the tower again.

The structure is tall and ominous, looming over the forest. At the top is a solid square enclosure with slits instead of windows, and around the enclosure is an open-air walkway. I don't see any guards on the walkway, but they're all probably inside, hiding from the stifling heat in the shade. There are no markings on the structure. It could be North Tower Two, or it could be some other one. There's no way for me to know.

I'll be passing right by it if I head west, and if the guards inside the enclosure look outside, I'll be caught in an instant.

For a moment, I consider turning back and trying to locate the road when I'm farther south, out of sight of this guard tower, but I decide against that. There could be more towers there. Plus, Rosa said the security software focuses on things *approaching* the estate. That means the computer might flag anything moving south from this point.

I have to either cross the river here, or turn west now and attempt to find the road where it intersects with this river.

I look at the river. With the thick bushes blocking my view, I can't tell how wide or deep it is. It could easily have a strong current or, since it's the Amazon rainforest, be teeming with crocodiles. If I were a particularly strong swimmer, I'd risk it, but crossing jungle rivers wasn't a big part of my training.

I glance at the tower again. Still no guards on the walkway. Could they be playing poker inside?

I vacillate between my two options for a minute, debating the pros and cons of each, but ultimately, it's the position of the sun that helps me make my decision. It's moving lower in the sky, signifying that the afternoon is wearing on. I don't have a watch, so I don't know the time, but it's probably getting close to three p.m.

If I don't locate the road soon, I risk missing the delivery truck, and then it won't matter if the guards in the tower spot me or not. Once Diego and Eduardo realize I'm missing, I'll be found in a matter of hours if I'm still in this jungle on foot.

Trying to steady my shaking hands, I place the M16 on the ground. I'm much more likely to get shot if I'm visibly armed, and one assault rifle won't help me against guards who are better armed and have the protection of the enclosure.

With one last look at the river, I leave the shelter of my tree and head west, toward the tower.

Thin tree. Thick tree. Root. Bush. A cluster of wild flowers. I stare at the plant life as I walk, the fear like icy fingers clawing at my chest. The tower looms closer—I can see it in my peripheral vision now—and I focus on not looking at it, on moving slowly and deliberately, just one foot in front of another.

Thick tree. Another thick tree. A small ditch that I have to jump over. My heart feels like it might leap out of my throat, but I keep moving, keep not looking at the tower. It's parallel to me, then slightly behind me, and I still keep my gaze trained ahead and walk at the same measured pace.

My skin crawls and the back of my neck tingles as I cross a small clearing, but there are still no shouts or gunfire.

They don't see me.

This must be North Tower Two.

I risk picking up my pace slightly, and when I glance back a couple of minutes later, the tower is no longer visible.

I stop and lean against a tree trunk, my knees going weak with relief.

I made it past the tower without getting shot.

When my frantic heartbeat slows a little, I force myself to straighten and keep going.

I don't know how long it takes before I reach the road, but the sun is hovering lower in the sky when I find it. The road is not much—it's just an unpaved path cutting through the jungle—but at the point where it meets the river, it widens onto a sturdy wooden bridge.

I stop and listen, but all is silent. No sounds of a car approaching, no signs of the guards.

I turn onto the bridge and start walking. Immediately, I realize I was right not to try crossing the river at the earlier location. The river is wide, and both banks are steep, almost cliff-like. Even if I made it across, I would've had trouble climbing up the other side.

I keep walking, and soon the bridge—and Esguerra's compound—is behind me. I try to keep to the tree line as much as I can while staying by the road. I don't want to be spotted by any drones that might be patrolling the area, but I can't chance missing the returning delivery truck.

I walk for what feels like hours before I finally hear the rumble of a car engine.

This is it.

I take out the knife I stole from Lucas's kitchen and stick it into the waistband of my shorts, covering the handle with the bottom of my tank top. I hope I won't have to use the knife, but it's best to be prepared.

Ignoring the frantic hammering of my pulse, I step out onto the road and wait for the vehicle to approach.

It's a van, not a truck as I supposed. It stops in front of me, and the driver—a short middle-aged man with darkly bronzed skin—jumps out, staring at me in surprise. He asks something in Spanish, and I shake my head, saying, "Tourist. I'm an American tourist, and I got lost. Please help me."

He looks even more surprised and says something in rapid-fire Spanish.

I shake my head again. "Sorry, I don't speak Spanish."

He frowns and looks around, as if expecting a translator to

jump out from the bushes. When nothing happens, he shrugs and motions for me to follow him to the car.

I climb into the passenger seat next to him, making sure to keep my hand close to the knife at my side. The delivery man could be Esguerra's employee, or he could be a civilian who just happens to deliver food to an arms dealer's estate.

Either way, if he tries anything—or attempts to call anyone —I'm ready.

The driver starts the car, and the van begins moving, heading north on the dirt road. After a few minutes, the man puts on some music and starts humming along under his breath. I smile at him and move my hand off the knife handle.

I made it.

I escaped.

Now I can warn Obenko and save my brother.

"Goodbye, Lucas," I whisper soundlessly as the van bumps along the unpaved road, carrying me away from my captor.

Carrying me away from the man I love.

CLAIM ME

CAPTURE ME: BOOK 3

I

THE ESCAPE

1

ucas

"SAY THAT AGAIN?" I GRIP THE PHONE TIGHTER, NEARLY CRUSHING IT as my disbelief morphs into burning fury. "What the fuck do you mean she escaped?"

"I don't know how it happened." Eduardo's voice is tense. "We came back to your house a half hour ago and found her missing. The handcuffs were on the floor of your library, and the ropes were sawed through with something small and sharp. We had the guards scour every inch of the jungle, and they found Sanchez unconscious by the northern border. He has a hell of a concussion, but we got him to wake up a few minutes ago. He says he came across her in the forest, but she surprised him and knocked him out. That was over three hours ago. We're getting the drone feeds now, but it's not looking good."

My rage deepens with every sentence the guard speaks. "How

did she get her hands on 'something small and sharp'? Or open the fucking handcuffs? You and Diego were supposed to watch her at all times—"

"We did." Eduardo sounds bewildered. "We checked her pockets after each meal, like you said, and we inspected the bathroom—the only place she's been alone and untied—several times. There was nothing there she could've used. She must've concealed the tools somehow, but I don't know how or when. Maybe she's had them for a while, or maybe—"

"Okay, let's suppose you didn't completely fuck up." I take a breath to control the explosive anger in my chest. The important thing now is to get answers and figure out where the holes in our security are. In a calmer tone, I say, "How could she have gotten out without triggering the alarms or any of the guard towers spotting her? We have eyes on every foot of that border."

There's a prolonged silence. Then Eduardo says quietly, "I don't know why none of the security alarms were triggered, but it's possible there were a couple of hours when we didn't have eyes on the border at all locations."

"What?" I can't hold back my anger this time. "What the fuck do you mean by that?"

"We did fuck up, Kent, but I swear to you, we had no idea the security software would let anything slide." The young guard is speaking quickly now, as if anxious to get the words out. "It was just a friendly poker game; we didn't know the computer wouldn't—"

"A poker game?" My voice goes deadly quiet. "You were playing poker while on duty?"

"I know." Eduardo sounds genuinely contrite. "It was stupid and irresponsible, and I'm sure Esguerra will have our hides. We just thought that with all the technology, it wouldn't be a big deal. Just a way to get out of the afternoon heat for a couple of hours, you know?"

If I could reach through the phone and crush Eduardo's windpipe, I would. "No, I don't know." I'm all but biting out the words. "Why don't you explain it to me, all nice and slow? Or better yet, put Diego on the line, so *he* can do it."

There's another bout of silence. Then I hear Diego say, "Lucas, listen, man… I don't even know what to say." The guard's normally upbeat voice is heavy with guilt. "I don't know why she decided to go past that tower, but I'm looking at the footage from the drones now, and that's exactly what she did. Just walked right by us, heading west, and then got on the bridge. It's like she knew where to go and when." A note of incredulity creeps into his tone. "Like she knew we'd be distracted."

I pinch the bridge of my nose. *Fuck.* If what he's saying is true, Yulia's escape is not dumb luck.

Someone gave my captive key security details—someone intimately familiar with the guards' schedule.

"Did she come in contact with anyone?" The most logical possibility is that the traitor is either Diego or Eduardo, but I know the young guards well, and they're both too loyal and too smart for this kind of double cross. "Did anyone talk to her besides the two of you?"

"No. At least, we didn't see anyone." Diego's voice tightens as he catches on to my suspicion. "Of course, she was by herself for a large portion of the day; someone could've come to the house when we weren't there."

"Right." Hell, the traitor could've even approached Yulia before I left for Chicago. "I want you to pull up the drone footage on any and all activity around my house in the past two weeks. If anyone so much as stepped a foot on my porch, I want to know."

"You got it."

"Good. Now get going and track down Yulia. She couldn't have gotten far."

Diego hangs up, clearly eager to make up for his and Eduardo's blunder, and I put the phone back in my pocket, forcing my fingers to unclench from around the object.

They'll catch her and bring her back.

I have to believe that, or I won't be able to function this evening.

~

WHILE I WAIT FOR AN UPDATE FROM DIEGO, I DO THE ROUNDS WITH the guards, making sure they're all in position at Esguerra's new Chicago vacation home. The mansion is in the wealthy private community of Palos Park and well situated from a security standpoint, but I still check the newly installed cameras for blind spots and confirm the patrol schedules with the guards. I do this because it's my job, but also because I need something to keep my mind off Yulia and the suffocating anger burning in my chest.

She ran. The moment I was gone, she ran to her lover—to this Misha, whose life she begged me to spare.

She ran even though less than two days ago she told me she loved me.

The fury that fills me at the thought is both potent and irrational. I don't even know if Yulia's words had been meant for me; she mumbled them while half-asleep, and I didn't have a chance to confront her. Still, the possibility that she might love me had kept me tossing and turning the night before my departure.

For the first time in my life, I'd felt like I was close to something… close to some*one*.

I love you. I'm yours.

What a fucking liar. My ribcage tightens as I recall Yulia's attempts to manipulate me, to butter me up so I'd agree to save her lover's life. From the very beginning, I've been just a means to an end for her. She slept with me in Moscow to get information, and she played the part of an obedient captive to facilitate her escape.

The time we spent together meant nothing to Yulia, and neither do I.

The buzzing of the phone in my pocket interrupts my bitter

thoughts. Fishing it out, I see the encrypted number that's our relay from the compound.

"Yes?"

"We have a problem." Diego's tone is clipped. "It looks like your girl timed her escape perfectly in more ways than one. There was a delivery of groceries to the compound this afternoon, and the Miraflores police just found the driver walking on the side of the road, a few kilometers outside town. Apparently, he picked up a beautiful American hitchhiker just north of our compound. He had no idea she was anything other than a lost tourist—that is, until she pulled out a knife and made him get out of the van. That was over an hour ago."

"Fuck." If Yulia has wheels, her chances of eluding us go up exponentially. "Search all of Miraflores and find that van. Get the local police to help."

"We're already on it. I'll keep you posted."

I hang up and head back into the house. Esguerra's in-laws are already pulling into the driveway for their dinner with my boss and his wife, and Esguerra is likely not in the mood to be bothered right now. Still, I have to let him know what happened, so I send a one-line email:

Yulia Tzakova escaped.

2

ulia

As soon as I'm in the city bounds of Miraflores, I pull into a gas station and ask the attendant to use the landline in the tiny store. He understands enough of my English to let me do so, and I dial the emergency number all UUR agents have memorized. As I wait for the call to connect, I watch the door, my palms slick with sweat.

Diego and Eduardo must know I'm missing by now, which means Esguerra's guards are looking for me. I felt bad threatening the van's driver and forcing him to get out of the car, but I needed the vehicle. As it is, I don't have long before Esguerra's men track me here—if they haven't already.

"Allo." The Russian greeting, spoken in a mellow female voice, brings my attention back to the phone.

"It's Yulia Tzakova," I say, giving my current identity. Like the operator, I'm speaking Russian. "I'm in Miraflores, Colombia, and need to speak to Vasiliy Obenko right away."

"Code?"

I rattle off a set of numbers, then answer the operator's questions designed to verify my identity.

"Please hold," she says, and there's a moment of silence before I hear a click signifying a new connection.

"Yulia?" Obenko's voice is filled with disbelief. "You're alive? The Russians' report said you died in prison. How did you—"

"The report was false. Esguerra's men took me." I keep my voice low, cognizant that the attendant is eyeing me with increasing suspicion. I told him I'm an American tourist, and my speaking Russian undoubtedly confuses him. "Listen, you're in danger. Everyone connected to UUR is in danger. You need to disappear and have Misha disappear—"

"Esguerra got you?" Obenko sounds horrified. "Then how are you—"

"There's no time to explain. I escaped from his compound, but they're looking for me. You need to disappear—you and everyone in your family. And Misha. They'll be coming for you."

"They cracked you?"

"Yes." Self-loathing is a thick knot in my throat, but I keep my voice even. "They don't know your current location, but they have the agency's initials and one former agent's real name. It's only a matter of time before they track you down."

"Fuck." Obenko goes silent for a moment, then says, "We need to get you out of there before you're recaptured." Before they have a chance to extract more information out of me, he means.

"Yes." The attendant is typing something on his cell phone while glancing at me, and I know I need to hurry. "I have a car, but I'll need help getting out of the country."

"All right. Can you get closer to Bogotá? We may be able to call in some favors with the Venezuelan government and smuggle you out across the border."

"I think so." The attendant puts down his phone and starts toward me, so I say quickly, "I'm on my way," and hang up.

The attendant is almost next to me, his forehead furrowed, but I hurry out of the store before he can grab me. Jumping into the van, I shut the door behind me and start the car. The attendant runs out behind me, but I'm already peeling out of the parking lot with a squeal of tires.

When I'm back on the road, I assess my situation. There's only a quarter tank of gas left in the van, and the attendant most likely reported me to the authorities—which means the vehicle became compromised faster than I expected.

I'll need a different set of wheels if I'm to make it out of Miraflores.

My heart hammers as I step on the gas, pushing the old van to its limits while keeping a careful eye on the road. One kilometer, one-point-five kilometers, two kilometers… My anxiety intensifies with every moment that passes. How long before Esguerra's men hear about the strange blonde at the gas station? How long until they start looking for the van via satellites? I can't have more than a half hour at this point.

Finally, after another kilometer, I see it: a small unpaved road that appears to lead to a farm of some kind. Praying that my hunch is correct, I turn onto it, leaving the main road.

A couple of hundred meters later, I spot a storage shed. It's a dozen meters to the right, and behind it is a thickly wooded area. I turn toward it and park the van behind the shed, under the cover of the trees. If I'm lucky, it won't be spotted for some time.

Now I need to locate another vehicle.

Leaving the shed, I walk until I come across a barn with an old, beaten-up tractor in front of it. I don't see any people, so I approach the barn and peek inside.

Jackpot.

Inside the barn is a small pick-up truck. It looks old and rusty, but its windows are clean. Someone uses it regularly.

Holding my breath, I slip into the barn and approach the truck. The first thing I do is search the nearby shelves for keys; sometimes people are stupid enough to leave them next to the vehicle.

Unfortunately, this particular farmer doesn't seem to be stupid. The keys are nowhere to be found. Oh, well. I glance around and see a rock holding down a piece of tarp. I grab the rock and use it to smash the truck's window. It's a brute-force solution, but it's faster than picking the locks.

Now comes the hard part.

Opening the driver's door, I climb onto the seat and remove the ignition cover under the wheel. Then I study the tangle of wires, hoping I remember enough of this to not disable the vehicle or electrocute myself. We covered hot-wiring in training, but I've never had to do it in the field, and I have no idea if it'll work. Every car is a little different; there's no universal color system for the wires, and older cars, like this pick-up truck, are particularly tricky. If I had any other option, I wouldn't risk it, but this is my best bet right now.

Here goes nothing. Steadying my breathing, I begin testing the different combinations of wires. On my third attempt, the truck's engine sputters to life.

I exhale a relieved breath, close the door, and drive out of the barn, heading back toward the main road.

With any luck, the truck's owner won't discover it missing for some time, and I'll make it to the next town before I have to get another vehicle.

~

As I drive, my thoughts turn to Lucas. Did the guards tell him about my escape? Is he angry? Does he feel like I betrayed him by leaving?

I love you. I'm yours. Even now, my cheeks flame as I remember those words, said in a dream that might not have been a dream.

Until that night, I didn't know how I felt, didn't realize how attached I'd become to my jailer. There was so much wrongness between us, so much fear and anger and mistrust that it took me a while to understand this strange longing.

To make sense of something so irrational and senseless.

I'll miss you. Lucas said that to me as he cuddled me on his lap the next morning, and it was all I could do not to burst into tears. Did he know what he was doing to me with his confusing words of caring? Was that incongruous tenderness part of his diabolical revenge? An even more sadistic way to wreck me without inflicting so much as a bruise?

The road blurs in front of me, and I realize the tears I held back that day are rolling down my face, the adrenaline from my escape sharpening the remembered pain. I don't want to think about how Lucas broke me, how he promised me safety and tore my heart to pieces instead, but I can't help it. The memories loop through my mind, and I can't shut them off. Something about Lucas's behavior that last day keeps nagging at me, some discordant note I registered but didn't process fully at the time.

"Do not fucking beg for him," Lucas snapped when I pleaded for my brother to be spared. "I decide who lives, not you."

There were other things he said, too. Hurtful things. Yet when he took me that night, there hadn't been anger in his touch. Lust, yes. Insane possessiveness, definitely. But not anger—at least not the kind of anger I would've expected from a man who hates me enough to let my only family be murdered. And that "I'll miss you" the following morning. It just didn't fit.

None of it fit—unless that's how Lucas wanted it.

Maybe he wasn't done mind-fucking me yet.

My head begins to ache from the confusion, and I wipe the tears off my face before tightening my grip on the wheel. Whatever Lucas planned for me no longer matters. I escaped, and I can't keep looking back.

I have to keep moving forward.

3

ucas

I WAKE UP FRIDAY MORNING WITH A THROBBING HEADACHE THAT adds to my fury. I've barely slept—Diego and Eduardo kept sending me hourly updates on their search for Yulia—and it takes two cups of coffee before I start feeling semi-human.

As I'm getting ready to leave the kitchen, Rosa walks in, dressed in jeans instead of her usual conservative maid's outfit.

"Oh, hi, Lucas," she says. "I was just looking for you."

"Oh?" I try not to glower at the girl. I still feel bad that I had to squash her little crush on me. It's not Rosa's fault that my prisoner escaped, and I don't want to take out my shitty mood on the girl.

"Señor Esguerra said I can explore the city today if I take a guard with me," Rosa says, watching me warily. She must've picked up on my anger despite my attempts to look calm. "Is there anybody you could spare?"

I consider her request. Truthfully, the answer is no. I don't want to take any guards away from Nora's parents' house, and fifteen minutes ago, Esguerra texted me that he's taking Nora to a park, which means he'll need at least a dozen of our men to be in position there.

"I'm going to Chicago today," I say after a moment of deliberation. "I have a meeting there. You can come with me if you don't mind waiting for a bit. Afterwards, I'll take you wherever you want to go, and by lunchtime, one of the other guys will be available to replace me—assuming you want to stay in the city longer than a couple of hours, that is."

"Oh, I…" A flush darkens Rosa's bronzed skin, even as her eyes brighten with excitement. "Are you sure I wouldn't be imposing? I don't have to go today if—"

"It's all right." I remember what the girl told me on Wednesday about having never been to the United States before. "I'm sure you're eager to see the city, and I don't mind."

Maybe her company will get my mind off Yulia and the fact that my prisoner is still on the loose.

~

ROSA CHATTERS NONSTOP AS WE DRIVE TO CHICAGO, TELLING ME ALL about the various Chicago trivia she's read online.

"And did you know that it's named the Windy City because of politicians who were full of hot air?" she says as I turn onto West Adams Street in downtown Chicago and pull into the underground parking garage of a tall glass-and-steel building. "It has nothing to do with the actual wind coming off the lake. Isn't that crazy?"

"Yes, amazing," I say absentmindedly, checking my phone as I get out of the car. To my disappointment, there's no new update from Diego. Putting the phone away, I walk around the car and open the door for Rosa.

"Come," I say. "I'm already five minutes late."

Rosa hurries after me as I walk to the elevator. She takes two steps for every one of mine, and I can't help comparing her bouncy walk to Yulia's long-limbed, graceful stride. The maid is not quite as petite as Esguerra's wife, but she still looks short to me—especially since I've gotten used to Yulia's model-like height.

Fucking stop thinking of her. My hands clench in my pockets as I wait for the elevator to arrive, only half-listening to Rosa chattering about the Magnificent Mile. The spy is like a splinter under my skin. No matter what I do, I can't get her off my mind. Compulsively, I pull out my phone and check it again.

Still nothing.

"So what is your meeting about?" Rosa asks, and I realize she's staring up at me expectantly. "Is it something for Señor Esguerra?"

"No," I say, slipping the phone back into my pocket. "It's for me."

"Oh." She looks deflated at my curt reply, and I sigh, reminding myself that I shouldn't take out my frustration on the girl. She has nothing to do with Yulia and the whole fucked-up situation.

"I'm meeting with my portfolio manager," I say as the elevator doors slide open. "I just need to catch up on my investments."

"Oh, I see." Rosa grins as we step into the elevator. "You have investments, like Señor Esguerra."

"Yes." I press the button for the top floor. "This guy is his portfolio manager as well."

The elevator whooshes upward, all sleek steel and gleaming surfaces, and less than a minute later, we're stepping out into an equally sleek and modern reception area.

For a twenty-six-year-old guy born in the projects, Jared Winters certainly leads a good life.

His receptionist, a slim Japanese woman of indeterminate age, stands up as we approach.

"Mr. Kent," she says, giving me a polite smile. "Please, have a seat. Mr. Winters will be with you in a minute. May I offer you and your companion some refreshments?"

"None for me, thanks." I glance at Rosa. "Would you like anything?"

"Um, no, thank you." She's staring at the floor-to-ceiling window and the city spread out below. "I'm good."

Before I have a chance to sit down in one of the plush seats by the window, a tall, dark-haired man steps out of the corner office and approaches me.

"Sorry to keep you waiting," Winters says, reaching out to shake my hand. His green eyes gleam coolly behind his frameless glasses. "I was just finishing up a call."

"No worries. We're a bit late ourselves."

He smiles, and I see his gaze flick over to Rosa, who's still standing there, seemingly mesmerized by the view outside.

"Your girlfriend, I presume?" Winters says quietly, and I blink, surprised by the personal question.

"No," I say, following him as he walks back toward his office. "More like my assignment for the next couple of hours."

"Ah." Winters doesn't say anything else, but as we enter his office, I see him glance back at Rosa, as if unable to help himself.

4

ulia

"YULIA TZAKOVA?"

My heart leaps into my throat as I spin around, my hand automatically clutching the knife tucked into my jeans.

There is a dark-haired man standing in front of me. He looks average in every way; even his sunglasses and cap are standard issue. He could've been anyone in the busy Villavicencio marketplace, but he's not.

He's Obenko's Venezuelan contact.

"Yes," I say, keeping my hand on the knife. "Are you Contreras?"

He nods. "Please follow me," he says in Spanish-accented Russian.

I drop my hand from the knife handle and follow the man as he begins winding through the crowd. Like him, I'm wearing a cap and sunglasses—two items I stole at another gas station on the way here—but I still feel like someone might point at me and yell, "That's her. That's the spy Esguerra's men are looking for."

To my relief, nobody pays me much attention. In addition to the cap and sunglasses, I acquired a voluminous T-shirt and baggy jeans at that same gas station. With the shapeless clothes and my hair tucked into the cap, I look more like a teenage boy than a young woman.

Contreras leads me to a nondescript blue van parked on the street corner. "Where's the vehicle you used to get here?" he asks as I climb into the back.

"I left it a dozen blocks from here, like Obenko instructed," I say. I've spoken to my boss twice since my initial contact at Miraflores, and he gave me the location of this meeting and orders on how to proceed. "I don't think I was followed."

"Maybe not, but we need to get you out of the country in the next few hours," Contreras says, starting the van. "Esguerra is expanding the net. They already have your picture at all the border crossings."

"So how are you going to get me out?"

"There's a crate in the back," Contreras says as we pull out into the traffic. "And one of the border guards owes me a favor. With some luck, that will suffice."

I nod, feeling the cold air from the van's AC washing over my sweaty face. I drove all night, stopping only to steal another car and get the clothes, and I'm exhausted. I've been on the lookout for the sound of helicopter blades and the whine of sirens every minute I've been on the road. The fact that I've gotten this far without incident is nothing short of a miracle, and I know my luck could run out at any moment.

Still, even that fear is not enough to overcome my exhaustion. As Contreras's van gets on the highway, heading northeast, I feel my eyelids closing, and I don't fight the drugging pull of sleep.

I just need to nap for a few minutes, and then I'll be ready to face whatever comes next.

~

"WAKE UP, YULIA."

The hushed urgency of Contreras's tone yanks me out of a dream where I'm watching a movie with Lucas. My eyes snap open as I sit up and quickly take in the situation.

It's already twilight, and we appear stuck in some kind of traffic.

"Where are we? What is this?"

"Roadblock," Contreras says tersely. "They're checking all the cars. You need to get in the crate, now."

"Your border guard isn't—"

"No, we're still some twenty miles from the Venezuelan border. I don't know what this roadblock is about, but it can't be good."

Shit. I unbuckle my seatbelt and crawl through a small window into the back of the van. As Contreras said, there is a crate back there, but it looks far too small to fit a person. A child, maybe, but not a woman of my height.

Then again, in magic acts, they fit people into all kinds of seemingly too-small containers. That's how the cut-in-half trick is often done: one flexible girl is the "upper body" and a second one is "legs."

I'm not as flexible as a typical magician's assistant, but I'm far more motivated.

Opening the crate, I lie down on my back and try to fold my legs in such a way that I'd be able to close the lid over me. After a couple of frustrating minutes, I concede that it's an impossible task; my knees are at least five centimeters above the edge of the crate. Why did Contreras get a crate this small? A few centimeters deeper, and I would've been fine.

The van begins moving, and I realize we're getting closer to the checkpoint. At any moment, the doors at the back of the van will open, and I'll be discovered.

I need to fit into this fucking crate.

Gritting my teeth, I turn sideways and try to wedge my knees into the tiny space between my chest and the side of the crate. They don't fit, so I suck in a breath and try again, ignoring the burst of pain in my kneecap as it bumps against the metal edge. As I struggle, I hear raised voices speaking Spanish and feel the van come to a stop again.

We're at the checkpoint.

Frantic, I turn and grab the lid of the crate, pulling it over me with shaking hands.

There are footsteps, followed by voices at the back of the van.

They're going to open the doors.

My heart pounding, I flatten myself into an impossibly tiny ball, squashing my breasts with my knees. Even with the numbing effects of adrenaline, my body screams with pain at the unnatural position.

The lid meets the edge of the crate, and the van doors swing open.

5

ucas

My meeting with Winters takes just under an hour. We go over the current state of my investments and discuss how to proceed given the recent froth in the market. In the time that Jared Winters has been managing my portfolio, he's tripled it to just over twelve million, so I'm not particularly concerned when he says he's liquidating most of my equity holdings and getting ready to short a popular tech stock.

"The CEO is about to get in some serious legal trouble," Winters explains, and I don't bother asking how he knows that. Trading on insider information may be a crime, but our contacts at the SEC ensure that Winters's fund is nowhere on their radar.

"How much are you putting behind the trade?" I ask.

"Seven million," Winters replies. "It's going to get ugly."

"All right," I say. "Go for it."

Seven million is a sizable sum, but if the tech stock is about to drop as much as Winters thinks, it could easily be another triple or more.

We go over a few more upcoming trades, and then Winters walks me out to the reception area, where Rosa is reading a magazine.

"Ready to go?" I ask, and she nods.

Getting up, she places the magazine back on the coffee table and beams at me and Winters. "Definitely ready."

"Thanks again," I say, turning to shake Winters's hand, but he's not looking at me.

He's staring at Rosa, his green gaze oddly intent.

"Winters?" I prod, amused.

He tears his eyes away from her. "Oh, yes. It was a pleasure," he mutters, shaking my hand, and before I can say another word, he strides back into his office and shuts the door behind him.

As I promised Rosa, after the meeting I take her shopping on the Magnificent Mile—also known as Michigan Avenue. As she tries on a bunch of dresses at a department store, I take a seat next to the fitting room and check my email again. This time, there's a short message from Diego:

Located the stolen pick-up truck at a gas station near Granada. No other cars reported stolen for now. Blockades up at all the major roads as per your instructions.

I put the phone away, frustrated anger churning in my gut. They still haven't found Yulia, and by now, she could be in another country. She has undoubtedly made contact with her agency, and depending on how resourceful they are, it's entirely possible that they've smuggled her out.

For all I know, she's already on a plane, flying to her lover.

"How do you like this?" Rosa asks, and I turn to see that she's come out of the fitting room in a short, form-fitting yellow dress.

"It's nice," I say on autopilot. "You should get it." Objectively, I can see that the dark-haired girl looks good in that dress, but all I can think about right now is the fact that Yulia may be on her way to Misha… to the man she truly loves.

"All right." Rosa gives me a huge smile. "I will."

She hurries back into the fitting room, and I pull out my phone to fire off an email to the hackers looking into UUR.

Even if Yulia managed to get away, she won't stay free for long.

No matter what it takes, I'll find her, and she'll never escape again.

6

ulia

"Sorry about that," Contreras says, pulling the lid off my crate. "I didn't expect you to be this tall. I'm glad you were able to fit in there."

I groan as he pulls me out, my muscles cramping from being stuck in the tiny crate for the last hour. My knees feel like two giant bruises, and my spine is throbbing from being squashed against the side of the crate. I am, however, alive and across the Venezuelan border—which means it was all worth it.

"It's okay," I say, rotating my head in a semi-circle. My neck is painfully stiff, but it's nothing a good massage won't cure. "It fooled the police and border patrol. They didn't even try looking into the crate."

Contreras nods. "That's why I brought it. It looks too small to fit a person, but when one is determined…" He shrugs.

"Yeah." I rotate my head again and stretch, trying to get my muscles working. "So what's the plan now?"

"Now we get you to the plane. Obenko has already arranged everything. By tomorrow, you should be in Kiev, safe and sound."

~

OUR DRIVE TO THE SMALL AIRSTRIP TAKES LESS THAN AN HOUR, AND then we're pulling up in front of an ancient-looking jet.

"Here we are," Contreras says. "Your people will take it from here."

"Thank you," I say, and he nods as I open the door.

"Good luck," he says in his Spanish-accented Russian, and I smile at him before jumping out of the van and hurrying to the plane.

As I walk up the ladder, a middle-aged man steps out, blocking the entrance. "Code?" he says, his hand resting on a gun at his side.

Eyeing the weapon warily, I tell him my identification number. Technically, eliminating me would accomplish the same thing as getting me away from Esguerra: I wouldn't be able to spill any more UUR secrets. In fact, it would be an even neater solution...

Before my mind can travel too far down that path, the man lowers his hand and steps aside, letting me enter the plane.

"Welcome, Yulia Borisovna," he says, using my real patronymic. "We're glad you made it."

7

ucas

By Saturday morning, I'm convinced that Yulia must be back in Ukraine. Diego and Eduardo were able to track her as far as Venezuela, but her trail seems to have gone cold there.

"I think she left the country," Diego says when I call him for an update. "A private plane registered to a shell corporation filed a flight plan to Mexico, but there's no record of it landing anywhere in that country. It must've been her people, and if that's the case, she's gone."

"That's not a fact. Keep looking," I say, even though I know he's most likely right.

Yulia got away, and if I'm to have any hope of recapturing her, I'll have to widen the net and call on some of our international contacts.

I consider bringing Esguerra up to speed on the whole situation, but decide to postpone it until Sunday. Today is his wife's twentieth birthday, and I know he's not in the mood to be bothered. All my boss cares about is giving Nora everything she wants —including a trip to a popular nightclub in downtown Chicago.

"You do realize guarding that place will be a nightmare, right?" I tell him when he brings up the outing at lunchtime. "It's too many people. And on a Saturday night—"

"Yes, I know," Esguerra says. "But this is what Nora requested, so let's figure out a way to make it happen."

We spend the next two hours going through the club schematics and deciding where to station all the guards. It's unlikely that any of Esguerra's enemies will catch wind of this, since it's such a spur-of-the-moment event, but we still decide to position snipers in the buildings nearby and have the other guards within a one-block radius of the club. My role will be to stay in the car and keep an eye on the club's entrance, in case there's any threat coming from that direction. We also work out a plan for securing the restaurant where Esguerra and his wife will have dinner before going to the club.

"Oh, I almost forgot," Esguerra says as we're wrapping up. "Nora wants Rosa to join us at the club. Can you have one of the guards drive her there?"

"Yes, I think so," I say after a moment of consideration. "Thomas can bring the girl to the club before taking his position at the end of the block."

"That would work." Esguerra rises to his feet. "I'll see you tonight."

He leaves the room, and I go outside to assign the guards their tasks.

~

Esguerra's dinner outing passes without an incident, and afterwards, I drive him and Nora to the club. Rosa is already waiting there, dressed in the yellow dress she bought on our shopping trip. The moment Nora steps out of the car, Rosa runs up to her, and I hear the two young women chattering excitedly as they head into the club. Esguerra follows them, looking mildly amused, and I stay in the car, settling in for what promises to be a long, boring night.

After about an hour, I eat a sandwich I packed earlier and check my email. To my relief, there's an update from our hackers.

Finally broke through the Ukrainian government's firewalls and deciphered some files, the email reads. *UUR is an acronym for Ukrainskoye Upravleniye Razvedki, which roughly translates to "Ukrainian Intelligence Bureau." It's an off-the-books spy group that was established in response to their main security agency's corruption and close ties to Russia. We're now working on decoding a message that may point to two UUR field operatives and a location in Kiev.*

Smiling grimly, I write a reply and put away the phone. It's only a matter of time before we take down Yulia's organization. And once we do, she'll have nowhere to run, no one to help her.

No lover she could return to.

My teeth clench as violent jealousy spears through me. Yulia could be with him already, with this Misha of hers. He could be holding her at this very moment.

He could even be fucking her.

The thought fills me with blazing fury. If I had the man in front of me right now, I'd kill him with my bare hands and make Yulia watch. It would be her punishment for this latest betrayal.

A buzzing vibration from my phone cuts into my vengeful thoughts. Grabbing it, I read Esguerra's text, and my blood turns to ice.

Nora and Rosa attacked, the message says. *Rosa taken. I'm going after her. Alert the others.*

8

ulia

THE FAMILIAR SMELL OF CAR EXHAUST AND LILACS FILLS MY NOSTRILS as the car weaves through the busy Kiev streets. The man Obenko sent to pick me up at the airport is someone I've never seen before, and he doesn't talk much, leaving me free to take in the sights of the city where I lived and trained for five years.

"We're not going to the Institute?" I ask the driver when the car makes an unfamiliar turn.

"No," the man replies. "I'm taking you to a safe house."

"Is Obenko there?"

The driver nods. "He's waiting for you."

"Great." I take a steadying breath. I should be relieved to be here, but instead, I feel tense and anxious. And it's not just because I screwed up and compromised the organization. Obenko doesn't deal kindly with failure, but the fact that he extracted me from Colombia instead of killing me eases my worry in that regard.

No, the main source of my anxiety is the empty feeling inside me, an ache that's growing more acute with every hour without Lucas. I feel like I'm going through a withdrawal—except that would make Lucas my drug, and I refuse to accept that.

Whatever I had begun to feel for my captor will pass. It has to, because there's no other alternative.

Lucas and I are over for good.

"We're here," the driver says, stopping in front of an unassuming four-story apartment building. It looks just like every other building in this neighborhood: old and rundown, the outside covered with a dull yellowish plaster from the Soviet era. The scent of lilacs is stronger here; it's coming from a park across the street. Under any other circumstances, I would've enjoyed the fragrance that I associate with spring, but today it reminds me of the jungle I left behind—and, by extension, the man who held me there.

The driver leaves the car by the curb and leads me into the building. It's a walk-up, and the stairwell is as rundown as the building's exterior. When we walk past the first floor, I hear raised voices and catch a whiff of urine and vomit.

"Who are those people on the first floor?" I ask as we stop in front of an apartment on the second floor. "Are they civilians?"

"Yes." The driver knocks on the door. "They're too busy getting drunk to pay us much attention."

I don't have a chance to ask more questions because the door swings open, and I see a dark-haired man standing there. His wide forehead is creased, and lines of tension bracket his thin mouth.

"Come in, Yulia," Vasiliy Obenko says, stepping back to let me enter. "We have a lot to discuss."

~

Over the next two hours, I go through an interrogation as grueling as anything I'd experienced in the Russian prison. In addition to Obenko, there are two senior UUR agents, Sokov and Mateyenko. Like my boss, they're in their forties, their trim bodies honed into deadly weapons over decades of training. The three of them sit across from me at the kitchen table and take turns asking questions. They want to know everything from the details of my escape to the exact information I gave Lucas about UUR.

"I still don't understand how he broke you," Obenko says when I'm done recounting that story. "How did he know about that incident with Kirill?"

My face burns with shame. "He learned about it as a result of a nightmare I had." And because I had confided in Lucas afterwards, but I don't say that. I don't want my boss to know that he had been right about me all along—that when it mattered, I couldn't control my emotions.

"And in this nightmare, you what… spoke about your trainer?" It's Sokov who asks me this, his stern expression making it clear that he doubts my story. "Do you usually talk in your sleep, Yulia Borisovna?"

"No, but these weren't exactly *usual* circumstances." I do my best not to sound defensive. "I was held prisoner and placed in situations that were triggers for me—that would be triggers for any woman who'd undergone an assault."

"What exactly were those situations?" Mateyenko cuts in. "You don't look particularly maltreated."

I bite back an angry response. "I wasn't physically tortured or starved, I already told you that," I say evenly. "Kent's methods of interrogation were more psychological in nature. And yes, that was in large part due to the fact that he found me attractive. Hence the triggers."

The two agents exchange looks, and Obenko frowns at me. "So he raped you, and that triggered your nightmares?"

"He…" My throat tightens as I recall my body's helpless

response to Lucas. "It was the overall situation. I didn't handle it well."

The agents look at each other again, and then Mateyenko says, "Tell us more about the woman who helped you escape. What did you say her name was?"

Calling on every bit of patience I possess, I recount my encounters with Rosa for the third time. After that, Sokov asks me to go through my escape again, minute by minute, and then Mateyenko interrogates me about the security logistics of Esguerra's compound.

"Look," I say after another hour of nonstop questions, "I've told you everything I know. Whatever you may think of me, the threat to the agency is real. Esguerra's organization has taken down entire terrorist networks, and they're coming after us. If you have any contingency measures in place, now is the time to implement them. Get yourselves and your families to safety."

Obenko studies me for a moment, then nods. "We're done for today," he says, turning toward the two agents. "Yulia is tired after her long journey. We'll resume this tomorrow."

The two men depart, and I slump in my chair, feeling even emptier than before.

9

ucas

As soon as I read Esguerra's message, I radio the guards and order half of them to head to the club. None of them had noticed any suspicious activity, which means that the threat, whatever it was, had come from within the club, not outside as we'd expected. I'm about to rush into the club myself when I get another text from Esguerra:

Recovered Rosa. Follow the white SUV.

I instantly radio the guards to do so, and at that moment, another message comes in:

Bring the car to the alley out back.

I start the car and zoom around the block, nearly running over a couple of pedestrians in the process. The alley at the back of the club is dark and stinks of garbage mixed with piss, but I barely register the ambience. Stepping out of the car, I wait, my hand on the gun at my side. A few seconds later, the men radio me that they located the white SUV and are following it. I'm about to give them further instructions when the door to the club swings open, and Nora comes out, her arms wrapped around Rosa. Esguerra follows them, his face twisted with rage. As the light from the car illuminates their figures, I realize why.

Both women are shaking, their faces pale and streaked with tears. However, it's Rosa's state that sends my blood pressure through the roof. Her bright yellow dress is torn and stained with blood, and one side of her face is grotesquely swollen.

The girl had been violently assaulted, just like Yulia seven years ago.

A crimson fog fills my vision. I know my reaction is disproportional—Rosa is little more than a stranger to me—but I can't help it. The images in my mind are of a fragile fifteen-year-old, her slender body torn and bleeding. I can see the shame and devastation on Rosa's face, and the knowledge that Yulia went through this makes my guts churn.

"Those fuckers." My voice is thick with rage as I step around the car to open the door. "Those motherfucking fuckers. They're going to fucking die."

"Yes, they will," Esguerra says grimly, but I'm not listening. Reaching for Rosa, I carefully pull her away from Nora. Esguerra's wife doesn't appear to be hurt as badly, but she's still clearly shaken. Rosa sobs as I shepherd her into the car, and I do my best to be gentle with her, to comfort her as I couldn't comfort Yulia all those years ago.

As I buckle her in, I hear Esguerra say his wife's name, his voice strangely tense, and I turn to see Nora double over next to the car.

The baby, I realize in an instant, remembering her pregnancy, but Esguerra is already bundling her into the car and yelling for me to drive to the hospital, now.

~

We get to the hospital in record time, but long before Esguerra comes out into the waiting room, I know that the baby didn't make it. There was too much blood in the car.

"I'm sorry," I say, taking in my boss's shattered expression. "How's Nora?"

"They stopped the bleeding." Esguerra's voice is hoarse. "She wants to go home, so that's what we'll do. We'll take Rosa, too."

I nod. I told the hospital I'm Rosa's boyfriend, so I've been getting regular updates on her condition. As expected, the girl has refused to talk to the police, and since none of her injuries are life-threatening, she doesn't need to stay overnight.

"All right," I say. "You take care of your wife, and I'll get Rosa."

Esguerra goes back to Nora, and I follow up with our cleanup crew, giving them instructions on what to do with the guy they found knocked out at the club. From the little I pieced together via Rosa's hysterical explanations, the maid had been attacked in the back room of the club by two men she'd danced with earlier. Nora came to her rescue, knocking out a third guy who had been guarding the room. Esguerra made it there in the nick of time, killing one of the assailants, but the other one dragged Rosa outside and would've taken his turn in the car if Esguerra hadn't saved her. It was that man who got away in the white SUV—the SUV whose license plate I'm tracking now.

Once we know his identity, the driver of that SUV is as good as dead.

Putting the phone away, I go to get Rosa. When I walk into her room, I find her sitting on the bed in nurse's scrubs; the hospital staff must've given them to her to replace her torn dress. Her knees are drawn up to her chest, and her face is bruised and pale. An image of Yulia flashes through my mind again, and I have to take a deep breath to suppress a swell of rage.

Keeping my movements slow and gentle, I approach the bed. "I'm sorry," I say quietly, clasping Rosa's elbow to help her to her feet. "I really am. Can you walk, or would you like me to carry you?"

"I can walk." Her voice is thin, high-pitched with anxiety, and I drop my hand when I realize my touch is upsetting her. "I'm fine."

It's an obvious lie, but I don't call her out on it. I just match my pace to her slower one, and lead her out to the car.

AN HOUR AFTER WE GET BACK TO ESGUERRA'S MANSION, MY BOSS comes down to the living room, where I'm waiting to fill him in on the developing situation.

"Where's Rosa?" he asks. His voice is calm, betraying nothing of the hollow agony I see in his gaze. He's compartmentalizing to cope with what happened, choosing to focus on what needs to be done rather than dwelling on what can't be fixed.

"She's asleep," I answer, rising from the couch. "I gave her Ambien and made sure she took a shower."

"Good. Thank you." Esguerra crosses the room to stand in front of me. "Now tell me everything."

"The cleanup crew took care of the body and captured the kid Nora knocked out in the hallway," I say. "They're holding him in a warehouse I rented on the South Side."

"Good. What about the white car?"

"The men were able to follow it to one of the residential high-rises downtown. At that point, it disappeared into a parking garage, and they decided against pursuing it there. I've already run the license plate number."

"And?"

"And it seems like we might have a problem," I say. "Does the name Patrick Sullivan mean anything to you?"

Esguerra frowns. "It's familiar, but I can't place it."

"The Sullivans own half of this town," I say, recounting what I just learned about our newest enemy. "Prostitution, drugs, weapons—you name it, they have their fingers in it. Patrick Sullivan heads up the family, and he's got just about every local politician and police chief in his pocket."

"Ah." There's a flicker of recognition on Esguerra's face. "What does Patrick Sullivan have to do with this?"

"He has two sons," I explain. "Or rather, he *had* two sons. Brian and Sean. Brian is currently marinating in lye at our rented warehouse, and Sean is the owner of the white SUV."

"I see," Esguerra says, and I know he's thinking the same thing I am.

The rapists' connection complicates matters, but it also explains why they attacked Rosa in such a public place. They're used to their mobster father getting them out of trouble, and it never occurred to them that they might be crossing someone just as dangerous.

"Also," I say while Esguerra is digesting everything, "the kid we've got strung up in that warehouse is their seventeen-year-old cousin, Sullivan's nephew. His name is Jimmy. Apparently, he and the two brothers are close. Or *were* close, I should say."

Esguerra's blue eyes narrow. "Do they have any idea who we are? Could they have singled out Rosa to get at me?"

"No, I don't think so." A fresh wave of anger makes my jaw clench. "The Sullivan brothers have a nasty history with women. Date-rape drugs, sexual assault, gang bangs of sorority girls—the list goes on and on. If it weren't for their father, they'd be rotting in prison right now."

"I see." Esguerra's mouth twists coldly. "Well, by the time we're done with them, they'll wish they were."

I nod. The minute I learned about Patrick Sullivan, I knew we'd be going to war. "Should I organize a strike team?" I ask, gripped by familiar anticipation. I haven't been in a good battle in a while.

"No, not yet," Esguerra says. He turns away and walks over to stand by the window. I don't know what he's looking at, but he's silent for well over a minute before he turns back to face me.

"I want Nora and her parents taken to the estate before we do anything," he says, and I see the harsh resolve on his face. "Sean Sullivan will have to wait. For now, we'll focus on the nephew."

"All right." I incline my head. "I'll begin making the arrangements."

10

ulia

I SLEEP FITFULLY MY FIRST NIGHT AT THE SAFE HOUSE, WAKING UP every couple of hours from nightmares. I don't remember the exact details of those dreams, but I know Lucas is in them, and so is my brother. The scenes are a blur in my mind, but I recall bits and pieces involving trains, lizards, gunfire, and underneath it all, the delicate scent of lilacs.

Around five in the morning, I give up trying to fall back asleep. Getting up, I put on a robe and wander into the kitchen to make myself some tea. Obenko is there, reading a newspaper, and as I enter, he looks up, his hazel eyes sharp and clear despite the early hour.

"Jet-lagged?" he asks, and I nod. It's as good of an explanation for my state as any.

"Want some tea?" I offer, pouring water into a tea kettle and setting it on the stove.

"No, thanks." He studies me, and I wonder what he's seeing. A traitor? A failure? Someone who's now more of a liability than an asset? I used to care what my boss thought, craving his approval as I once craved my parents', but right now, I can't work up any interest in his opinion.

There's only one thing I care about this morning.

"My brother," I say, sitting down after I make myself a cup of Earl Grey. "How is he? Where's your sister's family now?"

"They're safe." Obenko folds his newspaper. "We've relocated them to a different location."

"Do you have any new pictures for me?" I ask, trying not to sound too eager.

"No." Obenko sighs. "We thought you were gone, and when you contacted us, I'm afraid taking photos wasn't our main priority."

I take a scalding sip of tea to mask my disappointment. "I see."

Obenko lets out another sigh. "Yulia... It's been eleven years. You need to let go of Misha. Your brother has a life that doesn't involve you."

"I know that, but I don't think a few pictures every now and then is too much to ask." My tone is sharper than I intended. "It's not like I'm asking to see him..." I pause as the idea takes hold of me. "Well, actually, since you don't have the pictures, maybe I can just view him from a distance," I say, my pulse accelerating in excitement. "I could use binoculars or a telescope. He would never know."

Obenko's gaze hardens. "We've talked about this, Yulia. You know why you can't see him."

"Because it would deepen my irrational attachment," I say, parroting his words to me. "Yes, I know you said that, but I disagree. I could've died in that Russian prison, or been tortured to death by Esguerra. The fact that I'm sitting here today—"

"Has nothing to do with Misha and the agreement we made

eleven years ago," Obenko says. "You fucked up on this assignment. Because of you, your brother has already been uprooted, forced to change schools and give up his friends. You don't get to make demands today."

My fingers tighten on the tea cup. "I'm not demanding," I say evenly. "I'm asking. I know it was my mistake that led to this situation, and I'm sorry. But I don't see how that's relevant to the matter at hand. I spent six years in Moscow doing exactly what you wanted me to do. I sent you a lot of valuable intel. All I want in return is to see my brother from a distance. I wouldn't approach him, wouldn't speak to him—I would just look at him. Why is that a problem?"

Obenko stands up. "Drink your tea, Yulia," he says, ignoring my question. "There will be another debriefing at eleven."

11

ucas

I SPEND THE NIGHT COORDINATING WITH THE CLEANUP CREW AND preparing for our departure. If there's any silver lining to this disaster, it's that we're going home early, and I will soon be able to hunt down Yulia with no distractions.

First, though, I need to take care of the situation here.

I begin by making breakfast for Rosa, who hasn't come out of her room this morning. At first, I'm tempted to slap together a sandwich, but then I decide to try my hand at one of the omelets I've watched Yulia make. It takes me two attempts, but I succeed at producing something that resembles one of Yulia's delicious confections. It doesn't taste half-bad either, I decide, trying a bite before putting half of the omelet on a plate for Rosa.

Holding the plate with one hand, I knock on the door of Rosa's bedroom. After a couple of minutes, I hear footsteps, and she opens the door. She's dressed in a long, shapeless T-shirt, and to my relief, her eyes are dry, though the bruising on her face looks even worse.

"Hi," I say, forcing a smile. "I made an omelet. Would you like some?"

The maid blinks, looking surprised. "Oh… Sure, thanks." She accepts the plate and glances at it. "That looks great, thank you, Lucas."

"You're welcome." I study her injuries, my stomach tightening at the sight. "How are you feeling?"

Her face flushes, and she looks away. "I'm fine."

"Okay." I can tell she doesn't want company, so I say, "If you need anything, just let me know," and then I head back into the kitchen.

I need to eat my own breakfast before tackling the next task.

By the time Esguerra comes out of the house, everything is ready for him.

"I brought the cousin here," I say when my boss steps out onto the driveway. "I figured you might not want to go all the way to Chicago today."

"Excellent." Esguerra's eyes gleam darkly. "Where is he?"

"In that van over there." I point at a black van I parked behind the trees farthest from the neighbors.

We walk toward it together, and Esguerra asks, "Has he given us any info yet?"

"He gave us access codes to his cousin's parking garage and building elevators," I say. "It wasn't difficult to get him to talk. I figured I'd leave the rest of the interrogation to you, in case you wanted to speak to him in person."

"That's good thinking. I definitely do." Approaching the van, Esguerra opens the back doors and peers into the dark interior.

I know what he's seeing: a skinny teenager, gagged and with his ankles tied to his wrists behind his back. He's the third guy, the one Nora knocked out at the club yesterday. I've already had a couple of guards work him over, and now he's ready for Esguerra.

My boss doesn't waste time. Climbing into the van, he turns around and asks, "Are the walls soundproof?"

I nod. "About ninety percent." I can smell the urine and sweat inside the van, and I know these odors will soon be overwhelmed by the coppery stench of blood.

"Good," Esguerra says. "That should suffice."

He closes the van doors, locking himself in with the boy, and a minute later, the sound of his victim's pleas and screams fills the air. I tune them out, letting Esguerra have his fun while I read the latest update from Diego and Eduardo. They found a record of the private plane landing in Kiev, so Yulia is definitely out of Colombia.

I forward Diego's findings to the hackers, and when Esguerra is done, I wrap the teenager's body in a plastic sheet and message the cleaning crew to come in.

~

HALF AN HOUR LATER, I'M WALKING BACK TOWARD THE HOUSE WHEN my phone vibrates with another text from Esguerra.

New development. Need to expedite the departure.

My adrenaline spikes. Entering the house, I intercept Esguerra in the hallway. "What happened?"

"Frank, our CIA contact, emailed me," Esguerra says, pushing back his wet hair. He must've taken a shower to get rid of the Sullivan kid's blood. "An artist's sketch of myself, Nora, and Rosa is being circulated in the local FBI's office. It had to have come from the Sullivan brother who got away in that white SUV. I'm guessing it won't be long before the Sullivans find out who we are, and given what I did to the other Sullivan brother in the club and the cousin just now..." He doesn't finish, but he doesn't have to.

Esguerra and I both know Patrick Sullivan will be out for blood.

"I'll send Thomas to prepare the plane," I say. "Do you think Nora's parents can be ready to go in the next hour?"

"They'll have to be ready," Esguerra says. "I want them and the women away before we do anything."

"How many guards should we send on the plane with them?"

"Four, just in case," Esguerra says after a moment of deliberation. "The rest can stay to be part of our strike team."

"All right. I'll go tell the others and make sure Rosa is ready to go."

~

We arrive at Esguerra's in-laws' house in full force, our limo followed by seven armored SUVs transporting twenty-three guards. The neighbors gape at us, and I feel a twinge of amusement at the thought of Nora's parents trying to explain this to their suburban acquaintances. I'm sure the good people of Oak Lawn have heard rumors about Nora's arms dealer husband, but hearing and seeing are two different things.

Predictably, the parents aren't ready yet, so Esguerra and his wife go in to round them up. Rosa stays in the car, explaining to Nora that she doesn't want to be in the way.

When we're alone, I turn around and look at Rosa through the limo partition.

"Would you like some music?" I ask, but she shakes her head. She's not speaking, just staring out the window, and I'm sure she's thinking about what happened yesterday.

Not wanting to discomfit her, I roll up the partition and use the time to check on the plane. Thomas assures me that it's ready to go, so I double-check my weapons—an M16 slung across my chest and a Glock 26 strapped to my leg. I'd like to be even better armed, but I'm driving. Fortunately, Esguerra has an entire arsenal in the back under one of the seats. I'm hoping we won't need it, but we're prepared in case we do.

Some forty minutes later, Esguerra comes out of the house, hauling a huge suitcase. He's followed by Nora's father with another suitcase, and finally, Nora and her mother.

Though there's plenty of room in the back, Rosa comes to sit at the front with me, explaining that she wants to give the four of them more room.

"You don't mind, do you?" she asks, glancing at me, and I give her a reassuring smile.

"No, please have a seat." I roll up the partition again, separating us from the main cabin, and start the car. "How are you doing?"

"Fine." Her voice is quiet but steady. I don't press her for more, and we drive in comfortable silence for some time. It's not until we pull off the interstate onto a two-lane highway that Rosa speaks again. "Lucas," she says quietly. "I'd like to ask you for a favor."

Surprised, I glance at her before directing my attention back to the road. "What is it?"

"If there's ever a chance—" Her voice breaks. "If you ever get them, I want to be there. Okay? I just want to be there."

She doesn't spell it out, but I understand. "You got it," I promise. "I'll make sure you see justice served."

"Thank you—" she begins, but at that moment, I catch a glimpse of movement in the side mirror, and my pulse leaps.

On the narrow highway behind our SUVs is an entire cavalcade of cars, and they're gaining on us quickly.

I floor the gas pedal with a surge of adrenaline. The limo jerks forward, accelerating at a mad pace, and I lower the partition to meet Esguerra's gaze in the rearview mirror.

"We have a tail," I say tersely. "They're onto us, and they're coming with everything they've got."

12

ulia

"Bayu-bayushki-bayu, ne lozhisya na krayu..." My mom is singing a Russian lullaby to me, her voice soft and sweet as I snuggle deeper into the blanket. *"Pridyot seren'kiy volchok, i ukusit za bochok..."*

Her crooning is off-key and the words are about a gray wolf that will bite my side if I lie too close to the edge of the bed, but the melody is warm and comforting, like my mom's smile. I bask in it, savoring it for as long as I can, but with each word, my mom's voice gets fainter and softer, until there's only silence.

Silence and cold, empty darkness.

"Don't go, Mom," I whisper. "Stay home. Don't go to Grandpa tonight. Please, stay home."

But there's no response. There's never a response. There's only darkness and the sound of Misha crying. He's feverish and wants our parents. I pick him up and rock him back and forth, the sturdy weight of his toddler's body anchoring me in the sea of darkness. "It's okay, Mishen'ka. It's okay. We'll be okay. I'll take care of you. We'll be okay, I promise."

But he doesn't stop crying. He cries all through the night. His screams get hysterical when the headmistress comes for him in the morning, and I know she did something to him. I saw the bruises on his legs when he came out of her office last evening. She hurt him somehow, traumatized him. He hasn't stopped crying since.

"No, don't take him." I struggle to hold on to Misha, but she pushes me away, taking my brother with her. I come after her, but two older boys block my way, forming a human wall in front of me.

"Don't do it," one of the boys says. "It won't help."

His eyes are pitch black, like the darkness around me, and I feel myself spinning. I'm lost, so lost in that darkness.

"I have a proposition for you, Yulia." A man dressed in a suit smiles at me, his hazel eyes cold and calculating. "A deal, if you will. You're not too young to make a deal, are you?"

I lift my chin, meeting his gaze. "I'm eleven. I can do anything."

"Bayu-bayushki-bayu, ne lozhisya na krayu..."

"It's your fault, bitch." Cruel hands seize me, dragging me into the darkness. "It's all your fault."

"Pridyot seren'kiy volchok, i ukusit za bochok..."

The melody trails off again, and I'm crying, crying and fighting as I fall deeper into the darkness.

"Tell me about the program." Strong arms catch me, imprisoning me against a muscular male body. I know I should be terrified, but when I look up and meet the man's pale gaze, I'm suffused with heat. His face is hard, every feature carved from stone, but his blue-gray eyes hold the kind of warmth I haven't felt in years. There's a promise of safety there, and something else.

Something I crave with all my soul.

"Lucas..." I'm filled with desperation as I reach for him. "Please fuck me. Please."

He drives into me, his thick cock stretching me, spearing me, and the heat of him dispels the lingering coldness. I'm burning, and it's not enough. I need more. "I love you," I whisper, my nails digging into his muscled back. "I love you, Lucas."

"Yulia." His voice is cold and distant as he says my name. "Yulia, it's time."

"Please," I beg, reaching for Lucas, but he's already fading away. "Please don't go. Stay with me."

"Yulia." A hand lands on my shoulder. "Wake up."

Gasping, I sit up in bed and stare into Obenko's cool hazel gaze. My heart is drumming in my throat, and I'm covered in a thin layer of sweat. Turning my head, I take in the sight of peeling wallpaper and gray light seeping through a dirty window. There's no Lucas here, nobody to catch me in the darkness.

I'm in my bedroom at the safe house, where I must've fallen asleep before the debriefing.

"Was I... Did I say anything?" I ask, trying to get my shaky breathing under control. The dream is already fading from my memory, but the bits and pieces I recall are enough to knot my insides.

"No." Obenko's face is expressionless. "Should you have?"

"No, of course not." My frantic heartbeat is beginning to slow. "Give me a minute to freshen up, and I'll be right out."

"All right." Obenko walks out of my room, and I pull the blanket tighter around myself, desperate for what little comfort I can find.

13

ucas

AT THE EXPLOSION OF GUNFIRE, I GLANCE AT THE SIDE MIRROR AND see our guards in the SUVs shooting at the pursuing vehicles. A bullet dings against the side of our car, and I swerve, making the limo a more difficult target. In the back, Nora's parents scream in panic, and Esguerra jumps off the seat to get to his weapons stash.

Fucking hell. My hands tighten on the wheel. This shouldn't be happening. Not while we have civilians with us. Esguerra and I can handle this, but not Rosa and Nora—and certainly not Nora's parents. If anything were to happen to them… I press harder on the gas pedal, pushing the speedometer past 100 miles per hour.

More gunfire. In the side mirror, I see our men exchanging fire with the pursuers. All the way in the back, one of Sullivan's cars careens into one of ours, trying to force it off the road, and there's another burst of gunfire before the pursuers' SUV skids off the road and flips over.

Another car gains on one of our SUVs, smashing into its side. Behind it are at least a dozen vehicles—a mix of SUVs, vans, and Hummers with grenade launchers mounted on their roofs.

No, not a dozen.

They have as many as fifteen or sixteen cars versus eight of ours.

Motherfucking fuck. I push the gas pedal again, and the speedometer climbs to 110. We need to go faster, but the armored limo is too heavy. It's built for protection, not speed.

One of our SUVs in the back flies up, exploding in mid-air. The blast is deafening, but I ignore it, all my attention on the road ahead. I can't think about the men we just lost or their families.

If we're to survive, I can't afford the distraction.

"Lucas." Rosa sounds panicked. "Lucas, that's—"

"A police blockade, yes." I have to raise my voice to be heard over the din of gunfire and explosions. There are four police cars blocking our way, and they're surrounded by SWAT teams. They're here for us—which means they must be in Sullivan's pocket.

In the back, Julian is shouting something at Nora, and in the rearview mirror, I see him dragging out bulletproof vests and a handheld grenade launcher.

"We have to go through them," I yell, keeping my foot on the gas. We're seconds away now, rocketing toward the blockade at full speed. I aim the limo at the narrow gap between two police cars. For this, the heavy weight of the armored limo is an advantage.

"Hold on!" I shout at Rosa, and then we're crashing into the cars, the impact of the collision throwing me forward. I feel the seatbelt cutting into me, hear the SWAT team's bullets hitting the side and windows of our car, and then we're through, the limo barreling ahead as two more cars behind us collide and explode.

Sullivan's cars, I determine with relief a moment later. From what I can see in the side mirror, our SUVs are still intact. Beside me, Rosa is white with fear but seemingly uninjured.

Before I can catch my breath, I hear a deafening *boom* and see the police cruiser behind us fly up, exploding in the air. It lands on its side, burning, and one of Sullivan's Hummers slams into it. There's another explosion, followed by a Sullivan van careering off the road. I grin savagely as I catch sight of Esguerra standing in the middle of the limo, his head and shoulders sticking out of the opening in the roof.

My boss must be using the handheld grenade launcher from our stash.

There's another explosive *boom* as he fires the next shot, but no enemy vehicle goes belly-up this time. Instead, one of the Hummers swerves, ramming into one of our SUVs, and I see the guards' car flip over, rolling off the road.

Shit. My elation dissipates. Esguerra better get his aim straight, or we're fucked.

As if in response to my thoughts, there's another boom, followed by a Sullivan van exploding behind us. Two Sullivan SUVs crash into it, but my satisfaction is short-lived as I hear the ding of bullets against the side of our car. Swearing, I yank the wheel and begin zigzagging from side to side.

Unlike the limo, Esguerra's head is not bulletproof.

"Come on, Esguerra," I mutter, squeezing the wheel. "Fucking shoot them."

Boom! Another Sullivan SUV explodes, taking out the one behind it in the process.

"He's doing it," Rosa says in a shaking voice. "They have only six cars left now."

I steal a glance in the mirror and verify that she's right. Six enemy vehicles versus five of ours.

We might make it yet.

Suddenly, I see a flash of fire in the mirror. Two of our SUVs fly up in the air, and I realize the Hummers took them out. *Fuck. Fuck, fuck, fuck.*

"Come on, Esguerra." My knuckles turn white on the steering wheel. "Just fucking do it."

Boom! One of the Hummers veers off the road, smoke rising from its hood.

"Señor Esguerra did it!" Rosa's voice is filled with hysterical glee. "Lucas, he got it!"

I don't have a chance to reply before one of the enemy cars swerves and crashes into another. Our men must've shot the driver.

"Three of them left, Lucas. Only three!" Rosa is all but jumping in her seat, and I realize she's high on adrenaline. Past a certain point, one stops feeling fear, and it all becomes a game, a rush unlike any other. It's what makes danger so addictive—for me, at least.

I feel most alive when I'm close to death.

Except that's not true anymore, I realize with a jolt. The buzz is muted today, dulled by my worry for our civilians and my fury over our men's deaths. Instead of excitement, there's only a grim determination to survive.

To live so I can catch Yulia and feel alive in a whole different way.

"Lucas." Rosa sounds tense all of a sudden. "Lucas, are you seeing that?"

"What?" I say, but then the sound reaches my ears.

It's the faint but unmistakable roar of chopper blades.

"It's a police helicopter," Rosa says, her voice shaking again. "Lucas, why is there a helicopter?"

I floor the gas pedal instead of answering her. There are only two possibilities: either the authorities heard about what's happening, or it's more dirty cops. My money's on the last one, which means we're beyond fucked. By my calculations, Esguerra only has one shot left in that grenade launcher of his, and there's no way he can take down that chopper.

"What are we going to do?" Rosa's panic is evident. "Lucas, what are we—"

"Quiet." I floor the pedal, focusing on the structure looming ahead of us. We're almost to the private airport now, and if we can get inside, we stand a chance.

"I'm going for the hangar!" I yell to Esguerra, and take a sharp right turn toward the structure. At the same time, I floor the gas pedal, pushing the limo to its limits. We're all but rocketing toward the hangar now, but the roar of the helicopter is getting inexorably louder.

Boom! My ears ring from an explosion, and I swerve instinctively before righting the car and pressing on the gas again. Behind us, one of our SUVs careens into another, and they collide with a squeal of tires before rolling off the road.

"They shot it." Rosa sounds dazed. "Oh my God, Lucas, the helicopter shot it."

I shake my head, trying to get rid of the ringing in my ears, but before the noise dies down, there's another deafening explosion.

The Hummer behind us goes up in flames, leaving two enemy SUVs and the helicopter.

Esguerra came through with one last shot.

Before I can take a breath, a blast rocks the limo. My vision goes dark and my head spins, the ringing in my ears turning into a high-pitched, dizzying whine. Only decades of training enable me to keep my hands on the wheel, and as my vision clears, I register what Rosa is screaming.

"We're hit, Lucas! We're hit!"

Fuck, she's right. There's smoke rising from the back of the car, and the rear window is shattered.

"Are Esguerra and his family—" I begin hoarsely, but then I see Esguerra pop up in the rearview mirror. He's covered in blood but clearly alive. Pulling Nora up from the floor, he hands her an AK-

47. Behind them, her parents look dazed and bloody, but conscious.

We're almost to the hangar now, so I take my foot off the gas. I can hear Esguerra giving his wife instructions in the back. He wants her to take her parents and run for the plane as soon as we stop.

"You run with them too, Rosa, you hear me?" I say, not taking my eyes off the road. "You get out, and you run."

"O-okay." She sounds like she's on the verge of hyperventilating.

We plow through the open gates of the hangar, and I slam on the brakes, bringing the limo to a screeching holt.

"Run, Rosa!" I yell, unbuckling my seatbelt, and as she scrambles out of the car, I jump out on my side, grabbing my M16.

"Now, Nora!" Esguerra yells behind me, throwing open the passenger door. "Go now!"

Out of the corner of my eye, I see Rosa running after Nora and her parents, but before I can verify they got to the plane, a Sullivan SUV squeals into the building.

I open fire, and Esguerra joins in.

The SUV's windshield shatters as it screeches to a stop in front of us and armed men pour out.

"Get back! Behind the limo!" I yell at Esguerra, covering his retreat. Then he covers me as I dive behind the limo myself.

"Ready?" I say, and he nods. Synchronizing our movements, we pop up on each side of the limo and unleash a volley of shots before ducking back.

"Four down," Esguerra says, reloading his own M16. "I think there's only one left."

"Cover me," I say and crawl around the limo. I can feel the sweat dripping into my eyes as I slither on my stomach while Esguerra fires at the SUV to distract the guy. It takes almost a minute before I see an opening and fire at the shooter.

My bullets hit him in the neck, setting off a geyser of blood.

Breathing hard, I climb to my feet. After the nonstop racket of the battle, the silence feels like I've gone deaf.

"Good job," Esguerra says, coming out from behind the limo. "Now if our remaining men got the—"

"Julian!" On the other side of the hangar, Nora is waving her AK-47 above her head. She looks overjoyed. "Over here! Come, let's go!"

A huge smile lights up Esguerra's face as she begins running toward him—and then a blast of searing heat sends me flying.

14

ulia

The second "debriefing" is even more grueling than the first. Obenko and the two agents want me to go over every conversation with Lucas and describe each of our encounters in detail. They want to know how he kept me tied up, at what point he gave me clothes, what kind of meals I cooked, and what his sexual preferences are. I cooperate at first, but after a while, I begin stonewalling them. I can't bear to have my relationship with my former captor dissected by these men. I don't want them knowing about my feelings for Lucas or my fantasies about him. Those softer moments between us and the things he promised me—those are mine alone.

What happened during my captivity was wrong and twisted, but it also meant something—to me, at least.

"Yulia," Obenko says after I evade yet another one of his questions. "This is important. The man with whom you spent two weeks is Esguerra's second-in-command. From what you're telling us, it sounds like he, not Esguerra, is the driving force behind them coming after us. It's crucial that we understand exactly what he wants and how he thinks."

"I've already told you everything I know." I try not to let my frustration bleed into my voice. "What more do you want from me?"

"How about the truth, Yulia Borisovna?" Mateyenko gives me a penetrating look. "Did Kent send you here? Are you working for him now?"

"What?" My jaw falls open. "Are you serious? I'm the one who warned you. Do you honestly think I would betray my brother's adoptive family?"

"I don't know, Yulia Borisovna." Mateyenko's expression doesn't change. "Would you?"

I rise to my feet. "If I were working for him, why would I tell you that he got this information from me? A double agent wouldn't warn you that she'd cracked—she'd come to you as a hero, not a failure."

Next to Mateyenko, Sokov crosses his arms. "That would depend on how clever the double agent is, Yulia Borisovna. The best ones always have a story."

I turn to Obenko. "Is that what you believe as well? That I betrayed you?"

"No, Yulia." My boss doesn't blink. "If I did, you'd already be dead. But I do think you're hiding something. Aren't you?"

"No." I hold his gaze. "I've told you everything. I don't know anything else that could help us."

Obenko's mouth tightens, but he nods. "All right, then. We're done for the day."

~

When Mateyenko and Sokov leave, I go back to my room, a tension headache throbbing in my temples. I have no doubt Obenko meant what he said: if he thought I was a double agent, he would've killed me.

After surviving Russian prison and Esguerra's compound, I might die at the hands of my colleagues.

Strangely, the thought doesn't upset me much. The hollow chill that has settled in my chest numbs everything, even fear. Now that I'm here—now that I've done everything I can to ensure my brother's safety—I can't work up more than a smidgeon of interest in my own fate. Even the memory of Lucas's cruelty feels distant and muted, as if it happened years ago instead of days.

When I'm back in my room, I lie down and pull the blanket around me, but I can't get warm.

Only one thing could chase away this cold—and he's thousands of miles away.

15

ucas

Rat-tat-tat!

The sharp crackle of gunfire cuts through the darkness, bringing me back to my senses. My brain feels like it's swimming in a thick, viscous fog.

Groaning, I roll over onto my stomach, almost puking from the agony in my skull. Where's Jackson? What happened? We were out on patrol and then… *Fuck!*

Ignoring the throbbing in my head, I begin crawling on the sand, away from the gunfire. My whole body hurts, the sand particles pelting my eyes and filling my lungs. I feel like I'm made of sand, my skin ready to dissolve and blow away in the harsh, stinging wind.

More gunfire, then a pained cry.

Fear squeezes my chest. "Jackson?"

"I'm hit." Jackson's voice is filled with shock. "Oh, fuck, Kent, they got me."

"Hang on." I crawl back toward the gunfire, dragging my useless rifle. I ran out of ammo five minutes after we were ambushed, but I don't want to leave the weapon for the hostiles. "I called it in. They're coming for us."

Jackson coughs, but the sound turns into a gurgle. "Too late, Kent. It's too fucking late. Get back."

"Shut up." I crawl faster, the dim light of the moon illuminating a small mound next to our overturned Humvee. Jackson's voice is coming from that direction, so I know it must be him. "Just hang on."

"They're not… They're not coming, Kent." Jackson is wheezing now. The bullet must've hit his lungs. "Roberts… He wanted this. He ordered this."

"What are you talking about?" I finally reach him, but when I touch him, all I feel is wet meat and fractured bone. I yank my hand away. "Fuck, Jackson, your leg—"

"You have to"—Jackson sucks in a gurgling breath—"go. They'll blow this place if they come. Roberts, he… I caught him. I was going to expose him. This isn't Taliban. Roberts knew"—he coughs wetly—"knew we'd be here. This is his doing."

"Stop. We're going to get through this." I can't think about what Jackson is saying, can't process the implications of his words. Our commanding officer couldn't have betrayed us like that. It's impossible. "Just hang on, buddy."

"Too late." Jackson gurgle-wheezes as I reach for him again. "Roberts…" He chokes, and I feel hot liquid coating my hands as I press them over his stomach.

"Jackson, stay with me." My heart beats in a sick, erratic rhythm. Not Jackson. This can't be happening to Jackson. I increase the pressure on his wound, trying to stop the bleeding. "Come on, buddy, just stay with me. Help will be here soon."

"Run," Jackson mumbles inaudibly. "He'll kill…" He shudders, and I feel the moment it happens. His body goes limp, and the stench of evacuated bowels fills the air.

"Jackson!" Keeping my hand on his stomach, I reach for his neck, but there's no pulse.

It's over. My best friend is dead.

Rat-tat-tat!

The gunfire is back, and so is the syrupy fog in my brain. It's also hot—far hotter than it should be at night in the desert. The heat is consuming me, eating away at me like—

Fucking hell, I'm burning!

Throwing myself to the side, I roll, not stopping until the burning heat recedes. My ribs scream in pain and my head spins, but the flames licking at my skin are gone.

Panting, I open my eyes and stare at the tall ceiling above me.

Ceiling, not night sky.

My brain synapses finally connect and begin firing.

Afghanistan was eight years ago.

I'm in Chicago, not Afghanistan, and whatever took me down has nothing to do with my old commander.

Rat-tat-tat!

I turn my head to see a small figure running on the other side of the hangar. Four men in SWAT gear are running after her. As I watch in disbelief, Esguerra's wife turns and fires her AK-47 at the pursuers before darting behind one of the planes.

Shit. I have to help Nora. Groaning, I roll over onto my side. There's burning rubble all around me, and the limo is on fire. In the hangar wall behind the limo is a gaping hole through which I can see the police chopper. It's sitting on the grass outside, its blades no longer turning.

Sullivan's henchmen must've taken out the guards in our last SUV before coming for us.

As I struggle to my feet, I see Esguerra leap toward the burning limo. He survived, I realize with relief. Fighting a wave of dizziness, I take a step toward the car, ignoring the agonizing pain in my ribs.

Before I can get there, Esguerra jumps out of the limo, holding two machine guns, and sprints after Nora's pursuers. I'm about to go help him when I spot movement near the helicopter.

Two men are climbing out, clearly intent on getting away.

I react even before I consciously realize who they are. Lifting my weapon, I pepper them with bullets, purposefully aiming my shots away from critical organs. When I stop, the hangar is silent again, and I look back to see Esguerra embracing Nora, both of them seemingly unhurt.

A vicious smile curves my lips as I turn and make my way to the two men I injured.

It's time for the Sullivans to get their due.

~

"Is that who I think it is?" Esguerra asks hoarsely, nodding toward the older man, and my smile widens.

"Yes. Patrick Sullivan himself, along with his favorite—and last remaining—son Sean."

I shot Patrick through the leg and his son through the arm, and both men are rolling on the ground, blubbering in agony. Their pain helps soothe some of my raging fury. For what they did to Rosa and Nora, and for the guards who died today, these men will pay.

"I'm guessing they came in the chopper to observe the action and swoop in at the right time," I say, holding my aching ribs. "Except the right time never came. They must've learned who you were and called in all the cops who owed them favors."

"The men we killed were cops?" Nora asks, visibly trembling. She must be coming down from an adrenaline high. "The ones in the Hummers and the SUVs, too?"

"Judging by their gear, many of them were." Esguerra wraps a supportive arm around her waist. "Some were probably dirty, but others just blindly following orders from their higher-ups. I have no doubt they were told we were highly dangerous criminals. Maybe even terrorists."

"Oh." Nora leans against her husband, her face suddenly turning gray.

"Fuck," Esguerra mutters, picking her up. Holding her against his chest, he says, "I'm going to take her to the plane."

To my surprise, Nora shakes her head. "No, I'm fine. Please let me down." She pushes at him with such determination that Esguerra complies, carefully setting her on her feet.

Keeping one arm around her back, he gives her a concerned look. "What is it, baby?"

Nora gestures toward our captives. "What are you going to do with them? Are you going to kill them?"

"Yes," Esguerra answers with no hesitation. "I will."

Nora doesn't say anything, and I remember my promise to her friend. "I think Rosa should be here for this," I say. "She'll want to see justice served."

Esguerra looks at his wife, and she nods.

"Bring her here," Esguerra says, and despite the grimness of the situation, I feel a twinge of amusement as I walk back to the plane.

Esguerra's delicate little wife has acclimated to our world quite well.

When I get to the plane, Rosa steps out to meet me, her face pale. "Lucas, are they—"

"Yes, come." Carefully taking her arm, I lead her out of the hangar. As we step outside, I see that Patrick Sullivan has passed out on the ground, but his son is still conscious and pleading for his life.

I glance at Rosa, and I'm pleased to see that her cheeks have regained some color. Approaching Sean Sullivan, she stares down at him for a couple of seconds before looking up at me and Esguerra.

"May I?" she asks, holding out her hand, and I smile coldly as I hand her my rifle. Rosa's hands are steady as she aims at her attacker.

"Do it," Esguerra says, and she pulls the trigger. Sean Sullivan's face explodes, blood and bits of brain matter flying everywhere, but Rosa doesn't flinch or look away.

Before the sound of her shot fades, Esguerra steps toward unconscious Patrick Sullivan and releases a round of bullets into the older man's chest.

"We're done here," Esguerra says, turning away from the dead body, and the four of us return to the plane.

II

THE LEAD

16

ucas

I SPEND THE WEEK AFTER OUR RETURN FROM CHICAGO DEALING WITH the aftermath of the trip and recuperating from my injuries. According to Goldberg, our estate doctor, I have cracked ribs and a few first-degree burns on my back and arms—injuries that are beyond minor in light of the battle we survived.

"You're one lucky son of a bitch," Diego says when I finally sit down with him and Eduardo to catch up on the Yulia situation. "All those guys..."

"Yeah." My teeth ache from clenching my jaw all day long. The faces of our dead men haunt me, just like those of the guards who died in the plane crash. Over the past couple of months, we've lost more than seventy of our people, and the mood on the compound is grim, to say the least.

Between organizing funerals, finding new recruits, and

cleaning up the mess in Chicago, I've been running on nothing but adrenaline fumes.

"I hope you made the fuckers pay," Eduardo says, his voice vibrating with fury. "If I'd been there—"

"You'd be dead just like the others," I say wearily. I'm in no mood to indulge the young guard's bluster; my burns are mostly healed at this point, but my ribs hurt with every movement. "Tell me what you've learned thus far. Did you figure out if anyone had contact with my prisoner prior to the escape?"

Diego and Eduardo exchange an odd look. Then Diego says, "Yes, but I don't think it's her."

I frown. "Her?"

"Rosa Martinez, the maid from the main house," Eduardo says hesitantly. "She… Well, the drone footage showed her coming to your house a couple of times during those two weeks."

"Oh, yeah." I chuckle humorlessly. "She had some kind of strange curiosity about Yulia." I'm not about to tell the guards about Rosa's possible crush on me. The girl seems to be past that now, and I don't think she'd appreciate the others knowing about her feelings.

She's been through enough.

"Oh, good. I'm glad you know about that." Diego blows out a relieved breath. "We figured it's unlikely to be her, but I wanted to let you know just in case. She's the only one who came by your house on Tuesday, so…" He shrugs.

"Wait, Tuesday? As in, the day before we left?" I'd warned Rosa away long before that, and I thought she'd listened. "She came to my house on Tuesday?"

"That's what the footage shows," Eduardo says cautiously. "But it can't be her. I know Rosa—we dated for some time. She's not… she wouldn't—"

I hold up my hand, cutting him off. "I'm sure she's not the one to blame," I say, even as a hard knot forms in my chest. If Rosa came to my house after I warned her away, that changes things.

My assumptions about the girl were wrong.

"You did well telling me about this," I say to the two guards. "But I'd appreciate it if you kept quiet about it for now. We don't want anyone getting the wrong idea—Rosa herself included."

If there's something more to her actions than a misplaced crush, I don't want anyone to tip her off.

Diego and Eduardo both nod, looking relieved as I dismiss them. When they're gone, I pick up the phone and call the men we sent to Chicago.

Esguerra's CIA contacts did their best to cover up our high-speed battle, but it was impossible to conceal it all, and now every news outlet in Chicago is blaring with speculation about the clandestine operation to apprehend a dangerous arms dealer. The "arms dealer" story originated with the police chief, who had been in cahoots with Sullivan. The man used the information that Sullivan uncovered about us to come up with the tale of an arms dealer smuggling explosives into Chicago. Under that pretext, he assembled the SWAT team that helped Sullivan, and told everyone that Sullivan's men were reinforcements from another division. The operation was kept secret from other law enforcement agencies—which is why we didn't have advance warning of the attack. So now there's a shitload of work to be done. The police chief and any remaining Sullivan moles have to be taken care of, and the remnants of Sullivan's organization must be wiped out before Nora's parents can return home.

As much as I'd like to tackle Rosa's betrayal, I have more pressing matters to deal with first.

It's not until I'm lying in my bed late that night that I have a chance to think about Rosa again. Could she have done it? Could she have helped Yulia escape? If so, why? Out of jealousy or because someone got to the maid?

Could Yulia's agency have bribed or threatened Rosa?

I mull over that possibility for a few minutes before deciding that it's unlikely. The compound is isolated, and all emails and phone calls with the outside world are monitored. Esguerra is the only one whose communications are private, which means there's no way UUR could've contacted Rosa without raising alarms in the system.

Whatever Rosa did, she did of her own initiative.

The knot in my chest tightens, the bitterness of betrayal mixing with the ever-present anger. Rage has been my companion since I learned of Yulia's escape, and now I have a new target for my fury. If it weren't for the fact that the maid has just been through an ordeal, I'd drag her in for questioning tomorrow. As it is, I'm going to give Rosa another week to heal and use the time to keep a close eye on her, just in case I'm wrong about her motivations.

If she *is* on someone's payroll, I'm going to find that out. In the meantime, I have to finish the cleanup in Chicago and locate Yulia, and I have to do it soon. Not having Yulia is messing with my head. Despite working to exhaustion, I can't sleep at night. There are dozens of urgent business matters that should occupy my thoughts, but it's not worry over finding new guards or containing media leaks that keeps me awake. No, what I think about when I lie in bed is her.

Yulia.

My beautiful, treacherous obsession.

The moment I close my eyes, I see her—her eyes, her smile, her graceful walk. I remember her laughter and her tears, and I ache for her in a way that goes beyond my cock's craving for her silky flesh. As much as I'd like to fuck her, I also want to hold her, to hear her breathing next to me and smell the warm peach scent of her skin.

I fucking miss her, and I hate her for it.

Does she think about me at all, or is she too busy with the man she loves? I picture her lying in his arms, drowsy and replete after sex, and my fury edges into agony, tightening my chest until I can't breathe. I'd take a dozen broken ribs, suffer a hundred burns to avoid this sensation.

I'd do anything to have her back with me.

I love you. I'm yours.

Motherfucker.

I turn on the bedside lamp and sit up, wincing at the pain in my ribs. Getting up, I walk to my library and grab a random book.

It's only when I return to my bed that I realize the book I took was the last one I saw Yulia reading.

The tightness in my chest returns.

I have to get her back.

I simply have to.

17

ulia

"I HAVE A NEW ASSIGNMENT FOR YOU," OBENKO SAYS, WALKING INTO the kitchen of the safe house apartment.

Startled, I look up from my plate of cream-of-wheat kasha. "An assignment?"

Over the past week, my boss has been busy erasing all traces of UUR's existence from the net and reassigning key agents to lower-profile operations whenever possible. He's also been studiously ignoring me—which is why I'm surprised to see him here this morning.

Obenko takes a seat across from me at the table. "It's in Istanbul," he says. "As you know, the situation with Turkey and Russia is beginning to heat up, and we need someone on the ground."

I consume another spoonful of kasha to give myself time to think. "What do you want me to do in Istanbul?" I ask after I swallow. I have no appetite—I haven't had one all week—but I force myself to eat to keep up appearances.

I don't want Obenko to know how listless I feel and speculate about the cause of my malaise.

"Your assignment is to get close to a key Turkish official. To do that, you'll matriculate at Istanbul University as part of a graduate student exchange program with the United States. We have already prepared your documents." Obenko slides a thick folder toward me. "Your name is Mary Becker, and you're from Washington D.C. You're working on your Master's in Political Science at the University of Maryland, and though your undergraduate degree is in Economics, you minored in Near Eastern Studies—hence your interest in a study abroad program in Turkey."

The kasha I've eaten turns into a rock in my stomach. "So it's another long-term play."

"Yes." Obenko gives me a hard look. "Is that a problem?"

"No, of course not." I do my best to sound nonchalant. "But what about my brother? You said you'd get me the pictures."

Obenko's mouth thins. "They're in that folder as well. Take a look and let me know if you have any questions."

He gets up and walks out of the kitchen to make a call, and I flip open the folder, my hands shaking. I'm trying not to think about what this assignment will entail, but I can't help it. My throat is cinched tight, and my insides churn with nausea.

Not now, Yulia. Just focus on Misha.

Ignoring the papers in the file, I find the photos clipped to the back of the folder. They're of my brother—I recognize the color of his hair and the tilt of his head. The pictures were clearly taken in a rush; the photographer captured him mostly from the side and the back, with only one photo showing his face. In that picture, Misha is frowning, his youthful face looking unusually mature. Is he upset because his family had to relocate, or is something else behind his tense expression?

I study the pictures for several minutes, my heart aching, and then I force myself to set them aside so I can look at my assignment.

Ahmet Demir, a member of Turkish Parliament, is forty-seven years old and known to have a weakness for blond American women. Objectively speaking, he's not a bad-looking man—a little balding, a little chubby, but with symmetrical features and a charismatic smile. Looking at his photo shouldn't make me want to throw up, but that's precisely how I feel at the prospect of getting close to him.

I can't imagine sleeping with this man—or any man who's not Lucas.

Feeling increasingly sick, I push the papers away and take several deep breaths. The last time I felt a dread this strong was before my first assignment, when I feared a man's touch in the wake of Kirill's attack. It was a phobia I battled through in order to do my job, and I'm determined to overcome whatever it is I'm feeling now.

For Misha, I tell myself, picking up his pictures again. *I'm doing it for Misha.* Except this time, the words ring hollow in my mind. My brother is no longer a child, no longer a helpless toddler abused in an orphanage. The face in the photo is that of a young man, not a boy. Because of my mistake, his life has already been disrupted. I don't know what reason his adoptive parents gave him for changing their identities, but I have no doubt he's stressed and upset. The carefree, stable life I wanted for him is no longer a possibility, and despite the black guilt gnawing at my chest, I'm aware of a sense of relief.

What I feared has come to pass, and I can't undo it.

For the first time, I consider what would happen if I left UUR—if I simply walked away. Would they let me go, or would they kill me? If I disappeared, would Obenko's sister and her husband continue treating my brother well? I can't imagine that they wouldn't; he's been their adopted son for eleven years. Only monsters would throw him out at this point, and by all indications, Misha's adoptive parents are decent people.

They love Misha, and they wouldn't harm him.

I pick up the documents in the folder and study them. They look authentic—a passport, a driver's license, a birth certificate, and a social security card. If I accept this assignment, I'll start over as Mary Becker, an American grad student. I'll live in Istanbul, attend classes, and eventually become Ahmet Demir's girlfriend. My interlude with Lucas Kent will fade into the past, and I'll move on.

I'll survive, like I always have.

"Do you have any questions for me?" Obenko asks, and I look up to see him walk back into the kitchen. "Did you have a chance to look through the file?"

"Yes." My voice sounds hoarse, and I have to clear my throat before continuing. "I'll need to brush up on a number of subjects before I go to Istanbul."

"Of course," Obenko says. "You have a week before the start of the summer semester. I suggest you get busy."

He leaves the kitchen, and I pick up my half-full plate with unsteady hands. Carrying it over to the garbage, I dump the remnants of my breakfast, wash the plate, and walk to my room, a ghost of a plan forming in my mind.

For the first time in my life, I may have a choice about my future, and I intend to seize the opportunity with both hands.

Over the next week, I learn the basics of Turkish language and culture. I don't need to know a lot, just enough to pass for an American graduate student interested in the subject. I also memorize Mary Becker's background and brush up on American college life. I prepare stories about my roommates and frat parties, read

Economics textbooks, and come up with Mary's interests and hobbies. Obenko and Mateyenko quiz me daily, and when they're satisfied that I make a convincing Mary Becker, they buy me a plane ticket to Berlin.

"You'll travel as Elena Depeshkova to Berlin," Obenko explains. "And as Claudia Schreider from Berlin to New York. Once you're in the United States, your identity as Mary Becker will go into effect, and you'll fly from there to Istanbul. This way, nobody will be able to connect you to Ukraine. Yulia Tzakova will disappear for good."

"Got it," I say, slicking on a bright red lipstick in front of a mirror. I'll be wearing a dark wig for Elena's role, so I'll need bolder makeup for that. "Elena, Claudia, then Mary."

Obenko nods and makes me repeat the names of all of Mary's relatives, beginning with distant cousins and ending with parents. I don't make a single mistake, and when he leaves that day, I know my hard work has paid off.

My boss believes I'll make an excellent Mary Becker.

The next morning, Obenko drives me to the airport, dropping me off at the Departures area. I'm Elena now, so I'm wearing the wig and high-heeled boots that go well with my dark jeans and stylish jacket. Obenko helps me load my suitcases onto a cart before driving away, and I wave him goodbye as he disappears into the airport traffic.

The minute his car is out of sight, I spring into action. Leaving my suitcases on the cart, I run to the Arrivals area and grab a cab.

"Head toward the city," I tell the driver. "I need to pull up the exact address."

He starts driving, and I take out my phone. Opening the tracking app I installed a couple of days ago, I locate a small red dot heading toward the city a kilometer or two ahead of us. It's the tiny GPS chip I surreptitiously placed in Obenko's phone back at the safe house.

I may have no intention of carrying out the Istanbul mission, but I certainly found use for the surveillance equipment UUR gave me.

"Take a left here," I instruct the driver when I see the red dot turning left off the highway. "Then keep going straight."

I give him directions like this until I see Obenko's dot come to a stop in the center of Kiev. Telling the driver to stop a block away, I take out my wallet and pay him; then I jump out and walk the rest of the way, keeping a close eye on my app to make sure Obenko doesn't go anywhere.

I find Obenko's car in front of a tall building. It looks like some kind of office space, with an international corporation's logo blazing at the top and the first floor occupied by businesses ranging from a trendy coffee shop to a high-end clothing boutique.

Slowly, I approach the building, scanning my surrounding every few seconds to make sure I'm not being watched.

What I'm doing is a long shot: there's zero guarantee Obenko will visit his sister any time soon. However, this is the only way I can think of to find Misha. Given their recent relocation, my brother's adoptive parents are still getting settled into their new lives, and there's a chance they might need something from Obenko, something that will necessitate him to visit them personally.

If I follow my boss long enough, he might lead me to my brother.

I know my plan is both desperate and borderline insane. Since I'm walking away from UUR, my best bet is to disappear somewhere in Berlin, or better yet, go all the way to New York. And I'm planning to do exactly that—*after* I see my brother with my own eyes.

I can't leave Ukraine without making sure Misha is okay.

Two days, I tell myself. *I will do this for a maximum of two days.* If I still haven't found my brother by then, I'll leave. They won't realize I didn't board the plane until I don't meet my handler in Istanbul in three days—which gives me a little over forty-eight hours to tail Obenko before getting out of the country.

The dot on my phone indicates that Obenko is on the second floor of the building. I'm curious what he's doing there, but I don't want to expose myself by following him in. I doubt my brother's family is here; Obenko would've relocated them out of the city—assuming they'd lived in the city before. My boss never disclosed their location to me for security reasons, but from the backgrounds in my brother's pictures, I gathered that they'd lived in an urban environment, like Kiev.

Entering the coffee shop, I order a pastry and a cup of Earl Grey and wait for Obenko's dot to start moving again. When it does, I grab another cab and follow him to his next destination: our safe house.

He stays at the apartment for several hours before the dot starts moving again. By then, I've had lunch at a nearby restaurant and swapped my dark wig for a red one I brought with me for this purpose. I've also changed my jeans for a long-sleeved gray dress, and the high-heeled boots for flat booties—the most comfortable option "Elena" had in her carry-on bag.

Obenko's next destination appears to be another office building downtown. He stays there for a couple of hours before heading back to the safe house. I follow him again, feeling increasingly discouraged.

This is clearly not the way to find my brother.

My phone is beginning to run low on batteries, so I go to another coffee shop to charge it while Obenko is at the safe house. I also get online and buy a plane ticket to Berlin for the next morning to replace the one that has gone unused today.

It's time to admit defeat and disappear for good.

Sighing, I order myself another tea and drink it as I read the news on my phone. Obenko seems to be settled in for the night, his dot sitting firmly in the safe house every time I check the app. Finishing my tea, I get up, deciding to go to a hotel and get some rest before the long journey tomorrow. Just as I step outside, however, my phone beeps in my bag, signifying movement on the app.

My heart leaps. Fishing out the phone, I glance at the screen and see that Obenko's dot is going north—possibly out of the city.

This could be it.

Instantly energized, I jump into a cab and follow Obenko. I know there's a 99.9 percent chance this has nothing to do with my brother, but I can't help the irrational hope that grips me as I watch Obenko's dot heading farther north.

"Are you sure you know where you're going, young lady?" the cab driver says when we're out of the city. "You said you were going to get directions from your boyfriend."

"Yes, he's texting me as we speak," I assure him. "It's not much farther."

I'm lying through my teeth—I have no idea how far we're going—but I'm hoping it's not far. With all my cab rides, I'm running low on cash, and I'll need whatever I still have to get to the airport tomorrow morning.

"Fine," the driver mutters. "But you better tell me soon, else I'm dropping you off at the nearest bus stop."

"Just another fifteen minutes," I say, seeing the dot turn left and stop a half-kilometer later. "Turn left at the next intersection."

The driver shoots me a dirty look in the rearview mirror but does as I ask. The road we end up on is dark and full of potholes, and I hear him curse as he swerves to avoid a hole wide enough to swallow our whole car.

"Stop here," I tell him when the tracker app says we're two hundred meters away. Exiting the car, I approach the driver's window and hand him a stack of bills, saying, "Here's half of what I owe you. Please wait for me, and I'll give you the rest when you bring me back to the city."

"What?" He glares at me. "Fuck, no. Give me the full amount, bitch."

I ignore him, turning to walk away, but he leaps out of the car and grabs my arm. Instinctively, I whirl around, my fist catching the underside of his chin as my knee hits him in the balls. He collapses to the ground, wheezing and clutching at his groin, and I bring my foot down on his temple, knocking him out.

I feel awful hurting this civilian, but I can't let him drive off in this cab. If he leaves, I'll have no way of getting back to the city and I'll miss my flight tomorrow morning.

Pushing aside my guilt, I check the driver's pulse to verify that he's alive, grab the keys from the car in case he wakes up, and then head toward the blinking red dot on my phone map.

A couple of minutes later, I come across what looks like an abandoned warehouse. Disappointed, I stare at it, debating whether I should even approach. Whatever Obenko is doing here is unlikely to involve my brother's adoptive parents; my boss wouldn't ask his sister to meet him in the middle of nowhere just to give her some documents. It's far more probable that he's in the middle of an operation, and the last thing I want is to stand in his way.

Despite that, I take a step closer. Then another and another. My legs seem to be carrying me of their own accord. I've come this far, I reason to justify my compulsion. What's another few minutes to confirm that I've wasted my time?

There is a faint glow of light visible on one side of the warehouse, so I make my way there and crouch in front of a small, dirty window. Inside, I hear voices, and I hold my breath, trying to understand what they're saying.

"—getting good," a man says in Russian. There's something familiar about his voice, but I can't place it. The wall is muffling the sound. "Really good. I think another couple of years, and they'll be ready."

"Good," another man replies, and this time, I recognize the speaker as Obenko. "We'll need all the help we can get."

"Would you like a demonstration?" the original speaker says. "They'll be happy to show you what they've learned thus far."

"Of course," Obenko says, and then I hear a grunt, followed by the *thump* of something falling. The noises repeat again and again, and I realize I'm listening to a fight. Two or more people are engaged in hand-to-hand combat, which, combined with the bits I overheard, means only one thing.

I've stumbled upon a UUR training facility.

That's it. I need to leave before I'm caught.

I turn around, about to head back, when the original speaker laughs loudly and exclaims, "Good job!"

I freeze in place, a sick feeling spreading through me. *That voice.* I know that voice. I've heard it in my nightmares over and over again.

Cold sweat breaks over my skin as I turn, drawn to the window despite myself.

It can't be.

It just can't be.

My pulse is a violent drumbeat, and my hands tremble as I place them on the wall next to the window.

I'm imagining this.

I'm hallucinating.

I have to be.

Sinking my teeth into my lower lip, I edge to the left until I can see through the window. I know I'm taking a terrible risk, but I have to know the truth.

I have to know if they lied to me.

The scene that greets my eyes is straight out of my own training sessions. There are several teenagers of both genders standing in a semi-circle. Their backs are to me, and in front of them is a wide mat on which two men—or, rather, a man and a boy—are wrestling. Obenko is standing to the side, watching them with an approving smile.

I notice all of this only briefly because my eyes are glued to the wrestling pair. With the two of them twisting and rolling on the mat, I can't get a good look at either of them—at least until they stop, with the man pinning his younger opponent to the mat.

"Good job," the man says, rising to his feet. Laughing, he extends his hand to help his defeated opponent. "You were excellent today, Zhenya."

The boy gets up as well, brushing the dirt off his clothes, but I'm not looking at him.

All I see is the man standing next to him.

He hasn't changed much. His brown hair is thinner and has more gray in it, but his body is as strong and broad as I remember. His shoulders strain the seams of his sweat-soaked T-shirt, and his arms are as thick as drain pipes.

Nobody could best Kirill in hand-to-hand combat seven years ago, and it seems he's still undefeated.

Alive and undefeated.

Obenko lied to me. They all lied to me.

My rapist wasn't killed for what he did to me.

He wasn't even removed from his role as a trainer.

A metallic taste fills my mouth, and I realize I bit through my lip.

"It's your fault, bitch. It's all your fault." Kirill's massive body presses me into the floor, his hands cruelly tearing at my clothes. "You're going to pay for what you did."

Acid rises in my throat, mixing with the bitterness of bile. I feel like I'm going to choke on my terror and hatred, but before the memories can suffocate me, someone else enters my field of vision.

"It's my turn," a blond-haired boy says, approaching the mat. "Uncle Vasya, I want you to watch this." He assumes a fighter's stance opposite Kirill, and the fluorescent lights illuminate his face.

It's a face I know as well as my own—because I've spent hours staring at it in photos.

Because every feature on that face is a masculine version of what I see in the mirror.

My brother is standing in front of me, ready to spar with Kirill.

18

 *ucas*

"It's done," I say, entering Esguerra's office. "Your in-laws can go home tomorrow if they're so inclined."

Over the past week, we've exterminated the remnants of Sullivan's crime family, and the CIA has finally agreed to let Nora's parents return to their home. After the media nightmare we caused, it took promises of major favors, but Esguerra's contacts came through for us.

"You got the police chief as well?" Esguerra asks.

I nod, approaching his desk. "His body is dissolving in lye as we speak. He was the last of the moles—Chicago PD is now squeaky clean and vermin-free. Other than a few CIA higher-ups, nobody knows your in-laws were involved in this mess."

"Excellent." Esguerra rubs his temples, and I see that he looks unusually tired. Like me, he's been working nonstop since our return from Chicago. He doesn't have to put in these hours—I'm overseeing most of the logistics of the cleanup—but work seems to be his way of coping with the miscarriage. "I'll tell Nora. In the meantime, I want you to assign another dozen men to watch over her parents for the next few months. I'm not expecting any trouble, but it's best to be safe."

"Got it," I say. "You might also want to tell them to stay away from crowded places for a while, just in case."

"That's a good idea." Esguerra gives an approving nod. "As long as they're able to return to work and resume their social lives, they shouldn't mind the restrictions too much."

"I'm sure you'll miss them," I say drily. Nora's parents have been our reluctant guests for the last two weeks, and I imagine Esguerra must've found their disapproving presence wearing.

To my surprise, my boss chuckles. "They're not so bad. You know, family and all that."

"Right." I try not to stare at him but fail. Esguerra's changed; it's obvious to me now. When I first met him, the word "family" would've never passed his lips. And now he's putting up with in-laws who can't stand his guts and bending over backward to keep his young wife happy.

It's both amusing and unsettling to observe, like seeing a jaguar playing with a house kitten.

"You'll understand someday," Esguerra says, and I realize my expression must've given me away. "There's more to life than this." He waves at the flatscreen monitors behind him and the stack of papers on his desk.

"Are you going to give it up then? Walk the straight and narrow?" I say, only half-kidding. Esguerra is certainly wealthy enough to do so. His net worth is in the billions; even if he never sold another weapon, he could live like a king for the rest of his life.

Still, I'm not surprised when Esguerra shakes his head and says, "You know I can't do that. Once in this life, always in this life.

Besides"—he bares his teeth in a sharp smile—"I'd miss it. Wouldn't you?"

"Definitely," I say, and we share a moment of grim understanding.

The jaguar may play with the kitten, and even love said kitten, but he'll always be a jaguar.

~

As I leave Esguerra's office, my phone vibrates with an incoming message. I open my email, and my lips curl in savage anticipation.

Message decoded, the email from the hackers reads. *A confirmed UUR black site is located twenty-five kilometers north of Kiev. They seem to be in the process of covering up their tracks, but they're not fast enough. We're getting closer to the two field operatives. Hope to have more news soon.*

At the bottom of the email is an attachment. It's a grainy satellite photo with an X marking a spot on the map where, I presume, the black site facility is located.

We have a place to start.

"Hi, Lucas," a softly accented female voice says, and I turn to see Rosa approaching from the direction of the main house. She's dressed in her usual maid's outfit, with her dark hair pinned in a sleek knot. "How are you?"

Rage surges through me, but I manage to say calmly, "I'm fine." Her casual friendliness grates on me like chalk on glass. I'm tempted to string her up in the shed and interrogate her this very moment, but it would be smart to wait a little longer. Taking a steadying breath, I mimic her friendly tone and ask, "How's everything with you?"

She shrugs, her eyes dropping lower for a moment. "You know. Day by day."

"Right." Despite everything, I feel a swell of pity. Though the bruises on Rosa's face have faded, I remember how the girl looked after the club, and some of my anger cools.

If I believed in karma, I'd be inclined to think she's already been punished.

"How are your ribs doing?" she asks, looking up at me again. There appears to be genuine concern in her gaze. "Are they still hurting?"

"No, not as much as before," I say, my anger easing a little. "It'll be at least another month before I can resume training normally, but I've gotten to the point where I can breathe without pain."

"Oh, good." Rosa smiles, then asks nonchalantly, "Any news on your escapee?"

My fury returns in full force; it's all I can do not to wring the girl's neck. "Why, yes," I say silkily. "I have just found her." It's a lie —I have no idea if the location the hackers uncovered will lead me to Yulia—but if Rosa is working with UUR, I want her to panic and reach out to them. "In fact," I add, deciding to really frighten the maid, "I'll be going after Yulia as soon as I drop off Nora's parents."

"Oh." Rosa blinks, and I see a shadow pass over her face. "That's good."

"Yes, it is, isn't it?" I give her my blandest smile. "I can't wait. Now if you'll excuse me, I have to check up on our new recruits."

And before she can respond, I turn away and head toward the training field.

If I stay in Rosa's presence a moment longer, I'll kill the girl with my bare hands.

19

ulia

My brother.

Kirill is training my brother.

I feel like I stepped into one of my nightmares. I need to back away, to leave before I'm seen, but I can't move. My feet have grown roots, and my lungs scream for suddenly scarce air.

Misha and Kirill.

Student and teacher.

I taste vomit and my vision darkens, fading at the edges.

Run, Yulia. Go before it's too late.

I want to obey the voice in my head, but I'm paralyzed, frozen in place.

Obenko didn't just lie to me about Kirill's death. He deceived me about everything.

I try to suck in oxygen, but my throat is too tight. The window wavers in front of me, like the lens of a shaking camera, and I realize it's because I'm trembling violently, my fingers icy and numb as my palms press against the wall.

Run, Yulia. Now.

The voice gets more insistent, and I force myself to take a tiny step back. But I still can't look away from the horror in front of me.

Go, Yulia! Run!

Before I can take another step, Misha glances at the window and freezes, staring straight at me.

I see his blue eyes widen, and then he shouts, "Intruder!" and leaps toward the window.

My paralysis finally breaks, and I turn and run.

My legs are like wooden sticks, stiff and clumsy, and I can't get enough air. It's as if I'm moving through quicksand, every step requiring desperate effort. I know it's shock weighing me down, but the knowledge doesn't help. My muscles feel like they belong to a stranger, and my feet are numb as they touch the ground.

The car. I need to get back to the car.

I focus on that one goal, on putting one foot in front of the other and not thinking. As I run, I feel the stiffness in my muscles fading, and I know adrenaline is finally kicking in, overpowering my shock.

"Yulia! Stop!"

It's Obenko. Hearing him fills me with such rage that all remnants of my sluggishness fade. Gritting my teeth, I pick up my pace, my legs pumping with increasing desperation. If they catch me, I'm dead, and then nobody will make Obenko pay for his monstrous betrayal.

I will rot in a nameless grave while Kirill turns my brother into a conscienceless killing machine.

"Yulia!"

It's a different voice calling my name. I recognize Kirill's deeper tones, and sick terror explodes in my veins. The memories snake around me like poisonous vines. I try to push them away, but bits and pieces slip through, flashing through my brain in a disjointed reel.

Entering my room in the dorm. A large hand closing over my mouth as I'm grabbed from behind.

I run faster, the ground blurring in front of my eyes. My breath is coming in wheezing gasps, and my lungs are about to burst.

Struggling. Falling to the floor. A man on top of me. Immobilized, helpless.

I'm a dozen meters from the car, and I grip the keys in my pocket, preparing to jump in.

Pop! Pop! The car window shatters, and I zigzag to avoid the next bullet.

"Do not shoot to kill!" Kirill roars behind me. His voice sounds closer; he's gaining on me. "I repeat, do not shoot to kill!"

The knowledge that he wants me alive is more terrifying than the idea of dying. Putting on another burst of speed, I leap for the car. The cab driver is on the ground, still unconscious, and I desperately hope none of the bullets hit him. I don't have time to worry about it, though, because as I'm about to jam the keys into the door, a hand grips my shoulder.

I whirl around, gripping the keys like a weapon, and jab upward, aiming at my attacker's eye. He jerks back, and I drop down and roll under the car, registering only dimly the smaller frame and light hair of my opponent.

It wasn't Kirill who caught up with me; it was Misha.

I scramble to my feet on the other side of the car and begin running again. Even through my terror, I'm aware of an illogical flash of pride. My brother is a fast runner. Obenko had never mentioned that.

I hear him sprinting behind me, and I wonder if he knows who I am, if he realizes he's killing his own sister. Is he in on Obenko's deception, or did they lie to him too?

"Grab her!" Kirill shouts, and a hard body hits me in the back, knocking me to the ground. I manage to twist in the air, so I land on top of Misha, and before he has a chance to act, I punch him in the jaw and jump up to resume running.

Only it's too late. As I turn, another body hits me, knocking me off my feet, and this time, I don't have a chance to land a punch.

In a flash, my arm is twisted behind my back, and my face is pressed into the gritty dirt as a massive weight presses me down.

"Hello, Yulia," my trainer whispers in my ear. "It's good to see you again."

20

ucas

ESGUERRA NOTIFIES ME THAT NORA'S PARENTS WISH TO FLY OUT first thing in the morning, and I decide to do exactly what I told Rosa: go to Ukraine directly after taking them home. I'm still not fully recovered, but the workload from the Chicago disaster is easing up, and my ribs can heal in Ukraine just as well as here.

Now I need to break the news to Esguerra and fill him in on everything I've learned about UUR.

"So let me get this straight," Esguerra says when I stop by his office and explain about the black site. "You want to take a dozen of our best-trained men to conduct an operation in Ukraine when we're still trying to recover from all the losses? What's the urgency on this?"

"They're in the process of covering their tracks," I say. "If we wait much longer, they'll be much harder to track down."

I keep silent about the fact that every day that passes without Yulia is fucking torture, and I can't sleep without her by my side.

"So what?" Esguerra says, frowning. "We'll get them eventually —when we're stronger and have rebuilt our security team. We can't spare a dozen guards right now. UUR is not an immediate threat to us the way Al-Quadar were. We're going to make the Ukrainians pay for the crash, but we'll do it when the time is right."

I take a deep breath. I know Esguerra has a point, but I can't stay on the estate while Yulia is out there with this Misha of hers.

"All right," I say. "How about I go to Ukraine by myself, with just a couple of guards? I could take Diego and Eduardo—surely you can spare the three of us."

Esguerra's gaze sharpens. "Why? Is it because of the girl who escaped?"

I hesitate for a moment, then decide to tell the truth. "Yes," I say, watching Esguerra's reaction. "I want her back."

"I thought you were just amusing yourself with her."

"I was—but I'm not done."

Esguerra stares at me. "I see."

"She's mine," I say, deciding it's time to lay it out there. "I'm going to get her back, and I'm going to keep her."

"Keep her?" Esguerra's expression doesn't change, but I see a muscle twitch in his jaw as he leans forward in his seat. "What exactly do you mean by that?"

I plant my feet wider apart and give him a level look. "It means I'm going to put trackers on her and keep her for as long as it suits me. I'm sure you won't object to that."

The twitch in Esguerra's jaw intensifies as we stare at each other, neither one backing down. The air thickens with tension, and I know that this is it: this is when I find out if my boss truly values my loyalty.

Esguerra breaks the silence first. "So that's it? You're ready to forget about the crash?"

"She was following orders," I say. "And besides, who said she's getting off scot-free?"

For this new betrayal—for running to her lover—Yulia *will* pay.

Esguerra holds my gaze for a few more seconds before getting up and walking around his desk. Stopping in front of me, he says quietly, "You and I both know I owe you for Thailand, and if this is what you want—if *she* is what you want—then I won't stand in your way. But she's bad news, Lucas. Do what you must to get her out of your system, but don't forget what she is and what she's done."

"Oh, don't worry." I give him a humorless smile. "I won't."

I haven't yet decided how I'm going to punish Yulia when I get her back, but I do know one thing.

Her lover's days are numbered.

THAT EVENING, I MAKE ARRANGEMENTS TO HAVE THOMAS—another guard I trust—keep an eye on Rosa. I don't tell him why; I just ask him to follow her discreetly and to monitor all her emails and calls. My top priority right now is finding Yulia, but I haven't forgotten about the potential danger Rosa poses to us.

When I'm back from Ukraine, I'm going to deal with her. First, though, I need to get Nora's parents home and figure out how to get into Ukraine undetected.

I start by reaching out to Buschekov, the Russian official we met with in Moscow. I don't mention Yulia's escape, but I do give him the information I've uncovered so far about UUR. The more pressure I can bring to bear on Yulia's agency, the better.

Unfortunately, Buschekov claims to be unable to help me with discreet entry into Ukraine, explaining that tensions are running too high between the two countries. I suspect he just doesn't want to risk whatever agents he has in place there, but I don't press him on this. If I had a firm lock on Yulia's location, it would be different, but this black site is just a lead, and I need to preserve whatever goodwill we have with the Russians. That means there's only one thing left to do.

I contact Peter Sokolov, Esguerra's former security consultant, and ask him for help.

Peter saved Esguerra's ass after the crash, but to do so, he let the terrorists take Nora, and my boss has sworn to kill him if he ever lays eyes on him again. I, however, do not share Esguerra's feelings. In fact, I'm grateful that Esguerra is alive and well. I haven't kept in touch with Peter, but I do have his email from before, so I send him a message explaining the situation. The Russian's contacts in Eastern Europe are unparalleled; he's the one who introduced us to Buschekov in the first place.

He doesn't respond right away, but I don't expect him to. I know he's busy with his vendetta against the people on his list. Still, I'm hoping he'll spare a moment to check his email. All I need is to have a couple of air control officials in Ukraine look the other way when I land in Kiev.

As one final step, I brief Diego and Eduardo on our upcoming mission.

"It's going to be just the three of us," I explain, "so we're going to keep a low profile. We don't want anyone catching wind of our presence there until we're gone. The goal is to find out what we can and get out of the county in one piece. Is that clear?"

They both nod, and early the next morning, we load the plane with weapons, body armor, falsified documents, and everything else we'd need in case things don't go according to plan.

Now I just need Peter to come through.

By the time we land in Chicago, there's still no answering email from Sokolov, so I hand Esguerra's in-laws off to our Chicago security crew and instruct the guards to see them safely home. Both of Nora's parents seem relieved to be back on US soil, and I suspect we won't be seeing them in Colombia again any time soon.

"So what's the plan?" Diego asks when I return to the plane. "Are we flying to Kiev right away?"

"We might stop over in London for a day or two," I say. "I'm waiting on a lead." As I speak, my phone vibrates with an incoming message. Opening my email, I read the response from Peter, and a smile spreads across my face.

"Never mind," I say, turning toward the pilot's cabin. "We're heading to Ukraine."

21

ulia

"So, tell us, Yulia," Obenko says, leaning on the table. "Why didn't you get on that plane?"

I remain silent and focus on taking small, even breaths. One inhale, one exhale. Then again and again. That's all I can do at the moment. Anything else is beyond me. Somewhere out there, lurking at the edge of my consciousness, is the pain of betrayal, the kind of monstrous pain that will destroy me if I let it, and so I focus on the mundane, like my breathing and the flickering fluorescent lights above my head.

My hands are handcuffed behind me, and my ankles are secured to my wrists with a long chain. I'm still wearing the dress they captured me in, but they took off my wig at some point. I have no idea when that happened or where I am, since I have only a vague recollection of the hours that followed my capture. I know this is an interrogation chamber of some kind, with a wall-sized mirror and hard metal furniture, but I don't know if we're still in Kiev. I think I was driven somewhere from the warehouse, so perhaps not, but either way, it doesn't matter.

I'm not getting out of here alive.

"Answer me, Yulia," Obenko says in a harsher tone. "Why didn't you fly out as you were supposed to, and how did you find the training facility? Are you working for Esguerra now?"

I don't respond, and Obenko's eyes narrow. "I see. Well, if you don't want to talk to me, perhaps you'll talk to Kirill Ivanovich." He rises to his feet and gives the mirror a small nod before stepping out of the room.

A minute later, my former trainer walks in, his thin lips curved in a hard smile. Despite my best efforts to remain calm, my throat closes and cold sweat dampens my armpits as he approaches the table and sits down across from me.

"Why are you being so stubborn?" His knee brushes across my bare leg under the table, and I have to swallow to contain the vomit rising in my throat. "Are you a double agent, like they think you are?"

I try to move my leg, to shift away from his touch, but the chain keeps me in place. From this distance, I can smell his cologne, and my breathing speeds up until I'm almost hyperventilating. Desperate to control myself, I look down at the table, focusing on the oily stains marring the metal surface. *Inhale. Exhale. Inhale. Exhale.*

"Yulia…" Kirill's hand grips my knee under the table, his fingers digging into my thigh. "Are you working for Esguerra?"

Inhale. Exhale. Inhale. Exhale. I can survive this. I can keep the pain at bay. *Inhale. Exhale.*

His hand moves higher up my thigh. "Answer me, Yulia."

Inhale. Exhale. I feel the darkness approaching, the blankness that shielded me during my capture, and I embrace it for once, letting my mind flit away from this room, away from the encroaching agony. It's not me chained to this chair—it's just my body. It's just bones and flesh that will soon cease to be animate. There's nothing they can do to hurt me because I'm not here.

I don't exist in this place.

~

"—CATATONIC," A MAN SAYS. HIS VOICE SOUNDS LIKE IT'S COMING through a thick wall of water. I have trouble making out the words, and I struggle to push away the darkness as he says, "You're not going to get any answers from her this way. Just end it. It's obvious she's gone rogue."

"We need to find out what she knows," another man replies, and I recognize this voice as Obenko's. "Besides, if she's not a double agent, maybe this can still be fixed."

"You're deluding yourself," the original voice responds, and this time, I recognize it as belonging to Mateyenko, one of the senior agents who interrogated me after my return. "She'll never forgive you for this."

"Maybe not, but I have an idea," Obenko says, and I hear the sound of retreating footsteps. My mind slowly begins to clear, and I open my eyes a sliver, peeking through my eyelashes.

I'm still in the interrogation room, but I'm no longer chained at the table. Instead, I'm lying on my side on the cold cement floor next to the chair, my wrists still handcuffed behind my back.

There are two men standing by the door—Kirill and Mateyenko. They're speaking in low tones, occasionally glancing in my direction, and nausea twists my insides as darkness presses in again. Did Kirill touch me while I was out? Was he the one who unchained me and put me here?

"She's awake," Mateyenko exclaims, striding toward me, and I stop fighting off the darkness.

I'm not here.

I don't exist.

~

"YULIA." A COOL HAND BRUSHES OVER MY FOREHEAD. "YULIA, ARE you awake?"

The wall of water is back, messing with my hearing, but something about that voice catches my attention. The darkness dissipates, the wall of water thinning, and I open my eyes.

A blond boy is crouching over me, his eyes piercingly blue in his handsome face.

We stare at each other for a second; then my brother jumps to his feet. "Uncle Vasya," he yells. "She woke up."

I hear footsteps, and then strong hands drag me off the floor and place me back in the chair. My pulse jumps, but before my panic spirals out of control, I realize that Kirill is nowhere in sight.

It's just Obenko and me.

"Where's Misha?" I ask hoarsely. My throat feels coated with sand, and my mouth is woolly and dry. I must've been out for a while.

"He stepped out so we could talk," Obenko says. "So, Yulia, let's talk."

"All right." I become aware that I'm shivering and the tips of my fingers are numb and frozen. Despite that, my voice is steady as I say, "What do you want to talk about? The fact that you lied to me for eleven years?" My voice strengthens as the residual fog in my brain clears. "That you stole my brother and are having him trained by a monster?"

Obenko lets out a weary sigh. "There's no need to be so dramatic. I didn't lie to you—not about Misha, at least. I just didn't tell you everything."

"What's 'everything'?"

"Up until two years ago, Misha led exactly the kind of life we showed you in those pictures. He was a normal, happy, well-adjusted boy. Then things began to change. He started skipping school, getting into fights, shoplifting cigarettes…" Obenko grimaces. "My sister didn't know what to do, so she reached out to me to see if I could talk some sense into him. But when I tried, I could see it wouldn't work. Misha was too restless, too bored with his life." Obenko looks at me. "Kind of like how I felt at his age."

"So you what?" My frozen hands clench behind my back. "Decided he should be a spy?"

Obenko doesn't blink. "He needed direction, Yulia. He needed a sense of purpose, and we could provide that. There are so many youths like him in our disillusioned country—boys who lose their way and never find it again. They don't know what they're doing with their lives, don't care about anything but a momentary thrill. I didn't want your brother to be like that."

"Right." I feel like I'm about to choke. "You wanted him to be like you and Kirill."

"Yulia, listen, about Kirill…" Something resembling guilt shadows Obenko's gaze. "You have to understand that we're a small covert organization. We couldn't afford to lose someone as skilled and experienced as Kirill. Not over one mistake."

"One mistake?" My voice cracks. "Is that what they're calling brutal assault now?"

Obenko sighs again, like I'm being unreasonable. "What happened with you was an isolated incident," he says patiently. "It was the one and only time he lost control like that. I understand that it was a traumatic experience for you, but he's an asset to our agency and our country. The best we could do was relocate him away from you—and make sure you could move past it."

"By telling me that he was dead? That you had him assassinated?"

Obenko nods. "It was for your own good. That way you could forget him and move forward."

"You mean, be of use to UUR."

Obenko doesn't respond, and I know that's exactly what he

means. In his mind, I'm not a person. I'm a pawn on a chessboard —one that could function either as an asset or a liability.

"Does Misha know?" I ask, staring at the man I'd once looked up to. "Does he know I'm his sister?"

Obenko hesitates, then says, "Yes, Misha knows. He remembered you from the orphanage, so we had no choice but to tell him about you. He also knows that you turned on us—that whatever happened to you at Esguerra's compound made you betray your own country."

My nails dig into my palms. "That's a lie. I didn't betray you."

"Then why did you follow me? Why did you slip me this?" Obenko places his hand on the table and uncurls his fist to show me the GPS chip I planted in his phone.

After a moment of consideration, I decide I have nothing to lose by telling the truth. I'm already a liability in Obenko's eyes. "Because I wanted to see Misha one last time," I say evenly. "Because I couldn't do this anymore."

"So you were going to walk away." Obenko gives me an assessing look. "You know, I suspected that might be the case. You weren't the same after you came back."

I shrug, not about to explain about my complex relationship with Lucas and my inability to take on another "assignment." Whatever guilt I'd felt at abandoning UUR is gone, vaporized by the crushing blow of Obenko's betrayal and Misha's eager abandonment of the life I fought so hard to give him.

I've spent eleven years protecting my brother, only to find out he's going to end up like me.

I suppose I should be devastated, but the pain is still distant, held at bay by a cold numbness that overpowers everything, even my fury.

"I want to talk to him," I say to Obenko. "I want to talk to Misha."

He studies me for a moment, then slowly shakes his head. "No, Yulia. You'll only confuse the boy. He's where he needs to be, mentally and emotionally, and whatever you plan to tell him will only make it harder for him. I don't think you want that."

My upper lip curls. "So he doesn't know what Kirill did or how you manipulated me all those years."

Obenko doesn't blink. "What Misha knows is that Kirill Ivanovich dedicated his life to this country, just like all of us at UUR—and that you left Misha when he was a baby. Everything else is a matter of opinion."

"Of course it is." I should be enraged that my brother believes I'm a traitor who abandoned him in the orphanage, but it's too much to absorb all at once. It feels like this is happening to someone else, like I'm watching a movie rather than living it. "So what will his opinion be of my disappearance?"

Obenko sighs. "Yulia..."

"Just tell me."

"You will have escaped," Obenko says. "Disappeared to South America to be with your lover."

"Ah, yes. My lover, of course." I think of Lucas and the way we parted, and sharp agony rips through me. "So when exactly am I going to make my grand escape?" I manage to say. "Today? Tomorrow?"

"It doesn't have to be this way, Yulia." There's genuine regret in Obenko's eyes. "It's not too late. We can start over and forget all this. If you prove yourself—"

"Prove myself?" I can't hold back a burst of bitter laughter. "By doing what? Fucking a few more men for you?"

Obenko's hand flexes on the table, but his tone remains unruffled. "By carrying out your assignment. You know how important what we do is—"

"Yes, I do." My mouth twists. "So important that you'd let a rapist train underage girls. So important that you'd lie, murder, and manipulate everyone... even your own adoptive nephew."

Obenko's gaze hardens, and he gets up. "Suit yourself," he says.

"You have until tomorrow morning. If you decide to do the right thing, let me know."

He walks out of the room, and I remain at the table, listening to the sound of his departing footsteps.

After about an hour, Mateyenko comes in to unlock my handcuffs and bring me to a windowless room that resembles a cell. It has a narrow cot with a thin blanket, a metal toilet without a lid, and a small rusted sink.

"Where is this place?" I ask, but the senior agent doesn't respond. He just steps out and locks the door behind him, leaving me alone.

I wait for a few minutes to make sure he doesn't return, and then I use the toilet and wash my hands with the rusty water trickling from the faucet in the sink. I also consider drinking some of that water to quench my thirst, but decide against it.

I'd rather not spend my last night puking my guts out.

I walk over to the cot and lie down, staring at the ceiling. I know I won't be able to fall asleep, so I don't even try. My mind spins and whirls, cycling between bitter rage and numb despair. Three facts repeat over and over:

Kirill is alive and training my brother to be a spy.

My brother has been fed a bunch of lies about me.

I will die tomorrow unless I agree to work for UUR.

There's nothing I can do about the first two problems, but the third one is within my control—if Obenko is to be believed, at least. Theoretically, I could agree to carry out my assignment, and if I prove myself, all will be forgiven.

I could also promise to carry out the assignment, but run instead.

It's a tantalizing idea, except it won't be easy. I admitted to wanting to disappear, so if they do decide to let me out into the field, I'll be kept under close observation. They might even put some kind of trackers on me, the way Lucas planned to.

My despair gives way to bitter amusement. It seems I'm destined to be a prisoner one way or another.

A shiver rattles my body, and I realize I'm cold again, my hands and feet frozen and stiff. Rolling up into a small ball, I pull the blanket over my head and pretend I'm in a cocoon where nothing bad can ever touch me, where I can sleep and dream of a different life—a life where Lucas looks at me the way he did that last morning before his trip, and I don't have to leave.

A familiar pain pierces my chest, and I close my eyes, letting the memories come. Our relationship had been wrong in so many ways, yet there had been so much right about it too. And now... now none of the wrongness matters.

All I'm left with are the memories and a potent, impossible longing to see him one last time before I die.

THE BLANKET IS PULLED OFF ME, AND STRONG HANDS TUG AT MY underwear, tearing it off as my dress is flipped up. A heavy male body presses me down, and my wrists are pinned above my head. At first, I think I'm dreaming of Lucas, but then I smell it.

Cologne.

Lucas never wears cologne.

My eyes snap open on a surge of panic, and a hoarse scream bursts from my throat—a scream that's instantly muffled by a large palm over my mouth.

"Quiet now," Kirill whispers as I writhe hysterically, trying to throw him off. "We don't want to disturb anyone, do we?"

His hand over my mouth is crushing my jaw, and his other hand is squeezing my wrists so hard I feel my bones grinding against one another. With his legs pinning mine to the bed, I can't move or kick, and nauseating terror rips through me as I feel his erection rubbing against my bare leg.

"We're going to have a little fun," he says, his dark eyes gleaming with cruel excitement. "For old times' sake."

And forcing his knee between my legs, he lowers his head.

22

ucas

I RAISE MY FIST, SIGNALING FOR DIEGO AND EDUARDO TO STOP AS I peer through my night vision goggles at the building in front of us. For a black site, it's surprisingly small—just a ramshackle one-story house in a heavily wooded rural area.

"Are you sure this is the place?" Diego whispers, crouching next to me. "It doesn't look like much."

"I'm guessing most of it is underground," I say, keeping my voice low. "I see two SUVs in the shed in the back, and I don't think Ukrainian villagers drive SUVs."

We left our own car in the woods a half-mile away to scope out the location and figure out our plan of action. Whatever we do, we need to be quick and discreet, so we can be out of the country before UUR realizes we were here. Thanks to Peter Sokolov's contacts, we landed at a private airport undetected, and we have to be able to leave the same way.

"Go around the back and keep an eye on the place from there," I tell Eduardo, who has come up behind Diego. "I'm going to try to hack into their computers remotely."

He nods and disappears into the bushes, and I take out the device I brought with me. One of the benefits of working with Esguerra is having access to cutting-edge military intelligence technology—like this remote data skimmer.

Opening my laptop, I sync it with the device and tell Diego, "Good news: we're within range. Now we just need to let the hacking program do its magic."

It takes more than an hour to break through the firewalls, but gradually, my screen fills with all kinds of data, including blueprints of the house and a live video feed of a dimly lit hallway.

"Is that from inside their building?" Diego asks, looking over my shoulder.

"You bet," I say, watching as two men walk past the camera. One of them looks unusually young, barely a teenager, which throws me for a moment—until I remember that UUR is in the habit of recruiting children.

I click on the next video feed and see what looks like an interrogation room. It's empty except for a metal table and two chairs. Next, I access a camera in what must be a security room. There's one heavily armed man sitting there in front of a row of computers. I click to the next feed, which shows yet another hallway, and several more feeds that reveal cell-like rooms. To my disappointment, all those rooms are empty.

This facility must not be heavily used.

I click through a few more camera feeds, comparing the rooms I see to the blueprints on my screen, and jot down notes on how everything is positioned. In the process, I come across two more men—one that's built like a heavyweight wrestling champion and a leaner one who appears to be in his forties.

"Only five agents so far, and one of them is a kid," Diego says over my shoulder. "If that's all, we might be able to take them."

"Right." I click through a few more feeds, making notes on the interior of each room, and pause when I come back to one of the empty cells—or at least a cell I'd thought empty before. Now I see I was wrong: there's a small mound on a cot covered by a blanket.

"Is that—"

"Yes, looks like they have a prisoner there," I say, peering at the grainy feed. It's definitely a person-sized mound; I should've noticed it the first time. "Hold on, let me see if I can get a clearer image."

Activating the hacking program's remote control feature, I isolate the portion of surveillance mechanism that controls the camera in that room. Carefully, I angle it so it's pointed directly at the cot. The person, whoever it is, is unmoving, as if passed out or asleep.

"Okay, so six people," Diego says, "if we count this prisoner as a threat. Pretty decent odds, especially if we catch them by surprise."

"Yes, I think so," I say, clicking over to the next image. Originally, I planned for us to just gather data and leave, but I can't pass up this opportunity. It's possible that one of these agents knows Yulia's whereabouts. My ribs choose that moment to twinge with pain, but I ignore the dull ache.

Even with me injured, we should be able to take five or six opponents.

Turning on my earpiece, I say, "Eduardo, I need you to plant some explosives on the northwest and southwest corners of the house. Use enough to take down the walls but not destroy the whole house. We want to capture as many of them alive as we can."

"Got it," Eduardo replies, and I turn to glance at Diego.

"We're going in right after the first blast," I say. "Get ready."

He nods, taking out his M16, and I turn my attention back to the computer. Within a minute, the hacking program takes control of the surveillance feeds outside, replacing the image of Eduardo stealthily approaching the house with a nonthreatening view of night-darkened trees and bushes.

Now we just need Eduardo to set the charges.

As we wait for that, I check all the internal video feeds again. On the hallway feed, I see one of the men walk toward the cell with the prisoner. It's the agent who's built like a wrestler, alone this time. With mild interest, I watch him enter the cell, place his gun in the sink on the other side of the room, and step toward the covered figure on the cot. He bends over it and, to my surprise, unzips his jeans.

What the fuck? My attention sharpens as he pulls the blanket off the figure—which I now see is female—and flips up her dress. With the way he's standing, the camera doesn't allow me to see much of the prisoner, yet my chest tightens with anxious premonition.

"Kent?" Diego says, but I'm not listening to him. All my attention is on the computer screen as I frantically work to angle the camera.

The man straddles the prisoner and grabs her wrists—thin, delicate wrists that look impossibly breakable in his bear-like grasp. The camera tilts, angling to the left, and I see tangled blond hair and a beautiful pale face.

My heart stops for a split second; then feral fury blasts through me.

Yulia.

She's here—and she's being attacked.

23

ulia

KIRILL'S BREATH IS HOT AND FETID ON MY FACE, AND HIS MASSIVE bulk is like a mountain on top of me, crushing me into the cot. My insides heave with horror and disgust, and I feel my mind sliding toward the dark place where I don't exist and can't feel this.

No. With stark clarity, I know that if I go there, I'm lost. I'll never emerge from that darkness. I have to stay conscious. I have to fight.

I can't let him destroy me again.

Suppressing my instinctive inclination to struggle, I let myself go limp, my wrists relaxing in Kirill's brutal grip. I don't react as he drags his tongue over my cheek, and I don't tense as he parts my legs, settling heavily between them. He needs to think me dazed and tamed.

It's my only chance.

I feel his cock, hard against my bare thigh, and nausea rises in my throat, my long-ago meal threatening to come up. *Just a second longer,* I tell myself, keeping my muscles relaxed. *Don't rush it. Wait for the right moment.*

The right moment arrives when he shifts on top of me and his face ends up directly over mine. I peer at him through a tiny crack between my eyelids, and when he lowers one hand to grab my breast, I strike.

With all my strength, I jerk my head up, smashing my forehead straight into his nose.

Blood spurts everywhere as Kirill recoils with a startled shout. Any other man would've clutched his broken nose, but he just rears up, snarling, "Bitch!" and smashes his fist into my jaw.

My head whips to the side, the blast of pain stunning me for a second. I see stars at the edge of my vision and taste coppery blood. But Kirill is not done with me yet.

"Fucking bitch!" The next blow is to my stomach, his fist like a wrecking ball hitting my kidney. "Always thought yourself too good for me, did you?"

I can't reply; I can only wheeze through the agony as I curl up to protect myself. He let go of my wrists to hit me, I realize dazedly, and as he raises his fist again, I twist my upper body to the side. His fist grazes my cheekbone instead of shattering it as he'd likely intended, but my ears still ring from the blow. I twist again, trying to throw him off, but his lower body is like a boulder on top of me.

Fight, Yulia, fight. The words are like a desperate chant in my mind. I strike upward with my fist and manage to hit his jaw, but his eyes just glitter brighter as he catches my wrists again. I can see the rage and madness in their dark depths, and I know I won't walk away from this alive.

"You're going to pay for that," he says in a low, guttural hiss, and I feel his hairy balls on my thigh as he forces my legs wider, his fingers cutting off all blood flow to my hands. His cock presses against my entrance, and I scream, bracing for the inevitable horror of violation.

Boom!

For a moment, I'm sure that he hit me again, that the deafening noise is my facial bones cracking, but the dust and plaster raining down on me dispel that impression. Kirill jumps off me with a curse, his cock sticking out of his unzipped pants, and staggers back a couple of feet as another explosion shakes the room.

Seizing the chance, I roll off the cot and scramble to my feet, ignoring the throbbing pain in my face and side. There is a sharp crackle of gunfire above us. Kirill freezes in place, his gaze swinging madly between me and the door. He has to realize the facility is being attacked, and I feel his hatred for me warring with his sense of duty. He should be out there, defending his colleagues, but what he really wants is to make me suffer.

The latter impulse seems to win out.

"You fucking traitor," he grits out, the veins in his forehead bulging, and then he steps toward me, his fist raised for a blow.

Reflexively, I duck, and at that moment, another blast rattles the room, throwing Kirill off-balance and causing more plaster to rain down on us. A creaking, groaning sound seems to emanate from the depths of the building itself, and one corner of the room suddenly crumbles, bricks and plaster falling in an avalanche less than a meter from me.

Gasping, I jump to the side—and then I see it.

A brick with a rusted metal rod embedded in it.

I leap for it, sliding on my stomach across the debris-littered floor. Bits of rock and plaster scrape my bare legs and belly, but my hands close around the metal rod, and I jump up just in time to smash the brick across Kirill's face as he rushes at me.

He staggers back, catching himself on the sink, and I again hear the furious staccato of automatic gunfire above us. This time, though, the deafening noise doesn't stop. Whoever the attackers are, they have serious firepower. I don't get a chance to wonder about their identity, though, because I see Kirill reach into the sink and pull out a gun.

Reacting in an instant, I let go of the heavy brick and throw myself to the side, rolling across the floor toward my attacker. I hear the shot, feel the burning sting of the bullet as it grazes my arm, and then I'm smashing into Kirill's knees at full speed.

He must not have fully recovered from my earlier hit, because he staggers back again, and his next shot goes wide. I scramble to my feet, my ears ringing from the shot and the gunfire above, and grab his right wrist, twisting it sideways in an effort to break his hold on the gun.

In the next instant, I'm flying across the room. He backhanded me with his other hand, I comprehend hazily as I slam into a wall. Air whooshes from my lungs, and I wheeze in paralyzed agony as Kirill points the gun at me, his face twisted with manic rage.

He's going to kill me.

The knowledge injects adrenaline straight into my brain. Without further thought, I throw myself at Kirill, my arms extended in a desperate grab, and my hand closes around the cold metal of the barrel. I feel it buck under my fingers, hear the deadly whine of the bullet, and then I'm falling.

I'm falling, but I'm not dead.

I land on top of Kirill, stunned, my hand still convulsively grasping the barrel. I can't believe I'm alive. Instinctively, I yank at the gun, trying to pull it out of his grasp, and to my shock, I succeed. Clutching the weapon, I crawl backward off Kirill's massive body, and it's only when I'm a couple of feet away that I understand what happened.

A portion of the ceiling collapsed on top of him, knocking him out. There's a thin trickle of blood on his temple, and plaster all around him.

Kirill is unconscious, maybe even dead.

Dizzily, I climb to my feet and point the weapon at him, trying to steady my violently shaking hand. My vision is blurry, and every thought seems to require inordinate effort. All I'm aware of is hatred. Black and potent, it pulses through my veins, taking away all rational thought. My finger tightens on the trigger, almost of its own volition, and I watch as the first shot rips a bloody hole in my rapist's side.

His body jerks, and I shoot again, pointing the gun between his legs. His deflated cock and balls explode in a spray of bloody meat. My dizziness intensifies, my head swimming with pain, and I clench my teeth, determined to remain conscious long enough to finish him off.

A fresh burst of gunfire above draws my attention, and I realize suddenly that I still have no idea what's happening or who the attackers are. Almost immediately, I recall something else.

Misha.

My brother was here earlier.

Icy terror cuts through my haze. Could Misha still be here? Could he be *upstairs,* in that war zone with the unknown enemies?

Before I can even process the thought, I'm already out the door, sprinting down the basement hallway.

I have to get to Misha.

If he's still alive, I have to save him.

As I round the corner to the stairs, I collide with a person running toward me. We crash into each other, and as we tumble to the floor, I realize with shock that it's Misha—that my brother was sprinting toward me. He lands on top of me, and before I can catch my breath, he climbs to his feet, breathing heavily.

"Misha!" Fighting my dizziness, I scramble to my feet. I'm still holding Kirill's gun, but I manage to grab Misha's arm before he can step away. "Are you hurt? Are you injured? What's happening?" My questions come out in a frantic mix of Russian and Ukrainian, but Misha just shakes his head, his eyes wide and uncomprehending. He seems to be in shock; under the dirt and blood covering his face, his cheeks look sickly pale.

My heart hammers as I run my free hand over him, looking for gunshot wounds or broken bones, but other than a few scratches, he seems to be in one piece. Relieved, I grab his arm again and tug him into one of the rooms off the hallway. "Come on. We have to get out of here."

"You… they…" He seems to have trouble speaking. "They just—"

"Yes, I know, come on." I drag him into a small cell that resembles the one I was just in and look for a place to hide. There isn't one, and my stomach sinks as the gunfire upstairs stops, and then resumes with even greater violence.

"Misha." Gripping my gun tightly in my right hand, I raise my left hand and gently touch his cheek. My baby brother is already a couple of inches taller than me, and if his lanky frame is anything to go by, he still has quite a bit of growing to do. He's also shaking uncontrollably, his skin icy under my touch. "Mishen'ka, do you know a way out of here?"

He swallows. "No."

"Okay." I'm shaking myself, but I keep my voice calm so as not to add to his terror. "Do you know what's going on upstairs? Who's attacking?"

"I don't know." His shaking intensifies. "They just… They killed Uncle Vasya and—"

"Obenko is dead?" Despite everything, I feel a slight pang in my chest. Pushing the illogical emotion aside, I lower my hand and ask, "How many are there? Did any of them say anything?"

Misha shakes his head again, his eyes brimming with tears. "They killed Uncle Vasya," he whispers, as if unable to believe it. "And Agent Mateyenko." His face crumples, just like it did when he was a toddler.

"Oh, Misha…" I step closer, swallowing my own tears. "I'm sorry." More than anything, I want to hug and console him, but there's no time, so I say, "We have to figure out a way out. There must be—"

I'm interrupted by the sound of heavy footsteps pounding

down the stairs. Misha tenses, and I see terror flash in his eyes. "They're coming for us. They're going to—"

"Shh." I hold up my finger to my lips as I step back and cast a desperate look around the room. I don't know if Kirill's gun was fully loaded when he got to my cell, but even if it was, there can't be more than a couple of bullets left. Still, I could potentially use those bullets as a distraction so Misha can get away.

"Come," I whisper, grabbing his arm. "The minute you see a chance to run, you run. Understand?"

"But they're—"

"Quiet," I hiss, towing him down the hallway. When we reach the next room, I shove my brother in there and whisper, "Don't make a sound."

And gripping the gun with both hands, I turn back toward the stairs, ready to meet my fate.

24

ucas

YULIA.

I have to get to Yulia.

The thought hammers in my brain as I run down the stairs, ignoring the blood dripping down my arm. A bullet had grazed my shoulder and my ribs ache from all the movement, but I'm barely cognizant of the pain. The fight turned out to be lengthy and brutal; even caught off-guard and dazed by the bombs we set, the UUR operatives weren't easy to take down. Being forced to exchange fire with them while Yulia was getting assaulted downstairs nearly drove me mad. As soon as we took out two of the three agents defending the house on the first floor, I sprinted to the basement stairs, leaving Diego and Eduardo to deal with the remaining shooter. I hope they're able to capture him instead of killing him like we did the other two, but either way, it's not worth me sticking around.

Saving Yulia beats gathering intelligence any day.

When I get to the bottom of the stairs, I force myself to slow down. The young agent ran this way after we killed the second shooter, and Yulia's assailant could be lying in wait for me here too. He couldn't have missed the shots and explosions upstairs. Or so I'm hoping, at least. I gave the order to detonate the bombs before we were optimally positioned for that exact reason: I figured the man was unlikely to continue with Yulia once he realized they were under attack.

Gripping my M16, I stop as I reach the corner. The hallway with all the rooms is to my right. If my recollection is correct, Yulia's cell should be the fourth one on the left.

This is going to be tricky. I can't shoot indiscriminately, like I did upstairs—not without risking Yulia's life.

Crouching, I risk a quick look around the corner.

The hallway is empty.

I risk a second glance, this time eyeballing the distance to the nearest cell with an open door.

Ten feet. I can make it.

Tightening my grip on the gun, I dive for the cell, rolling across the floor. I half-expect to feel the bite of bullets, but nothing happens as I throw myself through the open door and leap to my feet, scanning the room for danger.

Empty. No sign of anyone.

I inhale to steady my racing heartbeat. The knowledge that Yulia is only a few rooms away from me is like a fire in my blood, but I know I need to be patient. Somewhere down here are two potentially dangerous opponents, and I have to be cautious if I'm to survive and get her back.

Plastering myself against the wall next to the door, I study the hallway, all my senses on alert. I have no doubt they know I'm here, which means it's just a matter of time before someone gets impatient and tries to take me out. To combat my own urge to act, I mentally count to ten, then do so again.

By my third count, I hear a faint scrape and catch a flash of movement. It's almost nothing—just a shadow changing shape inside one of the other doorways—but I know.

This is the enemy.

The safest move would be to pepper that doorway with bullets, but I can't risk shooting Yulia by accident. As is, I can see that the bombs we set off did some damage down here. The floor is covered with plaster, and the ceiling lights are flickering madly. The idea of Yulia hurt in any way is intolerable, so I push the thought aside, along with the fear and rage clawing at my chest. I can't focus on any of that, not until I have Yulia safely with me.

Taking another breath, I mentally measure the distance to the other doorway.

Seven feet, give or take a few inches.

I allow myself one more steadying breath, and then I spring for it, covering the distance in three long strides. A shot rings out, but I'm already there, knocking the gun out of the shooter's hand as I tackle him to the floor and pin him with my assault rifle across his throat.

No, I realize a split second later.

Across *her* throat.

Yulia is on her back underneath me, her blue eyes huge with shock. Her pale face is dirty and bruised, marred with blood and bits of plaster, but there's no doubt that it's her.

"Lucas?" she chokes out, and I see her gaze suddenly flick to the right.

I react instinctively. Clutching Yulia with one hand and the M16 with the other, I throw myself to the side and roll, pulling her with me. My ribs hurt like hell, but the brick that was about to connect with my head crashes into the floor instead, and I jump up to meet the new threat—the young agent I saw in the video feed.

The boy has clearly had some training, and he's fast. As I swing my weapon at his head, he ducks and simultaneously kicks out with his right leg. I jump back, causing his foot to miss my side, and before he can regroup, I thrust the gun forward, ramming the barrel into his solar plexus.

His face turns ghostly white, and his knees buckle. He collapses to the floor, gasping for air, and I raise the gun to knock him out. But before I can bring the handle down on his head, I spot a flicker of movement at my side.

It's Yulia leaping at me, teeth bared.

"Get away! Don't hurt him!" Her scream verges on hysterical as I catch her mid-leap and twist to pin her against the wall. Her fist lands in my side, causing my ribs to scream in agony as I struggle to contain her without dropping my weapon. She grabs for the gun, trying to wrestle it away from me, and I grunt in pain as her elbow hits me in the ribs again.

"Fucking hell, Yulia, stop!" I don't want to hurt her, but I can't let her get that weapon. She's already shot at me once; there's no telling what she'd do with a fully loaded M16. As I'm wrestling with her, in my peripheral vision I see a shadow move across the hallway.

If it's the other agent joining the fight, I'm screwed.

Steeling myself, I twist and slam my elbow into Yulia's ribcage. It's a carefully controlled blow—I use just enough force to knock the air out of her—and then I jump back and turn to face the boy, who's still on the floor but beginning to recover from my hit.

His eyes widen as I raise the gun, pointing it straight at him, and for the first time, I get a good look at his features.

Features that are oddly familiar.

"No!"

Before I have a chance to process what I'm seeing, Yulia slams into me, tackling me with such force that I stagger back before I can catch myself. Her face is twisted with terrified anger as she wrestles with me for the weapon, and I begin to get an inkling of what's happening.

"Misha!" she yells at the top of her lungs, followed by some Russian word, and my suspicion crystallizes into certainty as I see the boy struggle to his feet and rush at me, his teeth bared in a grimace that's nearly identical to the one on Yulia's face.

Motherfucker.

"Stop," I snarl, yanking the gun out of Yulia's hands with one hard pull. "I'm not going to fucking hurt him!"

The boy crashes into me before I finish speaking, and I hit him in the throat, tempering the force of my blow to avoid crushing his trachea. Even with my light tap, he collapses, choking and gasping for air, and I'm left to deal with Yulia's attack.

She flies at me like a feral creature, all teeth and claws, her eyes wild with terror. She clearly didn't believe my promise not to hurt the boy, whoever he is to her, and is fighting like a mama bear protecting her cub. Cursing, I block her attempt to knee me in the balls, and duck to avoid her swinging fist. Before she can lash out again, I catch her and pin her arms to her sides, squeezing her tightly. The M16 is still in my hand, but I don't use it. I just hold Yulia against me, letting her tire herself out with her desperate struggles.

She weakens faster than I expected, likely because she's injured. Within a couple of minutes, she goes limp in my arms, her breathing fast and shaky. I feel her muscles quivering in exhaustion as I hold her, and despite the violent ache in my ribs, a familiar mix of lust and tenderness spreads through me, warming my chest and stiffening my cock.

Yulia.

I finally have my Yulia.

Her breasts are soft against me, her body slim and delicate in my embrace. She smells of fear, sweat, and blood, but underneath it all is the faint scent of peaches—a fragrance I'll forever associate with her. I breathe it in, indulging myself for a moment, but then I recall the shadow I saw moving earlier.

The other agent—Yulia's attacker—is still on the loose.

"Did he hurt you?" My voice thickens with spiking rage. "Did that bastard touch you?"

Yulia's whole body goes rigid, and then she starts struggling again. "Let me go." Her words are muffled against my shirt. "Let me go, Lucas!"

I tighten my arms around her, ignoring the pain the move causes me. "Answer me."

She stills, breathing rapidly, and I see the boy trying to get to his feet. I clench my jaw and turn Yulia so I have my M16 pointed at him. He freezes immediately, and I try to figure out how to proceed next. Everything in me demands that I rush into the hallway to capture the agent who assaulted her, but if I let go of Yulia, she'll attack me again, and I don't want to have to hurt her.

Also, there's the fucking kid.

As I wrestle with my dilemma, I realize that I'm no longer hearing any gunfire—that, in fact, it's been quiet for a couple of minutes. Just as the thought occurs to me, I hear running footsteps on the stairs, and a minute later, Eduardo bursts into the room, ready to take down our remaining opponents.

"Wait," I order as he points his weapon at the kid. "Don't shoot him."

Yulia begins to struggle again, so I squeeze her tighter and whisper in her ear, "Calm down. We're not going to hurt him. If I wanted him dead, he'd already be dead."

That seems to get through to her. She stops fighting, and I risk loosening my grip on her. When I see that she's still not attacking, I release her and step back. At the last moment, I change my mind and grab her wrist with my left hand, anchoring her to me.

There's no way I'm chancing her escaping me ever again.

"There's one more down here somewhere," I tell Eduardo in a hard voice. The thought of Yulia's attacker on the loose is intolerable. "Find him and bring him to me."

Eduardo nods and disappears, and Yulia stares at me, trembling all over. She looks like she's on the verge of either fainting or bolting. "You're not—" Her voice breaks. "You're not going to hurt Misha?"

I glance down at the boy, who's wisely remaining motionless on the floor. "If that's Misha, then no." I take a calming breath, trying not to wince at the pain in my ribs. "Who is he to you?"

Yulia's eyes widen. "You don't know? But you said—"

"I think it's possible I misunderstood," I say, keeping my voice even. "Who is he? Your cousin?"

She blinks. "My brother."

Now it's my turn to be taken aback. "You said you were an only child."

"I lied," she says. Then her forehead wrinkles in confusion. "But you said you knew. When I asked you not to kill him, you said you knew. What did you mean? Why did you—"

"I thought he was your lover, okay?" Anger—at myself this time—clips my words. "Why did you lie about being an only child?"

Yulia moistens her lips. "Because I didn't trust you."

Of course—and apparently, with good reason. I force myself to take another breath. In a calmer tone, I ask, "Are you hurt? Did that fucker hurt you?"

She stiffens again. "How do you—"

"I hacked into this facility's video feed," I say. Releasing her wrist, I raise my hand to run my fingertips over the swelling on the left side of her face. "Did he do this?" I ask, trying to suppress my fury. "Did he hit you?"

"He…" Yulia swallows. "I fought, so he hit me. Then you—" She stops. "How did you find this place?"

I narrow my eyes, refusing to be distracted. "Did he rape you?"

"He tried, but no." Her gaze drifts down. "Not this time."

"This time?" I all but explode on the spot. "He hurt you before?"

She looks up, seemingly startled. "I told you about that. You don't remember?"

"That was—"

"Kirill, yes." Her bruised lips flatten. "They lied to me about him. He was alive. Alive and training Misha…" She glances down at the boy, who's been utterly silent during our conversation. I don't know how much English he understands, but judging from the stunned look on his face, he must've gotten at least some of it.

I can see Yulia is about to start talking to him, so I grip her chin firmly to bring her attention back to me. "We're going to get him," I promise grimly. "He won't get away this time."

To my surprise, Yulia's mouth curves in a small smile as I lower my hand. "It's okay. I took care of him."

"What?"

"He's dead—or will be shortly, if he's not already." Yulia's smile sharpens. "He's in my cell. Or at least his body should be there."

I'm about to tell her to take me there when Eduardo enters the room. "He's gone," the guard says with evident disgust. "The bastard somehow made it to one of the SUVs in the backyard and squealed out of here. There must've been another exit down here. He bled the whole way to the car, though, so he's hurt pretty badly. Maybe he'll bleed out on his own."

Yulia's eyebrows draw together. "Who are you—"

"He's talking about Kirill." I fight to keep my voice level. "I saw a shadow move in the hallway earlier, when you and Misha were doing your best to bash my head in. He must not have been hurt as badly as you thought, or else—"

"I shot his cock and balls off." Yulia's curt statement makes me —and all the other males in the room—flinch instinctively. "Also, I put a bullet in his side," she says, and before anyone can respond, she rushes out of the room, running down the hallway toward her cell.

"Keep an eye on him," I tell Eduardo, nodding at Yulia's brother, and then I take off after her, determined not to let her out of my sight ever again.

25

ulia

Lucas is here. He promised not to hurt my brother. Kirill might have escaped.

I can't process any of it, so I don't even try. As I burst into the cell where Kirill attacked me, I see right away that Eduardo was right.

Kirill is gone.

There's blood all over the place. I turn to follow the trail leading out of the room, but Lucas is already there, looming in the doorway like a human mountain. His hard jaw is shadowed with blond stubble, and his eyes are the color of an iced-over lake. With his SWAT-like gear and machine gun, he looks like the ultimate merciless soldier.

I want to flee from him and jump into his arms at the same time.

I do neither. Instead, I say dully, "He's gone." I know I'm stating the obvious, but all forms of higher thinking seem to be beyond me at the moment. My head is throbbing with pain, and my knees feel like they might buckle at any moment. The adrenaline that sustained me during my fight with Lucas is gone, leaving me trembling in the aftermath.

Kirill almost raped me again. Lucas saved me. Lucas had thought Misha was my lover.

I shake my head, a hysterical laugh escaping my throat.

"Yulia…" Lucas reaches for me, frowning, and my laughter intensifies. I can't stop laughing, not when he pulls me into his embrace, his M16 digging into my back, and not when he rocks me against him, whispering soothing nothings into my ear. He promises that he'll find Kirill for me, that he'll make sure the fucker suffers, but I'm not listening to him. My mind is like a ping-pong ball, leaping from one insane fact to the next.

Lucas is in Ukraine. My brother is here with me. Lucas doesn't intend to kill him—though he did when he thought Misha was my lover.

My hysterical laughter turns into equally hysterical sobbing. I know it's pathetic, but I can't stop. All the heartache and stress of the past few hours coalesce into an expanding ball in my throat, and no matter how much air I draw in, I can't stop feeling like I'm suffocating.

Misha could've been killed. He could still be killed if Lucas changes his mind. I want to plead for my brother's life again, but all I can manage is a choked sound that devolves into another sob.

"Hush, sweetheart, it'll be all right…" Lucas's voice is a soft rumble in my ear. "I'll protect you from him, I promise."

Bending down, he picks me up, cradling me against his chest, and I wind my arms around his neck, pressing my face into his throat. Almost instantly, I feel calmer, my sobs easing as he carries me down the hallway.

When we pass by the room where I left my brother, however, I see that it's empty, and the choking sensation returns. "Where is he?" My voice takes on a higher pitch as I push at Lucas's shoulders. "Where's Misha?"

"I assume Eduardo brought him upstairs, which is where I'm taking you now," Lucas says, pressing me tighter against him. "Don't worry, baby. He's going to be fine, and so will you."

His words reassure me somewhat. I still don't trust Lucas, but I don't see what he has to gain by lying to me in this instance. As he told me, if he wanted Misha dead, he would've already killed him.

"What are you going to do with him?" My tone is a tiny bit calmer as I pull back to look at my captor. "With us, I mean?"

"You're coming with me, and so is your brother." Lucas's eyes glitter as he takes the stairs two at a time. "Now relax—we'll sort all the rest of it soon."

And before I can ask anything else, he steps out into the ruins of the first floor of the house.

~

THE NEXT SEVERAL HOURS ARE HAZY IN MY MIND. I RECALL SEEING Obenko's bloodied corpse as Lucas carried me out of the wreckage, but I must've passed out soon after that because I don't remember the drive to the airport or the plane taking off. My last semi-clear recollection is of my brother sitting in the car next to me, his eyes red and swollen and his hands handcuffed behind his back.

A few times during the flight, Diego shakes me awake and makes me tell him my name and how many fingers he's holding up. The first time that happens, I ask about my brother, and Diego points to a blanket-covered bundle on the couch across the cabin.

"We gave him a sedative so he wouldn't keep fighting us," the guard explains. "Your brother didn't take the other agents' deaths well."

I try to get up to make sure Misha is all right, but my whole body lodges a violent protest, beginning with my skull, and I fall back into my plush seat with a pained groan, fighting a wave of nauseating dizziness.

"Don't try to move," Diego says, buckling me in with the seat-belt. "Lucas thinks you might have a concussion. He said I'm to watch over you while he's flying the plane."

"But Misha—"

"He's fine." Diego walks over and pokes Misha's shoulder. My brother makes an incoherent noise, and the guard says, "See? He's sleeping. Now relax. We're already over the Atlantic and should be home soon."

"Home?" I try to think through the throbbing pain in my temples.

"Our compound." The young Mexican grins. "The wind is at our back, so we'll be landing in no time."

I want to argue that Esguerra's compound is not *my* home, but the pain in my head intensifies, and I fade into unconsciousness again.

~

"—A LOT OF BRUISING ON HER BACK, FACE, AND STOMACH, AND YES, A mild concussion. I'm going to give her some pain medication, so she can rest comfortably. There's no need to wake her up; it's not that severe of a head injury. Her body's just been through a trauma and needs to heal. The more she sleeps, the better. I suggest you take it easy as well; you're not doing your ribs any favors with all this activity."

The voice is somewhat familiar. Prying open my eyelids, I see Lucas standing next to a short, balding man—the doctor who inspected me when I was first brought to the estate. What was his name? Stifling a groan, I turn my head to take in my surroundings and realize I'm in Lucas's bedroom, lying on his large comfortable bed.

I'm also clean and naked under the blanket. Lucas must've undressed and washed me while I was passed out.

"Where's Misha?" My words come out in a barely audible croak. Clearing my throat, I try again. "Where's my brother?" Judging by drawn shades and bedroom lights being on, it's already evening or maybe even night.

Lucas and the doctor turn to face me at the same time. Lucas's mouth is set in a hard line, but the moment I try to sit up, he crosses the room in a couple of strides and sits down on the edge of the bed. "You are to rest." His tone is harsh, but his touch is gentle as he pushes me back down. "Don't move."

He starts to get up again, and I grab his hand in desperation. "I need to see Misha."

Lucas hesitates for a moment, then says gruffly, "Fine. I'll have him brought here. But you rest, understand?"

I tighten my grip on Lucas's hand. "Where are you holding him?" Now that we're out of immediate danger, a new fear takes hold of me. My brother is here, in Esguerra's compound, in the hands of men who can snuff out his life as easily as squashing a bug. If I hadn't stopped Lucas in that basement, he would've likely killed Misha—just as he'd killed Obenko and the other agents.

My captor is dangerous, and I can't forget that.

"Misha—or Michael, as he told us he prefers to be called—is staying in the guards' barracks," Lucas says, his jaw muscle flexing. He seems angry about something, but I have no idea what. "Diego and Eduardo are keeping an eye on him. Now if you'll excuse me, I'll call Diego and have your brother brought here."

I release Lucas's hand, and he gets up. "Give her the pain meds," he instructs the doctor. "I'll be back in a minute."

The man nods, and Lucas walks out after giving me one last hard look. Even with the pain squeezing my temples, I understand his silent warning:

Behave or else.

If he'd asked me, I could've told him that his caution is unwarranted. Not only am I feeling like a truck ran me over, but Lucas has my brother. Even if I wanted to run, I wouldn't go anywhere without Misha—which must be why Lucas had him brought here, I realize with a shudder.

"Here you go," the doctor says, extending his hand toward me, and I automatically accept the two pills he gives me.

"Thank you, Dr. Goldberg," I say, finally recalling his name.

The short man gives me a kind smile and helps me sit up, putting two pillows under my back as I clutch the blanket to my chest. He also gives me a bottle of water, which I use to wash down the pills. There's no point in resisting; the pills might cloud my mind, but the headache is doing that already. Even after sleeping the whole trip, I feel sluggish and exhausted, my body aching all over.

"You should rest," Dr. Goldberg says, then turns away to rummage in his bag as I tuck the blanket tighter around my naked chest, pinning it in place with my arms.

As if obeying his instruction, my eyelids get progressively heavier, my thoughts beginning to drift as the doctor stands there, quietly humming under his breath. I'm almost asleep when I suddenly remember something he said earlier.

"Is Lucas hurt?" I sit up straighter, my sleepiness fading in a rush of worry. "You mentioned his ribs."

Dr. Goldberg turns around, eyebrows arched in surprise. "Oh, that. Yes, cracked ribs take time to heal. He's supposed to abstain from physical activity, not run around like Rambo."

I frown. "When did he crack his ribs?" From the way the doctor is talking, it sounds like an older injury.

Dr. Goldberg gives me an owlish look. "You don't know?" Then his face clears, and he shakes his head. "Of course you don't know. What am I thinking?"

"Did something happen here?"

He hesitates, then says, "I think it's best if Kent fills you in."

"Fills her in on what?" Lucas asks, walking into the room, and I see my brother come in after him, his hands handcuffed in front of his body.

"Misha!" I almost jump from the bed, injuries be damned, but at the last moment, I remember that I'm naked under the blanket. Flushing, I tighten my arms at my sides and give my brother a smile instead. "How are you doing?" I ask in Russian. "Are you okay?"

Misha stares at me, and I see color creep up his neck as he glances from me to Lucas and then to Dr. Goldberg.

I turn to my captor. "Lucas, would it be possible—"

"You have five minutes," he growls and strides out of the room. The doctor follows him out, closing the door behind him, and I find myself alone with my brother for the first time in eleven years.

26

ucas

THE MOMENT THE DOOR TO THE BEDROOM CLOSES, I TURN TO Goldberg and say, “Prepare the trackers. I want them implanted before you leave.”

The doctor blinks at me. “Tonight? But—”

“She’s already on pain meds, and as banged up as she is, she’ll hardly feel the discomfort.” I fold my arms across my chest. “You can use a local anesthetic to make sure there’s no pain when they go in.” Pausing, I frown at Goldberg. “Unless you think this will impede her recovery?”

“No, but…” He gives me a wary look. “Don’t you think she’s been through enough?”

“Excuse me?”

Goldberg sighs and says, “Never mind. I can see you’re set on this. I’ll prepare for the procedure.”

He walks over to the couch and sits, opening his doctor's bag to take out a syringe with a thick needle and the sterilized implants I gave him earlier. The trackers are tiny, about the size of a grain of rice, but capable of transmitting a signal from anywhere in the globe. I watch him for a few moments, then walk over to the window and stare blindly outside, trying to contain the fury simmering in me.

Kirill escaped.

He hurt Yulia, and then he fucking escaped. I don't know how he managed it—if Yulia was right about the damage she inflicted, he should've been at death's door—but the fucker drove away in the SUV, and we couldn't give chase without alerting the authorities to our presence in their country. As is, given all the explosions and gunfire, it was bound to be only a matter of time before we got in trouble. Our safest bet had been to hightail it out of the country as fast as we could, and that's exactly what we did.

Of course, we only did that because Yulia had been injured, and I wanted to get her home as quickly as possible. Otherwise, I would've chased down the bastard and worried about getting out of the country later.

Thinking about that—about Yulia beaten and nearly raped—sends fresh rage surging through me. I don't know which one of us I'm angrier at: Yulia for lying about being an only child and running away, or myself for not doing proper due diligence before jumping to conclusions.

Misha is her brother, not her lover.

Her fucking teenage brother.

During the flight, I had time to think about everything, and in hindsight, it's obvious how my jealousy had blinded me to the truth. The idea of Yulia in love with another man had been so intolerable I refused to listen to her pleas.

My obsession with her nearly got her killed.

"Lucas?" Goldberg's voice cuts into my thoughts. When I spin around to glare at him, the doctor says cautiously, "I think their five minutes are up. If you want me to do the procedure, I'm ready."

"All right." I force my tone to even out. "Let's go."

Misunderstanding or not, Yulia won't escape from me ever again.

27

ulia

THE SECOND THE DOOR CLOSES BEHIND THE DOCTOR, I SCOOT closer to the edge of the bed, making sure the blanket covers my chest. My head pounds with the movement, but I say, "Mishen'ka—"

"It's Mikhail—or Michael, since you're so fond of the English language," my brother snaps, his light-colored eyebrows drawing together in a ferocious frown. "I'm not a child."

"No, I can see that." Ignoring the throbbing in my temples, I study his features, noticing the changes brought about by adolescence. At fourteen, he's already begun the transition into manhood, his face leaner and harder than I recall seeing in pictures as recent as from a few months ago.

Suppressing an irrational urge to cry, I begin again. "Michael"—the formal American version of his name feels foreign on my tongue—"I want to talk to you about... well, about everything."

He just stands there, looking tense and angry, so I plow on. "I'm sorry about Obenko—your uncle, that is. I know he meant a lot to you. And Mateyenko... They were good agents. They truly cared about their country, and I know Obenko cared about you..." I realize I'm rambling, so I take a breath and say, "Listen, I know the men holding us seem scary, but I promise you, I'll do everything in my power to protect you. Lucas said he won't hurt you, and I—"

"Is he your lover?" Misha's cheeks redden as he asks the question, but he doesn't look away, his gaze locked on me accusingly.

I feel my own face heat up. This is not a conversation I want to be having with my young brother. "He's... It's complicated. But you don't need to worry about that. I'll make sure you're safe, okay?"

"Yeah, like you made sure Uncle Vasya was safe." Misha's tone is harsh, but I sense the fear and grief underneath. The training he received in the last two years wouldn't have prepared him for this. My baby brother might know how to fight and shoot a gun, but I doubt he'd seen death up close before yesterday.

That part doesn't come until later in the training program.

"Michael..." I bite my lip, wondering how to best tackle Obenko's lies. "I know your uncle has told you some things about me, and—"

"Are you going to accuse him of being a liar too? Isn't it enough that he's dead because of you?" Misha's face tightens, and his eyes gleam a shade too brightly. "These killers, they came after *you*. This all happened because of you."

"No, Misha—Michael—that's not true." My heart aches at his pain. "I escaped so I could warn Obenko about—" I cut myself off, realizing I'm about to scare my brother further. In a calmer tone, I say, "Look, I know how it must seem to you, but I swear, I came with the best intentions. Everything I've done since leaving the orphanage was so that—"

"Oh, please." Misha steps toward me, his handcuffed hands stiff in front of his body. "You left me there to rot. One day you were promising you'd always be there for me, and the next you were gone."

Shocked, I open my mouth, but he doesn't give me a chance to reply. "You think I don't remember?" His voice rises as he takes another step toward me. "Well, I do. I remember everything. You lied to me. You said we'd always be together, and then you left!"

"That's enough." Lucas's voice freezes us both in place as the door opens and my captor steps in. He's followed by Dr. Goldberg, who's wearing latex gloves and carrying a surgical tray with various-sized syringes and needles.

My heart skips a beat, then leaps into overdrive. "What is this?" I can't hide my panic as I look at Lucas. "You said—"

"It's the trackers I mentioned to you before," Lucas says, crossing the room. Stopping in front of my bed, he glances at my brother, whose horrified gaze is locked on the tray. "She'll be fine," Lucas says, grabbing Misha's arm and dragging him away from the bed.

"No, wait." Cold sweat breaks out all over my body as Dr. Goldberg picks up a small syringe and comes toward me. I'm not ready for this battle. "Lucas, please, you don't need these," I plead as he tows my brother across the room, ignoring Misha's attempt to drop to the floor and kick out his knees. "I won't run, I promise. I'll do anything you want…"

Lucas stops in the doorway and pulls Misha against him in a chokehold. His muscled forearm is thicker than Misha's neck. "I know," he says, his arctic gaze pinning me in place. "You will. And right now, I want you to be a good girl and let the doctor give you some local anesthetic to make the insertion easier."

"But—"

Misha's face turns purple as Lucas tightens his arm, and I nod quickly, my eyes burning with helpless tears. "Okay, yes. I'll do it. Just let him go."

"I will—when the implants are in." Releasing Misha's throat, Lucas grabs his shirt and drags him out of the room, shutting the door on the way.

"I'm sorry," the doctor says, leaning over me. His brown eyes are filled with sympathy. "I know this isn't easy for you. If you could please lie down on your stomach..."

My bruises ache dully as I obey, stretching out and turning over onto my stomach. The doctor pulls the blanket off me, and I feel a small pinch between my shoulder blades as the needle sinks into my skin. It's followed by another pinch at my nape and a prick near my underarm. My skin grows numb, and I close my eyes, my tears dampening the sheets under my face.

My captor is as cruel as ever, and this time, there's no escape.

28

ucas

"WHAT DO YOU WANT FROM US?" THE BOY ASKS IN ENGLISH, RUBBING his throat with his handcuffed hands. His gaze swings between me and the bedroom door, and I know he's deciding whether he should attack me to try to save his sister. "Are you going to kill us?"

His English is good, nearly as good as Yulia's, which makes sense. UUR must've also taught him from an early age.

"No, Michael," I say. "Not if your sister does what she's told." I wouldn't kill him—and I certainly wouldn't kill Yulia—but it's best if the kid doesn't know that yet. He may be young, but he's strong and skilled for his age.

I'll need leverage to keep him in line.

Sure enough, the boy's chin juts out belligerently. "If you're not going to kill us, why did you bring us here? I'm not going to betray my country, so if you think you can get me to talk—"

"I doubt a trainee would know anything worthwhile, so you can relax. Torture is not on the agenda today."

He glares at me, and I see him weighing the odds of winning against me in a fight.

"I wouldn't if I were you." I step to the right so that I'm between him and the bedroom door. "I promised Yulia I wouldn't hurt you, but if you keep attacking me…" I leave the threat unsaid, but the boy blanches and takes a step back.

Satisfied, I gesture toward the couch. "Sit. You can watch some TV until Diego returns."

The kid doesn't move. "Why are you doing this to Yulia? What do you want from her?"

"That's none of your business." My words come out harsher than I intended. I overheard the two siblings talking when I came in, and though I don't understand Russian, it was obvious to me that Michael accused his sister of something. She'd looked hurt, devastated by whatever the boy said to her. It almost made me change my mind about forcing the implants on her today.

Almost, but not really.

The need to lock Yulia down, to chain her to me, is a compulsion I can't fight. Not having her with me these last couple of weeks has been the worst form of torture, and I won't put myself through it ever again. Esguerra definitely had the right idea when he used the implants on his wife. The trackers will keep me informed of Yulia's whereabouts at all times. With the devices embedded in her neck and back, only a highly skilled surgeon would be able to remove them safely.

"She's my sister," the boy snaps, his blue eyes—eerily like Yulia's—burning with fury. "If you hurt her—"

"You won't be able to do anything about it," I say, figuring it's best to establish that right away. "The only reason you're alive and well is because I'm keeping you that way. A lot of people on this compound died because of your agency, and my boss was nearly killed. Do you understand?"

The kid stares at me for a few moments, then walks over to the couch and sits down, his shoulders rigid with tension.

He gets it now.

If something were to happen to me, he and Yulia would be goners.

I suppose I should feel bad scaring the boy, but he needs to know the reality of his situation. So far, the kid has been nothing but trouble. He attacked Eduardo on the plane, landing a kick to his groin, and when Diego dropped him off at my house, the guard told me the boy tried to grab his weapon in the car on the way here.

For his own safety, Yulia's brother needs to accept his new circumstances.

"Listen, Michael..." I approach the couch and pick up the remote control. "I don't intend to harm Yulia—or you, for that matter. But you need to cooperate and stop fighting us."

The kid gives me a sullen look. "Fuck you."

I should probably castigate him for his language, but I've said worse when I was his age. "What do you want to watch?" I ask, waving the remote at the TV.

He doesn't reply for a moment, then says in a low voice, "You killed my uncle."

I turn toward him in surprise. "Your uncle?"

"Yeah." The boy jumps to his feet, his hands clenched. "You know, the man whose head you shot off yesterday?"

I frown. The story is more complicated than I thought. "He was one of the agents at the black site?"

"Fuck you." The kid plops down on the couch and stares straight ahead. "I hope you eat shit and die."

"*Modern Family* it is, then," I say, turning on the TV and selecting the popular comedy. "Diego should be here any minute, but for now, I think that should hit the spot."

The show starts playing, and I walk over to the bedroom door and lean against the wall, keeping an eye on the boy while listening for sounds from the bedroom. Everything is quiet in there, and a few minutes later, Diego shows up.

"Watch him carefully," I tell the guard, lowering my voice to just above a whisper. "It seems we might've killed some of his family. I have to talk to Yulia to make sense of it all, but for now, keep an eye on him. The kid wants blood."

Diego nods, his face set in grim lines, and I know he understands.

Nothing motivates quite like revenge.

I walk them to the door, making sure the boy doesn't try anything along the way, and then I return to the bedroom, where Goldberg is already packing up his bag.

Yulia is lying on her stomach, stiff and silent, with square bandages marking the insertion sites. The blanket is folded down to her waist, exposing her slim back and the elegant line of her spine. Her face is turned away from me, her hair spread in a tangled blond cloud across the sheets, and my chest aches as I see the scrapes and bruises marring her smooth skin.

Maybe I should've waited with the trackers after all.

No. Shaking off the uncharacteristic self-doubt, I look at the doctor. "Did it go okay?" I ask, and Goldberg nods, picking up his bag.

"Everything went fine," he says, heading for the door. "The bleeding should stop in about an hour, and you can replace the bandages with regular Band-Aids at that point if you want. If you keep the insertion points clean, there won't be any scarring."

"Good. Thank you." I approach the bed and sit down, waiting for the doctor to leave. As soon as I hear the front door close, I extend my hand and run my fingers over Yulia's naked back, avoiding the bruised areas. Her skin is cool and silky, and I feel her quiver under my touch. Instantly, my body comes to life, my hunger for her awakening with savage fury.

Cursing silently, I withdraw my hand, curling it into a fist to keep myself from reaching for her again. I can't take her yet.

She's traumatized and hurt, too weak to handle my pent-up desire.

I have to let her heal.

To my surprise, Yulia rolls over onto her back and stretches her arms above her head—a move that draws my gaze to the soft, round globes of her breasts. "Aren't you going to fuck me?" she murmurs, and I see her nipples hardening, as if from arousal.

My cock turns into a metal spike in my jeans. I know her nipples are most likely reacting to the cool air from the AC, but my mouth still waters with the urge to suck them, to lick the pale flesh around the pink aureolas and sink my teeth into the soft underside of her breasts. Only the black-and-blue marks on her face and stomach keep me from grabbing her then and there.

With effort, I tear my gaze away from her breasts. "No," I say hoarsely. I know I should get up, get away from the temptation, but I can't move. I want her, and not just for sex. The longing that consumes me emanates from deep within my being. We've only been apart for two weeks, but it felt like years. "I'm not going to touch you today."

Yulia's cracked lips twist, her eyes unnaturally bright, and I notice wet streaks on her cheeks. "No? I'm no longer pretty enough for you?" There's a dark taunt in her voice, and I realize that she's punishing me for the trackers, that this is her way of reclaiming control.

Even knowing that, I rise to her bait. "You're gorgeous, and you fucking know it," I say harshly. If tormenting me like this makes Yulia feel better, I'll allow it—if only to alleviate the uncomfortable prickling of guilt the sight of her tears generates.

I should've fucking waited.

"So do it. Fuck me," Yulia says, kicking off the rest of her blanket. She's naked underneath—I undressed and bathed her when we arrived an hour ago—and my body tightens at the sight of her flat stomach and slim, shapely legs that seem to go on forever. And between those legs… Heat rises in me, my breathing turning fast and heavy as I look at the glistening pink folds between her thighs.

"I'm not touching you," I repeat, but even to my own ears, my words lack conviction. She'd been unconscious when I bathed her, and even that simple act had brought me to painful arousal.

Yulia fully awake and taunting me with her body is like a defenseless mouse parading in front of a starved cat.

"Why not?" She arches her back, thrusting her breasts upward in a porn star pose, and I bite back a tortured groan as her nipples draw my attention once more. "Isn't this why you chased me down? So you could fuck me?"

She's right, except fucking is only part of it now. I want what we had before and more.

I want all of her.

Giving in to the vicious hunger riding me, I climb onto the bed and straddle her on all fours, caging her with my body without touching her. Her eyes widen, and I catch a glimmer of fear in her gaze.

She didn't expect me to take her up on her offer.

A dark smile forms on my lips. Leaning down, I whisper in her ear, "Yes, beautiful. I brought you here to fuck you—and I will. Soon. For now, we're going to do something different."

A shudder runs through her as my breath warms her neck, and she lets out a quiet moan as I kiss the tender spot under her ear, then nibble on her delicate earlobe. Her hair tickles my face, and her peach-like fragrance fills my nostrils, making me burn with the need to possess her, to slide down my zipper and thrust inside her, sheathing myself in her soft, wet heat.

The urge is almost unbearable, but I make myself move down her body, ignoring the insistent throbbing of my cock. I lick her neck, kiss her collarbone, and suck each erect nipple before tasting her flat, trembling belly. When my face is parallel to the V between her thighs, I bend my head and inhale deeply, breathing in her warm female scent. Yulia tenses, her thighs tightening to restrict my access to her sex, and I gently but firmly grasp her inner thighs, pulling her legs wide apart.

"Relax, I won't hurt you," I murmur, looking up at her. Her blue eyes are wide and uncertain, the porn-star act gone without a trace. I can sense her growing anxiety, and the image of Kirill attacking her flashes through my mind, cooling my lust by a small degree.

For all her bravado, my beautiful spy is nowhere near ready to play these games.

Keeping my gaze locked on her face, I press my mouth to her pussy, tasting her slick pink flesh. Yulia quivers, her slender hands knotting into fists at her sides, and I nibble on the soft folds around her clit, teasing and licking the sensitive area before swiping my tongue along her slit. She moans, closing her eyes, and I taste her growing arousal as her inner muscles clench helplessly under my tongue.

"Yes, sweetheart, that's it…" I breathe in her intoxicating scent again, then close my lips around her clit and lave the underside of it with my tongue before sucking on it with strong, pulling motions. She cries out, her hips lifting off the bed, and I feel the tension in her rising. My own body responds with a fresh surge of blood to my cock, and my balls tighten as I feel her contractions begin.

I lick her until she's limp and panting in the aftermath of her orgasm, and then I finally give in to my own need. Rising up on my knees, I unzip my jeans and close my fist around my swollen cock.

A few hard jerks of my hand, and I'm coming too, my seed splattering all over her white belly and breasts. It's not a particularly satisfying release—I'd much rather be inside her—but the sight of my cum on her body is erotic in its own way.

On some primitive level, it marks her as my property.

Yulia doesn't move or speak as I climb off the bed and walk to the bathroom. She just watches me, her eyes half-closed, and when

I return with a warm, wet towel a minute later, she remains silent, her expression unreadable as I clean her off.

When I'm done, I undress and climb into bed next to her. Carefully, I draw her against me, trying not to put pressure on her injuries as I curve my body around hers from the back. My ribs ache, but I ignore the nagging pain. It feels too good to have her in my arms, to hold her and know that she's mine.

Yulia is stiff at first, but after a few moments, I feel the tension in her muscles slowly ebbing. In another minute, her breathing evens out, and I know healing sleep has claimed her again.

My own eyelids grow heavy, and I brush my lips across her temple before closing my eyes. "Good night, beautiful," I whisper, euphoric contentment spreading through me as she snuggles closer with a sleepy mumble.

I have my Yulia back, and I'm never losing her again.

III

THE CARETAKER

29

ucas

THE SUN IS IMPOSSIBLY BRIGHT IN THE SKY AS I WALK TOWARD Esguerra's office, the humid air making me sweat despite the early hour. Still, I feel lighter than I have in weeks, the knowledge that Yulia is sleeping in my bed filling me with an incandescent mix of satisfaction and relief.

I found her. I have her.

Even the knowledge that Kirill escaped is not enough to spoil my mood this morning. I left Diego to watch over sleeping Yulia so I could start the process of hunting Kirill, but I feel infinitely calmer after eight hours of sleep.

So calm, in fact, that my pulse barely increases when I see Rosa walking across the lawn toward me. As she approaches, I see that she looks uneasy, her hands twisting fistfuls of her skirt at her sides.

"I heard you were in another shootout in Ukraine," she says, studying me with worried curiosity. "And that you found her. Is it true? Are you all right?"

I nod, my good mood slipping away with every word she speaks. Before leaving the house, I skimmed Thomas's report on Rosa and found that it contained no new information. The maid hasn't reached out to anyone outside the compound, nor has anyone tried to contact her. If the girl is working with UUR or any of our enemies, she's either really good at concealing it, or my original guess about jealousy was right.

It's time to deal with this problem once and for all.

"Rosa," I say softly, stepping closer to her. "Why did you help Yulia escape?"

The maid's bronzed face turns pale. "Wh-what do you mean?"

"Did someone pay you?"

She takes a step back, her eyes huge. "No, of course not! I—" She makes a visible effort to compose herself. "I don't know what you're talking about," she says in an almost steady voice. "Whatever she's told you is a lie. I had nothing to do with her escape."

I smile coldly. "Yulia didn't say a word, but I find it interesting that you think she would have."

Rosa pales even more, and I see her hands tighten convulsively as she continues to back away. "Please, Lucas, it's not what you think."

"No?" I close the distance between us and grab her upper arm before she can turn and run. "What is it then?"

"It's—" She clamps her lips shut and shakes her head, staring up at me. "I had nothing to do with her escape," she repeats, lifting her chin, and I see that she has no intention of admitting anything to me.

"All right," I say, tightening my grip on her arm. "Since you're Esguerra's maid, let's see what he has to say about all this."

And ignoring her terrified expression, I resume walking toward Esguerra's office, dragging Rosa along at my side.

Esguerra's face is rigid with fury as I present the drone footage. The videos are low resolution and obscured by trees in a few places, but there's no mistaking Rosa's curvy figure in her maid's outfit as she approaches my house. Rosa sits quietly, trembling from head to toe while Esguerra watches the videos on his computer. It's not until he turns toward her that she begins crying.

"Why?" His voice is like ice as he rises to his feet. "What did you hope to gain by this? You know what we do to traitors."

Rosa shakes her head, crying harder as Esguerra approaches her, and despite my own anger, I feel a flicker of pity for the girl. In the next second, however, I remember what almost happened to Yulia because of Rosa, and my pity disappears without a trace.

Whatever my boss chooses to do to the maid will be no less than she deserves.

"Please, Señor Esguerra," she begs as he grips her elbow and drags her off the chair where she was huddling. "Please, it wasn't like that…"

"What was it like, then?" I ask, fishing my Swiss knife out of my pocket and opening the blade. Stepping toward the maid, I twist my fist in her hair, pulling her head back as Esguerra holds her upright by her upper arms. "Why did you help my prisoner escape?"

Tears streak down Rosa's face and her mouth quivers as I press the blade against her throat, nicking her neck just enough for her to feel the first bite. "Don't, please…" Her terror washes over me, but this time, it leaves me cold. I'm in my interrogation mode, and so is Esguerra. I see it in the hard gleam of his eyes.

If the girl doesn't talk in the next couple of minutes, the tiny wound I left on her neck will be the least of her worries.

"Julian, did you see—" Nora freezes as she enters the office, her eyes widening as she takes in the scene.

"Fuck," Esguerra mutters, releasing Rosa abruptly. I barely

catch her as she stumbles backward, crashing into me. Before she can get away, I secure the sobbing maid with my forearm across her throat and lower my knife. At the same time, Esguerra steps toward his wife, saying, "Nora, baby, go home. This is a security matter."

"A security matter?" Nora's voice is thin as her gaze swings wildly between me and her husband. "What are you talking about?"

"Rosa helped Lucas's prisoner escape," Esguerra explains tersely, taking Nora's arm and putting his hand on her back to guide her out of the room. She digs in her heels, but her petite frame is no match for his strength, and he gently but firmly steers her toward the exit. "We're interrogating her to find out more. It's nothing you need to worry about, my pet."

"Are you insane?" Nora's voice rises as she begins to struggle, and Esguerra stops, wrapping his arms around her from the back as she tries to kick, then headbutt him. "She's my friend. Don't touch her!"

Esguerra's only response is to lift his tiny wife against his chest and hold her tightly to restrain her flailing. Nora screams, bucking in his arms, and Rosa's sobbing intensifies as Esguerra begins carrying Nora out. He's almost at the door when Nora yells, "Stop, Julian! She didn't do it. It was me—all me!"

Rosa's sobs cut off as suddenly as if she'd been muted, and Esguerra stops, lowering Nora to her feet.

"What?" His expression is thunderous as he grips his wife's narrow shoulders. "What the hell are you talking about?"

I very nearly ask the same question, but at the last moment, I keep my mouth shut. Given Nora's unexpected involvement, it's best if Esguerra handles it from here on.

He'd gut me for so much as looking at his wife the wrong way.

"I did it." Nora raises her chin to meet her husband's furious gaze. "I helped Yulia escape. So if you're going to interrogate anyone, it should be me. She had nothing to do with it."

"You're lying." Esguerra's voice is lethally soft. "I saw the drone footage. She went to Lucas's house right before our departure."

Nora doesn't miss a beat. "Right. Because I asked her to."

Rosa makes a choking sound, her hands clawing at my forearm, and I realize I inadvertently tightened my arm across her throat. Cursing silently, I lower my arm and push Rosa away from me, letting her collapse on the chair she was sitting on earlier. Esguerra's wife is lying—I'm almost certain she's lying—but I have no idea how to prove it. There was no reason for Nora to help Yulia; she doesn't know the Ukrainian spy, and she certainly doesn't have any feelings for me.

"Why would you do this?" Esguerra demands. He's clearly thinking along the same lines. "You despise this girl. You hate her for the crash, remember?" His eyes drill into Nora, but she doesn't back down.

"So what?" She twists out of Esguerra's hold and steps back, her small chest heaving. "You know I had a problem with Lucas torturing a woman at his house—even *that* woman."

Recognition flickers across Esguerra's face before his jaw tightens further, and I realize to my shock that Nora might've done it after all. Esguerra did mention that she and Rosa had been to my house the day Yulia arrived. If so, Nora might've seen Yulia sitting in my living room, naked and bound to a chair. It's not inconceivable that the sight bothered the girl; for all her newfound toughness, Nora is a product of her upbringing—her soft American middle-class background.

Most people new to this way of life would've objected to me torturing Yulia, and it's possible Nora did too.

Fucking hell. If Nora weren't Esguerra's wife…

Esguerra himself looks on the verge of murder as he catches Nora's arm and drags her closer to him. "Walk me through this." His blue eyes gleam with rage. "You instructed Rosa to do what, exactly?"

Rosa begins crying again, and I spare her a glance before

turning my attention back to the drama playing out in front of me. I've never seen Esguerra so mad at his wife before. If I were Nora, I'd be backpedaling right about now; the things I've seen her husband do would make serial killers squirm.

Nora's face is white as she stares up at Esguerra, but her voice barely shakes as she says, "I asked her to help Yulia escape. I didn't tell her how to do it—she knows this place better than me, so I left the exact method up to her. Rosa didn't want to do it, but I told her how much it bothered me, and with the baby and everything, she gave in to my request."

Manipulative little witch. I want to wring Nora's neck and applaud in admiration at the same time. Mentioning the baby they just lost was a low blow, but it had the desired effect. Esguerra's grip on Nora's arm slackens, and pain flits across his face before he composes himself. When he speaks again, some of the lethal bite is gone from his voice.

"Why didn't you talk to me about it? If it bothered you that much, why didn't you say something?"

"I didn't think it would've helped," Nora says, and I see her big dark eyes fill with tears. "I'm sorry, Julian. I wanted the girl gone by the time we returned, and I told Rosa to make it happen. I was sure you wouldn't go along with it." Her chin quivers as the tears spill over and roll down her cheeks. "Please, if you have to punish someone, it should be me, not Rosa. She was just being a good friend to me. Please, Julian." She reaches up to touch his face with her free hand, and I avert my gaze as Esguerra catches her wrist and pulls her flush against him, his nostrils flaring. The tension between them turns thickly sexual, and I suddenly feel like an intruder, a peeping tom observing an intimate moment.

Clearing my throat, I step toward Rosa and grab her upper arm, pulling her to her feet. "I'll let you two figure this out," I say, marching the maid toward the door. "In the meanwhile, I'll have Rosa watched by the guards."

Neither Esguerra nor his wife justify my statement with a

response, and as I exit the building, I hear the sound of something falling, followed by Nora's choked cry. Rosa sucks in her breath—she must've heard it too—and her shoulders shake with a fresh bout of tears.

"Don't worry," I say, giving the girl an icy look as I lead her away from the building. "Esguerra may be a sadist, but he won't hurt her—much. You, on the other hand, are still a question mark. If Nora lied to protect you..."

I don't complete my statement, but I don't have to.

We both know what Esguerra will do to Rosa if she allowed Nora to take the fall for her.

30

ulia

I WAKE UP GROGGY AND CONFUSED, HURTING FROM HEAD TO TOE. Groaning, I stumble out of bed and make my way to the bathroom. Still half-asleep, I take care of business, and it's only when I'm washing my face that it dawns on me that I'm alone—and untied.

A soreness at the back of my neck reminds me of the reason for that: the tracker implants. Lucas must be certain I won't be able to run away again.

I lift my hand and touch the bandage on my nape, then turn to peer at my back in the mirror. Besides the spot I'm touching—and amidst a mottled canvas of bruises—there are two more areas where the trackers went in. The bandages on the wounds are simple Band-Aids now; Lucas must've changed them while I was sleeping. I vaguely recall the doctor giving instructions about that.

I also remember what happened afterwards, and a violent blush sears my face, chasing away the remnants of my sleepiness. I'm not sure why I egged Lucas on like that, but at the time, it seemed to make sense. He clearly cares little about me as a person, and I wanted him to admit it. I wanted him to prove to me once and for all that I'm nothing more than a convenient body for him to fuck, a sexual object that he can and will hurt at will.

Except he didn't hurt me. He gave me pleasure, and then he took his own with his fist, leaving me covered with his seed.

"Yulia?" A knock on the door startles me, and I turn, my pulse jumping into the stratosphere. The voice is not Lucas's, and I'm completely naked.

"Yes?" I call out, grabbing a big fluffy towel off the rack and wrapping it around myself.

"Lucas asked me to watch you this morning," the man says, and I exhale in relief as I recognize Diego's voice. "I hope I didn't scare you. He said you might be sleeping for a while, and I was in the kitchen, grabbing myself a snack, when I heard the water running. You okay? Do you need anything?"

"No, I'm fine, thanks," I say, my heartbeat slowing a bit. "I'll just, um… I'll be right out."

"No problem. Take your time. I'll be in the kitchen." I hear retreating footsteps.

On autopilot, I brush my teeth and run a comb through my hair, untangling the wild blond mess. Honestly, I don't know why I'm even trying to look presentable. The face staring at me from the mirror is like something out of a nightmare. My lips are already beginning to heal, but the left side of my face, where Kirill hit me, is one giant ugly bruise. Smaller scrapes and bruises decorate the rest of my face and body—except for my back, which looks even worse than my face.

No wonder I'm still in pain.

Carefully, I rotate my neck from side to side, trying to ease the stiffness in my muscles. My head aches with the movement, but not as much as yesterday. The doctor had been right about the mildness of my concussion; I had passed out on the plane as much from shock and exhaustion as the head injury itself.

Feeling marginally better, I tighten the towel around myself and walk to the bedroom to change. All the skimpy outfits that Lucas got for me are still there, and I select a pair of shorts and a T-shirt at random, grimacing in pain as I put the clothes on.

When I finally make my way to the kitchen, I find Diego there, spreading cream cheese on a toasted bagel.

"Hey," he says, giving me his usual charming grin. "Are you hungry?"

My stomach chooses that moment to rumble, and the young guard's smile widens. "I'll take that as a yes," he says, putting his bagel down on his plate and getting up. "What would you like? Cereal, toast, fruit? Here, sit." He gestures toward the table. "I'm under strict orders to make sure you don't do anything strenuous today."

"Um, cereal would work." I walk over to the table and sit down, feeling disoriented. It seems like only minutes ago, I was in Ukraine amidst gunfire and explosions, and now I'm in Lucas's kitchen, talking about cereal with one of the mercenaries who killed my UUR colleagues.

My *former* UUR colleagues, I mentally correct myself. I ceased being part of the organization when I made the choice to disappear instead of carrying out my assignment.

"Where's my brother?" I ask, remembering what Lucas told me about the guards watching him.

Diego gives me another grin. "He's with Eduardo. The poor guy drew the short straw."

I blink. "Oh?"

"Let's just say your brother is not very happy to be here." Diego walks over to the fridge and takes out a carton of milk. Pouring cereal into a bowl, he adds the milk, grabs a spoon, and brings the bowl to me. Before I can ask, he says, "But he's okay, so don't worry. Nobody's going to hurt him."

I pick up my spoon, though I no longer feel hungry. My stomach is tight with anxiety. Of course Misha is not happy to be here. How could he be? His uncle was killed in front of his eyes, and he must be terrified out of his mind. And if Obenko didn't lie about Misha's relationship with his adoptive parents, they must be worried sick about him. Unless he lives at the UUR dorms, like other trainees? If that's the case, they might not be aware of what happened yet, though I'm sure someone is bound to notify them soon.

What a disaster—and it's all my fault. If I hadn't been so weak, Lucas wouldn't have known anything about UUR. I let my captor break me, and then I inadvertently led him to my brother—the very person I was trying to protect. I remember yesterday's argument with Misha, the accusations he threw at me, and I want to curl up and cry.

"Are you all right?" Diego sits down across from me and picks up his bagel. "You look really pale."

"I'm fine," I say automatically, dipping my spoon into the cereal and bringing the soggy corn flakes to my lips. "Just a bit out of it."

"Of course." Diego gives me a sympathetic grin. "Jet lag is a bitch, plus you got it pretty rough yesterday."

He focuses on his bagel, and I choke down a few bites of cereal before putting down my spoon. I didn't lie about being out of it; my thoughts are all over the place, my mind jumping from one question to another. The future—especially my brother's future—is like a terrifying black hole looming in the distance, so I try to focus on the present and the near past.

"How did you know where to find me?" I ask Diego when he's done with his bagel. "In general, how did you locate that facility?"

"Oh, yeah, that..." The guard gets up and takes his plate over to the sink. "I'm afraid your rescue was more or less luck on our end, but I'll let Kent fill you in on that."

Great. Another person stonewalling me. Does every person on

this compound regard me as Lucas's property to such an extent that they can't answer my questions on their own?

Suppressing my frustration, I force myself to eat another spoonful of cereal before getting up to dump the rest of it in the garbage.

"What are you doing? Here, I got it." Diego intercepts me before I can get to the sink, grabbing the bowl out of my hands. "You need to rest today."

"I'm fine," I say, then lean against the counter, the weakness in my knees belying my statement. "I want to see Misha—Michael, I mean. Can you bring him here or take me to him?"

"Nope," Diego says cheerfully. "Eduardo took him to the training gym an hour ago. Why don't you rest for now, and then we'll see what Kent says later?" The guard is smiling, but I can sense the steel underneath his easygoing facade. He's not about to let me do anything other than rest and wait for Lucas to come home.

I want to argue, but I know it'll be useless. Besides, getting back in bed doesn't sound all that unappealing.

"All right," I say. "Thank you for the breakfast."

Making my way back to the bedroom, I lie down, feeling as exhausted as if I just ran ten kilometers. My head is throbbing again, and my bruises ache. Even my throat is sore, and my skin feels tight and achy all over. On the nightstand next to the bed, I see the pain pills from yesterday, and after a moment of indecision, I reach for the bottle and extract two pills. Picking up a water bottle that someone thoughtfully left on the nightstand, I swallow the pills and wash them down with water before lying back and closing my eyes.

There's no point in fighting Lucas's orders today. I need to save my strength for when it matters.

31

ucas

After being away for several days, I have a shitload of work to catch up on, and I don't make it home until dinnertime. When I finally walk in, I see Diego watching TV on my couch.

"How is she?" I ask, glancing at the bedroom. "Still sleeping?"

Diego nods, rising to his feet. "Yeah. Like I told you in my texts, she slept through lunch, then woke up for an hour or so, read in bed, and then fell asleep again. I made a sandwich for her, but she left most of it untouched. Oh, and she kept asking to see her brother, but I said you have to authorize that."

"I see. Thank you for watching her. I'll let you know if I need you tomorrow."

Diego grins. "No problem, man."

He leaves, and I enter the bedroom to check on Yulia. Excessive sleeping is not an uncommon reaction to physical trauma and extreme emotional stress—it's the body's way of letting itself heal —but her lack of appetite worries me.

It's dark in the room, so I make my way over to the bed and turn on a bedside lamp. Yulia doesn't so much as twitch at the soft light. She's lying on her back, the blanket pulled up to her chest and her face turned toward me. My chest tightens at the sight of her swollen jaw and darkened eye. With her slender hand lying palm-up on the pillow, she looks achingly young and defenseless, a hurt child instead of a grown woman.

If Kirill is still alive, he'll wish he were dead ten times over by the time I'm done with him.

This morning, I sent out feelers to all our contacts in Europe and gave our hackers a new assignment: tracking down Kirill Luchenko. I also reached out to Peter Sokolov again to see if he knows anyone in Ukraine who can help. He responded right away, promising to look into it, so now it's just a matter of time before we locate the fucker.

Assuming he didn't croak from his wounds, that is. Since Yulia shot his dick off, it might be touch and go for a while.

Sitting down on the edge of the bed, I reach over and stroke her upturned palm with the tip of my finger, feeling the warm softness of her skin. Like the girl herself, her hand is deceptively delicate, an embodiment of elegant femininity. But I know how dangerous it can be—and now Kirill does too.

The fucking bastard will die a dickless eunuch. I really like that.

Yulia's fingers curl in response to my touch, and a small moan escapes her throat. She still doesn't wake up, though, and some instinct makes me reach over and touch her forehead with the back of my hand.

Fuck.

She's hot—much too hot. Her forehead is burning.

In the next instant, I'm on my feet, pulling out my phone. Goldberg doesn't pick up at first, so I call him again. Then again.

On the third attempt, he picks up the phone. "What is it?"

"Yulia is sick," I say without preamble. "Something's really wrong with her. I need you here. Now."

"On my way."

He hangs up, and I sit down on the bed and pick up Yulia's hand, noticing the dry heat coming off her skin. My heart thuds with a dull, heavy rhythm as I lift her wrist up to my face and press my lips against her palm.

"You'll be all right," I whisper, ignoring the sharp fear clawing at my insides. "You'll be all right, baby. You have to be."

"Looks like a type of flu," Goldberg says after examining Yulia. "It hit her hard, probably because her immune system was already under stress from her injuries and everything. I'll get her started on an antiviral and give her Tylenol to bring down the fever. Other than that, you just keep her comfortable and make sure she gets enough fluids."

As he speaks, Yulia's eyelids flutter open, and she stares at me in confusion. "Lucas?" Her voice is weak and raspy as she rolls over onto her side. "What—"

"It's okay, sweetheart. You're just feverish from the flu," I say, sitting down on the bed next to her. Picking up the water bottle from the nightstand, I slide my arm under her upper back and help her sit up, propping her up on the pillows. Handing her the bottle and the pills Goldberg gives me, I murmur, "Here, drink this. It'll make you feel better."

I can feel the doctor's amused gaze on me as he packs his bag, but I no longer give a fuck what he thinks or whom he tells about my weakness for Yulia.

She's mine, and it's time everyone knew that fact.

Yulia obediently swallows the pills and washes them down with all the water remaining in the bottle. "Where's Misha?" she asks when she's done, and I sigh, realizing this is going to be an ongoing battle.

"Your brother had a very nice day with Eduardo," I say, putting the empty bottle back on the nightstand as Goldberg discreetly slips out of the room. "They had a lengthy workout session where Michael worked off quite a bit of his aggression toward the guard, and now they're eating dinner, I believe—which is what we should be doing. Are you hungry? I can heat up some chicken noodle soup. It's canned, but—"

"I'm not hungry," she says, shaking her head. "I just want to see Misha."

"How about this: you take a shower, eat a little soup and drink some tea, and I'll see what I can do about getting Misha over here again?" I want her to eat so she can recover, and this seems like the best way to go about it.

"Okay." Yulia pushes the blanket off her legs and starts to get up, but I catch her and lift her against my chest before she can do more than take a couple of shaky steps. She gives me a startled look, but winds her arms around my neck, holding on to me as I carry her to the bathroom.

When I reach my destination, I carefully lower Yulia to her feet and begin to undress her, pulling off her T-shirt and shorts while she stands there mutely, her eyes glazed with fever. For some reason, I'm reminded of when she was first brought here, bedraggled and malnourished after the Russian prison. It seems impossible that only a month has passed since then—that I met her just three months ago.

It feels like I've been obsessed with my captive for a lifetime.

"Do you need a moment?" I ask, and Yulia nods, the unbruised parts of her face reddening with a flush.

"Okay. I'll be right outside. Call out if you feel dizzy or anything."

I step out to let her use the restroom, and when I hear the

shower turn on, I come back in. She's already standing inside the glass stall, her hand shaking as she reaches for shampoo.

"Here, let me help you," I say, swiftly stripping off my own clothes and joining her in the shower. "I don't want you to strain yourself."

"I'm okay," she protests, but I take the shampoo from her hand and pour a small amount into my palm, then step under the spray to keep the water from hitting her in the face. As I lather her hair, she leans against me, closing her eyes, and I suppress a groan as her firm, curvy ass presses against my groin, taking me from semi-erect state to full-blown hardness. Up until then, I'd managed to keep my eyes off her naked body, my libido taking a back seat to my concern for her health, but this is too much.

Even sick and hurt, she turns me on unbearably.

Down. Fucking go down, I will my cock. My blood feels like molten lava in my veins as I turn Yulia toward the spray and rinse the shampoo from her hair before applying conditioner to the long blond strands.

"Lucas…" Her voice is a shaky whisper as she turns to face me, her fever-bright eyes locking on my face. Water droplets cling to her brown lashes, emphasizing their length, and my lungs feel like I can't get enough air as she reaches for me, her hand brushing over my abs before traveling downward to curl around my hard, aching cock.

It takes all my strength to step out of her reach. "What are you doing?" I ask hoarsely, my stiff cock bobbing up to my navel as the water spray hits her in the chest. "You have the fucking flu."

She follows me, blinking the water out of her eyes. "Let me take care of you, at least like this." Her fingers brush against my erection again, but I catch her wrist before she can wrap her hand around the shaft.

"What the fuck, Yulia?" I stare down at her in disbelief, seeing the dark circles under her eyes and the unnatural pallor of her skin. She's about to collapse, and she wants to give me a handjob?

At my rejection, Yulia's lips tremble, and she drops her gaze, her wrist going limp in my grasp. She looks utterly dejected, and as I stare at her bent head, a dark possibility occurs to me.

"Are you doing this because you think you have to?" I ask, my voice roughening. "Are you afraid I'll hurt your brother if you don't have sex with me?"

She looks up, her eyes swimming with tears, and I realize that's exactly what she fears, that she thinks me capable of this. She's not entirely wrong—I would use her brother to control her if I had to—but not for this.

Not while she's in this condition.

"Yulia…" I gently cup her jaw, making sure I touch only the uninjured side of her face. "I'm not going to punish you for being sick, okay? I'm not that much of a monster. Your brother is safe. You can rest and recover without worrying about him."

"But—"

"Shh." I press the tips of my fingers to her lips. "He'll be fine on one condition: that you stop stressing and let yourself heal. Do you think you can do that?"

She nods slowly, and I lower my hand. "Good. Now, let's wash the rest of you and get you into bed. Tonight, I'm taking care of you, okay?"

Yulia nods again, and I rinse off her conditioner, then carefully wash her all over, ignoring my persistent arousal. I tell myself that I'm a doctor caring for a patient, that this is no different than washing a child, but my cock doesn't buy it. Nonetheless, I manage to get through the shower without jumping her, and by the time I towel her off and bring her back to bed, I'm almost back in control.

"Now soup and tea," I say, propping her up on the pillows again, and she gives me a listless look, her pallor even more pronounced.

"Okay," she murmurs. "And then my brother, right?"

"Yes," I say, but by the time I return with the soup and tea, she's already asleep, her skin burning even hotter.

32

ulia

THE NEXT SEVERAL DAYS PASS IN A FOG OF FEVER AND PAIN. MY bones ache, and my throat feels like I swallowed a ball of fire. Even the roots of my hair hurt, the heat of the fever consuming from within. The illness takes everything out of me, leaving me weak and shaking, and the simplest activities—like going to the bathroom and showering—require Lucas's help.

I sleep for what feels like twenty hours a day, and if it weren't for Lucas forcing water, tea, and soup on me at regular intervals, I'd sleep even more. But he keeps waking me up to spoon-feed me various liquids, and I'm too drained to resist his gentle but insistent brand of caregiving. He's with me at night, his big body curved protectively around mine as we sleep, and he's next to me during the day—all day.

"Don't you have someplace to be?" I croak out the first time I see my captor at my bedside, working on a laptop in an uncomfortable-looking chair. "You're usually gone at this time."

Lucas's hard mouth curves in a smile. "I'm taking a sick day. How are you feeling? Hungry? Thirsty?"

"I'm okay," I murmur, closing my eyes. "Just really, really tired." The exhaustion seems to have settled deep in my bones, weighing me down like an anchor. Even this brief exchange has depleted my nonexistent energy, and I'm already almost asleep again when Lucas makes me sit up and drink room-temperature water from a cup with a curved straw.

Swallowing hurts my throat, but the liquid invigorates me enough that I ask about my brother. Lucas assures me that he's fine, but when I continue to insist that I see Misha, Lucas makes Eduardo take an impromptu two-minute video of my brother and email it to us. On the video, my brother is eating a burger and arguing with Diego about the merits of Krav Maga versus Tae Kwan Do. He looks neither afraid nor abused, which reassures me quite a bit.

"I'll bring him by when you're a little stronger," Lucas promises. "Goldberg said you should be through the worst of it by tomorrow."

But I'm not. The next day is even worse, my fever spiking uncontrollably, and I wake up mid-day to hear Lucas arguing with the doctor about whether I need to be hospitalized.

Blearily, I open my eyes to see my captor pacing around the room, a thermometer clutched in his powerful fist. "Her fever is almost a hundred and four. What if it's pneumonia or something like that?"

"I told you, her lungs are clear," Dr. Goldberg says with a hint of exasperation. "As long as you keep giving her enough liquids, she'll be fine. You just need to let this illness run its course. The human body doesn't handle extreme stress well, and from what you've told me, she's been through more in the past three months than most people survive in a lifetime. She's traumatized physically and mentally, and she needs rest and sleep to heal. In a way, this flu is her body's way of telling her to slow down and take care of herself."

Lucas stops in front of the bed, his hands clenched. "If anything happens to her…"

"Yes, I know, you'll tear me limb from limb," the doctor says wearily. "So you've said. Now if you don't mind, I have a guard with a bullet in his leg who needs my attention. Call me if her fever goes higher, and for now, alternate her Tylenol with Advil."

He departs, and I close my eyes, sinking back into sleep.

THE FEVER CONTINUES FOR THREE MORE DAYS, SPIKING AND FALLING in an unpredictable manner. Every time I wake up, feeling like I'm dying, Lucas is by my side, ready to feed me liquids, put a wet towel on my forehead, or carry me to the bathroom.

"Are you sure you don't have a nursing degree?" I joke weakly when he places me back in bed, having changed the sheets and fluffed up my pillows. "Because you're really good at this."

Lucas smiles and tucks the blanket around me. "Maybe I'll look into it if this gig with Esguerra doesn't work out."

I manage a tiny smile in return, and then I'm out again, too exhausted to cling to wakefulness for long.

That night, the fever torments me nonstop, defying Lucas's efforts to bring it down with Tylenol and cool towels. I toss and turn, alternately shivering and sweating as troubled dreams invade my mind. The wolf of the children's lullaby comes to me, gnawing at my side, and I scream as his snout transforms into Kirill's face—a face that explodes into bits as I shoot him, over and over again. Lucas shakes me awake, holding me on his lap until my hysterical sobbing subsides, but as soon as I fall asleep again, I see a variation of the same dream, only this time, my bullets miss Kirill and hit my brother while Kirill laughs, holding his bloodied cock.

"Yulia, hush, sweetheart, don't. He's okay. Misha is okay." The assurance, delivered in Lucas's deep voice, calms me down until I'm swept into yet another twisted dream-memory, and the vicious cycle continues until my fever breaks in the morning.

"I'm sorry," I whisper when I wake up and see Lucas sitting next to me, his eyes ringed with dark circles and his hard jaw unshaven as he frowns at something on his laptop. "Did I keep you up all night?"

He looks up from the computer. "No, of course not." Despite his tired appearance, his pale eyes are sharply alert as he reaches over to the nightstand and hands me the cup with the straw. "How are you feeling?"

"Like I couldn't swat a fly," I say hoarsely after sucking down the full cup of water. "But overall, better." For the first time in days, my head doesn't ache, and my skin feels like it actually wants to stay attached to my body. Even my throat is almost back to normal, and there's a hollow sensation in my stomach that feels suspiciously like hunger.

Lucas's tense look eases as he places his laptop on the nightstand and gets up. "I'm glad. Another few hours like that, and I was flying you to a hospital, no matter what Goldberg said." Leaning over me, he carefully picks me up and brings me to the bathroom, where he runs a bath for me since I'm too weak to stand in a shower stall.

"Why are you doing this?" I ask when he's done washing me from head to toe. Now that I'm feeling marginally more human, it dawns on me just how extraordinary Lucas's actions over the past several days have been. I don't know many husbands who would've cared for their wives with such dedication.

"What do you mean?" Lucas frowns as he wraps me in a thick towel and picks me up. "You needed a bath."

"I know, but you didn't need to be the one to give it to me," I say as he carries me back to the bedroom. "You could've had one of the guards help or—" I stop as his expression darkens.

"If you think I'm letting another man touch you…" His voice is pure lethal ice, and despite myself, I shiver as he lays me back on the bed, stuffing two pillows under my back to prop me up to a half-sitting position. Leaning in, he growls, "You're mine and mine alone, understand?"

I nod warily. I'd let myself forget for a moment how dangerous —and insanely possessive—my captor can be.

Straightening, Lucas makes a visible effort to get himself under control. His chest expands with a deep breath, and he asks in a calmer tone, "Are you hungry? Do you want some chicken broth?"

I lick my cracked lips. "Yes. And maybe something like a sandwich?"

His eyebrows lift. "Really? A sandwich? You must be on the mend. How about eggs? I tried making an omelet recently, and it didn't come out awful."

"You did?" I stare at him. "Okay, sure, I'll gladly have some eggs."

Lucas smiles and disappears through the doorway. Twenty minutes later, he comes back carrying a tray with a delicious-smelling omelet and a steaming cup of Earl Grey.

"Here we are," he says, placing the tray on the nightstand and picking up the plate with the fork. Spearing a piece of omelet, he holds up the fork and commands, "Open up."

"I can feed myself," I begin, reaching for the plate, but he moves it out of my reach.

"Too weak to swat a fly, remember?" He gives me a steely look. "Now sit back and open your mouth."

Sighing, I obey, feeling uncomfortably like a two-year-old as Lucas sits on the edge of the bed and feeds me with the nonchalant efficiency of a nurse. However, the glint in his eyes is distinctly un-nurselike, and to my shock, I realize he's enjoying this on some level.

He likes me helpless and dependent on him.

To test my theory, I watch him closely the next time he brings the fork to my mouth. And there it is: the moment my lips close around the fork, his gaze dips to my mouth and lingers there, his hand tightening on the handle of the utensil. The blanket bunched around my lap is blocking his lower body from my view, but I suspect that if I checked, I'd find him hard, his thick cock bursting out of the confines of his jeans.

A spiral of heat snakes down my spine, and my nipples tighten under the blanket. My body's reaction catches me off-guard. I'm hardly in shape to be thinking about sex. Nonetheless, I'm cognizant of a growing slickness between my thighs as Lucas continues feeding me, leaning over me each time he brings the food to my lips.

The omelet is good—Lucas really did learn how to make it—but I barely register the rich, savory flavor, all my focus on the twisted eroticism of the situation. In a way, Lucas's insistence on taking care of me is an extension of his desire to possess me, to control me completely. Weak and ill, I'm at his mercy more than ever, and for some perverse reason, the knowledge turns both of us on.

Before long, the omelet is gone, and I slump back against the pillows, equal parts stuffed and exhausted by the simple act of eating. Arousal or not, I'm still not well. Lucas puts a straw in my tea and lets me drink down half a cup, and then I fade out again, my body demanding yet more rest.

~

When I wake up again, I feel moderately stronger, and I remember some of the nightmares I had during the night.

"Can I please see my brother?" I ask Lucas when he brings me a sandwich and a bowl of soup. "I'd really like to talk to him."

Lucas shakes his head. "You're not well enough yet."

"I'm fine. Please, I really need to talk to him." I put my hand on

Lucas's thigh, feeling the hard muscle through the rough material of his jeans. "I just want to see him with my own eyes."

"I don't want you to tire yourself out," Lucas says, but I can tell he's wavering.

"How about this?" I push myself up to a straighter sitting position. "I'll eat, and then if I don't fall back asleep, you'll let him come by. Just for a little while. Please, Lucas."

His eyes narrow. "You'll eat, and I'll think about it."

I nod eagerly and dig into my sandwich, consuming it in several big bites. Lucas insists on feeding me the soup himself, his pale eyes heavy-lidded as he brings the spoon to my mouth. I don't object; I'm too excited by the idea of seeing Misha, and I don't mind this weird kink my captor seems to have developed. Also, I don't want Lucas to realize that I'm not as recovered as I thought. Once again, eating has tired me out, and I'm beginning to feel uncomfortably warm, as though the fever is returning.

Fortunately, Lucas doesn't catch on to that, so when I don't fall asleep immediately after my meal, he messages Diego to bring Misha to see me.

"I'm going to give you ten minutes with him," Lucas says, dressing me in one of his T-shirts. "But the second you feel tired—"

"I'll end it and rest," I say, curving my lips in what I hope is a bright, healthy smile. "Don't worry. It's going to be fine."

Lucas frowns as he feels my forehead, but at that moment, there is a knock on the door.

My brother and Diego are here.

"Ten minutes," Lucas warns, tucking the blankets around me. "I'll be right outside, okay?"

I nod. "Can you please put a chair a few feet away from the bed? I don't want Misha to catch this bug."

Lucas does as I ask before leaving the room, and a few moments later, my brother walks in.

"How are you feeling?" he asks in Russian as soon as he enters the bedroom, and I put my hand up, not wanting him to get too close. Though I suspect I'm past the contagious stage of this illness, I still feel more like a germ-infested rag than a person.

"I've been better," I say, waving Misha toward the chair Lucas prepared for him. My skin is hurting again, but my brother doesn't need to know that. "How are you? How are they treating you?"

Misha hesitates, then shrugs. "All right, I guess." He sits down in the chair, and I notice that his hands are not handcuffed this time.

"They let you walk around untied?" I ask, surprised, and my brother nods.

"They don't leave me alone with weapons, and I'm handcuffed at night, but yeah, I have some freedom."

"Good." I rack my brain for a good place to start, then decide to just come out with it. "Michael," I say quietly, "where are your adoptive parents? How did you end up with UUR?"

He gives me a stony look. "Uncle Vasya said he told you everything."

"He told me... some things. But I'd like to hear it from you." After Obenko's betrayal, I have zero trust in my former boss's version of the story. "Do your parents know what you were doing? Did they agree to your training?"

Misha looks at me silently.

"Mishen'ka..." My bones ache as I sit up straighter. "All I want is to know a little bit about your life. You have no reason to believe me, but eleven years ago, I made a bargain with Vasiliy Obenko—your Uncle Vasya. I promised him I'd join UUR in exchange for his sister adopting you and providing you with a good life. That's why I left: because I wanted you to have the kind of life we had before our parents were killed, the kind of life I couldn't provide for you in the orphanage..."

As I speak, Misha shakes his head. "You're lying," he says, jumping to his feet. "You left. Uncle Vasya told me you joined the program because you didn't want the responsibility of a baby brother... because you were tired of being in the orphanage. He felt bad that you left me behind, and he told Mom about me and then…" He stops, his chest heaving. "He wouldn't have lied to me about this. He wouldn't have." He repeats that as if trying to convince himself, and I realize that my brother is not as sure of Obenko as he appears. Has he already had a chance to witness the man's ruthlessness?

"I'm sorry," I say, lying back against the pillows as my brief burst of energy wanes. "I wish that were true, but for your uncle, his country always came first. You know that, don't you?"

Misha's lips flatten, and he shakes his head again. "No. He said you're good at twisting things."

"Misha…"

"It's Michael." He folds his arms across his chest. "And I don't want to talk about this anymore."

"Okay." I'm still too sick to argue with a traumatized teenager. "Just tell me one thing… Are they good people, those adoptive parents of yours? Did they treat you well?"

After a moment's hesitation, Misha nods and sits down in the chair. "They did—they are." His gaze softens a little. "Mom makes potato pancakes on the weekends, and Dad plays table tennis. He's really good at it. I used to play with him every evening when I was little."

Tears of relief fill my eyes at the genuine emotion in his voice. Whatever caused him to end up in UUR, Misha loves his adoptive parents—loves them like I loved our Mom and Dad.

"Do you see them often?" Now that my brother is actually speaking to me, I find myself desperate to hear more about his life. "Since you started training, I mean? Are you staying at the dorms, or do you still live at home? What do your parents think of you doing this?"

Misha blinks at my rapid-fire questions. "I… I see them once a month now," he answers slowly. "And yes, I'm staying at the dorms. Mom didn't want that, but Uncle Vasya said it would be best, said it would help me with the transition and everything."

I nod encouragingly, and he continues after a brief pause. "They're mostly okay with me joining the agency. I mean, they understand that we serve our country." His gaze slides away as he fidgets in the chair, and I read between the words.

His parents might've understood, but they were less than happy to have their adolescent son recruited to the cause.

"Do you think they're worried about you?" Ignoring my growing exhaustion, I push myself to an upright sitting position again. "Would they have heard about what happened?"

"They—" His voice cracks as he looks back at me, blinking rapidly. "Yeah, I think they must know by now. Someone would've notified Mom about Uncle Vasya."

"I'm sorry, Michael." I bite my lip. "I'm really sorry that it happened like that. Believe me, if I could undo it—"

"Don't." Misha stands up, his hands clenched. "Don't pretend."

"I'm not—"

"That's enough." Lucas's voice is knife sharp as he enters the room, approaching my brother with furious strides. "I told you, you're not allowed to upset her." Grabbing Misha by the back of his shirt, he drags him toward the door, growling, "She's sick. Which part of that don't you understand?"

"Lucas, stop." I throw off my blanket, my pulse leaping in sudden fear. "Please, he didn't do anything."

Lucas instantly lets go of Misha and crosses the room toward me as I swing my feet to the floor, about to get up despite a wave of dizziness.

"What are you doing?" Glaring at me, he grabs my legs and places them back on the bed, forcing me back into the half-sitting position on the pillows before caging me between his arms. His eyes gleam with fury as he leans in, his face centimeters from mine. "You are to rest, understand?"

"Yes." I swallow the knot in my throat. "I'm sorry."

Apparently that satisfies Lucas, because he straightens and turns toward my brother. "Let's go," he says, jerking his thumb toward the door, and Misha shoots me an apologetic look before exiting the room ahead of Lucas.

Exhausted, I slide down the pillows and close my eyes.

My brother is all right for now, but this is no place for him. I need to get him back to his parents.

He has to go home.

33

ucas

AFTER I ESCORT MICHAEL OUT OF THE HOUSE AND HAND HIM OVER to Diego, I return to the bedroom to find Yulia asleep again. Though the bruises from Kirill's assault are barely visible now, deep blue shadows lie under her eyes, and her face is pale and thin. She lost weight during the illness, and she once again looks disturbingly fragile, like a glass figurine that could shatter at the slightest touch.

I must be a pervert, because I want her anyway.

Taking a deep breath, I undress and climb into bed beside her. The pillows are all bunched up, so I arrange them more comfortably and lie down, pulling her against me. She's still wearing the T-shirt, but I don't mind the barrier between our bodies.

It keeps my lust for Yulia under control, helps me maintain the illusion that I'm a dispassionate caretaker rather than a man who's had to jerk off twice a day for the past week.

Last night, I didn't sleep, so I should be out like a light, but I'm wide awake as I feel the heat rising off her skin again. The fucking fever is back. I knew I shouldn't have listened to Yulia, but I couldn't resist the plea in her big blue eyes. I still don't know the full story with her brother—the boy refuses to answer any questions—but I know she loves him.

She ran away to save him from me.

Closing my eyes, I berate myself for the hundredth time for not listening to her. Over the past several days, I've had a chance to replay our pre-escape conversations in my mind, and I see that I have no one but myself to blame for the misunderstanding. If I'd let Yulia speak, I would've known who Misha was, and I would've promised not to harm him.

Even *I* have limits.

Yulia mumbles something in her sleep, burrowing closer to me, and I kiss the delicate shell of her ear, my chest tightening as I feel her burning skin. She's not nearly as sick as last night, but she's still far from well.

Carefully disentangling myself from her, I go to the bathroom and return with a cool wet towel. When I remove the T-shirt and run the towel over her body, Yulia wakes up, blinking at me with dazed blue eyes, but before I'm done wiping her down, she falls asleep again.

I turn off the light and get in bed beside her again, pulling her into my arms. My body heat is not optimal right now, but I've noticed she sleeps better when I'm holding her. She's less prone to nightmares that way.

Closing my eyes again, I try not to think about the source of her nightmares, but it's impossible. Yulia's illness has derailed my normal work routine, but I've made sure that the search for Kirill is proceeding uninterrupted. Unfortunately, other than some vague rumors and a few false leads, there's been nothing in the past few days. It's like the bastard just vanished. It's feasible he didn't survive his wounds, but in that case, we should've found a body or heard something about a funeral.

No, my gut instinct tells me Yulia's former trainer is alive—likely in horrendous pain, but alive. I'll have to step up my efforts to find him when Yulia is well.

First, though, I need to get her well.

Kissing her temple, I snuggle her closer, ignoring the lust stiffening my cock. With any luck, Yulia's improved appetite means she's on the mend, and I will soon have her strong and healthy again.

If not, Goldberg will wish he'd never been born.

~

To my relief, over the next two days, Yulia's recovery continues with no further relapses. Her appetite returns with a vengeance, and I find myself scouring the Internet for simple but nutritious recipes. I'm still pretty terrible in the kitchen, but I've discovered that with enough focus and concentration, I can make basic dishes by following instructions and watching online videos —something I've never been motivated to do before. But with Yulia completely dependent on me, it feels wrong to feed her only sandwiches and cereal.

I want her to eat well so she regains her health.

"What are you doing, man?" Diego asks when he enters my kitchen and sees me chopping up vegetables for stew. "I've never seen you cook before."

"Yeah, well, I'm expanding my skill set," I say, depositing all the vegetables into a large pot before glancing at my open laptop for the next step in the process. "It's never to late to learn, right?"

"Uh-huh, sure." Diego gives me a dubious look. "Why didn't you just ask Esguerra's housekeeper to make some extra food for you? She usually doesn't mind."

"I'm not Ana's favorite person right now," I say, carefully measuring out a teaspoon of salt. "You know, with Rosa and all."

"Oh, right." Diego sits down at the table and watches me with evident fascination. "She's pretty upset about the whole thing, huh?"

"You could say that again."

Though Nora's intervention saved Rosa from our interrogation and subsequent punishment, the maid has been under house arrest for the past week while Esguerra is deciding what to do with her. If it weren't for Nora's friendship with the girl, it would've been easy, but Esguerra doesn't want to upset his wife by executing her close friend.

Besides, neither one of us is completely certain that Nora told the truth, which means there's still a chance the maid could've been working for someone else.

Now that Yulia is feeling better, I'm going to question her about that—and about everything else.

"So that's it? You're a master chef now?" Diego says as I pour the suggested amount of water into the pot and cover it before turning on the stove. "Does that mean Eduardo and I can come over for dinner?"

"Fuck, no. Make your own damned stew."

Diego bursts out laughing, but quickly sobers up when I turn to face him.

"Enough chitchat," I say, wiping my hands on a paper towel. "Fill me in on the new trainees and where we are with the recruiting efforts."

The guard launches into his daily report, and I sit down at the table, keeping an eye on the pot to make sure it doesn't boil over.

~

WHEN THE STEW IS DONE, I CHECK ON YULIA AND FIND HER NAPPING in the armchair in the library, dressed in another one of my T-shirts. I brought her here after lunch when she insisted on getting up, claiming she was tired of lying in bed all day. Judging by the book on her lap, she fell asleep while reading.

Frowning, I brush my hand over her forehead to check for fever. To my relief, her skin feels normal to the touch. She's still not fully recovered, but Goldberg was right not to let me panic.

I glance at the clock.

Four p.m. Plenty of time before dinner.

Making a decision, I quietly exit the room and head outside. I need to do my rounds with the guards and catch up with Esguerra. With any luck, Yulia will nap for the next couple of hours while I do some work, and then we'll have a nice meal together—our first normal meal since her return.

I can't fucking wait.

34

ulia

An unnerving sensation wakes me up. It's almost like someone's watching me, or—

Gasping, I sit up in the armchair and gape at the petite, golden-skinned girl standing in the middle of Lucas's library. She's wearing a light blue sundress, and her shiny dark hair streams over her slim bare shoulders. I'm pretty sure I've never seen her before, though something about her delicate features is familiar.

"Who are you?" I try to keep my voice level—not an easy feat with my heart pounding in my throat. I'm still weak from my illness, and though the doll-like creature in front of me doesn't seem like much of a threat, I know looks can be deceiving. "What are you doing here?"

"I'm Nora Esguerra," she says in unaccented American English.

Her dark, thickly lashed eyes regard me with cool derision. "You've met my husband, Julian."

I blink. That explains how she got into the house—she must have the same master keys as Rosa—and why she looks familiar. Her picture was in the files Obenko gave me in Moscow.

Also, I've seen those dark eyes once before.

"You were looking in the window the first day I was brought here," I say, tugging Lucas's T-shirt down to cover more of my thighs. Had I known I'd have visitors, I would've put on some real clothes. "With Rosa, right?"

The girl nods. "Yes, we looked in on you." She doesn't apologize or explain, just studies me, her eyes slightly narrowed.

"Okay, and you're here today because..." I let my voice trail off.

"Because I've been waiting for a chance to talk to you, and this is the first time Lucas has left the house in several days," she says, and approaches my armchair.

Feeling uneasy, I stand up. Though my legs still feel like cooked noodles, I'll be better able to protect myself on my feet—if the need arises.

"What did you want to talk about?" I ask, keeping a careful eye on the girl's hands. She doesn't appear armed, but something about her posture tells me she might not need weapons to inflict harm.

She's had some fighting training, I can tell.

"Rosa," the girl says. Her small chin lifts as she gives me a hard look. "Specifically, what you're going to tell Lucas and Julian about her."

I frown in confusion. "What do you mean?"

"They're going to want to know how you escaped and who helped you," Nora says evenly. "And you're going to say that it was Rosa acting on my instructions. Do you understand?"

"What?" That's the last thing I expected to hear. "You want me to blame you?"

"I want you to tell the truth," she says coolly. "And yes, that means telling everyone that Rosa was helping you on my request."

"She didn't say anything about it being your request," I say, my mind racing. It sounds like the maid is in trouble, and Esguerra's wife is trying to protect her by admitting her own involvement. Except—

"It doesn't matter what Rosa said or didn't say." Nora's voice tightens. "I'm telling you now that Rosa was acting on my orders, and that's what you will say when Lucas and Julian ask you about it. Understand?"

"Or what?" I can hear the threat in the girl's tone, but I want to see how far she'd go. "Or what, Mrs. Esguerra?"

"Or I will personally ensure that Julian flays every bit of flesh from your bones." She gives me a cool smile. "In fact, I may do it myself."

I stare at her, trying to recall what I know about the girl. She's young—a couple of years younger than me, according to Esguerra's file—and recently married to the arms dealer. Before that, she was supposedly kidnapped by him; there was an FBI investigation that lasted more than a year. But regardless of her background, it's obvious to me that she's not all that different from her husband now.

She's not making an idle threat.

"All right," I say slowly. "Let's presume you did suggest to Rosa that she help me. Why? What would've been your motivation? Lucas will want to know."

"He'll understand my motivation. All you need to do is tell the truth—the full truth, including my involvement."

My lips twist. "Right. And I assume the full truth doesn't include your visit to me today."

"Correct." Her dark gaze is unblinking. "There's no reason for Rosa to pay for my actions. I'm sure you agree with that."

"I do." If Esguerra's wife wants her notoriously ruthless husband to think the whole thing was her idea, I have no intention of standing in her way—especially given this little chat. "Now, is that all, or can I help you with something else?"

"That's all," she says, then turns and starts walking away. But before I can exhale in relief, she stops in the doorway and looks back at me. "Just one more thing, Yulia..."

I lift my eyebrows, waiting.

"From what Julian's said, Lucas seems... unusually enamored with you." Her voice is oddly flat. "It's fortunate for you, given what's occurred."

She's talking about the plane crash, I realize. Esguerra's wife would naturally blame me for that. At least I didn't succeed in seducing her husband; I have a feeling if Nora knew Esguerra was my initial assignment, I might've woken up with my throat slit.

"I'm sure you were just doing your job," she continues in that same flat tone. "Carrying out your superiors' orders."

I nod warily. I have no idea what she wants me to say. I didn't know that my intel would be used to bring down her husband's plane, but even if I did, I'm not sure that would've changed anything. I might've tried to get Lucas to stay off that plane, though he had still been a stranger to me at the time, but I wouldn't have lifted a finger to save Esguerra. I still wouldn't.

Given everything I know about the man, the world would be better off without him—and so would his wife.

"Good. That's what Lucas told Julian," Nora says. "It wasn't personal, so to speak."

I nod again, hoping she gets to the point soon. The lingering tiredness from the illness is making my legs tremble, and I'm sweating from the exertion of standing for so long. I don't want to show vulnerability in front of Esguerra's wife, though. It would be like baring one's throat to a small but deadly she-wolf.

"Okay, Yulia..." The she-wolf's eyes gleam with a peculiar light. "I guess what I'm trying to say is, for your sake, I hope you share Lucas's feelings. Because if he ever withdraws his protection..." She doesn't complete her sentence, but I understand her perfectly.

My brother is not the only one who doesn't belong on this estate.

"Understood," I manage to say calmly. "Anything else?"

She gives me a tight smile. "No. That's all. Hope you feel better soon."

She turns and disappears through the doorway, and I collapse back into the armchair, as exhausted as if I'd just fought a war.

35

Lucas

It takes me longer than expected to catch up on everything I've neglected over the past several days, and by the time I get home, it's almost seven-thirty.

The first thing I do upon entering the house is go to the library. To my surprise, Yulia is not there.

"Lucas?" she calls out, and I realize her voice is coming from the kitchen. Frowning, I backtrack and go there.

"What are you doing?" I say when I see her carrying two spoons to the kitchen table. Approaching her in two long strides, I grab the utensils from her hand and clasp her elbow. "You need to be resting."

"I'm all right," she protests as I guide her to the table. "Really, Lucas, I'm much better. I got tired of sitting on my butt all day and wanted to set the table for dinner."

"Tough shit." I pull out her chair. "Sit, and I'll take care of that. Your only job right now is to recover, got it?"

Yulia gives me an exasperated look but obeys. For the first time since her illness began, she's wearing her normal clothes—a pair of jean shorts and a tank top—but the skimpy outfit only emphasizes the severity of her weight loss. Her stomach is concave, and her arms are reed thin. I don't know why she's pushing herself so hard, but I don't like it.

"You are not to move a muscle," I say as I wash my hands and take out a pair of bowls. Yulia must've already turned on the stove to warm up the stew, because when I check, I find it simmering on a low setting. I pour each of us a generous portion and bring the bowls over to the table. "I don't want you to have another relapse," I say, sitting down across from her.

She sniffs at the stew instead of replying. "You made it?" she asks, looking up, and I nod, curious to see what she'll think. I tasted it earlier and liked it, though I still have far to go before I can rival Yulia in the cooking department.

She dips her spoon in and tries a little of the broth surrounding the veggies. "It's good, Lucas," she says, and I can't suppress a smile at the surprise in her voice.

"I'm glad you like it," I say, digging into my own portion. "It wasn't difficult to make, so I should be able to repeat it."

Yulia begins eating with evident enthusiasm, and I watch her, pleased to see her enjoying my efforts. There's something oddly satisfying about seeing her at my kitchen table, eating the food I made and wearing the clothes I got for her. I never thought of myself as the nurturing type, never considered that I might want to take care of someone, but that's precisely what I want to do with her. It's particularly strange because, this illness aside, Yulia is one of the most capable women I've met.

She's quiet as we make quick work of the stew, and I let her eat in peace, worried that even this meal might be too taxing for her.

When we're done, I clean up and make Yulia a cup of her favorite Earl Grey.

"How are you feeling?" I ask when I bring it to the table, and she smiles, patting her flat belly.

"Extremely full. The stew was amazing. Thank you for making it."

"My pleasure." I grin as she stifles a yawn before sipping her tea. "Sleepy?"

"Just food coma, I think," she says with another almost-yawn. "I can't possibly want to sleep. I've slept enough for a lifetime."

"Your body needed it," I say, my amusement fading as I recall her near-catatonic state after Kirill's attack. "You've been through a lot."

She looks down at her cup. "Yeah, I guess."

"Yulia..." I sit down and reach across the table to cover her hand with mine. "What happened? How did you end up with Kirill?"

Her slender fingers twitch under my palm, but she doesn't look up.

"Yulia." I squeeze her hand lightly. "Look at me."

She reluctantly meets my gaze.

"Do you have any other siblings you're hiding from me?"

She shakes her head.

"Anyone else you're trying to protect?"

She blinks. "No."

"Then tell me what happened. Why were you in that cell? Did they think you double-crossed them?"

"They... it... It's complicated, Lucas." Her lips tremble for a second before she presses them together.

"I see." I get up and walk around the table. Yulia gives me a startled look when I pull her to her feet, but I just pick her up and walk to the living room, carrying her cradled against my chest.

"What are you doing?" she asks when I sit down on the couch, holding her on my lap. She's disturbingly light in my arms, as breakable as after her stint at the Russian prison.

"I'm getting comfortable so you can tell me your complicated story," I say, settling her more securely on my lap. Even after her weight loss, her ass is soft and curvy, and her hair smells sweet, like peaches mixed with vanilla. My body reacts instantly, but I ignore the spike of lust. Keeping one arm around her back, I tuck a strand of hair behind her ear with my free hand and say softly, "Talk to me, sweetheart. I won't hurt you or your brother, I promise."

Yulia looks at me for a few moments, and I know she's debating how much to trust me. I wait patiently, and finally, she murmurs, "Where do you want me to start?"

"How about at the beginning? Tell me about Michael. When did you both get recruited by the agency?"

Yulia takes a deep breath and launches into her story. I listen, my chest aching as she tells me about a ten-year-old girl whose parents left her to watch her two-year-old brother on an icy winter night and never returned, about the police visit the next morning and the horrors of the orphanage that followed.

"Nobody paid much attention to me—like I told you, I was skinny and awkward at that age, a real ugly duckling. But Misha was beautiful," she says in a raw voice. "He could've starred in baby-product commercials. And I wasn't the only one who thought so. The headmistress kept bringing him to her office, and I'd see men, different men each time, go in. I don't know what they did to him, but there would be bruises on him, and blood occasionally. And he wouldn't stop crying for days afterwards. I tried to report it, but nobody would listen. The country was in disarray —it still is—and nobody cared about the orphans. We were out of the way, and that was all that mattered." Her eyes glitter fiercely as she says, "I would've done anything to get Misha out of there. Anything."

Fury is a pulsing beat in my skull, but I keep quiet and continue listening as Yulia tells me about a visit from a well-dressed man whose cold hazel eyes both scared her and gave her hope.

"Vasiliy Obenko offered me a deal, and I took it," she says. "It was the only way I could save Misha. We'd been at the orphanage for less than a year, and he was already a mess: acting out, crying at random times, disobeying his teachers… Even if a good family had come along, they wouldn't have wanted to adopt a child with those kinds of behavioral issues, no matter how beautiful he was. I was so desperate I considered taking Misha and running away, but we would've starved on the streets or worse. The world isn't kind to homeless children." She draws in a shuddering breath, and I stroke her back, trying to keep my own hands from trembling with rage.

I'm going to find the headmistress of that orphanage and make the child-pimping bitch pay.

"So yeah," Yulia continues after a moment, "when Obenko came to recruit me in exchange for his sister and brother-in-law adopting Misha and providing him with a good home, I jumped at the opportunity. I knew there was a chance I was making a deal with the devil, but I didn't care. I just wanted Misha to have a shot at a better life."

Of course. That explains so fucking much: her bizarre loyalty to an organization that abused her, her willingness to carry out "assignments" after what happened with Kirill. It was never about patriotism; all along, she'd been doing it for her brother.

"And did Obenko uphold his part of the bargain?" My tone is relatively calm.

"Sort of—well, I don't know." She bites her lip. "I'm still trying to untangle the truth from the lies. Misha was supposed to have a normal life, and it seems like he did—at least until a couple of years ago. His adoptive parents have nothing to do with the agency; Obenko's sister is a nurse, and her husband is an electrical engineer. Part of the bargain was that I stay away from Misha and his new family, so I only saw him in pictures. I didn't realize my brother had been recruited by UUR until I followed Obenko to a warehouse on the outskirts of Kiev and saw Misha there, being trained by Kirill along with the other youths."

"The Kirill you thought was dead?" My rage intensifies as I picture her reaction to this double blow—to a betrayal so cruel even I can't fathom it.

Yulia nods, her gaze hardening as she tells me about her capture and subsequent interrogation at the hands of her own agency. "They thought I'd been turned, you see," she says. "That I betrayed *them*."

"I don't understand something." I slide my hand under her hair and rest it on her nape, managing to keep my fury under control. "What prompted you to follow Obenko to that warehouse? Did you suspect something?"

"No, not at all." Her blue eyes are shadowed. "I started following Obenko in the hopes that he might eventually lead me to his sister's family—to my brother. I wanted to see Misha just this once before—" She stops, her teeth sinking into her bottom lip.

"Before what?"

Yulia doesn't respond.

"Before what, beautiful?"

"Before I left for another assignment," she whispers, blinking rapidly.

Her words fill me with such violent jealousy that I almost miss it when she adds, almost inaudibly, "And disappeared for good."

"What?" My hand tightens on the back of her neck. "What the fuck do you mean by that?"

She winces, and I gentle my grip, massaging the area I just abused. She still doesn't say anything, however, and the seconds tick by, each one adding to my fury.

"Yulia..." Only the knowledge of what happened the last time I let jealousy blind me stops me from exploding on the spot. "What the fuck do you mean by that?"

"Nothing. I was just—" She closes her eyes for a second before opening them to meet my gaze. "I was going to walk away, okay?"

Her voice shakes. "I couldn't do it anymore, couldn't carry out another assignment for them. I was going to use the plane tickets and the identities they gave me to disappear and start over fresh."

"You were?" I lower my hand to the small of her back, some of my anger cooling. "Why? Why after all these years?"

She gives a tiny shrug and looks down, avoiding my gaze. "I figured my brother was safe at this point—it's not like his adoptive parents would put him back in the orphanage after eleven years."

"I'm sure they wouldn't have put him back after five years either." I grip her chin to force her to look at me. I can feel her discomfort with the topic, and it makes me even more determined to unravel this mystery. "You didn't know about Kirill and your brother yet. So why did you decide to run?"

She remains silent.

"Yulia..." I lean forward until our noses are almost touching. This close, her sweet scent is intoxicating. I breathe it in, feeling like I'm on the verge of losing control. My heart pounds heavily in my chest, and when I speak, the words come out rough and strained. "Why did you decide to run, beautiful? What changed?"

Her lips part as she stares at me, and the temptation to kiss her, to taste the pink, lush softness of her mouth is unbearable. I'm hyperaware of her, of everything about her. The shallow, uneven rhythm of her breathing, the warmth of her soft, smooth skin, the way her long brown lashes tangle with one another at the far corners of her eyes—it all lures me in, intensifying the hunger burning in my veins. Only the conviction that I must have this answer—that it's something truly important—keeps me from giving in to my need.

"Tell me, baby," I whisper, moving my hand to stroke her cheek. "Why couldn't you do it anymore?"

Yulia's breath hitches, her eyes filling with tears as she pushes at my shoulders, trying to twist away. Her distress is such that I almost let her go, but some instinct makes me hold on.

"Shh," I soothe, tightening my arm around her back to hold her still. "It's okay. You're okay. Just tell me, sweetheart. Tell me why you were going to leave."

"Lucas, please…" Her tears overflow, spilling down her cheeks as she stops pushing at me. "Please, don't."

"Don't what?" I feel like I'm tormenting a helpless kitten, but I can't stop. Leaning closer, I kiss away the salty moisture on her cheeks and murmur, "Don't ask? Why not? What don't you want to tell me? What are you hiding?"

Yulia closes her eyes, and I brush my lips across her trembling eyelids. "Come on, sweetheart," I whisper, pulling back. "Just tell me. What changed for you? Why didn't you want to do this?"

"Because I couldn't." Opening her eyes, she gazes at me, her eyes swimming with fresh tears. "I just couldn't do it anymore, okay?"

"Why?"

She tries to pull away, but I tighten my arm again, keeping her in place.

"Why, Yulia?" I press. "Tell me."

"Because I fell in love with you!" With shocking strength, she pushes at my chest, and I'm so stunned that I loosen my grip, letting her scramble off my lap. The momentum propels her backward, nearly causing her to fall, but before I can grab at her, she catches her balance and sprints into the bedroom, slamming the door behind her.

36

ulia

Dura! Idiotka! Imbecile! Debilka!

Sobbing, I shove a chair against the bedroom door, wedging the back under the doorknob to keep it jammed. My arms shake from overexertion and adrenaline, and regret is like a sledgehammer beating against my skull. How could I have been so stupid? How could I have admitted my feelings to Lucas *again*? The last time, at least, I thought I was dreaming, but I have no such excuse today.

Fully awake and conscious, I gave in to Lucas's relentless tenderness, crumpled under the merciless pull of his gentle demands.

"Yulia!" The doorknob rattles as he pushes against the door. "What the fuck are you doing? Let me in."

My chest heaving, I back away from the door, pressing my fist against my mouth to muffle my sobs. Why did I do this again? Am

I some kind of masochist? I know what I am to him: a sex toy, someone he wants to own and possess. If I had any doubts on that front, the trackers would've dispelled them. What he's done is the closest thing to putting a dog leash on a human being, and no amount of sickroom care can make up for his intention to keep me prisoner until he tires of me.

Love and captivity don't mix—for most sane people, at least.

"Yulia." Lucas bangs his fist on the door. "Fucking let me in!" He kicks at it, and the chair makes a creaking sound as it moves a couple of centimeters across the carpet, letting the door open a crack.

I cast a desperate glance around the room. I don't know what I'm looking for, but there's nothing, so I continue edging backward as Lucas starts kicking at the door in earnest. The crack widens with each violent blow, and just as my trembling legs touch the bed behind me, the chair breaks and the door flies open.

"Lucas, I—" I'm not sure what I'm planning to say, but he doesn't give me a chance. Before I can gather my scattered thoughts, he's on me, and my world goes topsy-turvy as I tumble backward onto the bed. He lands on top of me, and in a blink of an eye, he grabs my wrists, stretching my arms above my head. His pale eyes burn into mine as he presses me into the mattress, his muscular body hot and heavy on top of me. He's already aroused— I can feel the hard swelling in his jeans— and I know there's only one way this evening will end.

My flu-induced respite is over.

His hands tighten around my wrists, and dark anxiety beats at me, mixing with perverse excitement. I'm viscerally aware of my captor's strength, of the power of his large male body. When Kirill had been on top of me like this, all I'd felt was terror and revulsion, but with Lucas, it's infinitely more complicated. Underneath the instinctive fear and distrust, there's a potent animal attraction mixed with a deeper longing, a desire for connection that makes no sense in the context of who and what we are.

I'm in love with a man who has every reason to despise me—a man who scares me to my very soul.

"Yulia..." he murmurs, staring down at me, and I draw in a shaking breath, feeling like I can't get enough air. I feel torn in two: a part of me wants to run and hide, pretend this isn't happening, but another part, the weaker part, wants to give in to him again, tell him how much he means to me and beg him to keep me forever.

Beg him to love me like I love him—like I will always love him.

"Yulia, sweetheart..." His gaze softens, and I realize I'm crying again, my entire body shaking with gasping sobs. "Hush, baby, it's not that bad... You're okay. Everything is going to be okay."

But I can't stop crying—not even when he kisses me, his tongue sweeping over my lips, and not when he releases my wrists and rolls off me to strip off my clothes. I can't stop crying because he's wrong. It won't be okay. There's no future for us, no hope for anything resembling a normal life. He's an arms dealer's second-in-command, a man with no conscience, and I'm his prisoner.

There are no happily-ever-afters for people like us.

The pain of that knowledge is so consuming that I barely feel it when Lucas tears off my thong and climbs on top of me after taking off his own clothes. My chest is agonizingly tight, my vision blurred with tears. It's only when he settles between my legs, his powerful thighs spreading mine apart, that the animal awareness returns, my body responding to him despite my distress. The tip of his cock nudges against my dampening folds, but instead of pushing forward, he stills, holding himself propped up on his elbows as he cradles my face between his large palms.

"Yulia..." His eyes burn with dark hunger, his sun-bronzed skin stretched tight over his sharp cheekbones. "You're mine," he says, his voice low and guttural. "Nothing and no one will take you from me. No more lies, no more running, no more hiding. I'm going to take care of you and protect you. You and your brother both, do you understand?"

I manage a small nod, my hands moving up to clutch at his sides. His hard body is vibrating like a string, his muscles coiled as if for a fight, and I know he's struggling to control himself. On any other night, he would've already been inside me, but he's trying to hold back, to go slowly because of my recent illness.

Something about that loosens the tight knot in my chest, chases away the panic I was feeling. Maybe I'm not just a toy to him.

He wouldn't hold back if he didn't care.

"It's okay, Lucas," I whisper, blinking to clear away the tears. Given what he's promising, letting him have my body is the least I can do. "I'm okay."

His pupils expand, darkening his blue-gray eyes, and then he lowers his head, capturing my lips in a deep, feral kiss. His tongue sweeps into my mouth, conquering and caressing at the same time, and my lower belly tightens as I feel the hard, insistent pressure of his cock. Heat builds inside me, centering between my legs, but a flutter of panic returns too. Despite my reassurances, I'm far from ready for this—emotionally, at least.

Sex with my captor is never casual and easy.

But it's too late to express my hesitations. Lucas's lips and tongue devour me, taking away my breath, and one of his hands moves down my body, kneading my breasts before traveling lower to touch my sex. His fingers find my clit, playing with it until I'm slick and throbbing, and then he grips his cock and guides it to my entrance, lifting his head to look at me at the same time.

His eyes glitter as he holds my gaze, and we both inhale sharply as the smooth, broad head of his cock breaches me, stretching my tight flesh. I'd forgotten how thick he is, how large all around. Despite my arousal, my inner muscles need to adjust to the feel of him inside me, and my breathing turns shallow as he presses deeper, his penetration slow and controlled but inexorable. When he's all the way in, he pauses, holding himself still above me, and I see sweat droplets forming on his forehead. He's still trying to rein himself in, to be as gentle as someone like him can be.

"I love you," I whisper, unable to hold back the words. At this moment, it doesn't matter that he might not return my feelings, that the odds are stacked against us in every way. "I love you, Lucas, so much."

His gaze fills with volcanic heat, his powerful muscles bunching even tighter, and I see the last of his self-control disintegrate. "Yulia," he groans, and then he withdraws and surges into me, thrusting so hard that air whooshes out of my lungs. It should've been too much, too overwhelming, but somehow it's just right, and I wrap my legs and arms around him, holding on tight as he starts hammering into me, claiming me with feral intensity.

"Lucas..." His name comes out on a ragged moan as the heat inside me coils and grows, transforming into an unbearable tension. "Oh God, Lucas..." Every muscle in my body vibrates from the agonizing pleasure, my heartbeat pounding audibly in my ears. The moment seems to stretch on forever, and then I climax with startling violence, my muscles clamping down on his shaft as every nerve ending in my body explodes with sensations.

Lucas lowers his head, swallowing my cry with his mouth, and continues thrusting into me, riding me through the orgasm. He fucks me like a man possessed, his hand sliding into my hair to hold me in place for his voracious kiss, and I feel another orgasm building, each merciless stroke of his cock bringing me closer to the edge. But before I can go over, he stops and raises his head to look at me.

"Say it again," he rasps out, his eyes boring into mine. His skin glistens with sweat, his chest heaving with harsh breathing as his cock throbs deep inside me. "Tell me you love me."

"I love you," I gasp, lifting my hips in a desperate attempt to reach the peak. "Please, Lucas, I love you!"

He sucks in an audible breath, and I feel him swell inside me, growing even thicker and harder as he thrusts in one last time before throwing back his head with a savage groan. His cock jerks inside me, his seed spurting out in several warm bursts, and then he rolls his hips in a circular motion, grinding his pelvis against my sex. To my shock, his movements push me over the edge, and I cry out, my nails digging into his back as a shattering wave of pleasure sweeps through me again, leaving me limp and shaking in its wake.

"Fuck, baby," Lucas groans, and I feel his cock spasm one last time before he withdraws and rolls off me. Like me, he's covered in sweat and breathing hard, but somehow he finds the strength to pull me toward him, embracing me from behind.

As my heartbeat slows and the post-orgasmic bliss begins to fade, I close my eyes, trying not to think about what I've done.

Trying to ignore the terrifying power Lucas holds over me now.

37

ucas

When my breathing slows and my muscles start obeying my instructions, I get up and carry Yulia to the bathroom for a quick rinse. She's silent and withdrawn, all but swaying on her feet as I wash her, and I know I pushed too hard, took her too roughly too soon. I should've given her at least a couple more days to regain her strength, but instead, I attacked her like a rampaging caveman, making no allowances for her fragile state.

Regret gnaws at me, mixing with worry for her health, but underneath the heavy press of guilt is a glow of hot, dark satisfaction. Beyond the aftermath of stunning pleasure, beyond the physical relief of sex, it's a feeling that warms me from the inside out, making me feel like I'm on top of the world.

Yulia loves me. There's no doubt of that now. She loves *me,* not some dream phantom or lover I'd made up.

It's ridiculous, but I feel like I won a fucking lottery.

When we're both clean, I help Yulia out of the shower and towel her off before picking her up again. Taking care of her this way feels like the most natural thing now, and the glowing sensation intensifies when she wraps her arms around my neck and trustingly lays her head on my shoulder as I carry her back to the bedroom.

"How are you feeling?" I ask, stopping next to the bed. Bending down, I place her gently on the sheets and clarify, "I didn't hurt you, did I?"

"No," Yulia whispers, closing her eyes. She looks exhausted, and worry spears through me again. What if this causes her to relapse? I should've held back, should've controlled myself better. Hell, I should've waited to get answers until she was completely well instead of giving in to my impatience.

Pushing the guilt away, I turn off the light and climb into bed beside her, pulling her into my arms. The feel of her warm, slim curves turns me on again, but this time, I'm able to ignore my body's reaction.

"Goodnight, beautiful," I whisper, reaching down to pull the blanket over us. "Sleep well."

Within a minute, Yulia's breathing takes on the steady rhythm of sleep, and I close my eyes, the glow returning as I hold her tight.

She loves me, and she's mine.

Life couldn't get any better.

TO MY RELIEF, THE NEXT MORNING YULIA WAKES UP WITH NO SIGNS of a relapse. I'm in the kitchen making breakfast when she walks in, already dressed in a pair of shorts and a T-shirt, her hair brushed and her eyes bright and alert.

"Hi," she says softly, stopping in the doorway. A delicate flush colors her cheeks as she looks at me. "Are you home again today?"

"Just for a bit," I say, smiling at her. "How are you feeling?"

"I'm okay." She gives me a tentative smile in return. "Just a little hungry."

"Good. The omelet's almost ready."

"Do you want some help?" she asks, coming up to the stove. "I can—"

"Thank you, but I got it." I wave her away. "If you want, make us both some tea, and I'll have this on the table in no time."

Yulia does as I suggest, and five minutes later, we're sitting down to eat.

"I want to see Misha today," she says after consuming half of her portion in record time. "Since I'm well and everything."

"I'm sure that can be arranged," I say. "I'll ask Diego to bring him over this afternoon." I'm still mad at the little punk for upsetting her the other day, but I know I can't keep her from him—not after what she told me last night.

Yulia puts down her fork, her expression unreadable. "Lucas…" She reaches up to brush her fingers over the back of her neck. "Am I still a prisoner in this house, even with the trackers?"

I frown. "No, you're not." I'd already decided that I would give her freedom to roam around the estate once the trackers were in. "I told you that."

"Then why does Diego need to bring my brother over? Can't I go see him on my own?"

I hesitate, looking at her. Though in theory, I like the idea of granting Yulia some independence, now that the moment is here, I feel uneasy at the thought of her walking around the estate by herself.

"You can," I say finally. "But not today. I need to introduce you to more people here first. They need to know who you are and what you mean to me."

"Because of my connection to the crash," she says, and I nod, relieved she understands. Though some of my unease stems from irrational possessiveness, there's a reason to be cautious.

The guards who died in the plane crash had friends and families, some of whom reside on the compound. And though Esguerra and I have done our best to keep the details of the crash under wraps, I know there are rumors about Yulia's involvement.

Until I publicly claim her as mine, she's not safe on her own.

"What about my brother?" she asks, picking up her tea, and I notice that she stopped eating, her blue eyes trained on me intently. "Is he in danger?"

"No," I reassure her. "Diego or Eduardo are with him at all times."

"So *he* is a prisoner?"

I sigh. "Yulia, your brother is… well, it's a fluid situation. Once we're sure he won't shoot anyone or try to run away, we'll give him more freedom as well, okay? It'll just take some time."

She takes a few sips of her tea and resumes eating, but I see a small frown etched into her forehead. She's worried about Michael —the brother who doesn't seem to appreciate the sacrifices she made for him.

"What were you two arguing about?" I ask when we're done with our food. "Your brother seemed angry with you for some reason."

Yulia finishes her tea, then says quietly, "He's confused. Obenko fed him a bunch of lies about me when he recruited him, and he was his uncle, so…" She shrugs, as if it doesn't matter, but I see the shadow of pain in her eyes.

UUR's betrayal goes deeper that I thought.

"So Michael doesn't know what you did for him?" My hand tightens around my cup as I picture all the things I'm going to do to Yulia's former colleagues.

"I don't think so, but it doesn't matter." She attempts a smile. "Misha's here now, so I just need to talk to him, straighten it all out."

"All right," I say, coming to a decision. Rage beats in my chest, but I keep my voice level as I say, "Let's go. I'll take you to see him myself."

Yulia's eyes widen. "Now? Don't you have work?"

"It'll wait." Putting down my cup, I stand up and walk around the table. "Do you feel up for a walk?"

She immediately jumps to her feet. "Definitely," she says, beaming. "Let's go."

~

We leave the house through the front door. As we step outside, I take Yulia's hand, squeezing her fingers lightly, and she gives me a wry look.

"I'm not going to run, you know," she says, and I smile, some of my anger fading.

"It's not to prevent you from running," I say, tightening my grip on her hand. Yulia is mine now, and nobody's going to hurt her again—not without answering to me, at least.

"Ah." She looks around at the guards and other passersby, most of whom are surreptitiously staring at us. "So this is strategic?"

"Partially." I'm holding Yulia's hand because I want to, but broadcasting our relationship to others is a definite bonus, especially since a few of the guards are eyeing her long, slender legs with obvious appreciation.

I glare at them, and they swiftly turn away.

Fuckers.

Yulia glances up at me and steps closer, all but pressing herself against my side as we walk. I give her an approving nod. She's smart to publicly accept my protection. As soon as everyone on the estate knows she's mine, she'll be safe.

We pass by the guards' barracks, and Yulia looks up at me again. "Where are we going?" she asks. "I thought Michael was staying here."

"He is, but Diego told me he's at the training field with him this morning. So that's where we're heading."

"Oh, I see." Yulia falls silent as we walk past a small group of guards. As soon as we're out of earshot, she slows down and turns her head to look at me. "Lucas…" she says quietly. "There's something I've been meaning to ask you."

"What is it?"

"When we first returned, Dr. Goldberg mentioned you'd been injured recently. What happened? Was there some trouble on your trip?"

"Trouble?" With my free hand, I absentmindedly touch my ribs, which bother me less each day. "Yeah, you could say that." And as we walk, I tell Yulia about the events in Chicago, from the nightclub assault on Rosa to the chase and its aftermath. I try to gloss over the more gruesome details, but even so, by the time I'm done, Yulia is ghost white, her hand icy in my grasp.

"You could've been killed," she whispers in horror. "And Rosa… Oh God, poor Rosa…"

"Yes, about that…" We're not far from the training field, so I stop and turn to face Yulia. "Why don't you tell me about Rosa? I want to know how she helped you escape."

Yulia's hand stiffens in my hold before she relaxes it again. "What do you mean?" she says, her eyebrows pulling together in seeming confusion. Her expression is the perfect imitation of sincere cluelessness; if I hadn't felt her hand twitch, I would've never known that my question gave her pause. "She didn't—"

"No more lies, remember?" I interrupt. "We had an agreement."

Yulia licks her lips. "Lucas, I…"

"You won't be ratting her out, if that's what worries you," I say, releasing her hand. Stepping closer, I grasp Yulia's chin, tilting her head up to meet my gaze. "We know what Rosa did, and we have the video to prove it."

"You do?" Yulia's slim throat works. "Did you— Is she okay?"

"For now." I drop my hand but don't bother elaborating further. "Now tell me exactly what happened. How did you escape?"

She stares at me, and I know she's deciding whether she can believe me about the video. Finally, she says quietly, "On the day before your departure, Rosa came by and gave me a razor blade and a hair pin. She also told me a little bit about the guards' schedules, including the fact that the ones at North Tower Two play poker on Thursday afternoons."

"I see." That explains why Yulia walked by that tower at that exact time. "And why was she helping you? Did your agency get to her?"

"No, of course not." Yulia seems surprised. "How could they have?"

"I don't know. But then why would she do this?"

Yulia hesitates again, then says slowly, "It was strange. She acted like she didn't like me, so I didn't understand at first, but then…"

"Then what?" I prompt when she doesn't continue.

"Then she mentioned something about Nora," she says, staring at me with wide, unblinking eyes. "It sounded like she asked her to do this. Rosa wouldn't tell me why, though."

Well, fuck. I want to punch someone.

Esguerra's wife didn't lie after all.

"Do *you* know why this Nora helped me?" Yulia asks, and I realize I'm just standing there, seething with silent rage. "She's Esguerra's wife, right?"

"She is," I say grimly, turning to resume walking. "Unfortunately, she is."

If she weren't, she'd already be dead. But as things stand, unless Esguerra chooses to punish Nora, she's untouchable, and if Rosa acted on her orders, the maid might be too.

38

ulia

As we resume walking toward the training field, I sneak a cautious glance at Lucas, trying to see if he bought my story. So far, it looks like he has. His square jaw is taut with anger, his mouth set in a hard, thin line. He looks like he's ready to murder someone, and to my surprise, I feel a tiny spurt of guilt for lying to him about Nora.

It's as if I'm betraying his trust.

No. I shake off that ridiculous feeling. There's never been trust between us. Lust, yes, and even some incongruous tenderness, but not trust. I may no longer be handcuffed, but with the trackers embedded in my body, I'm still Lucas's captive, and falling for him didn't make me blind. I know what kind of man he is and what he's capable of. If Lucas knew that Nora told me to implicate her in my escape, it's highly probable that the maid would be killed—which,

I'm guessing, is why Esguerra's wife took the fall for her. *If* she took the fall, that is. It's possible the petite girl simply owned up to the truth, and if that's the case, I didn't lie to Lucas. I just didn't mention Nora's visit, which is a completely different matter.

Besides, when I think about what happened to Rosa, I feel sick inside. I know how horrible she must be feeling. The last thing I want is for her to be hurt more.

Thankfully, as we walk, Lucas's anger seems to dissipate, and by the time we approach a large, grass-covered field, he appears to have gotten over it completely.

"Is this it?" I ask, looking around the field. It's divided equally between a shooting range and an obstacle course. There's also a flat-roofed building—an indoor gym, maybe?—on one side and what looks like a supply shed in the corner.

"Yes, this is the training area," Lucas says as we walk past a few guards practicing mixed martial arts. "And I think that's your brother over there." He points toward a small cluster of men on the obstacle course.

Sure enough, my brother's bright blond hair stands out like a beacon among the mostly Latino guards. He's doing pushups on the grass next to a slim, brown-haired guard who looks to be only a few years older than him.

As we get closer, I realize they're having a competition. The other men are standing in a semi-circle, cheering them on and placing bets in a colorful mixture of Spanish and English. Both Misha and the guy he's competing against are shirtless and dripping with sweat, and I wonder how long they've been at it. Not that it takes much exertion to sweat in this weather; my own shirt is sticking to my back just from walking here.

"Looks like Michael is ahead," Lucas comments, and I hear a note of dark amusement in his voice. "I'll have to boost the new recruits' training regimen. This simply won't do."

I shush him, not wanting to interrupt my brother's concentration. Misha's face is red, and his arms are shaking as if they're going to give out. The other guard, however, is in even worse shape, and as I watch, the young man collapses on his stomach, unable to do another pushup.

"Go, Michael!" someone shouts, and I turn to see Diego clapping. He's grinning from ear to ear. Turning to the other guards, he holds out his hand and says smugly, "Told you the kid could do it. Now pay up."

While he speaks, my brother collapses on the grass as well. Panting, he rolls over onto his back, and I see a huge, bright smile on his face. He looks as happy as in those photos.

I hurry toward him, my own face split in a joyous smile. "Good job, Michael," I call out, feeling like I might burst from pride. "That was amazing."

He sits up, his eyes widening as he sees me approach. "Yulia?" he says in Russian. "How are you feeling?"

"I'm much better, thank you," I respond in the same language. Then, cognizant that some of the other guards have started frowning, I say in English, "Glad to see you boys are having fun."

Misha climbs to his feet, brushing off bits of dirt and grass from his shorts. "Um, yeah," he says in English, casting an embarrassed glance at the others. "We were just, you know..."

"Yeah, she knows," Lucas says, coming up behind me. Crossing his arms in front of his chest, he looks at the guards, and they quickly scatter, mumbling something about having a job to do.

Only Diego stays behind, a big grin lighting up his face. "We should hire him," he says. "He's already better than some of these new guys, and with a bit more training—"

Lucas holds up his hand, interrupting Diego. "Michael's going to come with us for a bit," he says. "I'll call you when I need you."

"All right," Diego agrees easily. "I'll be around."

He lopes off to join the others, and Lucas turns to Misha, who's watching him warily.

"I have to speak to a few guards," Lucas says. "Can I trust you to stay on this field and not get into trouble if I leave you alone with your sister?"

Misha's face is stony, but he nods.

"Good." Lucas clasps my elbow and pulls me to him. Lowering his head, he presses a quick, hard kiss to my lips before stepping back. "I'll see you both soon. Stay within sight. Got it?"

"Yes," I say, trying to ignore the burn in my cheeks. "We'll be here."

Lucas walks away, and I turn to face Misha, my embarrassment intensifying when I see an identical flush on his face. I know why Lucas kissed me like that—it's all about claiming me in public today—but that doesn't mean I wanted my fourteen-year-old brother to witness it.

Misha already thinks poorly of me.

"Do you want to take a walk?" I offer, trying to pretend the kiss didn't happen. "I haven't seen this area before. Maybe you can show me around?"

"Sure." Misha seems glad to have something to do. Grabbing his shirt from the grass, he pulls it on and says, "Here, let's go this way."

He leads me toward the obstacle course, and I follow, ignoring the mix of hostile and curious looks coming our way from the guards.

"How are you?" I ask in English. I want to get used to speaking with Misha this way, so that Lucas and the others don't think we're trying to hide something from them. "Are they still treating you well?"

He nods. "They watch me all the time," he responds in English, "but other than that, it's okay."

"Good." I give him a relieved smile. "How are your accommodations?"

He shrugs as we walk around a pair of guards practicing scaling a barbed-wire fence. "They're fine. A little better than the dorms, I guess."

"That's good. And what about—"

"How long are they going to keep us here?" he interrupts, giving me a sidelong look. "The guards wouldn't tell me anything."

"Right. About that…" I take a deep breath. "I'm going to talk to Lucas, but before I do, I need to know a little bit more about your situation."

Misha frowns. "What do you mean?"

This is going to be tricky. "How did you end up in UUR, Michael?" I ask carefully, using his preferred name. "Did your uncle ask you to join?"

"No." Misha doesn't blink. "It was my idea."

I stop, staring at him in shock. "Yours?"

My brother gives me a level look. "I was in some trouble in school, and Uncle Vasya came to talk to me. He told me how stupid I was being, how many kids would've killed for a chance at my kind of life. And I told him that's not what I wanted. I didn't want to be an accountant or a lawyer or a nurse. I wanted to be an agent, like him."

I frown in confusion. "This was openly discussed in your family? UUR and everything?"

"No, of course not. My parents were very secretive about Uncle Vasya's job, but I kept overhearing things. Also, I knew I had a sister who was working for our country. My parents told me about that because I kept asking them why you left me." I wince, but he's already plowing ahead. "Anyways," he says, "I put two and two together, and on that visit, I confronted Uncle Vasya about it. He admitted that you'd joined his program, and then he told me how I came to be adopted by my parents."

"Michael, that's not—"

"Don't lie. He said you'd lie about it." Misha's tone sharpens. "He was a good man. He died for Ukraine."

"I know that, but…" I draw in a steadying breath. "Listen to me, Michael. Your uncle and I had a deal. Your adoption was part of it. You were supposed to be safe, not recruited into this life. It was only supposed to be me. I joined the agency because I wanted to protect you, and I couldn't do it at the orphanage. Obenko promised me—"

"Stop. I don't want to hear it." Misha steps back, shaking his head. "You're lying. I know you are."

"No, Mishen'ka." My heart squeezes at the anger and confusion in his gaze. "Your uncle didn't tell you everything. I didn't leave because I was tired of the orphanage. I left because that was the only way to keep you safe."

Misha keeps shaking his head, but he's no longer interrupting, so I tell him about the visit by the man in the suit and the bargain he offered me, including how I was supposed to stay away from Misha and the pictures I received every few months. As I speak, I see uncertainty replace some of the anger in my brother's eyes.

He doesn't know whom to believe, and I can't blame him.

"I still have all those pictures," I say when he remains silent. "I uploaded them to a secure cloud service a few months ago. I could show them to you one day, if you want."

Misha stares at me. "You kept them?"

"Of course." My chest is painfully tight, but I attempt a smile. "You're my only family, Michael. I kept every single one."

He swallows and looks away before resuming walking. I catch up with him, and we walk without speaking for a few minutes. There are a million things I want to tell him, a billion questions I want to ask, but I don't want to push us into another argument.

It's nice to just have my brother's company for now.

To my surprise, Misha breaks the silence first. "I didn't know it was you that day," he says quietly as we stop to observe two guards throwing knives.

"What?" I turn to look at him. "What are you talking about?"

"That day at the warehouse, when I helped them catch you. I didn't know that was you." Misha's forehead is creased with tension. "I only found out later."

"Oh, of course." It hadn't even occurred to me that he could've known. "You hadn't seen me since you were three, and I was wearing a wig. Besides, why would you ever expect your sister to be lurking outside your training facility?"

"Right." He folds his arms across his chest. "So why *were* you there? Uncle Vasya said that you'd turned on us, that you were no longer loyal to UUR."

"I never turned on the agency, but I *was* going to walk away," I say, deciding to be completely honest. "I was following Obenko because I was hoping he'd lead me to you, so I could see you one last time before I left."

Misha blinks. "You followed him to see me? But why were you going to walk away?"

"It's a long story, Michael."

"Is it because of him?" Misha glances toward the other side of the field, where Lucas is talking to a group of guards. "Because"—his cheeks redden—"you two are lovers?"

"It's…" God, why is this so difficult? It's not like *I'm* fourteen. "It's complicated between us," I finally manage to say. "His boss has been at odds with Ukraine for a while, and—"

"Is Kent forcing you?" Misha's eyes flash with blue fire. "Because I'll kill him if he is—"

"No, of course not," I interrupt, my pulse jumping. The last thing I need is Misha in defender mode. "I want to be with Lucas," I say firmly. "It's just a complicated situation because of UUR and everything."

My brother doesn't look convinced, so I add quickly, "And yes, us being lovers was a big part of why I was going to walk away."

Misha flushes again and looks away. "Okay," he mutters. "That's what I thought."

"Yes, and you were right." Pushing aside my discomfort, I give him a rueful smile. "You're very smart, and pretty much an adult now. I'll have to get used to that. The last time I saw you, your biggest achievement was going on the potty, so it's a bit of an adjustment for me, seeing you all grown up like this."

Misha grins, as pleased by that praise as any boy of fourteen, and I realize how mature my brother acts most of the time. I don't have much experience with teenagers, but I doubt many of them could've handled this situation as well as he has.

In fact, few *adults* could've kept their cool while being kidnapped, taken halfway around the world, and kept captive on an arms dealer's jungle compound.

As I ponder that, a flicker of motion from across the field catches my gaze.

"We should head back," I say, realizing Lucas is waving at me. "I think Lucas is calling us."

Misha nods, falling into step beside me, and as we walk back, I try to think of the best way to approach my captor about sending my brother home.

39

ucas

AFTER I TALK TO THE NEW RECRUITS ON THE FIELD, I CATCH YULIA'S eye and wave at her, motioning for her to return. She grabs her brother and starts walking back, and I head over to the pull-up bar, figuring I'd get some quick exercise in while I wait.

I'm midway through my first set of wide-grip pull-ups when I see Esguerra approach.

"What's up?" I ask, letting go of the bar to land on the grass. The sun is unbearably hot, and I use the bottom of my shirt to wipe the sweat off my face. "Were you looking for me?"

"We need to figure out the Rosa situation," he says without preamble. "Nora is after me to lift her house arrest, but we still don't know if—"

"We do, actually," I interrupt. "I was going to talk to you this afternoon. I just got confirmation from Yulia that Nora *was* involved."

Esguerra's face darkens. "What did your spy say, exactly?"

I convey my conversation with Yulia almost word for word. "So yeah," I conclude, "looks like it wasn't Rosa's own initiative—not that it means she should get away with it." Nor should Nora, in my opinion, but I know better than to say that.

"Fuck." Esguerra spins around, his posture rigid with fury, and I see the moment he spots the approaching figures. Turning back toward me, he says incredulously, "Is that—"

"Yes." I meet his gaze coolly. "That's Yulia and her brother, Michael. I told you we grabbed him during the trip to Ukraine, remember?"

The corner of his real eye begins to twitch. "Grabbed him, yes. Gave him free run of the compound alongside his treacherous sister, no. What the fuck are you doing, Lucas? You said she's not getting off scot-free."

"And I said I'm keeping her." The steel in my voice matches the iciness of his expression. "She's mine to punish or not. Just as Nora is yours."

For a moment, I'm sure Esguerra's going to hit me, and I tense, ready to strike back. But he takes a breath instead and steps back, his hands hanging loose at his sides. Turning, he looks at Yulia and her brother, who are now less than fifty feet away.

Yulia must've spotted him because she's moving slower now, her face white with anxiety. Her brother is walking next to her, but as they get closer, she grabs his wrist and steps in front of him, as if trying to hide him from Esguerra's view.

"She's mine," I repeat in a low, hard voice as Yulia comes to a complete stop some thirty feet away, her gaze flitting from me to Esguerra and back again. "If you do anything to them..."

Esguerra turns his head to look at me. "I won't." His eyes gleam coldly. "But, Lucas, do us both a favor. Keep her as far away from me as you can."

I incline my head, but he's already walking away, heading in the opposite direction from where Yulia and her brother are standing.

~

On our walk home, Yulia is silent, and I know she's worrying about Esguerra. Diego came back to get Michael shortly after my confrontation with Esguerra, and Yulia smiled and gave her brother a parting hug. Since then, however, she's barely said a word, her gaze distant and her shoulders tense as she walks next to me.

I want to reassure her, tell her that she's stressing over nothing, but the words stick in my throat. Esguerra's estate is large in terms of acreage, but population-wise, it's more like a small village. Everybody runs into each other on a regular basis, and keeping Yulia out of Esguerra's hair won't be easy—at least if I do as I promised and let her roam on her own.

Esguerra might not harm her in the near term, but he won't forgive her either.

As we get closer to the house, Yulia's gait slows, and I realize the long walk must've tired her out, depleting her body's all-too-recently replenished strength reserves. Without a second thought, I bend down and swing her up into my arms, ignoring her startled squeak and my ribs' faint twinge of pain.

"What are you doing?" she exclaims as I resume walking. "Lucas, you don't need to carry me—"

"Hush." I press her tighter against my chest, ignoring her half-hearted attempts to push me away. "I'm carrying you home."

She stops struggling, and after a moment, she winds her arms around my neck and lays her head on my shoulder. "Lucas…" Her voice is as weary as I've ever heard it. "It's not going to work, you know."

"What are you talking about?"

"You and I." She lifts her head to look up at me, and I see the dark shadow of despair in her gaze. "It's not going to work."

"Bullshit." I pick up my pace, a burst of fury propelling me forward. "It's going to work if I want it to."

Yulia slowly shakes her head. "No. Maybe in another life—"

"In another life, our paths would've never crossed, beautiful. This is the only way you could've been mine."

If her parents hadn't been killed in that car crash, if I hadn't been working for Esguerra, if UUR hadn't given her that assignment... The number of ways I could've *not* met her is endless, but I did meet her, and there's no fucking way I'm giving her up.

Yulia sighs and places her head back on my shoulder, letting me carry her without further protests. I know she's not convinced, however.

Like me, she's seen too much of this world to believe in happy endings.

"LUCAS, I THINK MISHA SHOULD GO HOME."

I pause with the spoon halfway to my mouth. "Home?"

"To his parents," Yulia clarifies, putting down her own utensil. Her bowl of soup steams in front of her, mostly eaten. "His adoptive parents."

"I thought he was with your agency." I put down my spoon and wipe my mouth with my napkin.

I've been expecting something like this since the incident this morning, and I'm not looking forward to this conversation.

"He was with UUR of his own free will, yes, but by all indications, he's also close to his parents." Yulia's gaze is unflinching. "They let him join against their better judgement, and I'm sure they're going crazy with worry for him now."

I drum my fingers on the table. "So you want me to what, bring him back to them? What about the fact that you haven't seen him in eleven years? Don't you want to spend some time with your brother?"

Yulia's face tightens. "Of course I do, but I can't be that selfish. Misha doesn't belong here, and he's not safe. I saw the way Esguerra was looking at him… at us both. He hates us, Lucas. I know you said you'll protect us, but—"

"He won't lay a finger on either one of you," I say, and mean every word. As much as I respect Esguerra, I'll kill him before I let him harm Yulia. "You're safe, and so is your brother."

"But for how long?" She leans forward. "Until you get tired of me? And then what? We're at Esguerra's mercy?"

"I won't get tired of you." I can't picture a day I wouldn't want her. I've lusted after women before, but never like this. My craving for Yulia feels like a part of me now, like something imprinted on my DNA. "You don't have to worry about that."

"You can't expect me to believe that, but okay, let's assume for a moment that it's true." She pushes her bowl aside. "That still leaves us with the fact that your job is dangerous, Lucas. Your *life* is dangerous. Just look at what happened when you went to Chicago. If there's a bullet coming at Esguerra, it's more than likely to hit you first."

I look at her silently, knowing she's right. I'd said as much to Michael. If something were to happen to me, Yulia and her brother would be on their own, in a place where nobody will raise a finger to help them.

No, it's worse than that. If I were gone, they'd likely be killed on the spot.

"I can't send Michael back right now," I say after a couple of moments. Leaning back, I lace my fingers behind my head and give Yulia an even look. "Not if you want him to remain safe, at least."

All color drains from her cheeks. "Why?"

"Because Operation UUR is in full swing." The hacking

program we used during our raid on the black site downloaded and transmitted a lot of confidential data from the agency's computers. We now have names and cover identities of just about every UUR operative, and we're systematically taking them out. I don't explain that to Yulia, though. All I say is, "It would be too dangerous for your brother."

She understands, and her face turns impossibly paler. "What about his parents? Are they—"

I lower my arms and lean forward. "I already put out word that Obenko's sister's family is not to be touched." I did that as soon as I realized Michael's connection to them. "However, their names *are* in our files," I continue before Yulia can say anything, "and given your brother's very direct involvement with the agency, it's best if he stays here for now."

"Oh God." She pushes her chair back and stands up, her hand pressed to her mouth. She's visibly shaking. "You're murdering them all, aren't you?"

My eyebrows snap together. "You asked me to spare Michael, and that's exactly what I'm doing." I rise to my feet and walk around the table. Reaching Yulia, I curl my fingers around her wrist and pull her hand down, away from her trembling lips. "That's what you wanted, isn't?" I tug her closer to me. "Your brother left unharmed, even though he's connected with the agency? And I'm even extending the courtesy to his adoptive parents. So you see, it's all going to work out."

Tears glisten in Yulia's eyes as she shakes her head, but she doesn't move away as I let go of her wrist and grasp her hips, molding her lower body against mine. My growing erection presses against her belly, and my breathing picks up as molten heat moves through my veins. Our unfinished dinner, UUR, her brother—none of that matters right now.

All I can focus on is the beautiful girl in my arms and the pain in her big blue eyes.

"Yulia…" I breathe in her scent, my hunger intensifying as her tongue flicks out to moisten her lips. I'm leaning in to taste the glossy softness of those lips when she presses her palms against my chest, pushing with all her strength to keep me at bay.

"Lucas, please, listen to me…" Her chest rises and falls in a shallow rhythm. "Most of the agents had nothing to do with the crash. It was Obenko's idea, and he's now dead. You don't need to—"

"Forget about them," I growl, my hands tightening on Yulia's hips when she tries to pull away. My frustrated lust adds to my anger, and my tone sharpens as I say, "The agency is not your problem anymore. You're with me now, understand?"

"But, Lucas, they're—"

"Living on borrowed time," I say harshly. "Those who are still living, that is. Your agency killed dozens of our men, and they're going to pay for that. The only ones who'll be spared are your brother and you."

The tears are streaking down her cheeks now, but the sight doesn't sway me. There's nothing she can say that would convince me to forgive our enemies. They chose to strike at us, and now they're reaping the consequences of their actions. It's just that simple.

Still, I don't like seeing Yulia upset.

Letting go of her hips, I raise my hand to brush away her tears. "Don't cry for them," I say in a slightly softer tone. "They don't deserve it. You know that."

"That's not true." Her voice is strained. "Some of them might not deserve it, but many are guilty of nothing more than wanting to serve their country and—"

"And the forty-five men who died on that plane were guilty of nothing more than working for Esguerra." I drop my hand, my anger returning in full force. "Nobody is innocent in this business, beautiful—not even you."

Yulia takes a step back, but I catch her arm before she can back away.

"You haven't asked about Kirill," I say coldly. My cock throbs in my jeans, but I push the lust aside, knowing I need to deal with this once and for all. "Don't you want to know what measures we're taking to find him?"

She blinks. "I assumed he died. His wounds—"

"There's no body and no burial record of any sort. No sign of him, period. Dead men aren't that good at covering up their tracks."

Yulia draws in an unsteady breath. "So what are you saying?"

"I'm saying the bastard is most likely alive—and hiding with help from others in your agency." I pause, trying to rein in my rage. When I speak again, my voice is moderately calmer. "The people whose lives you're trying to save are the same ones who let that monster keep his job and lied to you about it. Our operation in Ukraine is not just about retaliation anymore. It's also about tracking him down."

Yulia stares at me, and I see the torturous conflict in her gaze. She wants Kirill dead just as much as I do, but she doesn't want UUR agents to die in the process. I understand that on some level; she must've gotten to know many of them during her training, maybe even become friends with a few, so she doesn't want their deaths on her conscience.

Unfortunately for those agents, *my* conscience can handle their deaths just fine.

"So what do I tell Misha?" Yulia finally asks. Her voice is still hoarse, but the tears are drying on her face. "Is he supposed to sit tight and wait while you exterminate everyone in UUR? Train with the guards and hope his parents survive the purge?"

"What you tell him is up to you," I say, refusing to rise to her bait. "I'd be more diplomatic if I were in your shoes, but he's your brother and you know best. Now"—I use my grip on her arm to tug her closer—"where were we?"

Yulia looks like she's about to say something else, but I'm done with this discussion.

Wrapping my arms around her slender frame, I bend my head and slant my mouth across her lips.

40

ulia

Lucas's kiss holds an edge of anger, his lips and tongue punishing as he invades my mouth, and fear-tinged arousal heats my core, adding to my turmoil.

The man I love is killing my former colleagues, and it's all my fault. If I hadn't let Lucas break me that time, if he hadn't come after me, none of this would be happening. Rationally, I understand there were other factors at play—Obenko's ill-advised attack on Esguerra's plane, for one—but I still feel responsible for the current mess.

If my brother's adoptive family dies, it'll be on me.

It doesn't help that underneath the crushing press of guilt, I'm not entirely sorry. Somewhere along the way, a root of hatred had taken hold within me, and I didn't know it until Lucas brought up Kirill's name. I'd suppressed all thoughts of my former trainer, telling myself that I'd already gotten my revenge, but as soon as Lucas mentioned him, I realized the damage I inflicted wasn't enough.

I want Kirill dead, wiped off the face of the Earth—along with anyone who might be helping him.

Lucas deepens the kiss, his arms tightening around me, and my head falls back under the pressure of his mouth. His tongue explores me with a hunger that borders on brutality, his teeth tugging at my lower lip, and I moan helplessly, my hands moving up to clutch at his muscled shoulders as he backs me up against the kitchen wall, trapping me there. He's wearing jeans and a T-shirt, and I'm dressed too, but even through our layers of clothing, I can feel the heat of his large body and smell the clean musk of his skin. His erection is like a rock pressing into my stomach, and my nipples tighten, my body responding to his need.

"Fuck, Yulia, I want you," he mutters, raising his head, and I gasp as one of his big hands slides down my body and cups my sex through my shorts, palming it hard. The heel of his hand puts pressure on my clit, and moisture rushes to my core as he moves his palm in a semi-circle, the rough rhythm shockingly erotic.

"Yes." My heartbeat thunders in my ears, my muscles tensing with intensifying pleasure. "Oh God, yes..." I don't know what I'm saying; all I know is I want him—this man, this ruthless killer who's wrong for me in so many ways. I want him, and I fear him. I hate him, and I love him. The dichotomy of my emotions tears at me, slicing me into pieces, yet it all feels right too, like I'm supposed to be here, in his arms.

Like I belong with him.

He lowers his head to kiss me again, and I latch on to his mouth, responding with the same fierce need. My teeth sink into his lower lip until I taste blood, and it unleashes something violent inside me, a wildness I never knew was there. I'm trapped in his embrace, yet at that moment I feel free—free to rage, free to hurt him as I've been hurt. It feels like a chain snapping, and I revel in the sensation, my helplessness giving way to triumph as he tears his mouth away and I see the smear of blood on his lips. His broad chest heaves with labored breaths as he stares down at me, his pale eyes slitted with burning need, and the wildness inside me grows, crowding out fear and reason.

I want him, and I'm not going to deny myself.

Reaching up, I clasp Lucas's face with both hands and pull his head down, reclaiming his mouth. He's still palming me between my legs, the hard pressure of his hand keeping me on the edge, but it's not enough, and I bite his lip again, as desperate for his pain as I am for release.

He shudders in response, and with startling swiftness, spins me around, backing me up against the edge of the table. His arm sweeps out in a violent arc, and my pulse leaps as I hear the bowls shatter, the remnants of our dinner splattering on the floor. It almost jolts me out of my trance-like state, but he's already laying me on the table, and heat rushes through me again, centering in a pulsing ache between my thighs as he drags my shorts off my legs and yanks down the zipper of his jeans.

We're still kissing, our lips and tongues dueling with feral hunger, when he drives into me, his thick cock splitting me open. I gasp into his mouth, tensing at the shockwave of sensations. My flesh quivers around him, trying to adjust, but he doesn't stop, doesn't slow down. He just starts pounding into me, and I tear my mouth away, my breath coming in pained gasps as his thrusts drag me back and forth on the hard table. His possession is violent, overwhelming, yet I want more. More of his roughness, more of this dark, savage heat.

I want him to match the animal inside me, to hurt me as I'm hurting him.

My legs come up, wrapping around his hips, and I sink my teeth into the corded muscle of his neck, reveling in the taste of salt and man. His big body shudders, and he rasps out a curse, his pace picking up until he's all but drilling into me. My hands fist in his sweat-drenched shirt, and the tension inside me grows, the heat between my legs swelling and intensifying. It seems to be taking over all my senses, crowding out everything but the need to come.

"Lucas," I gasp, feeling the swell begin to crest. "Oh, fuck, Lucas!"

Impossibly, his thrusts pick up speed, and I'm hurled over the edge, the orgasm hitting me with massive force. The pleasure blasts through my nerve endings, so sharp it's almost painful, and I cry out, my muscles clenching and releasing in pulsing waves. My heart hammers uncontrollably as aftershocks ripple through my body, but Lucas is not done yet. Before I can so much as draw in a breath, he pulls out and flips me onto my stomach, bending me over the table.

"Is this what you want?" he bites out, driving into me again. Gripping my hair, he forces my upper body to arch off the table. "For me to fuck you? To use you and make you hurt?"

"Yes." Oh God, yes. His cock is thick and burning hot inside me, a threat and a promise all at once. I didn't know I wanted this, but I do. I want the pain he inflicts to be the only one in my mind, his touch the only one in my memory. It's sick and utterly illogical, but I want Lucas to hurt me so I can forget about Kirill.

"All right." My captor's voice is dark and strained. "Remember, you asked for this."

My pulse spikes, but he's already pulling my hair harder, making my neck bend at an impossible angle. I cry out, my hands flying up to grab at his wrist, but he ignores my flailing arms and thrusts two fingers of his free hand into my mouth, making me gag from the sudden assault. His fingers are faintly salty, and they feel huge and rough in my mouth, almost as big as a cock. He pushes them in so far that I gag again and spit up saliva—which is apparently what he's after.

Pulling his wet fingers out of my mouth, he uses his grip on my hair to push me down, flattening my face against the table.

"Wait, Lucas..." Panic explodes in my brain as he moves the hand from my mouth to my ass and starts working one finger into the tight ring of muscle. "I don't... this isn't..." I reach back blindly, my hands pushing at his hips, but I have no leverage in this position. I'm bent over the table with his cock deep inside me; even if he weren't built of solid muscle, there'd be little I could do.

"Shh... It's going to be okay." Lucas accompanies the words with a shallow thrust of his cock, and I suck in a breath as his finger presses deeper, the slick coating of my saliva easing the way. "You're going to be okay, baby." His hand releases my hair, his palm splaying on my upper back to keep me in place. "We've done this before, remember?"

It's true; he used his finger, and I enjoyed it on some level, but he wants to go further today. I can sense his hunger, and it terrifies me. I want to push away the bad memories, replace them with a hurt of my choosing, but this is too much, too close to my nightmares. I clench my buttocks, trying to keep him out, but the second finger is already pushing into me, making my flesh stretch and burn at the invasion.

"Wait, not like this..." Beyond the burn is a strange, uncomfortable fullness, a feeling of being overstuffed and overtaken. His cock flexes inside me, adding to the sensation, and my breathing turns shallow as sweat trickles down my back. "Please, Lucas..."

He ignores my begging, slowly working his slick fingers into my ass, and my body gives in to his inexorable advance, the muscles stretching because they have to. Panting, I lie with my face pressed against the hard surface of the table and feel his cock throb in my pussy. His fingers are all the way in now, and it *is* too much. My body wasn't made for this. Everything about this penetration feels wrong and unnatural, like the time when—

Lucas begins to thrust, distracting me from my thoughts, and I realize that somewhere along the way, my straining muscles relaxed slightly, the burn from the invasion lessening. He's not moving his fingers—he's just keeping them inside me—and with his cock pumping in and out in a slow, careful rhythm, the sensation isn't as uncomfortable as it was.

I close my eyes and try to steady my breathing. His fingers still feel too large, but there's no actual pain, and the realization calms me further, drawing my attention to the slowly gathering tension in my core. The thrusting motions of his cock are reigniting my arousal, and the invasive fullness in my ass doesn't seem to take away from that. In some perverse way, it's even adding to the intensity.

I may survive this after all.

"Yulia." Lucas's voice is hoarse as he withdraws almost all the way. "I'm going to fuck you hard now."

My heart lurches, all illusion of calm fleeing. "Wait—"

But it's too late. Before I can finish speaking, he rams his cock back in, pushing me into the edge of the table. I cry out, my hands sliding forward to brace myself, but he's already withdrawing and thrusting back in. The hard battering of his hips moves me on his fingers, and I cry out again, tensing at the overwhelming sensations. But he doesn't stop. He keeps thrusting, keeps fucking me, and the discomfort morphs into something else: a dark, throbbing heat that spreads through my whole body. My heart gallops in my chest, my breathing turns frantic, and I feel myself rocketing to the edge again, the dual invasion of my body intensifying all my senses. The hot musk of sex in the air, the quivering of my overstretched flesh, the restraining pressure of his big hand on my back—it all adds to my sensory overload, winding me tighter and tighter. My cries grow louder, transforming into screams, and then I shatter, exploding with a force that steals my breath and dims my vision. My muscles spasm, milking his cock and fingers, and I hear his raspy groan as he thrusts in one last time and stops, pulsing deep inside me in release.

Dazed and trembling, I lie there, unable to say or do anything as Lucas slowly pulls his fingers out and lifts his hand from my back. His cock is still inside me, but after a moment, he withdraws that too. Cool air washes over my heated flesh as he steps back, and I feel the slickness coating my folds—my own moisture combined with his seed.

"Hang on, baby," he murmurs, stepping away, and I hear the sink running.

A minute later, he returns, holding a wet paper towel. By then, I've recovered enough to push myself off the table and stand on shaking legs, and I take the towel from him, using it to mop at the wetness between my legs. Lucas watches me with hooded gaze, his jeans already zipped up, and a hot flush crawls through my hairline as I see my shorts on the floor, lying next to the mess of broken bowls and spilled food.

Swallowing, I ball the used paper towel in my hand and turn toward my shorts, but Lucas catches my arm.

"I've got it," he says, his pale eyes gleaming. "Go take a shower. I'll join you in a moment."

I don't argue, and a minute later, I'm standing under the hot spray, my mind mercifully blank. True to his word, Lucas joins me in a bit, and I close my eyes, leaning against him as he washes me from head to toe, taking care of me yet again. I'm glad he doesn't say anything or ask me any questions. I'm not sure I'll ever be able to articulate why I wanted something so dark from him… why even now, after he pushed me far beyond my limits, I feel grateful for the experience.

When we're both clean, Lucas leads me out of the shower and wraps a towel around me before grabbing one for himself. He's still silent, his gaze oddly watchful, and finally, I feel the urge to speak.

"You didn't fuck me in the ass," I say, my hands twisting in the towel. "Why?"

"Because you weren't ready." He finishes drying himself and casually hangs up his towel, revealing his body in all its powerful masculinity. "Not to mention, we'd need some real lube for that.

You're tight, and, well..." He glances down at his cock, which, even soft, is impressively sized.

"Right." I swallow the sudden lump of fear in my throat. "You're bigger than your two fingers."

"Yes, somewhat," he says drily, and I see a glimmer of amusement in his eyes.

For some reason, knowing he finds this funny makes me flush again. Turning, I step toward the door to exit the bathroom, but Lucas steps in front of me, his expression turning serious.

"Don't worry, beautiful," he murmurs, cupping my chin. His thumb brushes over my lower lip in a gentle caress. "Every part of you will be mine eventually. You're going to forget him, I promise you that."

I stare at him, equal parts startled and terrified by his perceptiveness, but Lucas is already lowering his hand and turning away.

"Come," he says, opening the door. "Let's go get dressed. We'll make something else for lunch."

He heads down the hallway, and I follow, my thoughts in disarray.

I'm not sure what I expected from my new captivity, but this—whatever this is—wasn't it.

IV

THE NEW CAPTIVITY

41

 *ulia*

Over the next couple of weeks, Lucas and I go back to something resembling our old routine. With my strength rapidly returning, I take over the cooking and other domestic chores, and Lucas resumes his normal working schedule, returning home only in the evenings and for mealtimes. While he's gone, I read books and do body-weight exercises to stay fit, and when we're together, we discuss the books I've read. We also go on morning walks together. The main difference between now and before is the presence of my brother on the estate and that, technically, I'm allowed to walk around on my own.

I say "technically," because the first time I'm about to take advantage of that opportunity, Lucas cautions me to avoid Esguerra as much as possible.

"He won't do anything to you, but it's best if you don't draw his attention unnecessarily," Lucas says, and I read between the lines.

If it weren't for Lucas, Esguerra would gladly do as his wife threatened and flay every bit of flesh from my bones.

Given this, I rethink my idea of strolling over to the guards' barracks to chat with my brother. Instead, I request that Diego bring him over to Lucas's house. I'm not afraid for myself—I've been living on borrowed time since my capture in Moscow—but I can't bear the thought of anything happening to Misha. That possibility worries me so much that when Diego comes over, I surreptitiously pull the young guard aside and ask him to keep my brother away from his boss.

"From Esguerra?" Diego gives me a surprised look. "Why? He's doesn't care about Michael. He's seen the kid half a dozen times since your arrival, and he's never shown any interest in him."

That reassures me somewhat. On the training field, Esguerra looked at me with unmistakable hatred. If he feels differently about my brother—or, rather, is indifferent toward him—it's a good thing. Still, the core of my fear remains. Even if the arms dealer's animosity is reserved solely for me, I know what he's capable of. If Esguerra decides to hurt me, it won't matter to him that Misha is fourteen, or that he had nothing to do with the crash.

My brother could end up paying for my sins.

"Are you sure Misha is safer here than in Ukraine?" I press Lucas that evening. "Maybe if his parents moved to a different part of the country, or—"

"Ukraine is a battle zone right now," Lucas says bluntly. "We've got three dozen men on the ground there now, and more are getting sent in as we speak. I can't guarantee your brother won't get caught in the crossfire. Do you want to take that risk?"

"No, of course not." I chew the inside of my cheek, trying to block out mental images of the massacre that must be taking place. "But what about Misha's adoptive parents? They're probably worried sick about him—not to mention terrified, if they have any clue about what's going on."

"The best I can do is send them word that Misha's alive and well," Lucas says. "That, and remind our men that they're off-limits. But like I said, I can't make any guarantees. The situation is volatile, and since I'm not there to oversee the operation in person, the men have been given a lot of autonomy to carry out the mission as they see fit."

I swallow. "I understand... and thank you. Anything you can do to keep Misha's parents safe would be greatly appreciated," I say, and mean it. I may not be able to prevent Lucas and Esguerra from getting their vengeance, but if I can keep my brother's family out of harm's way, then I won't feel quite so conflicted about it—helpless and complicit all at once.

I'm not only sleeping with a monster; I'm in love with him.

And the monster knows it. He revels in it, making me admit my feelings almost every day. I don't know why Lucas gets such a kick out of it—I can't be the first woman to have fallen for him—but he definitely enjoys hearing the words from me. He forces me to scream them as he fucks me roughly, and to whisper them as he cradles me gently in his embrace. The constant juxtaposition of violent possessiveness and tender care confuses me, keeping me off-balance. I have no idea where my captor stands. One minute, I'm certain he views me as his sex toy, and the next, I find myself hoping it's something more.

I find myself dreaming that someday he may love me too.

It doesn't help that Lucas keeps doing things that make me feel like we're in a real relationship. Every time he learns about a food or drink I like, he surprises me by getting it for me. Over the past week, we've received deliveries of hard-to-find Russian candy, a box of ripe persimmons from Israel, five exotic varieties of Earl Grey tea, and freshly baked loaves of German rye bread. He's also ordered me a wider variety of clothes—some of which he allowed me to choose for myself online—and all kinds of toiletries and bath products, including my favorite peach-scented shampoo.

I'm so pampered it scares me.

And it's not just about the things Lucas buys for me. It's everything he does. If I so much as get a scratch, he bandages it for me. If my muscles ache after a workout, he gives me a full body rub. We've started watching TV together in the evenings, and he's gotten into the habit of stroking my hair or playing with my hand as I sit curled up next to him. It's an absentminded sort of affection, like petting a cat, but that doesn't lessen its impact on me. It's what I've been starving for, what I've wanted for so long. Every time my captor kisses me goodnight, every time he holds me close, the dry, empty fissures around my heart heal a bit, the pain of my losses fading.

With Lucas, the terrifying loneliness of the past eleven years seems like a distant memory.

What touches me most, however, is that Lucas understands my devotion to my brother and doesn't try to interfere with the rebuilding of our relationship. Despite Misha's continued antagonism toward him, he lets me invite my brother over as often as I want, and the three of us start having meals together—meals that often brim with awkward tension.

"Your brother doesn't like me much, does he?" Lucas says drily after our first joint lunch. "For a few moments there, I thought he was going to pull a Yulia and try to stab me with a fork."

"I'm sorry," I apologize, worried that he'd want Misha to stay away. "I'll talk to him. It's just that with his uncle and what happened in Ukraine—"

"It's okay, baby. I understand." Lucas's gaze softens unexpectedly. "He's still a kid, and he's been through a lot. He has every reason to hate me. I'm not going to hold it against him."

I blink. "You're not?"

"No. He'll come around. And if he doesn't… Well, he's your brother, so I'll deal."

My throat swells with emotion. "Thank you," I manage to say. "Really, Lucas, thank you for that and… and everything."

It's not lost on me that by hunting me down in Ukraine, Lucas most likely saved my life—and he certainly saved my sanity. I don't know if I could've survived a second assault from Kirill, so in a way, my recapture had also been my rescue.

"Of course," Lucas says, stepping toward me. The warmth in his gaze transforms into a familiar dark heat. "It's my pleasure, believe me."

And as he sweeps me up in his arms, I forget all about my worries—for the time being, at least.

~

"Are you in love with him?" Misha asks after we've been on the estate for almost six weeks. "Is he your boyfriend for real?"

"What?" I glance at my brother in surprise. We're walking in the forest to minimize the chances of running into Esguerra, and up until this moment, we were discussing utterly innocuous subjects: Misha's old school, his best friend Andrey, and the types of movies boys his age are into. This came out of nowhere. "Why do you ask?" I say cautiously.

Misha shrugs. "I don't know. In the beginning, I thought maybe you were playing him so it would be easier for us to get away, but the more I see you two together, the less that seems to be the case." He shoots me an indecipherable look. "Do you even want to leave?"

"Michael, I…" I take a breath, knowing I need to tread carefully. Our relationship has been going so well. Last week, I finally convinced Lucas to let me get online, and I showed Misha the pictures I'd uploaded to the cloud. He viewed them silently, with no accusations of lies or manipulations, and I thought we were finally making progress. The last thing I want is to push us back to our adversarial beginnings.

"Listen, Michael," I say finally, "I'm working on getting you back to your family. I told you, your parents were notified that you're okay, and as soon as things in Ukraine settle down a bit—"

"That's not what I'm asking." Misha stops and turns to face me. "Do you want to leave? If you had a chance to get away from him, would you take it?"

I stop too, struck by the question. In the last month, I haven't thought about escape at all. Even if I didn't have the trackers embedded under my skin, the fact that Lucas found me in Ukraine showed me there's nowhere I can run. Even if I somehow managed to escape again, Lucas would just come after me and bring me back.

That's not what Misha wants to know, though.

"No," I say quietly, holding my brother's gaze. "I wouldn't leave if I could."

He nods. "That's what I thought."

He resumes walking, and I hurry to catch up with his long strides. Misha seems to have grown another inch or two since we've been here, his shoulders broadening and filling out. I suspect when he's fully grown, he'll have Lucas's height and build. For now, though, he's still a boy—and I'm still his big sister.

"Michael, listen to me." I fall into step beside him. "Just because I don't want to leave doesn't mean I'm not working to make it happen for you. Please believe me. I'm doing everything I can to get you home."

"I know." He glances at me, his brow furrowed with a frown. "I just wish you'd come with me when I leave. A lot of people here hate you, you know."

"I know." I smile to chase away the stressed look on his face. "But don't worry about me. I'm going to be fine."

"Because you have *him*."

"Lucas? Yes." I've noticed that my brother doesn't like to refer to Lucas by his name, preferring to just say "he." "He'll keep me safe."

Misha is still frowning, so on impulse, I reach over and ruffle his hair playfully. "You know, this mop on your head is getting long. Want me to give you a haircut, or are you trying to grow a ponytail?"

"Eeww, no." Misha grimaces and reaches up with his hand. His fingers disappear in the thick blond strands. "Yeah, I guess I do need to cut it," he says grudgingly. "Are you good at giving haircuts?"

"I'm sure I'll manage." I grin at his dubious expression. "If I screw it up, we'll just ask Lucas to fix it—he gives himself a buzz cut every other week."

At the mention of Lucas, Misha tenses again, and his gaze slides away. "That's okay," he mutters, suddenly fascinated by an ant hill to our left. "I'm sure whatever you do will be fine."

I sigh but let it go. I can't force my brother to like Lucas. The brutal attack on the black site and Obenko's death left an indelible impression on his young psyche. Misha regards Lucas as the enemy, and rightly so.

If Lucas hadn't realized who Misha was, my brother would've been one of the casualties of that attack.

We walk without talking for a few minutes, but as we approach the edge of the forest, I touch Misha's arm, bringing him to a halt. "I'm sorry about what happened that day," I say when he turns to face me. "Truly, I am. If I could go back and change things, I would. The last thing I wanted was to endanger you or the others, believe me."

Misha stares at me, then says slowly, "It wasn't your fault… not really. I'm sorry I said that before. Besides, if they hadn't come—" He stops, his Adam's apple bobbing.

"What?"

"You probably would've been killed." His words are barely audible. Turning away, he continues walking, and I hurry after him, my stomach knotted tight.

"Who told you that, Michael?" Catching up with him, I grab his arm, bringing him to a stop again. "Why did you say that?"

"Because it's true." Misha's face is shadowed, his forearm tense in my grip. "I overheard Uncle Vasya talking about it with Kirill Ivanovich. I didn't want to believe it at first—I thought maybe I misunderstood, or took their words out of context—but the more I thought about it, the clearer it became. They were going to kill you and tell me you ran off with your lover." He draws in an unsteady breath. "They were going to lie, like they've lied about you all along."

"Oh, Michael…" I release his arm, my heart clenching at the pain in his eyes. I can't even fathom how agonizing this betrayal must be for him. Obenko had been my boss and mentor, but for my brother, he had been so much more. Misha must've fought so hard against this knowledge, seeking to deny the truth for as long as he could. "Maybe you did misunderstand," I say, unable to bear his distress. "Maybe it was—"

"No, don't. You've been saying this all along, and I was too stupid to believe you. And then when you showed me those pictures last week…" Shaking his head, Misha takes a step back. "I should've listened to you from the start. I just didn't want to believe what you were saying, you know?" His face contorts. "He was dead and—"

"And he was your uncle, a man you looked up to, and I was the sister who left you when you were three." I keep my voice soft and even. "You had no reason to believe me over him. I understand… and I understood then too." I inhale to ease the constriction in my throat. "And I'm sorry, Michael. I'm really, truly sorry that things worked out this way."

Misha's expression doesn't change. "You have nothing to be sorry for," he says, his voice strained. "Uncle Vasya—Obenko—is a liar, and I'm an idiot for believing him. Kent said—" He stops again, his face reddening for some reason.

"Lucas?" I stare at Misha blankly. "You talked to him?"

"Yesterday," Misha mumbles, and begins walking again. "When he took me back to the barracks after dinner."

"What did he say?" I ask, falling into step beside him. Misha doesn't respond, so I say more firmly, "What did he say, Michael?"

"He said Kirill Ivanovich hurt you when you were my age," he says reluctantly. "And that Obenko told you they took care of him and they didn't." He glances at me, his face now pale. "Is it true? Did he"—he stops, blocking my way—"do something to you?"

Oh God. The rush of blood to my brain almost makes me dizzy. My cheeks turn hot, then cold as rage fills my stomach. How dare Lucas tell this to a fourteen-year-old? I never wanted Misha to know about Kirill. From what I've been able to pry out of him, it seems my brother has suppressed most of what happened to him at the orphanage. He remembers that it was bad, but he doesn't know the extent of it. Something like this could bring back those horrible memories, and even if it doesn't, I don't want him exposed to that kind of ugliness. It's bad enough that Misha's uncle deceived him; now my brother is going to think the whole world is made up of awful people.

For a moment, I'm tempted to deny everything, but that would make me just one more person who's lied to Misha. "Yes," I say, my voice strained. "It's true. But I was a little older than you—fifteen—and they did keep him away from me after they learned what happened."

Misha's hands curl as I speak. "Are you making excuses for them?" His voice rises incredulously. "For these… these *monsters*? After everything they've done to you? I thought Kent was making it up so I'd hate him less, but he wasn't, was he? That's what the two of you were talking about back at the black site. I heard you, but there was so much going on I didn't really register it. Kirill hurt you, and I…" His face twists painfully. "Oh, fuck, I trained with the guy. I liked him."

"Mishen'ka…" Pushing my anger at Lucas aside, I reach out to touch Misha's shoulder, but he steps away, shaking his head.

"I'm such an idiot." Stumbling over a root, he catches himself on a tree and continues to back away, muttering bitterly, "I'm such a fucking idiot..."

"Michael." Pushing my concerns about his suppressed memories aside, I make my voice stern. "I don't want you to use that kind of language. Do you understand? You're not an idiot, and you're certainly not a fucking anything. There was no way you could've known this, just like you couldn't have known that Obenko was lying. Nothing about this situation is your fault."

Misha blinks. "But—"

"No buts." Wiping all emotion from my face, I come closer and stop in front of him. "I don't want to hear any more whining. What's done is done. It's in the past. This, here and now, is the present. We're here, and we're not going to look back. Yes, we've been through some bad things, and we've known some bad people, but we survived and we're stronger now." Softening my voice a little, I reach out and squeeze his hand. "Aren't we?"

"Yes," Misha whispers, his fingers tightening around mine. "We are."

"Good." I release his hand and step back. "Now let's go. Diego told me he might take you to shooting practice this afternoon, since you've been good and all. You don't want to be late for that."

I turn and begin walking, and Misha trails next to me, the bitterness on his face replaced by a look of bewilderment. I've never spoken to him like that before, and he doesn't know what to make of it.

Despite my simmering fury at Lucas, I smile as we approach his house.

I'm Misha's big sister, and it feels good to act like one.

42

ucas

"HOW COULD YOU DO THIS?"

The minute I walk through the front door, Yulia stalks toward me, all long legs and flowing blond hair. Her blue eyes are narrowed into slits, her nostrils all but breathing fire.

"Do what?" I ask, confused. I did receive a rather gruesome update from Ukraine this morning, but I don't see how Yulia could've found out about that. "What are you talking about?"

"Misha," she hisses, stopping in front of me. Her hands are clenched at her sides. "You told him about Kirill."

"Oh." I almost smile but think better of it. Yulia looks ready to deck me, and given her restored health, she might land a blow or two before I subdue her. Keeping my expression carefully neutral, I say in a reasonable tone, "Why shouldn't I have told him? He deserves to know the truth. You know that part of his anger is because he feels deceived, right? Nobody likes to be manipulated."

Yulia's teeth snap together. "He's fourteen. He's still a child. You don't tell children about brutal rape—especially children with his kind of background. Kirill was his trainer. Misha admired him—"

"Yes, exactly." I catch her wrists as a preemptive defense measure. "Your brother kept talking about the bastard and all the things he taught him. Do you think that was good for him? Healthy? How do you think Michael would've felt when he found out that you let him respect your rapist? And he would've found out, believe me. Truth has a way of coming out."

Yulia's wrists are stiff in my grasp, but she doesn't kick me or try to get away. I take it as a sign that I'm getting through to her and say, "Also, he's not a child. Not really. You know your brother already slept with a girl, right?"

"What?" Yulia's mouth drops open.

"Yes, he told Diego about it." I use her shock to pull her closer, molding her lower body against my hardening cock. "The trainees went out to a club a few months ago, and he hooked up with an older girl there. He's crazy proud of it, like any teenage boy would be."

Her throat works. "But—"

"Don't worry. He used protection. Diego asked."

And before Yulia can recover from that, I lower my head and kiss her, enjoying the way she struggles before melting against me.

It takes a long time before we sit down to dinner that evening, but I don't regret a minute of the delay.

As our new life together continues, I find myself increasingly obsessed with all things Yulia. Everything about her fascinates me: the way she hums under her breath when she's cooking, how she stretches in the morning, the purring moan that escapes her lips when I kiss her neck. Her body has filled out again, her sickly pallor fading, and one look at her golden beauty is all it takes to get me hard these days. I fuck her every chance I get, and it's not enough. I want her constantly, with a need that consumes me. Every time I take her, it's the best feeling ever, yet I'm still left craving more.

Sometimes I think I'll go to my grave wanting her.

If it were just a sexual itch, I might've been able to handle it. But my hunger runs deeper. I want to know everything about her, every tiny detail of her life. I don't like thinking of my past, so I've never had much interest in that of other people, but with Yulia, my curiosity knows no bounds.

"You know, you never told me your real name," I say as we're eating lunch one day. "Your last name, I mean."

"Oh." She blinks. "Why do you care about that?"

"Because I do." I put down my fork and stare at her intently. "You have no one to protect anymore, so please, tell me, baby."

She hesitates, then says, "It's Molotova. I was born Yulia Borisovna Molotova."

Molotova. I make a mental note of that. I haven't forgotten what she told me about the headmistress of her orphanage, and I intend to use this information to track the woman down. I debate disclosing this to Yulia, but I'm not sure how she'd react, so I decide to keep quiet for now.

Changing the topic, I ask, "Have you ever killed anyone? Not in a fight or as self-defense, but outright."

To my surprise, Yulia nods. "Yes, once," she murmurs, looking down at her plate.

"When?" I reach across the table to cover her slender hand with my palm. "How did it happen?"

"It was during training, as the last part of the program," she says, her gaze veiled as she looks up at me. "None of us were supposed to be assassins, but they wanted to make sure we'd be able to pull the trigger if it came to that."

"So what did they do? Have you kill someone?"

"In a way." She wets her lips. "They brought in a dying homeless man. He had Stage Four liver cancer. He only had a few days to live at best, and he was in terrible pain. They shot him full of drugs, and then, instead of a paper target, they strung him up. Our goal was to make a killing shot."

"So all of you shot at this one guy?"

"Yes." Yulia's fingers twitch under my palm. "We used marked bullets, and he was autopsied afterwards to see whose bullets hit the target. A couple of trainees couldn't bring themselves to shoot."

"But you could."

"Yes." She pulls her hand out of my grasp but doesn't look away. "The autopsy revealed that three bullets hit his heart."

"Was yours one of them?" I ask, leaning back.

"No." Her gaze is unflinching. "Mine was found in his brain."

THAT NIGHT, YULIA CLINGS TO ME WITH A PASSION BORDERING ON desperation, and I realize my questioning brought back some bad memories. I know I should leave her alone, let her live in the present the way she clearly wants to do, but the questions keep gnawing at me, and I finally give in.

"Have you ever slept with a man of your own initiative?" I ask as we lie tangled together after a long bout of sex. By all rights, I should be sinking into sleep, but my body hums with energy and my thoughts keep returning to this topic.

Yulia stiffens in my arms. Turning over, she pulls back to look at me. "What do you mean? I was only forced that one time—"

"I mean, did you ever date anyone who wasn't an assignment?" I say, placing my hand on her hip. "Go to bars, clubs? Hook up with a guy just for fun?" I'd intended the question to be a casual one, but as I say the words, I realize that Yulia with another man will never be a casual topic for me.

I want to commit murder at the mere thought that someone who wasn't me touched her.

Yulia's gaze lights with comprehension. "No," she says softly. "I never dated. It wouldn't have been fair to the guy."

"So there was a guy?" My jealousy sharpens. "Someone you wanted?"

"What?" To my relief, she seems startled by the notion. "No, there was no one. I just meant that I was always on assignment, so I would've been a terrible girlfriend."

"So not even a casual hook-up?" I press.

"No." She bites her lip. "I didn't see the point. I had classes and school assignments on top of my job, and I didn't have much free time."

"So you're telling me that other than your three assigned lovers and myself, you've never been with anyone else?"

Her face tightens. "You're forgetting Kirill."

"I'm not forgetting him." The fact that we still haven't found him or his body is like a festering splinter under my skin. Suppressing the flare of rage, I say evenly, "He was your assailant, not your lover."

"In that case, yes." Yulia's blue eyes are clear and guileless as she looks at me. "I've had four lovers, including you."

I stare at her, hardly able to believe my ears. My seductive spy —the beautiful girl who used her body to get information—has slept with fewer men than an average college student.

"What about you?" she parries, propping herself up on one elbow. "How many women have *you* slept with?" The look in her eyes is a mirror image of my earlier jealousy.

"Probably not as many as you think," I say, pleased by her possessiveness. "But definitely more than four. Like your brother, I started fairly young, and… well, I wasn't much of a relationship guy back then."

Her eyes narrow. "Really? And you are now?"

"I'm in a relationship with you, am I not?" I say, my cock stirring at the sight of her nipple peeking out from under the blanket. "So yeah, I'd say so."

Yulia opens her mouth to reply, but I'm already pulling the blanket away. Rolling on top of her, I push her legs apart with my knees and grip my cock, positioning it against her opening. She's slick from our earlier session, so I thrust in, invading her silky tightness with no preliminaries. She doesn't seem to mind, her arms and legs wrapping around me to hold me close, and I begin to fuck her in earnest, taking her hard and fast. It takes only a few minutes before my orgasm starts to build, and I force myself to slow down, wanting to prolong the moment.

"Tell me you love me," I demand, stroking deep into her body. "I want to hear you say it."

"I love you, Lucas," she breathes in my ear, her legs squeezing my hips. Her pussy is like a hot, slippery glove around my dick, and my balls pull tight against my body as I feel her spasms begin. We detonate together, and in that moment, I feel as if we're one, as if our ragged halves have fused, forming one unbroken whole. Our lungs work in tandem, our breaths intermingle, and when I raise my head and see Yulia looking at me, something hot and dense expands inside my chest.

"I'll always love you," she whispers, curving her hand around my cheek, and the feeling grows stronger, the dense heat spreading until it fills every hollow corner of my soul.

With Yulia, I feel complete, and I treasure the sensation.

43

ulia

In some bizarre way, it feels like Lucas and I are newlyweds, and this unusual period—this lengthy truce between us—is our honeymoon.

Part of it is definitely the sex. Far from fading with time, the attraction between us only burns hotter, the magnetic pull intensifying with each passing day. Our bodies are attuned to each other in ways I could've never imagined. A look, a breath, a touch, and the flames ignite. Neither one of us can get enough. As many times as Lucas reaches for me, I respond, my body craving his no matter how sore I get. His touch reduces me to someone I don't recognize, a primitive being of wants and needs. It's like I've been programmed to exist solely for his pleasure, to desire him in all ways. He pushes me past my limits, and I want more. Rough or gentle, my captor consumes me, my need for him tethering me tighter than any ropes.

Beyond the sex, however, there is a growing emotional intimacy between us. Every day, Lucas demands my love, and I give it, helpless to do anything else. It's not an equal exchange; Lucas never says the words back or gives me any indication of his feelings. However, after we have sex, he holds me close, as if afraid to let me stray to the other side of the bed, and I know those quiet, tender moments are as important to him as they are to me. They give me hope that one day, I might have more of him—that I might reach the man underneath the hard shell.

"You know, you never really told me how you ended up here... how you went from being a Navy SEAL to Esguerra's second-in-command," I murmur one night when we lie there like that, wrapped in each other so completely it's impossible to tell where one ends and the other one begins. Tracing a circle on his powerful chest with my finger, I say, "All I know is what I read in your file, and there was nothing that explained why you did it."

"Killed my commanding officer?" Lucas's voice doesn't betray any emotion, but his shoulder muscle flexes under my head. "Is that what you want to know? Why I killed the bastard?"

"Yes." I scoot back a little so I can look at him. In the dim light of the bedside lamp, my captor's face is as harsh as I've ever seen it. It doesn't deter me, though. "Why did you do it?" I ask softly.

"Because he killed my best friend." Cold, ancient anger creeps into Lucas's voice. "Jackson—my friend—caught Roberts selling weapons to the Taliban, and he was going to report him. But before he could, Roberts had him killed... made it look like an ambush by hostiles. I was there when it happened."

"Oh, Lucas, I'm so sorry..." I reach up to touch his face, but he intercepts my hand, catching it in a viselike grip.

"Don't." He glances at me, his eyes slitted. "It was in Afghanistan, a long time ago." His gaze returns to the ceiling, but he doesn't release my hand. Holding my fingers tightly, he says, "In any case, I survived. It took several days for me to return to the base, but I made it. And when I got there, I killed the bastard. I took his own gun and peppered him with bullets."

Of course he did. I stare at my captor with a mix of sadness and bitter understanding. Like me, he had been betrayed by someone he trusted, someone who was supposed to have had his back. I don't know what I would've done to Obenko had he lived, but it neither shocks nor appalls me that Lucas chose this brutal method of retaliation.

"So what happened then?" I prompt when Lucas remains silent, his gaze locked on the ceiling. "Were you arrested?"

"Yes." He still doesn't look at me."I was taken back to the States for a court martial. Roberts had friends in high places, and my allegations against him were swept under the rug faster than I could make a formal report."

"How did you escape then?"

Lucas finally turns to face me. "My parents," he says in a hard, flat voice. "They couldn't tolerate the embarrassment of having their son tried for murder, so they arranged for me to disappear. My father made a deal with me: he'd help me vanish in South America, and I'd never contact them again."

"They wanted you out of their lives?" I gape at him, unable to fathom any parent making such a deal. "Why? Because of the murder charge?"

"Because, according to my father, I'm a bad apple—'rotten to the core' is the way he put it."

"Oh, Lucas..." My heart shatters on his behalf. "Your father was wrong. You're not—"

"Not a bad man?" He quirks an eyebrow, a sardonic smile flitting across his face. "Come now, beautiful, you know what I am. My parents sent me to all the best schools, gave me every advantage they could, and what did I do? I threw it all away, joined the Navy so I could satisfy my urge to fight. That's pretty fucked up, no? Can you really blame my parents for wanting to have nothing to do with me?"

"Yes, I can." I swallow, holding his gaze. "You were still their son. They should've stood by you."

"You don't understand." Lucas's eyes glint with ice. "They never wanted a son. I was to be their legacy. A perfect extension of them… a culmination of their ambitions. And I ruined all of that when I became a soldier. The murder charge was just the last straw. My father was right to offer me that deal. I didn't fit into their lives—I never had—and they certainly didn't fit into mine."

I bite the inside of my cheek, trying to hold back the tears stinging my eyes. I can picture Lucas as a volatile, restless boy constantly pushed and prodded to be something he didn't want to be. I can also see how his corporate lawyer parents must've been out of their depths trying to raise a child who was, at his core, a warrior—a boy who, by some strange quirk of genetics, was utterly unlike them.

Still, to tell their son that they never wanted to see him again…

"So you haven't spoken to them since then?" I ask, keeping a steady tone. "Not even once?"

"No." His gaze is pure steel. "Why would I?"

Why would he, indeed? To me, family is sacred, but my parents were very different from Lucas's family. I can't imagine Mom and Dad walking away from either me or Misha, no matter what path we chose to follow in life. They would've stood by us no matter what, just like I would stand by my brother.

And by Lucas, I realize with a sudden jolt of shock. In fact, I *am* standing by him, even as he and Esguerra lay waste to the organization I worked for. His father wasn't completely wrong—Lucas is not a nice guy, by any means—but that doesn't alter how I feel about him.

Maybe I'm rotten to the core as well, but somewhere along the way, my ruthless captor has become something like my family.

I push the startling revelation aside to focus on the rest of the story. "So how did you end up with Esguerra, then?" I ask, propping myself up on one elbow. "Did you just run into him somewhere in South America, and he hired you?"

"It was... a bit more complicated than that." The corners of Lucas's mouth twitch. "I was actually hired by a Mexican cartel to guard a shipment of weapons that they purchased from Esguerra. But when I showed up to do my job, I discovered that one of the cartel leaders had gotten greedy and decided to steal the shipment for himself, double-crossing Esguerra and his own people in the process. There was a nasty shootout, and at the end of it, Esguerra and I were among the few survivors, each of us pinned behind cover. He was running low on ammunition, and I had only a few bullets left, so instead of us continuing to try to kill each other, he offered to hire me on a permanent basis. Needless to say, I agreed." He chuckles darkly before adding, "Oh, and then I shot a guy who was sneaking up behind Esguerra to try to gut him. That sealed the deal, so to speak."

"Is that why you said Esguerra owes you?" I ask, remembering his long-ago words. "Because you saved his life that time?"

"No. That was just me doing my new job. Esguerra owes me for something else."

I look at him expectantly, and after a moment, Lucas sighs and says, "Esguerra was hurt last year in a warehouse explosion in Thailand. I carried him out and got him to a hospital, but he was in a coma for almost three months. I kept things together for him during that time, made sure the business didn't fall apart, his wife was safe, et cetera."

"I see." No wonder Lucas was confident that Esguerra would let him keep me. True loyalty had to be rarer than unicorns in the arms dealer's world. "And you weren't once tempted to take it all for yourself? Esguerra's business has to be worth billions."

"It is, but Esguerra pays me quite well, so what would be the point?" Lucas gives me a wry look. "Besides, I kind of like the guy. He used his contacts to take my name off the wanted lists after I started working for him. Not to mention, he doesn't pretend to be anything other than what he is, and that works for me."

Of course. I can see how that would be appealing after his commander's betrayal in Afghanistan. Still, many men in Lucas's position would've been blinded by greed, and that he wasn't speaks volumes about his character.

My captor may not be close to his family, but in his own way, he's as loyal as I am.

As our extended pseudo-honeymoon continues, I find myself with a strange problem: I have an excessive amount of free time. I have no assignments or classes, no real responsibilities of any kind. Initially, it had been nice; the illness and the traumatic events that preceded it had taken a lot out of me, leaving me exhausted mentally as well as physically. For several weeks, I'd been content to read, watch TV, spend time with Misha, and putter leisurely around the house, but as the weeks turned into months, I began itching to do more. I'd always been busy—first as a student, then as a trainee, and the last few years as an active spy on assignment. Free time had been a luxury I treasured, but now I'm awash in it and I don't like it.

To fill up the hours, I begin experimenting with new recipes. Lucas grants me access to the Internet—on a monitored computer, since he still doesn't trust me completely—and I find myself browsing various websites in search of new and interesting dishes. Lucas is all for my new hobby—he enjoys the results of it at every meal—and I gradually develop a kitchen repertoire that ranges from classic Russian dishes like *borscht* to exotic fusion cuisine that incorporates elements from Asian, French, and Latino cooking. I even come up with my own variations, like cilantro-curry sushi topped with pickled beets, Peking duck stuffed with apple-flavored cabbage, and arepas with Russian eggplant spread.

"Yulia, this is phenomenal," Lucas says when I make delicate pastries layered with shiitake mushrooms and Camembert cheese. "Seriously, this is better than any high-end restaurant. You should've been a chef."

"It really is amazing," my brother chimes in, devouring his fourth pastry. He's taken to eating lunch with us almost every day, and I suspect my cooking is a big reason for that. He's even willing to tolerate Lucas these days, though they're still far from being best buddies.

"Good. I'm glad you're enjoying it," I say, getting up to carry my plate to the sink. I'm full to bursting after two pastries, but Misha and Lucas seem to have infinite room in their stomachs. I conceal a grin as Lucas reaches for the second-to-last pastry and my brother instantly grabs the last one, stuffing it into his mouth like he's afraid it'll run away.

"Do you have any extra?" Misha asks after he chews and swallows. "Diego and Eduardo begged me to bring back some leftovers."

"What the hell?" Lucas pauses mid-bite to give Misha a glare. "They can make their own pastries. We won't have any leftovers."

"Actually, I made an extra batch just in case," I say, heading over to the oven. This is not the first time the two guards have begged for food through my brother, and I suspect it won't be the last. If Lucas allowed it, they'd come over to eat here every day, but since he doesn't, they find other ways to benefit from my new hobby. "Just tell them to eat the pastries before they cool completely. They won't be as good reheated in the microwave."

"Of course," Misha says as I put plastic wrap over the foil tray and hand it to him. "I'll give it to them right away."

Lucas observes us with an unhappy frown. "But what about—"

"I'll make more soon," I promise, grinning. "For dinner, I'm making enoki pasta with cashew sauce, and chocolate bread pudding with yuzu-raspberry topping. If you're still hungry after that, I'll make these pastries again, okay?"

Misha listens with clear envy before asking, "Do you think you'll have some bread pudding left if I come by after dinner? The guards invited me to a barbecue tonight, but I'll probably have some room for dessert…"

"Yes, of course." I beam at him. "I'll be sure to save some for you."

"Yeah, him and half the guards," Lucas mutters, getting up to wash his plate. "Next thing you know, we'll be feeding the whole compound."

I laugh, but before long, Diego and Eduardo start finding various excuses to stop by, often bringing a couple of their friends with them. I don't mind cooking larger portions—it's a fun challenge for me—but Lucas gets irritated, especially when our meals get interrupted by frequent visitors.

"This is not a fucking restaurant," he roars at Diego when the young guard "just happens to swing by" with six of his buddies at lunchtime. "Yulia cooks for me and her brother, got it? Now get the fuck out before I give you an extra shift."

The guards leave, dejected, but the next day, Eduardo comes by right before Lucas is due to return for lunch. "You wouldn't happen to have any of that shrimp salad left, would you?" he asks, keeping a wary eye on the front door. "Michael mentioned that you made some last night, and—"

"Sure." I suppress a grin. "But you better hurry. I think Lucas and Michael are almost here."

I give him a container of the leftover salad, and he thanks me before rushing out the door. The next day, Diego copies Eduardo's maneuver, stopping by a half hour before dinner, and I give him a whole extra cranberry-and-rice stuffed chicken I made for just such an occasion. He thanks me profusely, and for the next week, I surreptitiously feed the guards that way. On the following Monday, however, Lucas catches me in the act, and he's not pleased.

"What the fuck is this?" he snarls, stalking into the kitchen just as I'm giving a tray of freshly baked meat pies to Diego. Stopping next to us, he gives the guard a furious look. "I warned you—"

"Lucas, it's okay. I made enough for everyone," I assure him. "Really, it's fine. I don't mind cooking for them. I enjoy it."

"See? She's fine with it." Diego grins, snatching the tray out of my hands. "Thanks, princess. You're the best."

He sprints out of the kitchen, and Lucas turns toward me, jaw clenched. "What the fuck are you doing? It's not your job to feed the guards. They have a cafeteria in the barracks, you know."

"I know." Impulsively, I step toward him and lay my hand on his hard jaw, feeling the muscles working under the stubble-roughened skin. "It's okay, though. This is fun for me. I like it that the guards enjoy my cooking. It makes me feel…" I pause, searching for the right word.

"Useful?" Lucas says, his expression softening, and I nod, surprised that he pinpointed it so well.

He sighs and covers my hand with his before bringing my fingers to his mouth. Brushing his lips over my knuckles, he studies me, his expression now more troubled than angry. "Yulia, sweetheart… You are useful to *me*, okay? You don't need to feed every person on this estate to prove your worth."

I stare at him, my stomach inexplicably tight as he releases my hand. "What if I don't want to be useful just to you?" I whisper. "What if I need more than to warm your bed and take care of your house? You know I finished a university for real, right?" I can see Lucas's gaze darken as I speak, but I can't stop, my voice growing stronger with each word. "I have a degree in English Language and International Relations, and I was an excellent interpreter as well as a spy. For six years, I lived in one of the most cosmopolitan cities in the world and interacted with the highest-ranked officials in the Russian government. I was always going places, doing things, and now I barely step foot outside your house because I don't want Esguerra to remember that I exist." I stop to draw in a breath, and realize that a muscle is ticking in Lucas's jaw.

"Is that right?" he says, his voice deadly quiet. "You miss being a spy?"

I instantly curse my loose tongue. I should've known how Lucas would interpret my words. "No, of course not—"

"You miss fucking men on assignment?" He moves closer, backing me up against the kitchen counter.

My pulse spikes. "No, that's not what I—"

His hand grips my throat, tightening just enough to let me feel the steely strength in those fingers. Leaning in, he whispers in my ear, "Or is it that I'm not enough for you?" His breath heats my skin, making my arms erupt in goosebumps. "Do you need more variety, beautiful?"

"No," I choke out, my breathing turning shallow. A jealous Lucas is a terrifying thing. "That's not it at all. I just meant that—"

"You're mine," he growls, raising his head to pin me with an arctic stare. "I don't give a fuck what kind of life you led before. I caught you, tagged you, and you're fucking mine. No man will ever touch you again, and if I want to keep you in a fucking cage for the rest of your life, I will. Understand?"

His grip on my neck loosens, but my throat closes up, the pain like a tidal wave crashing through me. For weeks, I'd existed in a bubble of domestic bliss, playing house with a man who views me as nothing more than a possession, a glorified sex slave he "tagged" with the trackers. Any other woman would've fought tooth and nail for her freedom, but I embraced my captivity like I'd been born to it, letting myself imagine our messed-up relationship could someday turn into something real.

In my longing for my captor's love, I again built castles in the sand.

"I understand," I manage to whisper through numb lips. "I'm sorry."

Lucas releases me and steps back, his face still taut with anger, and I turn away, blindly reaching for some dishes to wash.

Our "honeymoon," such as it was, is over.

That night, Lucas doesn't come home until late, and Misha and I eat dinner by ourselves. I put on a happy mask for my brother, but I know he senses something off. It's a relief to usher him out of the house with a batch of leftovers for the guards; more than anything, I want to be alone to lick my wounds.

I'm already finishing my shower when Lucas returns. He enters the bathroom just as I'm stepping out of the stall, and without saying a word, he sweeps me up into his arms and carries me to the bedroom. His face is hard, his gaze shuttered as he walks, and the old unease slithers through me. I don't think he'll truly hurt me —physically, at least—but that doesn't lessen my anxiety. Lucas in this mood is unpredictable, and I'm barely keeping myself together as is. For a brief, insane moment, I consider fighting him, but instantly dismiss the idea. It's not like I stand a chance of actually winning. Besides, what would be the point of trying to resist? Like he said, I'm his to do with as he wants.

My life—and my brother's—is in his hands.

If I could cling to the numbness that encased me this afternoon, it would've been easier, but everything is sharp and bright in my mind, every sensation painfully vivid. I feel the heat of his skin through our clothes and the way his arm muscles flex as he places me on the bed; I see the pale glitter of his eyes and smell his warm male scent. He bends over me, and my body comes to life, a familiar heat brewing low in my stomach. My nipples peak, my breasts aching for his touch, and my sex grows slick as he kisses me, his tongue invading my mouth with rough, demanding strokes. His large hands catch my wrists, pinning them above my head, and I close my eyes, willingly sinking into the heated oblivion of lust. My hurt and anxiety dissipate, and animal instinct takes over. Moaning, I arch against Lucas, rubbing my hardened nipples against his T-shirt, and my insides clench as I feel the thick bulge in his jeans pressing against my naked hip.

Yes, take me, fuck me, make me forget... The erotic chant plays on a loop in my mind. For now, I don't need to worry about the future, about my life with a man who views me as his exclusive toy. I don't need to think about the fact that I may never be more than a vessel for his lust. I can just focus on his drugging kisses and the warm, heavy weight of his body on top of mine.

It's only when he transfers my wrists into one of his hands and rummages in the bedside drawer with the other that I resurface enough to feel a flicker of unease. Opening my eyes, I tear my lips away from his. "Lucas, what are you—"

He cuts me off with another deep, devouring kiss, and in the next moment, I have my answer. A cold metal touches my left wrist, and then I hear a click as the handcuff locks in place. Gasping, I turn my head to the side and try to twist my other wrist out of his grasp, but Lucas uses my motion to turn me over onto my side and drag my handcuffed arm toward the metal pole he'd installed by the bed during the early days of my captivity. Straddling me, he loops the handcuff around the pole and grabs my other wrist, cuffing it before I can put up any real resistance.

My unease transforms into real fear. I'm lying on my side, naked and with my wrists handcuffed to the pole—just like old times.

"Why are you doing this?" My voice turns high and thin as I turn my head to gaze at Lucas, who's now reaching for something else in the bedside drawer. "Lucas, don't, please." My hair is all over my face, interfering with my vision, and before I can shake it off, a soft dark cloth drops over my eyes.

"Shh," Lucas whispers, tying it around my head. "You're going to be fine, baby."

Fine? He just handcuffed and blindfolded me. My pulse drums in my ears, my arousal dampened by panic. "Lucas, please... What are you going to do?"

Still straddling me, he leans down, and I feel his warm breath on the side of my face. "Do you love me?" he murmurs. His lips brush the rim of my ear, his tongue tracing over the outer edge. "Do you love me, Yulia?"

I swallow thickly. "Yes. You know I do."

"Do you trust me?"

No. The truth almost slips out, but I clamp my lips shut just in time. I don't trust Lucas—I never have—but I'm certainly not about to admit it at the moment. I don't know the rules of this new game, and until I do, I'm not going to play along.

"I see," he murmurs, and I realize that my non-answer was an answer in itself. My heart rate speeds up further.

"Lucas, I—"

"It's okay." He bites my earlobe gently. "You don't have to lie." He moves off me, and I hear the sounds of clothes being removed, followed by that of the nightstand drawer being pulled out. I listen, straining, but I don't hear anything else, and a moment later, Lucas turns me so that I'm lying on my back, my handcuffed arms pulled to one side.

I'm about to ask again what he's planning to do, but he's already moving down my body and pushing my legs apart, his powerful hands pinning my thighs to the mattress.

The first touch of his tongue on my folds is startlingly soft, a caress rather than an assault. It both disorients and disarms me. I'd been prepared for something frightening and brutal, but the leisurely strokes of his tongue on my labia and at the rim of my opening are nothing of the sort. He licks me like he has all the time in the world, his lips and tongue toying with my sensitive flesh for what feels like hours before he gets anywhere near my pulsing clit. By then, I'm soaking wet and moaning his name, my hips moving uncontrollably as my arousal returns in full force. If it weren't for his hands holding down my thighs, I would've ground my sex against his mouth, forcibly taking the orgasm that shimmers just beyond my reach.

"Please, Lucas," I beg as his tongue circles my clit with maddeningly light strokes. "Just a little more, please..."

To my surprise, he obliges, latching on to my clit with a sucking pull that I feel all the way down to my toes. A choked cry escapes my throat as my inner muscles tighten, and then the orgasm washes over me, sweeping away everything but the devastating pleasure. I come so hard that I see flickers of light, my hips almost coming off the bed despite the restraining pressure of his hands. The pulsations continue for several long moments, and when it's all over, I'm left lying there, boneless and panting, wrung out by the sensations.

I know Lucas is not done with me yet, but I'm still startled when he flips me over onto my stomach, making the handcuffs clang against the metal pole. My arms are now stretched to the opposite side, and for the first time, the scary versatility of this kind of restraint dawns on me.

Lucas can do anything he wants to me, in any position, and I can't do anything to stop him.

He straddles my legs, immobilizing them against the bed, and fear prickles at me again, chasing away some of the post-orgasm endorphins. A second later, I feel something cool and wet trickle between my ass cheeks and realize my anxiety is justified.

Lucas poured some lube on me.

"Don't, please." I yank at the cuffs chaining me to the pole, my heartbeat skyrocketing. "Please… not like this."

"It's okay, beautiful." Ignoring my attempts to wriggle away, Lucas stuffs two thick pillows under my hips, propping me up so I'm almost on all fours. "I told you, you're going to be fine."

But I won't be. I know that from experience. He'll tear me, his cock too long and thick for my body to accept that way. He's played with my ass several times in recent weeks, using his fingers and a couple of small toys, but he's never pushed beyond that and I'd foolishly begun to hope that he wouldn't, that he'd respect my wishes in that regard. I should've known better, of course.

His lust knows no boundaries when it comes to me.

He leans over me, the heat of his body warming my chilled

skin, and I realize I'm trembling, my back covered with a layer of cold sweat. His hand strokes the side of my hip, and I flinch before I can control my reaction, my muscles locking tight in anticipation of the pain to come.

"Yulia..." He gathers my hair to the side, moving it off my sweat-dampened back, and I feel his lips brush over my nape at the same time as his stiff cock presses against my leg. "I won't hurt you, baby, I promise."

Not hurt me? I want to scream that it's a lie, that he wouldn't restrain and blindfold me if he intended to make love to me sweetly, but I don't get a chance because at that moment, Lucas's fingers slip between my legs and find my clit. Pressing on it gently, he kisses my neck again, and to my shock, I feel a twinge of something that's not fear... a hot, tight pleasure that somehow coexists with my panic.

"I won't hurt you," he repeats, his words whisper soft as his lips trail over my shoulder, and some of my anxiety ebbs, melting away in the heat that's starting to pulse through me. By now, Lucas knows everything about my body, and he uses that knowledge without qualms, his fingers teasing out sensations that should've been beyond my reach.

The second orgasm catches me by surprise, and I pant into the mattress as waves of pleasure ripple through me. I haven't forgotten what awaits me, but it's hard to cling to fear when one's brain is swimming in endorphins. And Lucas is not done pleasuring me yet. His hand finds my pussy entrance, and one long finger pushes inside, unerringly locating my G-spot. Before long, the tension coils in my core again, and another orgasm, albeit a weaker one this time, rocks my body.

"No more, please," I moan when his finger withdraws from my spasming channel and circles my swollen clit. "I can't do it again."

"Yes, baby, you can." His teeth graze my neck, and then he whispers in my ear, "Again and again, as many times as it takes."

It takes two more orgasms, as it turns out. Or at least that's how many Lucas forces on me before my muscles turn to mush and I'm too exhausted to come again. By that point, I've stopped worrying about the dangerous slickness between my ass cheeks—I've stopped thinking, period. So when his fingers withdraw from my dripping-wet pussy and slide up between my cheeks, I just lie there, dazed and limp, barely reacting as two of those long fingers push into my ass, one after another, gliding in with almost no resistance.

"That's it, sweetheart. There's a good girl," Lucas croons as I remain relaxed, accepting his two fingers without clenching. It's still not my favorite sensation; the fullness feels odd and invasive, but there's no pain and I'm too drained to resist as he begins to fuck my ass with those fingers, pumping them in and out slowly. "Such a good girl…" The smooth, gliding rhythm is strangely hypnotic, making me feel like my mind is disconnected from my body. Dimly, I'm aware that I should be afraid, that I should be protesting this violation, but it doesn't seem worth the effort, particularly when Lucas's other hand presses gently on my clit again, coaxing a twinge of pleasure from my overstimulated flesh.

I'm so immersed in that disconnected state that it doesn't frighten me when his fingers withdraw and something smooth and thick presses against my back opening instead. My body remains limp and relaxed, even when I feel a massive, stretching pressure and hear Lucas groan under his breath, "Fuck, baby, you're tight…" The pressure intensifies, edging into pain, and it's only then that some of my fear returns, along with the urge to tighten against the intrusion.

"No, sweetheart, don't tense. Just breathe through it." The command comes in a low, strained voice, and I realize what this self-restraint is costing Lucas, how tightly he's reining himself in to avoid hurting me. Oddly, the knowledge calms me somewhat, and I take slow, deep breaths, trying to keep my muscles relaxed.

"Yes, that's it," he praises hoarsely, and I feel him begin to penetrate me, the broad head of his cock stretching the tight ring of muscle at my entrance. It burns, the urge to clamp down almost unbearable, but I continue to breathe evenly, and slowly, he advances, working his massive cock into me millimeter by millimeter.

When the head is all the way in, he pauses, stroking my hip soothingly, and after a few moments, I feel the stinging burn subside. I'm able to relax a bit more, and Lucas resumes his slow advance. As he pushes deeper into me, however, my calm flees. He's big, far too big. My heartbeat picks up, my breathing turning shallow and frantic. The slickness of the lube reduces friction, but it doesn't alter his size, and my insides churn as Lucas forces more of himself into me, stretching me past my limits. Overwhelmed, I whimper into the mattress, and he kisses my nape, the tender gesture a stark contrast to the merciless invasion of my body.

"Just a little more," he murmurs, and I realize that I inadvertently tightened around him, trying to prevent him from going deeper. "You can take it, baby."

No, I can't, I want to protest, but all I can do is make an incoherent noise, something between a grunting moan and a whimper. I'm shaking and sweating, my hands clutching at the metal pole I'm handcuffed to. This is nothing like the horrific pain Kirill inflicted on me that day, but in its own way, it's just as agonizing. Lucas's slow, careful movements allow me to feel his length fully… to absorb the immense, overwhelming pressure forcing my insides apart. His cock seems to fill every part of me, violating and possessing me at the same time, taking me to a place where darkness and eroticism collide, twisting together in some perverse symphony.

"Fuck, Yulia, you feel amazing," Lucas groans, and I realize he's in me fully, his balls pressing against my sex. His hand is still between my legs, his fingers putting pressure on my clit, and I bite back a cry as he shifts inside me, my stomach roiling at the strange sensation. "You're tight… so fucking tight." He presses harder on my clit, two of his fingers catching it in a scissor-like grip, and sharp, unexpected pleasure jolts my core, making me gasp out loud.

"Yes, there it is, beautiful..." Lucas's voice brims with dark satisfaction. "You can do it. Come for me one more time." His fingers begin to move in that scissoring motion, and to my shock, my body tightens on a wave of heat. The extreme fullness inside me both hampers and enhances the sensations, the pulsing ache from my clit warring with the agony from my overstretched ass. His cock feels like a steel pipe inside me, but the way his fingers are touching me makes my insides cramp in a different, distinctly pleasurable way. I cry out, trembling at the impending rush of orgasm, and Lucas grips my clit harder, pinching it almost painfully.

"That's it, just like that, baby..." He pinches my clit again, and helplessly, I explode, my abused nerve endings electrified by his rough touch. My body spasms over and over again, clenching around his thick length, and I sob at the painful ecstasy, at the scorching wrongness of it all. The pleasure is dark and brutal, and when he begins to move inside me, the thrust and drag of his cock sends me spiraling higher, the foreign sensations enhanced by the blindfold and the cold steel around my wrists. I don't know how long it takes before Lucas comes, his hot seed flooding my raw insides, but by the time he withdraws from me and unlocks my handcuffs, all I can do is lie there, weak and shaking, my ass burning and my clit pulsing with residual aftershocks.

Silently, he draws me into his arms, and I cry against his chest, feeling both broken and freed.

The past with Kirill is officially behind me. Every part of me now belongs to Lucas, for better or for worse.

44

ulia

At breakfast, Lucas is unusually quiet, his gaze trained on me thoughtfully, and I have to fight a blush every time I look up from my plate and see those pale eyes watching me. I want to ask him what he's thinking, but some bizarre shyness keeps me silent. It doesn't help that I'm sore, my every movement a reminder of what occurred between us. He didn't tear me like I feared, but I'm still very much aware that something large and thick had been inside me, taking me places I never knew I could go… making me feel things I never knew I could feel.

To expedite the meal, I make quick work of my mushroom-spinach quiche and get up to take my plate to the sink. When I return to the table to get Lucas's plate, he surprises me by catching my arm, his long fingers closing around my wrist in an unbreakable grip.

"Yulia." His eyes glint with something indefinable. "That was delicious, thank you."

"Oh." I blink. "You're welcome." I expect him to let go of my wrist at that point, but he continues holding it without saying anything else.

"Um, let me get your plate…" Awkwardly, I reach for it with my other hand, but he moves it to the side, out of my reach.

"I'll get it myself, don't worry. Yulia…" He inhales deeply. "Are you all right?"

"I'm fine." My face burns all the way to the roots of my hair, but I force myself not to avert my gaze like some blushing virgin. "Everything's fine."

"Good." His eyes darken. "I didn't want to hurt you."

"You didn't." I swallow. "Not much, at least."

Lucas studies me for a few more moments, then nods, seemingly satisfied. Releasing my wrist, he stands up and carries his plate to the sink. He washes it along with my plate, and I just stand there, unsure whether this odd conversation is over. Finally, I decide to leave the kitchen, but before I can walk out, Lucas wipes his hands on a paper towel and turns toward me.

In a few long strides, he closes the distance between us, stopping less than a foot in front of me. "Just so you know," he says quietly, "I'd never truly harm you. You *are* mine, but that doesn't mean I'd ever abuse you. Your happiness matters to me, Yulia. You can believe me or not, but it's the truth."

I open my mouth, then close it, unable to form a coherent sentence. This is the closest Lucas has ever come to telling me how he feels—and to acknowledging hurtful things said in the heat of jealousy. Yet there's no regret on his face, no real apology in his words. What he said last night is the absolute truth—in this relationship, I have all the rights of a slave—and he's not about to deny it. What he's promising, however, is to be a good owner, and strangely, I do find that reassuring. Last night—any night, really—he could've hurt me badly, but he didn't, and as I look at the hard man in front of me, I know with sudden certainty that he never will.

It may be stupid of me, but I trust my captor—in this, at least.

Before I can formulate how to tell him this, Lucas bends his head, kissing me on the mouth, and walks out of the kitchen, leaving me standing there dazed… and filled with new, fragile hope.

We don't discuss the issue of me cooking for the guards again, but a week later, I get a delivery of restaurant-grade kitchen equipment, everything from an enormous oven to huge pots and pans. Diego and Eduardo spend two days remodeling the kitchen and installing everything, and when they're done, I have everything I need to cook for a small army.

And by the time the next week is through, that's exactly what I find myself doing. As soon as Lucas leaves for work, I get busy preparing for the madness that is lunch. Diego and Eduardo must've told the other guards that Lucas relented, and the kitchen teems with visitors from ten in the morning until late into the afternoon. And then the dinner rush begins. One day, seventy-nine guards stop by—I count, just to make sure I'm not exaggerating—and I realize I'm going to have to do something to manage the situation. Lucas is remarkably stoic about everything, putting up with the insane disruption of our routine without any complaints, but I'm sure he won't let this go on forever. And I myself miss having meals with just the two of us—or three, if Misha comes over. There's a huge difference between giving a few leftovers to the guards and running what is quickly becoming an all-day restaurant operation. By the time dinner is over, I'm exhausted to the point of passing out, and several times, I do pass out in the living room as we watch TV—a situation that usually results in Lucas carrying me to bed and fucking my brains out before letting me go back to sleep.

There's also another, more tricky concern.

"Lucas, are the guards defraying any of the food expenses?" I ask him one morning as I mix up batter for *blini*—Russian-style crepes. "Or is Esguerra paying for the ingredients?"

"No, and no," Lucas replies, watching me with a hooded stare from the table. I have no idea if he wants the crepes, or if it's my tiny shorts that have him intrigued, but there's a distinct look of hunger on his starkly masculine face.

Refusing to let it distract me, I put down the whisk on a paper towel and frown at Lucas. "No? But this is a lot of food—and some of the ingredients are really expensive."

"So what?" His gaze travels over my body, lingering on the sliver of stomach exposed by my tank top. "You're enjoying this, and we can afford it."

I tug down the shirt and wait for his eyes to meet mine again. "We?"

"Sure," Lucas says without blinking. "I told you, Esguerra pays me well, and I've accumulated a nice stash over the years."

"Right." I decide that he misspoke with that pronoun, and return to the topic at hand. "But that still doesn't mean you should pay out of pocket for everyone's food," I say. "I mean, we're talking hundreds of dollars a day."

Lucas shrugs. "All right. If you're worried, I'll tell the guards to start paying for their meals. Your food is certainly good enough for a high-end restaurant, so I think it's a good idea if you charged like one."

"Seriously?" I stare at him. "You want me to run a real restaurant?"

"Sweetheart, I don't know if you're aware of this, but you *are* running a real restaurant." Lucas gets up to walk over to me. His eyes gleam as he stops in front of me and says, "A very good restaurant, as evidenced by the fact that a third of the guards come by at least once a day. And the rest... Well, many are still stuck on the crash, but most who don't come simply can't—they have duties that prevent them from leaving their posts."

"Oh." I hadn't realized my food was that popular, though the seventy-nine visitors that one day should've given me a clue.

"Yes, oh." Lucas reaches out to brush a strand of hair off my forehead. "You've been having fun with this, so I haven't said anything, but now that we're talking about it, I think it's a good idea to make the fuckers pay, and pay well. That might weed out some of the cheaper bastards and reduce the workload for you."

"All right," I agree after a moment of deliberation. "If you think that would be okay, I'll try."

I FOLLOW LUCAS'S SUGGESTION WITH TREPIDATION, CERTAIN THAT no one in their right mind would want to pay for my cooking when they could eat in the cafeteria for free. The main reason I do it is because I don't want to bankrupt Lucas with my hobby. He's been beyond generous with me, but I can't ask him to subsidize everyone's meals forever. Also, I'm not exactly opposed to a reduced workload; as fun of a challenge as this has been, laboring in the kitchen for ten-plus hours a day is hard work. I'm so tired I'm having to wear concealer to hide my undereye circles, and I know if Lucas notices that, he might put a stop to the whole operation.

My health is still his top worry.

To my surprise, when I post the prices—genuine high-end restaurant prices, written in black marker on a sheet of paper pinned to the front door—nobody so much as voices a peep of protest. By the time the day is over, I make over six million Colombian pesos—nearly two thousand US dollars.

Stunned, I show the haul to Lucas. "They paid. Can you believe it? They actually paid."

"I can, unfortunately." He glowers at the pile of money on the table. "They're not as cheap as I'd hoped."

And so the madness continues. My business—and I have to think of it as such now—is very lucrative, but it's also exhausting. I do everything from the cooking to the serving to the cleaning. By the time another three weeks have gone by, I realize that if I'm going to operate as a restaurant, I'm going to need to either get help or limit the scope of what I'm doing.

"I think I'm going to serve only lunch," I say to Lucas as I scrub the pots and pans left over from dinner. "And if you don't mind, I'll put out a few tables in the back yard, make it into a sit-down cafe of sorts instead of giving everyone takeout. That way, if more people come than can be comfortably seated during open hours, they'll have to make a reservation for another day."

"That's an excellent idea," Lucas says, coming over to help me lift a heavy pan out of the sink. "For tonight, why don't you go to bed early? I'll finish up here and join you."

"No, that's okay, I can do it," I say, but he brushes me aside and goes to work scrubbing the remaining pots. Seeing that he has no intention of budging, I sigh and thank him before wearily trudging off to take a shower.

At this point, I'll take any help I can get.

The next day, I start implementing my ideas. At first, some guards grumble about being deprived of dinner, but when Lucas shows up and gives them a glacial stare, all the grumbling stops. By the time the week is over, I've successfully transitioned from a disorganized all-day takeout operation to a small and highly sought-after lunch cafe.

"I'm booked solid for the next three weeks," I tell Lucas in gleeful disbelief as we go on a morning walk—our first in almost two weeks. "Seriously, I'm having to take reservations for the next month."

"Of course, what did you expect?" He gives me a warm smile. "I've always told you your cooking is amazing."

I grin, delighted at the praise. I suspect Lucas is more excited about the return of our private dinners than my cafe's popularity, but that doesn't change the fact that he's been incredibly supportive of my venture. I'm sure the profit the cafe makes doesn't hurt, but he was on board with everything even when my hobby was a financial drain.

"What have you been doing with the money?" I ask, wondering for the first time what happens to the pile of cash I give Lucas every night. "Do you deposit it somewhere? Invest it?"

"I put it into your account, of course. What else?"

"My account?" My eyebrows crawl up. "What do you mean, my account?"

"The account I opened for you in the Cayman Islands," Lucas says casually, as if that sort of thing is done every day. "Well, technically, it's in both of our names, as per the advice of my accountant, but you're the primary account holder."

"What?" I stop and frown at him, certain I must be misunderstanding something. "You've been depositing that money into an account for me? Why?"

"Because it's your money," he says, as if it's obvious. "You earned it, so what else would I do with it?"

"Um, keep it, seeing as I'm cooking with the ingredients you buy using equipment that you paid for?"

"Yes, but I'm not the one doing the actual cooking," Lucas says reasonably. "Besides, I do deduct food expenses before making the deposits. The money going into the account is pure business profit —*your* business profit."

My head spins as I stare at him. "But what do you expect me to do with that money? And how much money is there by now, anyway?"

"As of yesterday, there's a little over forty thousand dollars." He resumes walking, and I hurry after him, feeling like I've fallen through a rabbit hole. "As to what you want to do with it, it's up to you. If you want, I can ask my portfolio manager to invest it for you, or if you feel like playing the stock market yourself, you can do that too. Or just leave it sitting there until you have a better idea of what you want to do with it."

My Alice-in-Wonderland feeling intensifies. "I can play the stock market?"

"If that's what you want to do. Or you can leave it to the professionals—Winters, my portfolio manager, is quite good."

Right. Because everyone knows captives have access to topnotch portfolio managers. My mind races as I try to work through the implications of this. "Lucas, are you…" I glance at him cautiously. "Are you going to set me free?"

He stops and turns to face me, his casual demeanor gone without a trace. "What do you mean by that?" His pale eyes glint dangerously. "Are you saying you want to leave?"

"No, but"—I swallow, my pulse kicking up—"would you let me if I did?" Could Lucas have changed his mind about our relationship? Is it possible he's grown to care about me enough to give me this choice?

He steps toward me, his broad shoulders blocking out the sun streaming through the trees. "Never," he says with harsh finality. "You're not leaving me. You can do whatever you want, run a thousand restaurants, make millions if you feel like it, but you'll do it by my side. I'm not letting you go, Yulia—not now, not ever."

I stare up at him, my heart pounding with a contradictory mixture of dismay and elation. "Never? But what if you get tired of me?"

"That's not going to happen."

"You can't say that for sure—"

"Yes, I can." He steps even closer, forcing me to back up against a tree. Bracing his palms on the thick trunk behind me, he leans in, his eyes gleaming. "I've never wanted another woman the way I want you. You're like a fire under my skin. I want you every minute of every day. It doesn't matter how often we fuck; the moment I pull out, I want to be in you again, feeling your wet, silky heat, smelling you... tasting you." He draws in a deep breath, his muscular chest expanding, and I feel my own breathing quicken as his hard pecs touch my peaked nipples. My palms press against the tree behind me, the rough bark digging into my skin. I'm caged by him, surrounded, the fire that he just talked about burning under my skin as well.

Involuntarily, my tongue comes out to moisten my lips, and I see Lucas's eyes darken.

"Yulia..." He presses his lower body against mine, and I feel the hard swell in his jeans. "I can't stop wanting you, no matter what I do," he says in a low, thick voice. "Every night, when I hold you, I think that maybe tomorrow will be the day when this obsession lessens, when I can go a few hours without thinking about you, without craving you like a fucking drug, but that's not what happens. I wake up just as addicted, and you know what, baby?"

"What?" I manage to whisper, my mouth dry and my pulse hammering. What Lucas is saying, the way he's looking at me...

"I kind of like it." He lowers his head until his mouth hovers less than a centimeter from mine. I can smell the bergamot of Earl Grey on his breath, see the darkness of his pupils and the blue-gray rings of irises surrounding them. "You give me something I didn't know I wanted, and I'm not about to let it slip away."

"What..." I inhale, prickles of heat racing up and down my spine. "What do I give you?"

"This." His lips ghost over mine, the tenderness of the kiss contrasting with the savage hunger I feel in him. "You. Whichever way I want." His mouth trails over my jaw, warm and soft on my skin, and I close my eyes, a moan escaping my lips as my head involuntarily tips back. I feel hot and dizzy, my body thrumming with a dark, pulsing heat that has nothing to do with the midmorning sun beaming down on the rainforest canopy above us. I'm drunk on Lucas, high on whatever chemical cocktail my brain cooks up in his presence. He's not telling me anything I didn't already know—his sexual obsession with me has been obvious from the beginning—yet the needy part of me searches for a deeper meaning in his erotically charged words, tries to decipher them like a puzzle. Could this be his way of telling me he cares about me? That he loves me, even?

I open my eyes, fighting the drugged sensation so I can find the courage to ask, and then I hear it.

A woman's peal of laughter, followed by the sound of twigs snapping under someone's feet.

Lucas must've heard it too, because he releases me and spins around, keeping me protectively behind him.

A second later, a small, dark-haired girl sprints out from behind the trees, her tanned face glowing with a smile and her white sports bra soaked with sweat. Two steps behind her is a tall, darkly handsome man. He's wearing nothing but a pair of gray running shorts, his bronzed, muscular body gleaming with perspiration and his white teeth bared in a grin.

His blue eyes meet mine from behind the shelter of Lucas's body, and the heat inside me turns to ice.

It's Julian and Nora Esguerra.

They must've been out for a run.

Seeing us, they stop, breathing heavily. Their smiles disappear without a trace.

"Hey there," Lucas says calmly, seemingly oblivious to the tension crackling in the air. "How's your run?"

"Hot. Humid. You know, the usual," Esguerra responds in the same casual manner, but I see the hard set of his jaw as he steps forward to stand next to Nora. He towers over her petite frame, his biceps almost the same width as her slender waist. A ray of sunlight falls across his face, and I notice a faint white scar on his left cheekbone. It runs all the way to the top of his eyebrow, crossing his left eye.

His fake left eye, I remember with a cold shudder. He lost the real one after the plane crash I'd caused.

"Sorry, we didn't mean to interrupt," Nora says, her cool tone belying her apology. Her dark eyes travel from me to Lucas, then back to me as she adds, "It's my fault. We don't usually run this way, but I went off our usual path today."

Lucas's massive shoulders rise in a brief shrug. "It's your estate. You can go wherever you wish." His voice is still unruffled, but the muscles in his arms tighten, and when I glance at Esguerra, I see him staring at me, his gaze menacing in its intensity.

The ice inside me spreads all the way down to my toes. I'm not afraid for myself, but I can't bear the thought of endangering Lucas, who's standing in front of me like a human shield. He's ready to fight for me, I can feel it.

To protect me, he'll go up against Esguerra and die—if not in the fight itself, then afterwards, at the hands of two hundred guards presumably loyal to their boss.

"Lucas," I say quietly, curling my fingers around his wrist. "Come. We should go."

He doesn't move, and neither does Esguerra. The two men appear to be rooted in place, their powerful muscles bunched tight as they glare at each other. Lucas is a couple of centimeters taller and slightly thicker in the chest than Esguerra, but I have a feeling they'd be evenly matched in a fight. Violence is the language they speak; it's there in the scars on their bodies and the savagery in their eyes.

If the line of trust is crossed, only one of them will leave this forest alive.

Apparently reaching the same conclusion, Nora says softly, "Yes, Julian, we should go." Parroting my gesture, she wraps her slim fingers around her husband's broad wrist, her tiny hand appearing childlike next to his. Esguerra tenses further, and for a moment, I'm certain he'll twist out of her grasp, shaking her off with the ease of an adult pushing away a clinging toddler, but he doesn't.

"Yes," he says, making a visible effort to relax. "You're right. Let's go. I have some work to do."

Nora nods and drops her hand, turning away. "Race you!" she yells at Esguerra over her shoulder, and with one last glance in our direction, she sprints away, disappearing into the trees. Her husband follows, and a few moments later, we're alone again.

Lucas turns to face me. "Are you all right?" he asks quietly.

"Of course." I force a smile to my lips. "Why wouldn't I be?" Stepping to the left, I slip around him and hurry toward his house, unwilling to stay in the forest even a moment longer.

I no longer have any doubts about my future here.

The next time Esguerra sees me, blood will be spilled.

45

ucas

The moment we get home, Yulia excuses herself and disappears into the bathroom to take a shower before starting lunch preparations. I consider joining her there, but decide against it.

As much as I want to comfort her after what happened, there's something I must do first.

Half an hour later, I walk into Esguerra's office. He must've just showered and changed, because his hair is wet as he stands up to face me, his eyes hard and his jaw stiff with anger.

I don't bother beating around the bush. "She's mine," I say harshly, approaching his desk. "Which part of that was unclear?"

Esguerra's gaze hardens even more. "I didn't touch her."

"No, but you want to, don't you?" I put my fists on the desk and lean forward. "You want to make her pay for what happened."

"Yes—and so should you." He mirrors my aggressive stance, the wide desk between us the only barrier to the violence simmering in the air. "Almost four dozen of our men died, and she's walking around like nothing happened… running a fucking restaurant on *my* property." His words drip with barely restrained rage. "Do you know that a reservation at 'Yulia's cafe' is the hottest commodity on the estate these days? The guards treat those slots like they're fucking gold."

I straighten, glaring at him. "Yes, of course I know." It was only yesterday that I had to break up a fight between two guards—a fight that resulted from a card game where the prize was an eleven-thirty reservation slot on Friday.

"And you're letting this happen?" Rounding the desk with sharp strides, Esguerra stops in front of me, fists clenched. "This is *my* estate. I'm letting her live because I owe you, but I do not want to be reminded of her existence every day, do you understand me?"

"Perfectly." I meet his furious look with one of my own. "Which is why I'm leaving."

Esguerra goes still, the anger transforming into something colder. "Excuse me?"

"That's what I came here to discuss," I say, folding my arms across my chest. Pushing down the rage boiling in my gut, I say in a steady tone, "You will never forgive her, and I will never give her up, so the way I see it, we have two options. We can kill each other over this, or I can take her—and myself—out of the picture."

"You're quitting?"

"If that's what you want." I give him a level look. "We work well together, but it may be time to go our separate ways. I'll train my replacement before I go, of course. Thomas is an excellent pilot, so you'll be fine there, and Diego is smart and loyal; he'll make a good second-in-command for you. Or…" I let my voice trail off.

Esguerra's eyebrows snap together. "Or what?"

"Or we can figure out a way for us to work together without me living here." I pause, letting that sink in. "Before you decided to make this compound your permanent home, we went wherever the business took us. It was nice to settle down here—and certainly safer for you and Nora, given that situation with Al-Quadar—but you know as well as I do that we've had to give up a few lucrative opportunities because you wanted to limit travel."

His nostrils flare. "What exactly are you suggesting?"

"When you were in a coma, I ran the whole organization. I handled everything from suppliers to customers, and I got to know every aspect of the business. If you want—if you trust me enough—I can be more than the second-in-command working by your side. I can represent us internationally, do whatever is necessary to grow the business abroad."

All emotion fades from Esguerra's face. "You want to be my partner."

"You could call it that, though an executive operations manager might be a more accurate label. You'd have the final say on major decisions, but I would run the new ventures and keep an eye on our existing operations in person. I could set up base someplace central, like Europe or Dubai, and do as much travel as necessary to keep things running smoothly."

"You've thought this through."

"Yes. I've known for some time that this won't work long term."

"Because of *her*."

"Yes, because of Yulia." I hold his icy gaze. "I'm not about to let anything happen to her."

"And if I don't agree to this?"

"Your business, your choice," I say. "I like working with you, but I have other options. For one thing, I can go legit and open a security firm somewhere. If you don't want this, just say the word, and I'll be gone."

He stares at me, and I know what he's thinking. He can't let me leave—I know too much about the inner workings of his business—so he has two choices: kill me or agree to my proposition. I gaze back at him calmly, ready for either possibility. I know I'm taking a risk, pushing him like this, but I don't see any other way to resolve this situation. Yulia can't spend the rest of her life hiding in my house and trying not to draw Esguerra's attention. At some point, something's going to go wrong, and when it does, things are going to get ugly.

I have to take her away before that happens.

Just when I think Esguerra has decided my loyalty isn't worth it, he sighs and steps back, his hands uncurling at his sides. "Does she really mean that much to you?" There's weary resignation in his voice. "Can't you find another pretty blonde to fuck?

I raise my eyebrows. "Could you find another petite brunette?"

A humorless smile stretches across his face. "It's like that, huh?"

"She's my everything," I say without blinking. "So yes, I guess it's like that."

Esguerra looks at me, his smile fading. Then he says abruptly, "Ten percent of profits from the new ventures, plus the same salary—that's my offer."

"Seventy percent," I reply without missing a beat. "I'll be doing all the work, so it's only fair."

"Twenty percent."

"Sixty."

"Thirty."

"Fifty, and that's my final offer."

"Forty-five."

I shake my head, though I couldn't care less about those five percent. "Fifty percent," I repeat. If Esguerra is to respect me as a partner, I need to stand my ground. It'll make for a better working relationship longer term. "Take it or leave it."

He studies me coolly, then inclines his head. "All right. Fifty percent of the new ventures' profit."

"Deal." I extend my hand, and we shake on it. "I'll get the ball rolling, so we can be out of your hair soon," I say, releasing his hand and stepping back. "Just one more thing..."

Esguerra's mouth tightens. "What is it?"

"You know as well as I do that our line of work is dangerous, especially out there, beyond the compound," I say. "Given that, I need your promise that you won't *ever* come after Yulia or her family. No matter what happens to me."

Esguerra nods curtly. "You have my word."

~

THAT EVENING, YULIA IS QUIET AND WITHDRAWN, HER GAZE TRAINED on her plate throughout most of the meal despite her brother's presence at our table. Several times, Michael tries to engage her in conversation, but after getting only monosyllabic responses, he gives up and quickly finishes his meal.

"What's up with her?" he mutters as I walk him to the guards' barracks while Yulia stays behind to clean up. "Is she mad at me or something?"

"It has nothing to do with you," I say. "She's just worried about something."

"What?" The boy shoots me an anxious glance. "Did something happen?"

"No." I smile reassuringly. I've grown to like Yulia's brother over the past few weeks, and I don't want him to worry either. "She thinks it has, but she's wrong."

The boy frowns in confusion. "So everything is fine?"

"Yes, Michael," I say as we approach the building. "Everything is fine, I promise."

He gives me a doubtful look, but when we stop in front of the entrance, he says gruffly, "Tell Yulia I said, 'Good night and stop worrying.' She's such a worrywart sometimes."

"She is, isn't she?" I grin at the kid. "And you tell Diego that I'm going to need to talk to him first thing tomorrow, okay?"

He nods and goes into the building, and I walk back home. When I get there, I find Yulia sitting in the lounge chair in the library, her nose buried in a book.

"Hey, beautiful," I say, crossing the room. "What are you reading?"

She looks up. "*Gone Girl.*" She puts down the book and stands up. "I should probably go shower. I'm tired."

"Yulia." I catch her wrist as she tries to walk past me. "We have to talk."

She hesitates, then says, "All right, let's talk. Lucas" She draws in an unsteady breath. "You know this can't go on forever. Sooner or later, you and Esguerra will come to blows because of me, and I can't bear that. If anything happened to you—" Her voice breaks. "You have to let me go."

"No." I pull her toward me, my gut clenching at the mere suggestion. "I'm not letting you go."

"You have to." Her gaze turns imploring. "It's the only way."

"No, baby." I move my hands up to clasp her upper arms. "There's another alternative. We're going to leave together."

"What?" Yulia's lips part in shock. "What do you mean?"

"I'm going to oversee the expansion of Esguerra's organization," I explain. "There will be quite a bit of travel involved, so we won't be living here. We'll set up base somewhere in Europe or the Middle East—you can help me figure out exactly where."

Her eyes are impossibly wide as she stares up at me. "You want to leave here? But it's your home. What about—"

"I've lived here less than two years," I say, amused. "Another place can be home just as easily. This is Esguerra's estate, not mine."

"But I thought you liked it here."

"I do—but I'll like it elsewhere too." Moving one hand to her chin, I tilt her face up. "Anywhere you are will be my home, beautiful."

She exhales shakily. "But—"

"No buts." I press my thumb to her soft lips. "I'm not sacrificing anything, believe me. I'll be Esguerra's fifty-percent partner on these new ventures, so if all goes well, we'll get filthy rich."

"We?" she whispers when I take my thumb away.

"Yes, you and me." And before she can ask, I add, "We'll take your brother back to his parents. Things are quieting down in Ukraine, so it's safe for him to return. We'll visit him as often as you want, of course, and if he wishes to stay with us, that's also an option."

"Lucas…" Her forehead creases in a frown. "Are you sure about this? If you're doing it for me—"

"I'm doing it for us." Lowering my hands, I cup her ass and pull her against me, my cock hardening as I feel her legs press against mine. Holding her gaze, I say, "I want to know that you're safe, that no one will ever be able to take you away from me. You'll have the best bodyguards money can buy, men who are loyal to me and me only. We'll build a fortress of our own, beautiful—a place where you won't have to fear anyone or anything."

Yulia's palms press against my chest. "A fortress?" Her eyes gleam with hope and a strange kind of unease.

"Yes." I tighten my grip on her ass, enjoying the feel of her firm flesh even through the thick material of her shorts. Forcing my mind off the lust pounding in my veins, I clarify, "Nothing as extreme as Esguerra's compound, but a safe place of our own. Nobody will be able to touch you there."

"Except you," she murmurs, her slender hands fisting in my shirt.

"Yes." My lips twist into a dark smile. "Except me." She'll never be safe from me, no matter where she goes or what she does. I will protect her from everyone else, but I will never set her free.

"When…" She runs her tongue over her lips. "When are we leaving?"

"Soon," I say, my eyes following the movement of her tongue. "Maybe in a month or less."

And before my balls can explode, I reach for the zipper of her shorts and capture her lips in a deep, hungry kiss.

46

ulia

THE NEXT MONTH ZOOMS BY IN A FLURRY OF WORK AND DEPARTURE preparations. I continue operating the cafe, figuring the extra money can't hurt, though I do stop ordering new food supplies and limit the menu as various products run out. The cafe keeps me busy, which is good because Lucas works nonstop, frequently putting in eighteen- and twenty-hour days. In a span of four weeks, he trains Diego to oversee the guards on the compound, sets up manufacturing facilities in Croatia, finds clients for the weapons that will be made at those facilities, and purchases a house on the Karpass Peninsula in Cyprus —a country we settled on as our home base due to its warm climate, strategic proximity to Europe and the Middle East, and relatively high percentage of population fluent in either English or Russian.

"The house is on a cliff overlooking a private beach," Lucas says when he shows me photos of the new property. "It has only five bedrooms, but there's an infinity pool, a balcony on the second floor, and a fully equipped gym in the basement. Oh, and I'm having them remodel the kitchen, so it'll be done exactly to your specifications."

"It's beautiful," I say, looking through each photo. Though "only" five bedrooms, the house is large and spacious, with an open floor plan and floor-to-ceiling windows facing the Mediterranean. And most importantly for Lucas, it's set on ten acres of land that he intends to fence in and protect via bodyguards, guard dogs, and a variety of surveillance drones.

We *will be* living in a fortress—albeit a gorgeous, beachfront one.

It seems so surreal that I often feel the urge to pinch myself. The life Lucas is planning for us is like nothing I could've imagined when Esguerra's men came to extract me from that Moscow prison. I'm still Lucas's prisoner—the faint white marks where the trackers went in are a daily reminder of that—but the lack of freedom bothers me less nowadays. Maybe it's the needy little girl within me, but Lucas's fierce, unapologetic possessiveness reassures me almost as much as it frightens me.

I belong to him, and there's a comforting stability in that.

Of course, even if I could leave Lucas, I wouldn't. With every kiss, with every caring gesture big and small, my captor ties me to him a little tighter, makes me love him a little more. And though he doesn't say the words back, I'm increasingly certain that he loves me too, as much as a man like him is capable of loving anyone. What we have together is not normal, but neither are we. My "normal" ended with my parents' crash, and Lucas's may never have existed in the first place. But as I'm fast discovering, I don't need normal. My ruthless mercenary is giving me everything I've ever wanted, and when I stop to think about it, I'm seized by equal parts joy and fear.

Things are going so well I'm terrified something will happen to snatch it all away.

"Is everything okay?" Misha asks during dinner one day. Lucas is working late again, so it's just the two of us for the third night in a row. "You look worried."

"Do I?" Pushing my mushroom risotto away, I make a conscious effort to relax the tense muscles in my forehead. "I'm sorry, Mishen'ka. I'm just thinking, that's all."

Misha frowns over his quickly emptying plate. "What about?"

"This, that... the transition," I say with a shrug. "Nothing in particular." I don't want to tell my teenage brother that the future, though bright and shiny, scares me to the point of nightmares every night, that a cold, hard fist seems to be permanently lodged inside my chest, squeezing my heart every time I think of how fragile and fleeting happiness can be. Pushing the dark thought aside, I smile at Misha and say, "What about you? Are you excited about going home?"

"Yes, of course." Misha's face brightens as he reaches for a second serving of the risotto. "Lucas let me speak to my parents yesterday. Mom was crying, but they were happy tears, you know? And Dad is already planning all the things we're going to do together."

"Oh, that's wonderful." The knowledge of my upcoming separation from my brother is like an acid burn on my heart, but the joy in his eyes makes it all worthwhile. "How are they?"

Lucas showed me the surveillance photos taken of Misha's parents, and I can now picture them in my mind. Natalia Rudenko, Obenko's sister and Misha's adoptive mother, is a slim, stylish brunette who resembles her brother, while Misha's father, Viktor, is plump and balding—a typical middle-aged engineer. He's almost ten years older than his forty-something wife, and he looks it, but he has a kind face, and in many of the pictures I've seen, he gazes at his wife with a worshipful smile.

"They're good," Misha says. "Same, you know." His expression turns somber as he adds, "Mom's been grieving for Uncle Vasya, but Dad said she's doing better now. They've always known that his job was dangerous, so what happened wasn't a huge surprise. It helped that Lucas contacted them back then and told them I'm okay."

"Right." Lucas's message explained that I, Misha's long-lost sister, had come out of a long-term undercover assignment to take Misha someplace safe for a while. "So what did they say about that?"

"Well, they had a million questions, as you would expect, but for the most part, they were just relieved I'm returning home and"—he gives me a slightly bashful look—"going back to school."

I smile, more than a little relieved myself. It seems that the recent events have cooled some of my brother's enthusiasm for nontraditional career paths—at least for a while. "Will you have to take any extra classes to catch up?" I ask. It's already October, so Misha has missed at least a few weeks of ninth grade.

"No, I don't think so," he says, chowing down on the risotto. "We covered most of the subjects taught in school during UUR training."

"Oh, yes, that's right." I'd almost forgotten that the reason why I'd been able to start college at sixteen was because the curriculum for trainees had included math, science, history, and language studies at levels far beyond those taught to kids that age. "So you're more than caught up."

Misha nods, reaching for a cup of water next to his plate. "Yeah, I should be fine." He gulps down the water, and I study him, noticing again the leaner, harder lines of his face. With every day that passes, my baby brother grows up a little more, maturing right in front of my eyes. Soon, he won't be a boy at all, just like he's no longer the toddler of my memories.

My throat grows tight as I think again about him leaving. "I'm going to miss you," I say, trying not to sound as choked up as I feel. "A lot."

Misha puts down his cup. "I'll miss you too, Yulia." His expression is even more somber than before. "You'll come to visit, though, won't you?"

"Of course." Unable to sit still, I get up, swallowing the tears stinging the back of my throat. "We'll be just a three-hour flight away. Practically next door." At least when we're not traveling all over Europe, Asia, and the Middle East, as Lucas warned me we will have to. Pushing that knowledge aside, I say with forced brightness, "And you'll come visit us. During summers, school holidays, and such."

"Yeah, that's going to be great." Finishing his plate, Misha gets up too. "I'll be the envy of all my friends, vacationing in Cyprus like that."

"That's right." I smile, though all I want to do is cry. "You'll be the most popular boy in school."

"Oh, I was anyway," he says with a total lack of modesty. "So it's all good."

I laugh and walk around the table to hug him. He lets me, and even hugs me back, his sinewy arms sturdy and strong. When I pull away and look at him, I realize my baby brother has grown another couple of inches in the last month and get all choked up again.

"Oh, come on," Misha mutters as the tears I've been holding back spill out. Pulling me into another hug, he pats my back awkwardly. "Don't cry. Come on, it's going to be fine. We'll see each other often, and we'll email and Skype…"

"I know." I pull away and smile at Misha, wiping the wetness on my cheeks with the back of my hand. "It's just that I keep remembering how little you were, and now you're growing up so fast, changing into this young man…" I sniffle. "I'm sorry. I'm just being silly."

"Well, you are a girl," he says, scratching the back of his neck. "You're allowed, I guess."

I burst out laughing at that chauvinistic statement, and for the rest of the meal, we don't discuss the separation again.

ON THE AFTERNOON BEFORE OUR DEPARTURE, I THROW A BIG PARTY in Lucas's back yard, inviting all of my cafe's customers and anyone else who wants to come. Using the remaining food supplies, I make a variety of hors d'oeuvres and, with Lucas, Eduardo, and Diego's help, set up a couple of barbecue stations where I grill steaks, burgers, and lamb chops. Manning the grills is hot, sweaty work, but I feel elated as guard after guard comes up to me to say goodbye and express his gratitude for the gourmet meals.

"We're going to miss you here," one of the guards says gruffly. "Seriously, your cafe was the best food I've eaten."

"Thank you." I beam at him, then turn to smile at another guard who says something similar to me in Spanish. Most of these men are ex-soldiers of some kind, tough, scarred killers armed to the teeth, and to have them thank me like this touches me tremendously.

Of course, most guards here today are new recruits or those who didn't have friends among the victims of the crash, but I don't let that bother me. I know I'll never be fully accepted at Esguerra's estate—that's why we're leaving, after all—and to have so many people express regret at my departure is a gift beyond anything I could've expected.

"You're one lucky son of a bitch," a red-haired guard says to Lucas as I put a piece of medium-rare steak on his plate. "Seriously, man. Your girl's the best."

"I know," Lucas says and wraps a possessive arm around my waist. "Now move along, O'Malley. You're holding up the line."

After all the barbecue is eaten and the last of the hors d'oeuvres disappear off the plates, the party starts to wind down. Lucas leaves to get on yet another call with new suppliers, and Diego, Eduardo, and Misha carry the empty platters inside and collect all the trash. Exhausted, I go in to wash my hands, and when I come out, I see that all the guards are gone. Only one person is standing in the middle of Lucas's yard, her curvy figure clad in her usual black dress.

Stunned, I stare at the maid who helped me escape. "Rosa? What are you doing here?"

She casts a nervous glance at the house, where Misha and the two guards are still cleaning up, then says hesitantly, "Do you have a moment? I was hoping to talk to you alone."

I automatically scan her for weapons. Finding nothing suspicious, I say, "Okay, sure. Want to take a little walk?"

She nods and disappears into the trees. I follow, both curious and uneasy. I'm fairly certain she won't physically attack me, but I don't know what she's after and that makes me nervous. At the same time, I recall what Lucas told me about the events in Chicago, and sympathy tempers my wariness.

I may not know Rosa's motivations, but I certainly understand what she's been through.

When I catch up to Rosa, she stops and turns to face me. "Yulia, I..." She takes a breath. "I wanted to thank you for what you told Lucas. Nora said she spoke to you, but I wasn't sure if you'd do it or not."

"Well, Nora didn't leave me much choice," I say drily, recalling the petite girl's graphic threat. "But you're welcome. I assume you and Nora are both okay?"

Rosa nods, flushing. "Yes. I was under house arrest for a while, and I don't have access to those keys anymore, but Señor Esguerra reinstated my position in the main house a few weeks ago."

I smile, genuinely happy on her behalf. "Good, I'm glad. And I guess I should thank you for helping me that time. It was very nice of you—"

To my surprise, Rosa shakes her head. "It wasn't nice," she mutters. "It was stupid. *I* was stupid."

The smile dies on my lips. "What do you mean?"

Rosa's face is now dark red. "I had a crush on Lucas, and I thought that if you were gone..." Her hands twist in her skirt. "I'm sorry. I don't know what I was thinking. It was just that I wanted to believe that he was different. But then he was keeping you like that and—" She stops, pressing her lips together.

"And it was ruining the image you had of him," I say, finally beginning to understand. "You thought that if you let me go, you'd be doing something good while increasing your chances with the man you want." Seeing the stricken look on her face, I stop, then say gently, "Except he's not really the man you want, is he?"

"No." Her brown eyes darken. "He's not. He never was. I made up the man I wanted, and I pinned him on the nearest handsome face."

"Oh, Rosa..." Giving in to a sudden impulse, I step forward and give her hand a comforting squeeze. "Listen to me," I say softly. "You're going to find the right person for you, and he might not be whom you imagined, but you'll want him anyway, flaws and all. It won't be perfect, but it will be real, and you'll know it—you'll feel it. You'll both feel it."

She swallows thickly and pulls her hand away. "Is that what it's like for you and Lucas?"

"Yes," I say, and the truth of that sears through me. "It's not tender and pretty like I thought it would be. Some might even say it's ugly. But it's us. It's our reality, our version of perfect. And you will also have that one day—your own version of perfect. It might not be what you expect, or with whom you expect, but it *will* make you happy."

The girl's lips tremble for a second; then her face goes blank and she steps back. "You should go," she says, her hands once again playing with the skirt of her dress. "They'll be looking for you if you don't return soon."

"Right."

I'm about to turn and go back when Rosa says quietly, "Goodbye, Yulia. I wish you and Lucas all the best. I really do."

"Thank you—and the same to you," I say, but Rosa is already walking away, her black-clad figure melting into the greenery of the rainforest and disappearing out of sight.

47

ucas

I EXPECTED YULIA AND HER BROTHER TO SLEEP ON OUR FLIGHT TO Ukraine, but they spend the entire time talking. Whenever I stick my head out of the pilot's cabin to check on them, they're deep in conversation, and I go back, not wanting to intrude on their sibling time.

I'll have Yulia to myself soon enough.

When we approach Ukrainian airspace, I make contact with our men on the ground. Last week, they finally tracked down the last three known UUR associates and eliminated them as per my orders. To my disappointment, none of them were harboring Kirill, which means Yulia's former trainer is either completely off the grid or, as Yulia thought, the fucker ended up expiring from his injuries and we just haven't found his body. The latter possibility brings me little joy—I wanted to kill the bastard with my own hands—but it's better than the alternative. The men also tracked down the headmistress of Yulia's orphanage. The woman was already in jail for child abuse and trafficking, so I had to settle for sending in an assassin who cornered her in a bathroom and demonstrated just how much her victims suffered. The video of her death—all three hours of it—was the highlight of my Wednesday last week. Someday, I might show it to Yulia, but for now, I've decided not to, to avoid bringing back bad memories for her.

"You've been cleared to land," Thomas reports when I get him on the phone. I smile, satisfied that the bribe campaign we've been conducting is proving so effective. Despite the bloody war we've waged against UUR, most of Ukrainian bureaucrats are more than willing to look the other way—especially since Yulia's former agency was strictly off the books.

Nobody cares about a few officially nonexistent spies when fat checks are in play.

When we land at the private airport, there's an armored SUV waiting for us, and we go straight to Michael's parents' place. Thomas and two other guards ride along, while a dozen more of our men follow in other cars. I'm not expecting any trouble, but it's always good to be cautious when in hostile territory.

Bribes or not, Ukraine has little love for anyone connected to the Esguerra organization.

"Are you sure my brother will be safe?" Yulia asked me last night, and I assured her that thanks to our hacking and subsequent destruction of UUR's files, it's all but impossible to connect the adoptive son of two civilians to her, and by extension, to me and Esguerra. Just in case, though, I personally hired two bodyguards to watch over Michael and his family over the next few months. I don't think he's in danger, but I know how much the kid means to Yulia. And, to be honest, he's grown on me too. Yulia would probably be upset to hear this, but there's something about Michael that reminds me of myself at that age.

Vasiliy Obenko hadn't been entirely wrong to recruit him; the boy would've made an excellent agent had he completed his training.

On the ride from the airport, Yulia and Michael are both silent, and I know they're thinking of the upcoming separation. Theoretically, I could've hired more men to ensure Michael's safety and let him go home earlier, but I wanted to give Yulia more time with her brother, and I'm glad I did. The boy has come a long way from the defiant, sullen teenager who'd been fed lies about his sister. The two siblings are now as close as any I've seen, and I know that makes Yulia happy—which makes me happy in return.

If I could turn back the clock and wipe away all the pain in her past, I'd do it in a heartbeat. But since I can't, I have to settle for making sure she never has to suffer again.

She's mine, and I'm going to take care of her for the rest of our lives.

MICHAEL'S PARENTS LIVE ON THE FIFTH FLOOR OF AN APARTMENT building on the outskirts of Kiev. The two bodyguards I hired greet us at the entrance to the building and report that all is quiet. I thank them and give them the rest of the day off before instructing Thomas and the others to wait downstairs. There's no elevator, so Yulia, Michael, and I take the stairs.

Yulia walks a couple of steps ahead of me. She's wearing flat boots and stylish skinny jeans—both are her recent online purchases—and I can't tear my eyes away from her shapely ass, which flexes with every step she climbs.

"Dude, keep a lid on it for at least a few more minutes," Michael mutters, climbing the stairs next to me, and I shoot him a grin, not the least bit embarrassed that he caught me lusting after his sister.

"Why?" I reply in a low voice. "Your sister is hot. You didn't know that?"

"Ugh." He grimaces in disgust, and Yulia gives us a suspicious look over her shoulder.

"What are you guys talking about?" she asks as we clear the third-floor landing.

"Nothing," Misha says quickly, his face turning red. "Just guy stuff."

"Uh-huh." She gives us an exasperated look but doesn't press further, and we clear the remaining two flights in silence. I'm glad we don't run into any neighbors, because I have my M16 with me.

After what happened in Chicago, I don't go anywhere without a weapon.

When we reach the fifth floor, Yulia stops in front of apartment 5A and rings the doorbell.

My first hint that something is wrong is the white face of the trim, dark-haired woman who opens the door. It's Natalia Rudenko, Michael's adoptive mother—I recognize her hazel eyes from the surveillance photos. Instead of smiling and stepping forward to embrace her son, she swings the door wide and steps back, her lipsticked mouth trembling.

Instantly, I see why.

Wrapped around her stomach and partially concealed by the apron she's wearing is a tangle of wires and a black box with a blinking light.

"Mama?" Michael says uncertainly, stepping forward, and I instinctively grab his arm, yanking him back as I step in front of Yulia, shielding her from the bomb. My pulse jumps with a blast of adrenaline, terror and rage swamping me in a toxic shockwave.

Yulia, Misha, and a bomb.

Motherfucking fuck.

"It's okay, let the boy in," an accented male voice drawls in English. "He's not any safer out there than in here. There's enough to blow this whole building."

I don't move, though every instinct screams for me to rush in and attack, to protect Yulia and her brother. Only the knowledge that doing so means certain death for them keeps me still.

Calling upon all my years of battle experience, I block out the hammering beat of fear and assess the situation.

In addition to the woman, there are two men standing in the hallway. One of them, a portly, middle-aged man, is wired the same way as Michael's mother. I recognize his terrified face too. It's Viktor Rudenko, Michael's adoptive father. But he's not the one who holds my attention.

It's the massively built man standing behind him, his thin lips curled in a snarl of a smile.

Kirill Ivanovich Luchenko, the man we've been hunting.

He found us instead.

48

ulia

I'VE NEVER KNOWN TERROR THIS INTENSE, THIS ALL-CONSUMING. Lucas is a human wall in front of me, but I can see around his powerful body, and the surreal tableau makes my stomach drop to my feet.

Kirill is standing in the brightly lit hallway behind Misha's parents, who are wrapped in tangled wires. There's a gun in his right hand, and in his left, he's clutching something small and black.

A detonator, I realize with nauseating panic.

He's got his thumb on the detonator.

"Come on in," he says in English, looking at Lucas and Misha before focusing on me. A grotesque smile stretches his mouth as his gaze meets mine. "Make yourself at home. We're all one happy family here, aren't we?"

Lucas doesn't move a muscle, even when Misha tries to shove him aside, his young face contorted with the same terror that holds me paralyzed. I know what's going through my brother's mind; like me, he's probably seen this kind of detonator in explosives training.

It's UUR's version of a suicide vest, one designed to be used only in the most desperate of circumstances. Kirill doesn't need to press a button for the explosive to go off; he just needs to take his thumb *off* the button.

If his thumb slips—if he's shot, for instance—the bomb will be triggered.

Lucas must've realized this too, because he's not reaching for the M16 slung across his back.

"Let me through," my brother hisses when Lucas still doesn't budge. "It's my parents. Fucking let me through!"

This time, I'm the one to catch Misha's arm. "Don't," I say quietly, and he freezes in place. I don't know if my brother thinks I have a plan, or if it's the false calmness of my voice, but he stops shoving at Lucas and stands still, staring fixedly into the hallway.

"You don't want to come in?" Kirill says. "Fine, we can do it the hard way."

In a blur of motion, he lifts his right hand and fires. The shot is muffled—Kirill's gun has a silencer on it—but the screams that follow are unmistakable. I convulsively leap forward, terrified for Lucas, but he's still standing there, refusing to budge even as my brother renews his efforts to get into the apartment.

The bullet hit Misha's father in the leg, I realize as I peer around Misha's struggling figure. The older man is on the floor, screaming as he clutches his bleeding leg, and Misha's mother is kneeling next to him, weeping hysterically.

"The next bullet goes into his head," Kirill says, and Misha stills again. "And the one after that, into her brain." He waves the gun at the crying woman. "Oh, and if any of you try to run, I'm going to shoot both of them immediately, and the bombs will go off before you make it down a single flight of stairs." His smile widens as he takes in our expressions. "Like I said, come in and make yourself at home."

"Lucas, please," I whisper when he still doesn't move. Bile churns thickly in my throat. "Please, we have to do this. We can't let him kill them in front of Misha." I have no idea if Kirill is crazy enough to sacrifice himself by setting off the explosives, but I have no doubt he'll shoot Misha's parents without a second thought.

"You. Drop your weapon before you come in," Kirill says, gesturing at Lucas with the gun. "You don't want this to go off by mistake." He lifts his left hand—the one with the detonator—to illustrate exactly what he means.

Without saying a word, Lucas reaches for the strap of his M16 and drops the weapon on the floor. Then, just as silently, he steps into the hallway.

Misha and I follow. My brother's face is deathly pale, his eyes wild with fear. I have no doubt I look the same way. Terror is a hollow, icy pit in my stomach. When Kirill had captured me before, I'd been on my own, and I could escape into the dark corners of my mind. But there's no escape here, not when the only two people I love are in danger next to me—in danger *because* of me.

I know why Kirill is doing something so reckless and insane. He's after me. He wants to punish me for what I did to him, and he doesn't care who gets hurt in the process. Lucas is still in front of me, his body forming a shield between me and my former trainer, but he won't be able to save me.

We have the numbers advantage and men on the ground, but Kirill has his thumb on that detonator.

"Come here, bitch," my former trainer says, his gaze swinging toward me. His dark eyes glint with rage and something close to madness. "You're the one I want."

Ignoring the sickening terror twisting my insides, I step around my brother, pushing him behind me, but Lucas blocks my way.

"She's not going anywhere." His voice is lethal steel.

"No?" Kirill lifts his gun, pointing it at Viktor Rudenko's temple. The man freezes, his screams dying down, and Kirill's eyes cut back to me as Natalia's weeping grows in volume. "Don't make me repeat myself."

"Lucas, let me go." I try to squeeze past him, but the narrow hallway is stuffed with furniture, and I almost trip on a stool placed in front of a tall mirror. Chills of horror race up and down my spine as Kirill's jaw hardens at Lucas's uncompromising stance. Frantically, I grip Lucas's arm and try to push him aside. "Please, Lucas, let me through."

He ignores me. Every muscle in his body is locked tight, and when I glance at his face, the subzero fury in his pale eyes spikes my terror even more.

He's not going to listen to reason.

To protect me, he's going to let Misha's parents die—and get himself killed in the process.

"Why do you want her?" he asks Kirill, his tone incongruously calm. "You know you're going to die here today."

"Do I?" Kirill laughs, the sound oddly high pitched, and for the first time, I notice the changes in his appearance. His hair is now more gray than brown, his face is bloated, and the body that had always been hard muscle looks merely thick instead. It's as if he's aged ten years over the last few months. "And what makes you think I care?"

Lucas's expression doesn't change. "I know you don't. That's why you're here, aren't you? To go out in a blaze of glory rather than live like the pathetic half-man you've become?" Contempt seeps into his voice. "You should've just come to us from the beginning. I could've made it so much simpler for you, put you out of your dickless misery that much sooner."

What is Lucas doing? My heart pounds in horror as I watch Kirill's face contort with rage and his right hand come up, the gun pointing straight at Lucas's chest.

It's as if Lucas is trying to get himself shot.

And in the next instant, I realize that's exactly what he's doing. My captor is hoping to sacrifice himself and buy us some time. To do what, I'm not sure. We're on the fifth floor of a walk-up building. Even if the guards on the ground heard the shot—unlikely, given the silencer Kirill is using—they'd never get here in time. And even if they did, there'd still be the matter of explosives.

Regardless, even if Lucas does have a plan, I can't let him do this.

In a split second, I come up with the only solution I can.

"Oh, yeah, that's right," I say loudly. Behind me, I hear Misha suck in a breath, but I ignore him. "I almost forgot that I shot your balls and cock off," I continue, imbuing my tone with as much derision as I can. "What's that like, huh? Must be rough not being able to rape fifteen-year-olds."

The fury that twists Kirill's features is demonic. His bloated face turns a blotchy purple, and the gun swings toward me. Lucas moves to block me from Kirill's view, but I jump to the other side, exposing myself again.

I'm the one my former trainer wants. If I can get him to kill me, there's a chance the others might walk away.

"Go ahead," I taunt the man, jumping from side to side to avoid Lucas's attempts to shield me. "Shoot me like the coward you are, like the miserable slug that you've become." The words spill out of my mouth faster and faster. "Just look at yourself. The famous Kirill Luchenko, never defeated in combat. And what happened to you? Got your dick blown away. I bet that must've hurt. I bet you can't take a piss without crying like a baby. I wouldn't know how that feels, of course, but—"

The shot rings out, the noise deafening despite the silencer. Something slams into me, and I go flying.

My last thought is a desperate hope that Misha and Lucas survive.

49

ucas

Everything happens in an instant. The second the shot rings out, I'm already in motion, leaping at Kirill. I don't dare look back because if I see Yulia dead or dying, I'll lose the last shreds of my sanity, and I can't let that happen.

I have to save her brother.

We crash into the wall, and Kirill twists to protect the gun, but that's not what I'm after. With both hands, I grab his left fist and squeeze tight, forcing his fingers to remain closed and his thumb to stay on the detonator. At the same time, I pull back and slam into him again, twisting so that my shoulder hits his right arm. The gun clatters to the floor, but before I can celebrate my victory, he uses his bulk to push me back and smashes his right fist into my temple.

My vision goes dark for a second, my ears ringing, but I hang on to consciousness and force him back against the wall. The rage and grief boiling in my chest give me superhuman strength. *The motherfucker shot Yulia.* With a roar, I squeeze my fingers harder and hear his bones breaking. He bellows and swings his right fist at me, but I duck this time, keeping my hands locked around his left hand. Distantly, I'm aware that Michael's parents are scrambling to get out of the way, but I block out their panicked cries. The fight is happening with blurring speed; even a second of inattention could be fatal.

My ears ring and I taste blood as another blow connects with my jaw, but I move my leg in time to block Kirill's knee coming at my groin. Simultaneously, I jerk back to avoid a third blow and turn sideways to elbow him in the ribs. I hit him hard, but he doesn't even grunt this time. The bastard is built like a tank, and though his reflexes aren't as good as mine, he knows what he's doing. Under normal circumstances, it would've been a difficult fight, but with both of my hands squeezing his left fist, I'm at a severe disadvantage. I can't let go of his hand, however, because I'm certain he'll trigger that bomb.

At this point, all the fucker cares about is revenge, and he'll die to obtain it.

He raped Yulia at fifteen. He shot her.

The fury is like rocket fuel for my muscles. Spinning around, I slam the back of my head into his nose, crushing bone and cartilage, and before he can recover, I use my grip on his fist to swing him around and throw him against the opposite wall.

His eyes roll backward as his head hits the hard surface, but he manages to land a kick, his boot crashing straight into my kidney. My breath hisses out, my grip on his fist slackening for a moment, and he throws himself on the floor, dragging me along as I tighten my grip again. We collide and roll, and in the next moment I see what he was after.

The gun he dropped earlier.

He's grabbed it with his right hand, and he's aiming it straight at my head.

I see his finger start to tighten on the trigger, and things seem to slow. I register everything with vibrant clarity, as if my brain decided to take one last snapshot by sending my senses into overdrive. In that split second before I die, I see Kirill's victorious snarl, smell the rank sweat dripping down his face, and hear Michael's parents' screams at the back of the hallway. I also think of Yulia and how desperately I hope she survives.

I'd die a thousand deaths to keep her living.

The gun goes off with a deafening blast.

Only I don't die.

Instead, Kirill jerks with a scream, his right arm exploding into bloody bits. Stunned, I look up to see Michael holding my M16. The boy is panting, his pale face streaked with sweat and blood, and in the next instant, he squeezes the trigger again, releasing a round of bullets into Kirill's right shoulder.

Howling, Kirill kicks out at Michael, and I refocus on my opponent.

It's time to finish this thing.

Keeping my fingers locked tightly around Kirill's left fist, I slam my forehead into his bleeding nose, again and again, reveling in the crunch as I hammer the bone fragments into his brain. This isn't how I wanted the bastard to go, but it'll have to do.

When he's lying there unmoving, his face a bloody mess, I look up at Michael, my head throbbing. "Shoot his left arm," I order hoarsely, and the kid gets it right away.

Without hesitation, he unleashes another volley on the dead man's upper arm. The bullets cut the bone clean through. All I have to do is yank on the fist, and the arm separates from the body.

Ignoring the blood gushing from the stump, I climb to my feet, holding the severed appendage by the fist wrapped around the detonator. My heart thumps in a hollow, uneven rhythm as I turn toward the entrance. Behind me, Michael's mother is sobbing and his father is groaning in pain, but I don't give a fuck.

All I care about is Yulia.

She's lying unmoving amidst shards of broken mirror, her body crumpled like a rag doll's. Her long blond hair covers her face, but there's blood everywhere, all over her slim frame.

The hollowness in my chest spreads.

No. Fuck, no.

She can't be dead. She can't be.

"Yulia," I whisper, sinking to my knees beside her. I feel like I'm suffocating, like my lungs are collapsing in my ribcage. "Yulia, sweetheart…"

She doesn't move.

Numbly, I tighten my left hand around Kirill's fist, pressing down on the thumb to secure the detonator inside, and with my right hand, I reach for her. My fingers are drenched with Kirill's blood, and as I brush aside her hair, I have a sudden horrible feeling that I'm polluting her with my touch, that I'm destroying something pure and beautiful… an angel who doesn't belong in my ugly world.

Her lashes are brown half-moons on her pale cheeks, her mouth slightly parted. It's as if she's sleeping, except there's blood.

So much fucking blood.

"Yulia…" My hand shakes as I touch her face, leaving bloody fingerprints on her porcelain skin. The hollowness inside me expands, my very bones creaking under the pressure of the emptiness within. I can't picture a life without her. Fuck, I can't picture a single week without her. In a few short months, she's become my entire world. If she's dead, if she's gone… My fingers graze the side of her neck, feeling for her pulse, and I freeze, a violent shudder rippling through me.

There is a beat. A faint, but unmistakable beat.

"Yulia!" I bend down, gathering her against me with my free

arm. She's soft and warm, unmistakably alive. I feel the puffs of her breath on my neck, and my pulse roars with fierce joy.

She's alive.

My Yulia is alive.

For a moment, it's enough, but as my head clears, a new fear seizes me.

Why is she unconscious, and where did all the blood come from?

Lowering her to the floor, I frantically pat her down, looking for the bullet wound. She has numerous small cuts from the broken glass, and there's a bloody gash on the side of her head, but I don't see where the bullet went in.

"Is she okay?" Michael says, and I glance up to see him standing there. He's swaying on his feet, his face greenish white. For a moment, I think he's going to puke from the sight of the severed arm I'm still holding, but as I watch, he sinks to his knees next to me—or, more precisely, collapses to his knees.

Frowning, I start to reach for him and stop.

Blood is dribbling from under Michael's dark T-shirt.

"Misha?" Yulia croaks hoarsely, and I turn my head to see her eyelids open. As she focuses on us, horror crosses her face, and I know she's reached the same conclusion.

Her brother has been shot.

50

ulia

In the next ten minutes, everything seems to happen at once. There's blood everywhere: on Misha, who lies down beside me, on Lucas, around Kirill's mangled body, and on the severed arm Lucas is holding. A couple of meters away, Misha's father is groaning in agony, his leg bleeding uncontrollably, and Misha's mother is weeping and rushing back and forth between her wounded husband and son. Lucas's men—who must've heard the unsilenced gunshots—burst in, weapons ready, and Lucas starts barking orders at them. Within a minute, he has two men working on disarming the explosives, and two more trying to stem Misha's and his father's bleeding. I try to get up to help, but every time I move, a wave of nausea hits me and I have to lie down, my skull throbbing where I split my head open on the mirror. My frantic questions go unanswered in the chaos, but by the time we're back in the armored SUV and speeding toward a hospital, I piece together what happened.

It wasn't a bullet that slammed into me. It was my brother. Misha knocked me out of the way, pushing me headfirst into the mirror that shattered. In the process, he took the bullet meant for me. According to Lucas, it went through the fleshy part of his shoulder, knocking him down on top of me. It's mostly Misha's blood that covers me, though I also bled from my head injury and the glass cutting into my skin.

"He'll be fine," Lucas says for the fifth time as I reach for Misha, who's passed out in the backseat next to me. "He lost a good amount of blood, but we stopped the bleeding and he'll be okay. He saved us all. If he hadn't gotten my M16—" He breaks off, but a chill streaks down my spine as I fill in the unspoken words.

We'd come within seconds of dying, all of us. In one fell swoop, I could've lost my brother and the man who's become my entire life.

My hand trembling, I squeeze Misha's palm, and then I reach for Lucas, who's sitting on the other side of me.

Only he doesn't let me hold his hand. The minute I touch him, Lucas pulls me into his lap, wrapping me tightly in his embrace, and buries his face in my hair. I can feel the shudders wracking his big body, and I can no longer restrain myself.

Clutching him with all my strength, I cry.

I just hold Lucas and cry.

A local hospital takes care of Misha's and Viktor's gunshot wounds and the gash on my head, and then we fly to Switzerland to recuperate at a private clinic Lucas has used before. Misha's parents come with us, not wanting to be separated from their son despite their fear of me and Lucas.

I do my best to reassure them that they're safe, but I know that to them, we're scary strangers from a violent world—a world that invaded their lives in the most brutal way. What Kirill did, the way he terrorized them, left scars that will never go away.

Before that awful day, they knew what Natalia's brother did for his country, but they didn't truly understand it.

"We woke up that morning, and he was there, holding a gun on us," Natalia sobs as she tells us what happened. "He tied Viktor up and strapped the bomb to me, and then he did the same thing to him. We thought he was a terrorist—we thought we were going to die—but then he started talking about you and how he was waiting for you, and that's when we realized what he was really after..." She breaks down in hysterics at that point, and Lucas has to call a nurse for a sedative to calm her down.

Viktor—Misha's adoptive father—is in a similar state, though he tries to put on a brave face for his wife. Whenever Natalia starts to cry, he comforts her, telling her that he's fine, but the nurses told me that he himself wakes up screaming from nightmares.

The bullet that entered Viktor's leg shattered his kneecap, and he may never again walk without a limp.

The only bright spot in the whole mess is that Misha's shoulder wound has indeed turned out to be as clean as Lucas said. My brother lost a lot of blood, but the doctors promised that he'll be back on his feet—albeit with an arm sling—within a week.

While we recuperate, Lucas's men tear apart Rudenkos' apartment to figure out how Kirill got in unseen, and what they find gives us all pause. It turns out that Misha's parents' new apartment —where they had been relocated after I returned—had originally been a UUR safe house. As such, it had a secret apartment concealed behind the living room wall—a place stocked with medical supplies, ammunition, and enough food to last for several months. It was there that Kirill must've gone to heal when he escaped from the black site. How he survived the trip and concealed his tracks will always be a mystery, but judging from the state of the apartment, he'd been hunkered down there the entire time we'd been searching for him. Misha's parents swear they had no idea he was there, and after questioning them extensively, Lucas decides they're telling the truth.

Apparently, they heard noises in their living room several times, but chalked them up to strange acoustics of their new apartment building.

"I thought it was a ghost," Natalia Rudenko whispers, her eyes red and swollen in her pale face. "Viktor told me I was being an idiot, and I shut up. But I should've listened to my instincts. I'll never forgive myself for what happened."

Lucas starts to fire another question at her, but I stop him by laying my hand on his arm. The poor woman is in no state for further interrogation. "It's not your fault," I assure her gently. "Kirill was a seasoned agent. If he wanted to stay hidden, you didn't stand a chance."

"That's what Viktor said, but still, I should've known." Squeezing her eyes closed, she pinches the bridge of her nose with trembling fingers. "There were little clues, like our computer getting hacked that time, and a few things seeming to get moved on occasion..."

Secretly, I agree that she should've found those things suspicious—I certainly would have—but she's a civilian, and I'm not. Regular people aren't trained to look for those types of patterns, and even though Natalia wasn't a complete stranger to the shadowy world of intelligence organizations, she couldn't have imagined that a secret agent would be hiding in her apartment.

"The hacking of the computer must be how Kirill learned we were coming," Lucas says grimly, and I nod in agreement. I don't know if my former trainer used Rudenkos' apartment because it was the best hiding spot, or because he suspected I might return with Misha one day, but either way, he was well positioned to strike when we least expected it.

The guards were keeping watch for danger from the outside, but the enemy had been inside all along.

To my relief, Misha seems far less traumatized than his parents. I don't know if it's his UUR training or what he's already lived through during Lucas's attack on the black site, but my brother is recovering quickly in more ways than one. Far from being distraught and remorseful about his role in Kirill's death, Misha seems proud that he got to participate in the takedown of the man who hurt me and nearly killed his parents.

"I'm glad I got to shoot the bastard," he says fiercely when Lucas and I visit his bedside. "It's the least he deserved."

"You did well, kid," Lucas says, patting his uninjured shoulder. "Your hands didn't even shake when you shot off his arm."

I wince at the graphic imagery, but Misha just nods, accepting the praise as his due. He and Lucas appear to be on the same wavelength now, as if fighting Kirill together brought them closer. I like that development, but it does disturb me to see my fourteen-year-old brother being so casual about a man's gruesome death.

"And why should he be upset?" Lucas says when I mention my concern to him later that evening in our private hospital room. "He's old enough to understand that you have to do what's necessary if you want to survive and protect those you care about. The kid's growing up, and whether you want to admit it or not, he's not a delicate flower."

"Neither is he a remorseless killer—or at least he shouldn't be," I retort, but Lucas just sits down on the edge of the bed and picks up my hand. His gaze is hard and shuttered, but his grip is gentle. He's been this way, caring yet distant, ever since we got to this clinic, and no matter how much I try, I can't figure out why he does nothing more than cuddle me at night.

The doctors cleared me for sex the day before yesterday, but Lucas still hasn't touched me.

"Sweetheart," he murmurs, squeezing my hand lightly, "your brother is not like you. He never was, and never will be. It was his choice to join UUR, and whether you want to admit it or not, he belonged there more than you ever did."

The conviction in Lucas's voice distracts me from the puzzle of his behavior. Frowning, I say, "I don't think so. Misha probably imagined it would be glamorous, being a spy and all. I'm sure that's why he joined: so he could play at being James Bond. But when he saw what it was really like—"

"He still wanted it," Lucas says quietly. "Or wants it, I should say."

Struck, I stare at him. "What do you mean? He's going back to school."

"He is—but only to make you and his parents happy."

"What? How do you know that?"

Lucas sighs, his thumb stroking the inside of my palm. "He told me. Yesterday. He wants to come work for me when he's older, but for now, he thinks it's a good idea to finish civilian school so he could 'blend better into the general population.'" He pauses, then adds softly, "Those are his words, not mine."

"I see." Pulling my hand from his grasp, I get up, my temples throbbing with a headache that has nothing to do with the half-healed gash across my skull. I should be surprised, but I'm not. On some level, I already knew this.

Like Lucas, my brother is drawn to danger, and he'll eventually embrace this kind of life.

The pain creeps up on me; it's just a faint ache at first, but with every second, it grows stronger, welling up until it chokes me from within. My throat constricts, and I feel myself start to hyperventilate, frantically sucking in air to fill my stiff and empty lungs. A hoarse sob bubbles up, followed by another and another, and then Lucas is on his feet next to me, drawing me into his embrace as raw, ugly sounds tear from my throat. It feels like I'm cracking inside, like I'm crumbling into bits. I try to stop, to control myself, but the sobs just keep on coming.

"Yulia, sweetheart, it's okay... Everything's going to be okay." Lucas's arms are around me, holding me tight, and the knowledge that he's here, that I'm no longer alone, opens the dam even more.

The tears pour out, burning and cleansing at the same time, a toxic flood that destroys and renews at once.

I cry for my brother's future and our past, for all the lies and losses and betrayals. I cry for what might've been and what has come to pass, for the cruelty of fate and its incongruous mercy.

I cry because I can't stop, and because I know I don't have to.

I trust Lucas to hold me as I break, to lend me his strength when I need it most.

Somehow we end up back on the bed, with me curled in his arms as he rocks me on his lap, cradling me like I'm the most precious thing in his world. And still I cry. I cry until my throat is raw and torn, until my agony drowns in exhaustion. I'm only half-aware when Lucas lays me down and removes my clothes, and by the time he slides in beside me, I'm asleep.

Asleep and purged of all my fears.

I WAKE UP TO FIND LUCAS SITTING ON THE EDGE OF THE BED, watching me. Instantly, the recollection of last night comes to me, and I flush, remembering my inexplicable breakdown.

"I'm sorry," I mutter, clutching the blanket to my chest as I sit up. "I don't know what came over me."

Lucas doesn't move. "You have nothing to be sorry for, baby." Despite the reassuring words, his gaze is inscrutable, his expression still closed off and distant. "You were due for a good cry."

"Yes, well, I had one, that's for sure." Feeling embarrassed, I slide from under the blanket and grab a robe, then slip into the adjoining bathroom to take a quick shower and brush my teeth before the nurses make their morning rounds.

When I come out, I see Lucas still sitting on the bed, unmoving. The bruises on his face—the mementos of his fight with Kirill—are faded now, and with the morning light spilling across his hard, masculine features, he resembles a warrior's statue more than a living, breathing human being. Only his eyes belie that impression; sharp and clear, they track my every movement the way a big cat watches its prey.

My breath catches, and I find myself walking toward him, my legs carrying me to the bed almost against my will.

When I'm next to him, he curls his hand around my wrist, pulling me down to sit next to him.

"Lucas..." I stare at him, feeling strangely nervous. "What are you—"

"Shh." He presses two fingers against my lips, his touch incredibly gentle. His eyes burn into mine, and to my shock, I see a dark shadow of agony in his pale gaze. "I'm only going to say it once, and I want you to listen," he says quietly, lowering his hand. "I've deposited some money into your account—about two million to start. Later, I'll add more, but that should be enough to get you settled in the beginning. Of course, if you ever need anything, you and Michael can always come to me—"

"What?" I reel back, certain I misheard. "What are you talking about?"

"Let me finish." His jaw is rigid. "I will also provide you with a set of bodyguards," he continues, his voice growing more strained with each word. "Their job will be to protect you, but I expect you to be smart and not do anything to endanger yourself. If you have to fly somewhere, I'll send someone to take you, and I'll personally oversee the security perimeter around your new house. Also—"

"Lucas, what are you talking about?" Shaking, I jump to my feet. "Is this some kind of joke?"

"Of course not." He stands up, his muscles all but vibrating with tension. "You think this is easy for me? Fuck!" He spins around and starts to pace, his every movement filled with barely controlled violence.

Stunned, I watch him for a couple of moments; then the neurons in my brain start to fire. Stepping forward, I catch his arm, feeling the coiled strength within. "Lucas, are you—" I swallow thickly. "Does this mean you're letting me leave?"

His eyes narrow dangerously. "What else would it fucking mean?"

My heart thuds heavily as I drop my hand. "But why? Is it this?" Self-consciously, I touch the narrow strip of shaved hair on my head, where the stitches from the gash are visible despite my best attempts to hide them. Like Lucas's, the bruises on my face are almost gone, but the scars from the broken glass are not. They're healing—the doctors assured me they'll be all but invisible one day—but for now, I'm far from beautiful, and it suddenly dawns on me that Lucas's distance may have a very obvious cause.

His desire for me has cooled.

"What?" Incredulity fills his voice as his eyes follow the movement of my hand. "Are *you* fucking joking? You think I don't want you because of this wound?"

"You didn't touch me last night." I know I sound like an insecure schoolgirl, but I can't help it. Lucas is a highly sexual man, and for him to forego a chance to fuck me…

"Of course I didn't touch you," he says through clenched teeth. "You're still healing, and I— Fuck." He twists as if to turn away again, but stops himself. Reaching over, he grips my arm. "Yulia… If I'd touched you, if I'd taken you again, I wouldn't have been able to do this, do you understand?" His voice roughens. "I'd keep you with me like the selfish bastard I am, and you'd never get a chance to leave."

All breath exits my lungs. "No, I don't understand. If you still want me, then why are you doing this?"

"Because you don't belong in this world… *my* world. They forced you into this life, made you into someone you never wanted to become. When I saw you lying there, hurt and bleeding—" He breaks off, then says raggedly, "You should've never been in that kind of danger, never met men like Kirill and Obenko…" He takes a deep breath. "Men like me."

I stare at him, a strange ache unfurling deep inside my chest. "Lucas, you're not—"

"Yes, I am." His hard mouth twists. "Let's not pretend. I'm like *them*—the men who hurt you and used you and manipulated you. You never had a choice about it all, and I didn't give you one either. I took you for my own because I wanted you, and I kept you because I couldn't picture a life without you. When you escaped, I would've torn the world apart looking for you, beautiful. I would've done anything to get you back."

A tingle ripples down my spine. "So why are you letting me go?" I whisper, my heart beating erratically. Could it be? Is Lucas—

"Because I can't bear to lose you," he says harshly. "When I saw you lying there, covered in blood, I thought you were dead. I thought he'd killed you." A visible shudder ripples over Lucas's skin before he steps closer, his hands moving up to grip my shoulders. Leaning in, he says with barely controlled fury, "What the fuck were you thinking anyway, taunting the bastard like that? You should've stayed quiet, let me—"

"Let you get shot?" Everything inside me recoils at the mere notion. "I would never. He was after me, not you or Misha—"

"So you tried to sacrifice yourself for us, like you've been doing for your brother all along? Did you really think there was a chance in hell I'd let you do that?" His fingers dig into my shoulders, but before I can so much as wince, his grip eases and his harsh expression softens. "Yulia," he whispers hoarsely, "don't you know that I'd take a thousand bullets, die a hundred deaths before I let anything hurt you?"

My pulse lurches. "Lucas…"

"You're my reason for existing now." His eyes glitter fiercely. "You're my everything. I want you in my bed, but I want you in my life even more. It's been that way from the very beginning. Even when I hated you, I loved you. If you were gone—"

"You love me?" My lungs seize as I latch on to those words. I'd suspected, hoped—I even told myself I knew—but up until he said it, I hadn't been certain. For Lucas to finally admit this…

"Of course I love you." His hands move up to frame my face, his big palms warm on my skin. Gazing down on me, he says roughly, "I've loved you from the moment I saw Diego carry you off that plane, thin and dirty and so gorgeous it made my chest hurt. I told myself it was only lust, pretended I could fuck you out of my system, but I ended up falling for you even more, wanting you more each day. Your loyalty, your bravery, your warmth—it was everything I never knew I needed. Before you came into my life, I didn't have anyone, didn't care about anyone, and I was fine that way. But when I met you…" He inhales. "Fuck, it was like I saw the sun for the first time. You made my world so much brighter, so much fuller…"

My throat is so tight I can barely speak. "So then why—"

"Because you were made for love and family, for pretty things and soft words." Pain laces his voice as he drops his hands. "You should've been adored by your parents and brother, worshipped by loving boyfriends and loyal friends, and instead—"

"And instead I fell for you." Reaching for him, I grip his powerful hand. Tears blur my eyes as I stare up at my ruthless captor, the man who's now *my* everything. "I fell in love with the man who saved me from Kirill and the Russian prison, who nursed me back to health and gave me my brother back. Lucas…" I curve my palm around his hard jaw. "You might be like them, but you've always given me more than you've taken. Always."

He stares at me, and I see the growing frustration on his face. "Yulia…" His voice is low and lethal. "If you're going to walk away, tell me now. I'm giving you this one chance, do you understand?"

"I do." A smile trembles on my lips as I lower my hand. "I understand."

His muscles coil, as though bracing for a blow. "And?"

"And I'm staying."

For a second, Lucas is still, as if frozen in disbelief, and then he's on me, his lips devouring me with a hunger that's both violent and tender. His hands roam over my body, his touch rough yet restrained, cognizant of my healing injuries. We tumble backward on the bed, our mouths fused together and our hands ripping at each other's clothes. Somewhere out there are nurses and doctors, my brother and his adoptive parents, the whole entire world, but here, in this private room, it's just us and the heat burning brighter with each moment.

"I love you," I gasp as Lucas thrusts into me, and he whispers the words back, his voice raspy and thick as he moves inside me, claiming me over and over again. We come together, our bodies shattering in perfect symphony, and as we lie tangled in the aftermath, Lucas holds my gaze. In his eyes are lust and possessiveness, hunger and need, and underneath it all, the warm tenderness of love.

In a few minutes, the nurses will come, and our little bubble will break. We'll work on healing and moving on, on building our new life and settling into our new home. For now, however, we don't need to worry about what the future holds.

What Lucas and I have together will never be pretty, but it's perfect.

Our own version of perfect.

BONUS EPILOGUE: NORA & JULIAN

APPROXIMATELY 3 YEARS LATER

SPOILER ALERT: If you haven't read the *Twist Me* trilogy, please stop and read that first (click HERE to get the book). What follows is for those of you who loved Nora & Julian's story and asked for a glimpse of their future beyond the epilogue of *Hold Me (Twist Me #3)*. Oh, and it gives a peek at Lucas & Yulia's future too.

~

Julian

NORA'S SCREAM ECHOES OFF THE WALLS, THE TORMENTED SOUND flaying me open. I lean against the door frame, shaking from the effort it takes to remain still and not attack the white-coated buzzards hovering over my wife. My shirt is soaked with sweat, and my hands flex convulsively at my sides, the urge to protect Nora battling with the knowledge that I'd only get in the doctors' way.

The baby is two weeks early, and I've never felt so fucking useless in my life.

"Do you want me to get you anything?" Lucas asks quietly, and I realize he came up from the hallway to stand next to me. "Water, coffee... a shot of vodka?" His expression is uncharacteristically sympathetic.

"I'm fine." My voice is like a rasp of sandpaper over wood, and I clear my throat before continuing. "They said it's not long now. That's why they've tapered off the epidural."

Lucas nods. "Right. I've been reading up on it."

"Oh?" The bizarre statement—and momentary absence of screams from Nora—awakens a twinge of curiosity. "Are you and Yulia...?"

"No, not yet, but Yulia's been talking about it ever since the wedding." He exhales audibly. "I was thinking it wouldn't be so bad, but now that I've seen this—"

"Julian!"

Nora's agonized cry cuts off whatever he was going to say next, and I forget about everything, all but leaping across the room in response to her call.

"Mr. Esguerra, please, you have to step back—"

"She needs me," I snarl at the doctor blocking my path. If he wasn't the best obstetrician in the Swiss clinic, he'd already be dead. Shoving the idiot aside, I step forward to grip Nora's trembling hand. Her palm is slippery with sweat, but her fingers curl around mine with startling strength, her knuckles turning white as her towering belly ripples with another contraction. Her small face is a twisted mask of pain, her eyes scrunched shut, and my chest heaves with helpless fury as another scream rips from her throat. I'd give anything to trade places with her, to take this pain from her, but I can't, and the knowledge shreds me into pieces.

"I'm here, baby." My voice is hoarse, my free hand unsteady as I reach over to brush the sweat-soaked hair off her forehead. "I'm here for you."

Nora opens her eyes, and my heart clenches as her gaze meets mine and she attempts a reassuring smile. "It's okay," she pants.

"It'll be fine. I just need to—" But before she finishes speaking, her face contorts again, and I hear the doctors yelling, telling her to push, to bear down. Nora's hand tightens around mine with unbelievable force, her delicate fingers almost crushing the bones in my palm, and her whole body seems to go into a massive spasm, her head arching back with a scream that cuts me like a thousand knives. Her agony shatters me, ripping away all pretense at calm and reason. Red mist edges my vision, blood pounding loudly in my temples, and I know I won't be able to bear this much longer.

Holding Nora's hand, I turn and roar at the doctors, "Fucking help her! Now!"

But none of them are paying attention to me. All three doctors are clustered at the foot of the bed where a sheet is shielding Nora's lower body from view. I see one of them bending and then...

"There she is!" The doctor who blocked my path earlier straightens, holding something small, wriggling, and bloody. He turns away, working with quick, efficient movements, and in the next instant, an infant's cry pierces the air. It's weak and uncertain at first, but soon, it gains strength. The shock of that high-pitched, demanding sound is like a percussive wave from an explosion, stunning me into paralysis. When I finally manage to turn my head to look at Nora, I realize that her hand is limp in mine, her features no longer contorted in agony. She's crying instead, and laughing at the same time, and then she pulls her hand away and reaches for the baby the doctor is handing to her—the tiny, wriggling creature whose cries are growing in volume.

"Oh my God, Julian," she sobs as the doctor places the newborn into her arms and raises the bed to a half-sitting position. "Oh God, just look at her..." She cradles it against her chest, her hospital gown falling open to reveal one pregnancy-swollen breast, and as I gape in mute shock, the little thing begins to root at the breast, its pink mouth opening and closing several times before it latches on to Nora's nipple.

No, not *it*. She. Our daughter.

Nora and I have a daughter. One who's nursing at her breast like a pro.

My vision narrows, the sounds of the hospital fading away. A nuclear bomb could've gone off next to us, and I wouldn't have noticed. All I see, all I'm aware of is my beautiful, precious pet, her tangled hair falling forward in a dark cloud as she leans over the nursing baby. Mesmerized, I step closer, trying to make out all the details, and my pulse takes on a strangely audible beat. It's like I'm listening to someone else's heartbeat through a stethoscope. *Thu-thump.* A tiny fist kneads the softness of Nora's plump breast. *Thu-thump.* The little mouth works industriously, small cheeks hollowing out with every sucking motion. *Thu-thump.* The hair on the tiny head is dark and downy, as soft-looking as her lightly golden skin.

"What color are her eyes?" I whisper when I can speak, and Nora lets out a shaky laugh, glancing up at me.

"What color do you think?" Her face is glowing with tenderness. "Blue, like yours."

Like mine. The words sear through me. I don't really care about the color of her eyes—many babies' eyes change as they get older—but knowing that this tiny being is mine, that she's *my* daughter, takes my breath away. My hand shakes as I reach forward and gently touch one tiny foot, my fingers shockingly huge next to the baby's minuscule toes. It seems impossible that something so little can exist; she looks like a doll… a living, breathing human doll.

My Nora in miniature, only infinitely more vulnerable and fragile.

My chest constricts, and I yank my hand away, sudden irrational fear flooding my mind. Is it normal for a newborn to be so little? She *is* two weeks early. What if I hurt that tiny foot by touching it? Looking up, I pin the doctor with a deadly glare. "Is she—"

"She's healthy," the doctor reassures me with a smile. "A little on the small side at two-point-seven kilograms, but perfectly normal."

"She *is* perfect," Nora murmurs, gazing down at the baby with a love so consuming and absolute that my breath leaves my lungs again.

My wife. My child. My family.

My vision blurs for a moment, my eyes stinging, and I have to blink to clear away the watery veil. I haven't cried since I was a small child, but if I'm remembering the sensations correctly, this burning behind my eyes means I'm on the verge.

"Come here," Nora whispers, glancing up at me again, and I step closer, unable to help myself. Slowly, I lift my hand and stroke the baby's head with one finger, everything inside me going still as the baby releases Nora's nipple and blinks up at me. Nora had been right, I register in the split second before her tiny face scrunches up angrily.

She does have blue eyes.

Opening her mouth, my daughter lets out a bellow, and Nora laughs before helping the baby find her nipple again. Instantly, the little creature quiets, sucking industriously, and I lower my hand, staring at the wonder of it all.

"What do you want to call her?" I ask in a hushed tone as the baby continues to feed. Because of Nora's miscarriage three years ago, we agreed not to name the baby until she was actually here, but I suspect my pet has given it some thought on her own.

Sure enough, Nora looks up at me and smiles. "How about Elizabeth?"

A bittersweet ache squeezes my chest. "For Beth?"

"For Beth," Nora confirms. "But I think we can call her Liz—or Lizzy. Doesn't she look like a Lizzy?"

"She does." I brush my fingers across the downy head. "She very much does."

~

NORA AND THE BABY FALL ASLEEP, BOTH WORN OUT BY THEIR ordeal, and I step out of the room to grab a bottle of water and stretch my legs. To my surprise, when I get to the end of the hallway, I see two blond heads bent together in the waiting area.

Lucas's wife—the Ukrainian girl who was involved in the crash—is with him.

As I approach, Yulia glances in my direction. Instantly, she leaps to her feet, her pale face turning even whiter. Lucas gets to his feet as well, stepping protectively in front of her.

I let out a sigh. I promised Lucas I won't hurt her, but he still doesn't trust me around her, even though Nora and I went to their wedding in Cyprus last year. I don't blame him for his overprotectiveness—usually, the mere sight of the former spy makes my blood pressure rise—but today, I'm not in the mood for conflict.

I'm too overjoyed to care about anything but Nora and our daughter.

Lizzy, I remind myself.

Nora and Lizzy.

My heart seizes. *I have a daughter named Lizzy.*

"Congratulations," Yulia says softly, gripping her husband's arm, and I realize she's talking to me. "Lucas and I are very happy for you."

To my surprise, I feel a weary smile tugging at my lips. "Thanks," I say, and mean it. I'll never forgive the girl for nearly killing me and endangering Nora as a result, but over the years, my fury at her has cooled to a tepid simmer. She makes Lucas happy, and Lucas makes me a lot of money on the new ventures, so I no longer fantasize about skinning her alive.

"How is Nora?" Lucas asks, sliding his arm around Yulia's slender waist and pulling her toward him. "She must be exhausted."

"She is. She fell asleep right after her video calls with her parents, Rosa, and Ana. They were all upset that they couldn't make it here in time, but they understood that the baby had her own timeline." Exhaling, I run a hand through my hair. "Nora is sleeping now, and so is Lizzy."

"Lizzy?" Yulia says, and I see her pretty face soften. "That's a beautiful name."

"Thanks. We like it." I love it, actually, but I'm not about to bond with Lucas's wife over baby names. Tolerance—as in, not killing her on the spot—is as far as I'm willing to go.

Turning my attention to Lucas, I say, "Thanks for flying out on such short notice and pulling the men off that Syria project. Things have been pretty quiet lately, but extra security never hurts." Especially where my wife and daughter are concerned. I picture Lizzy in danger, and my insides turn to dry ice.

I'm going to get the trackers on her as soon as the doctors allow it, and hire an extra dozen bodyguards to watch her at all times. If she so much as pricks her little finger, her security team will answer to me.

"No problem," Lucas says. "We were on our way to London anyway, for the opening of Yulia's new restaurant. Michael is already waiting for us there."

Ah, so that's why Yulia is here. I was wondering why Lucas brought her. If I recall correctly, this will be the fourth restaurant that Lucas's wife lends her brand and recipes to—an interesting business for a former spy.

"Anyways," Yulia says, giving me a wary look, "we didn't mean to hold you up. You probably have to return to Nora and the baby."

"I do," I say, not bothering to deny it. I'm still in a good mood, however, so I add, "If I don't see you again, good luck on your opening."

And without waiting for a reply, I continue heading down the hallway.

~

I'M GIVING NORA A FOOT RUB—THE ONLY PHYSICAL CONTACT allowed for now—when the nurses bring the baby back for a feeding. Lizzy is screaming like a banshee, but the moment she's placed in Nora's arms, she goes quiet and begins to root for a nipple. I watch, mesmerized, as her tiny mouth finds its target, and she begins to suck. Nora croons to her, stroking her softly, and I just stare, unable to look away. My beautiful pet is a mother—the mother of my baby. I didn't think it was possible for me to feel more possessive of Nora, but I do. She belongs to me on a whole different level now, and seeing her like this brings out emotions I never thought myself capable of feeling. It's as if my whole life has been leading up to this—to my wife and child, to this terrifyingly incandescent joy.

"Do you want to hold her?" Nora murmurs when the baby releases her nipple, and I freeze, all my muscles locking tight. I've faced terrorists and drug lords, dealt with generals and heads of state, and I've never been this intimidated.

"Are you sure?" My voice comes out strained. "You don't think I might hurt her?"

"No." Nora's soft lips curve in a smile. "Here you go." Carefully, she hands me the baby, and I do my best to hold her the way Nora did, settling her in the crook of my arm while supporting her little head with my hand. Lizzy is unbelievably light, a tiny, warm bundle of sweet-smelling baby, and as I watch, she blinks at me again and closes her eyes.

"She's sleeping," I whisper in amazement. "Nora, she's sleeping in my arms."

"I know," Nora whispers, and I look up to see her smiling even as tears roll down her cheeks. "The two of you... God, I could've never imagined this."

"Me neither." Careful not to jostle Lizzy, I clasp Nora's delicate fingers in my free hand and bring them to my lips. Kissing her knuckles, I murmur, "I love you, baby, so much."

Nora's lips quiver in a smile. "And I love you, Julian."

We sit and watch our daughter sleeping, and I know it's just the beginning.

Our real story is about to unfold.

AFTERWORD

Thank you for reading! If you would consider leaving a review, it would be greatly appreciated.

If you enjoyed *Capture Me,* you might enjoy these other books by Anna Zaires:

- *Twist Me: The Complete Trilogy* – Julian & Nora's story
- *Tormentor Mine* – Peter's story
- *The Mia & Korum Trilogy* – A dark sci-fi romance
- *The Krinar Captive* – A standalone sci-fi romance

Collaborations with my husband, Dima Zales:

- *Mind Machines* – An action-packed technothriller
- *The Mind Dimensions Series* – Urban fantasy
- *The Last Humans Trilogy* – Dystopian/post-apocalyptic science fiction
- *The Sorcery Code* – Epic fantasy

If you'd like to be notified when the next book is out, please sign up for my new release email list at www.annazaires.com.

And now please turn the page for a little taste of *Tormentor Mine.*

EXCERPT FROM TORMENTOR MINE

Author's Note: *Tormentor Mine* is the first book in Peter's dark romance series. The following excerpt is from Peter's POV.

~

He came to me in the night, a cruel, darkly handsome stranger from the most dangerous corners of Russia. He tormented me and destroyed me, ripping apart my world in his quest for vengeance.

Now he's back, but he's no longer after my secrets.

The man who stars in my nightmares wants me.

~

"Are you going to kill me?"

She's trying—and failing—to keep her voice steady. Still, I admire her attempt at composure. I approached her in public to make her feel safer, but she's too smart to fall for that. If they've told her anything about my background, she must realize I can snap her neck faster than she can scream for help.

"No," I answer, leaning closer as a louder song comes on. "I'm not going to kill you."

"Then what do you want from me?"

She's shaking in my hold, and something about that both intrigues and disturbs me. I don't want her to be afraid of me, but at the same time, I like having her at my mercy. Her fear calls to the predator within me, turning my desire for her into something darker.

She's captured prey, soft and sweet and mine to devour.

Bending my head, I bury my nose in her fragrant hair and murmur into her ear, "Meet me at the Starbucks near your house at noon tomorrow, and we'll talk there. I'll tell you whatever you want to know."

I pull back, and she stares at me, her eyes huge in her pale face. I know what she's thinking, so I lean in again, dipping my head so my mouth is next to her ear.

"If you contact the FBI, they'll try to hide you from me. Just like they tried to hide your husband and the others on my list. They'll uproot you, take you away from your parents and your career, and it will all be for nothing. I'll find you, no matter where you go, Sara… no matter what they do to keep you from me." My lips brush against the rim of her ear, and I feel her breath hitch. "Alternatively, they might want to use you as bait. If that's the case—if they set a trap for me—I'll know, and our next meeting won't be over coffee."

She shudders, and I drag in a deep breath, inhaling her delicate scent one last time before releasing her.

Stepping back, I melt into the crowd and message Anton to get the crew into positions.

I have to make sure she gets home safe and sound, unmolested by anyone but me.

~

Tormentor Mine is available everywhere. If you'd like to find out more, please visit my website at www.annazaires.com.

ABOUT THE AUTHOR

Anna Zaires is a *New York Times, USA Today,* and #1 international bestselling author of sci-fi romance and contemporary dark erotic romance. She fell in love with books at the age of five, when her grandmother taught her to read. Since then, she has always lived partially in a fantasy world where the only limits were those of her imagination. Currently residing in Florida, Anna is happily married to Dima Zales (a science fiction and fantasy author) and closely collaborates with him on all their works.

To learn more, please visit www.annazaires.com.

Made in the USA
Columbia, SC
30 November 2019

84133195R10387